KT-571-303

PENGUIN CLASSICS

THE CHARTERHOUSE OF PARMA

HENRI MARIE BEYLE, known through his writings as Stendhal, was born in Grenoble in 1783 and educated there at the École Centrale. A cousin offered him a post in the Ministry of War, and from 1800 onwards he followed Napoleon's campaigns in Italy, Germany, Russia and Austria. In between wars, he spent his time in Paris drawing-rooms and theatres.

After the fall of Napoleon, he retired to Italy, adopted his pseudonym, and started to write books on Italian painting, Haydn and Mozart, and travels in Italy. In 1821 the Austrian police expelled him from the country, and returning to Paris he finished his book *De l'Amour*. This was followed by *Racine et Shakespeare*, a defence of romantic literature. *Le Rouge et le Noir* was his second novel, and he also produced or began three others, including *La Chartreuse de Parme*, none of which was received with any great understanding during his lifetime.

Beyle was appointed Consul at Civita Vecchia after the 1830 revolution, but his health deteriorated and six years later he was back in Paris and beginning a life of Napoleon. In 1841 he was once again recalled for reasons of illness, and in the following year he suffered a fatal stroke. Various autobiographical works, his *Journal*, his *Souvenirs de l'Egotisme* and *La Vie de Henri Brulard*, were published later, as his fame grew.

MARGARET SHAW was born in 1890 and took a B.A. degree by correspondence course from London University before going up to St Hugh's College, Oxford, to gain a 'first' in languages. She was at the Sorbonne when the First World War broke out, and returned to teach in Bradford, but she later went back to Paris and spent a long time there. She did research on Laurence Sterne, and published a book about his 'Letter to Eliza'. She became a tutor at St Hugh's, and taught in Repton in the Second World War. She translated two other books, Stendhal's *Scarlet and Black* and the *Chronicles of the Crusades* of Joinville and Villehardouin, for the Penguin Classics, and had begun work on another when she died in 1963.

STENDHAL

THE CHARTERHOUSE OF PARMA

TRANSLATED
AND WITH AN INTRODUCTION BY
MARGARET R. B. SHAW

PENGUIN BOOKS

PENGUIN BOOKS

Published by the Penguin Group
27 Wrights Lane, London w8 5TZ, England
Viking Penguin Inc., 40 West 23rd Street, New York, New York 10010, USA
Penguin Books Australia Ltd, Ringwood, Victoria, Australia
Penguin Books Canada Ltd, 2801 John Street, Markham, Ontario, Canada L3R 1B4
Penguin Books (NZ) Ltd, 182–190 Wairau Road, Auckland 10, New Zealand

Penguin Books Ltd, Registered Offices: Harmondsworth, Middlesex, England

First published 1958
Reprinted 1968, 1972, 1974, 1976, 1978, 1980,
1982, 1983, 1986, 1988

Translation and Introduction copyright © Margaret R. B. Shaw, 1958
All rights reserved

Made and printed in Great Britain by
Richard Clay Ltd, Bungay, Suffolk
Set in Monotype Bembo

Except in the United States of America,
this book is sold subject to the condition
that it shall not, by way of trade or otherwise,
be lent, re-sold, hired out, or otherwise circulated
without the publisher's prior consent in any form of
binding or cover other than that in which it is
published and without a similar condition
including this condition being imposed
on the subsequent purchaser

CONTENTS

CONTENTS

INTRODUCTION

'THE true avocation of this particular beggar,' wrote Stendhal to his friend and cousin, Romain Colomb, in 1835, 'is to write a novel in a garret; for I prefer the pleasure of writing bits of nonsense to that of wearing an embroidered coat which costs 800 francs.' He was then French Consul at Civita Vecchia, growing weary of life in Italy, of the cares of office, and looking back with longing to the days when he wrote his famous novel, *Le Rouge et le noir* (the *Scarlet and Black* of this series), in his little flat in the rue de Richelieu, where money was lacking, but lively, intelligent conversation was not. Working with uncongenial companions, thrown back in his leisure hours on his own resources, he hit on the idea of writing a history of his life, as some way, no doubt, of relieving his feelings; but all he achieved was a couple of fragmentary studies: *Souvenirs d'égotisme* (1832) and *La Vie de Henri Brulard* (1835–6). With the only novel of this period, *Lucien Leuwen* (1835), his invention or his courage seems to have failed him, for he flung it aside half-finished. It was not until May 1836, when he obtained a short leave of absence which was actually to last for a full three years, that the urge to write for the public once more possessed him, and spurred him on to fresh, and even feverish, activity.

At first he toyed with the idea of finishing *Lucien Leuwen*, but finally decided that, for a man who depended for his livelihood on a government appointment, the publication of a work so outspoken in its criticism of the existing social order was, to say the least, unwise. After considering various subjects, adapting a few stories based on old Italian manuscripts for the *Revue des Deux Mondes*, and even starting on a *Life of Napoleon*, he turned his attention to composing a work in which his love of travel and his interest in human beings would be equally expressed. He began, in short, to write an account of his native country, on much the same lines as his former picturesque study of people and places in *Rome, Naples et Florence*. Two volumes of his *Mémoires d'un touriste*, based on jottings made at various times in his life, on notes he had taken in journeys through the French provinces in 1837, and on ideas gleaned from books or from his friends, were published in the spring of 1838. He had originally meant to extend the work to several volumes, and went so far as to write a short sketch entitled *Voyage dans le Midi*, but in the meantime another idea had proved more tempting to him, and he set to work on it so eagerly and intently that from start to finish he took no more than seven weeks to write his second great novel – *La Chartreuse de Parme*.

It is true that the idea of it had long been germinating in his mind, though probably not so far back as 1830, as his Foreword to the novel seems to suggest. Indeed, the whole account he gives here of his experiences in Padua must be taken as drawn rather from imagination than from life. It can be affirmed, however, that round about 1833 to 1834 Stendhal had discovered some old Italian manuscripts which interested him greatly, and in which we can discover the germ of the story developed in *La Chartreuse de Parme*.

The Italian original relates how a certain Vandozza Farnese, with the aid of her lover Roderigo, furthered the fortunes of her nephew Alessandro. The latter, after being imprisoned for a long time in the Castel Sant'Angelo for having abducted a young Roman girl, succeeded in escaping, and subsequently became a cardinal. He continued however to lead a life of dissipation until the day when he fell in love with a girl of noble birth, named Cleria, whom he treated as his wife and by whom he had several children. His affair with Cleria lasted a long time, but was so discreetly conducted that it created no scandal.

Stendhal, in fact, builds up his novel *La Chartreuse de Parme* on a doubtfully authentic account of the youth of one who later became Pope Paul III, in much the same way as he built up the plot of *Le Rouge et le noir* on facts reported in a police gazette. Alessandro becomes Fabrizio; Vandozza Farnese, the Duchessa Sanseverina; Roderigo, Conte Mosca; the young actress, Marietta, replaces in some sort the Roman girl abducted by Alessandro. Fabrizio's imprisonment in the Farnese Tower, his secret love affair with Clelia, and his rise to high office in the Church are among the incidents which have their counterpart in the Italian story.

In this particular novel, however, Stendhal changes the time and setting of the story, transferring it from the sixteenth century to the period round about Waterloo, and choosing as its main background a city in a province to be found, indeed, on the map of Italy, but which, in fact, has little more existence in reality than the imaginary kingdom of Ruritania, or Shakespeare's Bohemia-by-the-Sea. He had at first, to judge from a note inserted in the volume containing his copies of the Italian documents, 'Turn this sketch into a *romanzetto*', intended to make the actual life of Alessandro Farnese his theme. But meanwhile it seems to have occurred to him that, in view of his position as French Consul in Italy, a story throwing a not too favourable light on the morals of a former Pope might well offend the Court of Rome, and create a scandal in which his own government would be involved. Moreover, the Battle of Waterloo had already attracted his attention. He had, indeed, before setting to work on his novel, embarked on a story of this battle, the hero of which, bearing the same name as the young Farnese, Alessandro, meets with adventures practically identical with those we find in the early chapters of *La Chartreuse de Parme*. On 3 September 1838, the idea of adapting the Italian theme to make a more modern story, and combining it with the tale of a young admirer of Napoleon, came into his mind like a flash. On 4 November, in his rooms on the fourth floor of a house in the rue Caumartin – the ideal writer's 'garret' – he sat down to write his novel, never breaking off his creative work except to dictate what he had written, or to correct what he had dictated. Writing at the rate of approximately twenty-four pages a day, by 15 November he had reached page 270 of his manuscript; by 2 December he was on to page 640. He completed the work on 25 December and handed it the very next day to his cousin Romain Colomb, who set about finding a publisher for it.

The book was accepted by Ambroise Dupont, and appeared in a two-volume edition at the beginning of April 1839. The publisher, however, thinking the work too long, had insisted on Stendhal's making it shorter. Exhausted by his seven feverish weeks of labour, and already engaged on another novel, *L'Abbesse de Castro*, Stendhal somewhat over-hastily agreed to shorten the end of the *Chartreuse*, a concession which he afterwards regretted, and which, indeed, his readers may also regret. The conclusion of this novel is carried through too rapidly, and even perfunctorily, to maintain its proper proportions in a work in which, up till then, each succeeding incident is developed with infinite carefulness of detail.

Readers of *Scarlet and Black* will find many resemblances to it in this later novel – the sparing use of the description, for instance, only admitted when it serves to establish the interrelation between the characters and their background, the many soliloquies by which the inner workings of the mind are revealed, the art with which the writer gives life to secondary actors in his story, even when they only make a passing appearance on the stage. Here also are to be found, in the two leading ladies of the drama, the same contrasted types of character, personified respectively as Madame de Rénal and Mathilde in *Scarlet and Black*, as Clelia and the Duchessa Sanseverina in the *Charterhouse of Parma*; the one type, gentle, sensitive, deeply religious, yielding to passion, but haunted by remorse, the other frankly passionate, bold and enterprising, obeying no law but her own inclinations, and recalling the women, such as Marguerite de Navarre, who belonged to a more adventurous, or, shall we say, a less conventional age.

In its general plan, however, this later novel differs greatly from *Scarlet and Black*. Whereas in the latter the action turns on the conflict between a man and the society in which he is to all intents an intruder, and the interest is therefore centred almost entirely on the character of the hero, in the *Charterhouse of Parma* we are presented with a young noble in a settled position, whose destiny is shaped by accidents in which his character, except in so far as it shows itself in his bearing under the various strokes of fate that fall upon him, plays a comparatively little part.

All the same, in spite of the sensational adventures that form the main plot of the *Charterhouse of Parma*, Stendhal himself was too much interested in people and in manners to write a novel in which chance, although strongly emphasized, is the all-controlling influence in his tale. Behind the accidents of which Fabrizio is the victim stands the court of Parma, ruled over by a Prince whose vanity, no less than his weakness of character, makes him a more or less willing accomplice in the intrigues of ambitious and envious men and women whose primary concern is to further their own ends. At the moment when their malevolence has brought about Fabrizio's imprisonment, and death on the scaffold or by poison seems to be his inevitable fate, an idyllic picture of young love, defying obstacles, transforms this tale of adverse chance into a story in which the characters of Clelia and her lover move into the foreground and the doom that overshadows the prisoner recedes. An accident brings about Clelia's vow to the Madonna; but that accident is due to the Duchessa's unbridled impetuosity, spurred on by jealousy of Clelia and a more than lawful passion for her nephew. The vow itself is as much inspired by

Clelia's instinctive filial piety as was Madame de Rénal's fatal letter by her remorse, and in the consequences of that vow the elements of chance and character are so intermingled that it is hard to say where the one begins and the other ends.

In the course of his novel, as in his foreword, Stendhal takes occasion to remind his readers that Italy, and not France, is the background of his story. From long residence in Italy he had come to know the people well, and had found them less rational, less sophisticated, less reticent, more unpredictable, passionate, and impulsive than the French. We must not therefore expect to find in his novel a priest with the sober good sense of the Abbé Chélan or the cold intellectuality of Father Pirard; nor when he paints the nobility must we look for a counterpart of the urbane Marquis de la Mole. Instead we have the eccentric Father Blanès, whose great concern is to read the future in the stars, and whom Stendhal's contemporary Balzac, while generously praising the novel, would have had his fellow novelist cut out as too fantastic to be true. As the most important character among the nobles, we have the vehement Conte Mosca, whose whimsical temerity and frankness of speech is never checked save by fear of offending his sovereign, and whose desperate love for the Duchessa finds vent in many a wild and passionate speech. None the less the exquisite art with which Stendhal paints his characters in the *Charterhouse of Parma*, as in his earlier great novel, enables us to feel the common ground of humanity beneath the different manifestations of climate and race. Exception of course must be made of the villains, male and female, in this story – the baseborn, sadistic Rassi, the equally base though highborn Fabio Conti, and that scheming factionary, the Marchesa Raversi. In the portrayal of these there is a varying degree of caricature, but, as Stendhal might reasonably have argued, in the measure that men become the puppets of their lower instincts so they become, perforce, a caricature of themselves.

The Duchessa Sanseverina, lovely, witty, intrepid, completely charming, and utterly amoral, possesses all the characteristics that Stendhal considered peculiarly Italian, with a special dose of Machiavellianism that is all her own. In a certain sense she is the real heroine of this novel, rather than Clelia Conti, who, for all she holds the first place in Fabrizio's affections, pales beside the lively Duchessa, and in her gentle, retiring nature resembles the quiet, convent-bred girl of any nationality; in short, a Juliet with none of Juliet's southern fire. The Jesuitical quibble, moreover, which she fastens on in order to keep her vow in the literal sense while breaking it in reality, makes her in some sort a less sympathetic figure than her more spontaneous and less scrupulous rival.

In more than one passage of his novel Stendhal insists on Fabrizio's *Italian* character. True, he is represented as more impulsive and more emotional than one might expect a Frenchman to be. On the other hand, compared with Conte Mosca, there is a certain 'northern' coldness in his nature, which is not perhaps surprising in view of unmistakable hints in the early chapters of the novel that his real father was the young French lieutenant who, in 1796, was billeted in the house of the del Dongo family in Milan. In fact, although stressing certain Italian traits in Fabrizio's character, as, for instance, his outburst of enthusiasm over a beautiful landscape, Stendhal has produced a very ingenious study of a young man, half French and half Italian, who acts usually on impulse, but all the same makes a not entirely unsuccessful attempt to understand, if not quite to rationalize, his own emotions.

Stendhal's choice of a title for his novel has often been the subject of comment, on the grounds that the Charterhouse of Parma to which Fabrizio retired after Clelia's death is only mentioned at the very end of the novel. Careful readers of this work will note, however, that the possibility of Fabrizio's ultimate retirement to a monastery is hinted at in more than one passage that goes before. His temporary withdrawal from society at the period of Clelia's marriage and his sojourn at the Carthusian monastery of Velleia are among other indications that his mind was tending that way. Unlike Julien Sorel, ambition was no temptation to him; at no time in his life, moreover, had he felt any interest in the kind of social life of a young man of independent means. Only the hope of meeting Clelia again, and later the somewhat modified pleasure of meeting her only after dark and never by day, had kept him from renouncing the world for ever. The shock of his son's death, quickly followed by Clelia's, left him desolate; suicide, to his mind, would have meant eternal separation; a monastery was his only refuge. Step by step, detaching him from worldly interests, his life had prepared him for this end. A title that gives the ultimate stage of a human journey is not perhaps so badly chosen after all.

Nearly nine years had passed since Stendhal wrote his bitter indictment of society in *Scarlet and Black*. Now, a tired man of fifty-six, grown gentler and more tolerant, perhaps, with age, he sat down to write a story in which there is hardly a trace of satire, but in which we can still catch glimpses of his own not uneventful life: his experience of campaigns with Napoleon's army, the magic spell of Italian scenery, the boredom and petty intrigues that so often vex a man in official position, the love affairs that seldom, if ever, came to a happy end. He weaves these memories into a tale of adventure, that touches on villainy, but not so bitterly as to make the story too painful, while from his own experience of love he draws material for a skilfully delicate analysis of different variations of this passion.

At this point I will leave the reader to discover for himself the many beauties of this novel: the vivid scenes on the fringe of Waterloo, where the noise of cannon comes from an invisible army, the charms of the Italian landscape on the shores of the Lake of Como, the glimpses of a vast horizon seen from the Farnese Tower, the gentle figure of Clelia at her aviary window, the thrill of Fabrizio's escape from prison; and all those touches of genius, in short, which redeem the somewhat melodramatic character of many incidents, and give life and colour to this exciting and pathetic tale.

BIOGRAPHICAL NOTE

HENRI MARIE BEYLE, the son of a lawyer at Grenoble, was born on 23 January 1783. His family were in comfortable circumstances, but, from the time of his mother's death when he was seven, the boy was unhappy at home. He was educated by private tutors until he was thirteen, and then went to the École Centrale at Grenoble. In 1799 he was offered a post at the Ministry of War by his cousin, Pierre Daru. From 1800 onwards he took part in most of Napoleon's campaigns: in Italy, as a second lieutenant in the 6th Dragoons and aide-de-camp to General Michoud; in Germany (1806) with a junior post in the commissariat; in Russia (1812); in Austria (1813). When the Allies invaded France he was helping to organize defence on the south-east frontier, and after the fall of Napoleon (1814) he retired to Italy and, taking the pseudonym of STENDHAL, began to write. His first works were a history of Italian painting, the lives of Haydn and Mozart, and a book of travels, *Rome, Naples et Florence*, in which his keen curiosity about men and manners begins to show itself. Expelled from Italy in 1821 by the Austrian police, he returned to Paris, where he finished *De l'amour* (1822), a semi-didactic, semi-autobiographical dissertation on love. He was friends with a small group of writers including Mérimée and Paul-Louis Courier, but his works were not popular. In *Racine et Shakespeare* (1822 and 1825) he defended the Romantics against attacks from their Classical opponents, but at the same time defined his own ideas of style in terms that showed him more of a realist than a romantic. His first novel, *Armance*, with the sub-title, 'a few scenes from a Paris drawing-room in 1827', marked the beginning of his campaign against society, continued with greater force and subtlety three years later in *Le Rouge et le Noir*. After the Revolution of July 1830, he was appointed Consul at Civita Vecchia. There he began another novel, but left it unfinished. From 1836 to 1839 he was on prolonged 'sick leave' in Paris, during which time he began a life of Napoleon, wrote *Les Mémoires d'un touriste*, and completed two more novels – *La Chartreuse de Parme* (presented here as *The Charterhouse of Parma*) which ranks with *Le Rouge et le Noir* as his greatest achievement in this line, and also *L'Abbesse de Castro*. He went on writing after his return to Civita Vecchia, but he found his isolation in that city deadening to his mind. He suffered from gout and fits of giddiness, and then in 1841 a slight stroke caused him to ask to be recalled to Paris. He was at work revising *La Chartreuse de Parme* in preparation for a second edition when, on 15 March 1842, he had another stroke, followed by yet another, this time fatal, on 23 March. He left many unpublished works, among them his *Journal*, the *Souvenirs d'égotisme*, and *La Vie de Henri Brulard*, from which is gathered much of what we know about the man himself, his likes and dislikes, his many unhappy love affairs, his unfulfilled ambitions. The dates of publication of these many works (from 1855 onwards) mark the growing esteem of his countrymen for a writer whose chief misfortune was to have been a realist in an age of Romantics.

M. R. B. S.

This translation follows the text of the first edition of *La Chartreuse de Parme*, as published by Ambroise Dupont, Paris, 1839, and reproduced by M. Henri Martineau in the Édition Garnier Frères.

For a number of details in the Introduction I am indebted to M. Martineau's admirable studies of the author in *L'Œuvre de Stendhal* and *Le Cœur de Stendhal* (Editions Albin Michel).

THE CHARTERHOUSE OF PARMA

THE POLITICAL OBJECT OF PLATO

FOREWORD

THIS novel was written in the winter of 1830, and in a place some three hundred leagues from Paris; it therefore makes no allusion to the events of 1839.

Many years before 1830, at the time when our armies were over-running Europe, I happened by chance to be given a billeting order on the house of a Canon. This was at Padua, a charming town in Italy; as my stay there was prolonged, the Canon and I became friends.

Passing through Padua again in 1830, I hastened to the worthy Canon's house. He himself, as I knew, was dead, but I wanted to see once again that drawing-room in which we had spent so many pleasant evenings, so often, since then, recalled with a sense of regret. I found there the Canon's nephew and that nephew's wife, who welcomed me as an old friend. A few people dropped in, and the party did not break up until a very late hour; the nephew sent out to the Caffè Pedrocchi for an excellent *zabaione*. What most of all kept us up was the story of the Duchessa Sanseverina, to which some-one made an allusion, and which the nephew was good enough to relate, for my benefit, from beginning to end.

'In the country to which I am going,' I said to my friends, 'I shall hardly meet with evenings like this one, and to while away the long hours after nightfall I shall make a novel out of your story.'

'In that case,' said the nephew, 'I will give you my uncle's journal, which, under the heading *Parma*, makes mention of certain intrigues of that court, in the days when the Duchessa was absolute mistress of it. But, let me warn you, this story is anything but moral, and now that in France you pride yourselves on your gospel-like purity, it may earn you a highly criminal reputation.'

I am publishing this tale without making any alteration to the manuscript of 1830, a course which may have two drawbacks.

The first affects the reader: the characters, being Italian, may possibly interest him less, since hearts in that country differ somewhat from hearts in France. The Italians are a sincere and simple-hearted people who, without any notion of taking or giving offence, say exactly what they think. They are only vain by fits and starts, and then vanity becomes a passion, and goes by the name of *puntiglio*. And lastly, poverty is not, with them, considered a subject for ridicule.

The second drawback concerns the author.

I will confess that I have been so bold as to leave my characters with their natural harsh traits unsoftened; but, on the other hand – I proclaim it openly – I cast the most moral censure on many of their actions. Where would be the use of endowing them with the high morality and pleasing graces of French characters, who love money above all things, and seldom sin from motives of love or hatred? The Italians in this tale are almost the opposite. And besides, it seems to me that, every time we move two hundred leagues northwards from the South, there is occasion both for a different scene and another kind of story. The Canon's charming niece had known and even been very fond of the Duchessa Sanseverina, and she has begged me to alter nothing in her adventures, which are certainly open to censure.

ON 15 May 1796, General Bonaparte made his entry into Milan at the head of that youthful army which but a short time before had crossed the Bridge of Lodi, and taught the world that after so many centuries Caesar and Alexander had a successor.

The miracles of gallantry and genius that Italy had been witness of in the space of a few months aroused a slumbering people. Only a week before the arrival of the French, the Milanese still regarded them as a horde of brigands, accustomed invariably to flee before the troops of His Imperial and Royal Majesty. That, at least, was what was reported to them three times weekly by a little news-sheet no larger than a man's hand and printed on grimy paper.

In the Middle Ages the republicans of Lombardy had given proof of a valour equal to that of the French, and had deserved to see their city razed to the ground by the German Emperors. Ever since they had become *loyal subjects* their main business had been the printing of sonnets upon little handkerchiefs of rose-coloured taffeta on the occasion of the marriage of some young lady belonging to a rich or a noble family. Two or three years after that great event in her life, this young lady would select a *cavaliere servente*: the name of the *cicisbeo* chosen by her husband's family sometimes occupied an honourable place in the marriage contract. It was a far cry from such effeminate manners to the deep emotions aroused by the unexpected arrival of the French army. Very soon a new and passionate standard of manners sprang into being. A whole nation became aware, on 15 May 1796, that everything it had respected up till then was supremely ridiculous and on occasion hateful. The departure of the last Austrian regiment marked the collapse of the old ideas; to risk one's life became the fashion. People saw that, in order to be happy after centuries of insipid sensations, they needs must love their country with genuine affection and seek to perform heroic actions. They had been plunged in darkest night by the continuation of the jealous despotism of Charles V and Philip II; they overturned these despots' statues and immediately found themselves flooded with light. For the last fifty years, and in proportion as the *Encyclopédie* and Voltaire had gained a reputation in France, the monks had been proclaiming aloud to the good people of Milan that to learn to read, or indeed to learn anything at all, was a waste of labour, and that by scrupulously paying one's tithe to one's parish priest, and giving him a faithful account of all one's petty transgressions, one was almost certain of having a fine place in Paradise. To complete the final enervation of this people once so formidable and so rational, Austria had sold them, on easy terms, the privilege of not having to furnish any recruits for her army.

In 1796, the Milanese army was composed of four-and-twenty jackanapes, in scarlet uniforms, who kept guard over the city together with four magnificent regiments of Hungarian Grenadiers. Freedom of morals was extreme, but passion very rare. Otherwise, apart from the inconvenience of having to tell one's curé everything, on pain of ruin even in this present world, the good people of Milan were still subjected to certain little monarchical restrictions which did not cease to vex them. For instance, the Archduke, who resided in Milan and governed it in the name of the Emperor, his cousin, had hit on the profitable idea of engaging in the corn trade. In consequence, the peasants were forbidden to sell their grain until His Highness had filled his own granaries.

In May 1796, three days after the entry of the French, a young miniaturist, slightly mad, named Gros, since become famous, who had arrived with the army, overhearing in the great Caffè dei Servi (which was then in fashion) some talk of the exploits of the Archduke, who by the way was enormously stout, picked up the list of ices which was roughly printed on a miserable slip of yellow paper. On the back of the sheet he drew the fat Archduke; a French soldier was sticking his bayonet into his stomach, and, instead of blood, an incredible quantity of corn was pouring out. The thing we call a skit or a caricature was unknown in this land of cold and cunning despotism. This drawing, left behind by Gros on the table in the Caffè dei Servi, seemed like a miracle fallen straight from heaven; it was engraved and printed during the night, and the next day twenty thousand copies of it were sold.

The same day, there were posted up notices of a war levy of six millions, effected for the needs of the French army which, having just won six battles and conquered twenty provinces, wanted nothing now but shoes, breeches, jackets, and caps.

The vast inrush of happiness and pleasure that poured into Lombardy in the wake of these extremely needy Frenchmen was such that only the priests and a small handful of the nobles were conscious of the heaviness of this levy of six millions, which was shortly after followed by others. These French soldiers laughed and sang the whole day long; they were all under twenty-five years of age, and their Commander-in-Chief, who was twenty-seven, was reckoned the oldest man in his army. This gaiety, this youth, this happy-go-lucky attitude of theirs, provided an amusing answer to the frenzied preaching of the monks who, for six months past, had been pro-claiming from the lofty eminence of their pulpits that the French were monsters, obliged, under pain of death, to burn down everything and to cut off everyone's head. With this intent, each regiment marched with a guillotine leading the van.

In the countryside, at the cottage doors, the French soldier could be seen dandling the housewife's baby, and almost every evening some drummer or other, striking up a tune on his fiddle, would improvise a ball. The set country dances proving a great deal too intricate and cunningly devised for the soldiers, who by the way hardly knew them themselves, to be able to teach them to the women of this region, it was the latter who showed the young Frenchmen the *monferrina*, the *salterello*, and other Italian dances.

The officers had been lodged, as far as possible, with wealthy families; they had every need to recruit their strength. A certain lieutenant named Robert, for instance, was given a billeting order on the *palazzo* of the Marchesa del Dongo. This officer, a young recruit of somewhat free and easy morals, possessed as his sole fortune, when he entered this *palazzo*, a scudo worth six francs he had just acquired at Piacenza. After the crossing of the Bridge of Lodi he had taken from a fine Austrian officer, killed by a cannon-ball, a magnificent pair of quite new nankeen breeches, and never did any garment come at a more opportune moment. His officer's epaulettes were of wool, and the cloth of his tunic was patched with the lining of his sleeves so as to make the different scraps of it hold together. But there was a matter even more distressing; the soles of his shoes were made out of fragments of soldiers' caps also picked up on the field of battle, on the far side of the Bridge of Lodi. These makeshift soles were attached to the uppers of his shoes with very visible pieces of string, so that when the butler of the house appeared at the door of Lieutenant Robert's room to invite him to dine with her ladyship the Marchesa the young officer was seized with the utmost embarrassment. His orderly and he spent the couple of hours that lay between them and this fatal dinner in trying to patch up the tunic a little and dying black, by means of ink, those unlucky strings on his shoes. At last the terrible moment arrived. 'Never in all my life did I feel more ill at ease,' so Lieutenant Robert told me. 'The ladies expected I would terrify them, but I was trembling far more than they. I looked down at my shoes, and did not know how to walk gracefully. The Marchesa del Dongo,' he added, 'was then in the full bloom of her beauty. You have seen her for yourself, with those lovely eyes of such angelic sweetness, and the beautiful auburn hair that made such a perfect frame for the oval of that charming face. I had in my room a *Herodias* by Leonardo da Vinci, which might have been her portrait. By heaven's grace, I was so overcome by such supernatural beauty that it made me forget my costume. For the past two years I had been seeing nothing but ugly and wretched things in the mountains in the regions of Genoa. I ventured to say a few words to her to express my utter delight.

'I had, however, too much sense to linger in a complimentary vein. All the while I was shaping my pretty phrases, I could see, in a dining-room panelled entirely in marble, a dozen lackeys and other menservants dressed in what seemed to me then the height of magnificence. Just imagine it! These rascals not only had good shoes, but silver buckles as well. I could see, out of the corner of my eye, all their stupid glances fixed on my tunic, and possibly on my shoes as well, a thing that cut me to the heart. I could have struck fear into all these fellows' hearts with a word, but how was I to put them in their place without running the risk of alarming the ladies? For the Marchesa, to give herself a little courage, as she has told me a hundred times since, had sent to fetch from the convent school where she was at that time a boarder, her husband's sister, Gina del Dongo, who later became that charming Contessa Pietranera. No one, in prosperous circumstances, surpassed her in gaiety and sweetness of character, just as no one surpassed her in courage and serenity of soul in an adverse turn of fortune.

'Gina, who might at that time have been thirteen, but looked eighteen, a frank and lively girl, as you know, was in such fear of bursting out laughing at the sight of my costume that she did not dare to eat. The Marchesa, on the other hand, overwhelmed me with polite, but constrained, attentions; she was very well aware of glimmers of nervous irritation in my eyes. In a word, I was cutting a very sorry figure, chewing the cud of my contempt, a thing which is said to be impossible for a Frenchman. At length, a heaven-sent idea cast its light into my mind: I set to work to tell these ladies of my poverty, and of what we had suffered for the past two years in the mountains in the region of Genoa, where two idiotic old generals had forced us to stay. There, I told them, we were paid in paper-money that was not legal tender in that province, and given three ounces of bread a day. I had not been speaking for two minutes before there were tears in the kind Marchesa's eyes, and young Gina had grown serious.

' "What, Lieutenant," she said to me, "three ounces of bread!"

' "Yes, Signorina: but on another hand the issue would run short three times in the week, and as the peasants with whom we lodged were even in worse poverty than ourselves, we used to give them a little of our bread."

'On leaving the table, I offered the Marchesa my arm as far as the door of the dining-room, then, hurriedly retracing my steps, I gave the servant who had waited on me at table the solitary piece of six francs upon the spending of which I had built so many castles in the air.

'A week later,' Robert went on, 'when it was well established that the French were not guillotining anyone, the Marchese del Dongo returned from his castle of Grianta on Lake Como in which he had gallantly taken refuge on the approach of the army, leaving his beautiful young wife and his sister exposed to the hazards of war. The hatred that this Marchese felt for us was equal to his fear, that is to say immeasurable; his pale and sanctimonious fat face was comical to see when he was paying me polite compliments. The day after his return to Milan I received three ells of cloth and two hundred francs out of the levy of six millions. I resumed my fine feathers and acted as cavalier to these ladies, for the season of balls had begun.'

Lieutenant Robert's story was much the same as that of every Frenchman; instead of making fun of the poverty of these brave soldiers people were sorry for them, and came to love them.

This period of unlooked-for happiness and wild excitement lasted only two short years. The outburst of folly had been so excessive and so general that it would be impossible for me to give any idea of it, except by this profound historic reflection – these people had been living in a state of boredom for the last hundred years.

The love of sensual pleasure natural in southern countries had prevailed in former days at the courts of the Visconti and the Sforza, those famous Dukes of Milan. But from the year 1635, when the Spaniards had taken possession of the dukedom of Milan, and had ruled it as taciturn, suspicious, and arrogant masters, for ever in dread of some revolt, all gaiety had fled. Its people, adopting the manners of their masters, thought rather of avenging the slightest insult by a dagger-thrust than of enjoying the pleasures of the moment.

Wild delight, gaiety, and sensual pleasure, and the thrusting aside of every sad or even reasonable feeling were carried to such a pitch between 15 May 1796, when the French entered Milan, and April 1799, when they were driven out again after the battle of Cassano, that instances could be cited of old millionaire merchants, money-lenders, and notaries who, during this interval, quite forgot to be surly and grim and intent on making money.

At the most it would have been possible to reckon a few families belonging to the higher ranks of the nobility, who had retired to their great houses in the country, as if in a fit of sulks against the general air of jollity and the light-heartedness all around. It is also true that these noble and wealthy families had been distinguished in a disagreeable manner in the allocation of the levies exacted for the French army.

The Marchese del Dongo, vexed by the sight of so much gaiety, had been one of the first to withdraw to his magnificent castle of Grianta, lying beyond the town of Como, to which the ladies brought Lieutenant Robert. This castle, standing in a position that is possibly unique in the world, on a plateau one hundred and fifty feet above that supremely beautiful lake, and commanding a view of a great portion of it, had once been a fortress. It had been built in the fifteenth century for the del Dongo family, as was everywhere attested by marble tablets bearing their arms. Its drawbridges and deep moats were still to be seen there, although the latter, it is true, had been drained of their water. But with its walls eighty feet in height and six in breadth this castle was safe from sudden assault; and for that reason was dear to the heart of the apprehensive Marchese. Surrounded by some twenty-five or thirty servants whom he supposed to be devoted to him – presumably because he never spoke to them without some insult on his lips – he was less tormented by fear than in Milan.

This fear was not entirely unwarranted. The Marchese was in active correspondence with an Austrian spy stationed on the Swiss frontier, three leagues from Grianta, to assist the escape of prisoners taken on the field of battle, and this might have been viewed in a serious light by the French generals.

The Marchese had left his young wife in Milan, where she had to take charge of family affairs and be responsible for meeting the levies imposed on the Casa del Dongo, as it was called in these parts. She was anxious to get the amount reduced, and this obliged her to call on certain noblemen who had accepted some public office, and even on a few highly influential persons not of noble birth.

A great event now occurred in this family. The Marchese had arranged the marriage of his young sister Gina with a personage of great wealth and of the highest birth; but he powdered his hair. On this account Gina received him with shrieks of laughter, and soon after she committed the folly of marrying Conte Pietranera. He was, it is true, a very worthy gentleman, and most handsome in appearance, but of a family ruined for generations past, and, as a crowning disgrace, a fervent supporter of the new ideas. Pietranera was a second lieutenant in the Italian Legion; this added further fuel to the Marchese's disappointment.

After these two years of mad excitement and happiness, the Directorate in Paris, giving itself airs like those of a well-established monarchy, began to show a deadly hatred of everything that was other than commonplace. The incompetent generals it imposed on the army in Italy lost a series of battles on those same plains of Verona which had witnessed but two years before prodigious feats performed at Arcola and Lonato. The Austrians once more drew near to Milan; Lieutenant Robert, who was now a major, and had been wounded at the battle of Cassano, came to lodge for the last time in the house of his friend the Marchesa del Dongo. Their parting was a sad one: Robert went off with Conte Pietranera, who was following the French in their retreat towards Novi. The young Contessa, whose marriage portion the Marchese had refused to pay, followed the army in one of the baggage waggons.

Then began that period of reaction and a return to the old ideas, which the Milanese call *i tredici mesi* (the thirteen months) because, in point of fact, their fate so willed it that this harking back to stupid ways and notions should last for thirteen months only, until Marengo.

Everyone who was old, or bigoted, or morose, reappeared at the head of affairs and resumed the leadership of society; and soon the people who had remained faithful to sound doctrines spread abroad a report in the villages that Napoleon had been hanged by the Mamelukes in Egypt, as he deserved to be on so many grounds.

Among those men who had retired to sulk on their estates and now came back athirst for vengeance, the Marchese del Dongo distinguished himself by his mad enthusiasm. The very extravagance of his feelings carried him naturally to the head of his party. These gentlemen, very decent folk when they were not in a state of panic, but who were still in a tremor, succeeded in getting round the Austrian general. Although a fairly kindly man, he let himself be persuaded that severity was a matter of high policy, and ordered the arrest of one hundred and fifty patriots, who were really quite the best men in all Italy at the time.

They were quickly deported to the Bocche di Cattaro, and being flung into subterranean caves, the damp, and even more the lack of food, did prompt and proper justice to all these scoundrels.

The Marchese del Dongo was given a high position, and as he combined the most sordid avarice with a host of other fine qualities he openly prided himself on not having sent a single scudo to his sister, Contessa Pietranera. Still madly in love, she refused to leave her husband, and was starving beside him in France. The kind-hearted Marchesa was in despair; finally she managed to abstract a few small diamonds from her jewel-case, which her husband took away from her every evening in order to lock it up in an iron coffer under his bed. The Marchesa had brought her husband a dowry of eight hundred thousand francs, and received from him eighty francs a month for her personal expenses. During the thirteen months in which the French were absent from Milan this extremely timid woman invented various pretexts for always wearing mourning.

We must confess that, following the example of many grave authors, we have begun the history of our hero a year before his birth. This essential personage is in fact none other than Fabrizio Valserra, *Marchesino*★ del Dongo, as they say in Milan. He had just taken the trouble to be born at the moment when the French were

★ By local custom, borrowed from Germany, this title is given to every son of a Marchese; *Contino* to every son of a Count, *Contessina* to all his daughters, etc.

driven out, and found himself, by accident of birth, the second son of that Marchese del Dongo, who was so great a lord, and with whose fat, pasty face, false smile, and boundless hatred for the new ideas you are already acquainted. The whole of the family fortune was entailed upon the elder son, Ascanio del Dongo, the worthy image of his father. He was eight years old, and Fabrizio two, when all of a sudden that General Bonaparte, whom everyone of good family understood to have been hanged a long time since, swooped down from the Mont Saint-Bernard. He entered Milan: that moment is still unique in history; imagine a whole populace madly in love! A few days later, Napoleon won the battle of Marengo. It is needless to say any more. The frenzied excitement of the Milanese was at its height; but this time it was mingled with thoughts of vengeance: these kindly people had been taught to hate. Shortly after they saw the arrival of all that remained of the patriots deported to the Bocche di Cattaro; their return was celebrated with national rejoicing. Their pale faces, great startled eyes, and emaciated limbs contrasted strangely with the joy that broke out on every side. Their arrival was the signal for the departure of the families most deeply compromised. The Marchese del Dongo was one of the first to flee to his castle of Grianta. The heads of the great families were filled with hatred and fear; but their wives and daughters remembered the joys of the former French occupation, and thought with regret of Milan and those gay balls, which were organized at the *Casa Tanzi*, immediately after Marengo.

A few days after this victory, the French general responsible for maintaining peace and order in Lombardy remarked that all the farmers on the noblemen's estates and all the old wives in the country-side, so far from still thinking of this amazing victory at Marengo, which had altered the destiny of Italy and recaptured thirteen fortified positions in a single day, had their minds solely occupied by a pro-phecy of San Giovita, the chief patron saint of Brescia. According to this holy man's pronouncement, the successful progress of France and of Napoleon would come to a stop exactly thirteen weeks after Marengo. What slightly excuses the Marchese del Dongo and all the nobles sulking on their estates is that really and truly and without any jesting they believed in this prophecy. Not one of these persons had read as many as four books in his life. They were making preparations quite openly for their return to Milan at the end of the thirteen weeks;

but time, as it sped by, noted new successes for the cause of France. On his return to Paris, Napoleon, by means of wise decrees, had saved the country from revolution at home as he had saved it from foreign enemies at Marengo. Then the Lombard nobles, sheltered in their castles, discovered that they had at first misunderstood the prophecy of the holy patron of Brescia; it was not a question of thirteen weeks, but rather of thirteen months. The thirteen months passed by, and the prosperity of France seemed to grow greater with every day.

We pass rapidly over ten years of progress and happiness, from 1800 to 1810. Fabrizio spent the first part of this decade at the castle of Grianta, giving and receiving many a pummelling among the peasant boys of the village, and learning nothing, not even how to read. Later he was sent to the Jesuit College in Milan. His father the Marchese insisted on his being taught Latin, not by any means from the works of those ancient authors who are always talking about Republics, but from a magnificent volume adorned with more than a hundred engravings, a masterpiece of seventeenth-century art. This was the Latin genealogy of the Valserra family, Marchesi del Dongo, published in 1650 by Fabrizio del Dongo, Archbishop of Parma. The fortunes of this house being pre-eminently military, the engravings represented a goodly number of battles, in which some hero of this name could always be seen dealing mighty blows with his sword. This book greatly delighted the young Fabrizio. His mother, who adored him, obtained permission, from time to time, to visit him in Milan; but since her husband never gave her any money for these journeys, it was her sister-in-law, the charming Contessa Pietranera, who used to lend her some. After the return of the French, the Contessa had become one of the most distinguished ladies at the court of the Viceroy of Italy, Prince Eugène.

After Fabrizio had made his First Communion, she obtained leave from the Marchese, still in voluntary exile, to invite him out, now and again, from his school. She found him an original, intelligent, and very grave little fellow, but a handsome lad who was not too much out of place in a fashionable lady's drawing-room; otherwise, as ignorant as you please and barely able to write. The Contessa, who brought her eager enthusiastic temperament to bear on everything, promised her patronage to the head of the institution provided that Fabrizio made outstanding progress, and carried off a good number of prizes at the end of the year. In order to put him in a position to deserve them, she used to send for him every Saturday evening, and often did not hand him back to his masters until the following Wednesday or Thursday. The Jesuits, although tenderly cherished by the princely Viceroy, were under sentence of expulsion from Italy by the laws of the realm, and the Rector of the college, an astute individual, was conscious of all the advantage he might draw from his association with a woman who was all-powerful at court. He was careful not to complain of the absences of Fabrizio, who, although more ignorant than ever, was awarded five first prizes at the end of the year. In these circumstances, the distinguished Contessa Pietranera, accompanied by her husband, now the General commanding one of the Divisions of the Guard, together with five or six of the most important personages at the vice-regal court, came to attend the prize-giving at the Jesuit College. The Rector was complimented by his superiors.

The Contessa took her nephew with her to all those brilliant festivities which marked the all too short reign of the kindly Prince Eugène. She had on her own authority created him an officer of Hussars, and Fabrizio, now twelve years old, wore their uniform. One day the Contessa, charmed by his handsome appearance, begged the Prince to give him a post as a page, a request which implied that the del Dongo family was coming round. The next day she had need of all her influence to obtain the Viceroy's kind consent to forget this request, which lacked nothing but the consent of the future page's father, and this consent would have been roundly refused. In consequence of this act of folly, which made him shudder, the sullen Marchese invented some excuse for recalling young Fabrizio to Grianta. The Contessa had a supreme contempt for her brother; she regarded him as a sorry fool, and one who would be malicious if ever it lay in his power. But she doted on Fabrizio, and, after ten years of silence, she wrote to the Marchese imploring him to send her nephew back to her. Her letter remained unanswered.

On his return to this formidable pile, built by the most bellicose of his ancestors, Fabrizio knew absolutely nothing at all except how to drill and how to sit on a horse. Conte Pietranera, as foolishly fond of the boy as was his wife, had often taken him out riding and made him accompany him on parade.

On reaching the castle of Grianta, Fabrizio, his eyes still very red from the tears he had shed on leaving his aunt's lovely rooms, was greeted with nothing save the passionate caresses of his mother and his sisters. The Marchese was closeted in his study with his elder son, the Marchesino Ascanio; there they were concocting letters in cipher which had the honour of being forwarded to Vienna. Father and son put in an appearance only at meal-times. The Marchese would repeat in a pompous way that he was teaching his natural successor to keep, by double entry, the accounts of the revenues from each of his estates. In actual fact, the Marchese was too jealous of his own power ever to mention these matters to a son who was the inevitable inheritor of all these entailed properties. He employed him in transcribing in cipher despatches of fifteen to twenty pages which two or three times a week he had conveyed into Switzerland, from whence they were sent on their way to Vienna. The Marchese claimed to inform his rightful suzerains of internal conditions within the kingdom of Italy, of which he himself knew nothing. His letters were all the same highly appreciated; and for the following reason: the Marchese would get some reliable agent to take a count on the high road of the number of men in a certain French or Italian regiment which was moving to other quarters, and, in reporting the fact to the court of Vienna he would take care to reduce by at least a fourth the number of soldiers involved. These letters, in other respects quite absurd, had the merit of contradicting others of greater accuracy, and thus gave pleasure. Consequently, a short time before Fabrizio's arrival at the castle, the Marchese had received the star of a famous order; it was the fifth to adorn his chamberlain's coat. He suffered, in truth, from the fact that he dared not sport this garment outside his study; but he never allowed himself to dictate a despatch without first putting on the gold-laced coat, bedecked with all his orders. He would have felt himself wanting in respect to have acted otherwise.

The Marchesa was amazed by her son's graceful ways. But she had kept up the habit of writing two or three times a year to General Comte d'A—, which was Lieutenant Robert's present title. The Marchesa had a horror of lying to people she was fond of. She questioned her son and was appalled by his ignorance.

'If to me who know nothing', she said to herself, 'he appears to have learnt very little, Robert, who is so clever, would consider his education an utter failure; and in these days one has to have some ability.' Another peculiarity, which astonished her almost as much, was that Fabrizio had taken quite seriously all the ideas on religion instilled into him at the Jesuit College. Although very pious herself, the boy's fanaticism made her shudder. 'If the Marchese has the wit to discover this means of influencing him, he will rob me of my son's affection.' She wept copiously, and her passionate love for Fabrizio was thereby increased.

Life in this castle, peopled by thirty to forty servants, was extremely dull; Fabrizio therefore spent all his days either shooting game or skimming round the lake in a boat. Soon he was on very intimate terms with the coachmen and the grooms; they were all of them madly enthusiastic supporters of the French and laughed openly at the pious valets who were the personal servants of the Marchese or of his elder son. The great subject of jest at the expense of these solemn individuals was that, in imitation of their masters, they powdered their hair.

CHAPTER 2: *Early Influences*

When evening casts its shadow o'er my eyes,
Musing on what's to come, I scan the skies,
Where God has written, clear for all to see,
The chequer'd course of human destiny.
For sometimes, leaning from His high abode,
By pity moved, He points us out our road,
Foretelling in the stars, His runic signs,
How good or ill this way or that inclines;
But men, by cares and fear of dying vex'd,
With eyes turn'd earthwards, scorn to read His text.

RONSARD

THE Marchese professed a vigorous hatred of enlightment. 'It is ideas,' he would say, 'that have been the ruin of Italy.' He did not know quite how to reconcile this holy horror of learning with his desire to see his son Fabrizio perfect the education so brilliantly begun with the Jesuits. In order to incur the least possible risk, he entrusted to the worthy Father Blanès, the parish priest of Grianta, the task of continuing Fabrizio's Latin studies. For this it was necessary that the priest should himself know that language; but as it happened it was to him an object of scorn. His knowledge in this field was limited to the recitation, by heart, of the prayers in his missal, the sense of which he could roughly convey to his flock. But this priest was none the less highly respected and even feared in the district. He had always said that it was not within thirteen weeks, nor even within thirteen months, that people would see the fulfilment of the famous prophecy of San Giovita, the patron saint of Brescia. He would further add, when speaking to friends whom he could trust, that this number *thirteen* would be interpreted in a manner that would astonish many people, if it were permissible for him to say all that he knew (1813).

The fact was that Father Blanès, a man of *primitive* honesty and virtue, and an intelligent man as well, spent all his nights up in his belfry; he was mad on astrology. After employing his days in calculating the conjunctions and the positions of the stars, he would spend the greater part of his nights in following their course through the sky. By reason of his poverty he had no other instrument save a long telescope with pasteboard tubes. One can judge what contempt a man who devoted his life to discovering the precise dates of the fall of empires and the revolutions that change the face of the world would feel for the study of languages. 'What more do I know about a horse,' he would say to Fabrizio, 'when I have been informed that in Latin it is called *equus*?'

The peasants held Father Blanès in dread as a great magician; for his part, with the help of the fear that his sessions in the belfry inspired, he kept them from stealing. His clerical brethren in the neighbouring parishes, very jealous of his influence, detested him; the Marchese del Dongo merely despised him, because he reasoned too much for a man of such humble station. Fabrizio adored him; to please him he sometimes spent whole evenings doing enormous sums of addition or multiplication. Then he would go up to the top of the belfry; this was a great favour and one that Father Blanès had never yet granted to anyone; but he loved this child for his simplicity. 'If you do not turn out a hypocrite,' he would say to him, 'perhaps you will turn out a man.'

Two or three times a year Fabrizio, dauntless and hotheaded in pursuit of pleasure, would come very near to drowning himself in the lake. He was the leader of all the great expeditions made by the peasant boys of Grianta and Cadenabbia. These boys had procured a few little keys, and on very dark nights would try to open the padlocks on the chains that fastened the boats to some big stone or a tree near the water's edge. It should be explained that on the Lake of Como the men engaged in the fishing industry place trawl-lines at a great distance from the shore. The upper end of each line is fastened to a small plank sheathed in cork, and a very flexible hazel twig, attached to this plank, bears a little bell that tinkles whenever a fish, caught on the line, makes the rope that ties it quiver.

The great object of these nocturnal expeditions, of which Fabrizio was commander-in-chief, was to go out and visit the trawl-lines before the fishermen had heard the warning note of the little bells. They used to choose stormy weather; and for these hazardous trips would embark in the early morning, an hour before dawn. As they climbed into the boat these youngsters fancied they were rushing headlong into the greatest danger – this was the fine side of their enterprise – and, following the example of their fathers, they would devoutly recite an *Ave Maria*.

Now it frequently happened that at the moment of starting, and immediately after the *Ave Maria*, Fabrizio would be seized with a foreboding. This was the fruit he had gathered from the astrological studies of Father Blanès, in whose predictions he had no faith whatsoever. According to his youthful imagination, this foreboding announced to him, with absolute certainty, the chances of success or failure; and, as he had more determination than any of his companions, the whole band gradually became so accustomed to these forebodings that if, at the moment of embarking, they caught sight of a priest on the shore, or observed a crow flying to the left of them, they would hasten to put the padlock back on the chain of the boat, and all of them would go off to bed. Thus Father Blanès had not imparted his rather difficult science to Fabrizio; but he had without knowing it inoculated him with unlimited confidence in the signs by which the future may be foretold.

The Marchese felt that any accident affecting his ciphered correspondence might put him at the mercy of his sister; and so every year, at the time of the feast of Sant'Angela, who was Contessa Pietranera's patron saint, Fabrizio was given leave to spend a week in Milan. The whole year through he lived either in expectation of this week or in regret that it was over. On this great occasion, for the carrying out of this diplomatic journey, the Marchese handed over four scudi to his son, and according to his usual custom gave nothing to his wife, who accompanied the boy. But a cook, six lackeys, and a coachman with a pair of horses, would set off for Como the day before, and every day while she was in Milan the Marchesa found a carriage at her disposal and a dinner for twelve persons.

The gloomy kind of life that the Marchese del Dongo led was certainly far from entertaining, but it had the advantage of permanently enriching the families who were good enough to give themselves up to it. The Marchese, who had an income of more than two hundred thousand lire a year, did not spend a quarter of it; he lived on hope. Throughout the thirteen years from 1800 to 1813, he constantly and firmly believed that Napoleon would be overthrown before six months had passed. Judge then of his rapture when, at the beginning of 1813, he learnt of the disasters of the Beresina! The taking of Paris and the fall of Napoleon almost sent him right off his head; he then allowed himself to make the most outrageous remarks to his wife and his sister. At last, after fourteen years of waiting, he had the inexpressible joy of seeing the Austrian troops re-enter Milan. In obedience to orders issued from Vienna, the Austrian general received the Marchese del Dongo with a consideration bordering on respect. They hastened to offer him one of the highest posts in the government, and he accepted it as the payment of a debt. His elder son obtained a lieutenancy in one of the smartest regiments of the Austrian Monarchy; but the younger could never be persuaded to accept a cadetship that was offered him.

This triumph, in which the Marchese exulted with peculiar insolence, lasted only a few months and was followed by a humiliating reverse. He had never had any gift for public affairs, and fourteen years spent in the country in the company of his menservants, his lawyer, and his doctor, added to the crabbedness of old age which had overtaken him, had turned him into an utterly incompetent man. Now it is not possible, in an Austrian country, to keep an important post without having the kind of talent required for the slow and complicated, but highly reasonable system of administration in this old monarchy. The blunders made by the Marchese del Dongo scandalized the staff of his department and even obstructed the course of public business. His ultra-monarchical utterances irritated the rank and file of the people, whom it was hoped to keep sunk in apathetic slumbers.

One fine day he was informed that His Majesty had been graciously pleased to accept the resignation he had submitted of his post in the administration, and at the same time conferred on him the office of *Second Grand Majordomo Major* of the Lombardo-Venetian Kingdom. The Marchese was furious at the abominable injustice of which he was the victim. He, who had so bitterly denounced the liberty of the press, now published an open letter to a friend. Finally, he wrote to the Emperor to say that his ministers were playing him false and were no better than Jacobins. Having done these things, he went sadly back to his castle of Grianta.

He had one consolation. After the fall of Napoleon, certain powerful personages in Milan had arranged for Conte Prina, a former minister of the King of Italy, and a man of the highest merit, to be brutally assaulted in the street. Conte Pietranera risked his own life to save the minister's, who died from blows received from umbrellas, after an agony of five hours' duration. A priest, who was the Marchese del Dongo's confessor, could have saved Prina by opening the iron gate of the Church of San Giovanni, in front of which the unfortunate minister was dragged, and even left for a moment lying in the gutter in the middle of the street. But this priest refused with jeers to open his gate, and six months later the Marchese had the happiness of securing a fine preferment for him.

The Marchese detested his brother-in-law, Conte Pietranera, who, while possessing an income of less than fifty louis, had the audacity to be quite content, presumed to show himself loyal to what he had loved all his life, and was insolent enough to preach that spirit of justice without respect of persons which the Marchese called an infamous piece of Jacobinism. The Conte had refused to serve in the Austrian army; great stress was laid on this refusal, and a few months after the death of Prina the same persons who had hired the assassins succeeded in getting General Pietranera thrown into prison. Thereupon the Contessa, his wife, obtained a passport and ordered post horses to take her to Vienna so as to tell the Emperor the truth. Prina's assassins took fright, and one of them, a cousin of the Contessa, came to her at midnight, an hour before she was to have started for Vienna, to bring her the order for her husband's release. Next day, the Austrian General sent for Conte Pietranera, received him with the greatest politeness, and assured him that his pension as a retired officer would be paid to him without delay and on most advantageous terms. The gallant General Bubna, an intelligent and warm-hearted man, appeared quite ashamed about the murder of Prina and the Conte's imprisonment.

After this sudden commotion, quelled by the Contessa's firmness of character, this couple lived as well as they could on the pension, which, thanks to General Bubna's recommendation, was not too long in coming.

Fortunately, it so happened that, for five or six years past, the Contessa had been on the most friendly terms with a very rich young man, who was also a close friend of the Conte, and who did not fail to place at their disposal the finest team of English carriage horses to be seen at that time in Milan, his box at the Scala theatre, and his house in the country. But the Conte was very conscious of his own valour; he was warm-hearted and impulsive by nature and easily moved to anger; on such occasions he would venture to make some very odd remarks. One day when he was out shooting with some young men, one of them, who had served under other flags than his own, began to make jesting allusions to the bravery of the soldiers of the Cisalpine Republic. The Conte slapped his face; immediately a fight began, and the Conte, who, among all these young men, was the only one of his way of thinking, was killed. This species of duel gave rise to a great deal of talk, and the persons concerned in it made up their minds to go on a journey into Switzerland.

That absurd form of courage which is called resignation, the courage of a fool who lets himself be hanged without saying a word, was not one of the Contessa's habits. Furious at the death of her husband, she would have liked Limercati, the rich young man who was her intimate friend, to take it into his head to journey likewise to Switzerland, and there to shoot or box the ears of Conte Pietranera's murderer.

Limercati thought this plan supremely ridiculous, and the Contessa realized that contempt had killed what affection she had felt for him. She redoubled her attentions to Limercati; she wanted to awaken love in him, and then leave him in the lurch and fill him with despair. To make this project of revenge intelligible to French readers, I should say that in Milan, in a country far removed from our own, people can still be driven to despair by love. The Contessa, who, in her widow's weeds, very easily outshone all her rivals, flirted with all the young men of the first rank in society, and one of these, a certain Conte N —, who, from the first, had said that he found Limercati's estimable qualities a trifle heavy, and rather too stiff and starchy for so witty and intelligent a woman, fell madly in love with her. She wrote to Limercati:

Will you for once act like an intelligent being? Pray imagine that you have never known me.

I am, with perhaps a little trace of contempt, your very humble servant.
                                        GINA PIETRANERA

After reading this note, Limercati set off for one of his country seats; his love rose to frenzy, he became quite mad and talked of blowing out his brains, a thing unheard of in countries where people believe in hell. On the very next day after his arrival he wrote to the Contessa offering her his hand and his income of 200,000 lire. She sent him back his letter, with the seals unbroken, by Conte N —'s groom. Whereupon Limercati spent three years on his estates, returning every other month to Milan, but without ever having the courage to remain there, and boring all his friends with his passionate love for the Contessa and the circumstantial account of all the favours she had formerly shown him. At first, he used to add that she was ruining herself with Conte N—, and that such a connexion was bad for her reputation. As a matter of fact, the Contessa felt no sort of love at all for Conte N — and she told him as much as soon as she was quite sure of Limercati's despair. The Conte, who was well acquainted with the ways of the world, begged her on no account to divulge the sad truth she had confided to him. 'If you will be so extremely kind,' he added 'as to continue to receive me with all the outward civilities accorded to a recognized lover, I may perhaps be able to find a suitable position.'

After this heroic declaration the Contessa declined to avail herself any longer either of Conte N —'s horses or of his opera box. But for fifteen years she had been accustomed to the most elegant style of living; she had now to solve that difficult, or rather impossible, problem: how to live in Milan on a pension of fifteen hundred francs. She left her *palazzo*, took a couple of rooms on a fifth floor, and dismissed all her servants, including even her personal maid, whom she replaced by a poor old woman who worked as a general servant. This sacrifice was in actual fact less heroic and less painful than it appears to us; in Milan poverty is not a subject for ridicule, and consequently does not present itself to timorous souls as the worst of evils. After some months of this noble poverty, during which she was besieged by incessant letters from Limercati, and indeed from Conte N —, who also wished to marry her, it happened that the Marchese del Dongo, who was as a rule most frightfully mean with money, got the idea that his enemies might find some cause for exultation in his sister's miserable plight. What ! a del Dongo reduced to living on the pension that this court of Vienna, which had given him so much cause for complaint, grants to the widows of its generals !

He wrote to tell her that a suite of rooms and an allowance worthy of his sister awaited her at the castle of Grianta. The Contessa's volatile mind embraced with enthusiasm the idea of this new mode of life. It was twenty years since she had lived in that venerable castle rising majestically from among old chestnut trees planted in the days of the Sforzas. 'There,' she said to herself, 'I shall find peace and quiet, and, at my age, is that not happiness?' (As she had now reached the age of thirty-one, she thought the time had come for her to retire.) 'On that heavenly lake where I was born, a happy and peaceful life at last awaits me.'

I do not know whether she was mistaken, but what is certain is that this passionate soul, which had just refused so lightly the offer of two huge fortunes, brought happiness to the castle of Grianta. Her two nieces were beside themselves with joy. 'You have given me back the happy days of my youth,' said the Marchesa as she embraced her, 'the day before you came, I felt a hundred years old.'

The Contessa set out to visit, in Fabrizio's company, all those enchanting spots in the neighbourhood of Grianta which have been so highly praised by travellers: the Villa Melzi on the other shore of the lake, opposite the castle, which commands a fine view of it; higher up, the sacred wood of the Sfondrata; and the bold promontory separating the two arms of the lake, that of Como, so luxuriantly beautiful, and the other that runs towards Lecco, so austere, a sublime and charming spectacle, which the most renowned site in the world, the Bay of Naples, equals, but does not surpass.

It was with a feeling of ecstasy that the Contessa recaptured the memories of her early childhood and compared them with her sensations at that moment. 'The Lake of Como,' she said to herself, 'is not surrounded, like the Lake of Geneva, with wide tracts of land enclosed and cultivated according to the most approved methods, calling up ideas of money and speculation. Here, on every side, I see hills of unequal height, covered all over with clumps of trees that chance has planted, and which the hand of man has never yet spoilt, and forced to *yield a return*. Among these hills so admirably shaped, pressing on towards the lake down slopes of a strangely curious formation, I can preserve all the illusions of Tasso's and Ariosto's descriptions. Everything is noble and tender, everything speaks of love; nothing recalls the ugly spectacles of civilization. The villages half-way up the slopes are hidden in tall trees, and above the tree-tops rises the charming architecture of their graceful spires. If some tiny field, fifty paces across, comes here and there to interrupt the clumps of chestnuts and wild cherries, my satisfied eye sees growing on it plants more vigorous and happier than elsewhere. Beyond these hills, whose summits offer hermitages in every one of which one would like to dwell, my astonished eye perceives the peaks of the Alps, for ever covered in snow, and their cold austerity recalls so much of the sorrows of life as is needed to increase one's present abounding joy.

The imagination is touched by the distant sound of church bells from some little village hidden among the trees; these sounds as they float across the water that softens their tone, take on a note of gentle melancholy and resignation, which seems to say 'Life is fleeting; do not therefore show yourself so hard to please in face of the happiness at hand; make haste to enjoy it.'

The language of these enchanting spots, which have not their like in all the world, restored to the Contessa the heart she had at sixteen. She could not conceive how she could have spent so many years without revisiting the lake. 'Can it then mean,' she thought, 'that happiness has chosen for its refuge the years in which we are beginning to grow old?' She bought a boat which Fabrizio, the Marchesa and she decorated with their own hands, for in the midst of the extreme splendour maintaining in the house, there was no money available for anything. Since his disgrace the Marchese del Dongo had been twice as keen on keeping up a show of aristocratic magnificence. For instance, in order to reclaim ten feet of land from the lake, near the famous avenue of plane trees, in the direction of Cadenabbia, he was building an embankment, the estimate for which amounted to eighty thousand lire. At the end of this embankment there gradually rose a chapel modelled on the design of the famous Marchese Cagnola and built entirely of huge blocks of granite, and inside this chapel Marchesi, the sculptor then in vogue in Milan, was erecting a tomb for him on which numerous bas-reliefs would represent the brave feats of his ancestors.

Fabrizio's elder brother, the Marchesino Ascanio, tried to join the ladies in their excursions. But his aunt flung water over his powdered hair, and every day found some new trick to play on his gravity. In the end he relieved the merry troop, who dared not laugh in his presence, of the sight of his fat, pasty face. They supposed him to be the spy of his father the Marchese, and it was necessary to humour that stern despot, who had been in a furious temper ever since his enforced retirement.

Ascanio swore to be revenged on Fabrizio.

There was a storm in which they were exposed to danger. Although they were extremely short of money, they paid the two boatmen generously to say nothing to the Marchese, who was already showing much ill-temper at their taking his two daughters with them. They ran into another storm; the storms on this beautiful lake are terrible and unexpected. Gusts of wind sweep suddenly out of the two mountain gorges situated on opposite sides of the lake and join battle on the water. The Contessa wished to land in the midst of the squall and the claps of thunder; she claimed that if she were on top of a rock that stood by itself in the middle of the lake and was the size of a small room, she would witness a strange spectacle; she would see herself assailed on all sides by tumultuous waves. But in jumping out of the boat she fell into the water. Fabrizio dived in after her to save her, and both of them were carried a considerable distance. Drowning, no doubt, is not a pleasant experience; but boredom, taken by surprise, was banished from the feudal castle.

The Contessa had become greatly enamoured of the primitive character of Father Blanès and his astrological pursuits. What little money remained to her after the purchase of the boat had been spent on buying a miniature telescope acquired as a bargain, and nearly every evening, with her nieces and Fabrizio, she would install herself on the platform of one of the Gothic towers of the castle. Fabrizio was the knowledgeable one of the party, and they spent many hours up there, very merrily, and out of reach of spies.

It must be admitted that there were days when the Contessa did not address a word to anyone. She would be seen strolling under the tall chestnut trees lost in sombre musing; she had too lively an intelligence not to feel at times the boredom that comes from having no opportunity for an interchange of ideas. But next day she would be laughing again as she had laughed the day before. It was the lamentations of her sister-in-law, the Marchesa, which made such a melancholy impression on this naturally active, eager mind.

'Are we then doomed to spend all the youth that is left to us in this gloomy castle!' the Marchesa would exclaim. Before the Contessa's arrival she had not even had the courage to feel such regrets.

They lived in this way throughout the winter of 1814 to 1815. On two occasions, in spite of her poverty, the Contessa paid a few days' visit to Milan. Her object was to see a marvellous ballet by Vigano, produced at the Scala, and the Marchese did not forbid his wife to accompany her sister-in-law. They went to draw the quarterly instalments of the Contessa's little pension, and it was the poor widow of the Cisalpine general who lent a few sequins to the enormously wealthy Marchesa del Dongo. These expeditions were delightful; they invited some of their old friends to dinner, and found consolation in laughing at everything, just like children. This Italian gaiety, so full of zest and whimsical light-heartedness, made them forget the atmosphere of sombre gloom which the countenances of the Marchese and his elder son spread around them at Grianta. Fabrizio, though barely sixteen, took the place of the master of the house very admirably.

On 7 March 1815, the ladies had been back for two days from a delightful little trip to Milan. They were walking along the fine avenue of plane trees which had recently been extended to the very edge of the lake. A boat appeared, coming from the direction of Como, and making very curious signals. One of the Marchese's agents sprang out on to the embankment. Napoleon had just landed in the Gulf of Juan. Europe was simple enough to be surprised at this event, which did not at all surprise the Marchese del Dongo. He wrote his sovereign a letter full of the most cordial effusions. He placed his talents at his service together with a million of money, and informed him once again that his ministers were Jacobins and in league with the ringleaders in Paris.

On 8 March, at six o'clock in the morning, the Marchese, wearing all his orders, was making his son dictate to him the draft of a third political despatch. He was solemnly occupied in transcribing it in his fine, careful hand, on paper bearing the Sovereign's effigy as a watermark. At the very same moment, Fabrizio was being shown into Contessa Pietranera's room.

'I'm going away,' he told her, 'I'm going to join the Emperor, who is also King of Italy; he was such a good friend to your husband. I shall go by way of Switzerland. Last night, at Menaggio, my friend Vasi, the dealer in barometers, gave me his passport. Now you must give me a few napoleons, for I've only a couple myself. But if necessary I shall go on foot.'

The Contessa wept with joy and anguish. 'Good gracious!' she cried, seizing Fabrizio's hands in her own, 'Why did you have to get that idea in your head?'

She got up and went to fetch from her linen-cupboard, where it was carefully hidden, a little purse embroidered with pearls; it was all she possessed in the world.

'Take it,' she said to Fabrizio, 'but in heaven's name, don't go and get yourself killed. What would your poor mother and I have left, if you were taken from us? As for Napoleon's succeeding, that, my poor boy, is impossible; our gentlemen here will know very well how to destroy him. Didn't you hear, a week ago, in Milan, the story of twenty-three plots to assassinate him, all so carefully planned, and from which he only escaped by a miracle? And at that time he was all-powerful. And you have seen that it wasn't the will to ruin him that was lacking in our enemies; France was no longer of any account at all from the moment he left it.'

It was in a tone of the keenest emotion that the Contessa spoke to Fabrizio of Napoleon's future destiny. 'In allowing you to go to join him,' she said, 'I am sacrificing to him what is dearest to me in the world.' Fabrizio's eyes grew wet, he shed tears as he embraced the Contessa, but his determination to leave was not for one moment shaken. He explained effusively to this beloved friend all the reasons which had decided him, reasons which we take the liberty of finding somewhat comical.

'Yesterday evening, it was just seven minutes to six, we were strolling, as you know, by the shore of the lake along the plane-tree avenue, below the Casa Sommariva, and we were walking in a southerly direction. It was there that I first noticed, in the distance, the boat that was coming from Como, bearing such great news. As I gazed at this boat without thinking of the Emperor, and only envying the lot of those who are free to travel, all at once I felt myself seized with a feeling of deep emotion. The boat touched ground, the agent said something in a low tone to my father, who changed colour, and took us aside to announce the *terrible news*. I turned towards the lake with no other object but to hide the tears of joy that were flooding my eyes. Suddenly, at an immense height in the sky and to my right, I saw an eagle, Napoleon's bird. He was flying majestically past on his way to Switzerland and consequently towards Paris. "And I too," I said to myself there and then, "I will cross Switzerland with the speed of an eagle, and I will go to offer that great man a very little thing, but after all, the only thing I have to offer, the support of my feeble arm. He wished to give us a country of our own and he loved my uncle." At that instant, while I was still gazing at the eagle, in some strange way my tears ceased to flow. And the proof that this idea is heaven-sent, is that at the same moment, without any need to deliberate, I made my decision and saw how I should make this journey. In the twinkling of an eye all the sorrows that, as you know, are poisoning my life, especially on Sundays, seemed to be swept away as by a breath from heaven. I saw the mighty figure of Italy raise herself from the mire in which the Germans keep her plunged;* she stretched out her mangled arms, still half loaded with chains, towards her King and Liberator. "And I, too," I said to myself, "the as yet unknown son of that unhappy mother, I will go forth to conquer or to die beside that Man of Destiny, who sought to cleanse us from the scorn that is heaped upon us by even the most enslaved and the vilest among the inhabitants of Europe."

'You know,' he added, dropping his voice, drawing nearer to the Contessa, and gazing fixedly upon her with eyes from which fire was darting, 'you know that young chestnut tree which my mother, in the winter in which I was born, planted herself on the edge of the big stream in our forest, two leagues from here. Before doing anything else, I wanted to visit it. "The spring is not too far advanced," I said to myself. "Well then, if my tree is in leaf, that shall be a sign for me. I too must emerge from that state of torpor in which I am languishing in this cold and dreary castle." Don't you feel that these old blackened walls, the symbols now as they were once the instruments of tyranny, are a true image of the dreariness of winter? They are to me what winter is to my tree.

'Would you believe it, Gina? Yesterday evening at half past seven I reached my chestnut; it had leaves upon it, pretty little leaves that were already quite big; I kissed them, but without harming them. I turned the soil reverently around this beloved tree. Immediately after, full of a new enthusiasm, I went over the mountain. I came to Menaggio; I needed a passport to enter Switzerland. The time had flown, it was already one o'clock in the morning when I found myself at Vasi's door. I thought I should have to knock for a long time to wake him; but he was still up with three of his friends. At the first words I uttered: "You are going to join Napoleon!" he cried, and fell on my neck. The others too embraced me with rapture. "Why am I married?" one of them remarked.'

Contessa Pietranera had grown thoughtful; she felt she ought to put forward a few objections. If Fabrizio had had the least experience of the world, he would have seen quite well that the Contessa herself had no faith in the sound reasons she hastened to give him. But, failing experience, he had determination; he did not condescend

* The speaker is a passionate individual; he is rendering in prose a few lines of the famous poet Monti.

even to listen to her arguments. The Contessa was soon reduced to making him promise that he would at least inform his mother of his intention.

'She will tell my sisters about it, and they will betray my secret without knowing it,' cried Fabrizio with a sort of heroic disdain.

'Please speak with more respect,' said the Contessa, smiling through her tears, 'of the sex that will make your fortune. For men will never find you sympathetic, you have too much fire to appeal to prosaic souls.'

The Marchesa burst into tears on learning of her son's strange plan; she could not appreciate its heroism, and did everything she could to keep him from going. When she was convinced that nothing in the world, except the walls of a prison, would prevent him from leaving, she handed over to him what little money she possessed. Then she remembered that she had in her keeping, since the day before, some eight or ten small diamonds worth perhaps ten thousand lire, which the Marchese had entrusted to her to take to Milan to be set. Fabrizio's sisters came into their mother's room while the Contessa was sewing these diamonds into our hero's travelling coat. He handed the poor women back their scanty store of napoleons. His sisters were so enthusiastic over his plan, they embraced him with such loud cries of joy that he picked up the few diamonds that still remained to be hidden and tried to go off there and then.

'You will give me away without knowing it,' he said to his sisters. 'Since I have so much money, there's no need for me to take any clothes; they can be got anywhere.' He embraced these people who were so dear to him and set off at once without even attempting to go back to his room. He walked so fast, in constant fear of being followed by men on horseback, that he reached Lugano that very evening. Thanks to God, he was now in a Swiss city, and no longer in dread of being assaulted on the lonely road by constables in his father's pay. From this place, he wrote him a finely worded letter, an act of childish weakness that gave substance to the Marchese's anger.

Fabrizio took the post, and travelled through the Saint-Gothard pass; his progress was rapid, and he entered France by way of Pontarlier. The Emperor was in Paris, and there Fabrizio's troubles began. He had started out with the firm intention of speaking to the Emperor; it had never crossed his mind that this might be a difficult thing to do. In Milan he used to see Prince Eugène ten times a day, and could easily have spoken to him. In Paris, he went every morning to the courtyard of the Tuileries to watch the reviews held by Napoleon; but he was never able to get anywhere near the Emperor. Our hero imagined that all the French were as deeply disturbed as himself by the extreme peril to which the country was exposed. At table in the hotel in which he was staying he made no mystery of his plans or his devotion. He met some young men who were very pleasant and kind, still more enthusiastic than himself, and who, in a very few days, succeeded in robbing him of all the money he possessed. Fortunately, out of sheer modesty, he had not mentioned the diamonds given him by his mother.

On the morning when, after an orgy of the night before, he found out that he had certainly been robbed, he bought a fine pair of horses, engaged an old soldier, one of the horse-dealer's grooms, as his servant, and, filled with contempt for the well-spoken young men of Paris, set out to join the army. He knew nothing except that it was mustering near Maubeuge. No sooner had he reached the frontier than he felt it would be absurd for him to stay in a house, busy warming himself in front of a good fire, while the soldiers were camping out of doors. In spite of all that his servant, who was not lacking in common sense, could say to him, he rashly hurried off to join the bivouacs on the extreme edge of the frontier, on the road into Belgium. No sooner had he reached the first battalion that was stationed by the side of the road than the soldiers began to stare at this young civilian about whose dress there was nothing that suggested uniform. Night was falling, a cold wind was blowing. Fabrizio went up to a fire and offered to pay for hospitality. The soldiers gazed at each other, amazed more than anything at the idea of payment, and good-naturedly made room for him by the fire. His servant constructed a shelter for him.

An hour later, however, the regimental sergeant-major happening to pass within range of the bivouac, the soldiers went to report to him the arrival of this stranger who spoke bad French. The sergeant-major questioned Fabrizio, who spoke to him of his enthusiasm for the Emperor in an accent that aroused grave suspicions. Thereupon this N.C.O. requested him to go with him to the Colonel, whose headquarters were in a neighbouring farm. Fabrizio's servant came up with the two horses. The sight of them seemed to impress the sergeant-major so forcibly that he immediately changed his mind, and began to question the servant. The latter, an old soldier, guessing at once what was his questioner's plan of campaign, spoke of the influential protection his master enjoyed, adding that no one, for sure, was going to *prig* his fine horses from him. At once a soldier summoned by the sergeant-major caught hold of the servant by the collar; another soldier took charge of the horses, and the sergeant-major, in a very stern manner, ordered Fabrizio to follow and not to answer back.

After making him cover a good league on foot in the darkness seemingly rendered more intense by the fires of the bivouacs which lit up the horizon on every side, the sergeant-major handed Fabrizio over to an officer of the constabulary who, with a solemn air, asked him for his papers. Fabrizio produced his passport, which described him as a dealer in barometers, *travelling with his wares.*

'What fools they are!' cried the officer. 'This really is a bit too thick!'

He put a number of questions to our hero, who spoke of the Emperor and of Liberty in terms of the keenest enthusiasm; whereupon the officer was seized with a fit of uncontrollable laughter.

'Upon my word; you're not too clever, my lad!' he cried. 'It's rather too much to believe they would venture to send us young simpletons like you!' And in spite of all that Fabrizio, who wore himself out explaining that he was not really a dealer in barometers, could say to him, the officer sent him to the prison at B —, a small town in the neighbourhood, where our hero arrived about three o'clock in the morning, beside himself with rage and half-dead with exhaustion.

Fabrizio, at first astounded and then furious, understanding absolutely nothing of what was happening to him, spent thirty-three long days in this wretched prison. He wrote letter after letter to the commandant of the place, and it was the gaoler's wife, a handsome Flemish woman of six-and-thirty, who undertook to deliver them. But as she had no desire whatever to get so nice-looking a young fellow shot, and as, moreover, he paid her well, she did not fail to throw all these letters into the fire. At a very late hour in the evening, she would deign to come in and listen to the prisoner's complaints. She had told her husband that the young greenhorn had money, whereupon the prudent gaoler had allowed her a free hand. She availed herself of this permission and received a few gold napoleons, for the sergeant-major had taken nothing except the horses, and the police officer had confiscated nothing at all.

One afternoon in the month of June Fabrizio heard a violent cannonade in the distance. So they were fighting at last! His heart leapt with impatience. He also heard a great deal of noise in the town; as a matter of fact a big movement of troops was being effected; three divisions were passing through B —. When, about eleven o'clock, the gaoler's wife came in to share his troubles, Fabrizio was even more pleasant to her than usual. Then seizing hold of her hands, he said: 'Help me get out of here, I swear on my honour to return to prison as soon as the fighting has stopped.'

'That's all my eye! Have you the *needful*?'

He looked troubled, he did not know what the word *needful* meant. The gaoler's wife, seeing his reaction, concluded that he must be in low water, and instead of talking of gold napoleons as she had intended talked now only of francs.

'Listen,' she said to him, 'if you can put down a hundred francs, I will place a double napoleon on each eye of the corporal who is coming to relieve the guard during the night. He won't be able to see you getting out of prison, and if his regiment is due to march to-morrow, he will agree.'

The bargain was quickly struck. The gaoler's wife even agreed to hide Fabrizio in her own room, from which he could more easily make his escape the following morning.

The next day, before dawn, the woman in a tender mood said to Fabrizio: 'My dear boy, you are still far too young to carry on this vile trade. Take my advice, don't go back to it again!'

'But for goodness' sake!' exclaimed Fabrizio. 'Is it then a crime to wish to defend one's country?'

'That's enough. Always remember that I saved your life. Your case was clear; you would have been shot. But don't say a word to anyone, or you will lose my husband and me our job. And above all, don't ever repeat your silly tale about being a gentleman of Milan disguised as a dealer in barometers, it's too stupid. Now listen well, I'm going to give you the uniform of a hussar who died two days ago in the prison. Open your lips as little as you possibly can, but if, after all, a sergeant or an officer questions you in such a way as to force you to answer, say that you've been lying ill in the house of a peasant who took you in out of charity when you were shivering with fever in a ditch by the roadside. If your answer doesn't satisfy them, then add that you are going to rejoin your regiment. You may perhaps be arrested on account of your accent; then say that you were born in Piedmont, that you're a conscript who was left behind in France last year and all that sort of thing.'

For the first time, after thirty-three days of blind fury, Fabrizio grasped the key to all that had happened to him. They took him for a spy! He argued with the gaoler's wife, who was in a very tender mood that morning: and finally, while armed with a needle she was taking in the hussar's uniform to fit him, he gave the astonished woman a very clear account of his adventures. She believed him for a moment; he had so innocent an air, he looked so handsome in his hussar's uniform.

'Since you are so very eager to fight,' she said to him at length, half-convinced, 'you really should have enlisted in a regiment the moment you reached Paris. You had only to stand a sergeant a drink and the whole affair would have been settled.' The gaoler's wife added much good advice for the future and finally, at the first streak of dawn, she let Fabrizio out of her house, after making him swear a hundred times over that he would never mention her name, whatever happened. As soon as Fabrizio had left the little town, marching jauntily along with the hussar's sabre under his arm, he began to feel some qualms. 'Here am I', he said to himself, 'with the uniform and the marching orders of a hussar who died in prison, to which he was committed, so they say, for stealing a cow and some silver spoons and forks. I have, so to speak, inherited his identity ... and that without wishing it or expecting it in any way! Beware of prisons! The omen is clear, I shall have much to suffer from prisons!'

Not an hour had passed since Fabrizio's parting from his bene-factress when the rain began to fall so heavily that the new hussar could scarcely manage to get along, encumbered as he was by a pair of clumsy boots which had not been made for him. Happening to meet a peasant mounted upon a sorry hack, he bought the animal, explaining that he wanted it by means of signs. The gaoler's wife had recommended him to speak as little as possible, on account of his accent.

That day the army, which had just won the battle of Ligny, was marching straight on Brussels. It was the eve of the battle of Waterloo.

Towards mid-day, with the downpour of rain still continuing, he heard the sound of the guns. This happy chance entirely drove out of his memory the frightful moments of despair in which so unjust an imprisonment had recently plunged him. He rode on until night was far advanced, and then, as he was beginning to gain a little common sense, he went to seek a lodging in a peasant's house a long way off the main road. This peasant wept and pretended that everything had been taken from him. Fabrizio gave him a crown, and he found some barley. 'My horse is no beauty!' Fabrizio said to himself, 'but what does that matter, he might easily take the fancy of some sergeant-major', and he went to lie down in the stable by its side. An hour before dawn the next day, Fabrizio was on the road, and by dint of patting and fondling his horse he succeeded in making it trot. About five o'clock he heard the cannonade; it was the prelude to Waterloo.

CHAPTER 3 : *The Guns of Waterloo*

FABRIZIO soon came upon some *vivandières*, and the deep gratitude he felt towards the gaoler's wife at B — moved him to speak to them. He asked one of them where he would find the 4th Regiment of Hussars, to which he belonged.

'You would do just as well not to be in such a hurry, young soldier,' said the *cantinière*, touched by Fabrizio's pallor and his attractive eyes. 'Your wrist is not yet strong enough for the sabre-thrusts they'll be giving today. All the same, if you had a musket, I don't say you couldn't perhaps let off your round as well as any of them.'

This advice did not please Fabrizio; but, however much he urged on his horse, he could go no faster than the *cantinière* in her cart. From time to time the sound of the guns seemed to come nearer and prevented them from hearing each other speak, for Fabrizio was so beside himself with enthusiasm and happiness that he had resumed the conversation. Each word from the *cantinière* increased his happiness twofold by making him understand it. With the exception of his real name and his escape from prison, he ended by confiding everything to this woman who seemed so kind. She was very much astonished and did not understand anything at all of what this handsome young soldier was telling her.

'I see what it is,' she exclaimed at length with an air of triumph. 'You're a young civilian who has fallen in love with the wife of some captain in the 4th Hussars. Your lady-love will have made you a present of the uniform you're wearing and you're hurrying after her. As sure as God's in heaven, you've never been a soldier, but, like the decent lad you are, since your regiment's under fire, you want to join it and not let them think you're a milksop.'

Fabrizio agreed with everything; it was his only way of getting good advice. 'I know nothing at all of the ways of these French people,' he said to himself, 'and if I'm not guided by someone, I shall manage to get myself thrown into prison again, and they'll steal my horse.'

'First of all, my lad,' said the *cantinière*, who was becoming more and more of a friend to him, 'confess that you're not yet twenty-one; at the very most you might be seventeen.'

This was the truth, and Fabrizio willingly admitted it.

'Then you're not even a conscript; it's merely because of Madame's bright eyes that you're going to get your bones broken. Bless my soul, she doesn't ask for much. If you've still got some of those *yellow-boys* she handed you, you must first of all buy yourself another horse. Look how your old screw pricks up its ears when the booming of the guns comes a little closer. That one there is a peasant's horse, it'll be the death of you the moment you reach the line. That white smoke you see over there above the hedge, that's the infantry firing, my boy! So get yourself ready to be in a fine stew when you hear the bullets whistling round you. You'd do as well too to have a bite while you have the time.'

Fabrizio followed this advice, and handing a napoleon to the woman, begged her to take what was owing.

'It makes your heart bleed to see him!' cried the woman. 'The poor lad doesn't even know how to spend his money. You'd well deserve it if, after grabbing your money, I made my Cocotte go off at a gallop. I'm damned if your screw could follow me. What would you do, you silly booby, when you saw me scampering off? You must learn that when the big brutes growl you should never show your gold. Look here,' she added, 'here's eighteen francs, fifty centimes, and your breakfast costs you thirty sous. Now, we shall soon have some horses for sale. If the animal is a small one, you'll give ten francs for it, and in any case not more than twenty, even if it should be the horse of the Four Sons of Aymon.'

Breakfast over, the *vivandière*, who was still holding forth, was interrupted by a woman who had come across the fields, and now stepped on to the road.

'Hi, there!' the woman shouted. 'Hullo, Margot! Your 6th Light Horse are over on the right.'

'I must leave you, my boy,' said the *vivandière* to our hero, 'but in honest truth I feel sorry for you. I've taken quite a liking to you, blow me if I haven't. You don't know a thing about anything, and you're going to get caught out, as sure as God's in heaven! Come along to the 6th Light with me.'

'I quite realize that I know nothing,' Fabrizio answered, 'but I want to fight, and I'm determined to go over there towards that white smoke.'

'Look how your horse is twitching his ears! As soon as he gets over there, however little strength he has, he'll prove too strong for you to handle, he'll start galloping, and heaven knows where he'll lead you. Will you be guided by me? As soon as you find yourself among the soldier boys, pick up a musket and a cartridge pouch, get down beside the men and do what they do, and do it exactly like them. But, good Lord, I bet you don't even know how to bite open a cartridge.'

Fabrizio, though stung to the quick, admitted all the same to his new friend that she had guessed rightly.

'The poor lad! he'll be killed straight off, and that's God's truth; it won't take long. You really must come with me,' went on the *cantinière* in a tone of authority.

'But I want to fight.'

'And you shall fight too; why the 6th Light is famous for that and there's fighting enough today for everyone.'

'But shall we soon get to the regiment?'

'In a quarter of an hour at the most.'

'With this good woman's recommendation,' said Fabrizio to himself, 'my ignorance of everything won't make them take me for a spy, and I shall get a chance of fighting.' At that moment the noise of the guns redoubled, each volley following straight on top of the last. 'It's like saying one's beads,' said Fabrizio.

'We're beginning to hear the infantry fire quite plainly now,' said the *cantinière*, giving a flick of her whip to her little horse, which seemed quite excited by the firing.

The *cantinière* turned to the right and took a side road that led through the fields; there was a foot of mud in it; the little cart seemed on the verge of getting stuck fast. Fabrizio gave a shove to the wheel. His horse fell twice. Soon the road, although less full of water, was nothing more than a path across the turf. Fabrizio had not gone five hundred paces when his nag stopped short. It was a corpse, lying across the path, which terrified horse and rider alike.

Fabrizio's face, which was naturally very pale, took on a very decidedly greenish tinge. The *cantinière*, after looking at the dead man, said, as though speaking to herself: 'That's not one of our Division.' Then, raising her eyes to look at our hero, she burst out laughing.

'Aha, my boy!' she cried. 'There's a titbit for you!' Fabrizio remained as if petrified by horror. What struck him most was the dirtiness of the feet of this corpse which had already been stripped of its shoes and left with nothing but a miserable pair of trousers all stained with blood.

'Come nearer,' said the *cantinière*, 'get off your horse, you'll have to get used to such things. Look,' she cried, 'he's got it in the head.'

A bullet, entering on one side of the nose, had come out by the opposite temple, and disfigured the corpse in a hideous fashion, leaving it with one eye still open.

'Get off your horse then, lad,' said the *cantinière*, 'and give him a shake of the hand, and see if he'll return it.'

Without hesitating, although almost ready to give up the ghost from disgust, Fabrizio flung himself off his horse and taking the hand of the corpse gave it a vigorous shake. Then he stood still as though no life was left in him. He did not feel he had the strength to mount his horse again. What most particularly horrified him was that still open eye.

'The *vivandière* will think me a coward,' he said to himself bitterly. But he felt it impossible to make any movement; he would have fallen down. It was a frightful moment; Fabrizio was on the point of going off into a dead faint. The *vivandière* noticed this, jumped lightly down from her little vehicle, and without saying a word, held out to him a glass of brandy which he swallowed at a gulp. He was able to remount his nag, and went on his way again without speaking. The *vivandière* glanced at him now and again out of the corner of her eye.

'You shall fight tomorrow, my boy,' she said at length, 'today you shall stay with me. You can see very well the business of soldiering is something you'll have to learn.'

'On the contrary, I want to start fighting at once,' said our hero in a sombre tone that seemed to the *vivandière* to augur well. The noise of the guns grew twice as loud and seemed to be coming nearer. The explosions were beginning to form a sort of figured bass; there was no interval between one explosion and the next, and above this figured bass, which resembled the roar of a torrent in the distance, the sound of musketry firing could be clearly distinguished.

At this point the road began to wind through a spinney. The *vivandière* saw three or four of our soldiers coming towards her as fast as their legs could carry them. She jumped briskly down from her cart and ran to hide herself fifteen to twenty paces from the road. She crouched down in a hole which had been left where a big tree had recently been uprooted. 'Now,' thought Fabrizio 'I shall see whether I am a coward!' He stopped by the side of the little cart which the woman had abandoned and drew his sabre. The soldiers paid no attention to him and passed at a run alongside the wood, to the left of the road.

'They're ours,' said the *vivandière* calmly, as she came back, quite breathless, to her little cart. 'If your horse could manage to gallop, I'd say to you: push on ahead to the end of the wood, and see if there's anyone on the plain.' Fabrizio did not wait to be told twice. He tore off a branch from a poplar, stripped off its leaves and began to beat his horse with all his might. For a moment the nag broke into a gallop, then fell back into its usual slow trot. The *vivandière* put her horse into a gallop. 'Stop, will you, stop!' she called out to Fabrizio. Soon they were both of them clear of the wood. As they reached the edge of the plain they heard the most frightful din, guns and muskets thundered on every side – to right, to left, and behind them – and as the spinney out of which they were emerging stood on a mound rising eight to ten feet above the plain, they had a fairly good view of a corner of the battle; but there was in fact no one to be seen in the meadow beyond the wood. This meadow was bordered, about a thousand paces away, by a long line of willows, with thickly clustering leaves. Above the willows appeared a cloud of white smoke which now and then rose whirling into the sky.

'If only I knew where the regiment was,' said the *cantinière*, somewhat at a loss. 'It won't do to go straight across this great meadow. By the way,' she said to Fabrizio, 'if you see one of the enemy, stick him with the point of your sabre, don't go and amuse yourself by slashing at him.'

At this moment the *cantinière* caught sight of the four soldiers we have just mentioned; they were coming out of the wood on to the plain to the left of the road. One of them was on horseback.

'There's just what you want,' she said to Fabrizio. 'Hi, there!' she called to the man on the horse, 'come over here and have a glass of brandy.' The soldiers approached.

'Where's the 6th Light?' she called out.

'Over there, five minutes away, across that canal which runs along by the willows; and by the way, their Colonel Macon has just been killed.'

'You there, will you take five francs for your horse?'

'Five francs! You're not half funny, my good woman. An

officer's horse I mean to sell for five napoleons within the next quarter of an hour.'

'Give me one of your napoleons,' said the *vivandière* to Fabrizio. Then going up to the mounted soldier, she said to him: 'Dismount quickly, here's your napoleon.'

The soldier dismounted, Fabrizio leapt gaily into the saddle and the *vivandière* unstrapped the little portmanteau which was on the nag.

'Give me a hand, you fellows!' she said to the soldiers. 'Is that the way you leave a lady to do all the work!'

But no sooner had the captured horse felt the weight of the portmanteau than he began to rear, and Fabrizio, who was an excellent horseman, had need of all his strength to hold him.

'That's a good sign,' said the *vivandière*. 'The gentleman is not used to being tickled by portmanteaus.'

'A general's horse,' exclaimed the man who had sold him, 'a horse that's worth ten napoleons if he's worth a farthing.'

'Here are twenty francs,' said Fabrizio, who was beside himself with joy at feeling his legs astride a really lively horse.

Just at that moment a round shot landed amongst the row of willows, striking them slantwise; and Fabrizio enjoyed the curious sight of seeing all the little branches flying to left and right as if they had been sliced off by a scythe.

'Look, there's the good old cannonade pushing forward,' said the soldier to him as he took the twenty francs. It was now about two o'clock.

Fabrizio was still under the spell of this strange spectacle when a group of generals, followed by a score of hussars, came galloping across one corner of the huge field on the edge of which he had halted. His horse neighed, reared two or three times in succession, then began jerking his head and tugging violently at the bridle that was holding him back. 'All right, here we go!' said Fabrizio to himself.

The horse, left to its own devices, dashed off at full speed to join the escort that was following the generals. Fabrizio counted four gold-laced hats. A quarter of an hour later, from a few words said by one hussar to his neighbour, Fabrizio gathered that one of these generals was the famous Marshal Ney. His happiness was at its height; he could not, however, make out which one of the generals was the Marshal. He would have given everything in the world to know, but he remembered that he ought not to speak. The escort pulled up to get across a wide ditch, left full of water from the rain of the previous day. It was bordered by tall trees and formed the left-hand boundary of the field on the farther side of which Fabrizio had bought the horse. Nearly all the hussars had dismounted; the bank of the ditch was very steep and extremely slippery, and the water lay quite three or four feet below the level of the field. Fabrizio, absent-minded in his joy, was thinking more of Marshal Ney and of glory than of his horse which, being highly excited, jumped into the canal, and sent the water spurting up to a considerable height. One of the generals was completely drenched by the column of water and swore aloud: 'Devil take the damned brute!' Fabrizio felt deeply hurt by this insult. 'Can I ask him to apologize?' he wondered.

Meanwhile, to prove he was not so clumsy after all, he tried to make his horse climb up the opposite bank of the ditch; but this rose perpendicularly up, and was five or six feet high. He had to abandon the attempt. Then he rode upstream, with the water coming up to his horse's head, and finally came upon a sort of drinking-place for cattle. By this gentle slope he was easily able to reach the field on the other side of the dike. He was the first man of the escort to appear there. He started to trot proudly along the bank. Down below, in the dike, the hussars were floundering about, somewhat embarrassed by their position, for in many places the water was five feet deep. Two or three horses took fright and tried to swim, thus making an appalling mess. A sergeant noticed the manoeuvre that this raw youngster, who looked so little like a soldier, had just carried out.

'Get back on your horses!' he called out. 'There is a drinking place on the left.' And gradually the whole party crossed over.

On reaching the farther bank, Fabrizio had found the generals there by themselves. The noise of the guns seemed to him to be getting twice as loud. He could hardly hear the general whom he had given such a soaking, and who now shouted in his ear:

'Where did you get that horse?'

Fabrizio was so agitated that he replied in Italian:

'*L'ho comprato poco fa.*' (I bought it a little while back.)

'What's that you say?' shouted the general.

But at that moment the din became so terrific that Fabrizio could not answer him. We must admit that our hero was very little of a hero at this juncture. However, fear came to him only as a secondary emotion, he was principally shocked by the noise, which hurt his ears. The escort broke into a gallop. They were crossing a large patch of tilled land which lay beyond the dike, and this field was strewn with bodies.

'The red-coats! the red-coats!' the hussars of the escort shouted gleefully, and at first Fabrizio did not understand. Then he noticed that as a matter of fact almost all these bodies wore red uniforms. One detail made him shudder with horror: he noticed that many of these unfortunate 'red-coats' were still alive. They were calling out, evidently asking for help, but no one stopped to give it to them. Our hero, being most humane, took infinite pains to see that his horse did not plant his hoof on any red uniform. The escort halted; Fabrizio, who was not paying sufficient attention to his duties as a soldier, went galloping on with his eyes fixed on one of these poor wounded wretches.

'Halt there, you infernal young ass!' the sergeant shouted to him.

Fabrizio discovered that he was twenty paces on the generals' right front, and precisely in the direction in which they gazing through their field-glasses. As he came back to take his place at the tail of the other hussars, who had halted a few paces to the rear, he noticed the stoutest of these generals speaking to his neighbour, also a general, in a tone of authority and almost of reprimand; he was swearing. Fabrizio could not restrain his curiosity; and, in spite of the warning not to speak, which his friend the gaoler's mate had given him, he prepared a short sentence in good French, quite correct, and said to him:

'Who is that general *making mincemeat* of the one next to him?'

'Why to be sure it's the Marshal!'

'What Marshal?'

'Marshal Ney, you blockhead! Why, where have you been serving up to now?'

Fabrizio, although extremely sensitive, had no thought of resenting this insult; he was gazing, lost in childish admiration, at this famous Prince de la Moskowa, the 'bravest of the brave'.

Suddenly they all moved off at a full gallop. A few minutes later Fabrizio saw, twenty paces ahead of him, a piece of tilled land that was being ploughed up in a singular fashion. The bottoms of the furrows were full of water, and the very damp soil that formed the ridges of these furrows was flying about in little black lumps flung three or four feet into the air. Fabrizio noted this curious effect as he was passing; then his mind turned to dreaming of the Marshal and his glory. He heard a sharp cry close by him; it was two hussars falling struck by shot; and when he looked round at them, they were already twenty paces behind the escort. What seemed to him horrible was a horse streaming with blood that was writhing on the ploughed land, its hooves entangled in its own entrails. It tried to follow the other horses; the blood ran down into the mire.

'Ah! so I am under fire at last,' he said to himself. 'I have seen the firing!' he repeated with a sense of satisfaction. 'Now I am a real soldier.' At that moment, the escort began to go at a tearing pace, and our hero realized that it was shot from the guns that was making the earth fly up all around him. He looked in vain in the direction from which the shots were coming. He saw the white smoke of the battery an enormous distance away, and, in the midst of the steady and continuous rumble produced by the firing of the guns, he seemed to hear volleys of shot much closer at hand. He could not make head or tail of what was happening.

At that moment, the generals and their escort dropped down into a lane filled with water which ran five feet below the level of the plain.

The Marshal halted and took another look through his glasses. This time Fabrizio could examine him at his leisure. He found him to be very fair, with a huge red face. 'We haven't any faces like that in Italy,' he said to himself. 'With my pale cheeks and my auburn hair, I shall never look like that,' he added sadly. To him these words implied: 'I shall never be a hero.' He looked at the hussars; with one exception, they all had fair moustaches. If Fabrizio was gazing at the hussars, they too were all of them looking at him. Their stares made him blush and, to get rid of his embarrassment, he turned his head towards the enemy. Here were widely extended lines of men in red, but what greatly surprised him was that these men seemed to be of very short stature. Their long files, which were regiments or divisions, appeared no higher than hedges. A line of red-coated cavalry was coming forwards at a trot and making towards the sunken road along which the Marshal and his escort had begun to make their way slowly, floundering in the mud. The smoke made it impossible to distinguish anything in the direction in which they were advancing. Now and then a few men moving at a gallop could be seen standing out against this background of white smoke.

Suddenly, from the direction of the enemy, four men could be seen approaching at a tearing pace. 'Ah! we are being attacked,' he said to himself; then he saw two of these men addressing the Marshal. One of the generals on the latter's staff set off at a gallop towards the enemy, followed by two hussars of the escort and by the four men who had just come up. On the other side of a little dike which their whole party crossed, Fabrizio found himself beside a sergeant who looked a good-natured sort of fellow. 'I must speak to this one,' he said to himself, 'then perhaps they'll stop staring at me.' He remained sunk in thought for a considerable time.

'Sir,' he said at length to the sergeant, 'this is the first time I have been present at a battle. But is this one a real battle?'

'You bet it is! But look here, who are you?'

'I'm the brother of a captain's wife.'

'And what is he called, your captain?'

Fabrizio was terribly embarrassed; he had never anticipated this question. Fortunately the Marshal and his escort set off again at a gallop.

'What French name shall I say?' he wondered. At length he remembered the name of the proprietor of the hotel in which he had stayed in Paris. He brought his horse close up to the sergeant's, and shouted to him at the top of his voice: 'Captain Meunier!' The other, not hearing properly on account of the roar of the guns, replied: 'Ah! Captain Teulier. Well, he's been killed.' 'Three cheers!' said Fabrizio to himself. 'Captain Teulier. I must play the mourner. Dear, dear!' he exclaimed aloud, assuming a woeful expression.

They had left the sunken road and were crossing a small meadow. They were tearing along at a breakneck speed, shots were coming over again, the Marshal headed towards a cavalry division. The escort found themselves surrounded by dead and wounded men; but this spectacle no longer made such an impression on our hero; he had other things to think of.

While the escort was halted, he caught sight of the little cart of a *cantinière*, and, his tender feeling towards this worthy sisterhood prevailing over everything else, he set off at a gallop to join her.

'Stay where you are, you blasted idiot,' the sergeant shouted after him.

'What can he do to me here?' thought Fabrizio, and he went on galloping towards the *cantinière*. When he put spurs to his horse he had had some hope that it might be his kind *cantinière* of that morning. The horse and the little cart were very much like hers, but their owner was quite different, and our hero thought she looked really unpleasant. As he came up to her Fabrizio heard her say: 'And he was such a good-looking fellow, too!' A very ugly sight awaited the new soldier. They were sawing off a cuirassier's leg at the thigh, a handsome young fellow of five foot ten. Fabrizio shut his eyes and drank four glasses of brandy one after the other.

'How you go about it, young whippersnapper!' cried the *cantinière*. The brandy gave him an idea: 'I must buy the goodwill of my comrades, the hussars of the escort.'

'Give me the rest of the bottle,' he said to the *vivandière*.

'But do you realize,' she answered, 'that what's left of it costs ten francs, on a day like this?'

As he rejoined the escort at a gallop the sergeant exclaimed: 'Ah! you're bringing us a drop o' drink. Was that why you deserted? Hand it over.'

The bottle went round; the last man to take it threw it up into the air after he had drunk. 'Thanks, pal!' he cried to Fabrizio. All eyes were gazing at him with goodwill. These glances lifted a hundred pound weight from Fabrizio's heart, it was one of those hearts of over-delicate make which require the friendship of those around them. So at last he was no longer looked at askance by his comrades; there was a bond between them!

Fabrizio drew a deep breath, then in a calm voice said to the sergeant: 'And if Captain Teulier has been killed where shall I find my sister?' He fancied himself a little Machiavelli to be saying Teulier so naturally instead of Meunier.

'You'll find that out to-night,' replied the sergeant.

The escort moved on again and made its way towards some infantry divisions. Fabrizio felt quite drunk; he had taken too much brandy, and was swaying slightly in his saddle. He remembered very opportunely a remark that his mother's coachman had often made to him: 'When you've been lifting your elbow, look straight between your horse's ears, and do like the man who's next to you.' The Marshal stopped for some time beside some cavalry units to whom he gave orders to charge; but for an hour or two our hero was barely

conscious of what was going on around him. He was feeling terribly
tired; whenever his horse started to gallop he slumped down over
the saddle like a lump of lead.

Suddenly the sergeant called out to his men: 'Can't you see the
Emperor, you blasted fools?' Whereupon the escort shouted, 'Long
live the Emperor!' at the top of their voices. It can well be imagined
that our hero stared till his eyes started out of his head, but all he saw
was some generals galloping, also followed by an escort. The long
floating plumes of horsehair which the dragoons of the bodyguard
wore on their helmets prevented him from distinguishing their faces.
'So I have missed seeing the Emperor on a field of battle, all because
of those cursed glasses of brandy!' This reflection quite roused him
out of his stupor.

They went down once more into a road filled with water; the
horses wanted to drink.

'So that really was the Emperor who went by just then?' he asked
the man beside him.

'Why, for sure, the one who had no braid on his coat. How was it
you didn't see him?' his comrade answered kindly. Fabrizio felt a
strong desire to gallop after the Emperor's escort and attach himself
to it. What happiness it would be to take a real part in a war in the
train of this hero! It was for this that he had come to France. 'I am
quite at liberty to do so,' he said to himself, 'for indeed I have no
other reason for carrying out my present duties save the will of my
horse, which started galloping after these generals.'

What made Fabrizio decide to stay where he was was that his new
comrades, the hussars, were treating him kindly. He was beginning
to fancy himself the intimate friend of all the soldiers with whom he
had been galloping for the last few hours. He saw springing up
between himself and them that noble friendship of the heroes of
Tasso and Ariosto. If he were to attach himself to the Emperor's
escort, there would be fresh acquaintances to be made; perhaps they
would frown upon him, for these other cavalry men were dragoons,
and he himself was wearing a hussar's uniform like all the rest who
were following the Marshal. The way in which they now looked at
him set our hero upon a pinnacle of happiness; he would have done
anything in the world for his comrades; his mind and his soul were
soaring aloft in the upper ether. Everything seemed to him to have
taken on a new aspect now that he was among friends, he was dying

to ask them all sorts of questions. 'But I'm still a little drunk,' he said to himself, 'I must remember what the gaoler's wife told me.'

He noticed on leaving the sunken road that the escort was no longer with Marshal Ney; the general they were following was tall and thin, with a severe expression and an awe-inspiring eye. This general was none other than Comte d'A —, the Lieutenant Robert of 15 May 1796. How delighted he would have been to meet Fabrizio del Dongo!

It was already some considerable time since Fabrizio had noticed the earth flying up in dark particles on being struck by shot. They now arrived at the rear of a regiment of cuirassiers; he could hear quite distinctly the rattle of the grape-shot against their breastplates, and he saw several men fall.

The sun was already very low, and it was on the point of setting when the escort, coming out of a sunken road, mounted a little slope three or four feet high to enter a ploughed field. Fabrizio heard a curious little sound quite close to him. He turned his head; four men had fallen with their horses; the general himself had been thrown off his horse, but he was getting up again, covered in blood. Fabrizio looked at the hussars who had been flung to the ground. Three of them were still making convulsive movements, the fourth cried: 'Pull me out from underneath!' The sergeant and two or three men had dismounted to assist the general, who, leaning upon his aide-de-camp, was attempting to walk a few steps. He was trying to get away from his horse, which lay on its back on the ground, struggling and lashing out furiously with its hooves.

The sergeant came up to Fabrizio. At that moment our hero heard someone behind him say quite close to his ear: 'This is the only one that can still gallop.' He felt himself seized by the feet; they were taken out of the stirrups at the same time as someone gripped his body under the arms. He was lifted over his horse's tail, and then let slip to the ground where he landed in a sitting position.

The aide-de-camp took Fabrizio's horse by the bridle; the general, with the help of the sergeant, mounted and rode off at a gallop; he was quickly followed by the six survivors of the escort. Fabrizio got to his feet in a furious rage, and began to run after them shouting: '*Ladri! Ladri!*' (Thieves! Thieves!) It was rather comical to be running after thieves in the middle of a battlefield.

The escort and the general, Comte d'A —, were soon lost to sight behind a row of willows. Fabrizio, mad with rage, also arrived at this same row; he found himself right up against a very deep dike, which he crossed. Then, on reaching the other side, he began to swear again as he saw once more, but far away in the distance, the general and his escort vanishing among the trees. 'Thieves! Thieves!' he cried, this time in French. Overcome with despair, not so much at the loss of his horse as on account of the treachery to himself, he let himself sink down by the side of the ditch, tired out and dying of hunger. If his fine horse had been taken from him by the enemy, he would not have given the matter another thought. But to see himself betrayed and robbed by that sergeant whom he liked so much and by those hussars whom he had looked upon as brothers! That was what broke his heart. He could find no consolation for such an infamous action, and, leaning his back against a willow, he began to shed hot tears.

He was abandoning one by one all those fine dreams of a sublime and knightly friendship, like that of the heroes of *Gerusalemme Liberata*. To see death come to one was nothing, when surrounded by heroic and tender hearts, by noble friends who clasped you by the hand at the moment when you breathed your last! But to keep your enthusiasm when surrounded by a pack of scoundrels! Like all men in a fit of anger Fabrizio exaggerated. At the end of a quarter of an hour of such self-pity, he noticed that the shot was beginning to arrive within range of the row of trees in whose shade he was meditating. He got up and tried to find his bearings. He scanned those meadows bordered by a wide dike and the row of leafy willows; he thought he knew where he was. He saw a body of infantry crossing the ditch and entering the fields about a quarter of a league in front of him. 'I was nearly falling asleep,' he said to himself, 'I must see that I'm not taken prisoner.' And he began to walk forward very quickly. As he advanced, his mind was set at rest; he recognized the uniforms. The regiments by which he had been afraid of being intercepted were French. He cut across to the right to join them.

After the mental anguish of having been so shamefully betrayed and robbed, there came another which, at every moment, made itself felt more keenly; he was really starving. It was therefore with the utmost joy that after walking or rather running for ten minutes, he saw that the infantry corps, which had also been moving very rapidly, was halting to take up a position. A few minutes later, he was in the midst of the nearest group of soldiers.

'My friends, could you sell me a bit of bread?'

'I say, this fellow here takes us for bakers!'

This unkind remark and the general jeers of laughter that followed it crushed Fabrizio's spirit. So war was no longer that noble and universal impulse of souls devoted to glory that he had figured it to be from Napoleon's proclamations! He sat down, or rather let himself sink down, on the grass; he turned very pale. The soldier who had spoken to him, and who had stopped ten paces off to clean the lock of his musket with his handkerchief, came nearer and threw him a piece of bread. Then, seeing Fabrizio did not pick it up, the soldier put a bit of this bread into his mouth. Fabrizio opened his eyes, and ate the bread without having the strength to speak. When at length he looked round for the soldier to pay him, he found himself alone; the men nearest to him were now a hundred paces distant and were marching. He got up mechanically and followed them. He entered a wood; he was well-nigh dropping with weariness, and was already looking round for a suitable spot to lie down in. But what was his joy on recognizing first of all the horse, then the cart, and finally the *cantinière* of that morning! She ran up to him and was alarmed at his appearance.

'Just walk a bit farther, my lad,' she said to him. 'You're wounded then? And where's your fine horse?' As she was speaking thus she led him towards her cart, and made him get up on it, supporting him under the arms. No sooner was he in the cart than our hero, utterly worn out, fell fast asleep.

NOTHING could wake him; neither the musket shots fired close by the little cart, nor the trotting of the horse which the *cantinière* was belabouring with all her might. The regiment, attacked unexpectedly by swarms of Prussian cavalry, after imagining all day that victory would be theirs, was now beating a retreat, or rather fleeing, in the direction of France.

The Colonel, a handsome young man, and a canny fellow, who had only just succeeded Macon, had been cut down. The major who had taken his place, an old man with white hair, ordered the regiment to halt. 'Damn you,' he said to his men. 'In the days of the Republic, we waited until we were forced to by the enemy before taking to our heels ... Defend every inch of ground, and let yourselves be killed!' he cried, swearing at them. 'It is the soil of your native land that the Prussians now seek to invade!'

The little cart pulled up; Fabrizio awoke with a start. The sun had set a long time back; he was quite astonished to see that it was almost dark. The troops were running in all directions in a state of confusion that amazed our hero; he thought they looked rather sheepish.

'What's up?' he asked the *cantinière*.

'Nothing at all. It's only that we've come a mucker, my lad; it's the Prussian cavalry, mowing us down, that's all. That idiot of a general thought at first it was ours. Come along, quick, and help me mend Cocotte's trace; it's got broken.'

A few musket shots rang out ten paces away. Our hero, now in good fettle, said to himself: 'But actually, I haven't done any fighting the whole of the day: I have only escorted a general. I must go and fight,' he said to the *cantinière*.

'Don't worry, you'll fight, and more than you want to! We're done for.'

'Aubry, my lad,' she called out to a corporal who was passing, 'just look and see how my little cart's getting on now and then.'

'Are you going to fight?' Fabrizio asked Aubry.

'Oh, no! I'm just putting on my pumps to go to a dance!'

'I'll follow you.'

'Take care of the little hussar, I tell you,' cried the *cantinière*. 'The young gentleman's plucky.' Corporal Aubry strode on without saying a word. Some eight or ten soldiers ran up and joined him; he led them behind a big oak surrounded by brambles. On reaching it he posted them along the edge of the wood, still without uttering a word, on a widely extended front with each man at least ten paces from the next.

'Now then, you fellows,' said the corporal, speaking for the first time, 'don't fire till I give you orders; remember you've only got three rounds each.'

'But what on earth's happening?' Fabrizio wondered. At length, when he found himself alone with the corporal, he said to him: 'I haven't got a gun.'

'Just hold your tongue, then. Go forward there; fifty paces in front of the wood you'll find one of those poor fellows of the regiment who've just been cut down. You will take his cartridge-pouch and his musket. Don't go and plunder a wounded man, however; take the musket and cartridge-pouch from one who's well and truly dead, and hurry up so you don't get shot by one of our fellows.' Fabrizio set off at a run and very quickly returned with a musket and a cartridge-pouch.

'Load your musket and post yourself behind this tree, and whatever you do don't fire until I give you orders to. God almighty!' said the corporal breaking off, 'he doesn't even know how to load his weapon!' He helped Fabrizio to do this while going on with his instructions. 'If one of the enemy's cavalry gallops at you to cut you down, get round behind your tree and don't let fly until your cavalryman's within short range, three paces from you. You must have your bayonet practically touching his uniform.'

'And do throw that great sabre away,' cried the corporal. 'Good God! do you want it to trip you up? A fine sort of soldier they're sending us nowadays!' As he spoke he himself took hold of the sabre and flung it angrily away.

'Now then you, wipe the flint of your musket with your handkerchief. But have you never fired a musket?'

'I'm used to hunting.'

'Thank God for that,' went on the corporal with a loud sigh. 'Now mind above all you don't fire until I give the order.' And he went off.

Fabrizio was full of joy. 'At last I'm really going to fight,' he said to himself, 'and kill one of the enemy! This morning they were sending cannon-balls at us, and I for my part was doing nothing but expose myself to the risk of getting killed; that's a fool's game.' He gazed all round him with extreme curiosity. Before long he heard seven or eight shots fired quite close at hand; but as he received no order to fire he kept quiet behind his tree. It was almost night; it seemed to him as if he were by some chance out bear-shooting on the mountains of Tramezzina, above Grianta. A hunter's dodge occurred to him; he took a cartridge from his pouch and removed the bullet. 'If I see him,' he said to himself, ' I mustn't miss him,' and he slipped the second bullet into the barrel of his gun. He heard two shots fired quite close to his tree. At the same moment he saw a horseman in a blue uniform passing at a gallop in front of him, going from right to left. 'He's more than three paces away,' he said to himself, 'but at that range I'm sure to hit him.' He kept his musket carefully pointing at the trooper and at last pulled the trigger; both horse and trooper fell.

Our hero fancied himself on a shooting party; he ran joyfully out towards the game he had just shot down. He was already touching the man, who seemed to him to be dying, when two Prussian troopers came charging at him with incredible speed to cut him down. Fabrizio dashed off as fast as his legs would carry him towards the wood, flinging down his musket in order to run more easily. The Prussian troopers were not more than three paces from him when he reached a newly planted clump of young oaks as thick as one's arm and standing very erect, which fringed the wood. These little oaks held up the troopers for a moment, but they passed through and continued their pursuit of Fabrizio along a clearing. Once again they were within an ace of reaching him when he slipped in among eight to ten big trees. At that moment his face came near to being scorched by the flame of five or six musket shots let off just in front of him. He ducked his head; when he raised it again he found himself face to face with the corporal.

'You killed your man?' Corporal Aubry asked him.

'Yes, but I've lost my musket.'

'It isn't muskets we're short of. You're a damn good fellow; though you do look as green as they make 'em. You've won through all right and these men here have just missed the two who were chasing you and coming straight towards them. I didn't see them myself. What we've go to do now is to do a quick bunk from here. The Regiment must be a quarter of a league away, and, what's more, there's a bit of open field in which we may find ourselves surrounded and taken.'

As he spoke the corporal went marching off at a brisk pace at the head of his ten men. Two hundred paces farther on, as they entered the little field he had mentioned, they met a wounded general who was being carried by an aide-de-camp and an orderly.

'You must give me four men,' he said in a faint voice to the corporal. 'I've got to be carried to the field hospital. One of my legs is shattered.'

'Go to hell!' answered the corporal, 'you and all your generals. You've all of you betrayed the Emperor today.'

'What!' cried the general, in a furious rage, 'you won't obey my orders! Do you know that I am General Count B —, commanding your Division,' and so on. He waxed rhetorical. The aide-de-camp rushed at the men. The corporal gave him a thrust in the arm with his bayonet, and then made off with all his party at the double. 'I wish they were all like you,' he repeated with an oath, 'with all their legs and their arms shattered! A pack of stupid measly rascals! All of them in the pay of the Bourbons and traitors to the Emperor!' Fabrizio listened thunderstruck to this frightful accusation.

About ten o'clock that night the little band came up with their regiment on the outskirts of a big village made up of several narrow streets, but Fabrizio noticed that Corporal Aubry avoided speaking to any of the officers. 'It's impossible to advance!' cried the corporal. All the streets were jammed with infantry, with cavalry, and, worst of all, with gun-carriages and wagons belonging to the artillery. The corporal made his way to the top of three of the streets; after walking twenty paces he had to stop. Everyone was swearing and getting out of temper.

'Yet another traitor in command,' exclaimed the corporal. 'If the enemy has the sense to surround the village we shall all be caught like rats in a trap. Follow me, you fellows.' Fabrizio looked round him; there were only six men left with the corporal. Through a big gate that stood open they passed into a huge courtyard; from this yard they made their way into a stable, the back door of which gave them entry into a garden. They lost their way there for a moment and wandered blindly round and round. But at last, after getting through a hedge, they found themselves in a huge field of buckwheat. In under half an hour, guided by the shouts and a medley of noises, they had come out again upon the high road beyond the village. The ditches along this road were filled with muskets that had been thrown down there; Fabrizio selected one of these. But the road, although very broad, was so encumbered with soldiers in flight and baggage-wagons that in the next half-hour the corporal and Fabrizio had barely advanced five hundred paces. They were told that this road led to Charleroi.

As the village clock struck eleven the corporal said: 'Let's cut across the fields again.' The little party was now reduced to three men, the corporal, and Fabrizio. When they were a quarter of a league from the high road, 'I can't go any farther,' said one of the soldiers. 'Ditto me,' said another.

'That's good news! We're all in the same fix,' said the corporal, 'but do what I tell you and you'll come out all right.' He caught sight of five or six trees alongside a little ditch in the middle of an immense cornfield. 'Over to the trees!' he told his men. 'Lie down there,' he added when they had reached them, 'and mind you don't make a sound. But before we go to sleep, who's got any bread?'

'I have,' said one of the men.

'Give it here,' said the corporal in a tone of authority. He divided the bread into five portions and took the smallest himself.

'A quarter of an hour before dawn,' he said as he was eating, 'you'll have the enemy's cavalry on top of you. The great thing is to see you're not cut down by their sabres. On these big plains a man by himself is done for with the cavalry on top of him, but on the other other hand five together can get away with it. All of you keep close together beside me, don't fire except at point-blank range, and by tomorrow evening I'll do my best to get you to Charleroi.' The corporal woke them up an hour before daybreak, and made them recharge their muskets. The terrific noise on the high road still continued; it had been going on all night: it was like the sound of a torrent heard in the distance.

'It's like a flock of sheep running away,' said Fabrizio in a naïve way to the corporal.

'Just you keep your mouth shut, you young whippersnapper!' said the corporal, greatly indignant. And the three soldiers who, with Fabrizio, made up the whole of his little army scowled angrily at the latter as though he had uttered blasphemy. He had insulted their nation.

'That's a bit strong,' thought our hero. 'I noticed this before at the Viceroy's in Milan: they never run away, oh, no! With these Frenchmen you're never allowed to speak the truth if it offends their vanity. But as for their scowls, I snap my fingers at them, and I must let them understand as much.'

They were marching forward, still keeping a hundred paces away from the torrent of fugitives that covered the high road. A league farther on, the corporal and his party crossed a lane that ran into the main road, and on which a number of soldiers were lying. Fabrizio bought a fairly good horse which cost him forty francs, and from among all the swords that had been flung down everywhere he carefully chose one that was long and straight. 'Since I'm told you've got to stick them,' he thought, 'this one is the best.' Thus equipped, he put his horse into a gallop and soon rejoined the corporal who had gone on ahead. He settled himself firmly in his stirrups, took hold of the scabbard of his sword with his left hand, and said to the four Frenchmen, 'Those men in flight along the high road look like a flock of sheep ... They are running like frightened sheep.'

Fabrizio stressed the word *sheep* to no purpose, his comrades no longer remembered that it had annoyed them an hour before. Here is revealed one of the contrasts between the Italian character and the French. The Frenchmen is doubtless the happier of the two; he slides lightly over the accidents of life and does not harbour grudges.

We shall not in any way try to conceal the fact that Fabrizio was highly pleased with himself after using the word *sheep*. They marched on, talking of trivial matters. Two leagues farther on, the corporal, still greatly astonished at seeing no sign of the enemy's cavalry, said to Fabrizio: 'You are our cavalry. Gallop over to that farm on that little hillock; ask the farmer if he will agree to *sell* us some breakfast; take care to tell him there are only five of us. If he hesitates, give him five francs of your own money in advance; but don't worry, we'll get the silver piece back again after breakfast.'

Fabrizio looked at the corporal. He saw an imperturbable gravity in his face, and an air of truly moral superiority; he obeyed. Everything fell out as the commander-in-chief had anticipated; only, Fabrizio insisted on their not taking back by force the five francs he had given to the peasant.

'The money is mine,' he said to his companions. 'I'm not paying for you, I'm paying for the oats he's given my horse.'

Fabrizio's French accent was so bad that his companions thought they detected in his words a hint of superiority. They were keenly offended, and from that moment the idea of a stand-up fight began to take shape in their minds for the end of the day. They found him very different from themselves, and this shocked them. Fabrizio, on the contrary, was beginning to feel very friendly towards them.

They had been walking without saying a word for a couple of hours, when the corporal, looking across at the high road, cried out in a transport of joy: 'There's the Regiment!' They were soon on the road, but, alas, not so much as two hundred men were mustered round the eagle. Fabrizio's eye soon caught sight of the *vivandière*. She was going on foot, her eyes were red and every now and then she burst into tears. Fabrizio looked in vain for the little cart and Cocotte.

'Plundered, ruined, robbed,' cried the *vivandière* in answer to our hero's inquiring glances. The latter, without a word, got down from his horse, took hold of its bridle and said to the *vivandière*, 'Get up!' She did not wait to be told twice.

'Shorten the stirrups for me,' she said.

Once she was comfortably in the saddle, she began to tell Fabrizio of all the disasters of the night. After a narrative of interminable length, eagerly listened to by our hero who, to tell the truth, could not make head or tail of what she was saying, but had a tender feeling for the *vivandière*, she went on:

'And to think that it was Frenchmen who robbed, and beat, and ruined me ...'

'What! it wasn't the enemy?' said Fabrizio with an air of innocence that made his pale, grave, handsome face look charming.

'What a great silly you are, my poor boy,' said the *vivandière*, smiling through her tears, 'but you're a very nice lad, all the same.'

'And such as he is, he brought down his Prussian very well,' said Corporal Aubry who, in the midst of the general crush of people, happened by chance to be on the other side of the horse on which the *cantinière* was sitting. 'But he's proud,' the corporal went on to say. Fabrizio made an impulsive movement. 'And what's your name?' added the corporal, 'for if there's a report I should like to mention you.'

'My name is Vasi,' replied Fabrizio, with a curious expression on his face. 'Boulot, I mean,' he added, quickly correcting himself.

Boulot had been the name of the possessor of the marching orders which the gaoler's wife at B— had given him. Two days before this he had studied them carefully as he was going along, for he was beginning to give a little thought to things and was no longer so easily surprised by them. In addition to the marching orders of the hussar, Boulot, he was keeping very carefully the Italian passport according to which he was entitled to the noble name of Vasi, dealer in barometers. When the corporal had accused him of being proud, he had been on the point of retorting: 'I proud! I Fabrizio Valserra, Marchesino del Dongo, who consent to go by a name like that of Vasi, a dealer in barometers!'

While he was making these reflections and saying to himself: 'I must remember that my name is Boulot, or look out for the prison fate threatens me with,' the corporal and the *cantinière* had been exchanging a few words with regard to him.

'Don't accuse me of being inquisitive,' said the *cantinière*, adopting a less familiar tone than usual, 'I'm only asking you questions for your own good. Who are you, now, really?'

Fabrizio did not reply at first. He was thinking that he could never find more devoted friends to apply to for advice, and he was in urgent need of advice from someone. 'We are soon to enter a fortified town. The governor will want to know who I am, and prison threatens me if I let him see by my answers that I know nobody in the 4th Hussars, whose uniform I am wearing!' In his capacity as an Austrian subject, Fabrizio was aware of all the importance necessarily attached to a passport. Members of his family, although noble and devout, although belonging to the winning side, had been subjected to annoyance more than a score of times in relation to their passports. He was therefore not in the least offended by the question which the *cantinière* had put to him. But as, before answering, he was trying to find a clear way of expressing himself in French, the *cantinière*, goaded by keen curiosity, added, to induce him to speak: 'Corporal Aubry and I are going to give you some good advice on the way you should behave.'

'I don't doubt it,' replied Fabrizio. 'My name is Vasi and I come from Genoa. My sister, who is noted for her beauty is married to a captain. As I am only seventeen, she got me to come and stay with her to show me something of France, and to give me a little polish. Not finding her in Paris, and knowing that she was with this army,

I came on here. I have looked for her everywhere without being able to find her. The soldiers, puzzled by my accent, had me arrested. I had money then, I gave some to the *gendarme*. He let me have some marching orders and a uniform, and said to me: "Be off now, and swear you'll never mention my name."'

'What was his name?' asked the *cantinière*.

'I've given my word,' said Fabrizio.

'He's right,' said the corporal, 'the *gendarme* is a rogue, but my pal here ought not to give his name. And this captain, now, your sister's husband, what name does he go by? If we knew what it was, we could try to find him.'

'Teulier, captain in the 4th Hussars,' replied our hero.

'So, from your foreign accent,' said the corporal rather shrewdly, 'the soldiers took you for a spy.'

'That's an abominable word!' cried Fabrizio, his eyes blazing. 'I, who love the Emperor and the French people so much! And it was that insult that annoyed me most.'

'There's no insult about it; that's where you're wrong,' replied Corporal Aubry gravely. 'The soldiers' mistake was quite natural.'

Then he explained to him with much pedantic precision that in the army a man has to belong to some corps and wear a uniform, failing which he may easily be taken for a spy. 'The enemy,' he said, 'sends us any number; everybody's a traitor in this war.' The scales fell from Fabrizio's eyes; he realized for the first time that he had taken a wrong view of everything that had happened to him during the last two months.

'But the boy must tell us the whole story,' said the *cantinière*, whose curiosity was more and more excited. Fabrizio obeyed. When he had finished the *cantinière* remarked in a serious tone to the corporal: 'The fact of the matter is, this lad is not a soldier at all. We're going to have a beastly sort of war now that we're beaten and betrayed. Why should he go and get his bones broken free, gratis, and for nothing?'

'Especially,' said the corporal, 'as he doesn't know how to load his musket, either on the word of command in twelve stages, or when he is firing on his own. It was I put in the bullet that brought down the Prussian.'

'And what's more,' added the *cantinière*, 'he shows everyone the colour of his money. He's sure to be robbed of all he has as soon as he's no longer with us.'

'The first cavalry sergeant he comes across,' said the corporal, 'will nab it from him to pay for his drinks, and maybe they'll enlist him on the enemies' side, for everyone you meet is a traitor. The first man he comes across will tell him to follow him, and he'll follow. He'd do much better to join our regiment.'

'No, not that, if it's all the same to you, corporal,' cried Fabrizio quickly. 'I'm much more comfortable on horseback; and besides, I don't know how to load a musket, and you've seen that I can manage a horse.'

Fabrizio was very proud of this little speech. We will not report the long discussion as to his future that followed between the corporal and the *cantinière*. Fabrizio remarked that in the course of it these two people repeated the details of his story two or three times over – the soldiers' suspicions; the gendarme selling him marching orders and a uniform; the way in which he had found himself part of the Marshal's escort on the previous day; his glimpse of the Emperor galloping past; the horse that had been scrounged from him, and so on.

The *cantinière*, with true feminine curiosity, kept harking back to the way in which he had been dispossessed of the good horse she had made him buy.

'You felt somebody seize your feet, you were gently lifted over your horse's tail, and left sitting on the ground.'

'Why on earth,' thought Fabrizio, 'keep repeating things that all three of us know perfectly well.' He was not as yet aware that this is the way in which the lower orders in France go about it when thrashing a matter out.

'How much money have you got?' the *cantinière* asked him suddenly. Fabrizio had no hesitation in answering. He was sure of the nobility of this woman's nature; that is the fine side of the French character.

'Altogether, I may have thirty gold napoleons left, and eight or nine five-franc pieces.'

'In that case, you have a clear field!' exclaimed the *cantinière*. 'Get right away from this mess of a defeated army. Clear off, take the first fairly beaten track that you meet with to the right; spur on your horse, and go on getting as far as you can from the army. At the first opportunity, buy yourself some civvies. When you've gone eight to ten leagues and there are no more soldiers in sight, take the mail-coach, and go and rest for a week and eat beefsteaks in some decent town. Never let anyone know that you've been in the army, or the gendarmes will pick you up as a deserter; and, nice as you are, my lad, you're not yet quite cunning enough to deal with the gendarmes' questions. As soon as you've got your civvies on your back, tear up your marching orders into a thousand, and return to your real name: say that you're Vasi. And where should he say he comes from?' she asked the corporal.

'From Cambrai on the Scheldt. It's a nice town, you know, and quite a small one. There's a cathedral there – and Fénelon.'

'That's it,' said the *cantinière*. 'Never let on to anyone that you've been in battle, don't breathe a word about B—, or the gendarme who sold you the marching orders. When you want to get back to Paris, make first for Versailles, and pass through the gates of Paris from that direction in a leisurely way, on foot, as if you were taking a stroll. Sew your napoleons into your breeches, and be specially careful when you have to pay for something only to produce the exact sum you need. What makes me sad is that people are going to fool you and crib from you everything you have. And whatever will you do without money, you who don't know how to look after yourself ...' and so on and so forth.

The worthy *cantinière* went on talking for some time still. The corporal backed up her advice by nodding his head, not being able to get a word in edgeways. Suddenly the crowd that was spread all over the road began first of all to double its pace; then, in the twinkling of an eye, crossed the little ditch which bounded the road on the left and fled hurry-scurry across country. Cries of 'The Cossacks! the Cossacks!' rose from every side.

'Take back your horse!' cried the *cantinière*.

'Heaven forbid!' said Fabrizio. 'Gallop off! Get away! I give him to you. Would you like something to buy another cart with? The half of what I have is yours.'

'Take back your horse, I tell you,' cried the *cantinière* angrily and she got ready to dismount. Fabrizio drew his sword. 'Hold on tight!' he shouted to her, and gave two or three blows with the flat of the blade to the horse, which set off at a gallop and followed the fugitives.

Our hero stood looking at the road. A short time before, three or four thousand people had been hastening along it, packed together like peasants in the tail of a procession. After the cry of 'Cossacks!' he saw precisely no one. The fugitives had thrown away shakos, muskets, sabres, etc.

Fabrizio, quite astounded, clambered up on to a field on the right side of the road and twenty or thirty feet above it. He scanned the length of the road in both directions, and also the plain, but saw no trace of the Cossacks. 'Queer people, these French!' he said to himself. 'Since I have to go to the right,' he thought, 'I may as well start off at once; it's possible these people have some reason for running away that I don't know of.' He picked up a musket, made sure that it was loaded, shook up the powder in the priming, cleaned the flint, then selected a well-filled cartridge-pouch, and looked round him again in all directions. He was absolutely alone in the middle of this plain which a short time back had been so crowded with people. In the far distance he could see the fugitives beginning to disappear behind the trees and still running. 'That's a very odd thing!' he said to himself, and, remembering the tactics employed by the corporal the night before, he went and sat down in the middle of a field of corn. He did not go farther away because he was anxious to see his good friends the *cantinière* and the corporal again.

In this cornfield, he ascertained that he had no more than eighteen napoleons left, instead of thirty as he had thought. But he still had some small diamonds, which he had stowed away in the lining of the hussar's boots that morning in the gaoler's wife's room at B —. He concealed his napoleons as well as he could, while pondering deeply over the sudden disappearance of the others. 'Is that a bad omen for me?' he wondered. His chief sorrow was that he had not asked Corporal Aubry the question: 'Have I really taken part in a battle?' It seemed to him that he had, and he would have been supremely happy if he could have been certain of this.

'Even so,' he said to himself, 'I took part in it bearing the name of a prisoner, I had a prisoner's marching orders in my pocket, and, what's more, his coat on my back! That's an unlucky portent for my future; what would Father Blanès say about it? And that wretched Boulot died in prison. It is all of the most sinister augury: my fate will lead me into prison.'

Fabrizio would have given everything in the world to know whether the hussar, Boulot, had been really guilty. When he examined his recollections, it seemed to him that the gaoler's wife at B — had told him that the hussar had been taken up not only for stealing some silver plate but also for robbing a peasant of his cow and beating the peasant unmercifully. Fabrizio had no doubt that he would be sent to prison one day for a crime that would bear some relation to that of the hussar Boulot. He thought of friend Father Blanès: what would he not have given for an opportunity of consulting him! Then he remembered that he had not written to his aunt since leaving Paris. 'Poor Gina!' he said to himself. And there were tears in his eyes when all of a sudden he heard a slight sound quite close to him. It was a soldier with three horses, whose bridles he had removed, which seemed almost dead with hunger, and which he was feeding on some of the corn, as he held them by the snaffle. Fabrizio rose up like a partridge; the soldier was frightened. Fabrizio noticed and yielded to the pleasure of acting the hussar for a moment.

'One of those horses belongs to me, confound you!' he cried. 'But I don't mind giving you five francs for the trouble you've taken in bringing it to me here.'

'Are you trying to make a b— fool of me?' cried the soldier. Fabrizio took aim at him from a distance of six paces.

'Give up the horse, or I'll blow your brains out.'

The soldier had his musket slung on his back, he swung his shoulder round to get hold of it.

'If you make the slightest movement, you're a dead man!' cried Fabrizio, rushing upon him.

'Oh well, give me the five francs and take one of the horses,' said the soldier, quite bewildered, after casting a rueful glance at the high road, on which there was absolutely no one to be seen. Fabrizio, keeping his musket raised in his left hand, flung him three five-franc pieces with his right.

'Dismount, or you're a dead man. Bridle the black, and get farther off with the other two. ... If you move, I fire.'

The soldier obeyed him sullenly. Fabrizio went up to the horse and slipped his left arm through the bridle rein without taking his eyes off the soldier, who was moving slowly away. When our hero saw that he was fifty paces away, he jumped nimbly on to the horse. He was hardly up and was feeling with his foot for the right stirrup when he heard a bullet whistle past him about a hair-breadth away; it was the soldier firing at him. Fabrizio, beside himself with rage, started galloping after the soldier who ran off as fast as his legs could carry him, and presently Fabrizio saw him mounted on one of his horses and galloping away. 'Good, he's out of range now,' he said to himself. The horse he had just bought was a splendid beast, but seemed half dead with hunger.

Fabrizio returned to the high road, where there was still no sign of any living soul. He crossed to the other side, and put his horse into a trot to reach a little fold in the ground on the left where he hoped to find the *cantinière*; but when he came to the top of the little rise he saw no one within a distance of more than a league, except a few scattered soldiers. 'It is written that I shall not see her again, that good, honest woman!' he said to himself with a sigh. He came to a farm which he had seen in the distance on the right of the road. Without getting off his horse, and after paying for it in advance, he made the farmer produce some oats for his poor horse, which was so famished that it began to gnaw the manger. An hour later, Fabrizio was trotting along the main road, still with a vague hope of finding the *cantinière* or at any rate Corporal Aubry. Pressing forward all the time and looking round him on every side, he came to a marshy stream, spanned by a fairly narrow wooden bridge. On the nearer side of the bridge, to the right of the road, was a solitary house bearing the sign of the White Horse. 'That's where I'll have dinner,' said Fabrizio to himself. A cavalry officer with his arm in a sling was posted at the head of the bridge; he was on horseback and looked very melancholy; ten paces away from him, three dismounted troopers were filling their pipes.

'Here are some people,' said Fabrizio to himself, 'who look to me very much as if they would like to buy my horse for less than it cost me.' The wounded officer and the three men on foot watched him approach and seemed to be waiting for him. 'I really ought not to cross by this bridge, but follow the river bank to the right; that would be the way the *cantinière* would advise me to take to get myself out of difficulties. ... Yes,' thought our hero, ' but if I take to flight now, I shall be heartily ashamed of myself by tomorrow. Besides, my horse has good legs, and the officer's horse is probably tired out; if he tries to make me dismount, I shall take to a gallop.' Reasoning thus with himself, Fabrizio checked his horse's speed and moved forward at the slowest possible pace.

'Come forward, you hussar!' the officer called out to him in a tone of authority.

Fabrizio advanced a few paces and then halted.

'Do you want to take my horse?' he cried out.

'Not in the least; come forward.'

Fabrizio looked at the officer. He had a white moustache, and seemed from his appearance the most honest fellow in the world. The handkerchief that supported his left arm was drenched in blood, and his right hand was also bound up in a piece of bloodstained linen. 'It's the men on foot who will spring at my horse's bridle,' thought Fabrizio. But on getting a nearer view of them he saw that they too were wounded.

'As you have a regard for honour,' said the officer, who wore the epaulettes of a colonel, 'stay here on guard, and tell every dragoon, light horseman, and hussar you see that Colonel Le Baron is in that inn over there, and that I order them to come and report to me.' The old colonel seemed as if broken-hearted with grief; from the first word he uttered he had made a conquest of our hero, who replied with great good sense: 'I am very young, sir, for people to listen to me. I ought to have a written order from yourself.'

'He's right,' said the colonel, studying him closely. 'Make out the order, La Rose; you can use your right hand.'

Without saying a word, La Rose took a little parchment-covered book from his pocket, wrote a few lines, and, tearing out a leaf, handed it to Fabrizio. The colonel repeated the order to him, adding that after two hours on duty he would be relieved, as was right and proper, by one of the three wounded troopers he had with him. Having said this, he went into the inn with his men. Fabrizio watched them go and remained motionless at the end of his wooden bridge, so impressed had he been by the dull, silent grief of these three persons. 'One would think they were spirits under a spell,' he said to himself. At length he unfolded the sheet of paper and read the order, which ran as follows:

Colonel Le Baron, 6th Dragoons, Commanding the 2nd Brigade of the 1st Cavalry Division of the 14th Corps, orders all troopers, dragoons, light horse, and hussars on no account to cross the bridge, and to report to him at the White Horse Inn, by the bridge, which is his headquarters. Headquarters, by the bridge of La Sainte, 19 June 1815.

For Colonel Le Baron, wounded in the right arm, and on his orders.

LA ROSE, Sergeant

Fabrizio had been on guard at the bridge for barely half an hour when he saw six light cavalry men approaching him mounted, and three on foot; he informed them of the colonel's orders. 'We're coming back', said four of the mounted men, and they crossed the bridge at a rapid trot. Fabrizio then spoke to the other two. During the discussion, which was becoming heated, the three men on foot crossed the bridge. One of the two mounted men who had stayed behind asked to see the order again and took it off with him, saying: 'I am taking it to my pals, who will come back sure enough; you can certainly expect them.' And he set off at a gallop, followed by his companion. All this had happened in the twinkling of an eye.

Fabrizio, furiously angry, called to one of the wounded soldiers, who appeared at one of the windows of the White Horse. This soldier, on whose arm Fabrizio saw a cavalry sergeant's stripes, came down and shouted to him as he was approaching: 'Draw your sword, man, you're on guard here.'

Fabrizio obeyed and then said to him: 'They've carried off the order.'

'They're in a bad mood after yesterday's affair,' replied the other gloomily. 'I'll give you one of my pistols. If anyone tries to force past you again, fire it into the air; I shall come, or the colonel himself will appear.'

Fabrizio had very clearly remarked the sergeant's start of surprise on hearing of the purloined paper. He realized that it was a personal insult to himself, and earnestly promised himself that he would not allow such a trick to be played on him again.

Armed with the sergeant's horse-pistol, Fabrizio had proudly resumed his guard when he saw coming towards him seven hussars, all mounted. He had taken up his position in such a way as to bar the bridge; he read them the colonel's order, which seemed to annoy them greatly; the boldest of them tried to cross. Fabrizio, acting on the wise advice of his friend the *vivandière* who, the morning before, had told him to thrust and not to slash, lowered the point of his long, straight sword and made as though to stick it into the man who was trying to force past him.

'Ah! he wants to kill us, the silly young shaver,' cried the hussars, 'as if we hadn't been killed quite enough yesterday!' They all drew their sabres at once and fell on Fabrizio; he gave himself up for dead, but he thought of the sergeant's surprise and did not want to earn his contempt again. Drawing back on to his bridge, he tried to thrust at them with his sword. He looked so odd as he wielded this huge, straight, heavy cavalry sword, which was much too ponderous for him, that the hussars soon realized what kind of man they had to deal with. They then endeavoured not to wound him but to cut his clothes off his body. In this way Fabrizio received three or four sabre-cuts on his arms. For his own part, still faithfully following the *cantinière's* precept, he kept thrusting the point of his sword at them with all his might. Unfortunately one of these thrusts wounded a hussar in the hand; highly indignant at being touched by such an inexperienced soldier, he replied with a downward thrust that caught Fabrizio in the upper part of the thigh. What made the blow more effective was that our hero's horse, so far from avoiding the scuffle, seemed to take a pleasure in it and to be flinging himself on the assailants. These, seeing Fabrizio's blood pouring all down his right arm, were afraid that they might have carried the game too far, and pushing him against the right parapet of the bridge they set off at a gallop. As soon as Fabrizio had a free moment he fired his pistol in the air to warn the colonel.

Four mounted hussars and two on foot, of the same regiment as the others, were coming towards the bridge, and were still two hundred paces away from it when the pistol went off. They had been watching very closely what was happening on the bridge, and thinking Fabrizio had fired on their comrades, the four mounted men rushed upon him at a gallop with their sabres raised; it was a regular charge. Colonel Le Baron, warned by the pistol shot, opened the tavern door and rushed on to the bridge just as the hussars galloped up to it, and himself ordered them to halt.

'There's no colonel in this business,' cried one of the men, and spurred on his horse. The colonel in exasperation broke off the reprimand he was giving them, and caught hold of the reins on the offside of the horse with his wounded right hand.

'Halt, you disgraceful soldier!' he cried to the hussar, 'I know you. You belong to Captain Henriot's company!'

'Well then, let the captain give me his orders himself! Captain Henriot was killed yesterday,' he added with a snigger, 'and you can go to the devil!'

As he spoke he tried to force a passage, and pushed the old colonel away, so that he fell in a sitting position on the roadway of the bridge. Fabrizio, who was a couple of paces farther along the bridge, but facing towards the inn, urged on his horse and, while the breast-plate on the hussar's horse struck the colonel, still clinging to the offside rein, and knocked him over, the young man, in indignation, delivered a downward thrust at the hussar. Luckily for the man, his horse, feeling itself dragged down towards the ground by the bridle to which the colonel was still clinging, swerved aside, so that the long blade of Fabrizio's cavalry sword slid along the hussar's waist-coat, and its whole length passed in front of his face. In a fury, the hussar turned round and delivered a blow with all his might which cut through Fabrizio's sleeve and went deep into his arm. Our hero fell.

One of the dismounted hussars, seeing the two defenders of the bridge on the ground, seized the opportunity, leapt on to Fabrizio's horse and tried to make off with it by urging it to gallop across the bridge.

The sergeant, as he hurried out of the inn, had seen his colonel fall, and believed him to be seriously wounded. He ran after Fabrizio's horse, and plunged the point of his sabre right into the robber's back: the man fell. The hussars, seeing no one now left standing on the bridge except the sergeant, crossed at a gallop and quickly made off. The one who was on foot fled off across the fields.

The sergeant came up to the wounded men. Fabrizio had already got to his feet; he was not in great pain, but he was losing a lot of blood. The colonel got up more slowly; he was quite dazed by his fall, but had not received any hurt.

'I feel no pain,' he said to the sergeant, 'except from the old wound in my hand.'

The hussar whom the sergeant had wounded was dying.

'May the devil take him!' exclaimed the colonel.' But,' said he to the two other troopers who came running up, 'look after this youngster whom I exposed to such improper risks. I shall stay on the bridge myself and try to stop these madmen. Take the lad to the inn and get his arm dressed. Use one of my shirts.'

CHAPTER 5 : *Cross-country Flight*

THE whole of this adventure had lasted but a mere fraction of time. Fabrizio's wounds were not in the least serious; they tied up his arms with bandages cut from the colonel's shirt. They wanted to make up a bed for him on the first floor of the inn.

'But while I am comfortably tucked up on the first floor,' said Fabrizio to the sergeant, 'my horse, who is down in the stable, will get bored all by himself and go off with another master.'

'Not bad for a raw recruit!' said the sergeant. And Fabrizio was installed on a nice clean litter of straw beside the very same manger to which his horse was tied.

Then, as Fabrizio was feeling very weak, the sergeant brought him a bowl of mulled wine and talked to him for a little. A few compliments included in this conversation carried our hero to the seventh heaven.

Fabrizio did not wake up until daybreak on the following morning. The horses were neighing loud and long, and making a frightful din; the stable was filled with smoke. At first Fabrizio could make nothing of this noise, and did not even know where he was. At length, half stifled by the smoke, he got the idea that the house was on fire; in the twinkling of an eye he was out of the stable and in the saddle. He raised his head; smoke was pouring violently out of two windows above the stable, and the roof was covered in black smoke that rose in whirls. A hundred fugitives had arrived during the night at the White Horse; they were all of them shouting and swearing. The five or six whom Fabrizio could see close at hand seemed to him to be completely drunk. One of them tried to stop him and called out to him: 'Where are you taking my horse?'

When Fabrizio was a quarter of a league away, he turned his head. There was no one following him; the building was in flames. Fabrizio caught sight of the bridge; he was reminded of his wound, and felt his arm tightly compressed by the bandages and very hot. 'And the old colonel, what has become of him? He gave his shirt to tie up my arm.' Our hero was that morning the coolest and most composed man in the world. The great amount of blood he had shed had liberated him from all the romantic element in his character.

'To the right!' he said to himself, 'and let's be off quickly.' He began quietly following the course of the river which, after passing under the bridge, flowed to the right of the road. He remembered the good *cantinière*'s advice. 'What a friendly soul!' he said to himself, 'what an open nature!'

After riding for an hour, he felt very weak. 'Ah now! Am I going to faint?' he wondered. 'If I faint, someone will steal my horse, and perhaps my clothes, and my money and diamonds with them.' He had no longer the strength to guide his horse, and was trying to keep his balance in the saddle when a peasant who was digging in a field by the side of the high road noticed his pallor, and came up to offer him a glass of beer and some bread.

'When I saw you look so pale,' said the peasant, 'I thought you were one of the wounded from the great battle.' Never did help come more opportunely. As Fabrizio was munching the piece of black bread his eyes began to hurt him when he looked straight ahead. When he felt a little better he thanked the man. 'And where am I?' he asked. The peasant told him that three quarters of a league farther on was the little market-town of Zonders, where he would be very well looked after. Fabrizio reached this town, not knowing quite what he was doing, and thinking only at every step of keeping himself from falling off his horse.

He saw a big door standing open. He entered; it was the Curry-comb Inn. The good mistress of the house, an enormous woman, came running out to him immediately; she called for help in a voice that trembled with pity. Two girls came and helped Fabrizio to dismount; no sooner had his feet touched the ground than he went off in a dead faint. A surgeon was fetched, who bled him. For the rest of that day and those that followed Fabrizio scarcely knew what was being done to him; he slept almost continually.

The sabre thrust in his thigh threatened to form a serious abscess. When his head was clear again, he begged them to look after his horse, and kept on repeating that he would pay them well, which offended the good hostess of the inn and her daughters. He had been admirably looked after for a fortnight, and was beginning to come to his senses a little, when he noticed one evening that his hostesses looked very worried. A short while after a German officer came into his room. In answering his questions they used a language which Fabrizio did not understand, but he realized clearly that they were talking about him and pretended to be asleep. A little later, when he thought that the officer had probably gone, he called his hostesses.

'That officer came to put my name on a list and to make me a prisoner, didn't he?' The hostess assented with tears in her eyes.

'Very well then, there's some money in my dolman!' he cried, sitting up in bed. 'Buy me some civilian clothes, and tonight I shall set off on my horse. You have already saved my life once by taking me in just as I was about to drop dead in the street; save it again by giving me the means of going back to my mother.'

At this point the landlady's daughters both burst into tears. They trembled for Fabrizio, and, as they hardly understood French, they came to his bedside to ask him questions. They argued things out with their mother in Flemish; but at every moment melting glances of pity were turned towards our hero. He thought he could make out that his flight would compromise them seriously, but that they would gladly run that risk. He thanked them profusely and with his hands clasped together.

A Jew in the district supplied a complete outfit, but when he brought it along towards ten o'clock that night, the girls saw, on comparing it with Fabrizio's dolman, that it would have to be severely taken in. They set to work at once ; there was no time to lose. Fabrizio pointed out a few napoleons hidden in his uniform, and begged his hostesses to sew them into the garments that had just been bought. With these had come a pair of new boots. Fabrizio did not hesitate to ask these kind girls to slit open his hussar's boots at the place he showed them, and they hid the little diamonds in the lining of the new pair.

One curious result of his loss of blood and the weakness that had followed it was that Fabrizio had almost entirely forgotten his French. He used Italian to address his hostesses, who spoke a Flemish dialect, so that they made themselves understood by each other almost entirely by signs. When the girls, who for that matter were perfectly disinterested, caught sight of the diamonds, their enthusiasm for Fabrizio knew no bounds; they imagined him to be a prince in disguise. Aniken, the younger and the more naïve of the two, embraced him without further ceremony. Fabrizio, for his part, found them charming, and towards midnight, when the surgeon, in view of the journey he was about to take, had allowed him a little wine, he felt almost inclined not to go. 'Where could I be better off than here?' he asked himself. Just as he was leaving his room, his good hostess informed him that his horse had been taken by the officer who had come to search the house a few hours before.

'Ah! the swine!' cried Fabrizio with an oath, 'to rob a wounded man!' He was not enough of a philosopher, this young Italian, to call to mind at what price he had himself acquired that horse.

Aniken told him, in the midst of her tears, that they had hired a horse for him. She would have liked him not to go. Their farewells were tender. Two tall young fellows, related to the good landlady, lifted Fabrizio into the saddle. During the journey they held him up on the horse, while a third, who walked a few hundred paces in front of the little convoy, scanned the roads to see if there was any suspicious patrol. After going for a couple of hours, they stopped at the house of a cousin of the landlady of the Curry-comb. In spite of anything Fabrizio could say to them, the young men who accompanied him persistently refused to leave him. They claimed that nobody knew the path through the woods better than they did.

'But tomorrow morning, when my flight is known, and you aren't to be seen anywhere about, your absence may get you into trouble.'

They started off again on their way. Fortunately, when it began to get light, the plain was enveloped in a thick fog. About eight o'clock they came within sight of a little town. One of the young men went on ahead to see if the post-horses there had been stolen. The postmaster had had time to spirit them away and to beat up a few wretched screws with which he had filled his stables. A couple of horses were fetched from the marches in which they had been hidden, and, three hours later, Fabrizio got into a little cabriolet, which was in a very shabby state, but had a pair of good post-horses harnessed to it. He had regained his strength. The moment of parting with his hostess's young kinsmen was pathetic in the extreme. On no account, whatever friendly pretext Fabrizio contrived to put forward, would they consent to take any money.

'In your condition, sir, you need it more than we do,' these worthy young fellows repeatedly insisted. Finally they set off with some letters in which Fabrizio, somewhat braced up by the excitement of the journey, had tried to convey to his hostesses all that he felt for them. Fabrizio wrote with tears in his eyes, and there was certainly some love contained in the letter addressed to little Aniken.

There was nothing out of the ordinary in the rest of his journey. On his arrival at Amiens he was suffering great pain from the cut he had received in his thigh; the country surgeon had not thought of lancing the wound, and in spite of the bleeding an abscess had formed. During the fortnight that Fabrizio spent in the inn at Amiens kept by an obsequious and money-grubbing family, the Allies were invading France, and so many and profound were the reflections he made on the things that had recently happened to him that he became another man. He had remained a child upon one point only: Was what he had seen a real battle? And, if so, was that battle Waterloo?

For the first time in his life he found some pleasure in reading; he was always hoping to find in the newspapers, or in published accounts of the battle, some description or other which would enable him to identify the ground he had covered with Marshal Ney's escort, and later with the other general. During his stay in Amiens he wrote almost every day to his good friends at the Currycomb. As soon as he was fit again, he went to Paris, where he found, at his old hotel, a score of letters from his mother and his aunt, who implored him to return home as soon as possible. The last letter from Contessa Pietranera had a certain enigmatic character which made him extremely uneasy; this letter drove away all his tender daydreams. His was a character for which a single word was enough to make him readily anticipate the greatest misfortunes; his imagination would subsequently undertake to depict these misfortunes to him in the most horrible details.

'Be very careful,' the Contessa wrote, 'not to sign the letters you write to give us news of yourself. On your return you must on no account come straight to the Lake of Como. Stop at Lugano, on Swiss soil.' He was to arrive in this little town under the name of Cavi; at the principal inn in that place he would find the Contessa's manservant, who would tell him what to do. His aunt ended her letter with the following words: 'Do everything you possibly can to keep your mad escapade a secret, and, above all, do not carry about you any printed or written papers. In Switzerland you will be surrounded by our friends of the Santa Margherita.* If I have money

* Signor Pellico has made this name known throughout Europe. It is that of the street in Milan in which the Ministry of Police and the prisons are situated.

enough,' the Contessa added, 'I will send somebody to the Hôtel des Balances, at Geneva, and you shall have details which I cannot put in writing, but about which you ought to know before you arrive. But, in heaven's name, not another day in Paris; our spies there would recognize you.'

Fabrizio's imagination began to conjure up the wildest surmises, and he was incapable of any other diversion save that of trying to guess what strange sort of information it could be that his aunt might have to give him. Twice, on his journey across France, he was arrested, but each time managed to get away. He owed these disagreeable experiences to his Italian passport, and that odd description of him as a 'dealer in barometers', which hardly seemed to tally with his youthful face and his arm in a sling.

Finally, in Geneva he met a man in the Contessa's service who told him, from her, that he, Fabrizio, had been reported to the Milanese police as having gone to convey to Napoleon certain proposals agreed on by a vast conspiracy organized in his late Kingdom of Italy. 'If this was not the object of his journey,' the report continued, 'what was his purpose in assuming a false name?' His mother, he was told, was endeavouring to establish the truth; firstly, that he had never gone beyond Switzerland, and, secondly, that he had left the castle hurriedly in consequence of a quarrel with his elder brother.

On hearing this story, Fabrizio felt a thrill of pride. 'So I'm considered to have acted as a sort of ambassador to Napoleon,' he said to himself; 'I'm supposed to have had the honour of speaking to that great man. Would to God I had!' He recalled his ancestor seven generations back, a grandson of the man who had come to Milan as one of Sforza's suite, and had had the honour of having his head cut off by the Duke's enemies, who surprised him as he was on his way to Switzerland to carry proposals to its praiseworthy Cantons, and to raise troops there. He saw in his mind's eye the engraving relating to this deed included in the genealogy of the family. On questioning the servant, Fabrizio found him utterly shocked by a particular detail which he finally blurted out, in spite of the express order of the Contessa, several times repeated, not to say anything about it. It was Ascanio, his elder brother, who had reported him to the Milan police. This cruel news almost drove our hero out of his mind.

To get into Italy from Geneva you have to pass through Lausanne. Fabrizio determined to set off there and then on foot, and thus cover ten to twelve leagues, although the mail-coach from Geneva to Lausanne was due to start in two hours' time. Before leaving Geneva, he picked a quarrel in one of those dreary cafés in the place with a young man who, so he said, was staring at him in a peculiar way. This was perfectly true; the young Genevan, phlegmatic, sensible, and with his mind on nothing but money, thought him mad. Fabrizio on coming in had glared furiously all round him, and then upset the cup of coffee that was brought to him over his trousers. In this quarrel, Fabrizio's first action was quite appropriate to the sixteenth century. Instead of proposing a duel to the young Genevan, he drew his dagger and rushed upon him to stab him with it. In this moment of passion, Fabrizio forgot everything he had ever learnt about the code of honour, and reverted to instinct, or more properly speaking to the memories of his earliest childhood.

The confidential agent whom he met at Lugano increased his fury by giving him fresh details. As Fabrizio was loved by the people of Grianta, no one there had mentioned his name, and, but for his brother's kind intervention, everyone would have pretended to believe that he was in Milan, and the attention of the police in this town would not have been drawn to his absence.

'No doubt the customs officers have a description of you,' said his aunt's envoy, 'and if we follow the main road, when we come to the frontier of the Lombardo-Venetian kingdom, you will be arrested.'

Fabrizio and his men were familiar with every little footpath over the mountain that divides Lugano from the Lake of Como. They disguised themselves as hunters – that is to say as smugglers – and as they were three in number and had a fairly resolute bearing, the customs officers they met only thought of passing the time of day with them. Fabrizio arranged things so as not to arrive at the castle before midnight; at that hour his father and all the powdered footmen had been a long time in bed. He climbed down without difficulty into the deep moat and entered the castle by the little window of a cellar. It was there that his mother and his aunt were waiting for him; presently his sisters came running in. Transports of tenderness alternated with tears for a considerable time, and they had hardly begun to talk sober sense when the first glimmer of dawn came to warn these people who thought themselves so unfortunate that time was flying.

'I hope your brother won't have any suspicion of your having come back,' Contessa Pietranera said to him. 'I have scarcely spoken to him since that fine prank of his, and his vanity has done me the honour of taking great offence at this. Tonight at supper I condescended to say a few words to him; I had to find some excuse to hide my wild delight, which might have roused his suspicions. Then, when I saw he was quite proud of this shammed reconciliation, I took advantage of his delight to make him indulge in a wild drinking-bout, and certainly he will not have thought of lying in wait to carry on his profession of spying.'

'We shall have to hide our hussar in your room,' said the Marchesa, 'he can't leave at once. At this first moment we haven't sufficient control of our reasoning faculties, and the important thing is to devise the best way of putting these terrible Milanese police off the scent.'

This plan was adopted. But the Marchese and his elder son noticed, next day, that the Marchesa was constantly in her sister-in-law's room. We will not stop to depict the transports of joy and tenderness which all that day continued to excite these extremely happy creatures. Italian hearts are much more tormented than ours by the suspicions and the wild ideas which a burning imagination presents to them, but on the other hand their joys are far more intense and more lasting. That day the Contessa and the Marchesa were absolutely out of their minds; Fabrizio was obliged to begin the whole tale of his adventures all over again. Finally, they decided to go away and hide the joy they shared in Milan, so difficult did it appear to them to keep things hidden any longer from the watchful eye of the Marchese and of his son Ascanio.

They took the boat ordinarily used by the household to get as far as Como; to have acted otherwise would have aroused innumerable suspicions. But on arriving at the harbour of Como the Marchesa remembered that she had left behind at Grianta some papers of the utmost importance. She hastened to send the boatmen back for them, and these men therefore could pass no remark on the way the two ladies were spending their time at Como. No sooner had they arrived than they casually engaged one of those carriages standing ready for hire near that tall medieval tower which rises above the Milan Gate. They set off at once without giving the coachman time to speak to anyone. A quarter of a league from the town they met a young sportsman of their acquaintance, who most obligingly, since they had no man with them, consented to act as their escort as far as the gates of Milan, whither he was bound, after shooting some game on the way.

Everything was going well, and the ladies were engaged in a most merry conversation with the young traveller, when at a bend which the road makes round the base of the charming hill and wood of San Giovanni, three constables in plain clothes sprang to grasp the horses' bridles. 'Ah! my husband has betrayed us!' cried the Marchesa, and fainted. A sergeant who had remained a little way behind came staggering up to the carriage, and said in a voice that reeked of the tavern: 'I am sorry for the commission I have to carry out, but I must arrest you, General Fabio Conti.'

Fabrizio thought the sergeant was playing a bad joke on him in calling him 'General'. 'You shall pay for this!' he said to himself. He watched the men in plain clothes and waited for a favourable moment to jump down from the carriage and dash across the fields.

The Contessa smiled – as a measure of precaution, I fancy – and then said to the sergeant: 'But, my dear sergeant, do you take this youngster of sixteen for General Conti?'

'Aren't you the General's daughter?' asked the sergeant.

'Look at my father,' said the Contessa, pointing to Fabrizio. The constables went off into loud fits of laughter.

'Show me your passports, and don't argue!' said the sergeant, nettled by the general atmosphere of merriment.

'These ladies never carry passports to go to Milan,' said the coachman with a cool and sagacious air. 'They have come from their castle at Grianta. This is her ladyship the Contessa Pietranera, and the other her ladyship the Marchesa del Dongo.'

The sergeant, quite put out of countenance, went forward to the horses' heads, and there consulted with his men. The conference had lasted fully five minutes when Contessa Pietranera begged these gentlemen to allow the carriage to be moved a few paces farther on into the shade; the heat was overpowering, although it was only eleven o'clock in the morning. Fabrizio, who was gazing intently in all directions, looking out for some way of escape, saw coming out of a path across the fields on to the main road, which was thick with dust, a young girl of fourteen or fifteen, shedding frightened tears under cover of her handkerchief. She was coming forward on foot between two constables in uniform, and three paces behind her, also flanked by gendarmes, came a tall, gaunt man who affected an air of dignity, like a prefect taking part in a procession.

'Where did you find them, then?' asked the sergeant, at that moment completely drunk.

'Running away across the fields, and not so' much as a scent of a passport about them.'

The sergeant appeared to lose his head completely; he had five prisoners in front of him, instead of the two he should have had. He went a little way off, leaving only one man to guard the male prisoner, who was putting on airs of majesty, and another to keep the horses from moving forward.

'Wait,' said the Contessa to Fabrizio who had already jumped out of the carriage, 'everything is going to be all right.'

They heard a constable exclaim: 'What does it matter! If they have no passports, it's right to arrest them anyhow.' The sergeant did not seem quite so certain. The name of Contessa Pietranera had made him feel a little uneasy; he had known the General, and had not heard of his death. 'The General,' he said to himself, 'is not the man to let things pass without getting back on me if I arrest his wife without good reason.'

During these deliberations, which were prolonged, the Contessa had entered into conversation with the young girl, who was standing in the road amid the dust by the side of the carriage. She had been struck by her beauty.

'The sun will be bad for you, Signorina. This good constable,' she added, addressing the man who was posted at the horses' heads, 'will surely be so kind as to allow you to step into this carriage.'

Fabrizio, who was strolling aimlessly round the carriage, came up to help the girl to get in. She had already darted forward and put her foot on the step, her arm supported by Fabrizio, when the imposing man, in a voice rendered louder by the desire to maintain his dignity, called out to her: 'Stay in the road! Don't get into a carriage which does not belong to you!'

Fabrizio had not heard this order; the girl, instead of getting into the carriage, tried to get down again, and as Fabrizio continued to hold her up, she fell back into his arms. He smiled, she blushed deeply; they remained for a moment looking at one another after the girl had disengaged herself from his arms.

'She would be a charming prison companion!' said Fabrizio to himself. 'What deep thoughts lie behind that brow! She would know how to love.'

The sergeant came up to them with an air of authority: 'Which of these ladies is named Clelia Conti?'

'I am,' said the girl.

'And I,' cried the elderly man, 'am General Fabio Conti, Chamberlain to His Serene Highness the Prince of Parma, and I consider it most improper that a man in my position should be hunted down like a thief.'

'The day before yesterday, when you embarked at the port of Como, didn't you send the police inspector, who asked for your passport, about his business? Well now, today he is preventing you from seeing to yours.'

'I was already getting my boat under way. I was in a hurry as the weather was stormy, a man not in uniform shouted to me from the quay to put back into harbour. I told him my name and continued on my way.'

'And this morning you slipped out of Como, didn't you?'

'A man like myself does not carry a passport with him when he goes from Milan to visit the lake. This morning, at Como, I was told that I should be arrested at the gate. I left the town on foot with my daughter; I hoped to find some carriage on the road that would take me to Milan, where, certainly, the first visit I shall pay will be to the General Commanding the Province, to lodge a complaint.'

A heavy load seemed to have been lifted off the sergeant's mind. 'Well, General, you are under arrest, and I shall take you to Milan. And you, who are you?' he said to Fabrizio.

'My son,' put in the Contessa. 'Ascanio, son of the Divisional General Pietranera.'

'Without a passport, your ladyship?' said the sergeant, now in a much gentler mood.

'At his age, he has never had one; he never travels alone, he is always with me.'

During this conversation General Conti was assuming more and more of an air of offended dignity in his attitude towards the constables.

'Not so much talk,' said one of them, 'you are arrested, that's enough!'

'You can count yourself too lucky,' said the sergeant, 'if we consent to let you hire a horse from some peasant! Otherwise, in spite of the dust and the heat and your rank as Chamberlain of Parma, you'll jolly well march on foot alongside our horses.'

The General began to swear.

'Will you stop it?' replied the sergeant. 'Where's your general's uniform? Couldn't anyone you please just say he is a general?'

The General became more than ever enraged at this. Meanwhile things were going much better in the carriage.

The Contessa got the constables going as if they had been her own servants. She had just given one of them a scudo to go and get some wine, and, better still, some cool drinking water from a hut that was visible two hundred paces away. She had found time to calm Fabrizio, who was determined, at all costs, to make his escape into the woods that covered the hill. 'I have a good brace of pistols,' he told her. She managed to persuade the infuriated General to let his daughter get into the carriage. On this occasion, the General, who loved to talk about himself and his family, told the ladies that his daughter was only twelve years old, having been born on 27 October 1803, but that, such was her intelligence, everyone took her for fourteen or fifteen.

'A thoroughly commonplace sort of man,' said the Contessa's eyes to the Marchesa. Thanks to the Contessa, everything was settled, after a discussion that lasted an hour. A constable, who discovered that he had some business to see to in a neighbouring village, lent his horse to General Conti, after the Contessa had said to him: 'You shall have ten francs.' The sergeant went off alone with the General. The other men stayed behind under a tree, accompanied by four huge bottles of wine, almost like small demijohns, which the constable who had been sent to the hut had brought back, with the help of a peasant.

Clelia Conti was given permission by the worthy chamberlain, to accept, for the journey back to Milan, a seat in the ladies' carriage, and no one dreamed of arresting the son of the gallant General Pietranera. After the first few minutes given up to an exchange of courtesies and to comments on the little incident that had just ended, Clelia Conti noted a certain degree of tender partiality in the way so beautiful a lady as the Contessa spoke to Fabrizio; certainly, she was not his mother. Her interest was particularly aroused by repeated allusions to something heroic, daring, and dangerous to a supreme degree, which he had recently done; but, for all her cleverness, little Clelia could not discover what it was all about.

She gazed with astonishment at this young hero whose eyes seemed still alight with all the fire of action. As for him, he was somewhat tongue-tied in face of the remarkable beauty of this girl of twelve, and her glances made him blush.

A league before they came to Milan, Fabrizio said that he was going to visit his uncle, and took leave of the ladies.

'If I ever get over my difficulties,' he said to Clelia, 'I shall go to look at the beautiful pictures in Parma. And will you then deign to remember this name: Fabrizio del Dongo?'

'Good!' said the Contessa, 'so that's how you conceal your identity. Signorina, be so kind as to remember that this young rascal is my son, and his name is Pietranera, and not del Dongo.'

That evening, at a very late hour, Fabrizio re-entered Milan by the Porta Renza, which leads to a fashionable promenade. The sending of their two servants to Switzerland had exhausted the very slender savings of the Marchesa and her sister-in-law. Fortunately Fabrizio had still some napoleons left, and one of the diamonds, which they decided to sell.

The ladies were highly popular, and knew everyone in the city. The most important personages in the Austrian and clerical party went to speak on behalf of Fabrizio to Baron Binder, the Chief of Police. These gentlemen could not conceive, so they said, how anyone could take a serious view of the foolish pranks of a boy of sixteen who ran away from his father's house after quarrelling with his elder brother.

'My business is to take everything seriously,' was the quiet reply of Baron Binder, a wise and melancholy-minded man. He was at that time engaged in organizing the famous Milan police, and had undertaken to prevent a revolution like that of 1746, when the Austrians were driven out of Genoa. This Milan police, since rendered so famous by the adventures of MM. Pellico and Andryane, was not precisely a cruel body; it carried out harsh laws in a logical and pitiless manner. The Emperor Francis II wished to strike terror into these overbold and imaginative Italian minds.

'Give me, in day to day record,' Baron Binder would reiterate to Fabrizio's protectors, '*proven* evidence of what the young Marchesino del Dongo has been doing. Take it from the moment of his departure from Grianta on 8 March to his arrival last night in this city, where he is hidden in one of the rooms of his mother's apartment, and I am prepared to treat him as the most well-disposed. and the most agreeable madcap of all the young men in town. If you cannot supply me with the young man's itinerary during all the days following his departure from Grianta, however exalted his birth may be, and however great regard I have for the friends of his family, is it not my duty to have him arrested? Am I not bound to keep him in prison until he has furnished me with the proof that he did not convey messages to Napoleon on the part of such disaffected persons as may exist in Lombardy among the subjects of His Imperial and Royal Majesty? Note further, gentlemen, that if young del Dongo succeeds in justifying himself on this point, he still remains guilty of having entered a foreign country without a passport properly issued to himself, and, in addition, of going under an assumed name and wilfully and knowingly making use of a passport issued to a common workman, that is to say to a person of a class greatly inferior to that to which he himself belongs.'

This declaration, cruelly logical, was accompanied by all the marks of deference and respect which the Chief of Police owed to the high position of the Marchesa del Dongo and of the important personages who were intervening on her behalf.

The Marchesa was in despair when she was told of Baron Binder's reply.

'Fabrizio will be arrested,' she sobbed, 'and once he is in prison, God knows when he'll get out! His father will disown him!'

Contessa Pietranera and her sister-in-law consulted with two or three intimate friends, and, in spite of anything these might say, the Marchesa was absolutely determined to send her son away that very night.

'But you can see quite well,' the Contessa said to her, 'that Baron Binder knows your son is here; he's not an ill-natured man.'

'No; but he is anxious to please the Emperor Francis.'

'But if he thought it would lead to his promotion to put Fabrizio in prison, the boy would be there now. It is showing an insulting defiance of the Baron to arrange his flight.'

'But his admission to us that he knows where Fabrizio is, is tantamount to saying: "Send him away!" No, I shan't breathe freely so long as I can say to myself: "In a quarter of an hour my son may be confined within four walls." Whatever Baron Binder's ambition may be,' the Marchesa added, 'he thinks it useful to his personal standing in this country to show open deference to a man of my husband's rank, and I see a proof of this in the singular frankness with which he admits that he knows where to lay hands on my son. Still more, the Baron obligingly gives us particulars of the two offences with which Fabrizio is charged; he explains that either of these two offences entails imprisonment. Isn't that as much as to say that if we prefer exile it is for us to choose?'

'If you choose exile,' the Contessa kept on repeating, 'we shall never set eyes on him again so long as we live.' Fabrizio, who was present at every one of their talks, together with an old friend of the Marchesa, now one of the councillors of the Austrian Tribunal, was very much in favour of running away. And, in fact, that very evening he left the *palazzo*, hidden in the carriage which was taking his mother and his aunt to the Scala theatre.

The coachman, whom they distrusted, went as usual to pass the time in a tavern, and while the footman, on whom they could rely, kept charge of the horses, Fabrizio, disguised as a peasant, slipped out of the carriage and left the town. The next morning he crossed the frontier with equal success, and a few hours later was safely installed on an estate which his mother owned in Piedmont, near Novara, or to be precise, at Romagnano, where Bayard was killed.

It can be imagined how much attention the ladies, on reaching their box at the Scala, paid to the performance. They had gone there solely to be able to consult a number of their friends who belonged to the Liberal party and whose presence at the Palazzo del Dongo might have been misconstrued by the police. In the box it was decided to approach Baron Binder again. There could be no question of offering a sum of money to this magistrate, who was a perfectly honest man. Moreover, the ladies were extremely poor; they had forced Fabrizio to take with him all the money that remained from the sale of the diamond.

It was, however, of the utmost importance that they should keep in touch with the Baron's latest pronouncements on the matter. The Contessa's friends reminded her of a certain Canon Borda, a most agreeable young man, who at one time had tried to make advances to her, and in a rather unpleasant way. Finding himself unsuccessful, he had reported her friendship for Limercati to General Pietranera, whereupon he had been sent about his business as a nasty fellow. Now, as it happened, this Canon was in the habit of going every evening to play tarot with Baroness Binder, and was naturally an intimate friend of her husband's. The Contessa made up her mind to take the horribly painful step of going to see this Canon; and the following morning, very early, before he had left the house, she had herself shown in.

When the Canon's one and only servant announced the Contessa Pietranera, his master was so overcome with emotion as to be almost incapable of speech; he made no attempt to repair the disorder of a very simple indoor attire.

'Show her in, and leave us,' he said in a very faint voice. The Contessa entered the room; Borda fell on his knees.

'It is in this position that a miserable crazy wretch should properly receive your orders,' he said to the Contessa who, in a simple, un-elaborate dress that was almost a disguise, was irresistibly attractive that morning. Her intense grief over Fabrizio's exile and the violence she was doing to her feelings in coming to the house of a man who had acted treacherously towards her combined to give incredible brilliance to her eyes.

'It is in this position that I wish to receive your orders,' cried the Canon, 'for it is obvious that you have some service to ask of me, otherwise you would not have honoured with your presence the poor house of an unhappy madman. Once before, carried away by love and jealously, he behaved towards you like a despicable scoun-drel, as soon as he saw that he could not win your favour.'

These words were sincere and all the more admirable since the Canon now enjoyed great power. The Countess was moved to tears by them. Humiliation and fear had chilled her heart; now in a moment they were replaced by tenderness and a slight feeling of hope. From a most unhappy state she passed, as quick as thought, to one of almost happiness.

'Kiss my hand,' she said, as she held it out to the Canon, 'and stand up.' (She used the second person singular. This in Italy, you should know, indicates a frank and open friendship just as much as a more tender feeling.) 'I have come to ask your favour for my nephew Fabrizio. Here is the whole truth of the matter without the slightest concealment, exactly as one would tell it to an old friend. At the age of sixteen and a half he has recently done a remarkably foolish thing. We were at the castle of Grianta on the Lake of Como. One evening at seven o'clock a boat from Como brought us news of the Emperor's landing in the Gulf of Juan. Next morning Fabrizio set off for France, after borrowing the passport of one of his lower-class friends, a dealer in barometers named Vasi. As he has not exactly the look of a dealer in barometers, he had hardly gone ten leagues in France before his handsome appearance got him arrested; his outbursts of enthusiasm in bad French seemed suspicious. After a short while he escaped and managed to reach Geneva; we sent someone to meet him at Lugano. ...'

'That is to say, Geneva,' said the Canon smiling.

The Contessa finished her story.

'I will do everything for you that is humanly possible,' said the Canon effusively. 'I place myself entirely at your disposal. I will even commit imprudences,' he added. 'But tell me, what have I to do as soon as this poor room is deprived of this heavenly apparition which marks an epoch in the history of my life?'

'You must go to Baron Binder and tell him that you have loved Fabrizio ever since his birth, that you saw him as a tiny baby when you visited our house, and that, in short, in the name of the friendship he shows you, you beg him to employ all his secret agents to find out whether, before his departure for Switzerland, Fabrizio had any sort of communication whatsoever with any of the Liberals whom the Baron has under supervision. Provided the Baron is well served by his agents, he will see that here is merely a question of a foolish youthful prank. You know that I used to have, in my lovely rooms in the Palazzo Dugnani, some prints of the battles won by Napoleon; it was by spelling out the inscriptions underneath these engravings that my nephew learnt to read. As soon as he was five, my poor husband began to tell him about these battles. We used to put my husband's helmet on his head, the child would drag his great sabre along behind him. Well then, one day he learns that my husband's god, the Emperor, has returned to France. He starts out to join him, like a thoughtless young fool, but does not manage to do so. Ask your Baron what penalty he wishes to inflict for this moment of folly?'

'I was forgetting one thing,' said the Canon, 'you shall see that I am not altogether unworthy of the pardon that you grant me. Here,' he said, hunting through the papers on his table, 'here is the accusation by that infamous *col-torto* (that is, hypocrite) – Look! it is signed *Ascanio Valserra del* DONGO – which was the beginning of all this business. I took it yesterday from the police headquarters, and went to the Scala in the hope of finding someone who was in the habit of going to your box, through whom I might be able to communicate it to you. A copy of this document was sent to Vienna a long time ago. Here is the enemy we have to fight.' The Canon read the accusation through with the Contessa and it was agreed that in the course of the day he would let her have a copy made by some trustworthy person. It was with a heart full of joy that the Contessa returned to the Palazzo del Dongo.

'No one could possibly be more of a gentleman than this reformed blackguard,' she said to the Marchesa. 'This evening at the Scala, at a quarter to eleven by the theatre clock, we are to send everyone away from our box, put out the candles and shut our door, and at eleven the Canon himself will come to tell us what he has managed to do. That's what we arranged as the least compromising course for him.'

The Canon was a very intelligent man. He was careful to keep the appointment; he showed on that occasion a perfect kindness and an unreserved openness of heart such as one hardly finds except in countries where vanity does not predominate over every other feeling. His denunciation of the Contessa to her husband, General Pietranera, was one of the things he most regretted in his life, and he had now found a means of getting it off his conscience.

That morning, when the Contessa had left his house, he had said to himself bitterly, 'There she is, in love with her nephew,' for he was by no means cured. 'Proud as she is, to have come to see me. ... After the death of that poor Pietranera she repulsed with horror my offers of service, though they were most polite and admirably presented to her by Colonel Scotti, her former lover. Imagine the beautiful Pietranera reduced to living on fifteen hundred francs!' added the Canon, striding vigorously up and down his room. 'And then to go and live in the castle of Grianta with that abominable *seccatore*, the Marchese del Dongo! ... Everything is now quite clear! After all, that young Fabrizio is full of charm, tall, well-built, and always with a smile on his face ... and, better still, a delightfully voluptuous expression in his eye ... like one of Correggio's faces,' the Canon added bitterly.

'The difference in age ... not too great ... Fabrizio born after the arrival of the French, about '98, I fancy. The Contessa might be twenty-seven or twenty-eight; impossible to be lovelier, or more adorable. Even in this country rich in beauties, she defeats them all – the Marini, the Gherardi, the Ruga, the Aresi, the Pietagrua – she is far and away superior to all these women. ... They were living happily together hidden from the world on that beautiful Lake of Como when the young man decided to join Napoleon. ... There are still noble souls in Italy ! And in spite of everything ! Dear Country ! ... No,' went on this heart inflamed by jealousy, 'it's impossible to explain in any other way her resigning herself to vegetating in the country, with the disgusting spectacle, every day, at every meal, of the horrible face of the Marchese del Dongo, and on top of it, that frightful pasty countenance of the Marchesino Ascanio, who is going to be worse than his father. Well, I will serve her faithfully. At least I shall have the pleasure of seeing her otherwise than through an opera-glass.'

Canon Borda explained the whole matter very clearly to the ladies. At heart, Binder was as well-disposed as they could wish. He was delighted that Fabrizio should have taken to his heels before any orders could arrive from Vienna; for Baron Binder had no power to make any decision, he was waiting for orders in this case as in every other one. Every day he sent to Vienna an exact copy of all the information he received; then he awaited a reply.

During his exile at Romagnano it was essential that Fabrizio should, in the first place, go to Mass every day, choose for his confessor a man of intelligence, devoted to the cause of the Monarchy, and never divulge to him, at the judgement-bar of penitence, any except the most irreproachable sentiments. Secondly, he should associate with no one who was reputed to have a mind of his own, and, on occasion, should speak of revolution with horror and as something never to be permitted to occur. Thirdly, he must never let himself be seen in a café, and never read any other newspaper other than the official *Gazette* of Turin or of Milan; in general he should show a distaste for reading and above all never open any book printed later than 1720, with the possible exception of the novels of Sir Walter Scott. And lastly, the Canon added, with a touch of malice, 'he must in particular pay court openly to one of the pretty women in the district – one of noble birth, of course. This will show that he has not the gloomy and discontented mind of an embryo conspirator.'

Before going to bed, the Contessa and the Marchesa each wrote Fabrizio an interminable letter in which they explained to him with a charming anxiety all the advice that had been given them by Borda.

Fabrizio had no wish to be a conspirator. He loved Napoleon, and in his situation as a young noble, believed that he was made to be happier than other sorts of men, and thought the middle classes ridiculous. He had never opened a book since leaving school, where he had only read works adapted by the Jesuits. He established himself at some distance from Romagnano, in a magnificent *palazzo*, one of the masterpieces of the famous architect San Michele. But for thirty years it had been uninhabited, so that the rain came into every room and not a single window shut properly. He took possession of the estate agent's horses, and rode them without ceremony at all hours of the day; he never spoke, and was constantly absorbed in thought.

The recommendation to choose a mistress from a family of *Ultras* took his fancy; he obeyed it to the letter. He chose as his confessor a young priest addicted to intrigues who wished to become a bishop (like the confessor of the Spielberg).* But he would go three leagues on foot, wrapped in what he believed to be impenetrable mystery, in order to read the *Constitutionnel*, which he thought sublime. 'It's as fine as Alfieri and Dante!' he would often exclaim. Fabrizio resembled young Frenchmen in this particular, that he was far more seriously taken up with his horse and his newspaper than with his politically right-minded mistress. But there was as yet no room for any imitation of others in that ingenuous and resolute nature, and he made no friends in the society to be found in the quiet country town of Romagnano. His simplicity passed for arrogance; people did not know what to make of his character. 'He's a younger son dissatisfied because he is not the elder', was the parish priest's verdict.

* See M. Andryane's curious memoirs, as entertaining as a novel and likely to last as long as the annals of Tacitus.

WE will frankly admit that Canon Borda's jealousy was not altogether unjustified. On his return from France Fabrizio appeared in the eyes of Contessa Pietranera like a handsome stranger whom she had known in days gone by. If he had spoken to her of love she would have loved him. Had she not already conceived, for his conduct and his person, a passionate admiration, and so to speak, without bounds? But Fabrizio embraced her with such an effusion of innocent gratitude and simple, honest affection that she would have been horrified with herself if she had looked for any other feeling in this almost filial friendship. 'After all,' said the Contessa to herself, 'some of my friends who knew me six years ago, at Prince Eugène's court, may still consider me pretty and even young, but for him I am a woman of good reputation ... and, if the truth must be told without sparing my vanity, a woman of a certain age.' The Contessa was under an illusion as to the period of life she had reached, but it was not the illusion of an ordinary woman. 'Besides, at his age, boys are apt to exaggerate in some slight degree the ravages of time; now a man of more advanced years ...'

The Contessa, who was pacing the floor of her drawing-room, stopped before a mirror, then smiled. It should be understood that, for some months past, Contessa Pietranera's heart had been besieged in a serious fashion, and by a man of singular character. Shortly after Fabrizio's departure for France, the Contessa, who, without altogether admitting it to herself, was already beginning to let her thoughts dwell on him a great deal, had fallen into a profound state of melancholy. All her occupations seemed to her to lack pleasure, and if one may venture to say so, savour. She told herself that Napoleon, wishing to attach the Italian people to himself, would make Fabrizio his aide-de-camp. 'He's lost to me!' she exclaimed, weeping, 'I shall never see him again! He will write to me, but what shall I seem to him in ten years time?'

It was in this frame of mind that she made a journey to Milan. She hoped to get more direct news of Napoleon in that place, and, possibly, some news of Fabrizio as a consequence. Without admitting it to herself, her active nature was beginning to be very weary of the monotonous life she was leading in the country. 'It is keeping oneself from dying,' she would say to herself, 'it is not living.' Every day to see those powdered heads, her brother's, her nephew Ascanio's, their footmen's! What would her excursions on the lake be without Fabrizio? Her sole consolation lay in the ties of affection that bound her to the Marchesa. But for some time now this intimacy with Fabrizio's mother, a woman older than herself and with no hope left in life, had begun to be less attractive to her.

Such was the curious position in which the Contessa was placed. With Fabrizio away, she had little hope in the future; her heart was in need of consolation and some new and interesting experience. On arriving in Milan she conceived a passion for the kind of opera then in vogue. She would go and shut herself up alone for hours on end at the Scala, in the box of her old friend, General Scotti. The men whom she tried to meet in order to get news of Napoleon and his army impressed her as coarse and vulgar. On returning home, she would improvise on her piano until three o'clock in the morning.

One evening, at the Scala, in the box of one of her friends to which she had gone in search of news from France, she made the acquaintance of Conte Mosca, Minister of Parma. He was an agreeable man who spoke of Napoleon and France in such a way as to give her heart fresh reasons for hope or fear. She returned to the same box the following evening; this intelligent man reappeared, and throughout the whole performance she talked to him with enjoyment. She had never found any evening so entertaining since Fabrizio went away. This man who amused her, Conte Mosca della Rovere Sorezano, was at that time Minister of War, of Police, and Finance to that famous Prince of Parma, Ernesto IV, so notorious for his severities, which the Liberals of Milan called acts of cruelty. Mosca might have been forty or forty-five. He had strongly marked features, with no trace of self-importance, and a simple and light-hearted manner which influenced people in his favour. He would have looked very well indeed, if a curious whim of his Prince's had not obliged him to wear his hair powdered, as a proof of his sound political views. As people in Italy have little fear of wounding another's vanity, they quickly adopt a tone of intimacy and make personal remarks. The antidote to this practice is to drop the acquaintance if one's sensibilities have been wounded.

'Tell me now, Conte, why you powder your hair?' the Contessa asked the third time they met. 'Powder! on a man like you, attractive and still young, who fought on our side in Spain!'

'Because in that country I looted nothing, and a man must live! I was madly eager for glory; a flattering word from Gouvion-Saint-Cyr, the French general who was commanding us, meant everything to me then. When Napoleon fell it so happened that while I had been eating up my fortune in his service, my father, a man of an imaginative turn of mind, who pictured me as a general already, had been building me a *palazzo* in Parma. In 1813 I found that my whole worldly wealth consisted of a huge, half-finished *palazzo*, and an officer's pension.'

'A pension? 3,500 francs like my husband's?'

'Conte Pietranera was a general commanding a division. My own pension, as a humble cavalry major, has never been more than 800 francs, and even that has been paid to me only since I became Minister of Finance.'

As there was no one in the box except the lady of strong Liberal views to which it belonged, the conversation continued with the same frankness. Conte Mosca, when questioned, spoke of his life in Parma. 'In Spain, under General Saint-Cyr, I braved the enemy's fire to win the Cross of the Legion of Honour and a little glory into the bargain. Now I dress myself up like some character in a comedy to keep up a great establishment and gain a few thousand lire. Once I had started a game on this sort of chessboard, the insolence of my superiors stung me and I determined to occupy one of the most important positions; I have reached it. But the happiest days of my life are always those which, now and again, I manage to spend in Milan; here, it seems to me, there still survives the spirit of your Army of Italy.'

The frankness, the freedom with which this minister of so dreaded a Prince spoke his mind piqued the Contessa's curiosity. From his title she had expected to find a stiff and affected personage, impressed with his own importance; what she saw was a man who blushed at the thought of occupying so high and solemn a position. Mosca had promised to let her have all the news from France that he could collect. This, in the month that preceded Waterloo, was a very grave indiscretion in Milan. The point in question at that time was whether Italy would or would not continue to exist; everyone in Milan was in a fever, a fever of hope or of fear. Amid this universal agitation, the Contessa began to make enquiries about a man who spoke so lightly of so coveted a position, and one that was his sole means of livelihood.

Certain curious and oddly interesting information was reported to the Contessa. 'Conte Mosca della Rovere Sorezano,' she was told, 'is on the point of becoming Prime Minister and acknowledged favourite of Ranuccio-Ernesto IV, absolute ruler of the state of Parma, and one of the richest princes in Europe besides. The Conte would already have attained to this exalted position if he had cared to show more gravity of manner; the Prince, it is said, often reads him a lesson on this point.

' "What do my manners matter to your Highness," he answers boldly, "so long as I conduct his affairs in a proper way?"

'The happy career of this favourite,' her informant added, 'is not without its thorns. He has to please a ruler who is, no doubt, a man of good sense and intelligence, but one who, since his accession to an absolute throne, seems to have lost his head, and shows, for instance, suspicions only worthy of the silliest old woman.

'Ernesto IV is courageous only in war. A score of times on the field of battle he has been seen leading a column to the attack like a gallant general; but since the death of his father Ernesto III, on his return to his dominions, over which, to his misfortune, he possesses unlimited power, he has set himself to inveigh in the maddest fashion against the Liberal party and liberty. Very soon he began to imagine that people hated him, and, finally, in a moment of ill temper, he had two Liberals hanged, who may or may not have been guilty, on the advice of a wretch called Rassi, a sort of Minister of Justice.

'From that fatal moment, the Prince's life has been changed; he is now to be seen tormented by the strangest suspicions. He is not yet fifty, and fear has so withered him, if one may use the expression, that the moment he begins to speak of Jacobins and the schemes of the Central Committee in Paris, his face becomes that of an old man of eighty; he reverts to the fantastic fears of early childhood. His favourite Rassi, the Lord Chief Justice (or chief magistrate) derives his influence solely from his master's fears; and whenever he is afraid that influence is waning, he hastens to discover some fresh conspiracy of the blackest and most fantastic kind. If thirty rash fellows meet together to read an issue of the *Constitutionnel*, Rassi declares them to be conspirators and sends them off to prison in that famous citadel of Parma, the terror of the whole of Lombardy. As it stands very high, a hundred and eighty feet up, so they say, it is visible from a long way off in the whole of that immense plain; and the outward appearance of this prison, about which horrible things are reported, makes it, through fear, the queen of all that plain which stretches from Milan to Bologna.'

'Would you believe it,' said another traveller to the Contessa, 'but at night, on the third floor of his palace, guarded by eighty sentinels who every quarter of an hour bawl out a whole sentence, Ernesto trembles in his room? With all the doors fastened by ten bolts, and the adjacent rooms, above as well as below him, filled with soldiers, he is afraid of the Jacobins. If a board in the flooring happens to creak, he snatches up his pistols and imagines there is a Liberal hiding under his bed. Immediately all the bells in the castle are set ringing, and an aide-de-camp goes to wake Count Mosca up. On reaching the castle, the Minister of Police takes good care not to deny the existence of a conspiracy; on the contrary, alone with the Prince, and armed to the teeth, he inspects every corner of the rooms, looks under the beds, and, in a word, applies himself to performing a whole heap of ridiculous actions worthy of an old woman.

'All these precautions would have seemed highly degrading to the Prince himself in those happy days when he was making war, and had never killed anyone except with a shot from his musket. As he is a man of infinite intelligence he is ashamed of these precautions; they seem to him ridiculous, even at the moment when he is giving himself up to them, and the source of Conte Mosca's enormous influence is that he employs all his skill in contriving that the Prince shall never have occasion to blush in his presence. It is he, Mosca, who, in his capacity as Minister of Police, insists upon looking under furniture, and even, so people say in Parma, inside the cases in which the double-basses are kept. It is the Prince who objects to this and chaffs his Minister about his excessive punctiliousness. "There's much at stake," Conte Mosca replies; "think of the satirical sonnets the Jacobins would heap upon our heads if we allowed you to be killed. It is not only your life we are defending, but our own honour." But it appears that the Prince is only half taken in by this, for if anyone in the city should take it into his head to remark that they have passed a sleepless night in the castle, Chief Justice Rassi sends the mischievous wag to the citadel, and once in that lofty abode and *in a good atmosphere*, as they say in Parma, it is a miracle if anyone re-members the prisoner's existence.

'It is because he is a soldier, and that in Spain he escaped a score of times, pistol in hand, from surprise attacks, that the Prince prefers Conte Mosca to Rassi, who has a much more flexible and abject nature. Those unfortunate prisoners in the citadel are kept in the most rigorously secret confinement, and all sorts of stories are told about them. The Liberals assert that, following a bright idea of Rassi's, the gaolers and confessors have orders to make them believe that, once a month, one of them is led out to die. That day the prisoners are given permission to go up on to the platform of the huge tower, a hundred and eighty feet high, and from there they see a procession wending its way with a spy who plays the part of some poor devil going to his death.'

These tales and a score of others of the same type and of no less authenticity keenly interested Contessa Pietranera. The next day she asked Conte Mosca, whom she chaffed in a lively way, for details. She found him entertaining, and maintained to his face that he was at heart a monster without suspecting it. One day, as he was going back to his inn, the Conte said to himself: 'Not only is this Contessa Pietranera a charming woman, but when I spend the evening in her box I manage to forget certain things in Parma, the memory of which cuts me to the heart.' This Minister, in spite of his light-hearted air and his lively manners, did not possess a soul of the French type; he could not *forget* the things that grieved him. When there was a thorn in his pillow, he was obliged to break it off and to blunt its point while getting many a prick from it in his trembling limbs. (I must apologize for this extract, which is translated from the Italian.)

The day after this discovery the Conte found that, in spite of the business that had summoned him to Milan, the hours seemed to him inordinately long; he could not stay in one place, he wore out his carriage-horses. Towards six o'clock he mounted his horse to ride to the *Corso*; he had some hope of meeting Contessa Pietranera there. Seeing no sign of her, he remembered that at eight o'clock the Scala Theatre opened; he went in there, but did not see so much as ten persons in that vast auditorium. He felt somewhat ashamed of himself for being there. 'Is it possible,' he asked himself, 'that at fully forty-five I should be committing follies that a second lieutenant would blush at? Fortunately nobody suspects them.' He rushed away and tried to pass the time by strolling through those charming streets that surround the Scala. They are lined with cafés, which at that hour are filled to overflowing with people. Outside each of these cafés crowds of inquisitive idlers installed on chairs in the middle of the street, sip their ices and criticize the passers-by. The Conte was a passer-by worthy of notice; thus he had the pleasure of being recognized and addressed. Three or four importunate individuals of the kind that cannot easily be snubbed seized this opportunity of obtaining an audience of so powerful a Minister. Two of them handed him petitions; the third contented himself with addressing some very long-winded advice to him on his conduct in politics.

'A man as intelligent as myself shouldn't be caught napping,' he said to himself, 'he oughtn't to walk about the streets when he is so powerful.' He went back into the theatre where it occurred to him to take a box in the third tier. From there his gaze could plunge, unnoticed, down to the box on the second tier where he hoped to see the Contessa arriving. Two full hours of waiting did not seem too long to this man in love; certain of not being observed he gave himself up with delight to the full extent of his folly. 'Is not old age,' he said to himself, 'above all things the time when one is no longer capable of such delightful puerilities?'

At length the Contessa appeared. Armed with his opera-glasses, he studied her with rapture. 'Young, sparkling, and light as a bird,' he said to himself, 'she doesn't look twenty-five. Her beauty is the least of her charms. Where else could I find a soul that is always sincere, that never acts *from prudent motives*, that abandons itself entirely to the pleasure of the moment, and asks only to be carried away by some new object? I can quite understand Conte Nani's follies.'

The Conte went on supplying himself with excellent reasons for behaving foolishly so long as he was thinking only of capturing the happiness which he saw before his eyes. He no longer hit upon such good arguments when he came to consider his age, and the cares and anxieties, sometimes of the saddest nature, that made up most of his life. 'A man of ability, driven out of his wits by fear, provides me with a fine existence and plenty of money for being his Minister. But were he to dismiss me tomorrow, I should be left old and poor, that is to say everything that the world most despises; and that's a fine sort of person to offer the Contessa!' These thoughts were too gloomy, his eyes strayed back to Contessa Pietranera. He could not tire of gazing at her, and, to be able to think of her better, he did not go down to her box.

'She took on Nani, so I have just learnt, for no other reason than to play a trick on that idiot Limercati, who would not agree to run his sword, or to get someone else to stick a dagger, into her husband's murderer. I would fight for her twenty times over!' cried the Conte in a transport of enthusiasm. Every moment he consulted the theatre clock which, with its brightly illuminated figures against a black background, warned the audience every five minutes of the approach of the hour when it was permissible to appear in a friend's box. The Conte said to himself: 'Since I am such a recent acquaintance, I shall only be able to spend half an hour at the most in her box. If I stay any longer, I shall attract attention, and at my age and still more with this accursed powder in my hair, I shall have all the seductive charm of an old fogy.' But one thought made him suddenly make up his mind: 'If she were to leave that box to pay a visit to another, I should be well rewarded for the miserliness with which I am hoarding up this pleasure.' He got up to go down to the box in which he saw the Contessa; all at once he felt he had almost lost his desire to present himself there. 'Ah, that's really charming,' he cried laughing at himself as he paused on the stairs. 'It's an impulse of genuine shyness! It must be a good twenty-five years since such an adventure happened to me.'

He entered the box, almost forcing himself to do so; and, taking advantage, like an intelligent man, of the accident that had happened to him, he made no attempt to appear at his ease, or to display his wit by plunging into some amusing story. He had the courage to be shy, he employed his wits in letting his agitation be guessed without making himself ridiculous. 'If she should take it amiss,' he said to himself, 'I am lost for ever. What! shy, with my hair all covered in powder, and which, without the help of the powder, would be visibly grey! But, after all, it is a fact; it cannot therefore appear ridiculous unless I exaggerate it or glory in it.' The Contessa had been so often bored at the castle of Grianta by the sight of the powdered heads of her brother, her nephew, and other politically orthodox persons of the neighbourhood, that it never occurred to her to give a thought to her new adorer's style of hairdressing.

The Contessa's mind thus having a protection against giving way to peals of laughter on his entry, she paid attention solely to the news from France that Mosca always had for her private ear on coming into her box; no doubt he used to draw on his invention. While discussing this news with him, she noticed that evening the expression in his eyes which was both attractive and kindly.

'I can imagine,' she said to him, 'that in Parma, surrounded by your slaves, you will not wear such an agreeable expression. That would ruin everything and give them some hope of not being hanged!'

The total absence of self-importance in a man who passed as the leading diplomat in Italy, seemed strange to the Contessa; she even found a certain charm in it. Indeed, since he talked well and with much animation, she was not at all displeased that he should have thought fit to play for one evening, and without prejudice, the part of an attentive admirer.

This was a great step forward, and highly dangerous. Fortunately for the Minister, who found no ladies cruel to him in Parma, the Contessa had only arrived from Grianta a few days before; her mind was still dulled by the boredom of life in the country. She had almost forgotten how to jest; and all those things that belong to a light and elegant way of living had taken on in her eyes, as it were, a tinge of novelty that sanctified them; she was in no mood to poke fun at anything, not even a lover who was forty-five and shy. A week later, the Conte's temerity might have met with a very different sort of welcome.

At the Scala, it is not usual to prolong for more than twenty minutes or so those little visits paid to other boxes. The Conte spent the whole evening in the box in which he had been so fortunate as to meet Contessa Pietranera. 'She is a woman,' he said to himself, 'who revives in me all the follies of my youth.' He was, however, well aware of the danger. 'Will my position as an all-powerful Panjandrum forty leagues away from here incline her to pardon me for this stupid behaviour? I get so bored in Parma!' Meanwhile, every quarter of an hour, he kept promising himself that he would take his leave.

'I must confess to your ladyship,' he said to the Contessa with a laugh, 'that in Parma I am bored to death, and I should be allowed to take heady draughts of pleasure whenever it comes my way. Therefore, in a casual way and for an evening only, permit me to play the part of lover in your company. Alas, in a few days I shall be far away from this box which makes me forget all my worries and even, so you will say, all my manners.'

A week after this prodigiously lengthy visit to the box at the Scala, and after various minor incidents too insignificant perhaps to interest the reader, Conte Mosca had fallen madly in love, and the Contessa had already begun to think that his age need be no objective if he proved attractive in other respects. Matters had reached this point when Mosca was recalled by a courier from Parma. It would seem that his Prince had grown afraid of being left alone. The Contessa went back to Grianta. That lovely spot, no longer embellished by her imagination, seemed to her a desert. 'Can I possibly have grown fond of this man?' she wondered. Mosca wrote to her, and found himself at a loss; separation had robbed him of the object that inspired his thoughts. His letters were amusing, and, prompted by a peculiar little notion, to which no exception was taken, of avoiding comments from the Marchese del Dongo, who was not fond of paying for the delivery of letters, he sent these missives by couriers who posted them at Como, Lecco, Varese, and other pretty little towns in the near neighbourhood of the lake. This was done in the hope that the couriers might bring back answers; and this hope was fulfilled.

Before long the days when the couriers arrived became eventful days for the Contessa. The couriers brought her flowers, fruit, and little presents of no intrinsic value, but which gave her pleasure as they did her sister-in-law. Her memories of the Conte began to be mingled with thoughts of his great power, and the Contessa became curious to know everything that was said about him. Even the Liberals paid tribute to his talents.

The main source of the Conte's evil reputation had its origin in the fact that he was considered the leader of the *Ultra* party at the Court of Parma, while the Liberal party had at its head a scheming woman capable of anything, even of succeeding – the Marchesa Raversi, who was immensely rich. The Prince made a great point of not discouraging that one of the parties which did not happen to be in power; he knew very well that he himself would always be master, even with a Ministry drawn from the Marchesa Raversi's circle. Endless details of these intrigues were reported at Grianta.

The absence of Mosca, whom everyone depicted as a Minister of the highest talent and a man of action, made it possible not to think any more about his powdered head, the symbol of everything that was dull and dreary. This was a detail of no consequence, one of the obligations imposed by the court at which he was playing so distinguished a part. 'A court,' said the Contessa to the Marchesa, 'is quite a ridiculous thing, but it is amusing. It's a game that interests you, but in which you have to conform to the rules. Whoever thought of protesting against the absurdity of the rules of whist? And yet, once you are accustomed to the rules, it is delightful to beat your opponent by winning all the tricks.'

The Contessa often thought about the writer of so many amusing letters; the days on which she received them were delightful to her. She would take her boat and go to read them at one of the beautiful spots by the lake, the villa Pliniana, Bellano, the woods of the Sfondrata. These letters seemed to console her a little for Fabrizio's absence. She could not, at all events, refuse to allow the Conte to be very much in love with her, and before a month had passed she was thinking of him with tender affection. For his part, Conte Mosca was almost sincere when he offered to hand in his resignation, to quit the Ministry and come and spend the rest of his life with her in Milan or elsewhere. 'I have 400,000 lire,' he added, 'which will always bring us in an income of 15,000.' 'A box at the theatre once more, horses, and so on,' thought the Contessa; these were pleasant dreams. The sublime beauty of the different views of the Lake of Como began to interest her anew. She went down to dream by its shores of this return to a brilliant and exceptionally pleasant existence, which, most unexpectedly, seemed now becoming possible once again. She saw herself on the Corso, in Milan, happy and light-hearted as in the days of the Viceroy. 'Youth, or at any rate a life full of activity, would begin again for me!'

Sometimes her eager imagination concealed the bare truth from her, but she never had any of those wilful illusions produced by a cowardly mind. She was above all things a woman who was honest with herself. 'Though I am a little too old to be doing foolish things,' she would say to herself, 'envy, which has self-illusions just the same as love, may poison my stay in Milan for me. After my husband's death, my noble poverty was a success, as was my refusal of two great fortunes. My poor little Conte Mosca has not a twentieth part of the riches cast at my feet by those two boobies, Limercati and Nani. The meagre widow's pension which I only obtained with great difficulty, the dismissal of my servants, which created a sensation, the little fifth-floor room which brought a score of carriages to the door, all that in its day went to form a striking spectacle. But I shall have some disagreeable moments, however skilfully I go about it, if, still possessing my widow's pension as my sole fortune, I go back to live in Milan on the comfortable little middle-class competency which may be provided by the 15,000 lire that Mosca will have left after handing in his resignation. One strong objection, out of which envy will forge a terrible weapon, is that the Conte, although long since separated from his wife, is still a married man. This separation is known in Parma, but in Milan it will come as news, and it will be put down to me. So adieu, my fine Scala theatre, my heavenly Lake of Como, adieu! adieu!'

In spite of all these forebodings, if the Contessa had had the smallest fortune of her own she would have accepted Mosca's offer to resign his office. She regarded herself as a woman of middle age, and the idea of a court alarmed her. But what will appear in the highest degree improbable on this side of the Alps is that the Conte would have handed in his resignation gladly. That at least, was what he managed to make his friend believe. In all his letters he begged, with an ever-increasing frenzy, for a second interview with her in Milan; this request was granted. 'To swear that I am madly in love with you,' said the Contessa one day to him in Milan, 'would be a lie. I should be only too happy to love today at thirty odd, as I used to love at twenty-two! But I have seen so many things decay that I had imagined would last for ever! I have the most tender regard for you, my trust in you knows no limits, and of all the men I know, you are the one I like best.' The Contessa believed herself to be perfectly sincere, and yet, towards the end, this declaration contained a slight prevarication. If Fabrizio had wished it, he might have prevailed over everyone else in her heart. But Fabrizio was nothing more than a boy in Conte Mosca's eyes. He himself arrived in Milan three days after this young spark's departure for Novara, and he hastened to intercede on his behalf with Baron Binder. The Conte came to the opinion that his exile was now irrevocable.

He had not come to Milan alone. He had in his carriage the Duca Sanseverina-Taxis, a handsome little old man of sixty-eight with dapple-grey hair, very polished, very trim, enormously rich, but not of the highest nobility. It was his grandfather only who had amassed millions in the office of Farmer-General of the Revenues of the State of Parma. His father had got himself appointed Ambassador of the Prince of Parma to the Court of — by advancing the following argument: 'Your Highness allowed 30,000 francs to your representative at the Court of —, where he cuts an extremely modest figure. If your Highness will deign to appoint me to this post, I will accept 6,000 francs as a salary. My expenditure at the Court of — will never fall below 10,000 francs, and my agent will remit 20,000 francs every year to the Treasurer for Foreign Affairs in Parma. With that sum it will be possible to attach to me whatever Secretary to the Embassy you please, and I shall show no sort of desire to acquaint myself with diplomatic secrets, if there are any. My object is to shed lustre on my family, which is still a new one, and to make it distinguished by holding one of the great offices in your dominions.'

The present Duca, the son of this Ambassador, had committed the blunder of appearing as a semi-Liberal, and for two years past had been in despair. In Napoleon's time, he had lost two or three millions by his obstinacy in remaining abroad, and even now, after the re-establishment of order in Europe, he had not managed to obtain a certain Grand Cordon which adorned the portrait of his father. For want of this Cordon he was gradually pining away.

At the degree of intimacy which in Italy follows on love there was no longer any obstacle in the nature of vanity between the two lovers. It was therefore with the most perfect simplicity that Mosca said to the woman he adored: 'I have two or three plans of conduct to offer you, all of them fairly well thought out. I have been pondering over nothing else for the past three months. First : I hand in my resignation and we go to live as good plain folk in Milan, Florence, Naples, or wherever you please. We have an income of 15,000 lire, apart from what we receive from the Prince's liberality, which will continue for some time, more or less. Secondly: You condescend to come to the place in which I have some influence. You buy a property, Sacca, for example, a charming house in the middle of a forest overlooking the river Po; you can have the contract signed within a week from now. The Prince will attach you to his court. But here I can see an enormous obstacle. You will be well received at court; nobody would presume to jib at this when I am there. Besides, the Princess imagines she is unhappy, and I have recently rendered her certain services with a view to your interest. But I must remind you of a paramount objection: the Prince is an extremely bigoted churchman, and, as you already know, as luck will have it I am a married man. From this will arise a million minor unpleasantnesses. You are a widow; that is a fine title that should be exchanged for another, and this forms the subject of my third proposal.

'One might find you a new husband who would not be too much in the way. But first of all he would have to be considerably advanced in years, for why should you deny me the hope of succeeding him one day? Well now, I have arranged this curious business with the Duca Sanseverina-Taxis, who, of course does not know the name of his future Duchessa. He knows only that she will make him an ambassador and will procure him the Grand Cordon which his father had, and the lack of which makes him the unhappiest of mortals. Apart from this, the Duca is not too much of a fool. He gets his clothes and his wigs from Paris; he is not in the least the sort of man to do anything deliberately spiteful, he seriously believes that honour consists in having a Cordon, and he is ashamed of his wealth. He came to me a year ago to suggest his founding a hospital, in order to get this Cordon. I laughed at him then, but he did not by any means laugh at me when I proposed a marriage to him. My first condition was, of course, that he should never set foot again in Parma.'

'But do you know that what you are proposing to me is highly immoral?' said the Contessa.

'No more immoral than everything else that is done at our court and a score of others. Absolute power has this advantage, that it sanctifies everything in the eyes of the public, and what thing can be absurd when nobody notices it? Our policy for the next twenty years is going to consist in feeling fear of the Jacobins – and what fear, too! Every year, we shall fancy ourselves on the eve of '93. You will hear, I hope, the fine speeches I make on that subject at my receptions! They are beautiful! Anything that can in some slight way reduce this fear will be *supremely moral* in the eyes of the nobles and the bigots. And in Parma, as it happens, everyone who is not either a noble or a bigot is in prison, or packing up to go there. You may rest assured that this marriage will not seem out of the ordinary at our court until the day on which I fall out of favour. This arrangement involves no dishonest trick on anyone; that, so it seems to me, is the essential thing. The Prince, on whose favour we are trading, has placed only one condition on his consent, which is that the future Duchessa shall be of noble birth. Last year my office, all told, brought me in 107,000 lire; my total income must have been 122,000; I invested 20,000 at Lyons.

'Well then, make your choice: either, a life of luxury based on our having 122,000 lire to spend, which, in Parma, will go at least as far as 400,000 in Milan; but with this marriage which will give you the name of a passable man whom you will never see once you leave the altar; or else a modest, comfortable existence on 15,000 lire in Florence or Naples, for I agree with you that you have been too much admired in Milan. Envy would make our lives a burden there, and that might possibly finish by souring our tempers. The splendid existence we shall lead in Parma will, I hope, have some touches of novelty, even in your eyes which have seen the court of Prince Eugène. You would be wise to become acquainted with it before shutting the door upon it. Don't think that I am trying to influence your opinion. As for me, my own choice is quite clear: I would rather live on a fourth floor with you than continue that grand existence by myself.'

The possibility of this strange marriage was thrashed out by the two lovers every day. The Contessa saw the Duca Sanseverina-Taxis at the Scala Ball, and thought him highly presentable. In one of their final conversations Mosca summed up his proposals in the following words: 'We must make a decisive choice, if we wish to spend the rest of our lives in an enjoyable fashion and not grow old before our time. The Prince has given his approval. Sanseverina is a person who might easily be worse; he possesses the finest *palazzo* in Parma, and has unlimited wealth. He is sixty-eight and has an insane passion for the Grand Cordon; but one great blot on his character ruins his life: he once paid 10,000 lire for a bust of Napoleon by Canova. His second sin, which will be the death of him if you do not come to his rescue, is that he lent twenty-five napoleons to Ferrante Palla, a lunatic of our province, but also something of a genius, whom we have since sentenced to death, fortunately by default. This man Ferrante has written a couple of hundred lines of poetry in his time which have not their like in the world. I will recite them to you, they are as fine as Dante's. The Prince is sending Sanseverina to the Court of —. He will marry you on the day of his departure, and in the second year of his travels, which he likes to call an embassy, he will receive the Grand Cordon of —, which he cannot live without. You will have in him a brother who will be no sort of nuisance to you. He is signing all the documents I require in advance, and besides, you will see him little or never, entirely as you choose. He asks for nothing better than never to show his face in Parma, where his grandfather the Farmer-General and his own reputed Liberalism are a source of embarrassment to him. Rassi, our hangman, makes out that the Duca has been a secret subscriber to the *Constitutionnel* by the intermediary of the poet Ferrante Palla, and this slander has for a long time been a serious obstacle in the way of the Prince's consent.'

Why should the chronicler who follows faithfully all the most trivial details of the story that has been told him be held up to blame? Is it his fault if his characters, led astray by passions which he, most unfortunately for himself, in no way shares, descend to actions that are profoundly immoral? It is true that things of this sort are no longer done in a country where the sole passion that has outlived all the rest is lust for money, that gives vanity its chance.

Three months after the events we have up till now recorded, the Duchessa Sanseverina-Taxis astonished the court of Parma by her easy affability and the noble serenity of her mind. Her house was beyond all comparison the most attractive in the city. This was what Conte Mosca had promised his master, Ranuccio-Ernesto IV, the reigning Prince, and the Princess his consort, to whom the Duchessa was presented by two of the greatest ladies in the principality, gave her a most marked welcome. The Duchessa was curious to see this Prince, master of the destiny of the man she loved; she was anxious, moreover, to please him, and in this she was more than successful. She found a man of tall stature, but rather thickset; his hair, his moustache, his enormous whiskers were of the finest golden hue, or so his courtiers said; elsewhere they might have provoked, by their faded tint, the ignoble epithet, *tow-coloured*. From the middle of a plump face a tiny, turned-up nose that was almost feminine projected slightly. But the Duchessa remarked that, in order to note all the elements of ugliness, one had first to attempt a detailed survey of each one of the Prince's features. Taken as a whole, he had the air of a man of sense and of determined character. The Prince's carriage, his way of holding himself, were not devoid of majesty, but he often tried to impress the person he was addressing; at such times he became embarrassed himself and fell into an almost continuous swaying motion, balancing first on one leg and then on the other. For the rest, Ernesto IV had a piercing and commanding gaze; there was nobility in the gestures of his arms, and his speech was at once both measured and concise.

Mosca had warned the Duchessa that in the large room in which he gave audiences the Prince had a full-length portrait of Louis XIV, and a very beautiful Florentine table encrusted with mosaic. She found the imitation striking; evidently he strove to copy the expression and the noble style of speech of Louis XIV, and he leant upon the mosaic table in such a way as to give himself the pose of Joseph II. He sat down immediately after his first words of greeting to the Duchessa, to give her an opportunity to make use of the tabouret befitting her rank. At this court, duchesses, princesses, and the wives of Spanish grandees alone have the right to be seated. All other ladies wait until the Prince or Princess invites them to sit down; and, to mark the difference in rank, these august personages always take care to let a short interval elapse before inviting those ladies who are not duchesses to be seated. The Duchessa found that at certain moments the imitation of Louis XIV was too strongly marked in the Prince; as, for instance, in his way of smiling affably as he threw back his head.

Ernesto IV wore a dress coat in the latest style from Paris. Every month he had sent to him from that city, which he abhorred, a dress coat, a frock coat, and a hat. But, by an odd blend of costume, the day on which the Duchessa was received he had put on red breeches, silk stockings, and very close-fitting shoes, models for which can be found in the portraits of Joseph II.

He received the Duchessa graciously; he made some shrewd and witty remarks to her; but she saw quite clearly that there was no effusiveness in his kind reception of her. 'Do you know why?' said Conte Mosca on their return from the audience, 'it's just because Milan is a larger and finer city than Parma. He would have been afraid, had he given you the welcome I expected and he himself had led me to hope for, of seeming like a provincial in ecstasies before the charms of a fine lady coming straight from the capital. No doubt, too, he is still upset by a particular detail that I hardly dare mention to you: the Prince sees at his court no lady who can vie

with you on the score of beauty. Last night, when he retired to
bed, that was the sole topic of his conversation with Pernice, his
chief valet, who has a soft spot for me. I foresee a minor revolution
in etiquette. My greatest enemy is a fool who goes by the name of
General Fabio Conti. Just imagine a freak who has been on active
service for possibly one day in his life, and sets out from that to
copy the bearing of Frederick the Great. In addition to which, he is
anxious also to reproduce the noble affability of General Lafayette,
and that because he is the head of the Liberal party here. (God knows
what sort of Liberals!)'

'I know that man Fabio Conti,' said the Duchessa. 'I had a glimpse
of him near Como; he was having a row with the police.' She related
the little adventure which the reader may possibly remember.

'You will learn one day, madam, if your mind ever manages to
penetrate the profundities of our etiquette, that young ladies do not
appear at our court until after their marriage. Well now, the Prince
has such a patriotic enthusiasm for the superiority of his city of Parma
over all others that I would bet he will find some way of having
little Clelia Conti, our Lafayette's daughter, presented to him. She
is charming, indeed; and was still considered, a week ago, the most
beautiful person in the Prince's dominions.

'I do not know,' the Conte went on, 'whether the horrors that
the enemies of our sovereign have published regarding him have
reached the castle of Grianta. They make him out a monster, a
veritable ogre. The fact is that Ernesto IV has his full complement of
nice little virtues, and, one may add that, had he been as invulnerable
as Achilles, he would have continued to be a model for potentates.
But in a moment of boredom and anger, and also a little in imitation
of Louis XIV, who cut off the head of some hero or other of the
Fronde who was discovered, fifty years after the Fronde, living
peacefully and insolently on an estate near Versailles, one fine day
Ernesto IV had two Liberals hanged. It appears that these rash fellows
used to meet on a certain day to speak ill of the Prince and address
earnest prayers to heaven that the plague might visit Parma and rid
them of the tyrant. The word *tyrant* was proved. Rassi called this a
conspiracy; and he had them sentenced to death, and the execution
of one of them, Conte L—, was atrocious. All this happened before
my time.

'Since that fatal hour,' the Conte added, lowering his voice, 'the

Prince has been subject to fits of panic *unworthy of a man*, but which are the sole source of the favour I enjoy. But for this overruling fear, I should have a kind of merit too abrupt, and too harsh for this court, where imbeciles abound. Would you believe that the Prince looks even under the beds in his apartment before retiring, and spends a million, which in Parma is the equivalent of four million in Milan, to maintain a good police force; and you see in front of you, madam, the Chief of that terrible police. By means of the police, that is to say by fear, I have become Minister of War and of Finance; and as the Minister of the Interior is my nominal chief, in so far as he has the police under his jurisdiction, I have had that portfolio given to Conte Zurla-Contarini, an imbecile who is a glutton for work and gives himself the pleasure of writing eighty letters a day. I have received one only this morning on which Conte Zurla-Contarini has had the satisfaction of writing the number 20,715 with his own hand.'

The Duchessa Sanseverina was presented to the doleful Princess of Parma, Clara Paolina, who, because her husband had a mistress (quite a pretty woman, the Marchesa Balbi), imagined herself to be the most unhappy woman in the universe, an idea which had made her the most boring one. The Duchessa found her a very tall and very thin woman, who was not yet thirty-six and who looked fifty. Her noble face, with regular features, might have passed for beautiful, though somewhat spoilt by large round eyes that could barely see, if the Princess had not given up taking care of her appearance. She received the Duchessa with a shyness so marked that certain courtiers, enemies of Conte Mosca, ventured to say that the Princess looked like the woman who was being presented, and the Duchessa like the sovereign. The Duchessa, surprised and almost disconcerted, could find no form of words that would put her in a place inferior to that which the Princess took for herself. To help this poor Princess, who in reality was not lacking in intelligence, to recover her self-possession in some slight measure, the Duchessa could think of nothing better than to begin, and carry on, a long dissertation on botany. The Princess was really an expert on this subject; she had some very fine hothouses with quantities of tropical plants. The Duchessa, while trying quite simply to find a way out of this difficult situation, made a lifelong conquest of Princess Clara Paolina, who, from being shy and speechless as she was at the beginning of the audience, found herself towards the end so much at her ease that, contrary to all the rules of etiquette, this audience lasted for no less than an hour and a quarter. Next day, the Duchessa sent out to buy some exotic plants, and gave herself out as a great lover of botany.

The Princess spent all her time with the venerable Father Landriani, Archbishop of Parma, a man of learning and even of intelligence, and a perfectly honest man too. But he presented a singular spectacle when he was seated in his chair of crimson velvet (this was the privilege of his office) opposite the Princess's armchair, around which were gathered her ladies-in-waiting and her two lady-companions. The old prelate, with his long white hair, was even shyer, if that were possible, than the Princess herself. They saw one another every day, and every audience began with a silence that lasted a good quarter of an hour. This had reached such a point that the Contessa Alvizi, one of the two ladies in attendance on the Princess, had become a sort of favourite, because she had the art of encouraging them to speak to each other and so break the silence.

To end the series of presentations, the Duchessa was admitted to the presence of his Serene Highness, the Crown Prince, a person of taller stature than his father, and even shyer than his mother. He was well up in mineralogy and was sixteen years old. He blushed excessively on seeing the Duchessa come in, and was so put off his balance, that he could not summon up a single word to say to this beautiful lady. He was a very handsome young man, and spent his whole life in the woods with a hammer in his hand.

At the moment when the Duchessa rose to bring this silent audience to an end: 'My god! madam, how pretty you are!' exclaimed the Crown Prince – a remark which was not considered to be in too bad taste by the lady presented.

The Marchesa Balbi, a young woman of five-and-twenty, could still (some two or three years before the arrival of the Duchessa Sanseverina in Parma) have passed for the most perfect model of the Italian type of beauty. Even now, she had still the finest eyes in the world, and the most charming little airs and graces; but, viewed close up, her skin was a network of countless fine little wrinkles, which made the Marchesa look like a woman in early middle age. Seen from a certain distance, at the theatre for instance, in her box, she was still a beauty; and the people in the pit thought that the Prince showed excellent taste. He used to spend every evening at the

Marchesa Balbi's house, but often without opening his lips, and the boredom she saw in the Prince's face had made this poor woman decline into a state of extraordinary thinness. She laid claim to an unlimited amount of subtlety, and there was always a tinge of malice in her smile. She had the prettiest teeth in the world, and on all occasions, since she had little or no sense, she would attempt, by smiling slyly, to convey some other meaning than that her words expressed. Conte Mosca declared that it was this continual habit of smiling, while inwardly she was yawning, that had given her so many wrinkles.

This woman Balbi had a finger in every pie, and the State never undertook a transaction involving a thousand lire without there being some little *souvenir* (this was the polite expression in Parma) for the Marchesa. Public report asserted that she had invested six millions in England, but her fortune, which in truth was of recent origin, did not in reality exceed 1,500,000 lire. It was to protect himself from her tricks and to have her dependent upon him that Conte Mosca had had himself appointed Minister of Finance. The Marchesa's sole passion was fear disguised as sordid avarice. '*I shall die upon straw!*' she would sometimes say to the Prince, who was utterly shocked by such a remark. The Duchessa noticed that the anteroom of the Marchesa Balbi's *palazzo*, resplendent with gilding, was lighted by a single candle with the wax dripping down on to a priceless marble table, while the doors of her drawing-room were black with dirt from her footmen's fingers. 'She received me,' the Duchessa told her lover, 'as if she were expecting me to offer her a tip of fifty lire.'

The Duchessa's triumphal progress was slightly interrupted by the reception given her by the shrewdest woman at the court, the celebrated Marchesa Raversi, a consummate intriguer who chanced to be at the head of the party opposed to that of Conte Mosca. She was anxious to overthrow him, and all the more so in the past few months, since she was the niece of the Duca Sanseverina, and was afraid of seeing her chances of a legacy endangered by the charms of the new Duchessa. 'The Raversi is not a woman to be disregarded,' the Conte remarked to his mistress, 'I consider her so far capable of resorting to any underhand measure that I separated from my wife solely because she insisted on taking as a lover Cavaliere Benti-voglio, a friend of the Marchesa.' This lady, a tall virago with jet black hair, remarkable for the diamonds which she wore all day, and the rouge with which she plastered her cheeks, had declared herself in advance the Duchessa's enemy, and on receiving her in her own house made it her business to open hostilities. The Duca Sanseverina, in the letters he wrote from —, appeared so delighted with his Embassy, and above all with the prospect of the Grand Cordon, that his family were afraid of his leaving part of his fortune to his wife, whom he loaded with little presents. The Marchesa Raversi, although a thoroughly ugly woman, had for a lover Conte Balbi, the handsomest man at court; as a general rule, she was successful in all her undertakings.

The Duchessa kept up a most sumptuous establishment. The Palazzo Sanseverina had always been one of the most magnificent in the city of Parma and the Duca, in view of his Embassy and his future Grand Cordon, was spending vast sums of money to make it still more splendid; the Duchessa had charge of the alterations.

The Conte had guessed rightly; a few days after the Duchessa had been presented to the Prince, Clelia Conti came to court; she had been made a Canoness. In order to parry the blow that this favour might be thought to have struck at the Conte's influence, the Duchessa gave a party under pretext of throwing open the gardens of her *palazzo* and, in her characteristic charming way, made Clelia, whom she called her young friend of the Lake of Como, the queen of the evening. Her monogram appeared as if by accident on the principal transparencies. Young Clelia, although somewhat pensive, talked in a pleasing way about the little adventure by the lake, and of her keen gratitude. She was said to be deeply religious and very fond of solitude. 'I'm ready to bet,' said the Conte, 'that she has enough sense to be ashamed of her father.' The Duchessa made a friend of this girl, she felt attracted towards her. She did not wish to appear jealous, and included her in all her pleasure parties. Her plan of action, in short, was to try and lessen all the enmities of which the Conte was the object.

Everything delighted the Duchessa. She was amused by this court existence where a sudden squall is always to be feared; she felt as if she were beginning her life anew. She was tenderly attached to the Conte, who was literally off his head with happiness. This pleasing situation had made him perfectly cool and composed with regard to everything that concerned his professional ambitions only. And so, barely two months after the Duchessa's arrival, he obtained the patent and honours due to a Prime Minister, which come very near to those accorded to the sovereign himself. The Conte had complete control of his master's mind and will; they had a proof of this in Parma by which everyone was impressed.

To the south-east, and ten minutes away from the city, rises that famous citadel, so renowned throughout Italy, the great tower of which stands one hundred and eighty feet high and is visible from such a great distance. This tower, constructed on the model of Hadrian's Tomb in Rome by the Farnese, grandsons of Paul III, towards the beginning of the sixteenth century, is so large in diameter that on the platform in which it ends it has been possible to build a *palazzo* for the governor of the citadel, and a new prison known as the Farnese Tower. This prison, erected especially for the eldest son of Ranuccio-Ernesto II, who had become the accepted lover of his own stepmother is regarded as something singular and fine throughout the principality. The Duchessa was curious to see it. On the day of her visit the heat down in Parma was overpowering, and up there, in that lofty position, she found the air fresh, a thing that so much delighted her that she stayed there for several hours. The officials were only too ready to throw open to her the rooms of the Farnese Tower.

On the platform of the great tower the Duchessa met a poor Liberal in confinement there, who had come to enjoy the half-hour's outing that was allowed him every third day. On coming down again into Parma, and not having yet acquired the discretion necessary in the court of an absolute sovereign, she spoke of this man, who had told her the whole story of his life. The Marchesa Raversi's party seized upon these remarks of the Duchessa and repeated them broadcast, hoping very much that they would shock the Prince. Ernesto IV, in fact, was in the habit of repeating that the essential thing was to impress people's imagination. 'Perpetual is a solemn word,' he used to say, 'and more terrible in Italy than elsewhere.' In consequence, he had never granted a pardon in his life.

A week after her visit to the fortress the Duchessa received a letter granting a remission of sentence, signed by the Prince and the Minister, with the name left blank. The prisoner whose name she chose to write would have his property restored to him and be given permission to spend the rest of his days in America. The

Duchessa wrote the name of the man who had spoken to her. Unfortunately this man turned out to be a bit of a rascal and a weak character; it was on the strength of his confessions that the famous Ferrante Palla had been sentenced to death.

The unprecedented nature of this pardon raised the pleasure of the Duchessa's position to its highest pitch. Conte Mosca was wild with delight; it was a great day in his life and one that had a decisive influence on Fabrizio's destiny. He, meanwhile, was still at Romagnano, near Novara, going to confession, hunting and shooting, reading nothing at all, and paying court to a lady of noble birth, as was prescribed by his instructions. The Duchessa was still a trifle shocked by this last requirement. Another sign that boded no good for the Conte was that while she would speak to him with the utmost frankness on any other subject, and would think aloud in his presence, she never mentioned Fabrizio to him without first carefully choosing her words.

'If you like,' the Conte said to her one day, 'I will write to that pleasant brother of yours on the Lake of Como, and I will duly force that Marchese del Dongo, at the cost of a little trouble to myself and my friends at —, to ask for the pardon of your charming Fabrizio. If it is true, as I should be loath to doubt, that Fabrizio is somewhat superior to those young fellows who ride their English thoroughbreds about the streets of Milan, what a life, at eighteen, to be doing nothing with no prospect of ever having anything to do! If heaven had endowed him with a real passion for anything whatever, were it only for fishing, I would respect it; but what will he do in Milan, even after he has obtained his pardon? At a certain hour of the day, he will get on a horse which he has had brought from England; at another, want of something better to do will take him to his mistress, for whom he will care less than for his horse. . . . But, if you ask me to do so, I will do my best to procure such a life for your nephew.'

'I should like him to be an officer,' said the Duchessa.

'Would you recommend a sovereign to entrust a post, which, at a given date, may become of some importance, to a young man who, in the first place, is liable to enthusiasm, and, secondly, has shown enthusiasm for Napoleon to the extent of going to join him at Waterloo? Just think what would have become of us all if Napoleon had won at Waterloo! We should have no Liberals to fear, it is true, but the heads of ancient royal families would not be able to reign unless they married the daughters of his Marshals. And therefore a military career for Fabrizio would be like the life of a squirrel in a revolving cage – a great deal of movement that gets you nowhere. He would have the vexation of seeing himself passed over in favour of all sorts of loyal plebeians. The first essential in a young man of the present day, that is to say for possibly fifty years to come, so long as we remain in a state of fear, and religion has not been restored to its proper place, is not to be liable to enthusiasm and not to have a mind of one's own.

'I have thought of one thing, but one that will begin by making you cry out in protest, and will give me infinite trouble for many a day to come; it is an act of folly I am ready to commit for your sake. But tell me, if you can, what act of folly would I not commit to win a smile?'

'Well?' said the Duchessa.

'Well! we have had as Archbishops of Parma three members of your family: Ascanio del Dongo who wrote a book in 16 ..., I forget the date; Fabrizio in 1699; and another Ascanio in 1740. If Fabrizio cares to become a prelate and distinguish himself by virtues of the highest order, I will make him a bishop somewhere or other, and then Archbishop here, provided my influence lasts. The real objection is this: Shall I remain Prime Minister long enough to carry out this fine plan, which will require several years? The Prince may die, he may have the bad taste to dismiss me. But, after all, it is the only way open to me of doing for Fabrizio something that is worthy of you.'

They discussed the matter at length; this idea was highly repugnant to the Duchessa.

'Prove to me once more,' she said to the Conte, 'that every other career is impossible for Fabrizio.' The Conte proved it.

'You regret the brilliant uniform,' he added. 'But as to that I don't know what I can do.'

At the end of a month which the Duchessa had asked for in order to think things over, she yielded with a sigh to the wise views of the Minister. 'Either to ride in a stiff and solemn manner on an English thoroughbred through the streets of some great city,' repeated the Conte, 'or else to adopt a calling that is not unbefitting to his birth; I can see no middle course. Unfortunately, a gentleman cannot become either a doctor or a lawyer, and this age is dominated by lawyers.

'Always bear in mind, madam,' the Conte went on, 'that you are giving your nephew, in the streets of Milan, the same lot enjoyed by the young men of his age who are accounted the most fortunate. Once his pardon is obtained, you will allow him fifteen, twenty, thirty thousand lire; it matters little, neither you nor I are anxious to save money.'

The Duchessa was susceptible to the idea of fame; she did not want Fabrizio to be a mere squanderer of money; she came round to her lover's plan.

'Note,' said the Conte, 'that I do not pretend to make him an exemplary priest, like so many you see. No, he is a great noble, first and foremost; he can remain perfectly ignorant if it seems good to him, and will none the less become a bishop and an archbishop, if the Prince continues to regard me as a man who is useful to him.

'If your orders deign to change my proposal into an immutable decree,' the Conte added, 'Parma must on no account see our protégé as a man in a humble position. His progress will create a scandal if people have seen him here as an ordinary priest. He must not appear in Parma until he has his *purple stockings*★ and a suitable establishment. Then everyone will guess that your nephew is destined to become a bishop, and nobody will be shocked.

'If you will be guided by me, you will send Fabrizio to have his training in theology and spend three years in Naples. During the vacations at his theological college he can go, if he likes, to visit Paris and London, but he must never show his face in Parma.' This last remark almost made the Duchessa shudder.

She sent a courier to her nephew, asking him to meet her at Piacenza. Need it be said that this courier was the bearer of all monetary requirements and all the necessary passports?

Arriving first at Piacenza, Fabrizio ran to greet the Duchessa on her arrival, and embraced her with transports of joy that made her burst into tears. She was glad the Conte was not present; this was

★ In Italy young men who have patrons or possess good intelligence become *Monsignori* or *prelati*, which does not mean bishop; they then wear purple stockings. A man does not take any vows to become *Monsignore*; he can discard his purple stockings and get married.

the first time since they had fallen in love with each other that she had experienced a like sensation.

Fabrizio was deeply touched, and also distressed, by the plans the Duchessa had made for him. It had always been his hope that once this affair of Waterloo was settled he might end by becoming a soldier. One thing struck the Duchessa and still further increased the romantic notion she had formed of her nephew: he absolutely refused to lead the life of an idle haunter of cafés in one of the big Italian cities.

'Can't you see yourself on the *Corso* in Florence or in Naples,' said the Duchessa, 'with thoroughbred English horses? For the evenings, a carriage, an attractive flat, and the like?' She dwelt with keen delight on the description of this ordinary, trivial sort of happiness which she saw Fabrizio reject with disdain. 'He is a real hero,' she thought.

'And after ten years of this pleasant existence, what shall I have done?' said Fabrizio. 'What shall I be? A young man getting on in life who will have to take second place to the first handsome youngster who makes his entry into society, also mounted upon an English horse.'

At first Fabrizio utterly rejected the idea of going into the Church. He spoke of going to America, of becoming an American citizen and a soldier of the Republic.

'What a wrong idea you have of things! You won't have any war, and you'll relapse into the life of a café-haunter, only it will be a life without elegance, without music, without love affairs,' replied the Duchessa. 'Believe me, for you as for myself, it would be a dreary existence in America.' She explained to him the cult of the 'almighty dollar', and the respect that had to be shown to ordinary men of the working-class, who by their votes decided everything. They came back to the idea of the Church.

'Before you fly into a passion,' said the Duchessa, 'please try to understand what the Conte is asking you to do. There's no question whatever of your being a poor priest of a more or less exemplary and virtuous life, like Father Blanès. Remember what your uncles the Archbishops of Parma were like; read over again the account of their lives in the appendix to the Genealogy. Before all things, it is fitting for a man of your name to be a great gentleman, noble, generous, an upholder of justice, destined from the first to find himself at the head of his order ... and in the whole of his life doing only one dishonourable thing, and that a very useful one.'

'So all my illusions come to nothing!' said Fabrizio, sighing deeply. 'It is a cruel sacrifice! I must admit I had not considered this horror of enthusiasm and a chivalrous spirit, even when exercised to their own advantage, which from now onwards is going to dominate the minds of absolute monarchs.'

'Bear in mind that a proclamation, an unreasoning impulse of the heart can suddenly impel the enthusiast to join a party opposed to the one he has served all his life!'

'I an enthusiast!' exclaimed Fabrizio. 'What a strange accusation! Why, I cannot even manage to fall in love!'

'What!' exclaimed the Duchessa.

'When I have the honour to pay my court to a beauty, even if she is of good birth and full of piety, I cannot think about her unless I have her in sight.'

This avowal made a strange impression on the Duchessa.

'I ask you to give me a month,' Fabrizio went on, 'in which to take my leave of Signora C— of Novara, and, what is still more difficult, to say goodbye to those castles in the air I have been building all my life. I will write to my mother, who will have the kindness to come and see me at Belgirate, on the Piedmontese side of Lake Maggiore, and in thirty-one days from now I shall be in Parma incognito.'

'No, you mustn't on any account do that!' cried the Duchessa. She did not want Conte Mosca to see her talking to Fabrizio.

The same two people met each other again at Piacenza. This time the Duchessa was in a great state of agitation; a storm had blown up at court. The Marchesa Raversi's party was on the brink of triumph; it was possible that Conte Mosca would be replaced by General Fabio Conti, the leader of what was known in Parma as the *Liberal Party*. With the exception of the name of the rival who was growing in the Prince's favour the Duchessa told Fabrizio everything. She discussed afresh the chances of his future career, even with the prospect of his having to do without the Conte's all-powerful patronage.

'I'm going to spend three years at the Ecclesiastical Academy in Naples,' exclaimed Fabrizio. 'But since I must above all things be a young gentleman, and am not obliged to lead the strict life of a virtuous seminarist, this stay in Naples holds nothing frightening for me. The life there will be quite as pleasant as life at Romagnano; the best society of the neighbourhood was beginning to consider me a Jacobin. During my exile I have discovered that I know nothing, not even Latin, not even how to spell. I had planned to begin my education over again at Novara; I shall willingly study theology in Naples; it's a very complicated branch of knowledge.'

The Duchessa was highly delighted. 'If we are driven out of Parma,' she said, 'we will come and see you in Naples. But since you accept, until further orders, the offer of *purple stockings*, the Conte, who is well acquainted with the Italy of today, has given me a message to convey to you. Believe or not, as you choose, the things they teach you, *but never raise any objection*. Imagine that you are being taught the rules of the game of whist; would you take objection in any way to the rules of whist? I told the Conte you were a believer, and he rejoiced to hear it; it is useful both in this world and the next. But though you are a believer, do not indulge in the vulgar habit of speaking with horror of Voltaire, Diderot, Raynal, and all those harebrained Frenchmen who ushered in government by two Chambers. Let these names be rarely on your lips; but if indeed you have to mention them speak of these gentlemen in a mild, ironic way: they are people long since refuted and whose attacks have ceased to be of any consequence.

'Believe blindly everything that they tell you at the Academy. Bear in mind that there are people who will make a careful note of your slightest objections. They will forgive you a little amorous intrigue if it is well handled, but certainly not an expression of doubt; age puts a stop to amorous scrapes, but adds more weight to doubt. Act on this principle when you go to confession. You shall have a letter of recommendation to a Bishop who is factotum to the Cardinal Archbishop of Naples; to him alone you should admit your escapade in France, and your presence on the 18th of June in the neighbourhood of Waterloo. Even so, cut out a great deal of this adventure and make it seem of less importance; confess it only so that they cannot reproach you for having kept it secret. You were so young at the time!

'The second idea which the Conte sends you is this: if a brilliant argument should occur to you, a triumphant retort that will change the course of the conversation, don't give way to the temptation to shine; remain silent; people of any discernment will read your cleverness in your eyes. It will be time enough to display your wit when you are a bishop.'

Fabrizio made his debut in Naples with an unpretentious carriage and four servants, good, simple Milanese folk whom his aunt had sent him. After a year of study no one would have said that he was clever; people looked upon him as a great nobleman, of a studious bent, very generous but with somewhat free and easy morals.

That year, amusing enough for Fabrizio, was terrible for the Duchessa. The Conte was three or four times within an ace of utter ruin. The Prince, more full of fears than ever because he was ill that year, believed that by dismissing him he could free himself from the odium of the executions carried out before the Conte became a Minister. Rassi was the prime favourite who must at all costs be retained. The Conte's perils made the Duchessa become passionately attached to him; she no longer gave a thought to Fabrizio. To lend colour to their possible retirement, it was discovered that the air of Parma, which was indeed a trifle damp, as everywhere else in Lombardy, did not agree with her. Finally, after intervals of disgrace which went so far as to make the Conte, even though Prime Minister, spend sometimes twenty whole days without seeing his master in private, Mosca won the day. He secured the appointment of General Fabio Conti, the reputed Liberal, as governor of the citadel in which the Liberals condemned by Rassi were imprisoned. 'If Conti shows any leniency towards his prisoners,' said Mosca to his mistress, 'he will be disgraced as a Jacobin whose political opinions make him forget his duty as a general. If he shows himself stern and pitiless, and that, to my mind, is the side to which he will incline, he ceases to be the leader of his own party, and alienates all the families that have a relative in the citadel. The poor man knows how to assume an air of deepest respect at the Prince's approach; if need be he can change his coat four times in a single day; he can discuss a question of etiquette, but he hasn't a head capable of following the difficult path by which alone he can escape disaster. And in any case, I am there.'

The day after the appointment of General Fabio Conti, which put an end to the ministerial crisis, it was learnt that Parma was to have an ultra-monarchical newspaper.

'What quarrels this paper will excite!' said the Duchessa.

'As for this paper, the idea of which is perhaps my masterpiece,' replied the Conte laughing, 'I shall gradually and quite against my will allow it to pass into the hands of the most rabid Ultras. I have had some fine salaries attached to the editorial posts. These posts will be solicited by people from every quarter; this business will carry us over a month or two, and people will forget the peril to which I have just now been exposed. Those solemn gentlemen P— and D— are already among the candidates on my list.'

'But this paper will be quite revoltingly absurd.'

'I am reckoning on that,' replied the Conte. 'The Prince will read it every morning and admire the doctrines emanating from me as its founder. As to the details, he will approve or be shocked by them; and there are two of the hours he devotes to work every day taken up. The paper will stir up some trouble for itself, but at the moment that serious complaints begin to come in, in eight or ten months time, it will be entirely in the hands of the ultra-rabids. It will be this party which is a nuisance to me that will have to answer them. As for me, I shall raise objections against the paper; but on the whole I prefer a hundred frightful absurdities to one hanging. Who remembers an absurdity two years after the publication of the official organ? On the other hand, I should have the sons and family of the man who is hanged vowing me a hatred that will last as long as I shall and possibly shorten my life.'

The Duchessa, always passionately interested in something or other, always active, never idle, had more intelligence than the whole of the court of Parma put together; but she lacked the patience and impassivity necessary for success in intrigues. However, she had managed to follow with keen excitement all the interests of the various cliques; she was even beginning to have some personal influence with the Prince. Clara Paolina, the Princess Consort, surrounded with honours but a prisoner to the most antiquated forms of etiquette, looked upon herself as the unhappiest of women. The Duchessa Sanseverina paid court to her and tried to prove to her that she was by no means so unhappy as she supposed.

It should be explained that the Prince never saw his wife except at dinner. This meal lasted for thirty minutes, and the Prince would spend whole weeks without addressing a word to Clara Paolina. The Duchessa tried to change all that; she amused the Prince, all the more so because she had managed to preserve all her independence. Even had she wanted to, she could not have succeeded in never wounding the feelings of any of the fools who swarmed about this court. It was this utter inability on her part that led to her being thoroughly detested by the common run of courtiers, everyone of them a Conte or a Marchese, enjoying an average income of about five thousand lire a year. She realized this unfortunate fact after the first few days, and devoted herself exclusively to pleasing the Prince and his Consort, the latter of whom had absolute influence over the Crown Prince. The Duchessa knew how to amuse her sovereign lord and master, and profited by the extreme attention he paid to her lightest word to set the courtiers who hated her in a highly ridiculous light. After the foolish actions that Rassi had made him commit, and for foolishness that leads to the shedding of blood there is no reparation, the Prince was sometimes afraid and was often bored, a state of mind that had filled him with brooding envy. He felt that he himself had little to amuse him, and fell into a gloomy mood when he saw other people amusing themselves; the sight of happiness made him furious. 'We must keep our love a secret,' the Duchessa remarked to her lover, and she allowed the Prince to gather that she was now only moderately fond of the Conte, a man who was in many respects so worthy of esteem.

This discovery had given his Highness a happy day. From time to time the Duchessa let fall a few words about her possible plan of taking a few months' holiday every year, which she would spend in seeing those parts of Italy with which she was not acquainted; she would go and visit Naples, Florence, and Rome. Now nothing in the world was more capable of distressing the Prince than such an apparent desertion. This was one of his most pronounced weaknesses; any steps that might be interpreted as showing contempt for his capital city pierced him to the heart. He felt that he had no way of holding the Duchessa Sanseverina, and the Duchessa Sanseverina was by far the most distinguished and interesting woman in Parma. A thing without parallel in view of the characteristic Italian indolence; people would drive in from the surrounding countryside to be present at her *Thursdays*; they were regular festivals; the Duchessa nearly always had something new and exciting for them. The Prince was dying to see one of these *Thursdays*; but how was he to manage it? A visit to the house of a private individual! That was a thing that neither his father nor he had ever done in their lives!

On a certain Thursday it was cold and rainy. All through the evening the Prince kept on hearing carriages rattling over the pavement of the square outside the palace, on their way to the Duchessa's house. A sudden feeling of impatience moved him. Other people were amusing themselves, and he, their sovereign Prince, their absolute master, who had more right to amuse himself than anyone in the world, he was only conscious of boredom!

He rang for his aide-de-camp. It took a little time to post a dozen trusty men in the street that led from his Highness's Palace to the Palazzo Sanseverina. At length, after an hour that seemed to the Prince a century, during which he had been tempted a score of times to brave the risk of assassins' daggers and go out on the offchance without any precautions, he made his appearance in the first of the Duchessa Sanseverina's drawing-rooms. A thunderbolt might have fallen in this drawing-room and not have produced so much surprise. In the twinkling of an eye, and as the Prince moved forward, a stupefied silence fell upon these gay and noisy rooms; every eye, fixed on the Prince, was immeasurably wide-open. The courtiers seemed taken aback; the Duchessa alone did not look in any way astonished. When at length people had recovered sufficient strength to speak, the great preoccupation of all present was to decide the important question: 'Had the Duchessa been warned of this visit, or had she like everyone else been taken by surprise?'

The Prince was amused, and the reader may now form some opinion of the utterly impulsive character of the Duchessa and the boundless power which certain vague hints of departure, adroitly thrown out, had enabled her to assume.

As she went to the door with the Prince, who was saying some very pleasant things to her, an odd idea came to her, which she ventured to put to him quite simply, and as though it were an entirely ordinary thing.

'If your Serene Highness would graciously address to the Princess three or four of those charming remarks which you have lavished on me, you would most certainly give me far more pleasure than by telling me at this moment that I am pretty. It is just that I would not for anything in the world have the Princess look with an unfriendly eye on the signal mark of favour with which your Highness has just honoured me.'

The Prince gazed intently at her and answered drily: 'I was under the impression that I was at liberty to go where I pleased.'

The Duchessa blushed.

'I wished only,' she went on at once, 'not to expose your Highness to the risk of a useless journey, for this Thursday will be the last. I am going away to spend a few days in Bologna or Florence.'

When she returned to the rooms, everyone imagined her to be at the height of favour, whereas she had just taken a risk which no one, in living memory, had ventured upon in Parma. She beckoned to the Conte, who left his whist-table and followed her into a little room that was lighted but empty.

'You have done a very bold thing,' he said to her, 'I shouldn't have advised it myself, but when hearts are really attracted to each other,' he added laughing, 'happiness increases love, and if you leave tomorrow morning, I will follow you tomorrow night. I shall be detained here only by that wearisome job as Minister of Finance which I was stupid enough to take over, but in four hours of useful toil one can hand over a good many treasury accounts. Let us go back, my love, and play the part of ministerial fatuity with all free-dom and without reserve; it is perhaps the last performance we shall give in this city. If he thinks he is being defied, the man is capable of anything; he will call it *making an example*. When these people have gone, we will decide on a way of keeping you safe against intruders for tonight. Your best plan perhaps would be to set off without delay for your house at Sacca, by the Po, which has the advantage of being not more than half an hour's distance from Austrian territory.'

This was an exquisite moment for the Duchessa's love and self-esteem. She gazed at the Conte and her eyes grew wet with tears. So powerful a Minister, surrounded by this horde of courtiers who loaded him with homage equal to that they paid to the Prince him-self, to leave everything for her sake, and so readily too!

When she returned to the drawing-room she was beside herself with joy. Everyone bowed down before her.

'How good fortune changes the Duchessa,' the courtiers were saying on every side, 'one would hardly recognize her. So that Roman spirit, so superior to everything, deigns after all to appreciate the grossly excessive favour that has just been shown her by the Sovereign!'

Towards the end of the evening the Conte came up to her: 'I must tell you the latest news.' Immediately the people who were standing near the Duchessa withdrew.

'The Prince, on his return to the palace,' the Conte went on, 'had himself shown in to his wife's room. Imagine the surprise! "I have come to tell you," he said to her, "about a really most delightful evening I have spent at the Duchessa Sanseverina's. It is she who has begged me to give you a detailed account of the way in which she has transformed that grimy old *palazzo*." Then the Prince, after taking a chair, began to give her a description of each of your drawing rooms in turn.

'He spent more than twenty minutes with his wife, who was weeping for very joy. For all her intelligence, she could not think of anything to say that would keep the conversation going in the light tone which His Highness had been pleased to give it.'

The Prince was by no means a really bad man, whatever the Liberals in Italy might say of him. In actual truth, he had had a fairly good number of them cast into various prisons, but that was out of fear, and he would repeat now and then as if to console himself for certain things he remembered: 'It is better to kill the devil than to let the devil kill you.' The day after the party we have just described he was full of joy; he had performed two good actions – going to the *Thursday*, and speaking to his wife. At dinner he addressed some remarks to her; in a word, this *Thursday* at the Duchessa Sanseverina's brought about a domestic revolution with which the whole of Parma rang. The Marchesa Raversi was in utter dismay, and the Duchessa was doubly delighted: she had contrived to be useful to her lover, and found him more in love with her than ever.

'All this on account of a thoroughly rash idea that suddenly occurred to me!' she said to the Conte. 'I should doubtless be freer in Rome or Naples, but should I find there so fascinating a game to play? No, indeed, my dear Conte, and you are the source of all my joy.'

CHAPTER 7: *Fabrizio in Parma*

IT is with little details of court life as insignificant as those we have just related that we should have to fill in the history of the next four years. Every spring the Marchesa came with her daughters to spend two months either at the Palazzo Sanseverina or on the estate of Sacca, by the banks of the Po. They spent many pleasant moments there, and used to talk of Fabrizio; but the Conte would never allow him to pay a single visit to Parma. The Duchessa and the Minister had indeed to make amends for certain acts of folly, but on the whole Fabrizio followed fairly steadily in the line of conduct that had been sketched out for him: that of a great nobleman who is studying theology and does not rely entirely on his virtues to advance him in his career. While in Naples he had acquired a keen taste for the study of antiquity. He engaged in excavations; this passion had almost taken the place of his passion for horses. He had sold his English thoroughbreds in order to carry on with excavations at Miseno, where he had come upon a bust of Tiberius as a young man which had been classed among the finest relics of antiquity. The discovery of this was almost the keenest pleasure he had experienced in Naples.

He had too proud a spirit to seek to copy other young men around him, and to wish, for instance, to play with any degree of seriousness the part of a lover. Certainly he by no means lacked for mistresses, but these were of no importance to him, and, in spite of his age, it might be said of him that he had no knowledge of love; he was only all the more loved on that account. Nothing prevented him from behaving with the utmost coolness, for to him one young and pretty woman was always the equivalent of another; only the latest one he had known always seemed to him the most enticing. One of the ladies among those who were most admired in Naples had committed various follies in his honour during the last year of his stay there. This had at first amused him and had ended by boring him to death, so much so that one of the happy things about his departure was that of delivering him from the attentions of the charming Duchessa d'A—. It was in 1821, after he had passed all his examinations tolerably well, that his director of studies received a decoration and a gratuity, and he himself set off at last to see that city of Parma of which he had often dreamed. He was now a *Monsignore*, and he had four horses for his carriage. At the post-stage before Parma he took only two of them, and after entering the city made them draw up in front of the church of San Giovanni. There was to be found the sumptuous tomb of the Archbishop Ascanio del Dongo, his great-great-uncle, the author of the Latin Genealogy. He prayed beside the tomb, then went on foot to the palazzo of the Duchess, who did not expect him until a few days later. There was a large crowd in her drawing-room; presently she was left alone.

'Well, are you satisfied with me?' he asked her as he flung himself into her arms. 'Thanks to you, I have spent four fairly happy years in Naples, instead of getting bored at Novara with the mistress allowed me by the police.'

The Duchessa could not get over her astonishment; she would not have known him if she had seen him passing in the street. She found him to be, what in fact he really was, one of the best-looking men in Italy; he had in particular a charming cast of face. She had sent him to Naples looking like a devil-may-care rough-rider; the horsewhip he invariably carried with him at that time seemed an inherent part of his person. Now he had the noblest and most restrained manner in front of strangers, while in private she found he had retained all the fire of his early youth. This was a diamond that had lost nothing by being polished.

Fabrizio had not been there an hour when Conte Mosca appeared; he arrived a little too soon. The young man spoke to him in such well-turned phrases of the Cross of Parma conferred on his tutor, and he expressed his keen gratitude for certain other benefits of which he did not venture to speak so explicitly, with such perfect discretion that at first glance the Minister formed a favourable impression of him. 'This nephew of yours,' he said to the Duchessa, 'is well fitted to grace all these high offices to which you will promote him in due course.' So far, everything was going wonderfully well, but when the Minister, who had been thoroughly pleased with Fabrizio, and up till then had been paying attention only to his actions and his gestures, turned to the Duchessa, he noticed a curious look in her eyes. 'This young man is making a strange impression here,' he said to himself.

This reflection was a bitter one; the Conte had reached the *fifties*; this is a very cruel word and one which possibly only a man who is desperately in love can feel in all its force. He was an extremely good-hearted man, very worthy to be loved, apart from his severities as a minister. But in his eyes that cruel word *fifties* cast a dark shadow over all his life and might well have had made him cruel on his own account. In the five years since he had persuaded the Duchessa to come to Parma, she had often aroused his jealousy, especially at the first, but she had never given him serious grounds for complaint. He even believed, and rightly too, that it was with the object of making herself more certain of his heart that the Duchessa had had recourse to those apparent marks of favour she bestowed on various young dandies at the court. He was sure, for instance, that she had rejected the Prince's advances; the latter, indeed, in that connexion, had made a significant remark.

'But if I were to accept your Highness's proposals,' the Duchessa had said to him with a smile, 'how should I ever dare to look the Conte in the face after that?'

'I should be almost as much embarrassed as you would. The dear Conte! My friend! But that is an obstacle easy enough to get round and to which I have given my attention; the Conte would be put in the citadel for the rest of his days.'

At the moment of Fabrizio's arrival the Duchessa was so beside herself with joy that she did not even give a thought to the ideas which the look in her eyes might put into the Conte's head. Its effect was profound, and the suspicions it aroused past hope of remedy.

Two hours after his arrival Fabrizio was received by the Prince. The Duchessa, foreseeing the good impression that this impromptu audience might make on the public, had been begging for it for the past two months. This favour put Fabrizio in an exceptional position from the outset; the pretext for it had been that he would only be passing through Parma on his way to visit his mother in Piedmont. At the moment when a charming little note from the Duchessa arrived to inform the Prince that Fabrizio was awaiting his orders his Highness was feeling bored. 'I shall see,' he said to himself, 'a saintly little simpleton, an uninteresting or sly face.' The Commandant of the city had already reported that first visit to the tomb of his uncle the Archbishop. The Prince saw coming into his room a tall young man whom he would have taken, had it not been for his purple stockings, for some young officer.

This little surprise drove away his boredom. 'Here is a jaunty fellow,' he said to himself, 'for whom they will be asking me heaven knows what favours, everything that it is in my power to bestow. He has just arrived, he is probably a little excited: I shall give him a taste of Jacobin politics, and we shall see a little how he replies.'

After the first gracious words on the Prince's part, he went on to say to Fabrizio: 'Well, *Monsignore*, the people of Naples, are they happy? Is the King beloved?'

'Your Serene Highness,' replied Fabrizio without a moment's hesitation, 'I used to admire, when passing by in the streets, the excellent bearing of the troops of the various regiments of His Majesty the King. The better classes are respectful towards their masters, as they ought to be; but I must confess that never in my life have I allowed the lower classes to speak to me about anything except the work for which I am paying them.'

'Confound it!' thought the Prince, 'what a *gamecock*! Here's a well-trained bird, here's the ingenuity of the Sanseverina.' Getting warmed to the game, the Prince employed great skill in leading Fabrizio to discuss this extremely ticklish subject. The young man, stimulated by the danger in it, was so fortunate as to hit on some admirable answers. 'It is almost insolence to make a display of one's love for one's King,' he said. 'What one owes him is blind obedience.' At the sight of so much caution the Prince almost lost his temper. 'Here, it seems, is a man with a clever brain arriving in our midst from Naples, and I don't like *that breed*. A man with a clever brain may try to follow the best principles and even apply them in good faith, all the same on one side or the other he is always first cousin to Rousseau and Voltaire.'

The Prince found himself as it were put on his mettle by such correctness of manner and such unassailable rejoinders on the part of a youth who had just left college. What he had expected to happen never occurred. In less than no time he assumed a tone of good-fellowship, and, going back, in a few brief words, to the first principles of society and government, he quoted, while adapting them to the occasion, a few phrases from Fénelon which he had been made to learn by heart in his boyhood for use at public audiences.

'These principles surprise you, young man,' he said to Fabrizio. (He had addressed him as *Monsignore* at the beginning of the audience, and intended to give him this title again when dismissing him, but in the course of the conversation he had thought it more adroit, and more likely to enhance certain moving turns of speech, to address him in a familiar and friendly style.) 'These principles surprise you, young man; I must admit that they bear little resemblance to the long-spun-out *twaddle on absolutism*' (this was the expression he used) 'which you can read every day in my official newspaper. ... But, good heavens, what am I saying now? These writers in my newspaper must be quite unknown to you.'

'I beg your Serene Highness's pardon; not only do I read the Parma newspaper, which seems to me to be very well written, but I also hold, with it, that everything that has been done since the death of Louis XIV, in 1715, has been at once criminal and silly. Man's greatest interest in life is his own salvation, there can be no two ways of looking at this matter, and that is a happiness which will last for ever. The words *Liberty, Justice, the Good of the Greatest Number* are infamous and criminal; they form in people's minds a habit of argument and mistrust. A Chamber of Deputies mistrusts what these people call *the Ministry*. This fatal habit of *mistrust* once contracted, human weakness applies it to everything. Men come to distrust the Bible, the Canons of the Church, traditions, and so on; from that moment they are lost. Even assuming – which it is abominably false and criminal to suggest – that this want of confidence in the authority of the Princes *by God established* were to secure us happiness during the twenty or thirty years of life which any of us may expect to enjoy, what is half a century, or even a whole century, compared with an eternity of torment?' And so on.

It was evident, from the way in which Fabrizio spoke, that he was trying to arrange his ideas so that they should be grasped as easily as possible by his listener; it was clear that he was not repeating a lesson.

Soon the Prince was no longer anxious to continue the contest with this young man, whose grave and simple manner was beginning to annoy him.

'Good-bye, *Monsignore*,' he said to him abruptly, 'I see that they provide an excellent education at the Ecclesiastical Academy in Naples and it is quite simple, when these good precepts fall upon so distinguished a mind, that they should produce brilliant results. Good-bye.' And he turned his back on him.

'I've quite failed to please that dull fellow,' said Fabrizio to himself.

'And now,' thought the Prince when he was once more alone, 'it remains to be seen whether this fine young man is capable of a passion for anything; in that case he would be a perfect paragon. ... Could any one repeat more cleverly the lessons he has learnt from his aunt? I felt I could hear her speaking. If we should have a revolution here, it would be she who would edit the *Monitore*, as the Marchesa San-Felice did once in Naples! But the San-Felice, for all her twenty-five years and her beauty, had a nice little hanging! A warning to women of too much intelligence.'

In supposing Fabrizio to be his aunt's pupil, the Prince was mistaken. People with brains who are born to sit on a throne, or beside it, soon loose all fineness of perception. They proscribe, in their immediate circle, all frankness of speech, which seems to them a breach of decorum; they refuse to look at anything but masks and pretend to judge the beauty of complexions; the amusing thing about it is that they imagine they have a great deal of perception. In this case, for instance, Fabrizio believed practically everything that we have heard him say; it is true, however, that he did not think more than twice in the month about all these great principles. He had keen appetites and desires, he had intelligence, but he also had faith.

The desire for liberty, the vogue and the cult of the *greatest good of the greatest number*, over which the nineteenth century has lost its head, were nothing in his eyes but a heresy that would pass like all the others, though not until destroying many souls, as the plague while it is prevalent in a country destroys many bodies. And in spite of all this Fabrizio read the French newspapers with keen enjoyment, and even took rash steps to procure copies of them.

When Fabrizio returned quite wrought up from his audience at the palace and told his aunt of the Prince's various skirmishes with him, she said to him: 'You must go at once to see Father Landriani, our excellent Archbishop. Go there on foot, slip softly up the stairs, and make as little noise as possible in the ante-rooms; if you are kept waiting, so much the better, a thousand times better! In a word, show an *apostolic discretion*!'

'I understand,' said Fabrizio, 'our man is a Tartuffe.'

'Not in the very least, he is virtue itself.'

'Even after the way he behaved at the time of Conte Palanza's execution?' Fabrizio retorted in amazement.

'Yes, my dear boy, even after the way he behaved. The father of our Archbishop was a clerk in the Ministry of Finance, a man of humble position, and that explains everything. Monsignore Landriani is a man of keen, extensive, and profound intelligence; he is sincere, he loves virtue. I am convinced that if another Emperor Decius were to appear in this world, he would undergo martyrdom like the Polyeucte in the opera that we saw last week. That is the good side of the picture, now for the other. As soon as he is in the presence of his Sovereign, or even of the Prime Minister, he is dazzled by the sight of so much greatness, he becomes confused, he grows red in the face; it is next to impossible for him to say no. This accounts for the things he has done, and which have earned him that cruel reputation he has throughout Italy. But what is not generally known is that, when public opinion succeeded in enlightening him as to the trial of Conte Palanza, he set himself the penance of living upon bread and water for thirteen weeks, the same number of weeks as there are letters in the name *Davide Palanza*. We have at this court a rascal of infinite cleverness named *Rassi*, a Chief Justice or Attorney General, who, at the time of Conte Palanza's death, cast a spell upon Father Landriani. During his thirteen weeks' penance, Conte Mosca, out of pity and also a little out of mischief, used to invite him to dinner once and even twice a week. The good Archbishop, in deference to his host, ate like everyone else. He would have thought it smacked of rebellion or Jacobinism to make a public display of his penance for an action approved by his Sovereign. But it was generally known that, for every dinner at which his duty as a loyal subject had obliged him to eat like everybody else, he inflicted on himself a penance of two days more on a diet of bread and water.

'Monsignore Landriani, a man of superior intellect, a scholar of the first rank, has only one weakness: *he likes to be loved*. Therefore, seem to grow more affectionate as you look at him. and on your third visit, show your love for him outright. This, added to your birth, will make him adore you at once. Show no sign of surprise if he accompanies you to the head of the stairs, look as if you were accustomed to such manners; he is a man who was born on his knees before the nobility. For the rest be simple, behave like the apostles – no cleverness, no brilliance, no quick repartee. If you don't startle him in any way, he will find your company pleasant. Bear in mind that it must be of his own accord that he makes you his Vicar-General.

The Conte and I will show ourselves surprised and even annoyed at such rapid preferment; that is essential in dealing with the Sovereign.'

Fabrizio hastened to the Archbishop's Palace. By a singular piece of good fortune, the worthy prelate's manservant, who was slightly deaf, did not catch the name *del Dongo*; he announced a young priest named Fabrizio. The Archbishop happened to be interviewing a parish priest of by no means exemplary morals, whom he had sent for in order to reprove him. He was in the act of delivering a reprimand, a thing that was most painful for him to do, and did not wish to have this distressing duty weighing on his heart for longer than was necessary. He therefore kept the great-nephew of the distinguished Archbishop Ascanio del Dongo waiting for three-quarters of an hour.

How can we depict his apologies and his despair when, after conducting the priest to the outer ante-room, and inquiring, on his way back, of the man who was waiting there *what he could do to serve him*, he caught sight of the purple stockings and heard the name Fabrizio del Dongo?

The incident appeared to our hero so entertaining that on this first visit he ventured to kiss the saintly prelate's hand in a transport of affection. You should have heard the Archbishop exclaiming over and over again in a tone of despair, 'A del Dongo kept waiting in my ante-room!' He felt himself obliged, by way of apology, to relate to him the whole story of the parish priest, his misdeeds, his replies, and so forth.

'Is it really possible,' Fabrizio asked himself as he made his way back to the Palazzo Sanseverina, 'that this is the man who hurried on the execution of that poor Conte Palanza?'

'What is your Excellency's impression?' Conte Mosca inquired laughingly, as he saw him on his return to the Duchess's. (The Conte would not allow Fabrizio to call him 'Your Excellency'.)

'I'm utterly astounded; I know nothing at all about human nature. I would have bet, if I hadn't known his name, that this man could not bear to see even a chicken bleed.'

'And you would have won your bet,' replied the Conte. 'But when he is in the Prince's presence, or merely with me, he cannot say no. True, in order for me to produce my full effect upon him I have to slip the yellow ribbon of my Grand Cordon over my coat; in plain morning dress he would contradict me, so I always put on a uniform to receive him. It is not for us to destroy the prestige of the powers that be, the French newspapers are demolishing it fast enough. It is doubtful whether the *mania of reverence* will last out our time, and you, my dear nephew, will outlive reverence. You, for your part, will be just an ordinary simple man!'

Fabrizio found great pleasure in the Conte's society. He was the first man of superior quality who had condescended to talk to him frankly, without make-believe; besides they had a taste in common, that for antiquities and excavations. The Conte, for his part, was flattered by the extreme attention with which the young man listened to him; but there was one vital objection: Fabrizio occupied a set of rooms in the Palazzo Sanseverina, spent all his time with the Duchessa and let it be seen that this intimacy was his whole delight. And Fabrizio had eyes and a complexion of a freshness that drove the older man to despair.

For a long time Ranuccio-Ernesto IV, who rarely encountered any unkind beauty, had been piqued to find that the Duchessa's virtue, which was well known at court, had not made an exception in his favour. As we have seen, Fabrizio's intelligence and presence of mind had shocked him at their first meeting. He took in bad part the friendship which his aunt and he recklessly displayed in front of everyone; he listened with extreme attention to the comments of his courtiers, which were endless. The arrival of this young man and the unprecedented audience he had obtained provided the court with news and a sensation for a whole month; this gave the Prince an idea.

He had among his guard a private soldier who carried his wine in the most admirable way. This man spent his whole time in public houses, and reported the spirit of the troops direct to the Sovereign. Carlone lacked education, otherwise he would long since have obtained promotion. Now his orders were to present himself at the Palace every day at midday as soon as the great clock struck the hour. The Prince would go in person a little before noon to arrange in a certain way the shutters in a room on a slightly lower level, but communicating with the one in which his Highness dressed. He returned to this *entresol* shortly after twelve had struck and found the soldier there. The Prince had in his pocket a sheet of paper and some writing materials; he dictated the following letter to the soldier:

Your Excellency has doubtless great intelligence, and it is thanks to your profound sagacity that we see this State so well governed. But, my dear

Conte, such great success is never unaccompanied by a little envy, and I am very much afraid that people will be laughing a little at your expense if your capacity does not fathom that a certain handsome young man has had the good fortune to inspire, though it may be unintentionally, a love of the most singular kind. This happy mortal is, so they say, only twenty-three years old, and, my dear Conte, what complicates the question is that you and I are both considerably more than twice that age. In the evening, at a certain distance, the Conte is charming, scintillating, a man of wit, as attractive as one can possibly be; but in the morning, in the privacy of his home, all things rightly considered, the newcomer may seem to have more charms. Now we women set great value on this youthful freshness, especially when we ourselves are over thirty. Is there not some talk already of settling this charming youth at our court, by giving him some fine position? And who indeed is the person who speaks of it most frequently to your Excellency?

The Prince took the letter and gave the soldier two scudi. 'This is in addition to your pay,' he said to him morosely. 'Not a single word of this to anyone, or you will find yourself in the dampest underground cell in the citadel.' The Prince had in his desk a collection of envelopes bearing the addresses of most of the people at his court in the handwriting of this same soldier, who passed as unable to write, and who never even wrote out his own police reports. The Prince picked out the envelope he required.

A few hours later Conte Mosca received a letter through the post. The hour of its delivery had been calculated, and at the very moment the postman who had been seen going in with a small envelope in his hand came out of the ministerial buildings, Mosca was summoned to his Highness's presence. Never had the favourite appeared to be in the grip of a darker mood of melancholy. To enjoy this all the more freely the Prince on seeing him called out: 'I want to relax a bit by talking to my friend, and not working with my Minister. I have a splitting headache this evening, and besides I am tormented by gloomy thoughts.'

Is it necessary to mention the abominable fit of temper that boiled up in the Prime Minister, Conte Mosca della Rovere, the moment he was permitted to take leave of his august master? Ranuccio-Ernesto IV was thoroughly skilled in the art of torturing a heart, and I could, without being too unfair to him, make the comparison here of the tiger which loves to sport with its prey.

The Conte had himself driven home at a gallop; he called out as he entered his house that not a living soul was to be allowed upstairs, sent word to the junior civil servant on duty that he was free to leave (the idea that there was a human being within earshot was hateful to him) and rushed to shut himself up in the great picture gallery. There, at last, he could give full vent to his fury; and there he spent the evening in the dark, pacing aimlessly up and down the room like a man who is out of his mind. He was trying to impose silence on his heart, so as to concentrate all the power of his attention upon what line of action he should take. Plunged in an anguish that would have moved his cruellest enemy to pity, he said to himself: 'The man I loathe is living in the Duchessa's house, he spends every moment of his time with her. Should I try to make one of her women speak? Nothing could be more dangerous – she is so kind, she pays them well, they all adore her (and who, good God, does not adore her?). Here is the question,' he continued, in a fresh access of fury. 'Ought I to let her guess what jealousy consumes me, or ought I to keep it quiet?

'If I hold my peace, she will hide nothing from me. I know Gina; she is a woman who always acts on a first impulse; her behaviour is unpredictable, even to herself; if she tries to plan out a line of conduct beforehand, she gets muddled; invariably, when the time comes for action, she gets some new notion into her head which she follows rapturously as though it were the best idea in the world, and which, in fact, upsets everything.

'If I say nothing to her of the tortures I am suffering, she will keep nothing from me, and I shall see everything possible happen ...

'Yes, but by speaking I create a new set of circumstances: I make her reflect, I ward off a number of those horrible things which might otherwise happen ... Perhaps she will send him away.' (The Conte breathed a sigh of relief.) 'Then I've almost gained the day ... Even if she shows a little temper at first, I could calm her down ... And as for temper, what could be more natural? ... She has loved him like a son for the last fifteen years. There lies all my hope – *like a son.* But she had not seen him since his flight to Waterloo; on his return from Naples, moreover, and to her especially, he is now a different man! *A different man!*' he repeated, raging, 'and a charming man, too! Above all, he has that artless, tender air and those smiling eyes that hold out such a promise of happiness. And the Duchessa cannot be accustomed to seeing such eyes at our court! ... Their place is taken here by morose or sardonic glances. I myself, harassed by the cares of office, governing only by virtue of my influence over a man who would like to make me appear ridiculous – what sort of look must I often have in mine! Ah! whatever care I take, it is in my eyes, above all, that I bear the marks of my age. As for my gaiety, doesn't it always border on irony? ... I will go further, for here I must be honest, doesn't my gaiety allow a glimpse to be caught of something as it were closely connected with absolute power ... and malevolence? Do I not sometimes say to myself, more especially when people vex me: "I can do what I like?" And even go on to add the foolish idea: "I should be happier than other men, since I possess what others have not – supreme power in three things out of four." Well then, let me be just. This habit of thought must spoil my smile ... must give me a look of selfishness ... a self-satisfied air ... And how charming is that smile of his! It breathes the easy happiness of early youth, and engenders it.'

Unfortunately for the Conte, the weather that evening was hot, oppressive, the forerunner of a storm – the kind of weather, in short, which in these parts leads men to make extreme decisions. How shall I give account of all the arguments, all the ways of looking at what was happening to him, which, for three mortal hours on end, kept this passionate man on the rack? At length the side of prudence prevailed, solely as a result of this reflection: 'In all probability I am out of my mind. When I think I am using my reason, I am not reasoning at all. I am simply turning round and round to find a less painful position, I pass close to some decisive argument without seeing it. Since I am blinded by excessive grief, let me obey the rule approved by every sensible man, which goes by the name of *prudence*.

'Besides, once I have uttered the fatal word *jealousy*, the part I must play is laid down for good and all. On the other hand, if I say nothing today I can speak tomorrow; I remain master of the situation.' His paroxysm of rage had been too acute; the Conte would have gone mad had it lasted any longer. For a few moments he felt relieved as he turned his attention to the anonymous letter. From whom could it have come? There followed then a search for names, and a personal judgement of each, which created a diversion. In the end, the Conte remembered a gleam of malice that had darted from the Sovereign's eyes when it had occurred to him to say, towards the end of the audience: 'Yes, my dear friend, let us agree to it, the pleasures and cares of the most successful ambition, even of unlimited power, are as nothing compared with the intimate happiness afforded by tender and loving relationships. I am a man before I am a prince, and when I am happy enough to be in love, my mistress speaks to the man and not to the Prince.'

The Conte compared that moment of malicious glee with the phrase in the letter: 'It is thanks to your profound sagacity that we see this State so well governed.' 'Those are the Prince's own words!' he exclaimed. 'In a courtier they would be a gratuitous piece of imprudence; the letter comes from his Highness.'

This problem solved, the slight joy caused by the pleasure of guessing the solution was soon effaced by the cruel vision of Fabrizio's charming graces, which flashed before him anew. It was like an enormous weight falling back on to the wretched man's heart. 'What does it matter from whom the anonymous letter comes?' he cried in rage. 'Does the fact it discloses to me exist any the less? This caprice of hers may alter my life,' he said, as if to excuse himself for being so mad. 'At the first opportunity, if she cares for him in a certain way, she will set off with him for Belgirate, for Switzerland, for some remote corner or other of the globe. She is rich, and besides, if she had to live on a few louis a year, what would that matter to her? Did she not admit to me, not a week ago, that her *palazzo*, so well arranged, so magnificent, bored her? Novelty is essential to so youthful a soul! And how simply does this new form of happiness present itself! She will be swept away before she has begun to think of the danger, before she has begun to think of being sorry for me! And yet I am so miserable!' cried the Conte, bursting into tears.

He had sworn to himself that he would not go the Duchessa's that evening, but he could not bear not to; never had his eyes felt such a longing to gaze at her. Towards midnight he presented himself at her house. He found her alone with her nephew; at ten o'clock she had sent all her guests away and given orders to close her doors.

At the sight of the tender intimacy that prevailed between these two creatures, and the artless joy of the Duchessa, a frightful difficulty loomed before the Conte's eyes, and one that was quite unforeseen. He had never thought of it during his long deliberations in the picture gallery: how was he to conceal his jealousy?

Not knowing what pretext to fall back on, he pretended that he had found the Prince that evening very ill-disposed towards him, contradicting all his statements and so forth. He had the pain of seeing the Duchessa hardly listening to him and paying no attention at all to those details which, barely two days ago, would have started her off on an endless discussion. The Conte looked at Fabrizio. Never had that handsome Lombard face appeared to him so simple and so noble! Fabrizio was paying more attention than the Duchessa to the troubles he was relating.

'Really,' he said to himself, 'that face combines extreme good nature with a certain expression of artless and tender joy which is quite irresistible. It seems to be saying: "Love and the happiness it brings are the only serious things on this earth." And yet when one happens to touch on some detail which requires thought, his eyes light up and astonish you, and you remain dumbfounded.

'Everything is simple in his eyes, because everything is seen from above. Good God! how is one to fight against an enemy like this? And after all, what is life without Gina's love? With what rapture she seems to be listening to the charming sallies of that mind which is so fresh and young and must, to a woman, seem without parallel in the world!'

A dreadful idea gripped the Conte like a sudden cramp; 'Shall I stab him here, in front of her, and then kill myself?'

He took a turn round the room, his legs barely supporting him, but his hand closed convulsively on the handle of his dagger. Neither of the others paid any attention to what he might be doing. He announced that he was going to give an order to his servant, they did not even hear him; the Duchessa was laughing tenderly at some remark Fabrizio had just made to her. The Conte went up to a lamp in the outer drawing-room and looked to see whether the point of his dagger was well sharpened. 'I must behave graciously, and with perfect manners towards this young man,' he said to himself as he came back and went up to them.

He was going quite mad; it seemed to him, that as they leant towards each other they were kissing, there, before his eyes. 'That is impossible in my presence,' he said to himself. 'I must be losing my reason. I must calm myself. If I behave churlishly, the Duchessa is quite capable, purely out of injured vanity, of following him to Belgirate; and there, or on the way there, chance may produce a remark that will give a name to what they feel for one another: and after that, in a moment, all the consequences will follow.

'Solitude will render that word decisive, and besides, with the Duchessa no longer near me, what will become of me? And if, after overcoming a host of objections on the Prince's part, I go and show my old and careworn face at Belgirate, what role shall I play in the company of these two people mad with happiness?

'Even here, what am I but the *terzo incomodo*? That beautiful Italian language is simply made for love: *terzo incomodo* (a third person who is a nuisance). What misery for a man of spirit to feel he is playing that odious part, and not able to make up his mind to get up and go away!'

The Conte was on the point of flying into a rage or at least of betraying his anguish by the discomposure of his features. When in one of his turns round the room he found himself near the door, he made his escape, calling out in a friendly and familiar way: 'Good-bye, you two! – One must avoid bloodshed,' he murmured to himself.

The day following this dreadful evening, after a night spent now in considering one by one each of Fabrizio's advantages, now in the frightful throes of the most cruel jealousy, it occurred to the Conte that he might send for a young servant of his own household. This man was keeping company with a girl by the name of Cecchina, one of the Duchessa's personal maids, and her favourite. As luck would have it this young manservant was very steady in his ways, even miserly, and was anxious to find a situation as hall porter in one of the public institutions in Parma. The Conte ordered the man to fetch his sweetheart Cecchina instantly. The man obeyed, and an hour later the Conte made a sudden appearance in the room where the girl was sitting with her young man. The Conte alarmed them both by the large amount of gold that he gave them; then he addressed these few words to the trembling Cecchina, looking her straight in the face: 'Is the Duchessa having a love affair with Monsignore?'

'No,' said the girl, making up her mind after a moment's silence; ... 'No, *not yet*, but he often kisses the Signora's hands, laughing, it is true, but very fondly.'

This evidence was fully supported by a host of replies to as many frenzied questions from the Conte. His uneasy passion made the poor couple earn to the full the money he had flung them; he ended by believing what they told him, and felt less unhappy. 'If ever the Duchessa has the slightest suspicion of our conversation,' he said to Cecchina, 'I shall send your young man to spend twenty years in the fortress, and you won't see him again until his hair is white.'

A few days elapsed, during which Fabrizio in his turn lost all his good spirits.

'I assure you,' he said to the Duchessa, 'Conte Mosca feels an antipathy to me.'

'So much the worse for His Excellency,' she replied somewhat petulantly.

This was by no means the real subject of anxiety that accounted for the loss of Fabrizio's good spirits. 'The position in which chance has placed me is untenable,' he said to himself. 'I am quite sure that she will never say anything, she would be as much horrified by a too significant word as by an act of incest. But if one evening, after a rash and foolish day, she should come to examine her conscience, if she believes I may have guessed the inclination she seems to have for me, what part should I then play in her eyes? Precisely that of the *casto Giuseppe*!' (An Italian saying, alluding to the ridiculous part played by Joseph with the wife of the eunuch Potiphar.)

'Should I give her to understand by a fine burst of confidence that I am not capable of feeling a serious passion? I haven't sufficient control of my ideas to announce this fact in such a way that it will not seem as like as two peas to a piece of impertinence. The sole resource that remains to me is to invent a great passion for someone left behind in Naples; in that case I must return there for twenty-four hours. Such a course is wise, but is it really worth the trouble? There still remains a minor affair with some one of humble rank in Parma. This might annoy her; but anything is preferable to the frightful part of a man who wilfully shuts his eyes to the truth. This second course might, it is true, compromise my future; I should have, by the exercise of prudence and by acquiring discretion, to minimize the danger.'

What was so cruel a thing among all these thoughts was that Fabrizio really loved the Duchessa far above anyone else in the world. 'I must be very clumsy,' he said to himself angrily, 'to have such misgivings as to my ability to convince her of what is too palpably true! Lacking the skill to extricate himself from this position, he grew sullen and sad. 'What in heaven's name would become of me if I quarrelled with the one being in the world for whom I feel a passionate affection?'

On the other hand, Fabrizio could not bring himself to spoil so highly delightful a happiness by an indiscreet word. His position had so many charms! Intimate friendship with so lovable and so beautiful a woman was so pleasant! To take things from the most vulgar point of view of life, her protection gave him so agreeable a position at this court, whose great intrigues, thanks to her who explained them to him, were as amusing to him as a play! 'But at any moment,' he thought, 'I may be awakened by a thunderbolt! If these evenings, so gay and so tender, passed in making intimate conversation with so alluring a woman, should lead to something more, she will expect to find in me a lover. She will call on me for transports of affection, for extravagant raptures, and I shall still have nothing more to offer her except the warmest affection, but no passion; nature has withheld from me that sort of sublime folly. What reproaches have I not already had to bear on that account! I still seem to hear the Duchessa d'A— speaking, and I even used to laugh at the Duchessa herself! She will think that I am wanting in love for her, whereas it is love that is wanting in me; she will never bring herself to understand me. Often after some amusing story about the court, told by her with that grace, with that extravagant verve which she alone in the world possesses, and which is, besides, an essential part of my education, I kiss her hand and sometimes her cheek. What shall I do if that hand presses mine in a certain fashion?'

Fabrizio put in an appearance every day at the most highly reputable and the least entertaining of the houses in Parma. Guided by the Duchessa's able advice, he paid clever court to the two Princes, father and son, to the Princess Clara Paolina, and to His Grace the Archbishop. He met with successes, but these did not in the least console him for his mortal fear of falling out with the Duchessa.

So, less than a month after his arrival at court, Fabrizio was burdened with all the cares of a courtier, and the intimate friendship which had made his life happy was poisoned. One evening, tormented by these thoughts, he left that drawing-room of the Duchessa's in which he had too much the air of a reigning lover. Wandering aimlessly through the town, he passed in front of the theatre, which he saw lighted up; he went in. It was wanton imprudence in a man of his cloth, and one that he had indeed promised himself to avoid in Parma, which, after all, is only a small town of forty thousand inhabitants. It is true that after the first few days he had got rid of his official costume; in the evenings, when he was not going out into the very highest society, he used simply to dress as a layman in mourning.

At the theatre he took a box on the third tier, so as not to be noticed. They were playing Goldoni's *La Locandiera*. He studied the architecture of the auditorium; he scarcely turned his eyes to the stage. But the crowded audience kept on bursting into laughter at every moment. He cast a glance towards the young actress who was playing the part of the landlady and thought her amusing. He looked more attentively, she seemed to him quite charming, and, above all, perfectly natural. She was a simple-minded girl, the first to laugh at the neat remarks Goldoni had put in her mouth, and she seemed to be quite surprised at uttering them. He asked what her name was, and was told: 'Marietta Valserra.'

'Ah!' he thought, 'she has taken my name; that's odd.' In spite of his intentions he did not leave the theatre until the end of the play. The following evening he returned; three days later he had discovered Marietta's address.

On the very evening of the day on which, with a certain amount of trouble, he had got hold of that address, he noticed that the Conte was looking at him in a very friendly way. The poor jealous lover, who had all the trouble in the world in keeping within the bounds of prudence, had set spies on the young man's track, and was pleased by this escapade of his at the theatre. How can we depict the Conte's joy when on the day following that on which he had managed to bring himself to be pleasant to Fabrizio, he learnt that the latter, only partially disguised, in truth, by a long blue overcoat, had climbed upstairs to the miserable rooms which Marietta Valserra occupied on the fourth floor of an old house behind the theatre. His joy was doubled when he heard that Fabrizio had presented himself under a false name, and had had the honour to arouse the jealousy of a scamp named Giletti, who in town played the part of Third Servant, and in the villages danced on the tight-rope. This noble lover of Marietta was lavish in his abuse of Fabrizio and said that he would like to kill him.

Opera companies are formed by an *impresario*, who engages, here and there, the actors whom he can afford to pay or finds out of a job, and the company collected at random remains together for one season, or two at the most. It is not so with a troupe of comedians. These, while travelling from one town to another and changing their address every two or three months, nevertheless form a family of which all the members either love or hate each other. There are in these companies certain couples living together in close union, whom the fashionable gallants of the towns in which the troupe appears find sometimes very difficult to split apart. This is precisely what happened to our hero. Little Marietta liked him well enough, but she was horribly afraid of Giletti, who claimed to be her sole lord and master and kept a close watch over her. He protested everywhere that he would kill the *Monsignore*, for he had followed Fabrizio and had succeeded in discovering his name.

This fellow Giletti was far and away the ugliest creature imaginable and the least fitted to be a lover. Disproportionately tall, he was also horribly thin, strongly pitted by smallpox, and inclined to squint. For the rest, possessing to the full the graces of his profession, he was in the habit of coming into the wings, where his fellow-actors were assembled, turning cart-wheels or indulging in some other pleasing trick. He triumphed in those parts in which the actor has to appear with his face whitened with flour, and to give or to receive a countless number of cudgellings. This worthy rival of Fabrizio drew a monthly salary of thirty-two lire, and thought himself extremely well off.

It seemed to Conte Mosca that he had been called back from the gates of death on receiving from his watchers the full proof of all these details. His old, kindly temper once more made its appearance; he seemed gayer and better company than ever in the Duchessa's drawing-room, and he took good care to say nothing to her of the little adventure that had restored him to life. He even took steps to ensure that she would be informed of everything that had occurred as late as possible. Finally he had the courage to listen to the voice of reason, which for a month past had been crying out to him in vain that whenever a lover's credit begins to dwindle, it is time for that lover to set out on his travels.

Urgent business summoned him to Bologna, and twice a day the ministerial couriers brought him not so much the official papers of his departments, as news of little Marietta's love affairs, the rage of the terrible Giletti and Fabrizio's various doings.

One of the Conte's agents asked several times for a performance of *Arlecchino fantasma e pasticcio*, one of Giletti's triumphs (he emerges from the pie at the moment when his rival Brighella is sticking his knife into it and gives him a cudgelling); this was a pretext for slipping him a hundred lire. Giletti, who was riddled with debts, took good care not to mention this windfall, but became amazingly arrogant.

Fabrizio's whim now developed into a matter of wounded vanity (at his age, his worries had already reduced him to a state of having *whims*!). Vanity drew him to the theatre; the girl acted with plenty of gaiety and amused him; on leaving the theatre, he was in love for quite an hour. The Conte returned to Parma on receiving the news that Fabrizio was in real danger. The man Giletti, who had served as trooper in Napoleon's fine regiment of Italian dragoons, spoke seriously of killing him and was making arrangements for a subsequent flight to Bologna. If the reader is very young, he will be shocked by our admiration for this fine trait of virtue. It meant, however, no slight effort of heroism on Conte Mosca's part to return from Bologna; for, after all, in the mornings, his face would often look pale and jaded, and Fabrizio was so fresh, and so serene! Who would ever have dreamed of holding him up to reproach for the death of Fabrizio, if it had occurred in his absence and from so stupid a cause? But he was one of those rare spirits who suffer eternal remorse for a generous action which they might have done and failed to do. Moreover, he could not bear the thought of seeing the Duchessa look sad, and by any fault of his.

On his arrival he found her taciturn and gloomy. This is what had happened: her young maid, Cecchina, tormented by remorse, and estimating the gravity of her misdeed by the enormous amount of money she had received for committing it, had fallen ill. One evening the Duchessa, who was very fond of her, went up to her room. The girl could not hold out against this mark of kindness; she burst out crying, tried to hand over to her mistress all that was left of the money she had received, and at length found courage to confess to her the questions the Conte had asked and her own replies. The Duchessa ran over to the lamp and put it out, then said to little Cecchina that she forgave her, but on condition that she never uttered a word about this strange incident to anyone in the world. 'The poor Conte,' she added, in a casual tone, 'is afraid of being laughed at; all men are the same.'

The Duchessa hurried downstairs to her own apartments. No sooner had she shut herself in her room than she burst into tears. There seemed to her something horrible in the idea of her having a love affair with Fabrizio, whom she had seen as a newborn babe; and yet what else could her behaviour imply?

This had been the primary cause of the dark mood of melancholy in which the Conte had found her plunged. The moment he arrived she suffered from fits of impatience with him, and almost with Fabrizio; she would have liked never to set eyes on either of them again. She was vexed by the part, a ridiculous one in her eyes, which Fabrizio was playing in little Marietta's company; for the Conte, like all true lovers, incapable of keeping a secret, had told her everything. She could not get used to this disaster; her idol had a flaw. At length, on an impulse of real, true friendship, she asked the Conte's advice; this was for him an exquisite moment and a handsome reward for the honourable impulse that had made him return to Parma.

'What could be more simple!' said the Conte, smiling. 'Young men want to have every woman they see, and the next day the whole thing goes out of their minds. Oughtn't he to be going to Belgirate, to see the Marchesa del Dongo? Very well, let him go. During his absence, I shall request the troupe of comedians to take their talents elsewhere and will pay their travelling expenses. But presently we shall see him in love with the first pretty woman that chance may put in his way; that's in the nature of things and I shouldn't care to see him otherwise. . . . If necessary, get the Marchesa to write to him.'

This idea, thrown out with an air of complete indifference, came as a ray of light to the Duchessa; she was frightened of Giletti. That evening the Conte announced, as though by chance, that a courier, on his way to Vienna, would be passing through Milan; three days later Fabrizio received a letter from his mother. He set off greatly annoyed at not yet having, thanks to Giletti's jealousy, profited by little Marietta's excellent intentions, the assurance of which she conveyed to him through a *mammaccia*, an old woman who acted as her mother.

Fabrizio found his mother and one of his sisters at Belgirate, a large village in Piedmont, on the right shore of Lake Maggiore; the left shore belongs to the State of Milan and consequently to Austria. This lake, running parallel to the Lake of Como and also stretching from north to south, is situated about ten leagues farther to the west. The air of the mountains, the calm and majestic aspect of this superb lake, that reminded him of the one beside which he had spent his childhood, all helped to transform into gentle melancholy Fabrizio's grief, which was next door to anger. It was with an infinite tenderness that the memory of the Duchessa now presented itself to him. It seemed to him that away from her he was beginning to feel that love which he had never yet felt for any woman. Nothing would have been more painful to him than to be separated from her for ever, and if, while he was in this frame of mind, the Duchessa had deigned to have recourse to the slightest coquetry, she would have conquered this heart by presenting him, for example, with a rival. But so far from taking any such decisive step, it was not without the keenest self-reproach that she found her thoughts constantly following in the young traveller's footsteps. She reproached herself for what she still called a wild freak of imagination, as though it had been something monstrous. She became twice as attentive and obliging in her manner towards the Conte, who, captivated by so much charm, did not listen to the sane voice of reason which prescribed a second journey to Bologna.

The Marchesa del Dongo, busy with preparations for the wedding of her elder daughter, whom she was marrying to a Milanese duke, could only spare three days for her beloved son. Never had she met with such tender affection from him. In the midst of the melancholy which was more and more invading Fabrizio's heart an odd, and even absurd, idea had occurred to him and he had suddenly decided to follow it up. Dare we say that he wished to consult Father Blanès?

This excellent old man was perfectly incapable of understanding the sorrows of a heart torn asunder by juvenile passions of more or less equal strength. Besides, it would have taken a week to make him have even a glimpse of all the conflicting interests that Fabrizio had to consider in Parma. Yet at the thought of consulting him Fabrizio recaptured the freshness of his sensations at the age of sixteen. Can you believe it? – it was not simply as to a sage, or as to a friend completely devoted to him, that Fabrizio wished to speak to him. The object of this expedition, and the feelings that agitated our hero during the fifty hours it lasted, are so absurd that doubtless, in the interests of our story, it would have been better to have suppressed them. I am afraid that Fabrizio's credulity may make him forfeit the sympathy of the reader. But after all, this it was. Why should I flatter him more than another? I have not flattered Conte Mosca, nor the Prince.

Fabrizio, then, since the whole truth must be told, escorted his mother as far as the port of Laveno, on the left shore of Lake Maggiore, the Austrian side, where she landed about eight o'clock in the evening. (The lake is regarded as neutral territory, and no passport is required of those who do not set foot on shore.) But scarcely had night fallen when he had himself landed on that same Austrian shore, in a little wood that juts out into the water. He had hired a *sediola*, a sort of rustic tilbury that goes very fast, by the help of which he was able to follow his mother's carriage, at a distance of five hundred paces. He was disguised as a servant of the *Casa del Dongo*, and none of the many police or customs officers ever thought of asking him for his passport.

A quarter of a league before Como, where the Marchesa and her daughter were to stop for the night, he took a path to the left which, after skirting the small town of Vico, ran into a little road recently made along the extreme edge of the lake. It was midnight, and Fabrizio did not anticipate meeting any of the police. The trees of the various thickets through which the little road constantly passed displayed the dark silhouette of their leafy branches against a sky with many stars, but veiled in a slight mist. Water and sky were marvellously serene, Fabrizio's soul could not resist this sublime beauty; he stopped, then sat down on a rock which jutted out into the lake, forming a kind of little promontory. The all-prevailing silence was broken only, at regular intervals, by the faint ripple of the lake as it died away upon the shore. Fabrizio had an Italian heart. I crave the reader's pardon for him; this defect, which will render him less attractive, consisted mainly in this: he was free from vanity, save by fits and starts, and the mere sight of sublime beauty inclined him to tenderness, and robbed his sorrows of their harsh and cruel sting. Seated on his lonely rock, no longer having any need to be on his guard against the police, protected by the deep night and the vast silence, gentle tears came to wet his eyes, and he found there, with little trouble to himself, the happiest moments he had experienced for many a long day.

He resolved never to tell the Duchessa any lies, and it was because he loved her to adoration at that moment that he vowed to himself never to tell her that *he loved her*; never would he utter the word *love* in her hearing, since the passion which goes by that name was a stranger to his heart. In the fervour of generosity and virtue which formed his present happiness, he made the resolution to tell her the truth at the very first opportunity – his heart had never known what it was to love. Once this courageous plan had been definitely adopted, he felt himself relieved of an enormous weight. 'She will possibly have something to say to me about little Marietta. Very well,' he assured himself light-heartedly, 'I will never see little Marietta again.'

The overpowering heat which had prevailed during the day was beginning to be tempered by the morning breeze. Already the dawn was outlining with a faint white glimmer the peaks of the Alps that rise to the north and east of the Lake of Como. Their massive shapes, white with the snow that covers them even in the month of June, stand out against the clear, deep blue of a sky which at those immense heights is always pure. A spur of the Alps stretching southwards into sunny Italy separates the sloping shores of the Lake of Como from those of the Lake of Garda. Fabrizio followed with his eye all the various ridges of these sublime mountains; the dawn as it grew brighter revealed the valleys that divide them, lighting up the delicate mist that rose from the depths of the gorges.

Some minutes before this Fabrizio had resumed his journey. He went over the hill that forms the peninsula of Durini, and at length there appeared before his eyes that belfry of the village of Grianta from which he had so often studied the stars in the company of Father Blanès. 'What boundless ignorance was mine in those far off days!'

he thought, 'I couldn't even understand the absurd Latin of those treatises on astrology which my master used to study, and I think I respected them mainly because, understanding only a few words here and there, my imagination took upon itself to give them meaning, and the most romantic one possible.'

Gradually his musings took another course. 'Would there possibly be some real meaning in this science? Why should it be different from all the rest? A certain number of fools and crafty people agree among themselves that they know, let us say, the Mexican language; they foist themselves by means of this qualification upon society which respects them and upon governments who pay them. Favours are showered upon them precisely because they have no real intelligence, and because the powers that be need not fear that they will rouse nations to revolt and stir men to pity by the aid of generous sentiments! Take, for instance, Father Bari, to whom Ernesto IV has just awarded a pension of four thousand lire and the Cross of his Order for having reconstituted nineteen lines of a Greek dithyramb!

'But, good heavens, have I the right to find such things ridiculous? Is it indeed for me to complain?' he said to himself suddenly, stopping short. 'Hasn't that same Cross just been given to my tutor in Naples?' Fabrizio experienced a sensation of tense uneasiness. The fine enthusiasm for virtue which had recently made his heart beat high was beginning to give way to the low pleasure of having had a pretty share of stolen goods. 'After all,' he said to himself at length, with the lack-lustre eyes of a man who is dissatisfied with himself, 'since my birth gives me the right to profit by these abuses, it would be a signal piece of folly on my part not to take my share; but I must never allow myself to speak against such abuses in public.' This reasoning was by no means unsound; but Fabrizio had fallen a long way from that height of sublime happiness to which he had found himself transported an hour before. The thought of privilege had withered that plant, always so delicate a growth, which we call happiness.

'If we are not to believe in astrology,' he went on, trying to divert his thoughts, 'if this science, like three-quarters of the non-mathematical sciences, is just a collection of enthusiastic boobies and cunning hypocrites who are in the pay of those they serve, how does it come about that I think so often and with such emotion of this fatal circumstance? Some time ago I got myself out of the prison at

B —, but in the uniform and with the marching orders of a soldier who had been flung into prison with good cause.'

Fabrizio's reasoning could never succeed in penetrating farther; he wandered a hundred ways round the difficulty without managing to surmount it. He was still too young. In his moments of leisure, his mind was occupied in rapturous enjoyment of those sensations evoked by the romantic circumstances with which his imagination was always ready to supply him. He was far from employing his time in a patient examination of the actual character of things in order to discover their causes. Reality still seemed to him dull and sordid. I can understand a person's not caring to look it in the face, but then he ought not to argue about it. Above all, he should not manufacture objections out of the various bits and pieces of his ignorance.

Thus it was that, although not lacking in intelligence, Fabrizio could not manage to see that his half-belief in omens was for him a religion, a deep impression received on his entry into life. To think of this belief was to feel, it was a happiness. Yet he persisted doggedly in an attempt to discover how this could be a *proved* a real science, in the same category as geometry, for example. He hunted eagerly amongst his memories for all the instances in which omens observed by him had not been followed by the lucky or unlucky events which they seemed to herald. But while believing himself to be following a logical course of argument and marching towards the truth, his attention would gladly linger over the memory of occasions on which the foreboding had been broadly speaking followed by the happy or unhappy accident which it had seemed to him to foretell, and his heart was filled with respect and stirred by emotion. And he would have felt an insuperable repugnance towards the person who denied the value of omens, especially if he had resorted to irony.

Fabrizio walked on without taking account of distances, and had reached this point in his futile reasonings when, raising his head, he saw the wall of his father's garden. This wall, which supported a fine terrace, rose to a height of more than forty feet above the road on the right-hand side. A string-course of hewn stone right at the top, next to the balustrade, gave it a monumental air. 'It's not bad,' said Fabrizio coolly to himself, 'it's good architecture, almost in the Roman style.' He was applying his recent knowledge of antiquities. Then he turned his head away in disgust; his father's harsh treatment of him, and more particularly his brother Ascanio's denunciation of him on his return from his wandering in France, came back to his mind.

'That unnatural denunciation was the origin of my present existence. I may detest it, I may despise it, but after all it has altered my destiny. What would have become of me once I was packed off to Novara and my presence barely tolerated in the house of my father's agent, if my aunt had not become engaged in a love affair with a powerful Minister? Or, if this aunt had happened merely to possess a cold, conventional nature instead of that warm, passionate heart which loves me with a sort of fervour that astonishes me? Where should I be now if the Duchessa had had the heart of her brother the Marchese del Dongo?'

Overwhelmed by these painful memories, Fabrizio now found his steps beginning to falter. He came to the edge of the moat immediately opposite the magnificent façade of the castle; he hardly cast a glance at this great building, which time had blackened. The noble language of its architecture left him unmoved; the memory of his brother and his father closed his heart to every sensation of beauty. He was attentive only to the necessity of keeping on his guard in the presence of hypocritical and dangerous enemies. He looked for a moment, but with marked distaste, at the little window of the bedroom on the third floor which he had occupied before 1815. His father's character had robbed the memories of his early childhood of all their charm. 'I have not set foot in it,' he thought, 'since 7 March, at eight o'clock in the evening. I left it to go and get the passport from Vasi, and next day my fear of spies made me hasten my departure. When I came back after my travels in France, I hadn't time to go upstairs to look at my prints again, and that thanks to my brother's denunciation of me.'

Fabrizio turned his head away in horror. 'Father Blanès is over eighty-three,' he said sadly to himself. 'He hardly ever comes to the castle now so my sister tells me; the infirmities of old age have had their effect on him. That heart, once so firm and noble, has grown icy cold with the years. Heaven knows how long it is since he last went up to his belfry! I shall hide myself in the cellar, under the vats or the wine-press, until he is awake. I shall not go in to disturb the good old man's slumbers; probably he will have even forgotten what I look like; six years make a great difference at his age! I shall find nothing now but the tomb of a friend! And it is really a childish folly on my part, to have come here to face the disgust that the sight of my father's castle rouses in me.'

By this time Fabrizio had reached the little square in front of the church. It was with an amazement bordering on delirium that he saw, on the second floor of the ancient belfry, the long, narrow window lit up by Father Blanès' little lantern. The priest was in the habit of leaving it there when he climbed up to the cage of planks which formed his observatory, so that its light should not prevent him from reading his planisphere. This chart of the heavens was stretched over a great jar of terra-cotta which had once contained one of the orange trees at the castle. In the opening at the bottom of the jar, the tiniest of lamps was burning, the smoke from which was carried away from the vase by a little tin pipe, and the shadow of the pipe indicated the north on the chart. All these memories of such simple things filled Fabrizio's mind with a flood of emotions and made him completely happy.

Almost without thinking he used both his hands to make the little, short, low whistle which had formerly been the signal for his admission. At once he heard several tugs given to the rope which, from the observatory above, lifted up the latch of the belfry door. He rushed up the staircase, in a veritable transport of excitement; he found the priest in his wooden armchair in his accustomed place, his eye was glued to the little window of a mural quadrant. With his left hand the priest signed to Fabrizio not to interrupt him in his observations. A moment later he wrote down a figure upon a playing card; then, turning round in his chair, he held out his arms wide open to our hero, who flung himself into them, bursting into tears. Father Blanès was his true father.

'I was expecting you,' said Blanès, after the first effusions of tenderness. Was the priest speaking in his character as a man who knew the future; or rather, since he often thought of Fabrizio, had some astrological sign, by pure chance, announced his return to him?

'My death is now near at hand,' said Father Blanès.

'What!' cried Fabrizio, overcome with emotion.

'Yes,' the priest went on in a grave but by no means sorrowful tone. 'Five months and a half, or six months and a half after I have seen you again, my life, having found its full complement of happiness, will be extinguished, *Come face al mancar dell'alimento* (as the little lamp when its oil runs dry).

'Before the supreme moment, I shall probably pass a month or two without speaking, after which I shall be received into Our Father's Bosom; provided always he finds that I have fulfilled my duty in the post in which he has placed me as a sentinel.

'But you yourself are worn out with exhaustion; your emotion makes you ready for sleep. Ever since I have been expecting you, I have kept a loaf of bread and a bottle of brandy stored away in the great chest which holds my instruments. Give yourself those things for sustaining life, and try to collect enough strength to listen to me for a few moments longer. It lies in my power to tell you a number of things before night shall have given place altogether to day; I see them a great deal more clearly now than I may possibly see them tomorrow. For, my son, we are all of us weak vessels, and we must always take this weakness into account. Tomorrow, it may be, the old man, the earthly man in me, will be occupied with preparations for my death, and tomorrow evening at nine o'clock, you will have to leave me.'

Fabrizio having obeyed him in silence, as was his wont, the old man went on: 'So then, it is true that when you tried to see Waterloo you found nothing at first but a prison?'

'Yes, Father,' replied Fabrizio in amazement.

'Well, that was a rare piece of good fortune, for, warned by my voice, your soul can prepare itself for another prison, far more painful, far more terrible! In all probability you will escape from it only by a crime; but, Heaven be thanked, that crime will not have been committed by you. Never fall into crime, however violently you may be tempted. I seem to see that it will be a question of killing an innocent man, who, without knowing it, has usurped your rights. If you resist this violent temptation which will seem to be justified by the laws of honour, your life will be most happy in the eyes of men ... and reasonably happy,' he added, after a moment's reflection, 'in the eyes of the sage. You will die, my son, like me, sitting on a wooden seat, far removed from all luxury, and with no illusions about it. And like me, without having any grave reproach upon your soul.

'And now consideration of your future state is at an end between us: I could not add anything of great importance. All in vain have I tried to see how long this imprisonment will last – is it a matter of six months, a year, or ten years? I have been able to discover nothing. I must, I suppose, have committed some sin, and it is the will of

Heaven to punish me by the distress of this uncertainty. All I have seen is that after your period in prison – but I do not know whether it is at the very moment of your leaving it – there will be what I call a crime; but, fortunately, I think I may be sure that it will not be committed by you. If you are weak enough to get yourself implicated in this crime, all the rest of my calculations are but one long mistake. Then you will not die with your soul at peace, on a wooden seat and dressed in white!'

As he uttered these words Father Blanès tried to rise, and then it was that Fabrizio became aware of the ravages of time. He took almost a minute to get up and turn towards Fabrizio. The young man watched him, while standing motionless and silent. The priest flung himself into his arms, and embraced him closely several times with the utmost tenderness. Then, regaining all his old cheerfulness, he said: 'Try to settle down among my instruments so as to sleep in moderate comfort. Take my fur-lined coats; you will find several of great value which the Duchessa Sanseverina sent me four years ago. She asked me for a forecast of your future, which I took care not to send her, while keeping her furs and her fine quadrant. Every fore-telling of the future is a breach of the rules, and contains this danger, that it may alter the event; in which case the whole science falls to the ground, as in one of those games that children play with cards or bricks. Besides, there would have been some very hard things to say to this Duchessa, who is always so lovely. By the way, don't let yourself be startled in your sleep by the bells, which will make such a terrible din close to your ear when the men come to ring for the seven o'clock mass. Later on, they will set the great bell going on the floor below, which shakes all my instruments. Today is the feast of San Giovita, Martyr and Soldier. As you know, the little village of Grianta has the same patron saint as the great city of Brescia, a thing which, by the way, led to a most amusing mistake on the part of my illustrious master, Giacomo Marini of Ravenna. On more than one occasion he announced to me that I should have a rather fine career in the church; he believed that I was to be the priest in charge of the magnificent church of San Giovita, in Brescia; I have been the parish priest of a little village of seven hundred and fifty houses! But every-thing has been for the best; I saw not ten years ago, that if I had been priest in Brescia, my destiny would have been to be cast into a prison on a hill in Moravia, the Spielberg.

'Tomorrow I will bring you all sorts of delicacies filched from the great dinner which I am giving to all the clergy of the district who are coming to sing at my High Mass. I shall leave them down below, but don't make any attempt to see me, don't come down to take possession of these good things until you have heard me go out again. You must not see me again *by daylight*, and as the sun sets tomorrow at twenty-seven minutes past seven, I shall not come to embrace you until about eight. And you must take your departure while the hours are still numbered by nine, that is to say before the clock has struck ten. Take care you are not seen at the windows of the belfry; the police have your description, and they are to some extent under the orders of your brother, who is a notable tyrant. The Marchese del Dongo is growing feeble,' added Blanès sadly, 'and if he were to see you again perhaps he would hand you over something secretly there and then. But such benefits, tainted by deceit, do not become a man like yourself, whose strength will one day lie in his conscience. The Marchese loathes his son Ascanio, and it is on that son that the five or six millions he possesses will devolve. That is right and proper. You yourself, at his death, will have an annuity of four thousand lire, and fifty ells of black cloth for your servants' mourning.'

Fabrizio's mind was in a state of nervous tension as a result of the old man's conversation, his own keen concentration on it, and his extreme fatigue. He had great difficulty in getting to sleep, and his slumber was disturbed by dreams, that were possibly presages of the future. The next morning, at ten o'clock, he was woken up by a general shaking of the whole belfry; a fearful noise seemed to be coming from outside. He got up in bewilderment, imagining that the end of the world had come. Then he fancied himself in prison; it took him some time to recognize the sound of the big bell which forty peasants were setting in motion in honour of the great San Giovita; ten would have been enough.

Fabrizio looked round for a convenient place in which to see without being seen. He discovered that from this great height he could look down into the gardens, and even into the inner courtyard of his father's castle. He had forgotten this. The thought of that father arriving at the ultimate bourne of life altered all his feelings. He could even make out the sparrows hunting for crumbs on the great balcony outside the dining-room. 'Those are the descendants of the ones I used to tame a long time ago,' he thought. This balcony, like the other balconies of the building, was covered with a great number of orange trees in earthenware tubs of a fairly large size. The sight of this moved him; the appearance of that inner courtyard thus adorned, with its shadows sharply defined and thrown into relief by the brilliant sunlight, was truly majestic.

The thought of his father's failing health came back into his mind. 'But it's really strange,' he said to himself, 'my father is only thirty-five years older than I am; thirty-five and twenty-three make only fifty-eight!' His eyes, fixed on the windows of the bedroom of that stern man who had never loved him, became filled with tears. He shuddered, and a sudden chill ran through his veins when he thought he saw his father crossing a terrace planted with orange trees which was on a level with his room; but it was only one of the menservants. Close to the foot of the belfry a number of girls dressed in white and split up into different groups were busy tracing patterns with red, blue, and yellow flowers on the paving of the streets through which the procession was to pass. But there was a spectacle that made a keener appeal to Fabrizio's soul. From the belfry, his gaze swept down to the two branches of the lake, for a distance of several leagues, and this sublime view soon made him forget all the others; it aroused in him the most lofty feelings. All the memories of his childhood came crowding in to besiege his mind; and this day which he spent imprisoned in a belfry was possibly one of the happiest days of his life.

Happiness carried him to heights of thought quite foreign to his nature; he considered the various incidents of life, he, still so young, as if he had already arrived at its furthest limits. 'I must admit,' he said to himself at length, after several hours of delightful musing, 'that since I came to Parma, I have known no such serene and perfect joy as that I used to find in Naples when galloping along the roads of Vomero or strolling by the shores of Miseno. All the extremely complicated interests of that evil-minded little court have made me evil-minded also. ... I take no pleasure at all in hating anyone, I even believe it would be a miserable sort of happiness for me to humiliate my enemies if I had any; but I have no enemy at all. ... Stop a moment!' he suddenly exclaimed. 'I have an enemy in Giletti ... And here's a curious thing,' he said to himself, 'the pleasure I would feel in seeing that intensely ugly fellow go to the devil has survived the very slight fancy I had for little Marietta ... She's far inferior to the Duchessa D'A —, whom I was obliged to make love to in Naples just because I had told her I was in love with her. Good God, how many times was I bored in the course of the long-drawn-out assignations which that fair Duchessa used to accord me. I never felt anything like that in that shabby bedroom, which served as a kitchen, in which little Marietta received me twice, and each time for two minutes only.

'Oh, good gracious! what do those people eat? It's pitiable! I ought to have settled on her and the *mammaccia* a pension of three beefsteaks payable daily. Little Marietta,' he went on, 'used to distract me from the evil thoughts which the proximity of the court put into my mind.

'I should perhaps have done well to adopt the café-haunter's life, as the Duchessa said; she seemed to incline that way, and she has far more intelligence than I have. Thanks to her kindness, or even merely with that annuity of four thousand lire and that capital fund of forty thousand invested at Lyons, which my mother intends for me,

I should always have had a horse and a few scudi to spend on excavating and forming a collection of ancient relics. Since it appears that I am never to know what love is, these will always be for me one of the great sources of joy. I should like, before I die, to go back to visit the battlefield of Waterloo, and try to identify the place where I was so gaily lifted off my horse and left sitting on the ground. That pilgrimage accomplished, I should often return to this sublime lake; nothing else as beautiful is to be seen in the world, for my heart at least. What is the use of going so far afield in search of happiness. It is there, right under my eyes!

'Ah!' thought Fabrizio, 'there is this objection: the police will drive me away from the Lake of Como, but I am younger than the people who direct the actions of the police. Here' he added, with a chuckle, 'I should certainly not find a Duchessa d'A —, but I should find one of those little girls down there who are making their pattern of flowers in the roadway, and, to tell the truth, I should love her just as much. Insincerity freezes me, even in love, and our great ladies aim at effects that are too sublime. Napoleon has given them ideas as to conduct and constancy.

'Hell and damnation!' he suddenly exclaimed, withdrawing his head from the window, as if he were afraid of being recognized in spite of the shadow cast by the enormous shutter that protected the bells from rain. 'Here comes a troop of police in full dress.' And indeed, ten policemen, four of whom were sergeants, had come into sight at the top of the main village street. The senior sergeant spaced them out at intervals of a hundred yards along the course which the procession was to take. 'Everyone knows me here; if they see me, it will only mean one jump for me from the shores of the Lake of Como to the Spielberg, where they will fasten to each of my legs a chain weighing a hundred and ten pounds. And what grief that will be for the Duchessa.'

It took Fabrizio two or three minutes to remind himself that first of all he was stationed at a height of more than eighty feet above the ground, that the place in which he stood was comparatively dark, that the eyes of the people who might be looking up at him were blinded by the dazzling sunlight, and finally they were walking about and staring with wide-open eyes in the streets where the houses had just been newly whitewashed in honour of the feast of San Giovita. In spite of such clear and simple arguments, Fabrizio's Italian soul would have been from that moment incapable of taking any pleasure in the scene if he had not interposed between himself and the police a tattered scrap of old linen which he nailed up against the window and in which he made two holes for his eyes.

The bells had been making the air quiver for ten minutes, the procession was coming out of the church, the sound of the *mortaretti* burst on the ear. Fabrizio turned his head and recognized that little terrace adorned with a parapet and overlooking the lake, where so often, when he was a boy, he had exposed himself to danger to see the *mortaretti* go off between his legs, with the result that on the mornings of public holidays his mother liked to see him by her side.

It should be explained that the *mortaretti* (or little mortars) are nothing other than gun-barrels which are sawn through so as to leave them only four inches long. That is why the peasants so greedily collect all the gun-barrels which, since 1796, Europe has been scattering broadcast over the plains of Lombardy. Once they have been reduced to a length of four inches, these little guns are loaded to the muzzle, they are placed on the ground in a vertical position, and a train of powder is laid from one to the next; they are drawn up in three lines like a battalion, and to the number of three or four hundred, in some emplacement near the route along which the procession is to pass. When the Blessed Sacrament approaches, a match is put to the train of powder, and then begins a running fire of sharp explosions, as irregular as anyone can imagine and altogether comical; the women go wild with joy. Nothing is so gay as the sound of these *mortaretti* heard from a distance across the lake and softened by the rippling motion of the water. This curious sound, which had so often been the delight of his childhood, drove away the somewhat too solemn thoughts by which our hero was assailed. He went and fetched the priest's big astronomical telescope, and recognized most of the men and women following the procession. Many of the charming little girls whom Fabrizio had last seen at the age of eleven or twelve, were now fine, handsome women in the full flower of vigorous youth. They revived our hero's courage and to speak to them he would readily have braved the police.

After the procession had passed and re-entered the church by a side-door which was out of Fabrizio's sight, the heat soon became intense even up in the belfry. The villagers returned to their homes, and deep silence reigned throughout the village. Several boats took on board a load of peasants returning to Bellagio, Menaggio, and other villages situated on the lake. Fabrizio could distinguish the sound of each stroke of the oars; so simple a detail as this sent him into an ecstasy. His present joy was made up of all the unhappiness, all the irritation that he found in the complicated life of a court. How happy would he have been at this moment to be sailing for a league over that beautiful lake which looked so calm and reflected so clearly the depths of the sky above!

He heard the door at the foot of the belfry open: it was the priest's old maidservant, bringing in a great hamper; he had all the difficulty in the world in restraining himself from speaking to her. 'She is almost as fond of me as her master,' he said to himself, 'and besides, I am leaving tonight at nine o'clock. Wouldn't she keep the oath of secrecy I should make her swear, if only for a few hours? But,' thought Fabrizio, 'I should be vexing my friend! I might get him into trouble with the police!' And he let Ghita go without speaking to her. He made an excellent dinner, then settled down to sleep for a few minutes. He did not wake up until half past eight in the evening; Father Blanès was shaking him by the arm, and it was dark.

Blanès was extremely tired, and looked fifty years older than the night before. He said nothing more about serious matters. Seated in his wooden chair, he said to Fabrizio: 'Embrace me.' He clasped him again and again in his arms. 'Death,' he said at length, 'which is coming to put an end to this extremely long life, will have nothing so painful about it as this parting. I have a purse which I will leave in Ghita's charge, with orders to draw on it for her own needs, but to hand over to you what is left should you ever come to ask for it. I know her; after these instructions, she is capable, from a wish to economize on your behalf, of not buying meat four times in the year, if you do not give her very strict orders. You may yourself be reduced to poverty and your old friend's mite will be of service to you. Expect nothing from your brother but abominable behaviour, and try to earn money by some work which will make you useful to society. I foresee strange storms; perhaps, in fifty years' time, the world will have no further use for idlers. Your mother and your aunt may fail you, your sisters will have to obey their husbands. ... Now go, away with you, fly!' cried Blanès earnestly. He had just heard a little whirring sound in the clock which warned him that ten o'clock was about to strike, and he would not even allow Fabrizio to give him a last embrace.

'Hurry, hurry!' he cried to him. 'It will take you a minute to get down the stairs. Take care not to fall; that would be a terrible omen.' Fabrizio rushed headlong down the stairs, and on reaching the square began to run. He had scarcely arrived in front of his father's castle when the clock chimed the hour of ten. Each stroke reverberated in his breast and occasioned strange anxiety there. He stopped to reflect, or rather to give himself up to the passionate feelings inspired in him by the contemplation of that majestic edifice which he had judged so coldly the night before. He was recalled from his musings by the sound of footsteps; he looked round and found himself surrounded by four of the police. He had a brace of excellent pistols, the priming of which he had renewed during dinner; the slight sound he made in cocking them attracted the attention of one of the constables, and he was within an inch of being arrested. He saw the danger he was in, and decided to fire the first shot; he would be justified in doing so, for it was the only way he had of resisting four well-armed men.

Fortunately for him, the constables, who were on their way round to clear the taverns, had not shown themselves altogether irresponsive to the polite attentions they had received in several of these friendly resorts; they did not make up their minds quickly enough to do their duty. Fabrizio took to his heels and ran. The constables went a few yards, also running, and shouting 'Stop! Stop!' Then all was silent again. After running about three hundred yards, Fabrizio stopped to recover his breath. 'The sound of my pistols nearly got me caught. For this once the Duchessa might certainly say, should it ever be granted me to see her lovely eyes again, that my mind takes pleasure in contemplating what is going to happen in ten years' time, and forgets to notice what is actually happening under my nose.'

Fabrizio shuddered at the thought of the danger he had just escaped. He quickened his pace, but presently found himself impelled to run, which was not over-prudent, as it attracted the attention of several peasants who were going back to their homes. He could not bring himself to stop until he had reached the mountain, more than a league from Grianta, and even when he had stopped, he broke into a cold sweat at the thought of the Spielberg.

'Here's a fine fright!' he said to himself aloud; on hearing the sound of this word, he was almost tempted to feel ashamed. 'But isn't my aunt always telling me that the thing I most need to learn is to make allowances for myself? I am always comparing myself with a model of perfection, which cannot exist. Very well, I forgive myself my fright, for, from another point of view, I was quite prepared to defend myself, and certainly all four of them would not have been left standing to carry me off to prison. What I am doing at this moment,' he went on, 'is not soldier-like. Instead of retiring rapidly, after obtaining my objective, and possibly giving the alarm to my enemies, I am amusing myself with a fancy more absurd perhaps than all good Father Blanès' predictions.'

For indeed, instead of retiring along the shortest line, and reaching the shore of Lake Maggiore, where his boat was awaiting him, he was making an enormous detour to go and visit *his tree*. The reader may perhaps remember the love Fabrizio bore for a chestnut tree planted by his mother twenty-three years earlier. 'It would be quite worthy of my brother,' he said to himself, 'to have had this tree cut down; but creatures of that sort are insensitive to delicate feelings; he will not even have thought of it. And besides, that would not be a bad omen,' he added firmly.

Two hours later his expression was one of consternation; some evil-minded men, or a storm, had broken off one of the main branches of the young tree, which hung down withered. Fabrizio cut it off reverently by means of his dagger, and smoothed the cut neatly, so that the rain should not get inside the trunk. Next, although time was very precious to him, for day was about to break, he spent a good hour turning up the soil around his beloved tree. All these acts of folly accomplished, he set off again rapidly on the road to Lake Maggiore. On the whole, he was not at all sad; the tree was well-grown; it was more vigorous than ever, and in five years had almost doubled its size. The branch was only an accident of no consequence. Once it had been cut off, it did no more harm to the tree, which would indeed shoot up straighter, since its branching began higher up.

Fabrizio had not gone a league when a gleaming band of white picked out to the east the peaks of the Resegone di Lecco, a mountain famous throughout the district. The road which he was following became crowded with peasants, but instead of thinking on military lines, Fabrizio let himself be moved by the sublime and touching aspect of these forests in the region of the Lake of Como. They are perhaps the finest in the world; I do not mean those which bring in more *new-minted money*, as they would say in Switzerland, but those that speak most eloquently to the soul. To listen to this language in such as a situation as that in which Fabrizio found himself, an object for the attention of those gentlemen, the Lombardo-Venetian police, was real childish folly.

'I am half a league from the frontier,' he said to himself at length. 'I am going to meet customs-officers and constables making their morning rounds. This coat of fine cloth will arouse their suspicions, they will ask me for my passport. Now that passport is inscribed at full length with a name that is marked down for prison; so here am I in the agreeable position of having perforce to commit a murder. If, as usually happens, the constables patrol in pairs, I cannot simply wait to fire until one of them tries to seize me by the collar; if as he falls he manages to keep his hold on me for even as much as a second, off I go to the Spielberg.'

Fabrizio, horrified most of all by the necessity of firing first, possibly on an old soldier who had served under his uncle, Conte Pietranera, ran to hide himself in the hollow trunk of an enormous chestnut tree. He was renewing the priming of his pistols when he heard a man coming towards him through the wood, singing very tunefully a delightful air by Mercadante, who was much in the fashion at that time in Lombardy.

'There's a good omen!' thought Fabrizio. This air, to which he listened with rapt attention, freed his mind from that little touch of anger which was beginning to mingle with his reasonings. He looked carefully along the main road in both directions, and saw no one. 'The singer must be coming along some side road,' he said to himself. Almost at the same moment he saw a manservant, very neatly dressed in the English style, who was coming towards him at a walking pace leading a fine thoroughbred, which was, however, perhaps a trifle too lean.

'Ah!' thought Fabrizio, 'if I reasoned like Mosca, when he tells me that the risk a man runs is always the measure of his rights over his neighbour, I would blow out that man's brains with a pistol-shot, and once I was mounted on that lean horse, I would certainly snap my fingers at all the police in the world. As soon as I was back in Parma, I would send some money to that man or to his widow. ... But that would be a monstrous thing to do!'

MORALIZING thus, Fabrizio sprang down on to the main road that runs from Lombardy into Switzerland. At this point it is a good four or five feet below the level of the forest. 'If my man takes fright,' said Fabrizio to himself, 'he will go off at a gallop, and I shall be left stranded here, looking the picture of a fool.' At this moment he found himself only ten yards from the man, who had stopped singing. Fabrizio could see in his eyes that he was frightened; he was possibly going to turn his horse. Without as yet having come to any decision, Fabrizio sprang forward and seized the lean horse by the bridle.

'My good man,' he said to the servant, 'I am not an ordinary thief, for I am going to begin by giving you twenty lire, but I am obliged to borrow your horse; I shall be killed if I don't get away pretty quickly. I have the four Riva brothers on my heels, those great hunters you probably know; they caught me just now in their sister's bedroom. I jumped out of the window, and here I am. They are out in the forest with their dogs and their guns. I had hidden myself in that great hollow chestnut because I saw one of them cross the road; their dogs will track me down. I am going to mount your horse and gallop a league beyond Como; I am going to Milan to throw myself at the Viceroy's feet. I shall leave your horse at the post-house with two napoleons for you, provided you consent with good grace. If you offer the least resistance, I shall kill you with these pistols you see here. If, after I have gone, you set the police on my track, my cousin, the brave Conte Alari, Equerry to the Emperor, will take care to break your bones.'

Fabrizio was inventing this speech as he went along, while delivering it in a wholly calm and peaceful tone.

'Besides,' he added, laughing, 'my name is no secret. I am the Marchesino del Dongo and my castle is quite close to here, at Grianta. Damn you!' he cried, raising his voice, 'let go the horse!' The servant, stupefied, did not utter a word. Fabrizio transferred the pistol to his left hand, seized hold of the bridle which the man had let go, sprang into the saddle and made off at a canter. When he was about three hundred yards away, he realized that he had forgotten to hand over the twenty lire he had promised. He stopped; there was no one on the road save the servant, who was following at a gallop. He signalled to him with his handkerchief to come on, and when he saw he was only fifty yards away, he flung a handful of small change on to the road, and went on again. From a distance, he could see the servant picking up the money. 'There's a really sensible man,' he said to himself with a laugh, 'not a single unnecessary word.'

He sped along rapidly towards the south, stopped for a time at a lonely inn, and started off again a few hours later. At two o'clock in the morning he was on the shore of Lake Maggiore. He soon caught sight of his boat which was drifting about on the water; at the agreed signal, it came to pick him up. He could see no peasant to whom he could entrust the horse; he turned the noble animal loose; three hours later he was at Belgirate. There, finding himself on friendly soil, he took a little rest; he was full of joy, everything had gone off perfectly. Dare we indicate the true causes of his joy? His tree showed a superb growth, and his soul had been refreshed by the deep and tender emotion he had felt in the arms of Father Blanès. 'Does he really believe,' he asked himself, 'in all the predictions he made to me? Or rather, since my brother has given me the reputation of a Jacobin, a man without law or honour, and utterly unscrupulous, was he simply seeking to persuade me not to yield to the temptation of breaking the head of some brute who may have done me a bad turn?' Two days later Fabrizio was in Parma, where he greatly amused the Duchessa and the Conte by relating to them with the utmost exactitude, as was his custom, the whole story of his travels.

On his arrival Fabrizio found the porter and all the servants of the Palazzo Sanseverina wearing the tokens of the deepest mourning.

'Whom have we lost?' he asked the Duchessa.

'That excellent man whom people called my husband has just died at Baden. He has left me this house; that had been arranged beforehand, but as a sign of true friendship he has added a legacy of 300,000 lire, which puts me in a serious quandary. I do not want to forgo it in favour of his niece the Marchesa Raversi, who plays the most abominable tricks on me every day. You are interested in art, you must find me a good sculptor; I shall erect a tomb to the Duca which will cost 300,000 lire.' The Conte began telling them some anecdotes about the Marchesa.

'I have tried to win her over by doing her good turns, but all to no purpose,' said the Duchessa. 'As for the Duca's nephews, I have had them all made colonels or generals. In return for which, not a month passes without their sending me some abominable anonymous letter. I have been obliged to engage a secretary to read missives of that sort.'

'And these anonymous letters are their mildest offence,' added Conte Mosca; 'they make a regular business of fabricating infamous accusations. A score of times I could have brought the whole of that set before the courts, and Your Excellency may imagine,' he went on, addressing Fabrizio, 'whether my worthy judges would have convicted them.'

'Well, that's what spoils all the rest for me,' said Fabrizio with an artlessness that was quite amusing in court circles. 'I should prefer to have seen them sentenced by magistrates judging according to their conscience.'

'You would give me great pleasure, seeing you travel with a view to improving your knowledge of things, if you would supply me with the addresses of such magistrates. I shall write to them before I go to bed.'

'If I were Minister, this absence of honest judges would wound my self-respect.'

'But it seems to me,' replied the Conte, 'that your Excellency, who is so fond of the French, and who even once lent them the aid of his invincible arm, is forgetting for the moment one of their great maxims: "It is better to kill the devil than to let the devil kill you." I should like to see how you would govern those passionate souls who spend the whole day reading the *History of the Revolution in France* by using judges who would acquit the people I accused. They would reach the point of not convicting the most obviously guilty scoundrels, and would fancy themselves a kind of Brutus. But I have a bone to pick with you. Does your extremely sensitive soul not feel a twinge of remorse with regard to that fine, but rather too lean, horse you have just abandoned on the shores of Lake Maggiore?'

'I fully intend,' said Fabrizio, with the utmost seriousness, 'to send the owner of the horse whatever sum is necessary to compensate him for the cost of advertising and other expenses he may incur to get it back from the peasants who may have found it. I shall read the Milan newspaper very attentively to see if it contains the announcement of a missing horse. I know very well what this one looks like.'

'He is truly *primitive*,' said the Conte to the Duchessa. 'And where would your Excellency be now,' he went on with a smile, 'if while you were galloping off at a furious rate on this borrowed horse, it had taken into its head to stumble? You would be in the Spielberg, my dear young nephew, and all my influence would barely have managed to get the weight of the chain attached to each of your legs reduced by thirty pounds. You would have spent ten years or so in that pleasure-resort; perhaps your legs would have become swollen or gangrened; then they would have duly cut them off.'

'Oh, for pity's sake,' cried the Duchessa with tears in her eyes, 'don't go any farther with such a gloomy fairy-tale! Here he is back again. ...'

'And I am more delighted than you, I assure you,' replied the Minister, with the greatest seriousness. 'But why didn't this tiresome boy ask me for a passport in a suitable name, since he was anxious to penetrate into Lombardy? At the first news of his arrest I would have set off for Milan, and the friends I have in those parts would have kindly shut their eyes and pretended to believe that their police had arrested a subject of the Prince of Parma. The story of your adventures is charming, amusing, I readily agree,' the Conte went on, resuming a less sinister tone. 'Your bursting out of the wood on to the high road pleases me well enough; but between ourselves, since that servant held your life in his hands, you had the right to take his. We are about to arrange a brilliant future for Your Excellency; at least that is what my lady here orders, and I do not believe that my worst enemies can accuse me of having ever disobeyed her commands. What terrible grief for her and for me if, in that sort of steeplechase which you have just engaged in on that lean horse, it had chanced to stumble. It would almost have been better for you,' the Conte added, 'if that horse had made you break your neck.'

'You are very tragic this evening, my dear,' said the Duchessa, deeply moved.

'It is because we are surrounded by tragic events,' replied the Conte, also with emotion. 'We are not in France, where everything ends in a song or in a year or two's imprisonment, and really it is wrong of me to speak of all this to you in a joking way. Now then, my young nephew, I suppose I shall find some way of making you a bishop, for quite frankly, I cannot begin with the Archbishopric of Parma, as is desired, most reasonably, by Her Grace the Duchessa here present. In that bishopric, where you will be far removed for our wise counsels, tell us roughly what your policy will be?'

'To kill the devil rather than let him kill me, as my friends the French have so sensibly said,' replied Fabrizio with shining eyes; 'to keep, by every means in my power, including a pistol-shot, the position you will have secured for me. I have read in the Genealogy of the del Dongo family the story of that ancestor of ours who built the castle of Grianta. Towards the end of his life, his good friend Galeazzo Sforza, Duke of Milan, sent him to visit a fortress on our lake; there was fear of another invasion by the Swiss. "I must just write a few civil words to the Governor," the Duke of Milan said to him as he was bidding him goodbye. He wrote and handed to our ancestor a note of a couple of lines; then he asked for it back to seal it. "It will be more polite," said the Prince. Vespasiano del Dongo started off, but as he was sailing over the lake he called to mind an old Greek tale, for he was a man of learning. He opened his good lord and master's letter, and found it contained an order addressed to the Governor of the castle to put him to death as soon as he should arrive. Sforza, too much intent on the joke he was playing on our ancestor, had left a space between the end of the letter and his signature. In this space, Vespasiano wrote an order proclaiming himself Governor General of all the castles on the lake, and suppressed the beginning of the letter. After arriving at the fortress and being duly acknowledged, he flung the Governor down a well, declared war on Sforza, and after a few years exchanged his fortress for those vast estates which have made the fortune of every branch of our family, and which will one day provide me with an income of four thousand lire.'

'You talk like an academician!' exclaimed the Conte laughing. 'That was a marvellous stroke of inspiration you have just related, but it is only once in ten years that one has the amusing chance to do exciting things of that sort. A half brainless individual, but one who keeps his eyes open and day in day out acts with prudence, will often enjoy the pleasure of triumphing over men of imagination. It was by a foolish error of imagination that Napoleon was led to surrender to the prudent *John Bull* instead of seeking to escape to America. John Bull, in his counting-house, had a good laugh over that letter of his in which he quotes Themistocles. In all ages, the base Sancho Panzas will, in the long run, triumph over the sublimely noble Don Quixotes. If you are willing to agree to do nothing out of the ordinary, I have no doubt that you will be a highly respected if not a highly respectable Bishop. None the less, my comment holds good: your Excellency acted very thoughtlessly in the affair of the horse, and was within an ace of imprisonment for life.'

This statement made Fabrizio shudder. He remained plunged in deep amazement. 'Was that,' he wondered, 'the prison with which I am threatened? Is that the crime which I was not to commit?' The predictions of Blanès, which, as prophecies, he had utterly disregarded, assumed in his eyes the importance of authentic forecasts.

'Why, what's the matter with you?' the Duchessa asked him in amazement. 'The Conte has infected you with his own dark thoughts.'

'I am enlightened by a new truth, and, instead of rebelling against it, my mind accepts it. It is true that I came very near to being imprisoned for ever! But that servant looked so nice in his English suit! It would have been such a pity to kill him!'

The Minister was charmed by his little air of wisdom.

'He's excellent from all points of view,' he said, looking towards the Duchessa. 'I may tell you, my dear fellow, that you've made a conquest, and one that is perhaps the most admirable of all.'

'Ah!' thought Fabrizio, 'now for some joke about little Marietta.' He was mistaken. The Conte went on to say: 'Your *evangelic* simplicity has won the heart of our venerable Archbishop, Father Landriani. One of these days we are going to make a Vicar-General of you, and what constitutes the cream of the jest is that the three existing Vicars-General, all most worthy men, and hard-working, two of whom, I fancy, were Vicars-General before you were born, will request, in a finely worded letter addressed to their Archbishop, that you shall rank first among them all. These gentlemen base their request in the first place on your virtues, and next on the fact that you are the great-nephew of the famous Archbishop Ascanio del Dongo. When I learnt of the respect they had for your virtues, I immediately made the senior Vicar-General's nephew a captain; he had been a lieutenant ever since the siege of Tarragona by Marshal Suchet.'

'Go right away now, dressed as you are, and pay an affectionate visit to your Archbishop,' exclaimed the Duchessa. 'Tell him about your sister's marriage; when he learns that she is going to be a Duchessa, he will find that you have more "apostolic" virtues than ever. But, by the way, remember you know nothing of all the Conte has just told your about your future appointment.'

Fabrizio hastened to the Archbishop's palace. There he behaved with modesty and simplicity; it was a manner he could assume only too easily, he had to make an effort to play the great nobleman. As he listened to the somewhat lengthy stories of Monsignore Landriani, he kept saying to himself: 'Ought I to have fired my pistol at the man who was leading that lean horse?' His reason said 'Yes', but his heart could not accustom itself to the cruel picture of the handsome young man falling off his horse, all disfigured.

'That prison in which I should have been swallowed up, if my horse had stumbled, was that the prison with which I am threatened by so many omens?'

This question was of the utmost importance to him, and the Archbishop was pleased by his air of deep attention.

O^N leaving the Archbishop's palace, Fabrizio hurried off to little Marietta's lodgings. From some distance away he could hear the loud voice of Giletti who had sent out for wine and was regaling himself with his friends and prompter and the candle-snuffers. The *mammaccia*, who did duty as a mother, came alone in answer to his call.

'A great deal new has happened since you were here,' she cried. 'Two or three of our actors are accused of celebrating the great Napoleon's feast-day with an orgy, and our poor company, which they say is a crowd of Jacobins, has been given orders to quit the States of Parma, so three cheers for Napoleon! But the Prime Minister, so they say, put his hand in his pocket. One thing certain is that Giletti has some money, I don't know how much, but I've seen him with a handful of scudi. Marietta has had five scudi from our manager to pay for the journey to Mantua and Venice, and I have had one. She is still very much in love with you, but she's frightened of Giletti. Three days ago, at the last performance we gave, he really tried to kill her; he boxed her ears hard twice, and what was abominable of him, he tore her blue shawl. If you would care to give her a blue shawl, you'd be a very decent fellow, and we would say we had won it in a lottery. The drum-major of the carabineers is giving an assault-at-arms tomorrow; you will find the hour posted up at all the street corners. Come and see us. If he has gone off to the assault, and we have any reason to hope he will stay away for some little time, I shall be at the window, and I'll give you a signal to come up. Try to bring us something really nice, and Marietta will be head over heels in love with you.'

As he made his way down the winding staircase of this foul hovel, Fabrizio was filled with compunction. 'I haven't altered in the least,' he said to himself. 'All those fine resolutions I made on the shore of our Lake, when I looked at life with so philosophic an eye, have taken wing. My mind at the time was not in its normal condition; the whole thing was a dream, and vanished in the face of stern reality.'

'Now would be the time to act,' he said to himself as he entered the Palazzo Sanseverina about eleven o'clock that evening. But it was in vain that he sought in his heart for the courage to speak with that sublime sincerity which had seemed to him so easy on the night he had spent by the shore of the Lake of Como. 'I am going to vex the person whom I love best in the world. If I speak, I shall simply seem to be a humbug. I'm not worthy of anything really, except in certain moments of exaltation.

'The Conte has treated me remarkably kindly,' he said to the Duchessa after giving her an account of his visit to the Archbishop's Palace. 'I appreciate his conduct all the more in that I think I am right in believing that he is only moderately pleased with me; my own behaviour towards him ought therefore to be strictly correct. He has excavations at Sanguigna about which, to judge at least from the journey he made two days ago, he is still madly keen; he went twelve leagues at a gallop to spend a couple of hours with his workmen. If they find fragments of statuary in the ancient temple, the foundations of which he has just laid bare, he is afraid of their being stolen. I have a mind to suggest to him that I should go and spend about a couple of days at Sanguigna. Tomorrow, about five, I have to see the Archbishop again. I can start that evening and take advantage of the cool night air for the journey.'

The Duchessa did not at first reply.

'One would say you are looking for some excuse for leaving me,' she said to him at length in an extremely affectionate tone. 'No sooner have you come back from Belgirate than you find a reason for going off again.'

'Here is a fine opportunity for speaking,' thought Fabrizio. 'But by the lake I was slightly off my balance, I didn't realize, in my enthusiasm for sincerity, that my pretty speech would end by becoming a piece of impertinence. It was a question of saying: "I love you with the most devoted affection, etc., etc., but my heart is not susceptible to passionate love." Isn't that as much as saying: "I see that you are in love with me; but I warn you, I cannot pay you back in the same coin?" If she really is in love, the Duchessa may be annoyed at its being guessed; and she will be revolted by my impudence, if what she feels for me is no more than plain and simple friendship ... and that is the kind of offence that people never forgive.'

While he was weighing these important considerations in his mind, Fabrizio, without noticing what he did, was pacing up and down the drawing-room, with the grave and dignified air of a man who sees disaster staring him in the face.

The Duchessa gazed at him with admiration. This was no longer the child she had seen come into the world, no longer the nephew always ready to obey her. Here was a man of serious character, and one by whom it would be an exquisite pleasure to be loved. She got up from the ottoman on which she was sitting, and flinging herself with rapture into his arms, she said to him: 'So you want to run away from me?'

'No,' he replied with the air of a Roman Emperor, 'but I should like to act wisely.'

This remark was capable of various interpretations. Fabrizio did not feel that he had the courage to go any farther and run the risk of offending this adorable woman. He was too young, too easily stirred to emotion; his brain could not supply him with any pleasing turn of speech to convey what he wished to say. In an instinctive burst of feeling, and in defiance of all reason, he took this charming woman in his arms and smothered her with kisses. At that moment, the Conte's carriage could be heard coming into the courtyard, and almost immediately the Conte himself entered the room: he seemed greatly moved.

'You inspire the most singular passions,' he said to Fabrizio, who stood there almost thunderstruck by this remark.

'The Archbishop,' went on the Conte, 'went this evening to the audience that his Highness grants him every Thursday. The Prince has just told me that the Archbishop, who seemed greatly troubled, began with a speech learnt by heart, and extremely scholarly, of which at first the Prince could understand nothing at all. Landriani ended by declaring that it was important for the Church in Parma that *Monsignore* del Dongo should be appointed as his chief Vicar-General, and subsequently, as soon as he had completed his twenty-fourth year, his Coadjutor, *with eventual succession*.

'These terms alarmed me, I must admit,' said the Conte. 'It is going a little too fast, and I was afraid of an outburst of temper on the Prince's part. But he looked at me with a smile and said to me in French: "*Ce sont là de vos coups, monsieur*". (I recognize your hand in this, sir.)

' "I swear before God and your Highness," I cried with all possible fervour, "that I knew absolutely nothing about the words 'eventual succession'." Then I told him the truth, that is to say what we were discussing here in this room two hours ago. I added, with some animation, that I should regard myself as more than satisfied with his Highness's favours if, in the course of time, he would deign to grant me a minor Bishopric to begin with. The Prince must have believed me, for he thought it fit to be gracious. He said to me with the greatest possible simplicity: "This is an official matter between myself and the Archbishop; you are in no way concerned in it. The worthy man delivered me a kind of report which was very lengthy and rather tedious, at the end of which he came to an official proposal. I answered · him very coldly that the person in question was very young and, moreover, a very recent arrival at my court; that I should almost look as if I were honouring a bill of exchange drawn on me by the Emperor, in holding out the prospect of so great a dignity to the son of one of the high officials of the Lombardo-Venetian Kingdom. The Archbishop protested that no recommendation of that sort had been made. That was a pretty stupid thing to say to *me*. I was surprised to hear it come from a man of his intelligence; but he always loses his head whenever he speaks to me, and this evening he was more confused than ever, which gave me the idea that he was passionately anxious to settle this matter. I told him that I knew better than he that there had been no recommendation from any high quarter in del Dongo's favour, nobody at my court denied his capability, that they did not speak at all too badly of his morals, but that I feared he might be given to *enthusiasm*, and I had promised myself never to promote to important positions any lunatics of that particular species, with whom a Prince can never be sure of anything.

' "And then," continued his Highness, "I had to submit to hearing a fresh appeal to my feelings that was almost as lengthy as the first; the Archbishop sang me the praises of enthusiasm for the House of God. 'Clumsy fellow,' said I to myself, 'you are going astray, you are endangering the appointment which was almost granted. You should have cut your speech short and thanked me effusively.' Not a bit of it; he continued his homily with ridiculous intrepidity. I tried to think of a reply that would not be too unfavourable to young del Dongo: I hit on one, and a fairly apt one, as you shall judge for yourself: 'Monsignore,' I said to him, 'Pius VII was a great Pope and a great saint. Among all the sovereign princes, he alone dared to say *No* to the tyrant who saw all Europe at his feet! Well, he was liable to enthusiasm, which led him, when he was Bishop of Imola, to write his famous Pastoral of the *Citizen-Cardinal* Chiaramonti, in support of the Cisalpine Republic.'

' "My poor Archbishop was left dumbfounded, and to complete his stupefaction, I said to him, with a very serious air: 'Goodbye, *Monsignore*, I shall take twenty-four hours to consider your proposal.' The poor man added a few more entreaties, rather badly expressed and hardly opportune after the word 'Goodbye' had been uttered by me. Now, Conte Mosca della Rovere, I charge you to inform the Duchessa that I have no wish to delay for another twenty-four hours a decision which may be agreeable to her. Sit down there, and write the Archbishop the letter of approval which will bring the whole matter to an end. " I wrote the letter, he signed it, and said to me: "Take it at once to the Duchessa." Here is the letter, madam, and it is this that has given me an excuse for affording myself the pleasure of seeing you again this evening.'

The Duchessa read the letter with rapture. While the Conte was telling his long story Fabrizio had had time to collect himself. He showed no sign of astonishment at this incident, he took the whole thing like a true aristocrat, who has always believed himself naturally entitled to these extraordinary promotions, these strokes of fortune which would unhinge a mere commoner's mind. He expressed his gratitude, but in well-chosen words, and ended by saying to the Conte: 'A good courtier should flatter a man's ruling passion. Yesterday you expressed a fear that your workmen at Sanguigna might steal any fragments of ancient sculptures they happened to bring to light. I myself am very fond of excavations; if you will kindly allow me to do so, I will pay a visit to these workmen. Tomorrow evening, after suitably expressing my thanks at the Palace and to the Archbishop, I will set off for Sanguigna.'

'But can you guess,' the Duchessa asked the Conte, 'what may have given rise to this sudden passion on our good Archbishop's part for Fabrizio?'

'I have no need to guess. The Vicar-General whose nephew I made a captain said to me yesterday: "Father Landriani starts from this sound principle, that the titular archbishop is superior to the coadjutor, and is beside himself with joy at having a del Dongo under his orders and of having done him a favour. Everything that brings Fabrizio's birth before the public eye adds to his own personal happiness, since he has such a man for his aide-de-camp! In the second place, Monsignore Fabrizio has taken his fancy, he does not feel at all shy in front of him. Lastly he has been cherishing for ten years past a very healthy hatred of the Bishop of Piacenza, who openly boasts of his claims to succeed him in the See of Parma, and is, moreover, the son of a miller. It is with a view to this eventual succession that the Bishop of Piacenza has established very close relations with the Marchesa Raversi, and now their connexion is making the Archbishop tremble for the success of his favourite scheme, that of having a del Dongo on his staff and of giving him orders." '

Two days later, at an early hour in the morning, Fabrizio was directing the work of excavation at Sanguigna, opposite Colorno (this is the Versailles of the Princes of Parma). These excavations extended over the plain close to the high road that runs from Parma to the bridge of Casalmaggiore, the first town on Austrian soil. The workmen were cutting a long trench across the plain, eight foot deep and as narrow as possible. They were engaged in seeking, alongside the old Roman road, for the ruins of a second temple which, according to local report, had still been in existence in the middle ages. Despite the Prince's orders, a certain number of the peasants viewed with some alarm these long trenches running across their property. Whatever one might say to them, they imagined that a search was being made for some treasure, and Fabrizio's presence was particularly opportune in view of any little disturbance that might arise. He was not in the least bored, he followed the work with really passionate interest. From time to time they turned up some medal or other, and he did his best to allow the workmen no time to arrange among themselves to smuggle it away.

The day was fine, it was about six o'clock in the morning; he had borrowed an old, single-barrelled gun, he shot a few larks. One of them, wounded, was on the point of falling down on to the high road when Fabrizio, as he went after it, caught sight of a carriage some way off, coming from Parma and making towards the frontier of Casalmaggiore. He had just reloaded his gun when, as this very ramshackle conveyance came towards him at a snail's pace, he recognized little Marietta. She was sitting between that huge, ungainly fellow Giletti and the old woman whom she passed off as her mother.

Giletti imagined that Fabrizio had posted himself there in the middle of the road, and with a gun in his hand, in order to insult him and perhaps even to carry off little Marietta. Like a man of valour, he jumped down from the carriage. He had in his left hand a large and very rusty pistol, and held in his right a sword that was still unsheathed, and which he used when the requirements of the company obliged them to cast him for the part of some Marchese.

'Hi there! you ruffian!' he shouted. 'I'm very glad to find you here a league from the frontier. I'll settle your hash for you in no time; here you're no longer protected by your purple stockings.'

Fabrizio was smiling inanely at little Marietta and paying little attention to Giletti's jealous cries, when suddenly he saw the muzzle of the rusty pistol within three feet of his chest. He had only time to aim a blow at this pistol, using his rifle as a club. The pistol went off, but did not wound anyone.

'Stop, will you, you —,' Giletti shouted to the *vetturino*. At the same time he was shrewd enough to spring to the muzzle of his adversary's gun and to hold it so that it pointed away from his own body. Fabrizio and he both tugged at the gun, each with all his might. Giletti, who was a great deal the stronger of the two, placing one hand in front of the other, kept sliding them forward towards the lock and was on the point of snatching away the gun when Fabrizio, to prevent him from using it, fired it off. He had first taken care to see that the muzzle of the gun was more than three inches above Giletti's shoulder; the report went off close to the latter's ear. He was somewhat startled at first, but recovered himself in a fraction of a minute.

'Ah! so you want to blow out my brains, you scum! I'll show you how I'll deal with you!' Giletti flung away the scabbard of his Marchese's sword, and fell upon Fabrizio with admirable swiftness. The latter had no weapon, and gave himself up for lost.

He darted off towards the carriage, which was drawn up a few paces behind Giletti; he passed to the left of it, and, grasping the springs of the carriage in his right hand, made a quick turn which brought him quite close up to the door on the right hand side, which stood open. Giletti, who had rushed forward on his long legs and had not thought of checking himself by catching hold of the springs, went on for a few paces in the same direction before he could stop. Just as Fabrizio was passing by the open door, he heard Marietta say to him in a whisper: 'Take care of yourself; he will kill you. Here, take this!'

At the same moment, Fabrizio saw a sort of big hunting-knife fall out of the carriage door. He bent down to pick it up, but as he did so he was struck on the shoulder by a blow from Giletti's sword. As Fabrizio stood up again he found himself within six inches of Giletti, who aimed a terrific blow at his face with the hilt of his sword; this blow was delivered with such force that it left him completely dazed. At that moment he was on the verge of being killed. Luckily for him, Giletti was still too near to be able to deliver a thrust with the point of his sword. On coming to his senses Fabrizio took to flight and ran away as fast as his legs could carry him; as he ran, he flung away the sheath of the hunting knife, and then, turning smartly round, he found himself three paces away from Giletti, who was pursuing him. Giletti sprang forward, Fabrizio stuck at him with the point of his knife, Giletti had time to turn the knife slightly aside with his sword, but he received the point of the blade full in the left cheek. He passed close by Fabrizio, who felt his thigh pierced; it was Giletti's knife, which he had found time to open. Fabrizio sprang to the right; he turned round, and at last the two adversaries found themselves within proper fighting range.

Giletti was swearing like a lost soul. 'Ah! I'll slit your throat for you, you rascally priest,' he kept on repeating every moment. Fabrizio was quite out of breath and unable to speak; the blow on his face from the sword-hilt was causing him a great deal of pain and his nose was bleeding profusely. He warded off a number of strokes with his hunting knife and made several lunges without knowing quite what he was doing; he had a vague feeling that he was at some public contest. This idea had been suggested to him by the presence of his workmen, who, to the number of twenty-five or thirty, had formed a circle round the two combatants, but at a very respectful distance; for at every moment they saw them rush forward and spring at one another.

The fight seemed to be slackening a little; the strokes had ceased to follow each other with the same rapidity, when Fabrizio said to himself: 'To judge by the pain I feel in my face, the fellow must have disfigured me.' Filled with rage at this idea, he leapt upon his enemy with the point of his hunting-knife. The point entered Giletti's chest on the right side and came out near his left shoulder. At the same moment Giletti's sword passed right to the hilt through the upper part of Fabrizio's arm, but the blade slid along under the skin and made only a slight wound.

Giletti had fallen down. As Fabrizio advanced towards him, looking down at his left hand which was clasping a knife, that hand opened mechanically and let the weapon drop to the ground.

'The rascal is dead,' said Fabrizio to himself. He looked at Giletti's face; blood was pouring from his mouth. Fabrizio ran to the carriage.

'Have you a hand-glass?' he cried to Marietta. Marietta looked at him, white as a sheet, and made no answer. The old woman, with great composure, opened a green workbag and presented Fabrizio with a little glass with a handle that was no bigger than his hand. As he looked at himself Fabrizio ran his fingers over his face. 'My eyes are all right,' he said to himself. 'That's a good thing, at any rate.' He examined his teeth; not one of them was broken. 'Then how is it I am in such pain?' he asked himself, half aloud.

The old woman answered him: 'That's because the top of your cheek has been crushed between the hilt of Giletti's sword and that bone we all have there. Your cheek is frightfully swollen and quite black and blue. Put leeches on it at once and it will be all right.'

'Ah! leeches, at once!' said Fabrizio laughing, and he regained complete control of his nerves. He saw that the workmen had gathered round Giletti and were gazing at him without venturing to touch him.

'Do something to help this man, I beg you!' he called out to them. 'Take his coat off.' He was going to say more, but on raising his eyes he saw five or six men some three hundred paces away on the high road who were advancing on foot, at a moderate pace, towards the scene of the incident.

'They must be the police,' he thought, 'and as there has been a man killed, they will arrest me, and I shall have the honour of making a solemn entry into the city of Parma. What a story for the courtiers who are friends of that Raversi woman and who detest my aunt!'

Immediately, and as quick as lightning, he flung the gaping workmen all the money that he had in his pockets and leapt into the carriage.

'Stop the police from following me,' he called out to the men, 'and I'll make your fortunes. Tell them I am innocent, that this man *attacked me and wanted to kill me.*

'And you,' he said to the *vetturino*, 'make your horses gallop! You shall have four golden napoleons if you get across the Po before those people over there can overtake me.'

'Right you are,' said the man; 'but you've no need to fear. Those men over there are on foot, and my little horses have only to trot to leave them a proper distance behind.' So saying, he put the animals to a gallop.

Our hero was shocked to hear the word 'fear' used by the driver; but the fact is he had actually been in a great state of fear after the blow from the sword-hilt which he had received in the face.

'We may run into men on horseback coming towards us,' said the *vetturino*, a cautious man who had his mind on the four napoleons, 'and the people who are following us may call out to them to stop us.' This was as much as to say: 'Reload your weapons.'

'Ah! how brave you are, my darling Monsignore!' cried Marietta as she embraced Fabrizio. The old woman was looking out through the window of the carriage; after a short space of time she withdrew her head.

'No one is following you, sir,' she said to Fabrizio in a tone of complete equanimity, 'and there is no one on the road in front of us. You know how stiff and starchy the officials of the Austrian Police can be; if they see you arrive like this at a gallop along the embankment of the Po, they'll arrest you, you needn't doubt it.'

Fabrizio put his head out of the carriage window.

'Go at a trotting pace,' he said to the driver. 'What passport have you?' he asked the old woman.

'Three, instead of one,' she replied, 'and they cost us four francs apiece. Isn't that a dreadful thing for poor dramatic artists who are kept travelling the whole year round! Here is the passport of Signor Giletti, dramatic artist; that will be you. Here are our two passports, Marietta's and mine. But Giletti had all our money in his pocket; what is to become of us?'

'How much had he?' asked Fabrizio.

'Forty good scudi of five lire each,' said the old woman.

'You mean six scudi and some small change,' said Marietta laughing. 'I won't have my darling Monsignore cheated.'

'Isn't it only natural, sir, that I should try to rook you of thirty-four scudi? What's thirty-four scudi to you? As for us, we've lost our protector. Who is there now to find us lodgings, to beat down prices with the *vetturini* when we are on the road, and to put the fear of God into everyone? Giletti wasn't a handsome fellow, but he was very useful, and if this young woman here hadn't been a fool, and fallen in love with you from the first, Giletti would never have noticed anything, and you would have given us a nice lot of scudi. I can assure you we are very poor.'

Fabrizio was touched; he pulled out his purse and gave the old woman a few napoleons.

'You can see,' he said to her, 'that I have only fifteen left, so it's no good your trying to play any further tricks on me.'

Little Marietta flung her arms round his neck and the old woman kissed his hands. The carriage was moving forward all this time at a slow trot.

When they saw in the distance the yellow barriers striped with black which showed they were coming into Austrian territory, the old woman said to Fabrizio: 'You would do best to go through on foot with Giletti's passport in your pocket. As for us, we shall stop for a moment, on the excuse of tidying ourselves up a bit. And besides, the customs officers will want to inspect our things. You yourself, if you will take my advice, will go through Casalmaggiore as if you were a casual stroller; even go into the café and drink a glass of brandy; once you are past the village, take to your heels. The police are as alert as the devil on Austrian territory; they will soon get to hear that a man has been killed. You are travelling with a passport which isn't yours, that's more than enough to get you two years in prison. Make for the Po on your right as you leave the town, hire a boat and get away to Ravenna or Ferrara. Get out of the Austrian States as quick as you can. With a couple of louis you will be able to buy another passport from some customs officer; this one would be fatal to you. Don't forget that you've killed the man.'

As he walked towards the pontoon-bridge of Casalmaggiore Fabrizio carefully studied Giletti's passport a second time. Our hero was in a great state of fear; he remembered vividly all that Conte Mosca had told him of the risk he ran in entering Austrian territory; moreover he could see, two hundred paces in front of him, the terrible bridge which was about to give him access to that country, the capital of which, in his eyes, was the Spielberg. But what else could he do? The Duchy of Modena, which borders on the State of Parma to the south, returned its fugitives in virtue of a special convention. That frontier of the principality which extends into the mountains in the direction of Genoa was too far off; his misadventure would be known in Parma long before he could reach those mountains.

There remained therefore nothing but the Austrian States on the left bank of the Po. Before there was time to write to the Austrian authorities asking them to arrest him, thirty-six hours, or even two days, must elapse. Having duly considered all these things. Fabrizio set his own passport alight with his cigar; it was better for him, on Austrian soil, to be a vagabond than to be Fabrizio del Dongo, and it was possible that they might search him.

Quite apart from the very natural repugnance that he felt to entrusting his life to the passport of the unfortunate Giletti, this document presented certain material difficulties. Fabrizio's height was at the most five foot five, and not five foot ten as was stated on the passport. He was not quite twenty-four, and looked younger; Giletti was thirty-nine. We must confess that our hero paced for a good half-hour along the top of a dyke beside the Po, close to the pontoon-bridge, before making up his mind to step down on to it. 'What should I advise anyone else to do in my place?' he finally asked himself. 'Obviously, to cross. There is danger in remaining within the State of Parma; one of the police may be sent in pursuit of the man who has killed another man, even if it were in self-defence.' Fabrizio went through his pockets, tore up all his papers, and kept literally nothing but his handkerchief and his cigar-case; it was important for him to curtail the examination he would have to undergo. He thought of one terrible objection that might be raised, and to which he could find no satisfactory answer: he was going to say that his name was Giletti, and all his linen was marked F. D.

As can be seen, Fabrizio was one of those unfortunate people who are tormented by their own imagination; this is a fairly common fault with men of intelligence in Italy. A French soldier of equal or even inferior courage would have gone straight on and crossed the bridge at once, without thinking beforehand of any possible difficulties; but he would also have brought all his coolness to bear on it, and Fabrizio was far from feeling cool or composed when, at the end of the bridge, a little man dressed in grey said to him: 'Go into the police office and show your passport.'

This office had dirty walls studded with nails from which hung the pipes and the grimy caps of the officials. The big deal writing-table behind which they were entrenched was covered all over with spots of ink and wine. Two or three fat registers in green leather bindings bore stains of every sort of colour and the edges of their pages were black with finger-marks. On top of the registers, which were piled one upon another, there were three magnificent wreaths of laurel which had done duty a couple of days before for one of the Emperor's festivals.

Fabrizio was impressed by all these details; they gave him a tightening of the heart. This was the price he had to pay for the magnificent luxury and the freshness conspicuous in his charming rooms in the Palazzo Sanseverina. He was obliged to enter this dirty office and to appear in it as an inferior; he was about to undergo an examination.

The official who stretched out a sallow hand to take his passport was a short dark man; he wore a brass pin in his necktie. 'This is a low, ill-tempered fellow,' thought Fabrizio. The man seemed excessively surprised as he studied the passport, and his reading of it lasted a good five minutes.

'You have met with an accident,' he said to the stranger, casting a glance at his cheek.

'The *vetturino* flung us out on the ground against the embankment of the Po.' Then silence fell once more, while the official cast fierce glances at the traveller.

'I have it,' said Fabrizio to himself, 'he's going to tell me he's sorry to have bad news to give me, and that I am under arrest.' All sorts of wild ideas came into our hero's brain, which at that moment was not extremely logical. For instance, he thought of escaping by a door in the office which had been left open. 'I'll take off my coat, I'll jump into the Po, and no doubt I shall be able to swim across it. Anything's better than the Spielberg.'

The police official was staring fixedly at him all the while he was calculating the chances of success in this mad enterprise; they provided a good contrast in expression. The presence of danger gives a touch of genius to the man who reasons; it raises him, so to speak, above his own level; in the imaginative man it inspires romantic ideas, bold, it is true, but frequently absurd.

You should have seen the indignant air of our hero under the searching eye of this police official, adorned with his brass gew-gaws. 'If I were to kill him,' thought Fabrizio, 'I should be convicted of murder and sentenced to twenty years in the hulks, or to death. That is a great deal less terrible than the Spielberg, with a chain of a hundred and twenty pounds' weight on each foot and eight ounces of bread for my sole nourishment. And that would last for twenty years, so I should not get out again until I was forty-four.' In Fabrizio's reasoning he overlooked the fact that, since he had burnt his own passport, there was nothing to indicate to the police that he was the rebel, Fabrizio del Dongo.

Our hero, as we have seen, was sufficiently alarmed; he would have been a great deal more so could he have read the thoughts that were troubling the police clerk's mind. This man was a friend of Giletti's: one may judge of his surprise when he saw his passport in another man's hands. His first impulse was to have that other man arrested; then he reflected that Giletti might easily have sold his passport to this handsome young man who presumably had just committed some misdemeanour or other in Parma. 'If I arrest him,' he said to himself, 'Giletti will get into trouble; they will easily discover that he has sold his passport. On the other hand, what will my bosses say if it is proved that I, Giletti's friend, put a visa on his passport when it was in someone else's hands?' The police clerk got up with a yawn and said to Fabrizio: 'Just a minute, sir.' Then, following the usual custom of the police, he added: 'A difficulty has arisen.' Fabrizio said to himself, 'What will arise is my escape.'

And in fact, the clerk went out of the office, leaving the door open, and the passport was left lying on the deal table. 'I'm in obvious danger,' thought Fabrizio. 'I will pick up my passport and walk slowly back across the bridge. I will tell the constable, if he questions me, that I forgot to have my passport stamped by the superintendent of police in the last village in the State of Parma.' Fabrizio had already taken the passport in his hand when, to his inexpressible astonishment, he heard the police clerk with the brass jewellery say 'Upon my word, I'm all out; the heat is stifling me; I'm going over to the café to get a small cup of coffee. Go into the office when you've finished your pipe, there's a passport to be stamped. The foreigner's in there.'

Fabrizio, who was stealing out on tiptoe, found himself face to face with a good-looking young man who was saying to himself in a sort of sing-song: 'All right, let's stamp this passport, and I'll put my flourish on it.'

'Where do you wish to go, sir?'

'To Mantua, Venice, and Ferrara.'

'Ferrara it is,' replied the clerk, whistling. He took up a die, stamped the visa in blue ink on the passport, and rapidly wrote the words: 'Mantua, Venice, and Ferrara,' in the space left blank by the stamp. Then he waved his hand several times in the air, signed his name, and dipped his pen in the ink to make his flourish, which he executed slowly and with infinite pains. Fabrizio followed every movement of his pen. The clerk gazed at his flourish with satisfaction, added five or six dots to it, and finally handed the passport back to Fabrizio, saying in a casual tone: 'A pleasant journey to you, sir!'

Fabrizio was making off at a pace whose speed he was endeavouring to conceal when he felt someone clutch his left arm. His hand went instinctively to the hilt of his dagger, and if he had not observed that he was surrounded by houses he might perhaps have been guilty of some rash act. The man who was touching his left arm, seeing that he appeared quite startled, said to him by way of apology: 'But I called to you three times, sir, and you didn't answer. Have you anything, sir, to declare to the customs?'

'I have nothing on me but my handkerchief; I am going to shoot on the estate of one of my relations, quite close by!'

He would have been greatly embarrassed had he been asked to give the name of this relation. What with the great heat and his intense emotion Fabrizio was almost as wet as if he had fallen into the Po. 'I am not wanting in courage when dealing with strolling players, but clerks with brass gew-gaws send me out of my mind. I'll make a humorous sonnet upon this theme for the Duchessa.'

The moment he entered Casalmaggiore Fabrizio turned to the right, along a mean street which leads down to the Po. 'I am in great need,' he said to himself, 'of the succour of Bacchus and Ceres,' and he entered a shop outside which there hung a grey dishcloth attached to a stick; on the cloth was inscribed the word *Trattoria*. A tattered bed sheet supported on two very slender wooden hoops and hanging down to within three feet of the ground protected the door of the *Trattoria* from the direct rays of the sun. Inside, a half-undressed and very pretty woman received our hero with due respect, which gave him the keenest pleasure. He hastened to inform her that he was dying of hunger. While the woman was preparing the dinner, a man about thirty came in. He had given no greeting on entering, but suddenly he rose from the bench on which he had flung himself down with the air of one who was at home there, and said to Fabrizio: '*Eccellenza, la riverisco.*' (My humble respect to your Excellency.)

Fabrizio was feeling very gay at the moment, and instead of forming sinister plans he answered laughing: 'And how the devil do you know my Excellency?'

'What, doesn't your Excellency remember Lodovico, one of her Grace the Duchessa Sanseverina's coachmen? At Sacca, where we used to go every year, I always went down with fever; so I asked her Grace to give me a pension and I retired from service. Now I am rich; instead of the pension of twelve scudi a year which was the most I had a right to expect, her Grace told me that, to give me leisure for writing some little things in verses, for I am a poet in my own homely dialect, she allowed me twenty-four scudi; and his Lordship the Conte told me that if I was ever in difficulties I had only to come and tell him. I have had the honour of driving Monsignore for a stage, when he went to make his retreat, like a good Christian, with the Carthusians at Velleia.'

Fabrizio gazed at the man and seemed to have a faint recollection of him. He had been one of the smartest coachmen in the Sans-severina establishment; now that he was rich, as he called it, his entire clothing consisted of a coarse, tattered shirt and a pair of canvas breeches, dyed black some time ago, which barely came down to his knees. In addition to this, he had not shaved for a fortnight. As he ate his omelette Fabrizio carried on a conversation with him, ab-solutely as between equals; he thought he could detect that Lodovico was their hostess's lover. He finished his meal quickly and then said under his breath to Lodovico: 'I want a word with you.'

'Your Excellency can talk freely in front of her, she's a really good sort of woman,' said Lodovico in a tone of affection.

'Well, then, my friends,' Fabrizio went on without hesitation, 'I am in trouble and need your help. First of all, my case has nothing to do with politics. I have simply killed a man who wanted to murder me because I spoke to his mistress.'

'Poor young man!' said the landlady.

'Your Excellency can count on me!' cried the coachman, his eyes aflame with the most burning devotion. 'Where does your Ex-cellency wish to go?'

'To Ferrara. I have a passport, but I should prefer not to speak to the police, who may have received information of what has happened.'

'When did you despatch this fellow?'

'This morning at six o'clock.'

'Your Excellency hasn't any blood on your clothes, have you?' asked the hostess.

'I was thinking of that,' put in the coachman, 'and besides, the cloth of that coat is too fine. You don't see many like that in our countryside, it would attract people's attention. I will go and buy some clothes from the Jew. Your Excellency is about my size, only slimmer.'

'For goodness' sake, don't go on calling me your Excellency; it may attract attention.'

'Certainly, your Excellency,' answered the coachman as he left the tavern.

'Here, here, I say!' cried Fabrizio. 'And what about the money! Come back, do!'

'What's that talk about money!' said the landlady. 'He has sixty-seven scudi which are entirely at your service. I myself,' she added lowering her voice, 'have some forty scudi, which I offer you most gladly. One doesn't always have money on one when these accidents happen.'

On account of the heat, Fabrizio had taken off his coat on entering the *Trattoria*.

'You have a waistcoat there which might cause us some bother if anyone came in: that fine *English cloth* would attract attention.' She gave our fugitive a cloth waistcoat, dyed black, which belonged to her husband. A tall young man came into the tavern by an inner door; he was dressed with a certain touch of style.

'This is my husband,' said the landlady. 'Pietro Antonio,' she said to her husband, 'this gentleman is a friend of Lodovico's. He met with an accident this morning on the other side of the river; he wants to get away to Ferrara.'

'All right, we'll get him across,' said the husband very politely. 'We have Carlo-Giuseppe's boat.'

Owing to another weakness of our hero, which we will confess as naturally as we have related his fear in the police office at the end of the bridge, there were tears in his eyes. He was profoundly moved by the perfect devotion which he found among these country folk; he also thought of his aunt's characteristic kindness of heart; he would have liked to be able to make these people's fortunes. Lodovico came back again, laden with a bundle.

'We'll say goodbye to our friends here,' the husband said to him with an air of frank good-fellowship.

'There's no question of that,' replied Lodovico in a tone of great alarm. 'People are beginning to talk about you; they noticed that you hesitated before turning into our *vicolo* and leaving the high street, like a man who was trying to hide.'

'Go up quickly to the bedroom,' said the husband.

This room, a very large and very fine one, had grey canvas instead of glass in its two windows; it contained four beds, each six feet wide and five feet high.

'Quick! Quick now!' said Lodovico. 'There's a conceited ass of a constable just arrived here who tried to make love to the pretty woman downstairs; whereupon I told him I could foresee that when he goes on his rounds outside the village he may very probably find himself stopping a bullet. If the miserable cur hears anyone mention your Excellency, he'll want to do us a bad turn; he'll try to arrest you here to give Theodolinda's *Trattoria* a bad name.'

'What's this!' Lodovico went on, seeing Fabrizio's shirt all stained with blood and his wounds tied up with handkerchiefs, 'so the *porco* defended himself after all? Here's a hundred times more than you need to get yourself arrested. I didn't buy you a shirt.' He opened the husband's wardrobe without ceremony and gave one of his shirts to Fabrizio, who was soon attired like a well-to-do country-man. Lodovico took down a net that was hanging on the wall, placed Fabrizio's clothes in the basket where the fish are put, ran downstairs and went quickly out of the house by a door at the back; Fabrizio followed him.

'Theodolinda,' Lodovico called out as he passed close by the tavern, 'hide what's upstairs, we are going to wait among the willows. And you, Pietro Antonio, make haste and send us a boat. You will be well paid for it.'

Lodovico led Fabrizio across more than a score of ditches. There were very long and very supple planks across the widest of these which Lodovico pulled away after passing over them. When they arrived at the last runnel he took away the plank carefully. 'Now we have time to breathe,' he said. 'That cur of a constable will have more than two leagues to go to reach your Excellency. Why, you're quite pale,' he said to Fabrizio. 'I haven't forgotten the little bottle of brandy.'

'It comes at the right moment; the wound in my thigh is beginning to hurt me; and besides, I was in a fine fright in the police office at the end of the bridge.'

'I can well believe it,' said Lodovico. 'With a shirt drenched with blood like yours, I can't even imagine how you ever dared to enter such a place. As for wounds, I understand all about them. I'm going to put you in a nice cool place where you can sleep for an hour. The boat will come to look for us there, if there is any means of getting one. If not, when you feel a little rested we'll go on two short leagues, and I'll take you to a mill where I shall hire a boat myself. Your Excellency knows far more than I do; her Grace will be in despair when she hears of your misadventure. They will tell her that you are mortally wounded, maybe even that you killed the other man in an underhand way. The Marchesa Raversi won't fail to circulate all the evil reports that may grieve her Grace. Your Excellency might write.'

'And how should I get the letter delivered?'

'The lads at the mill where we are going earn twelve soldi a day; in a day and a half they can be in Parma, so four lire, say, for the journey; and two lire for the wear and tear of shoe-leather. If the errand were being done for a poor man like myself, that would be six lire; since it is in the service of a lord I shall give them twelve.'

When they had reached the resting-place, in a copse of alders and willows, very leafy and very cool, Lodovico went to a house more than an hour's journey away in search of ink and paper. 'By Jove, how comfortable I am here!' exclaimed Fabrizio. 'Fortune, farewell! I shall never be an Archbishop!'

On his return Lodovico found him fast asleep and did not like to wake him. The boat did not arrive until about sunset. As soon as Lodovico saw it appear in the distance he called Fabrizio, who wrote a couple of letters.

'Your Excellency knows far more than I do,' said Lodovico, looking worried, 'and I am very much afraid, whatever you may say, of thoroughly displeasing you if I make a certain additional remark.'

'I am not such a simpleton as you think,' replied Fabrizio, 'and, whatever you may say to me, you will always be in my eyes a faithful servant of my aunt's, and a man who has done everything in the world to get me out of a very awkward situation.'

Many more protestations still were required before Lodovico could be prevailed upon to speak, and when at last he had made up his mind, he began with a preamble that lasted for fully five minutes. Fabrizio grew impatient, then said to himself, 'After all, whose fault is it? It is due to our vanity, which this man has very clearly observed from his seat on the box.' Lodovico's devotion at last induced him to run the risk of speaking plainly.

'What would the Marchesa Raversi not give to the messenger you are going to send to Parma to get hold of these two letters? They are in your handwriting, and consequently furnish legal evidence against you. Your Excellency will take me for an inquisitive and indiscreet fellow; in the second place, you will perhaps feel ashamed of setting before her Grace the Duchessa's eyes the wretched scrawl of a poor coachman like myself. But after all, the thought of your safety opens my lips, even though you may think me impertinent. Couldn't your Excellency dictate those two letters to me? Then I am the only person compromised, and that very little; I can say, if need be, that you appeared to me in the middle of a field with an inkhorn in one hand and a pistol in the other, and that you ordered me to write.'

'Give me your hand, my dear Lodovico,' cried Fabrizio, 'and to prove to you that I have no desire to keep anything secret from a friend like yourself, copy these two letters just as they are.' Lodovico fully appreciated this mark of confidence and was deeply moved by it, but after writing a few lines, as he saw the boat coming rapidly towards them downstream, he said to Fabrizio: 'The letters will be finished sooner if your Excellency will take the trouble to dictate them to me.'

When the letters were written, Fabrizio added an A and a B to the final line, and, on a little scrap of paper which he afterwards crumpled up, he put in French: 'Croyez A et B.'. The messenger was to hide this crumpled bit of paper in his clothing.

The boat having come within hailing distance, Lodovico called to the boatmen by names which were not their own. They made no reply, and put into the bank a thousand yards farther down, looking round them on every side to make sure they had not been seen by some customs officer.

'I am at your orders,' said Lodovico to Fabrizio. 'Would you like me to take these letters to Parma myself? Or do you wish me to accompany you to Ferrara?'

'To come with me to Ferrara is a service which I hardly dared to ask of you. I shall have to land and try to enter the town without showing my passport. I may tell you that I feel the greatest repugnance to travelling under the name of Giletti, and I can think of no one but yourself who would be able to buy me another passport.'

'Why didn't you speak of it at Casalmaggiore! I know a spy there who would have sold me an excellent passport, and not dear at that, for forty or fifty lire.'

One of the two boatmen, who had been born on the right bank of the Po, and who consequently had no need of a foreign passport to go to Parma, undertook to deliver the letters. Lodovico, who knew how to handle an oar, guaranteed that he could get the boat along with the help of the other man.

'On the lower reaches of the Po,' he said, 'we shall meet several armed police-boats, and I shall manage to keep out of their way.' Ten times and more they were obliged to hide themselves among little islets flush with the water, covered with willows. Three times they set foot on shore in order to let the boat drift past the police vessels empty. Lodovico took advantage of these long intervals of leisure to recite to Fabrizio several of his little poems. Their sentiments were correct enough but were so to speak blunted by the expression, and were not worth the trouble of putting them on paper. The curious thing was that this ex-coachman had passions and points of view that were vivid and picturesque; but he became cold and commonplace as soon as he began to write. 'This is the opposite of what we see in good society,' thought Fabrizio. 'People nowadays know how to express everything gracefully, but their hearts have nothing to say.' He realized that the greatest pleasure he could give to this faithful servant would be to correct the mistakes in spelling in his verses.

'People laugh at me when I lend them my note-book,' said Lodovico; 'but if your Excellency would be so kind as to dictate to me the spelling of the words, letter by letter, the envious fellows would have nothing left to say. Spelling doesn't make a genius.'

It was not until the third night of his journey that Fabrizio was able to land in perfect safety in a wood of alder trees, a league below Pontelagoscuro. All the next day he remained hidden in a field of hemp, while Lodovico went on ahead to Ferrara. There he took some humble lodgings in the house of a poor Jew, who at once realized that there was money to be earned if one knew how to hold one's tongue. That evening, as the light was beginning to fail, Fabrizio entered Ferrara riding upon a pony. He was in great need of this assistance, for the heat on the river had affected him; the knife-wound in his thigh and the sword-thrust that Giletti had given him in the shoulder at the beginning of their fight had both become inflamed and had brought on a fever.

CHAPTER 12 : *Flight to Bologna*

THE Jew landlord of their lodgings had got hold of a discreet surgeon, who, realizing in his turn that there was money in the case, informed Lodovico that his *conscience* obliged him to make his own report to the police on the injuries of the young man whom he, Lodovico, called his brother.

'The law is clear,' he added. 'It is evident that your brother has not hurt himself, as he declares, by falling off a ladder while he was holding an open knife in his hand.'

Lodovico coldly replied to this worthy surgeon that, if he should decide to yield to the promptings of his conscience, he himself would have the honour, before leaving Ferrara, of falling upon him in precisely the same way, with an open knife in his hand. When he reported this incident to Fabrizio, the latter took him severely to task, but there was not a moment to be lost in getting away. Lodovico told the Jew that he wished to try the effect of a little airing on his brother. He went to fetch a carriage, and our friends left the house, never to return.

The reader is no doubt finding these accounts of all the measures that the absence of a passport renders necessary very tedious. This sort of preoccupation does not exist any longer in France; but in Italy, and especially in the neighbourhood of the Po, everyone's conversation turns on passports. Once they had left Ferrara without hindrance, as though they were merely taking a drive, Lodovico sent the carriage back, re-entered the town by another gate, and returned to pick up Fabrizio with a *sediola* which he had hired to take them a dozen leagues. When they came near to Bologna, our friends had themselves driven across country to the road which leads into that city from Florence. They spent the night in the most wretched inn they could find, and the next day, as Fabrizio now felt strong enough to walk a little, they entered Bologna as if they were taking a stroll. They had burnt Giletti's passport. The comedian's death must by now be common knowledge, and there was less danger in being arrested as people without passports than as bearers of the passport of a man who had been killed.

Lodovico knew two of three of the servants in great houses in Bologna; it was agreed that he should go and get the latest news from them. He told them that, while he was on his way from Florence and travelling with his young brother, the latter, feeling in need of sleep, had let him come on by himself an hour before sunrise. They were to have joined each other in the village where he, Lodovico, would stop to rest during the heat of the day. But, failing to see his brother arrive, he had decided to retrace his steps. He had found him injured by a blow from a stone and several knife-wounds, and robbed, into the bargain, by some men who had picked a quarrel with him. This brother was a handsome lad, who knew how to groom and handle horses, read and write, and was anxious to find a place with some good family. Lodovico reserved for use, if and when the need for it should arise, the fact that when Fabrizio was on the ground, the thieves had made off, taking with them the little bag which held their linen and their passports.

On arriving in Bologna, Fabrizio, feeling extremely tired and not daring to present himself at an inn without a passport, had gone into the huge church of San Petronio. He found it delightfully cool in there; soon he felt quite revived. 'Ungrateful wretch that I am,' he said to himself suddenly, 'I go into a church, simply to sit down, as if I were in a café.' He threw himself on his knees and thanked God fervently for the evident protection with which he had been surrounded ever since he had had the misfortune to kill Giletti. The danger which still made him shudder was that of being recognized in the police office at Casalmaggiore. 'How,' he asked himself, 'did that clerk, whose eyes were so full of suspicion, and who read my passport at least three times, fail to notice that I am not five foot ten inches tall, that I am not thirty-eight years old, and that I am not strongly pitted by smallpox? What thanks I owe to Thee, O my God! And yet I have delayed until this moment to lay my utterly unworthy self at Thy feet! My pride would fain have believed that it was to vain human prudence that I owed the good fortune of escaping the Spielberg, which was already opening its jaws to swallow me up!'

Fabrizio spent more than an hour in this state of extreme emotion in presence of the immense loving-kindness of God. Lodovico came up to him without his hearing him approach, and stood in front of him. Fabrizio, who had buried his face in his hands, raised his head, and his faithful servant could see the tears streaming down his cheeks.

'Come back in an hour,' Fabrizio said to him rather sharply.

Lodovico excused this tone on the score of piety. Fabrizio repeated several times the Seven Penitential Psalms, which he knew by heart; he lingered for some long time over the verses which had a bearing on his situation at the moment.

Fabrizio asked pardon of God for many things, but what is indeed remarkable is that it never entered his head to number among his sins the plan of becoming Archbishop simply and solely because Conte Mosca was Prime Minister and considered that office and all the social distinction it conferred to be suitable for the Duchessa's nephew. He had desired it without passion, it is true, but still he had thought of it exactly as one might think of being appointed either a minister or a general. It had never occurred to him to think that his conscience might be concerned in this project of the Duchessa's. This is a remarkable feature of the religion which he owed to the teaching of the Jesuits of Milan. That religion *deprives men of the courage to reflect on unusual matters*, and particularly forbids *self-examination*, as the most heinous of sins ... it is a step towards Protestantism. To know of what sins one is guilty, one must question one's priest, or read the list of sins as it is to be found printed in the books entitled, *Preparation for the Sacrament of Penitence*. Fabrizio knew by heart this list of sins, rendered into the Latin tongue, which he had learnt at the Ecclesiastical Academy of Naples.

Thus, on reciting this list and coming to the article, *Murder*, he had roundly accused himself before God of having killed a man, but in defending his own life. He had passed rapidly, and without paying them the slightest attention, over the various clauses relating to the sin of *Simony* (the procuring of ecclesiastical offices with money). If anyone had suggested that he should pay a hundred louis to become Chief Vicar-General to the Archbishop of Parma, he would have rejected such an idea with horror. But although he was not wanting in intelligence and above all in the power to reason, it did not once come into his head that the employment of Conte Mosca's influence on his behalf was a form of *Simony*. Herein lies the crowning achievement of a Jesuitical education; the formation of a habit of paying no attention to those things which are clearer than daylight. A Frenchman, brought up among the characteristic self-interest and irony of Paris might, without being deliberately unfair, have accused Fabrizio of hypocrisy at the very moment when our hero was opening his heart to God with the utmost sincerity and the very deepest emotion.

Fabrizio did not leave the church until he had prepared the confession which he proposed to make the very next day. He found Lodovico sitting on the steps of the huge stone peristyle which rises above the great square in front of the façade of San Petronio. Just as after a great storm the air is purer, so Fabrizio's soul was serene and happy, and, so to speak, refreshed.

'I feel extremely well, I hardly feel my wounds just now,' he said as he came up to Lodovico. 'But first of all I must beg your forgiveness; I answered you crossly when you came to speak to me in the church; I was examining my conscience. Well now, how is our business progressing?'

'It's going very well indeed. I have taken lodgings – to tell the truth not very worthy of your Excellency – with the wife of one of my friends, who is very pretty, and, what's more, on the best of terms with one of the chief police agents. Tomorrow I shall go and declare how our passports came to be stolen. This declaration will be taken in good part, but I shall pay the postage of the letter which the police will write to Casalmaggiore to find out whether there exists in that commune a certain Lodovico San Micheli, who has a brother named Fabrizio in service with Her Grace the Duchessa Sanseverina in Parma. All is settled, *siamo a cavallo*.' (A proverbial expression in Italy meaning: 'We are saved'.)

Fabrizio had suddenly assumed a very serious air. He begged Lodovico to wait for him a moment, went back into the church almost at a run, and was hardly inside before he flung himself down on his knees, and humbly kissed the stone slabs of the pavement. 'It is a miracle, Lord,' he cried, with tears in his eyes. 'When Thou didst see my soul disposed to return to the path of duty, Thou didst save me. Almighty God! It is possible that one day I may be killed in some quarrel; in the hour of my death remember the state in which my soul is at this moment.' It was in an ecstasy of keenest joy that Fabrizio recited afresh the Seven Penitential Psalms. Before leaving the church he went up to an old woman who was seated in front of a large·statue of the Madonna and beside an iron triangle set upright on a stand of the same metal. The sides of this triangle bristled with a great number of spikes intended to support the little candles which piety of the faithful keeps burning before the famous

Madonna of Cimabue. Seven candles only were alight when Fabrizio approached; he registered this fact in his memory with the intention of reflecting on it more at his leisure.

'What do the candles cost?' he asked the woman.

'Two baiocchi each.'

As a matter of fact they were hardly thicker than a quill pen and were not a foot in length.

'How many more candles can still go on your triangle?'

'Sixty-three, since there are seven alight.'

'Ah!' said Fabrizio to himself, 'sixty-three and seven make seventy; that is another thing to note.' He paid for the candles, placed the first seven in position himself, and lit them; then he knelt down to make his oblation, and said to the old woman as he rose: 'It is for *grace received.*'

'I am dying of hunger,' said Fabrizio to Lodovico as he rejoined him.

'Don't let's go to a tavern, let's go to our lodgings,' said his servant, 'the mistress of the house will go out and buy you what you want for a meal. She will rob you of a score of soldi, and will feel all the more kindly disposed towards her new lodger.'

'All this means simply that I shall have to go on dying of hunger for a good hour longer,' said Fabrizio, laughing as light-heartedly as a child, and he went into a tavern close to San Petronio. To his extreme surprise, he saw, at a table near the one at which he had taken his seat, Peppe, his aunt's first footman, the same who had once come to meet him at Geneva. Fabrizio made a sign to him to say nothing; then after making a hasty meal, he got up, with a smile of happiness flickering on his lips. Peppe followed him, and, for the third time, our hero entered San Petronio. Out of discretion, Lodovico remained outside, strolling up and down the square.

'Oh, good heavens, Monsignore! How are your wounds? Her Grace the Duchessa is terribly upset. For a whole day she thought you were left for dead on some island in the Po. I will go and send a messenger off to her this very instant. I have been looking for you for the past six days. I spent three at Ferrara, going round all the inns.'

'Have you a passport for me?'

'I have three different ones. One with all your Excellency's names and titles; the second with your name only, and the third under an assumed name, Giuseppe Bossi. Each passport serves a double purpose, according to whether your Excellency chooses to have come from Florence or from Modena. You have only to go for a stroll outside the town. His Lordship the Conte would be glad if you would lodge at the Albergo del Pellegrino, the landlord of which is a friend of his.'

Fabrizio, as if he were taking a casual look round, went up the right aisle of the church to the place where his candles were burning. He fixed his eyes on the Madonna of Cimabue, then said to Peppe as he knelt down: 'I must just give thanks for a moment.' Peppe followed his example. When they left the church, Peppe noticed that Fabrizio gave a twenty-franc piece to the first beggar who asked him for alms. This beggar uttered cries of gratitude which attracted round the charitable donor the swarms of poor people of every sort who generally adorn the Piazza San Petronio. All of them were anxious to have a share in the napoleon. The women, despairing of making their way through the crowd that surrounded him, pounced on Fabrizio, shouting to him to inform them whether it was not a fact that he had given his napoleon to be divided among all God's poor. Peppe, brandishing his gold-headed cane, ordered them to leave his Excellency alone.

'Oh, your Excellency!' all these women started to cry, in still more strident tones, 'give another gold napoleon for us poor women!' Fabrizio increased his pace; the women followed him screaming and a number of male beggars, running in from every street, created, as it were, a sort of minor riot. The whole of this horribly filthy and lively crowd kept crying out: 'Your Excellency!' Fabrizio had a great deal of difficulty in ridding himself of this unruly mob. The uproar brought his imagination down to earth. 'I've only got what I deserve,' he thought, 'for rubbing shoulders with the rabble.'

Two women followed him as far as the Porta Saragozza by which he left the town; Peppe stopped them by threatening them seriously with his cane and flinging them some small coins. Fabrizio climbed the charming hill of San Michele in Bosco, walked round part of the town outside the walls, and took a path, which five hundred paces farther on brought him out on to the main road from Florence; then he re-entered Bologna and solemnly presented to the police clerk a passport in which his description was minutely recorded. This passport gave him the name of Giuseppe Bossi, student in theology. Fabrizio noticed a little spot of red ink, dropped, as if by accident, at the foot of the page, in the right-hand corner. Two hours later he had a spy on his heels, on account of the title of 'Excellency' which his companion had given him in front of the beggars of San Petronio, although his passport bore none of the titles which give a man the right to have himself addressed as 'Excellency' by his servants.

Fabrizio saw the spy, and thought it a very good joke. He was no longer concerned either with passports or the police, and was as amused as a child by everything round about him. Peppe, who had orders to stay beside him, seeing that he was very well pleased with Lodovico, thought it better to go back in person to carry such good news to the Duchessa. Fabrizio wrote a couple of very long letters to the persons who were dear to him; then it occurred to him to write a third to the venerable Archbishop Landriani. This letter, which contained a very exact account of his fight with Giletti, produced a marvellous effect. The good Archbishop, quite overcome with emotion, did not fail to go and read the letter to the Prince, who was very willing to listen to it, being rather curious to see how this young Monsignore went to work to excuse so shocking a murder. Thanks to the many friends of the Marchesa Raversi, the Prince, as well as the whole city of Parma, believed that Fabrizio had obtained the help of twenty or thirty peasants to slaughter a third-rate actor who had had the insolence to quarrel with him over little Marietta. In despotic courts, the first skilful intriguer manages to arrange the *truth*, just as fashion manages to do in Paris.

'But, devil take it!' exclaimed the Prince to the Archbishop, 'one gets things of that sort done by somebody else; to do them oneself is not good form. And besides, one doesn't kill a mere player like Giletti, one buys him.'

Fabrizio had not the slightest suspicion of what was going on in Parma. As a matter of fact, the question there was whether the death of this comedian, who in his lifetime had earned a monthly salary of thirty-two lire, would not bring about the fall of the *Ultra* Ministry, and of its leader, Conte Mosca.

On learning of the death of Giletti, the Prince, annoyed by the independent airs which the Duchessa was giving herself, had ordered his Lord Chief Justice, Rassi, to treat the whole case as though the person concerned were a Liberal. Fabrizio, for his part, believed that a man of his rank was above the law; he did not take into account the fact that, in countries where bearers of great names are never punished, intrigue can do anything, even against such persons. He often spoke to Lodovico of his perfect innocence, which would very soon be proclaimed; his great argument was that he was not guilty. Whereupon Lodovico said to him one day: 'I cannot imagine why your Excellency, who has so much intelligence and so much education, takes the trouble to say that sort of thing to me, who am his devoted servant. Your Excellency takes too many precautions. That is the kind of thing one says in public, or before a court of justice.' 'This man believes me to be a murderer, and loves me none the less for it,' thought Fabrizio quite downcast.

Three days after Peppe's departure, he was greatly astonished to receive an enormous letter, tied up with silken braid as in the days of Louis XIV, and addressed to '*His Most Reverend Excellency Monsignore Fabrizio del Dongo, First Vicar-General of the See of Parma, Canon, etc.*'

'But am I still all that?' he said to himself laughing. Archbishop Landriani's letter was a masterpiece of logic and lucidity. It covered no less than nineteen large pages, and gave an extremely good account of all that had happened in Parma in connexion with Giletti's death.

A French army commanded by Marshal Ney, and marching upon the town, would not have produced a greater effect [wrote the good Archbishop]. *With the exception of the Duchessa and myself, my dearly beloved son, everyone believes that you killed the actor Giletti wantonly. Had such a misfortune befallen you, it is one of those things that one hushes up with two thousand lire or so, and six months' absence abroad. The Marchesa Raversi, however, is bent on overthrowing Conte Mosca with the help of this incident. It is by no means the terrible sin of murder for which the public blames you, it is simply and solely for your* clumsiness, *or rather your insolence it not condescending to have recourse to a* bulo [a sort of inferior bully]. *I am conveying to you in plain terms the talk I hear all around me, for since this ever deplorable misadventure, I have gone every day to three of the most important houses in the city, so as to have an opportunity of vindicating you. And never have I felt that I was making a more righteous use of what little eloquence Heaven has deigned to bestow on me.*

The scales fell from Fabrizio's eyes. The Duchessa's many letters, brimming over with transports of affection, never condescended to tell him anything. The Duchessa swore to him that she would leave Parma for ever, if he did not soon return there in triumph.

The Conte [she wrote to him in the letter that accompanied the Archbishop's] *will do everything that is humanly possible on your behalf. As for myself, you have changed my nature with this fine escapade of yours; I am now as great a skinflint as the banker Tombone. I have dismissed all my workmen, I have done more – I have dictated the inventory of my fortune to the Conte, and I find it is far less considerable than I thought. After the death of the excellent Conte Pietranera – whose death, by the way, you would have done far better to avenge, instead of exposing your life to a creature of Giletti's sort – I was left with an income of twelve hundred lire and five thousand lire of debts. I remember, among other things, that I had two and a half dozen pairs of white satin slippers, and only a single pair of shoes to wear in the street. I have almost made up in my mind to take the three hundred thousand lire which the Duca left me, the whole of which I intended to use in erecting a magnificent tomb for him. For the rest, it is the Marchesa Raversi who is your principal enemy, that is to say mine. If you feel bored all by yourself in Bologna, you have only to say the word, I will come and join you. Here are four more bills of exchange* [and so on].

The Duchessa did not say a word to Fabrizio of the opinion that people in Parma had of his affair. She was anxious above all things to console him, and in any case the death of a ridiculous creature like Giletti did not seem to her the sort of thing for which a del Dongo could be seriously blamed. 'How many Gilettis have our ancestors not sent into the next world,' she said to the Conte, 'without anyone ever taking it into his head to reproach them for it?'

Fabrizio, filled with amazement, and getting for the first time a glimpse of the true state of things, applied himself to studying the Archbishop's letter. Unfortunately the Archbishop himself believed him to be better informed than he actually was. Fabrizio gathered that what contributed most of all to the Marchesa Raversi's triumph was the fact that it was impossible to find any eye-witnesses of this fatal combat. The manservant who had been the first to bring news of it to Parma had been inside the village inn at Sanguigna when the fight occurred; little Marietta and the old woman who acted as her mother had vanished, and the Marchesa had bought over the *vetturino* who drove the carriage and who now had made a deposition of an abominable kind.

Although the proceedings are enveloped in the most profound mystery [wrote the good Archbishop in his Ciceronian style] and under the direction of the Lord Chief Justice, Rassi, of whom Christian charity alone restrains me from speaking evil, but who has made his fortune by ruthlessly pursuing his wretched prisoners as the greyhound pursues the hare; although this man Rassi, I say, whose turpitude and venality your imagination could not possibly exaggerate, has been appointed to take charge of the case by an angry Prince, I have been able to read the three depositions made by the vetturino. By a signal piece of good fortune the wretch contradicts himself. And I will add, since I am addressing my Vicar-General, the man who, after myself, is to have the charge of this Diocese, that I have sent for the priest of the parish in which this lost sheep resides. I will tell you, my dearly beloved son, but under the seal of the confessional, that this priest already knows, through the wife of the vetturino, the actual number of scudi that her husband has received from the Marchesa Raversi. I will not venture to say that the Marchesa insisted on his slandering you, but that is probable. The scudi were transmitted to him by a miserable priest who performs functions of a hardly exalted order in the Marchesa's household, and whom I have been obliged, for a second time, to prohibit from saying Mass.

I will not weary you with an account of various other steps you might have expected me to take, and which, indeed, are a part of my duties. A canon, a colleague of yours at the Cathedral, who by the way is a little too ready at times to remember the influence he derives from his family fortune, to which, by divine sanction, he is now the sole heir, ventured to say in the house of Conte Zurla, the Minister of the Interior, that he regarded this paltry matter (he alluded to the killing of the unfortunate Giletti) as proved against you. I summoned him to appear before me, and there, in the presence of my three other Vicars-General, of my Chaplain, and of two priests who happened to be in my waiting-room, I requested him to communicate to us, his brother-clerics, the details of the complete conviction which he professed to have acquired of the guilt of one of his colleagues at the Cathedral. The poor wretch could only stammer out a few hardly conclusive reasons. Every voice was raised against him, and although I did not think it necessary to add more than a very few words, he burst into tears and made us the witnesses of a confession of his complete error. Whereupon I promised him, in my own

*name and in the name of all the persons who had been present at this con-
ference, to keep the matter secret, on condition, however, that he would use
the utmost zeal in correcting the false impressions that might have been
created by remarks he had been making during the previous fortnight.*

*I shall not repeat to you, my dear son, what you must for a long time past
have known, namely that of the thirty-four labourers employed on the
excavations undertaken by Conte Mosca and whom the Marchesa Raversi
alleges to have been paid by you to assist you in a crime, thirty-two were at
the bottom of their trench, wholly taken up with their work, when you
seized hold of the hunting-knife and used it to defend your life against the
man who attacked you unawares. Two of their number, who were outside
the trench, shouted to the others: 'Monsignore is being murdered!' This cry
alone is a striking vindication of your innocence. Well now, the Lord Chief
Justice, Rassi, maintains that these two men have disappeared; on the other
hand, they have found eight of the men who were at the bottom of the
trench. At their first interrogation six declared that they heard the cry: 'Monsignore is being murdered!' I know, through indirect channels, that at their
fifth examination, which took place yesterday evening, five of them declared
that they could not remember exactly whether they had heard the cry themselves or whether it had been reported to them by one of their companions.
Orders have been issued for me to be informed of the place of residence of
these navvies, and their parish priests will make them understand that they
will incur eternal damnation if, for the sake of earning a few scudi, they let
themselves be persuaded to distort the truth.*

The good Archbishop went into endless details, as may be judged
from those we have just reported. Then he added, using the Latin
tongue:

*This affair is nothing less than an attempt to bring about a change of
government. If you are sentenced, it can be only to the galleys or to death,
in which case I shall intervene by declaring from my archiepiscopal throne
that I know you are innocent; that you simply defended your life
against a ruffian; and that finally I have forbidden you to return to Parma
so long as your enemies triumph there. I even propose to stigmatize the Lord
Chief Justice as he deserves; the hatred felt for that man is as common as
esteem for his character is rare. But after all, on the eve of the day on which
this administrator of justice is to pronounce so unjust a sentence, the Duchessa
Sanseverina will leave the city, and possibly even the State of Parma. In
that event, no one has any doubt that the Conte will hand in his resignation.*

Then, very probably, General Fabio Conti will come into office, and the Marchesa Raversi will be triumphant.

The great disadvantage about your affair is that no skilled person has been appointed to take charge of the procedure necessary to bring your innocence to light and to foil the attempts being made to suborn witnesses. The Conte believes he is playing this part; but he is too great a gentleman to stoop to certain details; besides, in his capacity as Minister of Police, he was obliged to issue, in the first instance, the severest orders against you. Lastly – dare I say it – our Sovereign Lord believes you to be guilty, or at least pretends to have such a belief, and has introduced a certain bitterness into this affair.

The words corresponding to 'our Sovereign Lord' and 'pretends to have such a belief' were in Greek, and Fabrizio felt infinitely obliged to the Archbishop for having dared to write them. He cut this line out of the letter with a pen-knife and destroyed it on the spot.

Fabrizio broke off a score of times while reading this letter. He was stirred by feelings of the keenest gratitude, and replied at once in a letter of eight pages. Often he was obliged to raise his head so that his tears should not fall upon the paper. The next day, just as he was about to seal this letter, he thought it seemed too worldly in tone. 'I shall write in Latin,' he said to himself, 'that will make it appear more seemly to the worthy Archbishop.' But while seeking to construct fine Latin phrases of great length, carefully modelled on Cicero, he remembered that one day the Archbishop, in speaking to him of Napoleon, had made a point of calling him 'Buonaparte'. Immediately all the emotion that on the previous day had moved him to tears completely vanished. 'O King of Italy!' he cried, 'that loyalty which so many swore to you in your lifetime, I shall preserve for you after your death. The Archbishop is no doubt fond of me, but that is because I am a del Dongo and he a commoner's son.' So that his fine letter in Italian should not be wasted, Fabrizio made a few necessary alterations to it, and addressed it to Conte Mosca.

That same day Fabrizio came across little Marietta in the street. She blushed for joy and made a sign to him to follow her without speaking. She went quickly towards a deserted archway; there, she pulled forward the black lace kerchief, which according to local custom covered her head, so that she could not be recognized; then turning sharply round she said to Fabrizio: 'How is it that you are walking so freely about in the street?' Fabrizio told her his story.

'Good gracious! You've been to Ferrara! And there was I looking for you everywhere in that town! You must know that I quarrelled with the old woman because she wanted to take me to Venice, where I knew quite well that you would never go, because you are on the Austrian black list. I sold my gold necklace to get to Bologna. I had a presentiment that I should have the happiness of meeting you here. The old woman arrived two days after me, so I won't advise you to come and see us, she would make more of those horrid demands for money which make me feel so ashamed. We've lived very comfortably since that fatal day you know of, and we haven't spent a quarter of what you gave us. I would rather not come and see you at the Albergo del Pellegrino; that would make people talk. Try to find a little room in an unfrequented street, and at the *Ave Maria* [nightfall] I shall be here, under this same archway.' Having said this, she slipped quickly away.

THE unexpected appearance of this charming young person drove every serious thought from his mind. Fabrizio now settled down to live in Bologna with a feeling of deepest joy and security. This artless predisposition to take delight in everything that came to fill his life crept into the letters which he wrote to the Duchessa, and to such an extent that she began to feel annoyed. Fabrizio hardly noticed this; he wrote, however, in abbreviated form on the glass of his watch: 'When I write to the D. never say: *When I was a prelate, when I was in the Church; that annoys her.*' He had bought a pair of ponies with which he was greatly pleased: he used to harness them to a hired barouche whenever little Marietta wished to pay a visit to one of those enchanting spots in the neighbourhood of Bologna; nearly every evening he drove her to the *Cascata del Reno*. On their way back, he would call on the kindly Crescentini, who regarded himself to some extent as Marietta's father.

'Upon my word,' said Fabrizio to himself, 'if this is the café-haunter's life that seemed to me so ridiculous for a man of any worth, I did wrong to spurn it.' He overlooked the fact that he never went near a café except to read the *Constitutionnel* and that, since he was quite unknown to anyone in fashionable circles in Bologna, the gratification of vanity had nothing to do with his present state of happiness. When he was not with little Marietta, he was to be seen at the Observatory, where he was taking a course in astronomy. The Professor there had taken a great fancy to him, and Fabrizio used to lend him his horses on Sundays, to cut a figure with his wife on the *Corso della Montagnola*.

He had a horror of making anyone unhappy, however little worthy of esteem that person might be. Marietta was absolutely set against his seeing the old woman, but one day, when the former was in church, he went up to visit the *mammaccia*, who reddened with anger when she saw him enter the room. 'This is a case where one plays the del Dongo,' said Fabrizio to himself.

'How much does Marietta earn in a month when she has an engagement?' he cried, with the air of a self-respecting young Parisian taking his seat in the dress-circle at the Italian Opera.

'Fifty scudi!'

'You are lying, as usual. Tell me the truth or, by God, you'll not get a single centesimo.'

'Well then, she was earning twenty-two scudi in our company in Parma, when we had the bad luck to meet you. I myself was getting twelve scudi, and we used to give Giletti, our protector, a third of what each of us earned. Out of that, almost every month, Giletti would make Marietta a present; this present might be worth a couple of scudi.'

'You're lying again; you yourself got no more than four scudi. But if you are good to Marietta I will engage you as if I were an *impresario*. Every month you shall have twelve scudi for yourself and twenty-two for her; but if I see her with red eyes, you'll get nothing.'

'You give yourself airs, but let me tell you, your fine generosity will be the ruin of us,' replied the old woman in a furious tone. 'We are losing our *avviamento* [our connexion]. When we have the enormous misfortune to be deprived of your Excellency's protection, we shall no longer be known to any of the companies, and they will all be full up. We shall not find any engagement, and, thanks to you, we shall starve to death.'

'Go to the devil,' said Fabrizio as he was leaving the room.

'I shall not go to the devil, you impious wretch! but merely to the police station, where they'll learn from me that you are a Monsignore who has flung his cassock on the scrap-heap, and that you are no more Giuseppe Bossi than I am.' Fabrizio had already gone a little way down the stairs. He came back again.

'In the first place, the police know better than you what my real name may be. But if you take it into your head to denounce me, if you do anything so infamous,' he said to her very gravely, 'Lodovico will have a word to say to you, and it won't be six stabs with a knife that your old carcase will get, but two dozen, and you will be six months in a hospital, and without snuff.'

The old woman turned pale, snatched at Fabrizio's hand and tried to kiss it. 'I accept with gratitude the life you propose for Marietta and me. You look so soft-hearted that I took you for a simpleton; and, bear in mind, others besides myself might make the same mistake. I would advise you to make a habit of adopting a more lordly air.' Then she added with the most admirable impudence, 'You will reflect upon this good advice and, since winter is not far off, you will make both Marietta and me a present to two good coats of that fine

English stuff which they sell at that big draper's shop on the Piazza San Petronio.'

The love affair with pretty Marietta offered Fabrizio all the charms of the most delightful friendship, and this made him think of the happiness of the same order which he might have found in the Duchessa's company.

'But isn't it a very comical thing,' he asked himself at times, 'that I am not susceptible to that exclusive and passionate preoccupation which men call love? Among the liaisons chance supplied me with in Novara or in Naples, have I ever met a woman whose company, even in the first few days of intimacy, I preferred to a ride on a fine horse that I did not know? Can it be,' he went on, 'that what men call love is just another illusion? I certainly feel myself in love, just as I feel I have a good appetite at six o'clock in the evening. Can it possibly be that out of this somewhat uncouth propensity these liars have created the love of Othello, the love of Tancred? Or should I rather believe that I am fashioned in a different way from other men? That my soul should be lacking in one passion? And why should that be? It would be a singular stroke of fate!'

In Naples, and especially towards the close of his stay, Fabrizio had met certain women who, proud of their rank, their beauty, and the position held in society by the admirers whom they had sacrificed to him, had tried to bend him to their will. On perceiving their intention, Fabrizio had broken with them in the most abrupt and most scandalous fashion. 'Well now,' he said to himself, 'if I ever allow myself to be carried away by the pleasure, no doubt a keen one, of being on friendly terms with that charming woman known as the Duchessa Sanseverina, I shall be exactly like that ass of a Frenchman who one day killed the goose that laid the golden eggs. It is to the Duchessa that I owe the sole happiness I have ever derived from sentiments of tender affection. My friendship for her is my life, and, besides, without her, what am I? A poor exile reduced to living from hand to mouth in a tumble-down country-house on the outskirts of Novara. I remember how during the heavy autumn rains I used to be obliged, for fear of accidents, to fix up an umbrella over the tester of my bed at night. I rode the agent's horses, which he was good enough to allow out of respect for my blue blood (for my powerful influence, that is), but he was beginning to find my stay there a trifle long. My father had made me an allowance of twelve hundred lire, and thought himself damned for supporting a Jacobin. My poor mother and my sisters let themselves go without new clothes to enable me to make a few little presents to my mistresses. This generous behaviour wrung my heart. And besides, people were beginning to suspect my poverty, and the young noblemen of the district were on the point of pitying me. Sooner or later some coxcomb would have shown his contempt for a poor Jacobin whose plans had come to grief, for in those people's eyes I was nothing more. I should have given or received some effective sword-thrust which would have brought me to the fortress of Fenestrelle, or possibly I should have had to take refuge again in Switzerland, still on my allowance of twelve hundred lire. I have the good fortune to be indebted to the Duchessa for the absence of all these evils; furthermore, it is she who feels for me those transports of affection that I ought to be feeling for her.

'Instead of that ridiculous, mean existence which would have turned me into a sorry, witless sort of creature, for the past four years I have been living in a big city, and have an excellent carriage, which things have kept me free from envy and all such low provincial sentiments. This too indulgent aunt is always scolding me because I don't draw enough money from the banker. Do I wish to wreck so admirable a situation for good and all? Do I wish to lose the one friend I have in the world? I have only to tell a lie, I have only to say to this charming woman, who is possibly without her like in the world, and for whom I feel the most passionate friendship: "*I love you*", I who do not know what it is to love with my whole heart and soul. She would spend the whole day reproaching me for the absence of those transports to which I am a stranger. Now Marietta, on the other hand, who cannot read my heart and who takes a caress for a transport of the soul, thinks me madly in love with her, and regards herself as the most fortunate of women.

'As a matter of fact, the only time I ever experienced in some slight degree that tender obsession which, I believe, is known as *love*, was for that girl Aniken, in the inn at Zonders, near the Belgian frontier.'

It is with regret that we are about to record at this point one of Fabrizio's worst actions. In the midst of this tranquil life, a sorry impulse of excited vanity took possession of this heart which was refractory to love and led him to extremes. In Bologna at the same time as himself there happened to be the celebrated Fausta F —, unquestionably one of the finest singers of the day, and perhaps the most capricious woman ever seen. The excellent poet Buratti, of Venice, had composed the famous satirical sonnet about her, which at that time was to be heard on the lips alike of princes and of the meanest street Arabs.

To wish and not to wish [it runs], *to adore and on one and the same day to detest, to find satisfaction only in inconstancy, to scorn everything the world worships, while the whole world worships her, Fausta has these defects and many more. Therefore never look upon this serpent. If, rash man, you look upon her, you forget her caprices. If you have the happiness to hear her voice, you forget yourself, and love, in a moment, makes of you what Circe in far-off days once made of Ulysses' companions.*

For the moment this miracle of beauty had come under the spell of the enormous whiskers and haughty insolence of the young Conte M — to such an extent as not to be revolted by his frightful jealousy. Fabrizio saw this Conte in the streets of Bologna and was shocked by the air of superiority with which he took possession of the pavement and deigned to parade his charms in the public eye. This young man was extremely rich and imagined himself free to take any liberties, and as his *prepotenze* had brought threats of punishment on his head, he hardly ever appeared in public save with an escort of nine or ten *buli* (a sort of cut-throat) clad in his livery, whom he had brought from his estates in the region of Brescia. Fabrizio had once or twice exchanged glances with this terrible Conte when chance led him to hear Fausta sing. He was astonished by the angelic sweetness of her voice; he had never imagined anything like it. He was indebted to it for sensations of supreme delight, which made a pleasing contrast to the *placidity* of his life at that time. Could this at last be love? he wondered. Exceedingly curious to experience such a feeling, and amused moreover by the thought of braving this Conte M —, whose bearing was more terrifying than that of any drum-major, our hero indulged in the childish folly of passing a great deal too often in front of the Palazzo Tanari, which Conte M — had taken for Fausta.

One day, as night was beginning to fall, Fabrizio, while trying to catch Fausta's eye, was greeted by very loud roars of laughter issuing from the Conte's *buli*, who were standing round the door of the Palazzo Tanari. He ran home, snatched up some useful weapons and passed once again in front of the house. Fausta, hiding behind her shutters, was awaiting his return and accounted it to his credit. M—, who was jealous of everyone on this earth, became especially jealous of Signor Giuseppe Bossi, and gave vent to all sorts of ridiculous utterances. Whereupon every morning our hero had a letter delivered to him containing nothing save these words: 'Signor Giuseppe Bossi destroys noxious insects and is staying at the Pellegrino, Via Larga 79.'

Conte M —, accustomed to the respect which his enormous fortune, his blue blood, and the valour of his thirty menservants assured him everywhere, refused entirely to understand the purport of this little note.

Fabrizio wrote other notes to Fausta. M— set spies upon this rival, who was not perhaps unpleasing to the lady. First of all he found out his real name, and next, that for the present he could not show his face in Parma. A few days later, Conte M —, his *buli*, his magnificent horses, and Fausta set off for that city.

Fabrizio, warming to the game, followed them the next day. In vain did the good Lodovico utter pathetic remonstrances; Fabrizio sent him about his business, and Lodovico, who was himself extremely brave, admired him for it; besides, this journey would bring him nearer to that pretty mistress of his at Casalmaggiore. Through Lodovico's efforts, nine or ten veterans of Napoleon's regiments attached themselves to Signor Giuseppe Bossi, under the guise of servants.

'Provided,' said Fabrizio to himself, when committing the folly of going after Fausta, 'I have no communication either with the Minister of Police, Conte Mosca, or with the Duchessa, I expose no one to risk but myself. I shall explain to my aunt later on that I was going in search of love, that beautiful thing which I have never encountered. The fact is that I think of Fausta, even when I'm not looking at her ... But is it the memory of her voice that I love, or her person?'

As he had given up all thoughts of an ecclesiastical career Fabrizio had grown a moustache and whiskers almost as terrifying as Conte M —'s, and these disguised him to some extent. He set up his headquarters, not in Parma – that would have been too imprudent – but in a village on the outskirts, in the midst of woods, on the road to Sacca, where his aunt had her country-house. Acting on Lodovico's advice, he gave himself out in this village as the valet of a great English nobleman of very eccentric tastes, who spent a hundred thousand lire a year in providing himself with the pleasures of the chase, and would arrive shortly from the Lake of Como, where he was detained by the trout-fishing.

Fortunately for him, the charming little *palazzo* which Conte M — had taken for the fair Fausta was situated at the southern extremity of the city of Parma, right on the road to Sacca, and Fausta's windows looked out on to the fine avenues of tall trees which extend beneath the high tower of the citadel. Fabrizio was not known in this little frequented quarter.

He did not fail to have Conte M — followed, and one day when the latter had just left the marvellous singer's house Fabrizio had the audacity to appear in the street in broad daylight. He was mounted, it is true, on an excellent horse, and well-armed. A party of musicians, of the sort that frequent the streets in Italy, and are sometimes very fine performers, came and planted their double-basses under Fausta's windows: after playing a few opening bars they sang, and not at all badly, a cantata composed in her honour. Fausta came to the window and had no difficulty in distinguishing a very polite young man who, stopping his horse in the middle of the street, bowed to her first of all, and then began to cast glances at her in a way that could hardly be misunderstood. In spite of the exaggeratedly English costume adopted by Fabrizio she soon recognized the author of the passionate letters that had brought about her departure from Bologna. 'This is a very curious creature,' she said to herself, 'it seems to me that I am going to fall in love with him. I have a hundred louis in hand, I can quite well give that terrible Conte M — the slip. As a matter of fact, he's wanting in wit, and never does anything unexpected, and is only slightly amusing because of the horrible appearance of his escort.'

On the following day Fabrizio, having learnt that every morning at eleven o'clock Fausta went to hear mass in the centre of the town in that same church of San Giovanni which contained the tomb of his great-uncle, the Archbishop Ascanio del Dongo, ventured to follow her there. I must admit that Lodovico had procured him a fine English wig with hair of the most becoming red. In reference to the colour of this hair, which was that of the flames which were devouring his heart, he composed a sonnet which Fausta thought charming; an unknown hand had taken care to place it upon her piano. These skirmishes went on for quite a week, but Fabrizio found that in spite of all kinds of efforts, he was making no real progress; Fausta refused to see him. He was overworking his vein of eccentricity; she admitted afterwards that she had been afraid of him. Fabrizio was no longer held except by faint hope of coming to feel what is known as *love*, but he frequently felt bored.

'Sir, let us leave this place,' Lodovico kept on saying to him. 'You are not in the least in love; I find you are hopelessly cool and full of common sense. Besides, you are making no progress; for very shame, let us take ourselves off.' Fabrizio was getting ready to leave in a first impulse of ill-temper, when he learnt that Fausta was to sing at the Duchessa Sanseverina's. 'Perhaps that sublime voice will succeed in setting my heart on fire,' he thought, and he actually ventured to penetrate in disguise into that *palazzo* where everyone knew him by sight.

We may imagine the Duchessa's emotion, when right at the end of the concert, she noticed a man in *chasseur's* livery standing by the door of the big drawing-room; his appearance reminded her of someone. She went to look for Conte Mosca, who only then informed her of Fabrizio's extraordinary and really incredible folly. He himself took it extremely well. This love for someone other than the Duchessa pleased him greatly. The Conte who, apart from politics, was a perfect gentleman, acted upon the maxim that he could himself find happiness only so long as the Duchessa was happy too. 'I will save him from himself,' he said to his mistress. 'Imagine the delight of our enemies if he were to be arrested in this house! I have, moreover, a hundred of my own men here, and that is why I sent to ask you for the keys of the great reservoir. He gives out that he is madly in love with Fausta, and up till now has not been able to get her away from Conte M —, who gives the foolish creature the life of a queen.'

The Duchessa's features betrayed the keenest grief. Fabrizio was then nothing more than a libertine, utterly incapable of any tender or serious feeling. 'And not to come and see us! That is what I shall never be able to forgive him,' she said at length. 'And here am I writing every day to him in Bologna!'

'I greatly admire his self-restraint,' replied the Conte. 'He does not want to compromise us by this prank, and it will be amusing to hear him tell us about it.'

Fausta was too senseless a creature to be able to keep quiet about what was on her mind. The day after the concert, every aria of which her eyes had addressed to that tall young man in *chasseur's* livery, she spoke to Conte M—, of an unknown admirer. 'Where do you see him?' asked the Conte in a fury. 'In the streets, in church,' replied Fausta, quite confused. At once she attempted to make amends for her imprudence, or at least to remove from it any idea that might remind him of Fabrizio. She rambled off into an endless description of a tall young man with red hair; he had blue eyes; no doubt he was some Englishman, very rich and very gawky, or else some prince or other. At that word, Conte M —, who was not distinguished for the accuracy of his perceptions, jumped to the conclusion, delightfully flattering to his vanity, that this rival was none other than the Crown Prince of Parma. This poor melancholy young man, guarded by six tutors, assistant tutors, preceptors etc., etc., who never allowed him out of doors until they had taken counsel together, was in the habit of casting strange glances at every fairly good-looking woman he was permitted to approach. At the Duchessa's concert, his rank had placed him in front of all the rest of the audience, in an isolated armchair three paces away from the fair Fausta, and his glances had excessively annoyed Conte M—. This mad notion born of keenest vanity, the idea of having a prince for a rival, greatly amused Fausta, who took delight in confirming it with a hundred details artlessly presented.

'Your family,' she asked the Conte, 'is as old, is it not, as that of the Farnese to which this young man belongs?'

'What do you mean? As old? I have no bastardy* in my family.'

As luck would have it, Conte M — was never able to study this supposed rival at his leisure, and this confirmed him in the flattering idea of his having a prince as his opponent. The fact was that whenever the interests of his enterprise did not summon Fabrizio to Parma, he remained in the woods near Sacca and on the banks of the Po. Conte M — had grown very much prouder, but also more prudent, since he had come to imagine himself to be a fair way to disputing the heart of Fausta with a prince. He begged her very seriously to observe the utmost discretion in everything she did. After flinging himself

* Pietro Luigi, the first sovereign prince of the Farnese family, so renowned for his virtues, was, as is generally known, the natural son of His Holiness Pope Paul III.

on his knees like a jealous and impassioned lover, he told her very plainly that his honour was concerned in her not being made the dupe of this young Prince.

'Excuse me, I should not be his dupe if I loved him; as for me, I have never yet seen a prince at my feet.'

'If you yield,' he replied with a haughty glare in his eyes, 'I may not perhaps be able to avenge myself on the Prince, but I will, most certainly, have my revenge.' With that he went out, slamming the doors behind him. Had Fabrizio presented himself at that moment, he would have won his suit.

'If you value your life,' Conte M — said to her that evening as he took leave of her after the performance, 'see to it that I never find out that the young Prince has been inside your house. I can do nothing to him, confound it, but do not make me remember I can do anything I like to you!'

'Ah, my darling Fabrizio,' cried Fausta, 'if I only knew where to find you!'

Wounded vanity can lead a young man very far when he is rich and has always been surrounded by flatterers from his cradle. The very real passion that Conte M — felt for Fausta was stirred to new fury. He was not in the least deterred by the dangerous prospect of coming into conflict with the only son of the Sovereign in whose dominions he happened to be; at the same time he had not the sense to try and see this Prince, or at any rate to have him followed. Not being able to attack him in any other way, M — dared to entertain the idea of making him look ridiculous. 'I shall be banished for ever from the State of Parma,' he said to himself. 'Well, what does that matter?'

Had he attempted to reconnoitre the enemy's position, Conte M — would have learnt that the young Prince never went out without an escort of three or four old men, the tiresome guardians of etiquette, and that the one and only pleasure of his free choice allowed him in the world was mineralogy.

By day, as by night, the little *palazzo* occupied by Fausta and to which the best society in Parma flocked, was surrounded by men on the watch; M — knew, from hour to hour, what she was doing and, more important still, what others were doing round about her. This at least can be said in praise of this jealous lover's precautions – this eminently capricious woman had no idea at first of this increased supervision. The reports of all his agents informed Conte M — that a very young man, wearing a wig of red hair, appeared very often beneath Fausta's windows, but always in a different disguise. 'Evidently it is the young Prince,' said M — to himself, 'otherwise why should he appear in disguise? Well, by Jove, I'm not the sort of man to give way before him. But for the usurpations of the Venetian Republic, I too should be a sovereign prince myself.'

On the feast of San Stefano the reports of the spies took on a gloomier tone; they seemed to indicate that Fausta was beginning to respond to her unknown admirer's advances. 'I can go away this instant and take this woman with me,' said M — to himself. 'But stop! In Bologna I fled from a del Dongo; here I should be fleeing before a prince! But what would the young man say about it? He might think that he had succeeded in making me afraid! And, by Jove! I come of as good a family as he.'

M — was furious, but, as a final touch to his misery, he was particularly anxious not to appear in the eyes of Fausta, whom he knew to be given to mocking, in the character of a jealous lover. Therefore on San Stefano's day, after spending an hour in her company, and being welcomed by her with an ardour that seemed to him the very height of insincerity, he left her, shortly before eleven o'clock, as she was dressing to go and hear mass in the Church of San Giovanni.

Conte M — went back to his house, put on the shabby black coat of a young student in theology, and hurried off to San Giovanni. He chose a place behind one of the tombs which adorn the third chapel on the right. He could see everything that went on in the church from beneath the arm of a cardinal who is represented in a kneeling posture on his tomb; this statue kept the light away from the back of the chapel and gave him sufficient concealment. Presently he saw Fausta arrive, more beautiful than ever. She was dressed in all her finery, and a score of admirers, drawn from the best society, formed an escort for her. Smiles of joy shone on her lips and in her eyes. 'It's clear,' thought the poor jealous wretch, 'that she's counting on meeting here the man she loves, whom for a long time, thanks to me, she has not perhaps been able to see.'

Suddenly, the look of keenest happiness in her eyes seemed to double in intensity. 'My rival is here,' thought M —, and the fury of his wounded vanity knew no bounds. 'What sort of figure am I cutting here, serving as pendant to a young prince in disguise?' But however hard he tried he could never succeed in identifying this rival, whom his eager gaze kept seeking in every direction.

At every moment Fausta, after letting her eyes wander round every part of the church, would end by bringing her gaze, charged with love and happiness, to rest on the dim corner in which M — was concealed. In a passionate heart, love is apt to exaggerate the slightest shades of meaning, and draws from them the most ridiculous conclusions. Did not poor M — end by persuading himself that Fausta had seen him, and that having, in spite of all his efforts, become aware of his deadly jealousy, she wished to reproach him and at the same time console him for it by these very tender glances?

The tomb of the cardinal, behind which M— had posted himself to observe her, was raised four or five feet above the marble floor of San Giovanni. When, towards one o'clock, the fashionable mass had ended, the majority of the worshippers left the church, and Fausta dismissed the city gallants, on a pretext of wishing to perform her devotions. As she remained kneeling on her chair, her eyes, which had grown more tender and shone more brightly, were fixed on M —. Since there were now only a few people remaining in the church, she no longer took the trouble to let her eyes range over the whole building before coming happily to rest on the cardinal's statue. 'What delicacy!' thought Conte M —, imagining that she was gazing at him. At length Fausta rose and quickly left the church, after first making some odd gestures with her hands.

M —, off his head with love and almost entirely relieved of his mad jealousy, had left his post to fly to his mistress's *palazzo* and thank her a thousand, thousand times, when, as he passed in front of the cardinal's tomb, he noticed a young man all in black. This ominous being had remained until then on his knees, close up against the epitaph of the tomb, in such a position that the jealous lover's eyes, in their search for him, had managed to pass right over his head without seeing him at all.

This young man rose to his feet, moved quickly away, and was immediately surrounded by seven or eight rather awkward and odd-looking fellows, who seemed to belong to him. M— rushed after him but, without there being any too noticeable effort to this effect, was stopped in the narrow passage formed by the wooden lobby at the door by these same clumsy men who were protecting his rival. When at length he came out.after them into the street, all he could see was someone shutting the door of a rather shabby-looking carriage, which, by a curious contrast, was drawn by a pair of excellent horses, and in a moment had passed out of sight.

He returned home, breathless with rage. Presently his spies arrived and reported coolly that that morning the mysterious lover, disguised as a priest, had been kneeling in an attitude of great devotion up against a tomb which stood at the entrance to a dark chapel in the church of San Giovanni. Fausta had remained in the church until it was almost empty and had then rapidly exchanged certain signs with the unknown man; she seemed to be making some kind of crosses with her hands. M— hurried off to the faithless woman's house. For the first time she was unable to hide her confusion. She told him, with the artless mendacity of a passionate woman, that she had gone to San Giovanni as usual but that she had seen no sign there of the man who was persecuting her. On hearing these words, M—, quite beside himself, treated her as the vilest of creatures, told her all he had seen himself, and, as the boldness of her lies increased with the vehemence of his accusations, drew his dagger and flung himself upon her.

With the utmost coolness Fausta said to him: 'Very well then, everything you complain of is perfectly true, but I have tried to keep it from you so as not to provoke your boldness into carrying out wild plans of vengeance which may ruin us both. For let me tell you once and for all, that, according to what I imagine, the man who is persecuting me with his attentions is of a sort to meet with no opposition to his wishes, in these dominions at any rate.' Having very skilfully reminded M— that, after all, he had no legal authority over her, Fausta ended by saying that probably she would not be going to San Giovanni any more. M— was desperately in love, a touch of coquetry may perhaps have been mingled with prudence in this young woman's heart; he felt himself disarmed. He thought of leaving Parma; the young Prince, however powerful he might be, could not follow him, or if he did follow him would cease to be anything more than his equal. But pride once more reminded him that his departure must still have the appearance of a flight, and Conte M— forbade himself to think of it.

'He has no suspicion of my darling Fabrizio's presence here,' thought the singer with delight. 'And now we can make a fool of him in the most priceless fashion!'

Fabrizio had not the least idea of his good fortune. Finding next day that the singer's windows were tightly closed, and not seeing her anywhere, he began to feel that the joke was lasting rather too long. He felt some pangs of conscience. 'In what sort of position am I putting that poor Conte Mosca, and he the Minister of Police! People will think he is my accomplice, I shall have come to this place to ruin his career! But if I abandon a project I have been following for so long, what will the Duchessa say when I tell her of my essays in love!'

One evening, when on the point of giving up the game, he was moralizing in this way with himself, as he strolled up and down under the tall trees which divided Fausta's *palazzo* from the citadel, he noticed that he was being followed by a spy of very diminutive stature. In vain did he endeavour to shake him off by turning down several streets, this microscopic being seemed always to cling to his heels. Growing impatient, he dashed into a lonely street which ran alongside the river Parma, where his men were lying in wait. At a signal from him they leapt out upon the poor little spy, who flung himself at their feet; it was Bettina, Fausta's maid. After three days of boredom and seclusion, disguised as a man to escape the dagger of Conte M——, of whom both she and her mistress were in great dread, she had undertaken to come and tell him that Fausta loved him passionately and was burning to see him, but that she could not appear any more in the church of San Giovanni. 'It was high time,' thought Fabrizio. 'Hurrah for obstinacy!'

The little lady's maid was extremely pretty, a fact which took Fabrizio's mind away from his musings on moral topics. She told him that the public promenade and all the streets through which he had passed that evening were being carefully watched, though quite unobtrusively, by M——'s spies. They had taken rooms on the ground floors and the first storeys of the houses; hidden behind the shutters and keeping absolutely silent, they observed everything that went on, even in the apparently deserted streets, and heard all that was said there.

'If those spies had recognized my voice,' said little Bettina, 'I should have been stabbed without mercy as soon as I got back to the house and perhaps my poor mistress with me.'

This terror rendered her charming in Fabrizio's eyes.

'Conte M——,' she went on, 'is furious, and my mistress knows that he will stick at nothing ... She told me to say to you that she would like to be a hundred leagues away from here and with you.'

Then she gave an account of the scene on San Stefano's day, and of the fury of M —, who had not missed one of the glances and signs of love that Fausta, on that day madly enamoured of Fabrizio, had sent his way. The Conte had drawn his dagger, had seized Fausta by the hair, and, but for her presence of mind, she would certainly have been killed.

Fabrizio took the pretty Bettina up to a little apartment which he had nearby. He told her that he came from Turin, and was the son of an important personage who happened at that moment to be in Parma, a fact that obliged him to act with the greatest precaution. Bettina replied with a smile that he was a man of far greater rank than he chose to let appear. It was some time before our hero realized that the charming girl took him for no less a personage than the Crown Prince himself. Fausta was beginning to get alarmed and was becoming fond of Fabrizio; she had made up her mind not to mention his name to her maid, but to speak to her of the Prince. Fabrizio ended by admitting to this pretty girl that she had guessed aright. 'But if my name gets out,' he added, 'in spite of the great passion of which I have given your mistress so many proofs, I shall be obliged to stop seeing her, and at once my father's Ministers, those mischievous rogues whom I shall one day dismiss from office, will not fail to send her an order to quit those dominions which up till now she has adorned with her presence.'

Towards morning, Fabrizio arranged with the little lady's maid a number of plans by which he might manage to obtain a rendezvous with Fausta. He sent for Lodovico and another of his servants, a very cunning fellow, who came to an understanding with Bettina, while he himself wrote the most extravagant letter to Fausta. The situation called for every sort of tragic exaggeration and Fabrizio was not sparing in his use of them. It was not until day was breaking that he parted from the little lady's maid, who went away highly satisfied with the behaviour of the young Prince.

It had been insisted on a hundred times over that, now that Fausta had come to an understanding with her lover, the latter was no longer to appear beneath the windows of the little *palazzo* except when he could be admitted there, and then a signal would be given. But Fabrizio, now in love with Bettina, and believing himself to be getting near to the final point with Fausta, could not confine himself to his village two leagues away from Parma. The following evening, about midnight, he came on horseback and with a good escort to sing under Fausta's windows an air then in fashion, to which he had put different words. 'Is not this,' he asked himself, 'the way in which the noble company of lovers always behave?'

Now that Fausta had expressed a desire to meet him, all this pursuit of her seemed to Fabrizio very tedious. 'No, I am not by any means in love,' he said to himself as he sang, in a none too tuneful way, beneath the windows of the little *palazzo*. 'Bettina seems to me a hundred times preferable to Fausta, and it is by her I should like to be received at this moment.' Fabrizio, feeling rather bored, was on the way back to his village when, about five hundred yards from Fausta's palazzo, some fifteen or twenty men flung themselves upon him. Four of them seized his horse by the bridle, two others took hold hold of his arms. Lodovico and Fabrizio's *bravi* were attacked, but managed to escape; several pistol-shots were fired. All this was the affair of a moment; fifty lighted torches appeared in the street in the twinkling of an eye, and as if by magic. All these men were well armed. Fabrizio, in spite of the men who were holding him, had jumped down from his horse and tried to force his way through. He even wounded one of the men who was gripping his arms with hands that were like vices; but he was greatly surprised to hear the fellow say to him, in the most respectful tone: 'Your Highness will give me a good pension for this wound, which will be better for me than falling into the crime of high treason by drawing my sword against my Prince.'

'Here indeed is the punishment I get for my folly,' said Fabrizio to himself. 'I shall have damned myself for a sin that did not seem to me in the least attractive.'

Scarcely had this little attempt at a battle come to an end when several lackeys in full livery appeared with a sedan-chair, gilded and painted in an odd fashion; it was of those grotesque chairs used by revellers at carnival time. Six men, with daggers in their hands, requested 'His Highness' to step into it, telling him that the sharp night air might be bad for his voice. They used the most respectful forms of address, the title 'Prince' every moment repeated and almost shouted. The procession began to move on. Fabrizio counted in the street more than fifty men carrying lighted torches. It was round about one o'clock in the morning; all the townspeople had come to the windows; the whole thing was conducted with a certain solemnity. 'I was afraid of dagger-thrusts on Conte M —'s part,' Fabrizio said to himself; 'he contents himself with making a fool of me. I had not suspected him of such good taste. But does he really think that he is dealing with the Prince? If he knows that I am only Fabrizio, look out for dagger-thrusts!'

These fifty men carrying torches and the twenty armed men, after stopping for some considerable time under Fausta's windows, went on to parade in front of the finest *palazzi* in the city. A couple of major-domos, posted on either side of the sedan-chair, inquired of 'His Highness' from time to time whether he had any orders to give them. Fabrizio did not lose his head. With the help of the light the torches shed around him, he could see that Lodovico and his men were following the procession as closely as they could. Fabrizio said to himself: 'Lodovico has only nine or ten men and does not dare to attack.' From the interior of his sedan-chair Fabrizio could see quite clearly that the men responsible for carrying out this vulgar joke were armed to the teeth. He made a show of laughing with the major-domos in attendance on him. After more than two hours of this triumphal march, he noticed that they were about to pass the end of the street in which the Palazzo Sanseverina stood.

As they turned the corner of the street that leads to it, he quickly opened the door in the front of the chair, jumped out over one of the carrying-poles, and felled with a blow from his dagger one of the flunkeys who thrust a torch into his face. He himself received a stab in the shoulder from a dagger; a second flunkey singed his whiskers with his lighted torch, and finally Fabrizio reached Lodovico, to whom he shouted: 'Kill! Kill everyone who is carrying a torch!' Lodovico laid about him with his sword and delivered his master from two men who were bent on pursuing him. Fabrizio rushed up to the door of the Palazzo Sanseverina. The porter, out of curiosity, had opened the little door, three feet high, that was cut in the big door, and was gazing in utter bewilderment at this great assembly of torches. Fabrizio leapt inside and shut this tiny door behind him; he ran to the garden and escaped by a gate which opened on to an unfrequented street. An hour later, he was out of the town; at daybreak he crossed the frontier of the State of Modena and was now in safety. That evening he entered Bologna.

'Here's a fine sort of expedition,' he said to himself. 'I never even managed to speak to my charmer.' He hastened to write letters of apology to the Conte and the Duchessa, cautious epistles which, while describing what was going on in his heart, could not give away any information to an enemy. 'I was in love with love,' he told the Duchessa. 'I have done everything in the world to gain some knowledge of it; but it appears that nature has refused to give me a heart that is capable of loving and feeling melancholy. I cannot raise myself above the level of trivial delights,' and so forth.

It would be impossible to give any idea of the stir that this adventure caused in Parma. Its mysterious character excited curiosity. A countless number of people had seen the torches and the sedan-chair; but who was this man who was being carried off and to whom every mark of respect was paid? No one of note was missing from the city on the following day.

The humble folk who lived in the street from which the prisoner had made his escape did indeed say that they had seen a corpse. But in broad daylight, when the townsfolk dared to venture out of their houses, they found no other traces of the shindy than quantities of blood spilt on the pavement. More than twenty thousand sightseers came to visit the street in the course of the day. Italian towns are accustomed to strange sights, but they always know the *why* and the *wherefore* of them. What amazed the people of Parma about this occurrence, was that even a month afterwards, when the torchlight procession had ceased to be the sole topic of conversation, nobody, thanks to Conte Mosca's prudence, had been able to guess the name of the rival who had wished to snatch Fausta away from Conte M—. This jealous and vindictive lover had taken flight as soon as the procession set out. By Conte Mosca's orders, Fausta was sent to the citadel. The Duchessa laughed heartily over a little act of injustice which the Conte had been obliged to indulge in to check the curiosity of the Prince, who might otherwise have managed to hit on Fabrizio's name.

There was to be seen in Parma a learned man, who had come there from the North to write a history of the middle ages. He was in search of manuscripts in the libraries, and the Conte had given him every possible facility. But this scholar, who was still very young, appeared to be very irascible; he imagined, for one thing, that everyone in Parma was out to make a fool of him. It was true that the urchins in the streets sometimes followed him on account of the huge shock of bright red hair which he displayed with pride. This scholar imagined that at his inn he was charged the most fantastic prices for everything, and he never paid for the smallest trifle without first looking up its price in the *Travels* of a certain Mrs Starke, a book which has now gone into its twentieth edition, because it indicates to the prudent Englishman the price of a turkey, an apple, a glass of milk, and so forth.

On the evening of the very day on which Fabrizio made this forced excursion, this scholar with the tawny mane flew into a furious temper at the inn, and drew from his pocket a brace of pocket pistols to avenge himself on the waiter who demanded two soldi for an indifferent peach. He was arrested, for carrying pocket pistols is a serious crime!

As this irascible scholar was tall and thin, the very next morning the Conte conceived the idea of passing him off as the foolhardy fellow who, having tried to steal away Fausta from Conte M—, had been made the victim of a joke. The carrying of pocket pistols is punishable in Parma with three years in the galleys; but this penalty is never applied. After a fortnight in prison, during which time the scholar had seen nobody save a lawyer who had put him in a terrible fright about the atrocious laws directed by the pusillanimity of those in power against the bearers of hidden weapons, another lawyer visited the prison and told him of the expedition inflicted by Conte M— on a rival whose identity remained unknown. 'The police do not wish to admit to the Prince that they have not been able to find out who this rival is. Confess that you were seeking to find favour with Fausta; that fifty ruffians carried you off as you were singing beneath her window, and that for a whole hour they took you round in a sedan-chair without saying anything to you that was not extremely civil. There is nothing humiliating in such a confession, you are only asked to make a short statement. As soon as, by making it, you have got the police out of a difficulty, you will be put into a post-chaise and driven to the frontier, where they will bid you goodbye.'

The scholar held out for a month. Two or three times the Prince was on the point of having him brought to the Ministry of the Interior and of being present in person at his examination. But he had finally forgotten all about it when the historian, weary of the whole business, made up his mind to confess everything, and was conducted to the frontier. The Prince remained convinced that Conte M—'s rival had a regular mass of red hair.

Three days after his forced airing, while Fabrizio, who was in hiding in Bologna, was planning with the faithful Lodovico how to get hold of Conte M—, he learnt that he too was in hiding in a village in the mountains on the road to Florence. The Conte had only two or three of his *buli* with him. Next day, just as he was returning home after taking a ride, he was carried off by eight men in masks who gave him to understand that they were police agents from Parma. They conducted him, after bandaging his eyes, to an inn two leagues farther up in the mountains, where he was treated with the utmost possible respect and given a very liberal supper. He was served with the best wines of Italy and Spain.

'Am I then a prisoner of State?' asked the Conte.

'By no means,' the masked Lodovico replied very civilly. 'You have insulted a private individual, by taking upon yourself to have him carried about in a sedan-chair. Tomorrow morning he wishes to fight a duel with you. If you kill him, you will find a pair of good horses, money, and relays prepared for you along the road to Genoa.'

'What is the name of this swashbuckler?' asked the Conte angrily.

'He is called *Bombace*. You will have the choice of weapons and good seconds, thoroughly honourable men; but one or other of you must die!'

'Why, it's murder, then!' said the Conte in alarm.

'Heaven forbid! It is simply a duel to the death with the young man whom you had carried through the streets of Parma in the middle of the night, and who would be for ever dishonoured if you remained alive. One or other of you is superfluous on this earth, therefore do your best to kill him. You shall have swords, pistols, sabres – all the weapons in short that we have managed to procure at a few hours' notice – for we have had to make haste. The police in Bologna are, as you perhaps know, very diligent, and they must not hinder this duel which is necessary to the honour of the young man whom you have made a fool of.'

'But if this young man is a prince …'

'He is a private individual like yourself, and even a good deal less wealthy than you. But he wishes to fight to the death, and he will force you to fight, I warn you.'

'I am not afraid of anything in the world!' cried M —.

'That is just what your adversary most passionately desires,' replied Lodovico. 'Tomorrow morning, very early, make ready to defend your life; it will be attacked by a man who has good reason to be extremely angry, and he will not spare you. I repeat that you will have the choice of weapons; and see that you make your will.'

Next morning, about six o'clock, breakfast was brought to Conte M —. A door was then opened in the room in which he had been confined, and he was invited to step out into the courtyard of a country inn. This courtyard was surrounded by hedges and walls of a certain height, and its gates had been carefully closed.

In a corner, on a table which the Conte was requested to approach, he found several bottles of wine and brandy, two pistols, two swords, two sabres, paper and ink. A score or so of peasants were at the windows of the inn that overlooked the courtyard. The Conte implored them to take pity on him. 'They want to murder me,' he cried. 'Save my life!'

'You deceive yourself, or else you wish to deceive others,' called out Fabrizio, who was at the opposite corner of the courtyard, beside a table strewn with weapons. He had taken off his coat, and his face was hidden by one of those wire masks which one finds in fencing-schools.

'I must ask you,' Fabrizio added, 'to put on the wire mask which you will find beside you, then to advance towards me either with a sword or with pistols. As you were told yesterday evening, you have the choice of weapons.'

Conte M — raised endless difficulties, and seemed much upset at having to fight. Fabrizio, for his part, was afraid of the arrival of the police, although they were in the mountains, quite five leagues from Bologna; he ended by hurling the most atrocious insults at his rival. Finally he had the satisfaction of infuriating Conte M —, who snatched up a sword and advanced upon him. The fight began rather tamely.

After a few minutes it was interrupted by a terrible clamour. Our hero had been well aware that he was rushing into an action which might be made a subject of reproach, or at least of slanderous imputations against him, for the remainder of his life. He had sent Lodovico out into the countryside to gather in witnesses. Lodovico gave money to some strangers who were at work in a wood nearby; and they came running up to the inn shouting, thinking that it was a matter of killing the enemy of the man who had paid them. When they reached the inn, Lodovico asked them to keep their eyes open and to notice whether either of the young men who were fighting acted treacherously or took any unfair advantage of the other.

The fight, which had been interrupted for a moment by the cries of 'Murder!' uttered by the peasants, was slow in beginning again. Fabrizio started to hurl fresh insults aimed to prick the Conte's self-conceit. 'My dear Conte,' he called to him, 'when a man is insolent he should also be brave. I feel that such a condition is hard for you; you prefer to pay other men to be brave.' The Conte, goaded to fresh fury, began to shout back that he had for years frequented the fencing-school of the famous Battistini in Naples, and that he was going to punish him for his insolence. Now that Conte M —'s anger had at last come up again to the surface he fought with a certain determination, which did not, however, prevent Fabrizio from giving him a fine thrust in the chest with his sword, which kept him several months in bed. Lodovico, while giving first aid to the wounded man, whispered in his ear: 'If you report this duel to the police, I shall have you stabbed in your bed.'

Fabrizio fled to Florence. As he had remained in hiding in Bologna, it was only when he got to Florence that he received all the Duchessa's letters of reproach. She could not forgive him for coming to her concert, and not making an attempt to speak to her. Fabrizio was delighted by Conte Mosca's letters; they breathed a sincere friendship and the most noble feelings. He gathered that the Conte had written to Bologna, in such a way as to clear him of any suspicions that might be held against him with regard to the duel. The police behaved with perfect justice. They reported that two strangers, only one of whom, the wounded man (that is, Conte M—), was known to them, had fought with swords in the presence of more than thirty peasants, amongst whom, towards the end of the fight, the priest of the village had made his appearance, and had vainly attempted to separate the two combatants. As the name Giuseppe Bossi had never been mentioned, less than two months afterwards Fabrizio ventured to return to Bologna, more convinced than ever that his destiny condemned him never to become acquainted with the noble and intellectual side of love. This was what he gave himself the pleasure of explaining at great length to the Duchessa. He was utterly tired of his lonely life and now felt a passionate longing to return to those

charming evenings such as he used to spend in the company of the
Conte and his aunt. He had not experienced the sweet delights of
good society since the time he was with them.

*I have suffered so much boredom in connexion with the love I hoped to
enjoy, and with Fausta* [he wrote to the Duchessa], *that at the present
moment, even if her fancy were still inclined my way, I would not go
twenty leagues to hold her to her promise. So have no fear, as you tell
me you have, of my going to Paris, where I see she is appearing and having
the most tremendous success. I would go any possible number of leagues to
spend an evening with you and with the Conte who is so good to his
friends.*

CHAPTER 14 : *Plot and Counterplot*

W HILE Fabrizio was in pursuit of love in a village close to
Parma, Chief Justice Rassi, who did not know that he was so
near at hand, continued to treat his case as though he had been a
Liberal. He pretended that he could not find any witnesses for the
defence, or rather, he intimidated them. At length, after the most
skilful manoeuvring for nearly a year, and about two months after
Fabrizio's final return to Bologna, on a certain Friday the Marchesa
Raversi, beside herself with joy, announced publicly in her drawing-
room that next day the sentence pronounced but an hour before on
young del Dongo would be presented to the Prince for his signature
and approved by him. A few minutes later the Duchessa learnt of
this remark made by her enemy.

'The Conte must be extremely ill served by his agents!' she said
to herself. 'Only this morning he thought the sentence could not
be pronounced for another week. Possibly he would not be sorry
to have my young Vicar-General kept at a distance from Parma.
But,' she added, on a note of exultation, 'we shall see him come
back again, and one day he will be our Archbishop.'

The Duchessa rang the bell. 'Collect all the servants in the ante-
room,' she said to her footman, 'including the cooks. Go to the
town commandant and get the necessary permit from him to
procure four post-horses, and, lastly, see that those same horses are
harnessed to my carriage within half an hour.' All the women of the
household were kept busy packing trunks; the Duchess hurriedly put
on a travelling costume, all without sending any word to the Conte.
The idea of having a little game with him made her wild with
delight.

'My friends,' she said to the assembled servants, 'I learn that my
poor nephew is to be condemned, in his absence, for having had the
audacity to defend his life against a raving lunatic; it was Giletti
who wished to kill him. Every one of you has been able to note how
gentle and inoffensive Fabrizio is by nature. Rightly indignant at
this atrocious outrage, I am setting off for Florence. I am leaving
each one of you ten years' wages. If you are in distress, write to me,
and so long as I have a sequin left there will be something for you.'

The Duchessa meant exactly what she said, and, at her closing words, the servants dissolved into tears; her own eyes too were wet. She added in a voice that trembled with emotion: 'Pray to God for me, and for Monsignore Fabrizio del Dongo, Chief Vicar-General of the Diocese, who tomorrow morning is going to be sentenced to the galleys, or, what would be less stupid, condemned to death.'

The tears of the servants redoubled in volume, and changed by degrees into cries that were almost seditious. The Duchessa stepped into her carriage and had herself driven to the Prince's Palace. Despite the unseasonable hour, she sent in a request for an audience by General Fontana, the aide-de-camp in waiting; she was not by any means in full court dress, a fact which filled this aide-de-camp with utter stupefaction. As for the Prince, he was not at all surprised, and still less annoyed, by this request for an audience.

'We are about to see tears shed by lovely eyes,' he said to himself, rubbing his hands. 'She comes to sue for mercy: this proud beauty is going to humble herself at last! She was really too insupportable with her little airs of independence! Those speaking eyes seemed always to be saying to me, whenever the slightest thing offended her: "Naples or Milan would be a far pleasanter place to live in than your little town of Parma." It is true I do not reign over Naples, nor over Milan; but anyhow this great lady is coming to ask me for something that depends on me alone, and which she ardently longs to obtain. I always thought that this nephew's coming here would give me some pull over her.'

While the Prince was smiling at these thoughts and giving himself up to all these pleasing anticipations, he walked up and down his room, at the door of which General Fontana remained standing erect and stiff, like a soldier presenting arms. Seeing the Prince's gleaming eyes, and calling to mind the Duchessa's travelling costume, he imagined a dissolution of the Monarchy. His amazement knew no bounds when he heard the Prince say: 'Ask her Grace the Duchessa to wait for a quarter of an hour or so.' The General Aide-de-Camp turned to the right-about, like a soldier on parade; the Prince continued smiling. 'Fontana is not accustomed,' he said to himself, 'to see that proud Duchessa kept waiting. His astonished face when he tells her of this *little moment of waiting* will pave the way for the touching tears which this room is going to see her shed.' This short interval was exquisitely delightful to the Prince; he walked up and down with firm and even step; he *reigned*. 'The main thing at this point is not to say anything that is not perfectly correct; whatever my feelings for the Duchessa may be, I must never forget that she is one of the greatest ladies of my court. How used Louis XIV to speak to the Princesses his daughters when he had occasion to be displeased with them?' And his eyes came to rest on the portrait of the Great King.

The amusing thing about it was that the Prince never thought of asking himself whether he should show clemency to Fabrizio and what shape this clemency should take. At length, at the end of twenty minutes, the faithful Fontana presented himself again at the door, but without saying a word. 'The Duchessa Sanseverina may enter,' cried the Prince in a theatrical manner. 'Now the tears will begin,' he said to himself, and as if to prepare himself for such a spectacle, he pulled out his handkerchief.

Never had the Duchessa looked so vivacious or so pretty; she did not seem five-and-twenty. Seeing her light and rapid little step hardly brush the carpet, the poor aide-de-camp was on the point of losing his head altogether.

'I have many apologies to make to your Serene Highness,' said the Duchessa in her light and gay little voice. 'I have taken the liberty of presenting myself before you in a costume which is not precisely fitting, but your Highness has so accustomed me to your kindnesses that I ventured to hope you would be also pleased to grant me pardon for this.'

The Duchessa spoke rather slowly, so as to give herself time to enjoy the expression on the Prince's face. It was an exquisite sight, on account of its profound astonishment and the traces of pomposity which the posture of his head and his arms still betrayed. The Prince remained still as if struck by lightning, exclaiming from time to time in a shrill and agitated little voice, and barely articulating the words: *What on earth! What on earth!* The Duchessa, as though out of respect, having finished paying her compliments, left him plenty of time to reply; then she went on: 'I venture to hope that your Serene Highness deigns to pardon the incongruity of my costume.' But, as she said the words, her mocking eyes shone with so bright a sparkle that the Prince could not endure it. He gazed up at the ceiling which with him was the final sign of the most extreme embarrassment.

'What on earth! What on earth!' he said again; then he had the

good fortune to think of a remark. 'Your Grace, pray be seated'; he himself drew forward a chair for her, and with a certain amount of graciousness. The Duchessa was by no means unmoved by this courtesy; she assumed a less petulant expression.

'*What on earth! What on earth!*' the Prince once more repeated, fidgeting in his armchair, in which one would have said that he could not settle comfortably.

'I am going to take advantage of the cool night air to travel by post,' went on the Duchessa, 'and as my absence may be of some duration, I did not wish to leave the dominions of His Serene Highness without thanking him for all the kindness which for the past five years he has condescended to show me.' At these words the Prince understood at last, and turned pale. He was the one man in the world who suffered most when he found himself mistaken in his calculations. Then he assumed an air of grandeur quite worthy of the portrait of Louis XIV which hung before his eyes. 'That's good,' thought the Duchessa. 'He can play the man.'

'And what is the motive behind this sudden departure?' asked the Prince in a fairly firm tone.

'I have had this plan in mind for some time,' replied the Duchessa, 'and a petty insult which has been offered to Monsignore del Dongo, who is going to be sentenced either to death or to the galleys to-morrow, makes me hasten my departure.'

'And what town are you going to?'

'To Naples, I think.' She added as she rose from her chair: 'It only remains for me to take leave of your Serene Highness and to thank you very humbly for your *former* kindnesses.' In her turn she spoke with so firm an air that the Prince plainly saw that in a couple of seconds all would be over. Once the scandal of her departure had occurred, he knew that no arrangement would be possible; she was not a woman to go back on what she had done. He hurried after her.

'But you know very well, my dear Duchessa,' he said, taking her hand, 'that I have always had a great liking for you, and a liking to which it only remained with you to give another name. A murder has been committed, that cannot be denied. I entrusted the investigation of the case to my best judges.'

At these words, the Duchessa drew herself up to her full height. Every semblance of respect and even of urbanity disappeared in the twinkling of an eye; the outraged woman appeared plainly before him, and an outraged woman addressing a creature whom she knows to be insincere.

It was with an expression of the keenest anger and even contempt that she said to the Prince, laying stress on every word:

'I am leaving your Serene Highness's dominions for ever, so as never to hear anyone speak of the Chief Justice Rassi, and of the other infamous assassins who have condemned my nephew and so many others to death. If your Serene Highness does not wish to introduce a feeling of bitterness into the last moments I shall pass in the presence of a Prince who is courteous and intelligent when he is not misled, I beg you most humbly not to remind me of those infamous judges who sell themselves for a thousand scudi, or a decoration.'

The admirable – and, above all, genuine – tone in which these words were uttered made the Prince shudder. He feared for a moment to see his dignity compromised by a more direct accusation, but on the whole his sensation soon turned to one of pleasure. He admired the Duchessa; her whole personality attained at that moment to a sublime beauty. 'Good God! How lovely she is!' thought the Prince. 'Something must be forgiven in a woman who is so unique and of such a sort that there is possibly not another like her in the whole of Italy... Well, with a little careful diplomacy, it might not be impossible one day to make her my mistress. Such a creature is far removed from that doll of a Marchesa Balbi, who moreover robs my poor subjects of at least three hundred thousand lire a year ... But did I really hear aright?' he thought suddenly. 'She said: "Condemned my nephew and so many others." ' Then his anger got the upper hand, and it was with a haughtiness befitting his supreme rank that the Prince said, after a moment's silence: 'And what must be done to keep your Grace from leaving us?'

'Something of which you are not capable,' replied the Duchessa, in a tone of the most bitter irony and the most open scorn.

The Prince was beside himself, but from constant exercise of his profession as an absolute sovereign he drew strength to conquer his first impulse. 'I must have this woman,' he said to himself. 'So much I owe myself, and then I must kill her with scorn. If she leaves this room, I shall never see her again.' But, wild with rage and hatred as he was at this moment, how could he find a formula that would at once meet the requirements of what he owed to himself and induce the Duchessa not to forsake his court immediately? 'A gesture,' he thought, 'can neither be reported nor turned to ridicule,' and he placed himself between the Duchessa and the door of his room. A few moments later he heard somebody tap on the door.

'Who is this damned booby,' he shouted, swearing with all the strength of his lungs, 'who is the damned booby who seeks to intrude his idiotic presence upon me here?' Poor General Fontana showed a pallid face of utter bewilderment, and it was with the air of a man at his last gasp that he uttered the ill-articulated words: 'His Excellency Conte Mosca craves the honour of an audience.'

'Let him come in,' said the Prince at the top of his voice; and as Mosca bowed, he said to him: 'Well now, here is the Duchessa Sanseverina who declares that she is leaving Parma immediately to go and settle in Naples, and who, into the bargain, is making impertinent remarks to me.'

'What!' said Mosca turning pale.

'What! you didn't know of this plan for departure?'

'Not a word; when I left her Grace at six o'clock, she was content and full of gaiety.'

These words had an incredible effect on the Prince. First of all he looked at Mosca, whose increasing pallor showed that he was speaking the truth and was in no way an accomplice in the Duchessa's sudden caprice. 'In that case,' he said to himself, 'she is lost to me for ever; pleasure and vengeance both vanish in a flash. In Naples she and her nephew Fabrizio will make up epigrams on the great fury of the little Prince of Parma.' He looked at the Duchessa; the most violent scorn and anger were contending for possession of her heart; her eyes were fixed at that moment on Conte Mosca, and the delicate curves of that lovely mouth expressed the bitterest disdain. Her whole face seemed to be saying: 'Vile courtier!'

'So,' thought the Prince, after studying her carefully, 'I lose this means of recalling her to my dominions. At this very moment, if she leaves this room, she is lost to me; God knows what she will say about my judges in Naples. And with that intelligence and that divine power of persuasion which heaven has bestowed on her, she will make everybody believe her. Thanks to her, I shall have the reputation of a ridiculous tyrant, who gets up at night to look under his bed ...' Then, by a skilful manoeuvre, and as though he were intending to walk up and down to reduce his agitation, the Prince took up his stand once more in front of the door of his room. The Conte was on his right, at a distance of three paces, pale, discomposed, and trembling so greatly that he was obliged to seek support from the back of the armchair in which the Duchessa had been sitting at the beginning of the audience, and which the Prince in a moment of anger had pushed away from him. The Conte was in love. 'If the Duchessa leaves, I shall follow her,' he was saying to himself. 'But will she want me in her train? That is the question.'

On the Prince's left, the Duchessa, standing with her arms folded and pressed to her bosom, was looking at him with fine impertinence. Complete and intense pallor had taken the place of the vivid colour which a short time before had animated that marvellous face.

The Prince's face, in contrast to those of the other two actors in this scene, had grown red and wore a troubled expression. His left hand fidgeted nervously with the cross attached to the Grand Cordon of his Order which he wore under the coat; with his right hand he stroked his chin.

'What is to be done?' he asked the Conte, without knowing quite what he himself was doing, and carried away by the habit of consulting this man on everything.

'I really don't know, your Serene Highness,' replied the Conte with the air of a man who is giving his last gasp. He could scarcely pronounce the words of his answer. The tone of his voice gave the Prince the first consolation that his wounded pride had received in the course of this audience, and this trifling stroke of luck supplied him with a remark or two that gratified his vanity.

'Well,' he said, 'I am the most sensible of us three. I am willing to set aside all thoughts of my own position in the world. I am going to speak *as a friend*, and,' he added, with a fine smile of condescension, beautifully copied from the happy times of Louis XIV, '*as a friend speaking to friends*. Your Grace,' he went on, 'what is to be done to make you forget this untimely decision?'

'To tell the truth, I don't know of anything,' replied the Duchessa, sighing deeply, 'to tell the truth, I don't know of anything, I have such a horror of Parma.' There was no intention of making an epigram in these words; it was clear that sincerity itself spoke through her lips.

The Conte turned sharply towards her; his courtier's soul was scandalized; then he cast an imploring glance towards the Prince.

With great dignity and composure the Prince allowed a moment to pass, then, addressing the Conte: 'I see,' he said, 'that your charming friend is altogether beside herself; that is quite natural, she *adores* her nephew.' And, turning towards the Duchessa, he added, with a glance of the utmost gallantry and at the same time with the air one assumes when quoting a remark from a play: '*What must one do to find favour in these fair eyes?*'

The Duchessa had had time to reflect. In a slow and steady tone of voice and as if she were dictating her *ultimatum*, she answered: 'Your Highness might write me a gracious letter, as you know so well how to do. In it you would say that, not being at all convinced of the guilt of Fabrizio del Dongo, First Vicar-General of the Archbishop, you will not sign the sentence when it is presented to you, and that these unjust proceedings shall have no consequences in the future.'

'What, *unjust*!' cried the Prince, reddening to the whites of his eyes, and becoming once more furious.

'That is not all,' replied the Duchessa with a Roman pride. '*This very evening*, and,' she added, looking at the clock, 'it is already a quarter past eleven – *this very evening*, your Serene Highness will send word to the Marchesa Raversi that you advise her to retire to the country to recover from the fatigue which must have been caused her by certain judicial proceedings of which she was speaking in her drawing-room in the early hours of this evening.' The Prince was striding up and down the room like a man beside himself with fury.

'Did you ever see such a woman?' he cried. 'She is wanting in respect for me!'

The Duchessa replied with the most perfect grace: 'Never in my life have I had a thought of showing want of respect for your Serene Highness. Your Highness has had the extreme condescension to say that you were speaking *as a friend to friends*. I have, moreover, no desire to remain in Parma,' she added, looking at the Conte with the utmost contempt. That glance decided the Prince, up till then extremely hesitant, although his words might have seemed to hold out some promise of action. He had, however, very little regard for words.

There was still some further discussion, but at length Conte Mosca received orders to write the gracious note solicited by the Duchessa. He omitted the sentence: *these unjust proceedings shall have no consequences in the future*. 'It is enough,' said the Conte to himself, 'if the

Prince promises not to sign the sentence which will be laid before him.' The Prince thanked him with a quick glance as he signed.

The Conte was greatly mistaken. The Prince was tired out, and would have signed anything. He considered he was getting well out of the difficulty and the whole business was overshadowed in his eyes by the thought: 'If the Duchessa leaves, I shall find my court boring in less than a week.' The Conte noticed that his master revised the date, and replaced it by that of the following day. He looked at the clock; it pointed almost to midnight. The Minister saw nothing more in this correction of the date than a pedantic desire to show a proof of exactitude and good government. As for the banishment of the Marchesa Raversi, he made no objection; the Prince took a particular delight in banishing people.

'General Fontana,' he called out, opening the door a little way.

The General appeared with a face showing so much astonishment and curiosity, that a swift glance of amusement was exchanged between the Duchessa and the Conte, and this glance made peace between them.

'General Fontana,' said the Prince, 'you will get into my carriage, which is waiting under the colonnade; you will go to the Marchesa Raversi's house, you will send in your name. If she is in bed, you will add that you come from me, and on entering her room you will say these precise words and no others: "Your Ladyship the Marchesa Raversi, His Serene Highness requests you to leave tomorrow morning, before eight o'clock, for your country house at Velleia. His Highness will let you know when you may return to Parma.'

The Prince's eyes sought those of the Duchessa, who, without thanking him, as he had expected, made him an extremely respectful curtsey, and swept quickly out of the room.

'What a woman!' said the Prince, turning to Conte Mosca.

The latter, highly delighted at the banishment of the Marchesa Raversi, which allowed him greater ease in his ministerial activities, talked for a full half-hour like a consummate courtier. He was anxious to console his Sovereign's wounded self-respect, and did not take his leave until he had convinced him that the historical anecdotes of Louis XIV included no fairer page than that which he had just provided for his future historians.

On reaching home the Duchessa shut her doors, and gave orders that no one was to be admitted, not even the Conte. She wished to be left alone with herself, and to consider for a little what idea she ought to form of the scene that had just occurred. She had acted at random and for her own immediate pleasure; but whatever action she had been induced to take, she would have clung to it firmly. She would not have blamed herself on regaining her composure, still less repented of what she had done. Such was the character to which she owed the position of being still, at the age of thirty-six, the prettiest woman at the court.

She was dreaming at that moment of what Parma might have to offer in the way of attractions, as she might have done on returning after a long journey, so firmly convinced had she been, from nine o'clock till eleven, that she was leaving this place for ever.

'That poor Conte,' she thought, 'cut a really comical figure when he learnt of my departure in the Prince's presence. ... After all, he is a likeable man and with a rare kindness of heart! He would have given up his Ministries to follow me. ... But on the other hand, for five whole years he has not had any lack of attention on my part to complain of. How many women married before the altar could say as much to their lords and masters? It must be admitted that he is not at all self-important, nothing of a pedant; he gives one no desire to be unfaithful to him; when he is with me he always seems to be ashamed of his power ... He cut a funny figure in the presence of his lord and master; if he were here now, I should give him a kiss ... But nothing on earth would make me undertake to amuse a minister who had lost his portfolio; that is a malady which only death can cure, and ... one that kills. What a misfortune it would be to become a Minister when you are young! I must write to him; it is one of the things he should know officially before he quarrels with his Prince ... But I was forgetting my good servants.'

The Duchessa rang. Her women were still busy packing trunks; the carriage had been driven round to the portico, and was being loaded; all the servants who had no work to do were gathered round this carriage, with tears in their eyes. Cecchina, who, on great occasions, had the sole right to enter the Duchessa's room, told her all these details.

'Tell them to come upstairs,' said the Duchessa. A moment later she went into the anteroom.

'I have been promised,' she told them, 'that the sentence passed on my nephew will never be signed by the Sovereign [this is the term

used in Italy]. I am postponing my departure. We shall see whether
my enemies will have enough influence to get this decision altered.'

After a moment's silence the servants began to shout: 'Long live
our lady the Duchessa!' and to clap their hands furiously. The
Duchessa, who had gone into the next room, reappeared like an
actress taking a curtain call, dropped a little curtsey full of grace to
her people and said to them: *My friends, I thank you.* Had she said a
word, all of them, at that moment, would have marched on the
Palace to attack it. She beckoned to a postilion, a former smuggler
and a most devoted servant, who followed her.

'You will dress yourself as a countryman in easy circumstances,
you will get out of Parma as best you can, you will hire a *sediola* and
go as quickly as possible to Bologna. You will enter Bologna as if
you were paying a casual visit, and by the Florence gate, and you
will deliver to Fabrizio, who is at the Pellegrino, a packet which
Cecchina will give you. Fabrizio is in hiding and is known there as
Signor Giuseppe Bossi. Don't go and give him away by any thoughtless action; don't appear to know him; my enemies may set spies
upon your tracks. Fabrizio will send you back here in a few hours or
in a few days; it is particularly on your way back that you must take
extra precautions not to give him away.'

'Ah! the Marchesa Raversi's people!' exclaimed the postilion.
'We are on the look-out for them, and if your Grace wished they
would soon be exterminated.'

'Some day, perhaps! but beware, on your life, of doing anything
without my orders.'

It was a copy of the Prince's note that the Duchessa wished to
send to Fabrizio. She could not resist the pleasure of giving him
amusement, and added a word or two about the scene which had
led up to the note. This word or two became a letter of ten pages.
She sent for the postilion again.

'You cannot start,' she said, 'before four o'clock, when the gates are
opened.'

'I was thinking of going out by the main conduit. I should be up
to my chin in water, but I should get through ...'

'No,' said the Duchessa, 'I do not wish to expose one of my most
faithful servants to the risk of catching fever. Do you know anyone
in the Archbishop's household?'

'The second coachman is a friend of mine.'

'Here is a letter for that saintly prelate: skip quietly into his Palace, get them to take you to his valet; I do not wish His Grace to be awakened. If he has already retired to his room, spend the night in his Palace, and, as he is in the habit of getting up at daybreak, tomorrow morning, at four o'clock, have yourself announced as coming from me, ask the holy Archbishop for his blessing, hand him the packet you see here, and take any letters that he may possibly give you to Bologna.'

The Duchessa was sending the Archbishop the actual original of the Prince's note; as this note concerned his chief Vicar-General she begged him to deposit it among the archives of the Palace, where she hoped that their Reverences the Vicars-General and the Canons, her nephew's colleagues, would be good enough to take cognizance of it – all this under seal of the utmost secrecy.

The Duchessa wrote to Monsignore Landriani with a familiarity that could not fail to please this worthy commoner. The signature alone took up three lines; the letter, written in a very friendly tone, was followed by the words: *'Angelina-Cornelia-Isola Valserra del Dongo, Duchessa Sanseverina.'*

'I don't believe I have written my name at such length,' thought the Duchessa laughing, 'since my marriage contract with the poor Duca. But one only gets an influence over these people by things like that, and in the eyes of the middle classes exaggeration passes for beauty.'

She could not let the evening pass without yielding to the temptation to write a chaffing letter to the poor Conte. She announced to him officially for his *guidance*, so she said, *in relations with crowned heads*, that she did not feel herself to be capable of amusing a Minister in disgrace. 'The Prince frightens you,' she wrote. 'When you are no longer able to see him, will it then be my business to frighten you?' She had this letter taken to him at once.

The Prince, for his part, on the stroke of seven o'clock the next morning, sent for Conte Zurla, the Minister of the Interior.

'Once more,' he said to him, 'give the most stringent orders to all the local magistrates to arrest Fabrizio del Dongo. We have been informed that possibly he may dare to reappear in our States. This fugitive being now in Bologna, where he seems to defy the judgements of our courts of law, post police officers who know him by sight: (i) in the villages along the road from Bologna to Parma; (ii) in the neighbourhood of the Duchessa Sanseverina's country house at Sacca, and of her villa at Castelnuovo; (iii) round Conte Mosca's residence. I venture to hope from your great sagacity, my dear Conte, that you will manage to conceal all knowledge of these, your Sovereign's orders, from Conte Mosca's penetrating eye. Understand that I wish to have Signor Fabrizio del Dongo arrested.'

As soon as this Minister had left him, a secret door introduced into the Prince's presence Chief Justice Rassi, who came towards him bent double, and bowing at every step. This rascal's face was a picture; it did full justice to the infamy of the part he played and, while the rapid and ill-controlled movements of his eyes betrayed his consciousness of his own merits, the arrogant and self-confident grin on his lips revealed that he knew how to put up a fight against scorn.

As this personage is going to exercise considerable influence over Fabrizio's destiny, we may say a word about him here. He was tall, he had fine and extremely shrewd eyes, but a face that was marked by smallpox. As for intelligence, he had it in plenty, and of the keenest sort; it was admitted that he had a perfect knowledge of the law, but it was by his gift of resourcefulness that he chiefly shone. In whatever way a case might be presented to him he easily, and in a few moments, discovered very sound legal means of arriving either at a conviction or an acquittal. He was above all things past-master in the subtleties of a prosecutor's logic.

In this man, whom great monarchs might have envied the Prince of Parma, one passion only was known to exist – to have familiar intercourse with great personages and to please them with buffooneries. It mattered little to him whether the powerful personage laughed at what he said, or at his own person, or made revolting jokes about Signora Rassi; provided that he saw him laugh and was himself treated as a familiar acquaintance, he was satisfied. Sometimes the Prince, not knowing how to insult the dignity of this great judge any further, would give him a kick or two; if the kicks hurt him, he would begin to cry. But the instinct of buffoonery was so strong in him that he might be seen every day preferring the drawing-room of a Minister who scoffed at him to his own drawing-room where he exercised despotic sway over the whole of the black-robed profession in the district. This fellow Rassi had above all made for himself a peculiar position, in that it was impossible for the most insolent noble to manage to humiliate him. His method of avenging himself for the insults he suffered the whole day long was to retail them to the Prince, in whose presence he had acquired the privilege of saying anything. It is true that the Prince's answer often took the form of a well-applied box on the ear, which hurt him, but he never took any exception to that. The presence of this great judge used to distract the Prince in his moments of ill-temper; then he amused himself by insulting him outrageously. It can be seen that Rassi was almost the perfect man for a court: without a sense of honour or of humour.

'Secrecy is above all things essential,' the Prince cried out to him without bidding him welcome, and treating him, although usually so courteous to everyone, as if he were nothing but some low fellow of no account. 'From when is your sentence dated?'

'From yesterday morning, your Serene Highness.'

'How many of the judges signed it?'

'All five.'

'And the penalty?'

'Twenty years in a fortress, as your Serene Highness told me.'

'The death penalty would have horrified people,' said the Prince as if speaking to himself. 'It's a pity! What an effect on that woman! But he is a del Dongo, and this name is revered in Parma, on account of the three Archbishops almost following each other ... You say twenty years in a fortress?'

'Yes, your Serene Highness,' replied Rassi, still standing and bent double, 'with, first of all, a public apology before your Serene Highness's portrait; and, in addition, fasting on a diet of bread and water every Friday, and on the eve of all the principal festivals, *the person concerned being notorious for his impiety*. This with a view to the future and in order to wreck his career.'

'Write this,' said the Prince: '"His Serene Highness having deigned to grant a gracious hearing to the most humble supplications of the Marchesa del Dongo, mother of the culprit, and of the Duchessa Sanseverina, his aunt, which ladies have represented to him that at the period of the crime their son and nephew was very young, and moreover led astray by a mad passion conceived for the wife of the unfortunate Giletti, has been graciously pleased, notwithstanding the horror inspired by such a murder, to commute the penalty to which Fabrizio del Dongo has been sentenced to that of twelve years in a fortress." Now give it to me to sign.'

The Prince signed the paper and dated it from the previous day. Then, handing the sentence back to Rassi, he said to him: 'Write immediately beneath my signature: "The Duchessa Sanseverina having once more cast herself at His Highness's feet, the Prince has given permission that every Thursday the prisoner may take exercise for one hour on the platform of the square tower, commonly known as the Farnese Tower."

'Sign that,' said the Prince, 'and mind you keep your mouth shut, whatever you may hear said in the city. You will tell Councillor De Capitani, who voted for two years in a fortress, and even held forth in support of this ridiculous opinion, that I advise him to read over the laws and regulations. Once again silence, and good-night to you.' With great deliberation, Chief Justice Rassi made three deep bows to which the Prince paid no attention.

This took place at seven o'clock in the morning. A few hours later the news of the Marchesa Raversi's banishment spread through the city and the cafés; everyone was talking at once of this important event. The Marchesa's banishment drove away for some little time from Parma that implacable enemy of little towns and little courts, known as boredom. General Fabio Conti, who had looked upon himself as already Prime Minister, feigned an attack of gout and did not set foot outside his fortress. Middle-class citizens, and consequently the common people, concluded from what was happening that it was clear that the Prince had decided to confer the Archbishopric of Parma on Monsignore del Dongo. The astute politicians of the cafés went so far as to assert that Father Landriani, the present Archbishop, had been advised to feign a serious illness and to send in his resignation; he was, they were sure of it, to be awarded a fat pension, charged on the tobacco duties. This rumour reached the Archbishop himself, who was greatly perturbed by it, and for several days his zeal for our hero was considerably paralysed. Two months later this fine piece of news appeared in the Paris newspapers, with the slight alteration that it was Conte Mosca, the nephew of the Duchessa Sanseverina, who was to be made Archbishop.

The Marchesa Raversi meanwhile was in a terrific rage in her country house at Velleia. She was by no means one of those weak little women who think they can avenge themselves by pouring out violent abuse against their enemies. The very day after her disgrace, Cavaliere Riscara and three more of her friends presented themselves before the Prince at her orders, and asked him for permission to go to visit her at her house in the country. His Highness received these gentlemen with the utmost graciousness, and their arrival at Velleia was a great consolation to the Marchesa.

Before the end of the second week she had thirty people in her house, all those who were to obtain office under a Liberal government. Every evening, the Marchesa held a regular council with the better informed of her friends. One day, on which she had received a number of letters from Parma and Bologna, she retired to bed early. Her favourite maid let into her room, first of all the reigning lover, Conte Baldi, a young man of very handsome appearance and complete insignificance, and, later on, Cavaliere Riscara, his predecessor. The latter was a little man, with a soul as dark as his visage, who having begun by being a teacher of geometry at the College of Nobles in Parma, now found himself a Councillor of State and Knight of several Orders.

'I have the good habit,' said the Marchesa to these two men, 'of never destroying any paper, and this is lucky for me. Here are nine letters that woman Sanseverina has written to me on different occasions. You will both of you set off for Genoa; you will look for an ex-notary among the convicts there, named Burati, like the great Venetian poet, or else Durati. You, Conte Baldi, sit down at my writing-table and write what I am going to dictate to you.

' "An idea has just occurred to me, and I am writing you these few lines. I am going to my cottage near Castelnuovo. If you would care to come over and spend a day with me, I shall be very delighted. There is, it seems to me, no great danger after what has just happened; the clouds are clearing away. All the same, stop before you enter Castelnuovo. You will meet one of my servants on the road; they are all madly devoted to you. You will, of course, keep the name Bossi for this little expedition. I am told you have grown a beard like the most perfect Capuchin, and no one has seen you in Parma except with the countenance becoming a Vicar-General." You understand, Riscara?'

'Perfectly; but the trip to Genoa is an unnecessary extravagance. I know a man in Parma who, in actual fact, has not yet been sent to the galleys, but cannot fail to get there. He will counterfeit the Sanseverina's writing to perfection.'

At these words, Conte Baldi opened those fine eyes of his inordinately wide. He had only just begun to understand.

'If you know this worthy personage of Parma, whose interests you hope to advance,' said the Marchesa to Riscara, 'presumably he knows you too. His mistress, his confessor, his best friend may be bought by that woman Sanseverina. I should prefer to delay this little jest for a few days, and not to expose myself to any risks. Start in a couple of hours like two good little lambs, don't see a living soul in Genoa, and come back very quickly.' Cavaliere Riscara made off laughing, and speaking through his nose like Punchinello. 'I must pack my traps,' he said as he skipped away in a burlesque fashion. He wished to leave Baldi alone with the lady.

Five days later, Riscara brought the Marchesa back her Conte Baldi, extremely stiff and sore. To cut off six leagues, they had made him cross a mountain astride a mule; he vowed that no one would ever persuade him to make any more *long journeys*. Baldi handed the Marchesa three copies of the letter she had dictated to him, and five or six other letters in the same hand, composed by Riscara, which might perhaps be put to some advantage later on. One of these letters contained some very pretty jests with regard to the fears the Prince felt at night, and on the lamentable thinness of the Marchesa Balbi, his mistress, who left, so it was said, a mark like the dint of a pair of tongs on the cushions of an armchair after she had sat in it for a moment. One would have sworn that all these letters had been written by the hand of the Duchessa Sanseverina herself.

'Now I know, beyond any doubt,' said the Marchesa, 'that the favoured lover, Fabrizio, is either in Bologna or in the immediate neighbourhood ...'

'I am too unwell,' cried Conte Baldi, interrupting her. 'I ask as a favour to be excused this second journey, or at least I should like to be given a few days' rest to recover my health.'

'I will plead your cause,' said Riscara. He rose and spoke in an undertone to the Marchesa.

'Oh, very well, I agree,' she answered smiling. 'Don't worry, you won't have to go,' said the Marchesa to Baldi, with a certain air of contempt.

'Thank you,' he cried in heartfelt accents.

Riscara, in fact, got into a post-chaise by himself. He had scarcely been a couple of days in Bologna when he caught sight of Fabrizio and little Marietta out riding in a barouche. 'I'll be damned!' he said to himself, 'our future Archbishop doesn't apparently trouble to keep up appearances. We shall have to let the Duchessa know about this, she will be charmed to hear it.' Riscara had only to follow Fabrizio to discover his address. The next morning our hero received through the post the letter fabricated in Genoa; he thought it a trifle short, but otherwise suspected nothing. The thought of seeing the Duchessa and the Conte again made him wildly happy, and in spite of anything Lodovico might say, he took a post-horse and went off at a gallop. Without his knowing it, he was followed at a short distance by Cavaliere Riscara, who, on arriving at the stage before Castelnuovo, some six leagues away from Parma, had the pleasure of seeing a great crowd of people on the square outside the local prison. They had just led in our hero, recognized at the post-house, as he was changing horses, by two police officers who had been selected and sent there by Conte Zurla.

Cavaliere Riscara's little eyes sparkled with joy. With the most exemplary patience, he checked the facts of everything that had occurred in this little village, then sent a courier off to the Marchesa Raversi. After this, strolling through the streets as though to visit the very interesting church, and then to look for a picture by Parmigianino which, so he had been told, was to be found in that place, he finally ran into the *podestà* [local magistrate], who hastened to pay his respect to a Councillor of State. Riscara appeared surprised that he had not immediately despatched to the citadel of Parma the conspirator he had had the good fortune to have arrested.

'There is reason to fear,' added Riscara coldly, 'that his many friends who were looking for him the day before yesterday to facilitate his passage through the States of His Serene Highness, may come up against the police. These rebels numbered quite twelve or fifteen, all mounted.'

'*Intelligenti pauca!*' cried the *podestà* with a knowing air.

CHAPTER 15: *The Citadel of Parma*

Two hours later, poor Fabrizio, fitted with handcuffs and attached by a long chain to the actual *sediola* into which he had been thrust, set off for the citadel of Parma, with an escort of eight constables. These had orders to bring with them all the constables stationed in the villages through which the procession had to pass; the *podestà* himself followed this important prisoner. About seven o'clock in the evening the *sediola*, escorted by all the street urchins in Parma and by thirty constables, drove across the fine public promenade, passed in front of the little palazzo in which Fausta had been living a few months earlier, and finally presented itself at the outer gate of the citadel just as General Fabio Conti and his daughter were on the point of coming out. The governor's carriage pulled up before reaching the drawbridge to allow the *sediola* to which Fabrizio was attached to enter. The General immediately called out orders to close the gates of the citadel, and hurried down to the porter's lodge to get some idea of what it was all about. He was not a little surprised when he recognized the prisoner, who had grown quite stiff after being fastened to his *sediola* during such a long journey; four constables had lifted him down and were carrying him into the turnkey's office. 'So I have in my power,' thought the self-important governor, 'that famous Fabrizio del Dongo, with whom one would say that for the past year high society in Parma had vowed to concern itself exclusively!'

The General had met him a score of times at court, at the Duchessa's and elsewhere; but he took good care not to show any sign that he knew him; he would have been afraid of compromising himself.

'Have drawn up,' he called out to the prison clerk, 'a fully detailed report of the prisoner's delivery into my hands by the worthy *podestà* of Castelnuovo.'

Barbone, the clerk, a most terrifying personage on account of his enormous beard and his military appearance, assumed an air of even greater importance than usual; he might have been taken for a German gaoler. Thinking he knew that it was chiefly the Duchessa Sanseverina who had prevented his master, the Governor, from becoming Minister of War, he behaved with a more than ordinary insolence towards this prisoner, addressing him in the second person plural, which in Italy is the form one uses in speaking to servants.

'I am a prelate of the Holy Roman Church,' Fabrizio said to him firmly, 'and Vicar-General of this diocese; my birth alone entitles me to respect.'

'I know nothing about that!' replied the clerk impertinently. 'Prove your assertions by showing the patents which give you a right to those very respectable titles.'

Fabrizio had no patents and did not answer him. General Fabio Conti, standing beside his clerk, watched him write without raising his eyes to look at the prisoner, so as not to be obliged to admit that he really was Fabrizio del Dongo.

Suddenly Clelia Conti, who was waiting in the carriage, heard a terrific uproar in the guard-room. The clerk, Barbone, in making an insolent and extremely lengthy description of the prisoner's person, had ordered him to undo his clothing so as to verify and note down the number and condition of the slight wounds received by him in his fight with Giletti.

'I cannot,' said Fabrizio, smiling bitterly. 'I am not in a position to obey the gentleman's orders; these handcuffs prevent me from doing so.'

'What!' cried the General with an air of innocence, 'the prisoner is handcuffed! Inside the fortress! That is contrary to regulations; it requires a special order. Remove his handcuffs.'

Fabrizio looked at him. 'Here's a pretty Jesuit,' he thought. 'For the last hour he has seen me with these handcuffs which are hurting me horribly, and he pretends to be surprised!'

The handcuffs were taken off by the constables. They had just learnt that Fabrizio was the nephew of the Duchessa Sanseverina, and hastened to show him a honeyed politeness which contrasted with the rudeness of the clerk. The latter seemed annoyed by this and said to Fabrizio, who stood there without moving: 'Now then, hurry up! Show us those scratches you received from poor Giletti at the time of his murder.'

With a single bound, Fabrizio sprang upon the clerk and gave him such a box on the ear that Barbone fell from his chair against the General's legs. The constables seized hold of Fabrizio's arms, while he remained there motionless. The General himself, and two constables who were standing by him, hastened to pick up the clerk, whose face was streaming with blood. Two other constables who stood farther off ran to shut the door of the office, thinking that the prisoner was trying to escape. The sergeant in command of them thought that young del Dongo could not make any serious attempt at flight, since after all he happened to be inside the citadel; all the same, prompted by his professional instincts, he went up to the window to prevent any disorder. Opposite this open window and a foot or two away from it, the General's carriage was drawn up. Clelia had shrunk back inside it, so as not to be a witness of the painful scene that was being enacted in the office; when she heard all this noise, she looked out.

'What is happening?' she asked the sergeant.

'Signorina, it is young Fabrizio del Dongo, who has just given that insolent Barbone a fine box on the ear!'

'What! it is Signor del Dongo whom they are taking to prison?'

'Why, for sure,' said the sergeant. 'It's on account of the poor young man's noble birth that they're making all this fuss. I thought the Signorina knew all about it.'

Clelia could not draw herself away from the carriage window. Whenever the constables who were standing round the table moved aside a little she could see the prisoner. 'Who would have said,' she thought, 'when I met him on the road to the Lake of Como, that I should meet him again for the first time in such a sad situation! ... He gave me his hand to help me into his mother's carriage ... He was even then in the Duchessa's company! Had their love affair already begun at that time?'

The reader should be informed that among the Liberal party, led by the Marchesa Raversi and General Conti, people affected to have no doubts as to the tender relations presumed to exist between Fabrizio and the Duchessa. Conte Mosca, whom they abhorred, was the object of endless pleasantries on account of his gullibility.

'So,' thought Clelia, 'there he is a prisoner, and a prisoner in the hands of his enemies. For after all Conte Mosca, however much one would like to think him an angel, will be delighted at this capture.'

A loud burst of laughter came from the guard-room.

'Jacopo,' she said to the sergeant, in a voice that trembled with emotion, 'whatever is happening?'

'The General asked the prisoner sharply why he had struck Barbone. Monsignore Fabrizio answered coldly: "He called me an *assassin*; let him produce the titles and patents which authorize him to give me that title." And everyone laughed.'

A gaoler who could write took Barbone's place. Clelia saw the latter emerge, mopping the blood that streamed in abundance from his hideous face with his handkerchief, and swearing like a trooper. 'That b — Fabrizio,' he shouted at the top of his voice, 'will never die but by my hand. I'll cheat the hangman,' and so on and so forth. He had stopped between the window and the General's carriage, and his oaths redoubled in volume.

'Shove off,' said the sergeant. 'You mustn't swear like that in front of the Signorina.'

Barbone raised his head to look into the carriage, his eyes met Clelia's and a cry of horror escaped her; never had she seen at such close range so atrocious an expression on anyone's face. 'He will kill Fabrizio!' she said to herself. 'I shall have to warn Don Cesare.' This was her uncle, one of the most respected priests in the city. General Conti, his brother, had obtained for him the post of steward and principal chaplain to the prison.

The General got back into his carriage. 'Would you rather go home,' he said to his daughter, 'or wait for me, perhaps for some long time, in the courtyard of the Palace? I must go and report all this to the Sovereign.'

Fabrizio was just coming out of the office escorted by three constables; they were taking him to the room which had been allotted to him. Clelia looked out of the carriage window, the prisoner was quite close to her. At that moment she answered her father's question with the words: '*I will go with you.*' Fabrizio, hearing these words uttered so close to him, raised his eyes and met the young girl's glance. He was particularly struck by the expression of melancholy on her face. 'How much more beautiful she has grown,' he thought, 'since our meeting near Como! What an air of deep thoughtfulness! ... People are right to compare her with the Duchessa. What an angelic face!'

Barbone, the blood-bespattered clerk, who had not taken up his stand beside the carriage without a purpose, with a wave of his hand stopped the three constables who were leading Fabrizio away, and, slipping round the back of the carriage so as to reach the window next which the General was sitting, said to him: 'As the prisoner has committed an act of violence within the precincts of the citadel, would it not be fitting, in virtue of Article 157 of the regulations, to put the handcuffs on him for three days?'

'Go to the devil!' cried the General, still considerably worried about this arrest. It was essential not to drive either the Duchessa or the Conte to extreme measures and besides, what interpretation would the Conte put on this affair? After all, the murder of a man like Giletti was a mere trifle, and intrigue alone had contrived to make it something of importance.

During this short dialogue Fabrizio stood superb amidst these constables. Nothing could have been prouder or nobler than his bearing. His delicate, clear-cut features, and the smile of disdain that hovered on his lips, made a charming contrast with the coarse appearance of the constables standing round him. But all this formed, so to speak, only the outward, superficial side of his expression; he was enraptured by the heavenly beauty of Clelia, and his eyes betrayed all his surprise. She herself, sunk in reverie, had not thought of withdrawing her head from the window. He bowed to her with a half-smile of the deepest respect; then, after a moment, said to her: 'It seems to me, Signorina, that long ago, near a lake, I have already had the honour of meeting you in the company of the police.'

Clelia blushed, and was so taken aback that she could not think of a single word in reply. 'How noble he looks amongst those coarse fellows,' she had been saying to herself at the moment when Fabrizio spoke. The deep pity, and we might almost say the tender emotion that overwhelmed her, deprived her of the presence of mind necessary to find any form of words whatever. She became conscious of her silence and blushed all the more deeply. At this moment the bolts of the great gate of the citadel were drawn back with a reverberating din; had not his Excellency's carriage been kept waiting for at least a minute? The noise was so loud beneath this vaulted roof that even if Clelia could have found something to say in reply Fabrizio could not have heard what she was saying.

Whirled away by the horses, which had broken into a gallop immediately after crossing the drawbridge, Clelia said to herself: 'He must have thought me very silly!' Then suddenly she added: 'Not only silly; he must have seen in me a very mean soul, he must have thought that I did not respond to his greeting because he is a prisoner and I am the governor's daughter.'

Such an idea made this naturally high-minded girl feel utterly dejected. 'What makes my behaviour absolutely degrading,' she went on, 'is that formerly, when we met each other for the first time, also *in the company of the police*, as he said just now, it was I who was the prisoner, and he did me a service and helped me out of a very awkward situation ... Yes, I must acknowledge it, my behaviour was the absolute limit, it was both rude and ungrateful. Alas, poor young fellow! Now that he is in trouble, everybody will be disagreeable to him. He did indeed say to me at that time: "Will you remember my name in Parma?" How he must be despising me at this moment! It would have been so easy to say a civil word! Yes, I must admit, my conduct towards him has been frightful. Long ago, but for the generous offer of his mother's carriage, I should have had to follow the constables on foot through the dust, or, what would have been far worse, ride pillion behind one of those men. It was my father then who was under arrest and I who was defenceless! Yes, my behaviour was utterly shocking. And how keenly a nature like his must have felt it! What a contrast between his noble features and my behaviour! What nobility! What serenity! How like a hero he looked, surrounded by his vile enemies! Now I understand the Duchessa's passion for him. If he is like that in a distressing situation and one that may have fearful consequences, what must he be like when he has a happy heart!'

The governor's carriage waited for more than an hour and a half in the courtyard of the Palace, and yet, when the General came down from his interview with the Prince, Clelia by no means felt that he had stayed there too long.

'What is His Highness's will?' asked Clelia.

'His lips said: "Prison!" and his eyes: "Death!" '

'Death! Good God!' exclaimed Clelia.

'Come now, hold your tongue!' said the General angrily. 'What a fool I am to answer a child's questions!'

Meanwhile Fabrizio was climbing the three hundred and eighty steps that led up to the Farnese Tower, a new prison built on the platform of the great tower, at a tremendous height from the ground. He never once thought, at least not explicitly, of the great change that had just occurred in his fortunes. 'What eyes!' he was saying to himself. 'How many things they expressed! What depths of pity! She looked as though she were saying: "Life is such a tangled web of misfortunes! Do not grieve too much over what happens to you!

Are we not placed here below to be unhappy?" How those lovely eyes of hers remained fastened on me, even when the horses were moving forward with such a clatter under the archway!'

Fabrizio completely forgot to feel miserable.

Clelia accompanied her father to various receptions. In the early part of the evening no one had yet heard the news of the arrest of the *great culprit*, for such was the name which the courtiers bestowed a couple of hours later on this poor, rash young man.

People noticed that evening that there was more animation than usual in Clelia's face. Now animation, the air of taking part in what was going on around her, was just what was chiefly lacking in this fair creature. When people compared her beauty with that of the Duchessa it was particularly that air of not being moved by anything, that manner of being as it were superior to everything, which inclined the balance in her rival's favour. In England or in France, those native homes of vanity, the opposite opinion would probably have prevailed. Clelia Conti was a young woman still a thought too slim and one who might have been compared to the exquisite figures of Guido Reni. We will not conceal the fact that according to Greek ideas of beauty, the objection might have been made that her face had certain features a little too strongly marked; her lips, for instance, though full of the most appealing charm, were all the same a trifle thick.

The delightful peculiarity of this face, distinguished by its artless grace and the heavenly imprint of a most noble soul, was that, although of the rarest and most singular beauty, it in no way resembled the heads of old Greek statues. The Duchessa, on the other hand, had a little too much of the *recognized* ideal type of beauty, and her truly Lombard head recalled the voluptuous smile and the tender melancholy of Leonardo da Vinci's lovely pictures of Herodias. Just as the Duchessa was sparkling, brimming over with lively and even mischievous wit, attaching herself passionately, if one may so express it, to every subject which the course of conversation presented to her mind's eye, so Clelia, to an equal extent, showed herself calm and slow in expressing or feeling emotion, whether out of disdain for what was going on around her, or out of regret for some departed dream. It had long been thought that she would end by embracing the religious life. At twenty she was observed to show some marked reluctance to attend balls, and if she accompanied her father to such entertainments it was only out of obedience to him and in order not to prejudice the interests of his ambitious dreams.

'So it is going to be impossible for me,' the vulgar-minded General would often say to himself, 'though heaven has given me as a daughter the most beautiful person in our Sovereign's dominions, and the most virtuous, to reap any advantage from it for the advancement of my career! I live in too great isolation, I have only her in the whole world, and I urgently need a family which will give me some social support, and procure me an entry into a certain number of fashionable drawing-rooms, where my merit and above all my aptitude for ministerial office would be established as unchallengeable grounds in any political argument. Well now, my daughter, beautiful, wise, and devout as she is, turns petulant whenever any young man in a good position at court attempts to win her favour. Once this suitor is dismissed, her temper becomes less moody, and I find her almost gay, until another would-be husband enters the lists. The handsomest man at court, Conte Baldi, presented himself and failed to please her; the richest man in his Highness's dominions, the Marchese Crescenzi, has now succeeded him; she declares he would make her miserable.

'Most certainly,' the General would say at other times, 'my daughter's eyes are finer than the Duchessa's, particularly as, on rare occasions, they are capable of assuming an expression of greater depth. But this exquisite expression of hers, when is it ever to be seen? Never in a drawing-room where it might do her credit, but rather out driving alone with me, when she will let herself be moved, for instance, to pity the sad state of some hideous churl. "Keep some trace of that sublime expression," I tell her at times, "for the drawing-rooms in which we shall be appearing tonight." Not a bit of it; if she condescends to go out with me into society, her pure and noble face assumes the rather haughty and somewhat discouraging expression of passive obedience.' The General, as can be seen, spared no attempts to find himself a suitable son-in-law; but what he said was true.

Courtiers, who have nothing worth looking at in their own souls, take careful notice of everything outside them. They had observed that it was particularly on those days when Clelia could not succeed in rousing herself from her beloved dreams and feigning interest in something or other that the Duchessa would choose to linger near her and try to make her talk. Clelia had light auburn hair, that stood out, in very soft relief, against the delicate colouring of cheeks that were, as a rule, a trifle too pale. The mere shape of her brow might have told an attentive observer that that very noble air, that demeanour so far above all kinds of vulgar grace, sprang from a profound indifference to everything that was commonplace or mean. It was the absence and not the impossibility of interest in anything.

From the time her father had become governor of the citadel Clelia had lived happily, or at least free from any sort of annoyance, in her lofty dwelling. The appalling number of steps that had to be climbed in order to reach the governor's palatial residence, standing on the platform of the great tower, kept away tiresome visitors, and Clelia, for this concrete reason, enjoyed a quite conventual freedom. She found there almost all the ideal of happiness which at one time she had thought of seeking in the religious life. She was filled with a sort of horror at the mere idea of placing her beloved solitude and her inmost thoughts at the disposal of a young man whom the title of husband would authorize to disturb all this inner life. If by solitude she did not attain to happiness, at least she had succeeded in avoiding sensations that would have been too painful.

On the day on which Fabrizio was taken to the fortress, the Duchessa met Clelia at the evening party given by the Minister of the Interior, Conte Zurla. Everyone gathered round them; that evening Clelia's beauty outshone the Duchessa's. There was a look in the girl's lovely eyes so strange and so profound as to make them almost indiscreet. There was pity, there was indignation, and anger too, in her gaze. The Duchessa's gaiety and her brilliant ideas seemed to plunge Clelia into sudden spells of distress that almost amounted to horror.

'What will be the cries and groans of this poor woman,' she thought, 'when she learns that her lover, that young man with so great a heart and so noble a countenance, has just been flung into prison! And that look in the Sovereign's eyes which condemns him to death! O absolute Power, when wilt thou cease to lie heavy upon Italy! O vile and mercenary souls! And I am the daughter of a gaoler! And I did nothing to contradict that noble character when I did not deign to reply to Fabrizio! And once he was my benefactor! What will he be thinking of me at this moment, alone in his room with no company save his little lamp!' Revolted by this idea, Clelia cast a look of horror at the magnificent illumination of the drawing-rooms of the Minister of the Interior.

'Never,' so they were saying to each other in the circle of courtiers who had gathered round the two reigning beauties and were seeking to join in the conversation, 'never have they talked to each other in so animated and at the same time so intimate a fashion. Can it be that the Duchessa, who is always bent on dispelling the animosities aroused by the Prime Minister, has thought of some great marriage for Clelia?' This conjecture was supported by a circumstance which until then had never presented itself to the notice of the court; the girl's eyes had more fire, and even, if one may say so, more passion than those of the beautiful Duchessa. The latter, for her part, was astonished, and, one may say it to her credit, delighted, by the discovery of charms so novel in the young recluse. For an hour she had been gazing at her with a pleasure that is fairly seldom felt at the sight of a rival.

'Why, what can have happened?' the Duchessa wondered. 'Never has Clelia looked so beautiful, and, one might say, so touching. Can it be that her heart has spoken? ... But in that case, certainly, it is an unhappy love, some dark grief lies beneath this new-found animation ... But unhappy love keeps silent! Can it be a question of recalling an inconstant lover by making a social success?' And the Duchessa gazed attentively at all the young men standing round them. Nowhere could she see any peculiar expression on the part of anyone, everywhere she saw the same appearance of more or less self-satisfied complacency. 'But there is some miracle here,' thought the Duchessa, vexed by her inability to discover the truth. 'Where is that very shrewd man, Conte Mosca? No, I am not mistaken, Clelia is looking at me closely, and as if I were for her the object of a quite new interest. Is it the result of some order given by that base courtier, her father? I thought that young and noble mind incapable of lowering itself to matters of pecuniary interest. Can General Fabio Conti have some decisive request to make to the Conte?'

About ten o'clock, a friend of the Duchessa came up to her and whispered a few words; she turned extremely pale; Clelia took her hand and ventured to press it.

'I thank you, and I understand you now ... You have a noble heart!' said the Duchessa, making an effort to keep control of herself; she had scarcely strength to utter these few words. She smiled profusely at the lady of the house, who rose to escort her to the door of the outermost drawing-room. Such honours were due only to Princesses of the Blood Royal, and were for the Duchessa in cruel contradiction to her position at the moment. She therefore continued to smile profusely at Contessa Zurla, but in spite of desperate efforts she could not succeed in saying a single word to her.

Clelia's eyes filled with tears as she watched the Duchessa pass through these rooms, thronged at the moment with all the most distinguished figures in society. 'What will be the state of that poor woman,' she wondered, 'when she finds herself alone in her carriage? It would be an indiscretion on my part to offer to accompany her, I don't dare to ... What a great consolation, however, it would be to the poor prisoner, sitting alone in some frightful cell, with only his little lamp for company, if he knew that he was loved to this extent! What an appalling solitude that must be into which they have plunged him! And we ourselves are here in these brilliantly-lighted rooms! How abominable! Can there be any way of conveying a message to him? Good God! that would be betraying my father; his position is so delicate between the two parties! What will become of him if he incurs the passionate hatred of the Duchessa, who controls the will of the Prime Minister, who has the upper hand in three-quarters of the affairs of State? On the other hand, the Prince takes a constant interest in what goes on at the fortress, and is very touchy on that subject; fear makes people cruel. ... In any case Fabrizio' (Clelia no longer thought of him as Signor del Dongo) 'is far more to be pitied. He has much more at stake than the risk of losing a lucrative post! ... And the Duchessa! ... What a terrible passion love is! ... and yet all those liars in society speak of it as a source of happiness! ... Never shall I forget what I have just seen; what a sudden change! How those beautiful, radiant eyes of the Duchessa became dull and dimmed after the fatal words which Marchese N — came to say to her! ... Fabrizio must indeed be worthy of love!'

In the midst of these highly serious reflections, which claimed entire possession of Clelia's mind and heart, the complimentary remarks which were continually being showered upon her seemed to her even more distasteful than usual. To escape from them she moved over to an open window, half screened by a taffeta curtain; she hoped that no one would be so bold as to follow her into this sort of retreat. This window opened on to a little grove of orange trees planted straight in the ground; as a matter of fact, they had to be protected by a covering every winter. Clelia inhaled the scent of the blossoms with keenest delight, and this pleasure seemed to restore a little peace to her soul ... 'I felt he had a very noble air,' she thought, 'but to inspire such passion in such a remarkable woman! ... She has had the honour of refusing the Prince's homage, and if she had deigned to consent she could have been Queen of his dominions ... My father says that the Sovereign's passion went so far as to think of marrying her if ever he had become free to do so! ... and this love of hers for Fabrizio has lasted so long! for it is quite five years since we met them beside Lake Como! ... Yes, five years,' she said to herself after a moment's reflection. 'I was struck by it even then, at a time when so many things passed unnoticed before my childish eyes! How those two women seemed to admire Fabrizio! ...'

Clelia remarked with delight that none of the young men who had been talking to her so eagerly had ventured to approach her balcony. One of them, the Marchese Crescenzi, had taken a few steps in that direction, and then had stopped beside a card-table. 'If only,' she said to herself, 'under my little window in our *palazzo* in the fortress, the only one that has any shade, I had some pretty orange-trees to look at, just like these, my thoughts would be less sad! But to have as one's sole outlook the enormous blocks of stone of the Farnese Tower ... Ah!' she cried, with a sudden nervous start, 'perhaps that is where they have put him. How I long to have a talk with Don Cesare! He will be less strict than the General. My father will certainly tell me nothing on our way back to the fortress, but I shall find out everything from Don Cesare ... I have money, I could buy a few orange-trees, which, planted under the window of my aviary, would prevent me from seeing that great wall of the Farnese tower. How much more hateful it will seem to me now that I know one of the people it hides from the light of day ...

'Yes, it is just the third time I have seen him; once at court, at the ball on the Princess's birthday; today, with three constables around him, while that horrible Barbone was asking for him to be handcuffed, and finally, beside Lake Como ... That's quite five years ago. What a young scamp he looked then! How he scowled at the constables, and what strange glances his mother and his aunt kept casting his way! There was certainly some secret between them that day, some private concern of their own; at the time I had some idea that he too was afraid of the police ...' Clelia shuddered. 'But how ignorant I was! No doubt, even then, the Duchessa had begun to take an interest in him ... How he made us laugh a few minutes later, when the ladies, in spite of their obvious anxiety, had grown a little accustomed to the presence of a stranger! ... And this evening I could not bring myself to reply to the remark he made to me! ... O ignorance and timidity, how often do you give the appearance of something far more foul! And I behave like that when I am over twenty! ... I was quite right to think of the cloister; really I am fit for nothing but retirement from the world. "Worthy daughter of a gaoler!" he will have been saying to himself. He despises me, and as soon as he is able to write to the Duchessa he will tell her of my lack of consideration, and the Duchessa will think me a very deceitful girl; for, after all, this evening she probably thought me full of sympathy for her in her trouble.'

Clelia noticed that someone was approaching, apparently with the intention of placing himself beside her on the iron balcony of this window. She felt annoyed at this, while reproaching herself for feeling so; the musings from which she had been thus rudely roused had not been entirely devoid of sweetness. 'Here's some tiresome creature who'll get a pretty reception!' she thought. She was turning her head round with a look of haughty disdain, when she caught sight of the timid figure of the Archbishop approaching the balcony by a series of little imperceptible movements. 'This saintly man has no manners,' thought Clelia. 'Why come and disturb a poor girl like me? My peace is the only thing I possess.' She was greeting him with respect, but at the same time with a haughty air, when the prelate said to her: 'Signorina, have you heard the terrible news?'

The girl's eyes had at once taken on an altogether different expression; but, following the instructions repeated to her a hundred times over by her father, she replied with an air of ignorance which the language of her eyes openly contradicted: 'I have heard nothing, my Lord Archbishop.'

'My chief Vicar-General, poor Fabrizio del Dongo, who is no more guilty than I am of the death of that ruffian Giletti, has been forcibly taken from Bologna where he was living under the assumed name of Giuseppe Bossi. They have shut him up in your citadel; he arrived there actually *chained* to the carriage that brought him. A species of gaoler, named Barbone, who was pardoned some time ago after having murdered one of his brothers, chose to attempt an act of personal violence against Fabrizio; but my young friend is not the man to brook an insult. He flung his infamous adversary to the ground, whereupon they led him off to a cell twenty feet below the earth, after first putting handcuffs on him.'

'No, not handcuffs!'

'Ah! So you do know something!' cried the Archbishop. And the old man's features lost their expression of deep despondency. 'But, before we can proceed, someone may come near this balcony and interrupt us. Would you be so charitable as to hand this pastoral ring of mine to Don Cesare yourself?'

The girl took the ring, but did not know where to put it so as not to run the risk of losing it.

'Put it on your thumb,' said the Archbishop; and he himself slipped it on. 'Can I rely on you to deliver this ring?'

'Yes, Monsignore.'

'Will you promise me to keep secret what I am about to say next, even supposing you should not find it right to agree to my request?'

'Why, yes, Monsignore,' replied the girl, trembling all over on seeing the grave and portentous air the old man had suddenly assumed ...

'Our revered Archbishop,' she went on, 'can give me no orders that are not worthy of himself and of me.'

'Tell Don Cesare that I commend my adopted son to him. I know that the police who carried him off did not give him time to take his breviary with him, I therefore beg Don Cesare to let him have his own, and if your worthy uncle will send tomorrow to my palace, I undertake to replace the book given by him to Fabrizio. I beg Don Cesare also to convey the ring which this pretty hand is now wearing to Signor del Dongo.'

The Archbishop was interrupted at this point by General Fabio Conti, who came in search of his daughter to take her to his carriage. A few brief minutes of conversation ensued, during which the prelate showed himself not lacking in adroitness. Without referring in any way to the newly made prisoner, he so arranged it that the course of the conversation led naturally up to his own utterance of certain moral and political maxims. For instance: 'There are certain critical moments in the life of a court which decide, for long periods, the fate of the most exalted personages. It would be singularly imprudent to change into *personal hatred* the state of coolness in the political sphere which is often quite simply the result of opposite standpoints.' The Archbishop, letting himself be carried away to some little extent by the profound grief which he felt at so unexpected an arrest, went so far as to say that a man must undoubtedly try to preserve the position he enjoys, but that it would be a quite gratuitous imprudence to bring down furious hatred on his own head as a consequence of this, by countenancing certain actions which are never forgotten.

When the General was in the carriage with his daughter, he remarked to her: 'This might be described as threats ... Threats, to a man of my sort!' No other words passed between father and daughter during the next twenty minutes.

On receiving the Archbishop's pastoral ring, Clelia had fully intended to speak to her father, as soon as she was in the carriage, of the little service which the prelate had asked of her. But after the word *threats*, uttered with anger, she took it for granted that her father would intercept the gift; she therefore kept the ring covered with her left hand and clasped it passionately. During the whole of the time it took them to drive from the Ministry of the Interior to the citadel, she was asking herself whether it would be a crime on her part not to speak to her father. She was extremely pious, extremely timorous, and her heart, usually so calm, was beating with unaccustomed violence. But in the end the 'Who goes there?' of the sentry posted on the ramparts above the door rang out on the approach of the carriage before Clelia had found a form of words calculated to incline her father not to refuse, so great was her fear of a refusal. As they climbed the three hundred and sixty steps which led to the governor's residence, Clelia still could think of nothing to say.

She hastened to speak to her uncle, who scolded her and refused to lend himself to anything.

CHAPTER 16: *Desperate Measures*

'WHAT do you think!' cried the General on catching sight of his brother. 'Here is the Duchessa going to spend a hundred thousand scudi to make a fool of me and help the prisoner to escape!'

But, for the moment, we are obliged to leave Fabrizio in his prison, right at the top of the citadel of Parma; he is well guarded, and we shall find him perhaps a little altered when we return to him. We are now going to turn our attention first of all to the court, where certain highly complicated intrigues, and more particularly the passions of an unhappy woman, are going to decide his fate. As he climbed the three hundred and ninety steps to his prison in the Farnese Tower, beneath the eyes of the governor, Fabrizio, who had so greatly dreaded this moment, found that he had no time to reflect on his misfortunes.

On returning home after the party at Conte Zurla's, the Duchessa signed to her women to leave her; then, flinging herself, fully dressed, upon her bed, she cried aloud: *'Fabrizio is in the power of his enemies, and perhaps out of spite against me they will poison him!'* How can one depict the moment of despair that followed this summing-up of the situation by a woman so little ruled by reason, so much a slave to the sensation of the moment, and, without admitting it to herself, so desperately in love with the young prisoner?

It was a series of inarticulate cries, paroxysms of rage, convulsive movements, but not a single tear. She had sent her women away so as to hide her tears. She thought she would burst into sobs as soon as she was left alone; but tears, this first relief in all great sorrows, were utterly denied to her. Anger, indignation, the sense of her own inferiority in comparison with the Prince, had too great mastery over this haughty soul.

'Am I not humiliated enough?' she kept on exclaiming. 'I am bitterly insulted, and, what is worse, Fabrizio's life is endangered! And shall I not avenge myself! Not so fast, my Prince! You may kill me, well and good, you have the power to do so; but afterwards I shall have your life. Alas, poor Fabrizio, what good will that do you? What a difference from the day when I was ready to leave Parma! And yet even then I thought I was unhappy ... what blindness! I was on the point of breaking with all the habits of a pleasant life.

Alas! without knowing it, I was on the brink of an event which was to decide my fate for good and all. Had not the Conte, urged by his vile and vulgar habits of toadying to the great, suppressed the words "unjust proceedings" in that fatal note which the Prince's vanity had granted me, we should have been saved. More by luck than by dexterity, I must acknowledge, I had managed to bring into play his personal vanity on the subject of his beloved city of Parma. Then I threatened to leave him, then I was free! Good God! What sort of slave am I now? Here am I now pinned down in this foul cesspool, and Fabrizio in chains in the citadel, that citadel which for so many eminent men has been the antechamber to death! And I can no longer keep this tiger cowed by the fear of seeing me leave his den!

'He has too much intelligence not to realize that I will never move from that infamous tower to which my heart is chained. And now this man's wounded vanity may suggest the wildest notions to him; their fantastic cruelty would only stimulate his astounding self-conceit. If he renews his former insipid, amorous advances, if he says to me: "Accept the homage of your slave, or else Fabrizio dies," ... well, there's the old story of Judith ... Yes, but if it means only suicide for me, it will be murder for Fabrizio; his nincompoop of a successor, our Crown Prince, and that infamous villain Rassi will have Fabrizio hanged as my accomplice.'

The Duchessa shrieked aloud: this dilemma, from which she could see no way of escape, was torturing her unhappy heart. Her distracted brain could see no other probability in the future. For ten minutes she turned and twisted restlessly like a woman out of her mind; then a sleep of utter exhaustion took, for a brief moment, the place of this horrible state; life was drained out of her. A few minutes later she woke up with a start, and found herself sitting on her bed; it had seemed to her as if, in her presence, the Prince was trying to cut off Fabrizio's head. With what wild eyes the Duchessa gazed round about her! When at length she was convinced that neither the Prince nor Fabrizio was actually before her eyes, she sank back on her bed and was on the point of fainting.

Her physical exhaustion was such that she could not summon up enough strength to change her position. 'Good God! If only I could die!' she said to herself ... 'But what cowardice! the very idea of my abandoning Fabrizio in his misfortune! My mind must be wandering ... Come, let us return to reality, let us coolly consider the abominable situation into which I have plunged so to speak wantonly. What a fatal act of stupidity! To come and live at the court of an absolute prince! A tyrant who knows every one of his victims! Whose every glance directed at him seems to him a defiance of his power! Alas! that is what neither the Conte nor I envisaged when I left Milan. I had in mind the attractions of a pleasant court; something inferior, it is true, but still something in the style of the happy days of Prince Eugène.

'Looking at it from a distance, we can form no idea of what the authority of a despot who knows all his subjects by sight is really like. The outward form of despotism is the same as that of other kinds of government. There are judges, for instance, but they are men like Rassi. The monster! He would see nothing out of the ordinary in having his own father hanged if the Prince ordered him to do so ... He would call it his duty ... Win over Rassi! Unhappy woman that I am! I possess no means of doing so. What can I offer him? A hundred thousand lire, perhaps! And they say that, after the last dagger-thrust which the wrath of heaven against this unhappy country allowed him to escape, the Prince sent him ten thousand golden sequins in a casket. Besides, what sum of money could possibly seduce him? That soul of mud, which has never read anything but contempt in other men's eyes, enjoys here the pleasure at this present time of seeing fear, and even respect, in them. He may become Minister of Police, and why not? Then three-quarters of the inhabitants of this principality will be his base courtiers, and tremble before him in as servile a fashion as now he trembles before his Sovereign Prince.

'Since I cannot flee from this detestable place, I must make myself useful here to Fabrizio. Living alone, in solitude, in despair – what can I then do for Fabrizio? Come, *forward march, unhappy woman*! Do your duty; go into society, pretend to think no more of Fabrizio ... Pretend to have forgotten you, my poor darling!'

At these words, the Duchessa burst into tears; at last she could weep. After an hour conceded to natural human weakness, she saw with some slight feeling of relief that her ideas were beginning to grow clearer. 'Oh to have the magic carpet,' she said to herself, 'to snatch Fabrizio from the citadel and seek refuge with him in some happy place where no one could pursue us – Paris, for instance. We should live there at first on the twelve hundred lire which his father's agent transmits to me with such amusing regularity. I could easily get together a hundred thousand more from the remains of my fortune!' The Duchessa's imagination passed in review, with occasional bursts of inexpressible delight, all the details of the life which she would lead three hundred leagues away from Parma. 'There,' she said to herself, 'he could enter the service under an assumed name ... Posted to one of the regiments of those gallant Frenchmen, the young Valserra would soon make a reputation for himself; at last he would be happy.'

These joyful visions brought on a second fit of weeping, but this time they were gentle tears. So happiness did indeed exist somewhere in the world! This state of mind lasted for some considerable time; the poor woman had a horror of coming back to the contemplation of the grim reality. At length, just as the dawning day was beginning to mark with a line of white the tops of the trees in her garden, she made violent efforts to rouse herself. 'In a few hours,' she told herself, 'I shall be on the field of battle, it will be a case for action, and if anything should occur to irritate me, if the Prince should take it into his head to say anything to me about Fabrizio, I cannot guarantee that I shall be able to keep entirely calm. I must therefore, here and how, *make plans*.

'If I am declared a prisoner of State, Rassi will see to it that everything in this house is seized. On the first of this month the Conte and I, according to our usual custom, burnt all papers of which the police might make improper use; and he is Minister of Police – that is the amusing part of it. I have three diamonds of some value. Tomorrow, Fulgenzio, my old boatman from Grianta, will set off for Geneva, where he will deposit them in a safe place. If ever Fabrizio should escape' ('Great God! be Thou propitious to me!' – and she crossed herself) 'the Marchese del Dongo, in his incredible meanness, will decide that it is a sin to provide subsistence for a man who is pursued by his lawful Prince. Then he will at any rate have my diamonds, and will have the means to live.

'Dismiss the Conte ... to find myself alone with him after what has happened, that is what I could not bear. Poor fellow! he is not really bad, far from it; he is only weak. That commonplace soul does not rise to the height of ours. Poor Fabrizio! Why can't you be here with me for a moment, so that we could consult together about our perils!

'The Conte's meticulous prudence would hamper all my plans, and besides, I must on no account involve him in my ruin ... For why should not this tyrant's vanity make him cast me into prison? I shall have conspired ... what could be easier to prove? If it should be to his citadel that he sent me, and I could manage, by a lavish use of gold, to speak to Fabrizio, if only for an instant, with what courage we would go to our death together! But a truce to these follies; his creature Rassi would advise him to make an end of me with poison. My appearance in the streets, standing in a cart, might touch the hearts of his dear citizens of Parma ... But what! still romancing! Alas! These follies must be forgiven in a woman whose actual lot is so sad! The whole truth of the matter is that the Prince will not send me to my death; but nothing could be easier than to cast me into prison and keep me there. He will have all sorts of compromising papers hidden in some corner of my *palazzo*, as was done in the case of poor L—... Then three judges, who needn't be too great rogues, for they will have what is known as *documentary evidence*, together with a dozen false witnesses, will be quite sufficient. Thus I may be sentenced to death as having conspired; and the Prince, in his boundless clemency, taking into consideration the fact that I have had the honour of being admitted to his court, will commute my punishment to ten years in a fortress. But I, so as not to fall short in any way of that violent character which has drawn so many silly comments from the Marchesa Raversi and my other enemies, will bravely take poison. So at least the public will be kind enough to believe; but I wager that Rassi will appear in my cell and politely offer me, in the Prince's name, a little bottle of strychnine or laudanum.

'Yes, I must have a very open rupture with the Conte, for I do not wish to involve him in my downfall. That would be a disgraceful thing to do; the poor man has loved me so sincerely! My folly lay in believing that there was enough heart left in a true courtier to be capable of love. Very probably the Prince will find some excuse for casting me into prison; he will be afraid of my perverting public opinion with regard to Fabrizio. The Conte is a man of perfect honour; at once he will do what the miserable creatures at this court, in their profound astonishment, will call an act of madness – he will leave the court. I defied the Prince's authority on the evening of the note; I may expect anything from his wounded vanity. Will a man who is born a Prince ever forget the sensation I gave him that evening? Besides, the Conte, once he has broken with me, will be in a better position to help Fabrizio. But what if the Conte, whom this decision of mine will drive to despair, should avenge himself? ... That, however, is an idea that would never occur to him; his is not a fundamentally base nature like the Prince's. The Conte may, while lamenting the necessity, countersign an infamous decree,' but he has some sense of honour. And then, avenge himself for what? Simply because, after loving him for five years without giving his love the slightest cause for offence, I say to him: "Dear Conte, I had the good fortune to be in love with you. Well now, this flame is dying down; I no longer love you, but I know all that is in your heart, I retain a profound regard for you, and you will always be the dearest of my friends."

'What answer can a gallant gentleman make to so sincere a declaration?

'I shall take a new lover, or so at least society will believe. I shall say to this lover: "After all, the Prince does right to punish Fabrizio's folly; but on his birthday our gracious Sovereign will no doubt set him free." Thus I gain six months. The new lover that prudence indicates should be that venal judge, that vile hangman, that fellow Rassi ... He would find himself ennobled and, in fact, I should give him the right of entry into high society. Forgive me, dear Fabrizio; such an effort, for me, is beyond the bounds of possibility. What! That monster still steeped in the blood of Conte P — and of D —! I should faint with horror whenever he came near, or rather, I should seize a knife and plunge it into his vile heart. Do not ask impossibilities of me!

'Yes, first of all, I must forget Fabrizio! and not show a shadow of anger against the Prince. I must behave again with my usual gaiety, which will seem all the more attractive to these vile and filthy souls, in the first place because I shall appear to be submitting myself with good grace to their Sovereign's will, and secondly because so far from making fun of them, I shall take pains to bring out all their pretty little qualities. For instance, I shall compliment Conte Zurla on the beauty of the white feather in his hat, which he has just had sent him by courier from Lyons, and which gives him great delight.

'I must choose a lover from the Raversi's party ... If the Conte goes, that will be the party in office; that is where the power will lie. It will be a friend of the Raversi who will be governor at the citadel; for Fabio Conti will become a Minister. How on earth will the Prince, a man of breeding, a man of intelligence, accustomed to the Conte's charming way of conducting business, be able to discuss affairs of State with that great lubber, that king of fools who, his whole life long, has been occupied with that fundamental problem: ought His Highness's troops to have seven buttons on the breast of their tunics, or nine? It is such dull brutes as these who are extremely jealous of me, and therein lies your danger, dear Fabrizio! It is such dull brutes who are going to decide my fate and yours!

'Well then, I must not allow the Conte to hand in his resignation. Let him remain, even if he has to suffer humiliations. He always imagines that resigning his office is the greatest sacrifice a Prime Minister can make; and each time his looking-glass tells him that he is growing old, he offers me that sacrifice. A complete rupture therefore; yes, and a reconciliation only in the event of its being the sole means of preventing him from going. I shall, of course, give him his dismissal in the friendliest possible way. But after his courtier-like omission of the words "unjust proceedings" in the Prince's note I feel that, if I am not to hate him, I need to spend some months without seeing him. On that decisive evening, I had no need of his intelligence; all he had to do was to write at my dictation. He had only to write those few words which *I had won* by my own strength of character; his vile habit of sycophancy prevailed. He told me next day that he could not make the Prince sign anything so ridiculous, that what was wanted was a *free pardon*. Why, good heavens! with people like that, with those monsters of vanity and rancour who bear the name *Farnese*, one takes what one can get.'

At the thought of this, all the Duchessa's anger revived. 'The Prince has deceived me,' she said to herself, 'and in how dastardly a way! ... The man has no excuse. He has brains, he is shrewd and capable of reasoning; there is nothing base in him except his passions. The Conte and I have noticed it a score of times; he is never vulgar-minded save when he imagines that someone has tried to insult him. Well, Fabrizio's crime has nothing to do with politics, it's one of those trifling cases of homicide such as are noted by the hundred every year in his happy dominions, and the Conte has sworn to me that he has taken pains to procure the most precise information, and that Fabrizio is innocent. That fellow Giletti was by no means lacking in courage; finding himself but a few steps away from the frontier, he suddenly felt the temptation to rid himself of a favoured rival.'

The Duchessa paused for a long time to consider whether it was possible to believe in Fabrizio's guilt. Not that she felt that it would have been a very grave sin on the part of a nobleman of Fabrizio's rank to rid himself of an impertinent mummer; but, in her despair, she was beginning to have a vague feeling that she was going to be obliged to fight to prove Fabrizio's innocence. 'No,' she said to herself at last, 'here is a decisive proof. He is like poor Pietranera, he always carried arms in all his pockets, and that day he had only a wretched single-barrelled gun in his hand, and that, too, borrowed from one of the workmen.

'I hate the Prince because he has betrayed me, and betrayed me in the most dastardly fashion. After the note signing his pardon, he had the poor boy carried off from Bologna, and all the rest. But that account will be settled.' About five o'clock in the morning, the Duchessa, utterly worn out by this prolonged fit of despair, rang for her women; they screamed aloud. Seeing her on her bed, fully dressed, wearing her diamonds, white as the sheets and with closed eyes, it seemed to them as though they saw her lying in state after her death. They would have supposed her in a dead faint, if they had not called to mind that she had just rung for them. A few stray tears trickled from time to time slowly down her lifeless cheeks; her women gathered from a gesture she made that she wished to be put to bed.

Twice that evening after Conte Zurla's party the Conte had called at the Duchessa's house; each time refused admittance, he wrote to her that he wanted her advice on a point concerning himself. Ought he to retain his post after the insult they had dared to offer him? The Conte went on to say: 'The young man is innocent, but even if he were guilty, ought he to have been arrested without informing me, his acknowledged protector?' The Duchessa did not see this letter until the following day.

The Conte had no moral principles; one can even add that what the Liberals understand by *morality* (seeking the happiness of the greatest number) seemed to him mere tomfoolery. He believed himself bound to seek first and foremost the happiness of Conte Mosca della Rovere. He was, however, thoroughly honourable and perfectly sincere when he spoke of his resignation. Never in his life had he told a lie to the Duchessa. She, however, paid not the slightest attention to his letter; her decision, and a very painful decision at that, had been taken: *to pretend to forget Fabrizio*. After that effort, everything else was a matter of indifference to her.

Next day, about noon, the Conte, who had called ten times at the Palazzo Sanseverina, was finally admitted; he was appalled at the sight of the Duchessa. 'She looks forty!' he said to himself, 'and yesterday she was so sparkling, so young! Everyone tells me that during her long conversation with the girl Clelia Conti, she looked every bit as young as the latter and far more attractive.'

The Duchessa's voice and her manner were every bit as strange as her personal appearance. This manner, divested of all passion, of all human interest, of all anger, made the Conte turn pale. It reminded him of the behaviour of a friend of his who, a few months earlier, when on the point of death, and having already received the Last Sacrament, had wished to have a talk with him.

After some minutes the Duchessa was able to speak to him. She gazed at him, but her eyes remained dead.

'Let us part, my dear Conte,' she said to him in a faint but quite articulate voice, which she did her best to make sound friendly. 'Let us part; we must! Heaven is my witness that, for the past five years, my behaviour to you has been irreproachable. You have given me a brilliant existence in place of the boredom that would have been my sad lot at the castle of Grianta; without you I should have reached old age some few years sooner ... For my part, my sole consideration has been to try to bring you happiness. It is because I love you that I propose to you this separation *à l'amiable*, as they would say in France.'

The Conte did not understand; she was obliged to repeat her words several times. He grew deadly pale, and flinging himself on his knees beside her bed, he said to her all the things that profound astonishment, followed by the keenest despair, can inspire in a man of spirit who is passionately in love. At every moment he offered to hand in his resignation and to follow his mistress to some retreat a thousand leagues from Parma.

'You dare to speak to me of departure, and Fabrizio is here!' she exclaimed at length, half rising to her feet. But seeing that the mention of Fabrizio's name made a painful impression, she added after a moment's pause, and gently pressing the Conte's hand: 'No, my dear, I am not going to tell you that I have loved you with that passion and that rapture which nobody, so it seems to me, can feel after thirty, and I am already a long way past that age. People will have told you that I was in love with Fabrizio, for I know that such a rumour has been current at this *spiteful* court.' As she uttered the word 'spiteful', her eyes sparkled for the first time during this conversation. 'I swear to you, before God, and on Fabrizio's life, that not the slightest thing has ever passed between him and me that could not have borne the eye of a third person. I will not tell you, on the other hand, that I love him exactly as a sister might do; I love him, so to speak, instinctively. I love that courage of his, so simple and so perfect that he may be said to be unaware of it himself. I remember that this sort of admiration began on his return from Waterloo. He was still a child then, for all his seventeen years. His great anxiety was to know whether he really had been present at the battle; and if that were so, whether he could say he had fought when he had not marched to the attack of any battery or column. It was during the solemn discussions we used to have on this important subject that I began to recognize his perfect charm. His greatness of soul was revealed to me. What skilful lies a well-bred young man, in his place, would have flaunted! In short, if he is not happy, I cannot be happy either. There now; that is a remark which exactly describes the state of my heart. If that is not the truth, it is, at any rate as much of it as I can see.'

The Conte, encouraged by this tone of frankness and intimacy, tried to kiss her hand; she drew it back with a sort of horror. 'The time for that has passed,' she said to him; 'I am a woman of thirty-seven, I am now on the threshold of old age, I already feel all its despondency, and possibly I am even drawing near to the grave. That is a terrible moment, from all I have heard, and yet it seems to me that I long for it. I feel the worst symptom of old age: my heart is dulled by this frightful calamity, I am no longer capable of love. I see nothing in you now, dear Conte, but the shade of someone who once was dear to me. I will say more; it is gratitude, and gratitude alone, that makes me speak to you in this way.'

'What is to become of me?' the Conte repeated, 'of me, who feel that I am attached to you more passionately than in the first days of our acquaintance, when I used to see you at the Scala?'

'Shall I confess one thing to you, dear friend? This talk of love wearies me, and strikes me as indecent. Come,' she said, trying to smile, but in vain, 'take courage! Act like a sensible man, a judicious man, a man of resource in all emergencies. Be with me what you really are in the eyes of those who regard you coolly, the most able man and the greatest politician that Italy has produced for centuries.'

The Conte rose and paced the room in silence for a few moments.

'Impossible, my dear,' he said to her at length, 'I am torn in pieces by the most violent passion, and you ask me to consult my reason. Reason no longer exists for me at present.'

'Let's not speak of passion, I beg you,' she answered curtly. And this was the first time, in the course of two hours conversation, that her voice took on any sort of expression whatever. The Conte, though in the depths of despair himself, endeavoured to comfort her.

'He has deceived me,' she cried, without responding in any way to the reasons for hope which the Conte was setting before her. '*He* has deceived me in the most dastardly fashion!' For a moment her face lost its deadly pallor; but, even in this moment of violent excitement, the Conte noticed that she had not the strength to raise her arms.

'Good God! can it be possible,' he thought, 'that she is merely ill? In that case, though, it would be the beginning of some very serious illness.' Then, overcome with anxiety, he suggested calling in the famous Razori, the best physician in the place and in the whole of Italy.

'So you wish to give a stranger the pleasure of knowing the whole extent of my despair? ... Is that the counsel of a traitor or of a friend?' And she looked at him with a strange expression in her eyes.

'It's all over,' he said to himself in despair. 'She no longer has any love for me, and worse still, she no longer reckons me among ordinary men of honour.'

'I may tell you,' the Conte went on, speaking with emphasis, 'that I have made the most special efforts to obtain details of the arrest which has driven us to despair, and the curious thing is that I still know nothing positive. I have had the constables at the nearest station questioned. They saw the prisoner arrive by the road from Castelnuovo and received orders to follow his *sediola*. I immediately sent off Bruno, whose zeal is as well known to you as his devotion, with orders to go on from station to station to find out where and how Fabrizio was arrested.'

On hearing Fabrizio's name uttered, the Duchessa was seized with a slight convulsion.

'Forgive me, my dear,' she said to the Conte as soon as she could speak. 'These details interest me greatly. Give me them all, let me have a clear understanding of the smallest particulars.'

'Well, madam,' the Conte went on, trying to assume a somewhat lighter air in the hope of easing the strain on her a little, 'I am rather inclined to send a confidential messenger to Bruno with orders to him to push on as far as Bologna. It is from there, perhaps, that our young friend was carried off. What is the date of his last letter?'

'Tuesday, five days ago.'

'Has it been opened in the post?'

'No trace of any opening. I should tell you that it was written on frightful paper. The address is in a woman's hand, and that address bears the name of an old washerwoman who is related to my maid. The washerwoman believes that it is something to do with a love affair, and Cecchina refunded her the charges of delivery without adding anything further.' The Conte, who had now adopted a quite businesslike tone, tried to discover, by talking things over with the Duchessa on what day Fabrizio might have been taken away from Bologna. It was only then that he, who was ordinarily so perspicacious, perceived that this was the right tone to adopt. These details interested the unhappy woman and seemed to distract her a little. If the Conte had not been in love, this simple idea would have occurred to him as soon as he entered her room.

The Duchessa sent him away so that he might dispatch fresh orders to the faithful Bruno without delay. As they touched briefly on the question of how to find out whether there had been a sentence passed before the moment at which the Prince had signed the note addressed to the Duchessa, the latter somewhat eagerly seized the opportunity to say to the Conte: 'I shall not reproach you at all for having omitted the words "unjust proceedings" in the note which you wrote and he signed. It was your courtier's instinct that had you in its grip; all unconsciously, you put your master's interest before your friend's. You have let your actions, my dear Conte, be governed by me, and that for a long time past, but it is not in your power to change your nature. As a Minister you have great talents, but you have also the instinctive reactions of that profession. The omission of the word "unjust" was my ruin; but far be it from me to reproach you for it in any way, it was the fault of your instinct and not of your will.

'You are to keep in mind,' she went on, changing her tone, and with the most imperious air, 'that I am not unduly grieved at Fabrizio's capture, that I have never felt the slightest inclination to leave this principality, and that I am full of respect for the Prince. That is what you are to say, and this is what I, for my part, wish to say to you: Since I intend, in the future, to have the entire control of my own behaviour, I wish to part from you *à l'amiable*, that is to say as one who has been a good and long-standing friend of yours. Consider me as sixty years old; the young woman I was is dead, in that I can no longer feel anything excessively, I can no longer love. But I should be even more wretched than I am if I should happen to compromise your future career. It may enter into my plans to make it seem as if I had taken a young lover, and I should not like to see you pained. I can swear to you by Fabrizio's happiness,' she paused for half a minute after these words, 'that I have never once been unfaithful to you, never in five whole years. That's a long time,' she said. She tried to smile, her pale cheeks quivered convulsively, but her lips refused to draw apart. 'I swear to you that I have never even either planned or wished such a thing. Now that I have made things clear to you, please go.'

The Conte left the Palazzo Sanseverina in despair. He could see in the Duchessa a firmly fixed intention to part from him, and never had he been so desperately in love. This is one of those things to which I am often obliged to revert, because, outside Italy, they seem improbable. On returning, he dispatched as many as six different people along the road to Castelnuovo and Bologna, and gave them letters. 'But that is not all,' said the unhappy Conte to himself. 'The Prince may get the mad idea into his head of having this wretched boy executed, just to revenge himself for the tone which the Duchessa adopted with him on the day of that fatal note. I felt that the Duchessa was exceeding a limit beyond which one should never go, and it was in order to patch things up a little that I was so incredibly foolish as to suppress the words "unjust proceedings", the only ones that bound the Sovereign ... What nonsense! does anything bind such people at all? There I undoubtedly made the greatest mistake of my life, I hazarded everything that makes life precious to me. The question now is to repair my blunder by dint of skilful and untiring efforts. But if, after all, I achieve nothing, even by sacrificing a little of my dignity, I shall leave that man in the lurch. With his dreams of high politics, with his ideas of making himself constitutional King of Lombardy, we shall see how he will fill my place ... Fabio Conti is an utter fool, all Rassi's talent amounts to is finding legal justification for hanging a man whom those in power dislike.'

Once he had thoroughly made up his mind to resign from the Ministry if the harsh treatment of Fabrizio went beyond that of ordinary confinement, the Conte said to himself: 'If rash defiance of one of that man's vain whims costs me my happiness, I shall at least have my honour left ... And by the way, since I am putting my portfolio on the scrap-heap, I can now allow myself to do a hundred things which, only this morning, would have seemed to me beyond the bounds of possibility. For instance, I am going to attempt everything that is humanly feasible to help Fabrizio to escape ... Heavens above!' exclaimed the Conte, breaking off suddenly and opening his eyes excessively wide as though at the sight of some unexpected happiness, 'the Duchessa never said anything about an escape. Can she have been wanting in sincerity for once in her life, and does her quarrel with me simply come from a desire that I should betray the Prince. Upon my word it's as good as done!'

The Conte's eyes had recovered their old expression of sarcastic shrewdness. 'That pleasant fellow Rassi is paid by his master for all the sentences which dishonour us in the eyes of Europe, but he is not the sort of man to refuse payment from me for betraying his master's secrets. The beggar has a mistress and a confessor, but the mistress is too low a creature for me to be able to contact; the next day she would relate our interview to all the greengrocer's wives in the neighbourhood.' The Conte, revived by this glimmer of hope, was already on his way to the cathedral. Amazed at the lightness of his step, he smiled in spite of his grief: 'That's what it is,' he said, 'to be no longer Minister.'

This Cathedral, like many of the churches in Italy, serves as a passage from one street to another: from some distance away the Conte saw one of the Archbishop's Vicars-General crossing the nave.

'As I have met you,' he said to him, 'will you be good enough to spare my gout the immense fatigue of climbing up to His Grace the Archbishop. I shall be infinitely obliged to him if he will be so kind as to come down to the sacristy.' The Archbishop was delighted by this message, he had a host of things to say to the Minister on the subject of Fabrizio. But the Minister guessed that these things were nothing but empty phrases and would not listen to any of them.

'What sort of man is Dugnani, the curate of San Paolo?'

'A small mind and a great ambition,' replied the Archbishop, 'few scruples and extreme poverty, for he has his vices!'

'By Jove! Monsignore,' exclaimed the Conte, 'you portray men as well as Tacitus,' and he took leave of him laughing. No sooner had he returned to his Ministry than he sent for Father Dugnani.

'You direct the conscience of my excellent friend Chief-Justice Rassi. Would he possibly have anything he would like to say to me?' And without any further speech or ceremony, he dismissed Dugnani.

THE Conte considered himself as already out of office. 'Let's see now,' he said to himself, 'how many horses we shall be able to keep after my disgrace, for that is what they will call my retirement.' The Conte examined his financial position. On coming into office he had had a fortune of eighty thousand lire; he now discovered, to his great amazement, that his present holdings, all told, did not amount to more than five hundred thousand lire. 'That means an income of twenty thousand lire at the most,' he said to himself. 'I must admit that I am a fearful simpleton! There's not a worthy citizen in Parma who does not credit me with an income of one hundred and fifty thousand lire; and the Prince, on that particular matter, is as middle-class-minded as you make them. When they see me in abject poverty, they will say that I'm very clever at concealing my wealth. By Jove!' he cried, 'if I'm still in office in three months' time, we shall see that fortune doubled!'

This idea seemed to him to give an opportunity for writing to the Duchessa, and he seized upon it eagerly; but to get himself forgiven for a letter, seeing the terms on which they were at present, he filled this up with figures and calculations. 'We shall only have twenty thousand lire as our income,' he told her, 'to live upon, all three of us, Fabrizio, you, and I, in Naples. Fabrizio and I shall have one saddle-horse between us.' The Minister had only just sent off his letter when Chief Justice Rassi was announced; he received him with a haughtiness of manner that bordered on rudeness.

'How is this, sir,' he said to him, 'you seize and carry off from Bologna a conspirator who is under my protection, and what's more you propose to cut off his head, and you say nothing to me about it! Do you at least know the name of my successor? Is it General Conti, or yourself?'

Rassi was struck dumb; he was too little accustomed to the ways of good society to be able to judge if the Conte was speaking seriously. He grew very red, and mumbled a few hardly intelligible words; the Conte watched him and revelled in his embarrassment.

All at once Rassi pulled himself together and exclaimed with perfect glibness and with the air of Figaro caught red-handed by Alma-viva: 'Upon my word, your Lordship, I'll not mince matters with your Excellency. What will you give me to answer all your questions as I would those of my confessor?'

'The Cross of San Paolo' (this is the Parmese Order) 'or a sum of money, if you can find me an excuse for granting it to you.'

'I prefer the Cross of San Paolo, because it gives me noble rank.'

'What, my dear Chief Justice, you still have some esteem for our poor nobility?'

'If I had been of noble birth,' replied Rassi with all the impudence of his calling, 'the families of the people I have had hanged would hate me, but they would not despise me.'

'Very well,' said the Conte, 'I will save you from contempt. Pray cure me of my ignorance. What do you intend to do with Fabrizio?'

'Well, to tell the truth, the Prince is greatly embarrassed. He is afraid that, bewitched by the lovely eyes of Armida – forgive this somewhat picturesque language, I use the Sovereign's own words – he is afraid that, bewitched by certain very lovely eyes which have affected him a little himself, you may leave him in the lurch, and there is no one but yourself capable of dealing with the question of Lombardy. I will even say,' added Rassi, lowering his voice, 'that there is a fine opportunity here for you, and one that is well worth the Cross of San Paolo which you are giving me. The Prince would grant you, as a reward from the State, a fine property worth six hundred thousand lire, which he would set apart from his own domains, or else a gratuity of three hundred thousand scudi, if you would agree not to concern yourself with what is going to happen to Fabrizio, or at least not to mention the matter to him except in public.'

'I expected something better than that,' said the Conte. 'Not to concern myself about Fabrizio means a breach with the Duchessa.'

'Well, that is just what the Prince says himself. The fact is that he is horribly enraged with the Duchessa, be it said between ourselves; and he is afraid that, to compensate yourself for your rupture with that charming lady, you may ask him, now that you are a widower, for the hand of his cousin, the elderly Princess Isotta, who is not more than fifty years old.'

'He has guessed aright,' exclaimed the Conte. 'Our master is the shrewdest man in the whole of his dominions.'

The fantastic notion of marrying this elderly Princess had never entered the Conte's head; nothing would have less suited a man whom court ceremonial bored to death.

He began rapping with his snuff-box on the marble top of a little table close to his armchair. Rassi saw in this gesture of embarrassment the possibility of a fine windfall; his eyes gleamed.

'I earnestly beg your Lordship,' he cried, 'if your Excellency agrees to accept either the estate worth six hundred thousand pounds or the grant of money, not to choose any other intermediary than myself. I would do my utmost,' he added, lowering his voice, 'to have the gratuity increased or else to have a fairly extensive forest added to the crown lands. If your Excellency would deign to introduce a little moderation and tact into his manner of speaking to the Prince about this young whippersnapper they've clapped into prison, it would perhaps be possible to create a Duchy out of these lands which a grateful State would offer you. I tell your Excellency again, the Prince, at this present moment, loathes the Duchessa, but he is extremely worried, and to such a point that I have sometimes thought there must be some secret circumstance which he does not dare confess to me. Actually we may find a perfect gold mine here, with me selling you his most intimate secrets, and quite easily too, since I am supposed to be your sworn enemy. After all, if he is furious with the Duchessa, he also believes, and so do we all, that you are the one man in the world who can bring to a successful end all the secret negotiations relating to the State of Milan. Will your Excellency permit me to repeat to him word for word what the Sovereign said?' asked Rassi, growing excited. 'There is often a character in the juxtaposition of words which no paraphrase can render, and you may be able to see more in them than I do myself.'

'I give you full leave,' said the Conte, continuing to rap in an absent-minded way on the marble table with his gold snuff-box. 'I give you full leave, and I shall be grateful.'

'Give me a patent of hereditary nobility independently of the Cross, and I shall be more than satisfied. When I speak of ennoblement to the Prince, he answers: "A scoundrel like you, noble! I should have to shut up shop the very next day; nobody in Parma would ever again wish to be ennobled." To come back to the Milanese question, the Prince said to me not three days ago: "That rogue is the only man who can follow the thread of our intrigues; if I dismiss him, or if he follows the Duchessa, I may as well give up all hope of seeing myself one day the Liberal and beloved ruler of all Italy." '

At these words the Conte breathed again. 'Fabrizio will not die,' he said to himself.

Never in his life had Rassi been able to secure an intimate conversation with the Prime Minister. He was beside himself with joy; he saw himself on the eve of being able to discard the name of Rassi, which had become synonymous throughout the principality with all that was base and vile. The common people gave the name Rassi to mad dogs; only recently certain soldiers had fought duels because one or other of their comrades had called them Rassi. Not a week passed, in short, in which this unlucky name did not figure in some outrageous little set of verses. His son, an innocent young schoolboy of sixteen, was hounded out of cafés on account of his name. It was the searing memory of all these little amenities of his office that made him commit an act of imprudence.

'I have an estate,' he said to the Conte, drawing his chair closer to the Minister's; 'it is called Riva. I should like to be Barone Riva.'

'Why not?' said the Conte. Rassi completely lost his head.

'Well then, your Excellency, I shall take the liberty of being indiscreet; I shall venture to guess the object of your desires. You aspire to the hand of the Princess Isotta, and that is a noble ambition. Once you are of the family, you are safe from disgrace, you have *nobbled* our man. I will not hide from you that he has a horror of this marriage with the Princess Isotta. But if your affairs were entrusted to some skilful and *well-paid* person there might be no need to despair of success.'

'I, my dear Barone, should despair of it. I disavow in advance everything you happen to say in my name; but on the day on which that illustrious alliance comes at length to crown my desires, and give me so exalted a position in the State, I will give you, myself, three hundred thousand lire of my own money, or else recommend the Prince to grant you some mark of his favour that you yourself will prefer to that sum of money.'

The reader will find this conversation somewhat lengthy; and yet we are sparing him more than half of it; it lasted for another two hours. Rassi left the Conte's presence mad with joy; the Conte remained with great hopes of saving Fabrizio and more than ever determined to hand in his resignation. He came to the conclusion that his credit stood in need of renewal by the succession to power of such persons as Rassi and General Conti. He dwelt with keen delight on a possible method of revenging himself on the Prince which had just occurred to him. 'He may send the Duchessa away,' he cried, 'but, by Jove! he will have to abandon the hope of becoming constitutional King of Lombardy.' (This was a ridiculous fantasy; the Prince was highly intelligent, but, by dint of dreaming of it, he had fallen madly in love with the idea.)

The Conte could not contain himself for joy as he hurried to the Duchessa's to give her an account of his conversation with the Chief Justice. He found the door closed against him; the porter hardly dared to tell him of this order received from his mistress's own lips. The Conte went sadly back to the ministerial residence; the misfortune that had just befallen him completely eclipsed the joy that his conversation with the Prince's confidant had given him. Having no longer the heart to devote himself to anything, the Conte was wandering sadly up and down his picture gallery when, a quarter of an hour later, he received a note which ran as follows:

Since it is true, my dear friend, that we are now no more than friends, you must only come to see me three times a week. In a fortnight's time we shall reduce those visits, always so dear to my heart, to two a month. If you wish to please me, give publicity to this sort of rupture. If you would like to pay me back for all the love I felt for you, you will choose a new mistress for yourself. As for me, I have great plans for amusing myself. I intend to go a great deal into society; perhaps I shall even find some man of intelligence to make me forget my misfortunes. Of course, in your capacity as a friend, the first place in my heart will always be kept for you; but I do not wish it to be said any longer that my actions have been dictated by your wisdom. I wish above all things for it to be clearly known that I have lost all influence over your decisions. In a word, dear Conte, rest assured that you will always be my dearest friend, but never anything else. Do not, I beg you, cherish any idea of a return to past conditions, it is all over. Count, always, upon my friendship.

This last stroke was too much for the Conte's courage. He wrote a finely worded letter to the Prince resigning all his offices, and addressed it to the Duchessa with the earnest request that she would forward it to the Palace. Very shortly after, his letter of resignation was returned to him, torn right across, and on one of the blank spaces on the paper the Duchessa had condescended to write: '*No, a thousand times, no!*'

It would be difficult to describe the poor Minister's despair. 'She is right, I quite agree,' he kept saying to himself at every moment. 'My omission of the words "unjust proceedings" was a terrible misfortune; it will perhaps involve the death of Fabrizio, and that will lead to my own.' It was with death in his heart that the Conte, who did not wish to appear at the Royal Palace before being summoned there, wrote out with his own hand the *motu proprio* which created Rassi Knight of the Order of San Paolo and conferred hereditary nobility upon him. The Conte appended to this a report of half a page setting forth for the Prince's benefit the reasons of state which made this measure advisable. He found a sort of melancholy pleasure in making a fair copy of each of these documents, which he addressed to the Duchessa.

His mind was lost in conjectures; he tried to guess what, for the future, would be the line of conduct of the woman he loved. 'She has no ideas about it herself,' he thought. 'One thing alone is certain – nothing in the world would induce her to go back on a decision once she has announced it to me.' What added still further to his misery was that he could not succeed in finding that the Duchessa was at fault. 'She conferred a favour on me by loving me. She ceased to love me after an error on my part, involuntary, it is true, but which may entail the most frightful consequences. I have no right to complain.' Next morning the Conte learnt that the Duchessa had begun to mix in society again; she had appeared the evening before in all the houses where they were holding receptions. What would he have done if he had come across her in the same drawing-room? How was he to speak to her? In what tone should he address her?

The following day was a day of gloom; it was generally rumoured that Fabrizio was going to be put to death; the whole city was stirred by it. It was added that the Prince, out of regard for his high birth, had condescended to give orders that his head should be cut off.

'It is I who am killing him,' said the Conte to himself. 'I can never aspire to see the Duchessa again.' In spite of this fairly simple conclusion, he could not refrain from calling three times at her house. However, he went there on foot so as not to attract attention. In his despair he even summoned up courage to write to her. He had sent twice for Rassi; but the Chief Justice had not appeared. 'The rogue is playing me false,' said the Conte to himself.

On the following day three important items of news set high

society and even the middle classes in Parma in a commotion. The execution of Fabrizio was more certain than ever; and, as a highly strange accompaniment to this news, the Duchessa did not seem too deeply in despair. To all appearances, she showed only moderate regret with regard to her young lover; at any rate she exploited, with infinite art, a certain pallor resulting from a rather serious indisposition, from which she had suffered at the time of Fabrizio's arrest. Middle-class citizens clearly recognized from these details the cold heart of a great lady of the court. Out of decency, however, and as a sacrifice to the shade of the young Fabrizio, she had broken with Conte Mosca. 'What immorality!' exclaimed the Jansenists of Parma. But already the Duchessa – and this was incredible – seemed disposed to listen to the blandishments of the handsomest young men at court. It was observed, among other peculiar features, that she had been very merry in a conversation with Conte Baldi, the Marchesa Raversi's reigning lover, and had chaffed him greatly over his frequent visits to the castle of Velleia. The lower middle class and the common people were indignant about Fabrizio's death, which these good folk put down to jealousy on the part of Conte Mosca. The society of the court was also greatly taken up with the Conte, but only to jeer at him.

The third of the great pieces of news to which we have referred was none other than the Conte's resignation. Everyone laughed at a ridiculous lover who, at the age of fifty-six, was sacrificing a magnificent position to his grief at being forsaken by a heartless woman, and one, moreover, who had long since preferred a younger man to himself. The Archbishop alone had the intelligence – or rather the heart – to divine that honour forbade the Conte to remain Prime Minister of a State where they were going to behead, and that without consulting him, a young man who was under his protection. The news of the Conte's resignation had the effect of curing General Fabio Conti of his gout, as we shall relate in due course when we come to speak of the way in which poor Fabrizio was spending his time in the citadel, while the whole city was agog to discover the hour of his execution.

On the following day the Conte had another visit from Bruno, the trusty agent whom he had despatched to Bologna. His master was greatly moved when the man entered his study; the sight of him recalled the happy state in which he had been when he had sent him off to Bologna, almost in concert with the Duchessa. Bruno had just come from Bologna where he had discovered nothing; he had not been able to get in touch with Lodovico, whom the *podestà* of Castelnuovo had locked up in his village gaol.

'I am going to send you back to Bologna,' said the Conte to Bruno. 'The Duchessa will value the sad pleasure of knowing all the details of Fabrizio's misadventure. Apply to the sergeant of police in charge of the station at Castelnuovo ...

'But no!' exclaimed the Conte, breaking off in his orders. 'Start at once for Lombardy, and distribute money lavishly among all our agents. My object is to obtain from all these people reports of the most encouraging nature.' Bruno, having clearly grasped the object of his mission, set to work to write out his letters of credit. As the Conte was giving him his final instructions, he received an entirely specious but admirably written letter; it might have been taken for a letter from one friend to another requesting a favour from him. The friend who wrote it was none other than the Prince. Having heard mention of some idea of resignation, he begged his friend, Conte Mosca, to continue in office. He asked him to do this in the name of friendship and of the *dangers that threatened the State*; and commanded him to do it as his master. He added that the King of —, having just placed at his disposal two Cordons of his Order, he was keeping one for himself and was sending the other to his dear Conte Mosca.

'That brute is the cause of my unhappiness!' cried the Conte in a fury, in front of the astonished Bruno, 'and he thinks to lure me with those same hypocritical phrases we have so many times concocted together to lime the twig for some fool.' He declined the proffered Order, and in his reply spoke of the state of his health as allowing him but very little hope of being able to carry on the arduous duties of the Ministry much longer. The Conte was infuriated. A moment later Chief Justice Rassi was announced; he treated him like the lowest menial.

'Well! because I have made you a noble, you are beginning to play the insolent! Why did you not come yesterday to thank me, as was your strict duty, Master Good-for-Nothing!'

Rassi was a long way beyond the reach of insults; it was in this tone that he was daily received by the Prince. But he was anxious to be a Barone and vindicated himself cleverly. Nothing was easier.

'The Prince kept me glued to a table all day yesterday; I could not leave the Palace. His Highness made me copy out in my wretched attorney's script a mass of diplomatic papers so silly and so long-winded that I really believe his sole object was to keep me a prisoner. When I was finally able to take my leave of him, about five o'clock, he ordered me to go straight home and not to go out again the whole evening. As a matter of fact I saw two of his private spies, well known to me, patrolling my street until nearly midnight. This morning, as soon as I could, I sent for a carriage which took me as far as the door of the Cathedral. I got down from the carriage very slowly, then passed at a quick pace through the church, and here I am. Your Excellency is at this moment the one man in the world whom I am passionately anxious to please.'

'And I, Master Rogue, am not in the least taken in by all these more or less well-concocted stories. The day before yesterday you refused to speak to me about Fabrizio; I respected your scruples and your oaths of secrecy, although oaths, to a creature of your sort, are at the most opportunities of evasion. Today, I require the truth. What are these absurd rumours according to which this young man is sentenced to death as the murderer of the actor Giletti?'

'No one can give your Excellency a better account of these rumours, for it was I myself who had them circulated by the Sovereign's orders. And, now I come to think of it, it was perhaps to prevent me from informing you of this incident that he kept me a prisoner all day yesterday. The Prince, who does not reckon me a fool, could have no doubt that I would come and bring my Cross to you and ask you to fasten it in my buttonhole.'

'Come down to facts!' cried the Minister, 'and no fine speeches.'

'No doubt the Prince would be glad to pass sentence of death on Signor del Dongo, but, as you probably know, he has been sentenced only to twenty years in irons, and this was commuted by the Prince himself, on the very day after the sentence, to twelve years in a fortress, with fasting on bread and water every Friday and other religious practices.'

'It's because I knew that this sentence was one of imprisonment only that I was alarmed by the rumours of an execution shortly to take place, which were current in the town. I remember the death of Conte Palanza, which was such a clever trick on your part.'

'That's when I ought to have had the Cross!' exclaimed Rassi, not in the least disconcerted. 'I ought to have put on the screw while I held it in my hand, and the man was anxious to secure this death. I was a fool then; and it is armed with this experience that I venture to advise you not to copy my example today.' (This comparison seemed in the worst of taste to his questioner, who was obliged to restrain himself forcibly from kicking Rassi.)

'In the first place,' the latter went on, with all the logic of an expert lawyer and the perfect self-assurance of a man whom no insult can offend, 'in the first place, there can be no question of the execution of the said del Dongo; the Prince would not dare, the times have greatly changed! And besides, I myself, who am noble and hope with your help to become a Barone, would not lend a hand to it. Now it is only from me, as your Excellency knows, that the official deputed to carry out the extreme penalty can receive his orders, and I swear to you that Cavaliere Rassi will never issue such orders against Signor del Dongo.'

'And you will be acting wisely,' said the Conte eyeing him sternly.

'Let us draw a distinction,' went on Rassi, smiling. 'My only concern is with officially authorized deaths, and if Signor del Dongo should happen to die of a colic, do not go and put it down to me. The Prince is furious, though I don't know why, with the Sanseverina.' (Three days earlier Rassi would have said 'the Duchessa', but, like everyone else in the town, he knew of her rupture with the Prime Minister.) The Conte was struck by the suppression of her title on such lips; it can be judged what sort of pleasure it caused him. He darted a glance of bitterest hatred at Rassi. 'My dear angel,' he said to himself the next moment, 'I can prove my love for you only by blind obedience to your orders.

'I must admit,' he said to the Chief Justice, 'that I do not take any very passionate interest in the various caprices of Her Grace the Duchessa. However, since it was she who introduced to me that young scapegrace Fabrizio, who would have done well to remain in Naples and not come here to complicate matters for us, I am anxious that he should not be put to death while I am in office, and I am quite ready to give you my word that you shall be a Barone within a week of his release from prison.'

'In that case, your Lordship, I shall not be a Barone till twelve whole years are out, for the Prince is furious, and his hatred of the Duchessa is so keen that he is trying to conceal it.'

'His Highness is too good! What need has he to conceal his hatred, since his Prime Minister is no longer protecting the Duchessa? Only I do not wish that any one should be able to accuse me of meanness, nor, above all, of jealousy. It was I who persuaded the Duchessa to come to this principality, and if Fabrizio dies in prison you will not be made a Barone, but you may possibly be stabbed to death. But let's not dwell on this trifle. The fact is that I have reckoned up my fortune; I find I have an income of barely twenty thousand lire, on the strength of which I propose to offer my resignation most humbly to the Sovereign. I have some hopes of being taken into the service of the King of Naples. That great city will offer me certain distractions which I need at this moment, and which I cannot find in a hole like Parma. I should stay here only in the event of your obtaining for me the hand of the Princess Isotta,' and so forth. The conversation on this subject was endless.

As Rassi was rising to leave, the Conte said to him in a very casual manner: 'You know it has been said that Fabrizio was playing me false, in the sense that he was one of the Duchessa's lovers. I decline to accept that rumour, and to give it the lie, I want you to get this purse delivered to Fabrizio.'

'But, your Lordship,' said Rassi in alarm, looking into the purse, 'there is an enormous sum here, and the regulations . . .'

'To you, my dear man, it may be enormous,' replied the Conte with an air of supreme disdain. 'When a commoner like yourself sends money to a friend in prison, he thinks he is ruining himself if he gives him ten sequins. I, for my part, *wish* Fabrizio to receive these six thousand lire, and am most particularly anxious that the Palace should know nothing of the matter.'

As the terrified Rassi was attempting to reply, the Conte impatiently shut the door upon him. 'People of that sort,' he said to himself, 'cannot recognize authority save under a covering of insolence.' After making this remark, the Minister indulged in an action so ridiculous that we find some reluctance in reporting it. He ran to take from his writing-table a miniature of the Duchessa, and covered it with passionate kisses. 'Forgive me, my dear angel,' he cried, 'if I did not fling out of the window with my own hands the miserable sneak who dares to speak of you with a touch of familiarity; but if I am acting with this excessive patience, it is to obey your wishes! And he will lose nothing by waiting!'

At the close of a long conversation with the portrait, the Conte, who felt his heart dead within his breast, was struck with the idea of performing a ridiculous action, and gave himself up to it with the eagerness of a child. He sent for a coat which bore his decorations and went to pay a call on the Princess Isotta. Never in his life had he gone to her apartments, except on New Year's Day. He found her surrounded by a number of dogs and tricked out in all her finery, including even diamonds, as though she were going to court. On the Conte's expressing some fear of upsetting Her Highness's arrangements, since she was probably going out, the great lady replied that a Princess of Parma owed it to herself to be always in such array. For the first time since misfortune had befallen him the Conte felt an impulse of gaiety. 'I did well to come here,' he thought, 'and I must make my declaration this very day.'

The Princess had been delighted on receiving a visit from a man so renowned for his wit, and a Prime Minister moreover; the poor old maid was hardly accustomed to such visitors. The Conte began his remarks with an artfully worded preamble, that touched on the immense distance that must always separate a mere nobleman from the members of a reigning family.

'One must draw some distinction,' said the Princess. 'The daughter of a King of France, for instance, has no hope of ever succeeding to the throne; but things are not like that in the House of Parma. That is why we Farnese must always maintain a certain dignity in external, and I, myself, poor Princess as you see me now, cannot say that it is absolutely impossible that one day you may be my Prime Minister.'

The odd unexpectedness of this remark gave the poor Conte a second momentary feeling of utter amusement.

On leaving the apartments of the Princess Isotta, who had blushed deeply on receiving the Prime Minister's avowal of his passion, the latter met one of the palace attendants. The Prince had sent for him to come with all due speed.

'I am unwell,' replied the Minister, delighted to have the chance of behaving rudely to his Prince. 'Ah ha!' he cried, raging inwardly, 'you drive me utterly distracted, and then you expect me to do you a service! But you should realize, my dear Prince, that to have been granted power by Providence is no longer sufficient at the present time. It requires great brains and a strong character to succeed in being a despot.'

After dismissing the messenger from the Palace, highly scandalized by the perfect health of this invalid, the Conte thought it an amusing idea to go and see the two men at court who had the greatest influence over General Fabio Conti. What most particularly made the Minister tremble, and robbed him of all his courage, was that the governor of the citadel was accused of having some time ago made away with a certain captain, who had been his personal enemy, by means of the *aquetta di Perugia.*

The Conte was aware that for the past week the Duchessa had been pouring out incredible sums of money with a view of procuring information from people in the citadel; but, in his opinion, she had little hope of success; all eyes were still too much on the alert. We shall not relate to the reader all the attempts at bribery made by this poor woman. She was in despair, and agents of every sort, all perfectly devoted, were aiding her efforts. But there is perhaps only one kind of business which is carried out to perfection in small despotic courts, and that is the custody of political prisoners. The Duchessa's gold had no other effect than to secure the dismissal from the citadel of nine or ten men of all ranks.

CHAPTER 18 : *From a Prison Window*

THUS, in spite of their complete devotion to the prisoner's interests, the Duchessa and the Prime Minister had been able to do but little for him. The Prince was in a furious temper; the court as well as the public had a spite against Fabrizio and were delighted to see him come to grief; he had been too fortunate. In spite of the gold she had scattered broadcast, the Duchessa had not managed to advance a single step in her siege of the citadel; not a day passed but the Marchesa Raversi or Cavaliere Riscara had some new report to communicate to General Fabio Conti, thus bolstering up his weakness.

As we have already said, on the day of his imprisonment, Fabrizio was taken first of all to the governor's residence. This was an attractive little building constructed in the previous century from plans designed by Vanvitelli, who erected it one hundred and eighty feet above the ground, on the platform of the huge Round Tower. From the windows of this little *palazzo*, standing out by itself like a camel's hump on the back of the enormous tower, Fabrizio could look right over the country to the Alps in the far distance. Down below the citadel, he followed with his eye the course of the Parma, a sort of torrent which, turning to the right four leagues from the city, empties its waters into the Po. Beyond the left bank of this river, which formed as it were a series of huge white patches in the midst of the fresh green of the countryside around it, his enraptured eyes picked out distinctly each of the peaks of the mighty wall formed by the Alps on the northern borders of Italy. These peaks, always covered in snow, even in the month of August, as it was then, impart something like a reflected coolness throughout this countryside parched with heat. The eye can follow each tiny detail of their surface, and yet they are more than thirty leagues from the citadel of Parma.

This extensive view from the governor's residence is interrupted at one corner towards the south by the Farnese Tower, in which a room was being hastily prepared for Fabrizio. This second tower, as the reader may perhaps remember, was erected on the platform of the great tower in honour of a certain Crown Prince who, much unlike Hyppolitus the son of Theseus, had nowise repelled the advances of a young stepmother. The Princess died within a few hours;

the Prince's son did not regain his liberty until seventeen years later, when he ascended the throne on the death of his father. This Farnese Tower, to which, after an interval of three quarters of an hour, Fabrizio was conducted, had a very unattractive exterior; it rises some fifty feet above the platform of the great tower and is adorned with a number of lightning conductors.

The Prince, who, in a fit of anger at his wife's conduct, built this prison visible from all the country round about, had the singular desire to persuade his subjects that it had stood there for many years: that is why he gave it the name of the Farnese Tower. It was forbidden to make any reference to this building; yet from all parts of the city of Parma and from the plains around it, people could clearly see the masons laying each of the stones which compose this pentagonal edifice. In order to prove its antiquity, there was placed above the door, two feet wide and four feet high, which forms its entrance, a magnificent bas-relief representing Alessandro Farnese, the famous general, forcing Henri IV to withdraw from Paris. This Farnese Tower, standing in so conspicuous a position, consists of a hall on the ground floor, at least forty paces long, broad in proportion and filled with extremely squat pillars, for this disproportionately huge room is not more than fifteen feet high. It is used as a guard-room, and in the middle of it the staircase winds upwards in a spiral round one of the pillars; it is a small openwork iron staircase, very light, and barely two feet wide. Up this staircase, which quivered under the weight of the gaolers who were escorting him, Fabrizio came to a set of huge rooms more than twenty feet high and forming a magnificent first floor. They had in times past been furnished with the greatest luxury for the young Prince who spent in them the seventeen best years of his life. At one end of these rooms the new prisoner was shown a chapel of the greatest magnificence. The walls and the vaulted ceiling were entirely covered in black marble; pillars, also black and of the noblest proportions, were placed in line along the black walls without touching them, and these walls were decorated with a number of skulls in white marble, of colossal proportions, elegantly carved and supported underneath by crossbones. 'Here indeed,' thought Fabrizio, 'is an invention of the hatred that cannot kill, and what a devilish idea to show that sort of thing to me!'

A very light open-work staircase, similarly winding round a pillar, gave access to the second floor of this prison, and it was in the rooms of this second floor, which were approximately fifteen feet in height, that for the past year General Fabio Conti had given proof of his genius. First of all, under his direction, solid bars had been fitted to the windows of these rooms, originally occupied by the Prince's servants, and standing more than thirty feet above the flag-stones which paved the platform of the great Round Tower. The approach to these rooms, each of which had two windows, was along a dark corridor, running through the centre of this building; and in this very narrow corridor, Fabrizio noticed three iron doors in succession, formed of enormous iron bars and reaching right up to the vaulted ceiling. It was the plans, the cross sections and eleva-tions of all these fine inventions that, for two years past, had secured the General an audience with his master every week.

A conspirator placed in one of these rooms could not appeal to public opinion on the grounds of being treated in an inhuman fashion, and yet he was unable to communicate with any living soul, or to make a movement without its being heard. In each of these rooms the General had placed huge planks of oak to form a sort of trestle-table three feet high, and this was his great invention, the one that gave him a claim to the Ministry of Police. On these trestles he had set up a cell of planks that gave back every echo, some ten feet high, and only touching the wall on the window side. Along the other three sides ran a narrow passage four feet wide, between the original wall of the prison, which consisted of huge blocks of hewn stone, and the wooden sides of the cell. These sides, formed of four thicknesses of walnut, oak, and deal, were firmly held together by iron bolts and by innumerable nails.

It was into one of these rooms, made ready a year earlier, and the masterpiece of General Fabio Conti's talent, which had received the fine title of *Passive Obedience*, that Fabrizio was ushered. He ran over to the windows. The view from these barred windows was sublime; one little corner of the horizon only was hidden, to the north-west, by the cornice on the roof of the governor's charming *palazzo*, which was only two storeys high. The ground floor was occupied by the offices of the staff; and Fabrizio's eyes were first drawn to one of the windows of the upper floor, in which were to be seen, in pretty cages, a great number of birds of all sorts and kinds. Fabrizio amused himself in listening to their song, and in watching them greet the last rays of the setting sun, while the gaolers were bustling round him. This aviary window was not more than twenty-five feet away from one of his, and some five or six feet below it, so that he looked downwards on the birds.

There was a moon that evening, and at the moment of Fabrizio's entry into his prison it was rising majestically above the horizon on the right, over the chain of the Alps in the direction of Treviso. It was only half past eight, and at the other extremity of the horizon, to the west, a brilliant orange-red sunset picked out in perfect relief the outlines of Monviso and the other peaks of the Alps, running inland from Nice towards the Mont Cenis and Turin. Without a thought of his misfortunes, Fabrizio was moved and enraptured by this sublime spectacle. 'So it is in this enchanting world that Clelia Conti dwells! With her pensive and serious nature she must particularly enjoy this view. Here it is just as if one were in the solitude of the mountains a hundred leagues from Parma.' It was not until he had spent more than two hours at the window, admiring this wide landscape which spoke to his soul, and often also letting his eyes rest on the governor's charming *palazzo*, that Fabrizio suddenly exclaimed: 'But is this really a prison? Is this what I have dreaded so intensely?' Instead of seeing discomforts and reasons for bitterness at every turn, our hero let himself be charmed by the amenities of his prison.

Suddenly his attention was rudely recalled to reality by a frightful uproar. His wooden cell, which was rather like a cage and particularly sensitive to sound, was violently shaken. The barking of a dog and a number of little shrill squeaks added their full quota to the most amazing din. 'What on earth is up? Am I going to escape so soon?' thought Fabrizio. A moment later he was laughing as possibly no one has ever laughed in a prison. By the General's orders, at the same time as the gaolers there had been sent up an English dog, extremely savage, which was set to guard the more important prisoners, and was to spend the night in the space so ingeniously contrived all round Fabrizio's cage. The dog and the gaoler were to sleep in the three foot gap left between the stone pavement of the original floor of the room and the wooden boards on which the prisoner could not take a step without being heard.

Now, at the time Fabrizio arrived there, the room named *Passive Obedience* happened to be occupied by a hundred rats which fled in all directions. The dog, a sort of cross between a spaniel and an English fox terrier, was no beauty, but on the other hand he showed

himself extremely alert. He had been tethered to the flagstones below
the floor of the wooden room; but when he smelt the rats passing
quite close by him he made such desperate efforts that he succeeded
in slipping his head out of his collar. Then began that marvellous
battle, the din of which had aroused Fabrizio, sunk in far from
melancholy dreams. The rats that had managed to escape the first
snap of the mongrel's teeth took refuge in the wooden room, while
the dog came after them up the six steps that led from the stone floor
to Fabrizio's cell. Then began a far more frightful racket; the cell
was shaken to its very foundations. Fabrizio laughed like mad, and
laughed till he cried. The gaoler Grillo, no less overcome by laughter,
had shut the door. The dog, in chasing after the rats, was not im-
peded by any furniture, for the room was completely bare; there
was nothing to check his bounds in the course of his hunt except an
iron stove in one corner. When the dog had triumphed over all his
enemies, Fabrizio called to him, patted him, and succeeded in making
friends with him. 'If ever this animal should see me jumping over a
wall,' he said to himself, 'he will not bark.' But such artful designs
were an affectation on his part: in the state of mind in which he was,
he found his happiness in playing with this dog. By some odd freak
which he did not stop to consider, a feeling of secret joy possessed
him deep down in his heart.

After getting quite out of breath by running about with the dog,
he said to the gaoler: 'What's your name?'

'Grillo, at your Excellency's service in all that is allowed by the
regulations.'

'Well then, my dear Grillo, a certain fellow named Giletti tried to
murder me on one of the highroads. I defended myself and killed
him. I would kill him again if it had to be done, but for all that I
wish to lead a merry life so long as I am your guest. Ask leave of
your chiefs, and go and ask for some linen for me from the Palazzo
Sanseverina; in addition, buy me a plentiful supply of *nebiolo d'Asti*.'

This is a quite good sparkling wine which is made in Piedmont in
Alfieri's native place, and is highly esteemed, especially by the class
of connoisseurs of wine to which gaolers belong. Nine or ten of
these gentlemen were engaged in transporting to Fabrizio's wooden
room a few antique and highly gilded pieces of furniture, which
they had taken from the Prince's apartments on the first floor; all
of them carefully treasured up in their minds the words spoken in

recommendation of the wine of Asti. In spite of all they could do, the fitting up of Fabrizio's abode for this first night was deplorable, but he himself appeared to be upset only by the absence of a bottle of good *nebiolo*. 'He seems a good sort of chap,' said the gaolers as they left him, 'there's only one thing to be hoped, that our bosses will let him have money sent in to him.'

When he was alone and had recovered a little from all this disturbance, Fabrizio, gazing at this vast horizon extending from Monviso to Treviso, at the long chain of the Alps, the snow-covered peaks, the stars, and so on, asked himself: 'Is it possible that this is really a prison, and this my first night in prison, too? I can well imagine that Clelia Conti enjoys this airy solitude. Here one is a thousand leagues above the pettinesses and the wicked, spiteful things which occupy our minds down there. If these birds over there below my window belong to her, I shall see her ... Will she blush when she catches sight of me?' It was while still debating this important question that sleep overtook the prisoner in the small hours of the night.

On the day following this night, the first spent in prison and in the course of which he had never once lost patience, Fabrizio was reduced to making conversation with Fox, the English dog. The gaoler Grillo certainly still continued to look at him with a very friendly eye, but a newly issued order made him dumb, and he brought neither linen nor *nebiolo*.

'Shall I see Clelia?' Fabrizio asked himself on waking. 'But are those birds really hers?' The birds were beginning to utter little chirps and to sing, and at that height this was the only sound that was carried on the air. It was for Fabrizio a sensation full of novelty and pleasure to experience the deep silence which reigned at this height. He listened with rapture to the little warblings, so shrill and fitful, with which his neighbours the birds were greeting the day. 'If they belong to her, she will appear for a moment in that room down there, beneath my window.' And while he gazed intently at the huge ranges of the Alps, against the first tiers of which the citadel of Parma seemed to rise like an outwork, his eyes kept glancing back every moment to the sumptuous cages of satin-wood and mahogany which, adorned with gilded wires, hung high up in the middle of the bright room which served as an aviary. What Fabrizio did not discover until later was that this room was the only one on the upper floor which had any shade between eleven o'clock and four. The Farnese Tower screened it from the sun.

'How grieved I shall be,' thought Fabrizio, 'if, instead of that heavenly, pensive countenance which I expect and which will possibly blush a little if she catches sight of me, I see appear the coarse face of some completely common chambermaid, sent in her place to see to the birds! But if I see Clelia, will she condescend to notice me? Upon my soul, I shall have to take some liberties so as to attract attention; my position should have some privileges; besides we are both alone here and so far removed from the world. I am a prisoner and presumably what General Conti and other wretches of his type call one of their inferiors ... But she has so much intelligence, or, I should rather say, so much heart, or so the Conte supposes, that possibly, just as he says, she despises her father's profession; that would account for her melancholy! A noble cause of sadness! But, after all, I am not exactly a stranger to her. With what entirely modest grace she greeted me yesterday evening! I remember quite well how, that time we met each other near Como, I said to her: "One day I shall come to see your beautiful pictures in Parma. Will you then remember this name: Fabrizio del Dongo?" Will she have forgotten it? She was so young at the time!

'But by the way,' Fabrizio said to himself in astonishment, suddenly interrupting the current of his thoughts, 'I am forgetting to be angry. Can I be one of those men of valour of whom antiquity has furnished the world with certain examples? Am I a hero without suspecting it? Can you believe it! I who was so much afraid of prison am now confined to one, and I cannot even remember to be sad! This is certainly a case where it can be said that the fear of evil is a hundred times greater than the evil itself. What! I actually have to argue with myself before feeling distressed at this imprisonment which, as Blanès said, may as easily last ten years as ten months? Can it be surprise at all these novel surroundings that is distracting me from the grief I ought to feel? Perhaps this cheerful humour, independent of my will and with little rational foundation, will leave me all of a sudden. Perhaps in a single moment I shall sink back into the dark despair that I actually ought to be feeling.

'In any case, it is highly surprising to be in prison and to have to reason with myself in order to feel sad! Upon my word, I come back to my former supposition, perhaps I have a great character, after all!'

Fabrizio's musings were interrupted by the carpenter of the citadel, who came to take the measurements of a shutter for his windows. It was the first time that this prison had been used, and they had forgotten to complete it in this essential detail.

'And so,' thought Fabrizio, 'I am going to be deprived of that exquisite view.' And he tried to feel sad about this deprivation.

'But, good heavens!' he cried suddenly, addressing the carpenter. 'Am I not to see those pretty birds any more?'

'Ah, the Signorina's birds, that she's so fond of!' said the man with a kindly air. 'Hidden, eclipsed, blotted out like all the rest.'

The carpenter was as strictly forbidden to talk as were the gaolers, but this man felt pity for the prisoner's youth. He informed him that these enormous shutters, resting on the sills of the two windows, and standing away from the walls as they rose upwards, were intended to leave the prisoners no view save that of the sky. 'It is done,' he was told, 'for the sake of their morals, to encourage a more wholesome feeling of sadness and the desire to amend their ways in the hearts of the prisoners. The General,' added the carpenter, 'has also hit on the idea of taking the glass out of their windows and putting oiled paper there instead.'

Fabrizio was much taken with the epigrammatic turn of this conversation, a thing extremely rare in Italy.

'I should very much like to have a bird to cheer me, I am madly fond of them. Buy me one from Signorina Clelia Conti's maid.'

'What, do you know her,' exclaimed the carpenter, 'that you say her name so easily?'

'Who has not heard tell of so famous a beauty? But I have had the honour of meeting her several times at court.'

'The poor young lady finds life very dull here,' continued the carpenter. 'She spends all her time over there with her birds. This morning she has just sent out to buy some fine orange trees, which have been placed by her orders at the door of the tower, under your window. If it weren't for the cornice, you could see them.' There were in this reply certain things very precious to Fabrizio; he found a tactful way of giving the carpenter some money.

'I am breaking two of the regulations at once,' the man told him; 'I am talking to your Excellency and I am taking money. The day after tomorrow, when I come back about the shutters, I shall have a bird in my pocket, and if I'm not alone, I'll make a pretence of letting it escape. If I possibly can, I'll bring you a prayer-book; it must be very painful to you not to be able to recite your Offices.'

'So those birds are hers,' said Fabrizio to himself as soon as he was alone, 'but in two days more I shall no longer see them.' At this thought his eyes became tinged with sadness. But at length, to his inexpressible joy, after so long a wait and so much gazing, towards midday Clelia came to attend to her birds. Fabrizio remained motionless and unable to breathe; he was standing up against the enormous bars of his window and quite close to them. He noticed that she did not raise her eyes in his direction, but there was an air of constraint about her movements, like those of a person who knows that she is being looked at. Even had she wished to do so, the poor girl could not have forgotten the delicate smile she had seen hovering over the prisoner's lips the day before, just at the moment when the constables brought him out of the guard-room.

Although to all appearances she was keeping the most careful watch on all her actions, at the moment when she drew near to the window of the aviary, she blushed quite perceptibly. Fabrizio's first thought, as he stood glued to the iron bars of his window, was to indulge in the childish trick of tapping lightly with his hand on those bars, and so making a slight noise; then the mere idea of such a want of delicacy horrified him. 'It would serve me right if for the next week she sent her maid to attend to her birds.' Such a delicate thought would never have occurred to him in Naples or Novara.

He followed her eagerly with his eyes. 'Obviously,' he said to himself, 'she is going to leave the room without deigning to cast a glance at this poor window, and yet she is just opposite me.' But, on coming back from the farther end of the room, which Fabrizio, thanks to his superior position, could see quite plainly, Clelia could not help casting a swift upward glance at him as she moved forward, and this was quite enough to make Fabrizio think himself authorized to bow to her. 'Are we not alone in the world up here?' he said to himself, to give himself the courage to do so. At this salute the girl stopped short and lowered her eyes. Then Fabrizio saw her raise them again very slowly; and, evidently forcing herself to respond, she greeted the prisoner with the most grave and *distant* gesture. She could not, however, impose silence on her eyes; without her knowledge, in all probability, they expressed for a moment the keenest pity. Fabrizio remarked that she blushed so deeply that the rosy tinge spread rapidly down to her shoulders, from which, as she entered the aviary, the heat had obliged her to remove a black lace shawl. The unconscious stare with which Fabrizio replied to her greeting increased the girl's agitation twofold. 'How happy that poor woman would be,' she said to herself, thinking of the Duchessa, 'if just for one moment she could see him as I see him now!'

Fabrizio had had some faint hope of saluting her again as she went away; but, to avoid this further courtesy, Clelia beat a skilful retreat by stages, from cage to cage, as if, at the end of her task, she had to attend to the birds that were nearest the door. At length she went out. Fabrizio stood motionless, gazing at the door through which she had just disappeared. He was another man.

From that moment the sole object of his thoughts was to discover how he might manage to go on seeing her, even after they had put up that horrible shutter in front of the window that overlooked the governor's *palazzo*.

On the previous evening, before going to bed, he had set himself the long and tedious task of hiding the greater part of the gold in his possession in several of the rat-holes which graced his wooden cell. 'Tonight,' he thought, 'I must hide my watch. Have I not heard it said that with patience and a jagged watch-spring one can cut through wood and even iron? So I may be able to saw through this shutter.' The work of concealing his watch, which took him two whole hours, did not seem to him at all long; he was pondering over the different means of attaining his end and reckoning what he himself could do in the way of carpentry. 'If I set about it properly,' he said to himself, 'I shall be able to cut a section clean out of the oak plank which will form the shutter, at the place where it will rest on the window sill. I will take this piece out and put it back according to circumstances. I shall give everything I possess to Grillo, so that he may be kind enough not to notice this little device.'

All Fabrizio's happiness from now on depended on the possibility of carrying out this task, and he could think of nothing else. 'If I can only manage to see her, I am a happy man ... But no,' he went on, 'she must also see that I see her.' All night long his head was filled with devices of carpentering, and possibly he never once gave a thought to the court of Parma, the Prince's anger, or anything of that sort. We must admit that he did not think either of the grief in which the Duchessa must be plunged.

He waited with impatience for the morning; but the carpenter did not appear again; evidently he was regarded by the prison authorities as too much of a Liberal. They took care to send another man, a sour-faced fellow who made no reply except a portentous growl to all the pleasant remarks which Fabrizio cleverly tried to address to him. Certain of the Duchessa's many attempts to enter into correspondence with Fabrizio had been discovered by the Marchesa Raversi's many agents, and through her means General Fabio Conti was daily warned, frightened, and put on his mettle. Every eight hours six soldiers of the guard relieved the previous six in the great hall with the hundred pillars on the ground floor. In addition to these, the governor posted a gaoler on guard at each of the three successive iron doors of the corridor, and poor Grillo, the only person who saw the prisoner, was condemned to leave the Farnese Tower only once a week, at which he grumbled terribly. He vented his ill-humour on Fabrizio, who had the good sense to reply with these words only: 'Plenty of good *nebiolo d'Asti*, my friend.' And he gave him money.

'Well now, even this, which consoles us in all our troubles,' exclaimed the indignant Grillo, in a voice barely loud enough to be heard by the prisoner, 'we are forbidden to take and I ought to refuse it, but I accept it. Anyhow, it's money wasted; I can tell you nothing about anything. Go on, you must be jolly guilty. The whole citadel is upside-down because of you. Her Grace the Duchessa's fine goings-on have got three of us dismissed already.'

'Will the shutter be ready before midday?' This was the great question that made Fabrizio's heart beat fast throughout the whole of that long morning. He counted each quarter as it sounded from the citadel clock. At length, when the clock struck a quarter to twelve, the shutter had not yet arrived; Clelia reappeared and attended to her birds. Cruel necessity had made Fabrizio's daring take such strides, and the risk of not seeing her again seemed to him so greatly to transcend all others, that he ventured, as he looked at Clelia, to make with his fingers the gesture of sawing through the shutter. It is true that as soon as she had remarked this gesture, so seditious in a prison, she half-inclined her head and withdrew.

'Goodness me!' thought Fabrizio in amazement, 'can she be so unreasonable as to see, in a gesture dictated by the most imperious necessity, a piece of senseless impertinence? I wanted to beg her

always to be so kind, when she is attending to her birds, as to cast a
glance now and then at the prison window, even when she finds it
masked by an enormous wooden shutter: I wanted to make her
understand that I shall do everything that is humanly possible to
contrive to see her. Good God! Does this mean that she will not
come tomorrow on account of this indiscreet gesture?' This fear,
which troubled Fabrizio's sleep, was entirely justified. By three
o'clock on the following day, when the two huge shutters were finally
installed in front of Fabrizio's windows, Clelia had not appeared.
The various sections of these shutters had been hauled up from the
platform of the great tower by means of ropes and pulleys attached
to the iron bars outside the windows. It is true that Clelia, hidden
behind one of the sun-blinds in her room, had followed with deep
distress every movement of the workmen. She had clearly noted
Fabrizio's desperate anxiety, but had none the less had the courage
to keep the promise she had made to herself.

Clelia was a little devotee of Liberalism. While still a child she
had taken seriously all the Liberal utterances she had heard in the
company of her father, who thought only of making a good position
for himself. From this she had come to feel a contempt and almost a
horror for the courtier's too compliant character; hence her antipathy
to marriage. Since Fabrizio's arrival she had been tormented by
remorse. 'See how my unworthy heart,' she said to herself, 'takes
sides with the people who wish to betray my father! He dares to
make signs to me as if he were sawing through a door! ... But,'
she immediately added, with an aching heart, 'the whole city is
talking of his approaching death! Tomorrow, perhaps, may be the
fatal day! With the monsters who govern us, what in the world is
not possible! What gentleness, what heroic serenity in those eyes
which are perhaps about to close for ever! Heavens! what must be
the Duchessa's anguish! They say, by the way, that she is in a state
of utter despair. If I were she, I would go and stab the Prince, like
the heroic Charlotte Corday.'

Throughout this third day of his imprisonment Fabrizio was beside
himself with rage, but solely at not seeing Clelia reappear. 'Even
if it made her angry, I ought to have told her that I loved her,' he
cried, for he had arrived at this discovery. 'No, it is not from greatness of heart that I am not thinking about prison and am making
Blanès' prophecy prove false; I cannot claim so much honour. In

spite of myself I keep thinking of that sweet, pitying glance that Clelia cast on me as the constables were leading me out of the guardroom; that glance has wiped out all my past life. Who would have said that I should find such sweet eyes in such a place! And at the very moment when my own sight was offended by the faces of Barbone and of his worship the General who governs this prison, Heaven appeared to me in the midst of those vile creatures. And how can one help loving beauty and not seeking to see it again? No, it is certainly not greatness of heart that makes me indifferent to all the petty vexations which prison heaps upon me.'

Fabrizio's imagination, running rapidly over every possibility in turn, arrived at that of his being set at liberty. 'No doubt the Duchessa's friendship will work miracles for me. Well, I shall thank her for my liberty with my lips only; this is not the sort of place to which one pays frequent visits! Once out of prison, moving as we do in different circles, I should hardly ever see Clelia again! And after all, what harm does being in prison do me? If Clelia would only deign not to overwhelm me with her anger, what more should I have to ask of Heaven?'

On the evening of that day on which he had not seen his pretty neighbour, a great idea occurred to him. With the iron cross of the rosary handed out to every prisoner on his admission to prison, he began, with some success, to bore a hole in the shutter. 'This is possibly an imprudence,' he said to himself, before he began. 'Didn't the carpenters say in front of me that from tomorrow the painters would be coming in their place? What will these men say when they find the shutter with a hole in it? But if I don't commit this imprudence, I shan't be able to see her tomorrow. What! Am I to remain, by my own fault, a whole day without seeing her; and that, too, after she parted from me in anger.'

Fabrizio's rashness was rewarded. After fifteen hours' labour he finally saw Clelia, and, by extreme good fortune, as she had no idea that he could see her, she stood for a long time without moving and with her gaze fixed on the enormous shutter. He had ample time to read signs of the tenderest pity in her eyes. Towards the end of her visit she was even neglecting her duty to her birds to spend whole minutes in motionless contemplation of his window. Her heart was deeply troubled; she was thinking of the Duchessa, whose extreme unhappiness had inspired her with so much pity, and yet she was beginning to hate her. She was utterly at a loss to understand the profound melancholy which had taken possession of her whole being, and was angry with herself. Two or three times during the course of her visit Fabrizio's impatience moved him to try to shake the shutter; he felt that he could not be happy so long as he could not show Clelia that he saw her. 'However,' he said to himself, 'with that shy and retiring nature of hers, if she knew that I could see her so easily, she would probably slip away out of my sight.'

He was far happier on the following day (out of what poor trifles does love create happiness!). While she was gazing sadly up at the huge shutter, he managed to poke a tiny piece of wire through the hole he had contrived with his iron cross, and make signs to her which she evidently understood, at least in the sense that they implied: 'I am here, and I can see you.'

For the next few days Fabrizio was unlucky. He wanted to remove from the colossal shutter a piece of board the size of his hand, which could be replaced when he chose, and which would enable him to see and to be seen, that is to say to speak, at least by signs, of all that was in his heart. But it happened that the noise of the very imperfect little saw which he had made by notching the spring of his watch with the cross disturbed Grillo, who came and spent long hours in his cell. He thought he could see, it is true, that Clelia's severity seemed to diminish in proportion as the material difficulties in the way of any communication between them increased. He noted quite plainly that she no longer affected to lower her eyes or to look at the birds whenever he tried to make her aware of his presence with the help of his wretched little bit of wire. He had the pleasure of seeing that she never failed to appear in the aviary exactly as the clock struck a quarter to twelve, and he was almost presumptuous enough to imagine himself to be the cause of this exact punctuality. Why so? Such an idea does not seem reasonable; but love detects shades invisible to the indifferent eye, and draws endless conclusions from them. For instance, now that Clelia could no longer see the prisoner, she would raise her eyes towards his window almost as soon as she entered the aviary.

This was during those mournful days when no one in Parma had any doubts that Fabrizio would shortly be put to death. He alone knew nothing. But the frightful thought was never for a moment out of Clelia's mind, and how could she therefore reproach herself for

the excessive interest she took in Fabrizio? He was about to perish –
and in the cause of freedom! For it was too absurd to put a del Dongo
to death for thrusting his sword into a strolling player. It was true
that this attractive young man was attached to another woman!
Clelia was profoundly unhappy, and, without admitting to herself
the precise nature of the interest she took in his fate, she said to
herself: 'If they lead him out to die, I shall certainly take refuge in a
convent, and never in my life will I reappear in court circles; they
horrify me. Honey-tongued murderers, everyone!'

On the eighth day of Fabrizio's imprisonment, she had good cause
to blush. Absorbed in her own sad thoughts, she was gazing intently
at the shutter that hid the prisoner's window. That day he had not as
yet given any sign of his presence. Suddenly a small piece of the shutter,
larger than a man's hand, was removed by him. He looked at her
with an air of gaiety and she read a greeting in his eyes. She had not
the strength to endure this unlooked-for ordeal; she turned quickly
round to her birds and began to attend to them; but she trembled so
much that she spilt the water she was pouring out for them, and
Fabrizio could perfectly well see her emotion. She could not face
this situation, and decided to escape from it by running out of the
room.

This was, beyond all comparison, the happiest moment of Fabrizio's life. With what rapture he would have refused his freedom,
had it been offered to him there and then!

The following day was the day of the Duchessa's great despair.
Everyone in the city took it as certain that it was all over with Fabrizio. Clelia herself had not the sad courage to show him a harshness
that was not in her heart. She spent an hour and a half in the aviary,
paid attention to all his signals, and often answered him, at least by
glances expressing the keenest and sincerest interest. Every now and
then she turned away from him so as not to let him see her tears.
Her instinctive feminine coquetry made her keenly aware of the in-
adequacy of the language they employed. If they could have spoken
to each other, in how many different ways could she not have tried
to discover the precise nature of the feelings which Fabrizio had for
the Duchessa. Clelia was hardly able to delude herself any longer;
her feeling for this lady was one of hatred.

One night Fabrizio began to think somewhat seriously of his aunt.
He was amazed to find he could hardly recognize the picture he had

formed of her; the memories he had of her were now completely altered; in his mind, at this moment, she seemed to him fifty years old.

'Good God!' he exclaimed with considerable feeling, 'how well advised I was not to tell her that I loved her!' He had reached the point of being barely able to understand how he had ever thought her so pretty. In that respect, his impressions of little Marietta had changed less perceptibly; this was because he had never imagined that his heart was in any way involved in his love for Marietta, whereas he had often believed that his whole heart belonged to the Duchessa. The Duchessa d'A — and Marietta now appeared to him as two young doves, whose whole charm possibly lay in their weakness and their innocence, whereas the sublime image of Clelia Conti, in taking entire possession of his heart, went so far as to inspire him with terror. He felt only too clearly that the happiness of his whole life would perforce depend on his relations with the governor's daughter, and that it lay in her power to make him the unhappiest of men. Every day he lived in mortal fear of seeing brought to some sudden end, by some caprice of her will against which there was no appeal, this strange and exquisitely delightful sort of life he led in her presence. In any event, she had already filled with joy the first two months of his stay in prison. This was the period during which, twice a week, General Fabio Conti would say to the Prince: 'I can give your Highness my word of honour that the prisoner del Dongo never speaks to a living soul, and is spending his life overwhelmed by the deepest despair, or else asleep.'

Clelia came two or three times a day to see her birds, sometimes for a few moments only. If Fabrizio had not loved her so well he would have clearly seen that he was loved; but he had very grave doubts about this matter. Clelia had had a piano put in the aviary. As she struck the notes, so that the sound of the instrument might account for her presence there, and engage the attention of the sentries marching up and down beneath her windows, her eyes would be replying to Fabrizio's questions. To one subject alone she never made any answer, and indeed, on certain grave occasions, she took to flight, and sometimes disappeared for the space of a whole day. This was when Fabrizio's signals indicated feelings whose import it was too difficult not to understand. On this point she was inexorable.

Thus, although straitly confined in a somewhat narrow cage,

Fabrizio's life was fully occupied. It was entirely taken up with seeking the solution of this important problem: 'Does she love me?' The result of innumerable observations, perpetually renewed, but as perpetually subject to misgivings, was as follows: 'All her deliberate gestures say "No", but every involuntary movement of her eyes seems to admit that she is becoming fond of me.'

Clelia hoped very much that she might never come to the point of an avowal of her feelings, and it was to avert this danger that she had refused, with an excessive show of anger, a request that Fabrizio had several times addressed to her. The poverty of the resources employed by the poor prisoner ought, it might seem, to have inspired greater pity in Clelia. He tried to communicate with her by means of letters which he traced upon his hand with a piece of charcoal he had been so fortunate as to discover in his stove; he would have formed the words letter by letter, one after the other. This invention would have doubled the means of conversation, in that it would have allowed him to express his ideas clearly. His window was about five-and-twenty feet away from Clelia's; it would have been too great a risk for them to talk to each other over the heads of the sentries patrolling in front of the governor's residence. Fabrizio was in doubt as to whether he was loved; if he had had any experience of love he would have been left with no doubts at all. But no woman had ever as yet possessed his heart; he had, moreover, no suspicion of a secret which would have filled him with despair if he had known of it. There was serious question of a marriage between Clelia Conti and the Marchese Crescenzi, the richest man at court.

CHAPTER 19: *Alphabetic Operations*

GENERAL FABIO CONTI'S ambition, excited to the verge of madness by difficulties that had just arisen to hamper the Prime Minister Mosca in his career and which seemed to presage his downfall, had led him into having violent scenes with his daughter. He repeated to her incessantly and angrily that she would ruin his prospects if she did not finally make up her mind to choose a husband. Now that she was over twenty it was time to come to some decision. This cruel state of isolation in which her unreasonable obstinacy was plunging the General must be brought to an end, and so forth.

It was originally to escape from such constantly recurring fits of temper that Clelia had taken refuge in the aviary. It could be reached only by an extremely awkward little wooden staircase, which his gout made into a serious obstacle for the governor.

For some weeks past Clelia's heart and mind had been so troubled, she herself knew so little what she ought to wish for, that, without giving any definite promise to her father, she had almost allowed herself to be bound by one. In one of his fits of rage the General had shouted at her that he could easily send her to mope in the dreariest convent in Parma and that he would leave her there kicking her heels until she condescended to make a choice.

'You know that our family, old as it is, cannot muster a rent-roll of six thousand lire, while the Marchese Crescenzi's fortune amounts to more than a hundred thousand scudi a year. Everyone at court agrees that he has the kindest disposition; he has never given anyone cause for complaint; he is a very handsome man, young, and high in the Prince's favour, and I maintain that a woman who would reject his suit is only fit for a madhouse. If this were your first refusal I might perhaps put up with it; but there are now some five or six suitors, all among the first men at court, whom you have rejected, like the little goose you are. And what would become of you, I ask you, if I were to be retired on half-pay? What a triumph for my enemies, if they saw me living in some second-floor apartment, when I have so often been talked of as a possible Minister! No, by jingo, my good nature has let me play the part of a foolish old grey-beard quite long enough. You will supply me with some valid objection to this poor Marchese Crescenzi, who is so kind as to be in love with you, to be willing to marry you without a dowry, and to settle on you a jointure of thirty thousand lire a year, which will at all events provide me with board and lodging; you will talk to me sensibly, or, by jingo, you will marry him in two months from now! ...'

One remark alone in the whole of this speech had struck Clelia; this was the threat to send her to a convent, and consequently away from the citadel, at a moment, moreover, when Fabrizio's life seemed to be hanging only by a thread; for not a month passed in which the rumour of his approaching death was not once more current in the city or at court. Whatever arguments she might use, she could not make up her mind to run this risk. To be separated from Fabrizio, and at the moment when she trembled for his life! This was in her eyes the greatest of evils; it was at any rate the most immediate.

This does not mean that, even in the fact of not being parted from Fabrizio, her heart envisaged any prospect of happiness. She believed him to be loved by the Duchessa, and her soul was torn by deadly jealousy. Her mind dwelt incessantly on the advantages possessed by this woman who was so generally admired. The extreme reserve which she imposed on herself with regard to Fabrizio, the language of signs to which she had restricted him, for fear of being led into some indiscretion, all seemed to combine to deprive her of the means of reaching some clear understanding as to his relations with the Duchessa. Thus, every day, she became more cruelly conscious of the frightful misfortune of having a rival in Fabrizio's heart, and every day she dared less and less expose herself to the risk of giving him an opportunity of telling her the whole truth about what was going on in that heart. But how delightful it would be, all the same, to hear him make an avowal of his true feelings! What a joy for Clelia to be able to clear away those frightful suspicions that were poisoning her life!

Fabrizio had a volatile disposition; in Naples he had had the reputation of changing his mistresses easily. Despite all the reserve obligatory on the part of a young unmarried lady, Clelia, since she become a Canoness and had gone to court, had succeeded without ever asking questions, but merely by listening attentively, in finding out about the reputation made for themselves by each of the young men who had in turn sought her hand in marriage. Well Fabrizio, when compared with all these young men, was the one regarded as being the most fickle in affairs of the heart. He was in prison, he was bored, he was paying court to the only woman to whom he had a chance of speaking. What could be more simple? What, indeed, more *usual*? And it was this that wrung Clelia's heart. Even if, by a full revelation of his feelings, she should learn that Fabrizio no longer loved the Duchessa, what confidence could she have in his words? Even if she believed in the sincerity of what he said to her, what confidence could she have in the lasting nature of his feelings? And finally, to fill her heart completely with despair, was Fabrizio not already far advanced in an ecclesiastical career? Was he not on the eve of binding himself by vows that would hold him for ever? Did not the highest dignities await him in that walk of life? 'If I had the slightest glimmer of sense remaining,' the unhappy Clelia said to herself, 'ought I not to take to flight? Should I not beg my father to shut me up in some far distant convent? And, to crown my misery, it is precisely the fear of being sent away from the citadel and shut up in a convent that is governing all my conduct! It is this fear that is forcing me to prevaricate, that is obliging me to act the hideous and shameful lie of pretending to accept the public attentions of the Marchese Crescenzi.'

Clelia was by nature extremely sensible; never once in her life had she had to reproach herself with a single ill-considered step, and her conduct on this occasion was the very negation of good sense. Her sufferings may be imagined. They were all the more cruel in that she let herself rest under no illusion. She was becoming attached to a man who was loved to distraction by the most beautiful woman at court, a woman who was superior in so many respects to Clelia herself! And this man, even had he been at liberty, was incapable of any serious attachment, whereas she, as she felt only too well, would never have but one attachment in her life.

It was, therefore, with a heart disturbed by the most frightful twinges of conscience that Clelia came every day to the aviary. Drawn to this spot as if in spite of herself, her uneasiness changed its object and became less cruel; her conscience ceased to trouble her for a few moments. She would watch, with indescribable pulsations of her heart, for the moments when Fabrizio could open the sort of hatch which he had made in the huge shutter that masked his window. Often the presence of the gaoler Grillo in his cell would prevent him from conversing by signs with his friend.

One evening, about eleven o'clock, Fabrizio heard the strangest sort of noises in the citadel. At night, by lying up against the window and poking his head out through the hatch, he could manage to distinguish the slightly louder noises made on the great staircase called the 'Three Hundred Steps', which led from the outer courtyard inside the Round Tower to the stone platform on which had been built the Governor's residence and the Farnese prison in which he was himself.

About half-way up, about one hundred and eighty steps above the ground, this staircase crossed over from the south side of a vast courtyard to the north side. At this point there was a very light and very narrow iron bridge, in the centre of which a turnkey was posted. This man was relieved every six hours; he had to get up and stand out of the way before anyone could pass across the bridge which he was guarding and which was the only means of access to the Governor's house and the Farnese Tower. Two turns of a spring, the key of which the governor carried on his person, were enough to drop this iron bridge down into the courtyard, more than a hundred feet below. This simple precaution once taken, as there was no other staircase in the whole of the citadel, and as every night, on the stroke of twelve, a sergeant brought to the governor the ropes of all the wells and placed them in a closet which was reached through his bedroom, he was left completely inaccessible in his *palazzo*, and it would have been equally impossible for anyone in the world to reach the Farnese Tower.

All this Fabrizio had clearly noticed, on the day of his arrival at the citadel, and Grillo, who like all gaolers loved to boast of his prison, had explained the matter to him on more than one occasion; thus he had but little hope of escape. All the same, he called to mind one of Father Blanès' maxims: 'A lover thinks more often of how to reach his mistress than a husband thinks of guarding his wife; a prisoner thinks more often of escaping than the gaoler of locking his door; thus, whatever obstacles there may be, lovers and prisoners are almost sure to succeed.'

That evening Fabrizio could hear quite distinctly a considerable number of men crossing over the iron bridge, known as the 'Slave's Bridge' because a Dalmatian slave had once succeeded in escaping by flinging its guardian down into the courtyard below.

'They are coming here to carry somebody off; perhaps they are going to take me out and hang me. There may, however, be some confusion; I must make the most of it.' He armed himself, he was already taking his gold out of some of his hiding-places, when he suddenly stopped short.

'We men are queer creatures I must agree,' he exclaimed. 'What would an invisible spectator say if he saw my preparations? Do I by any chance wish to escape? What would happen to me the day after my return to Parma? Shouldn't I be doing everything in the world to get back to Clelia? If there is any disorder, let's take advantage of it to slip into the governor's palazzo. Perhaps I may be able to speak to her; perhaps, under cover of the confusion, I may venture to kiss her hand. General Conti, highly suspicious by nature, and no less naturally vain, has his *palazzo* guarded by five sentries, one at each corner of the building, and a fifth outside the main door; but luckily it is a very dark night.' Fabrizio crept on tiptoe to find out what the gaoler Grillo and his dog were doing. The gaoler was fast asleep in an ox-hide suspended from four ropes and enclosed in a coarse net. Fox, the dog, opened his eyes, got up, and came quietly towards Fabrizio to fawn upon him.

Our prisoner went softly back up the six steps which led to his wooden cell. The noise at the foot of the Farnese Tower and immediately in front of the door was becoming so loud that he thought that Grillo might easily wake up. Fabrizio, armed with all his weapons and ready for action, was imagining that great adventures lay in store for him that night, when suddenly he heard the opening bars of the loveliest symphony in the world. He was seized with a violent fit of laughter. 'And there was I already thinking of laying about me with my dagger! As though a serenade were not infinitely more normal than either an abduction requiring the presence of eighty persons in a prison, or than a mutiny!'

The music was excellent and to Fabrizio, who for so many weeks had had no distraction for his spirit, it seemed exquisitely delightful. It made him shed very happy tears; in his rapture he addressed the most irresistible speeches to the fair Clelia. The following morning, however, he found her in such a sombre mood of melancholy, she looked so pale, she cast glances at him in which he read at times so much anger, that he did not feel he had sufficient justification for asking her any questions about the serenade; he was afraid of seeming discourteous.

Clelia had good reason to be sad; it was a serenade given her by the Marchese Crescenzi. So public a step was almost tantamount to an official announcement of their marriage. Until the very day of the serenade, and until nine o'clock that evening, Clelia had put up the bravest resistance; but she had had the weakness to give way before the threat of being sent immediately to a convent, which had been held over her by her father.

'What! I should never see him again!' she had said to herself, weeping. It was in vain that her reason had added: 'I should never see again that creature who will cause me every possible kind of unhappiness, I should never see again that lover of the Duchessa, that fickle being who is known to have had ten mistresses in Naples, and was unfaithful to them all. I should never see again that ambitious young man who, if he survives the sentence now weighing down upon him, is to take Holy Orders! It would be a crime for me ever to look at him again once he has left this citadel, and his natural inconstancy will spare me that temptation. For what am I to him? An excuse for spending less tediously a few hours of each of his days in prison.'

In the midst of all this abuse, Clelia happened to remember the way he smiled at the constables surrounding him when he came out of the turnkey's office on his way up to the Farnese Tower. Her eyes overflowed with tears. 'Dear friend, what would I not do for you? You will be my ruin, I know; such is my fate. I am working my own ruin in a terrible fashion by listening tonight to this frightful serenade; but tomorrow, at midday, I shall look into your eyes again!'

It was on the very morrow of that day on which Clelia had made such great sacrifices for the young prisoner, whom she loved with such deep passion; it was on the morrow of that day on which, seeing all his faults, she had sacrificed her life to him, that Fabrizio was driven to despair by her coldness. If, even while employing only the very imperfect language of signs, he had done the slightest violence to Clelia's feelings, she would probably not have been able to hold back her tears, and Fabrizio would have obtained an avowal of all that she felt for him. But he lacked the courage, he was in too deadly fear of offending Clelia; she might inflict too severe a punishment upon him. In other words, Fabrizio had no experience of the kind of emotion awakened by a woman whom one loves; it was a sensation he had never felt before, even in the faintest degree. It took him a week, from the day of the serenade, to place himself once more on the accustomed footing of simple friendship with Clelia. The poor girl, overcome with mortal fear of betraying her feelings, took refuge in severity, and it seemed to Fabrizio that with every day that passed he stood less high in her favour.

One day – and Fabrizio had by then been nearly three months in prison without holding any communication whatever with the outside world, and yet without feeling unhappy – Grillo had remained in his cell until very late in the morning. Fabrizio did not know how to get rid of him and was feeling desperate. It had already struck half past twelve before he was finally able to open the two little trap-doors, one foot high, which he had made in the fatal shutter.

Clelia was standing at the aviary window, her eyes fixed on Fabrizio's; her drawn features expressed the most violent despair. No sooner had she caught sight of Fabrizio than she signed to him that all was lost. She rushed over to her piano, and making a pretence of singing a recitative from the opera then in vogue, she said to him in sentences broken by her despair and the fear of being understood by the sentries who were patrolling beneath the window, 'Good God! You are still alive? How deeply grateful I am to Heaven! Barbone, that gaoler whose insolence you punished on the day of your arrival here, had disappeared, he was no longer in the citadel. The night before last he returned, and since yesterday I have had reason to believe he is seeking to poison you. He comes prowling through the private kitchen of the *palazzo*, where your meals are prepared. I know nothing for certain, but my maid believes that he only shows his hideous face in the *palazzo* kitchens with the object of making away with you. I was frightened out of my life with anxiety when I did not see you appear, I thought you were dead. Take care not to eat any kind of food until further notice. I shall do everything possible to see that a little chocolate reaches you. In any case, at nine o'clock tonight, if, by Heaven's grace, you should happen to have a bit of thread, or if you can make a line out of some of your linen, let it down from your window on to the orange-trees. I will fasten a cord to it which you can pull up, and by means of this cord I will let you have some bread and some chocolate.'

Fabrizio had carefully treasured up the piece of charcoal which he had found in the stove in his cell. He hastened to take advantage of Clelia's emotion, and wrote on his hand a series of letters which taken in order formed these words:

'I love you, and life is dear to me only because I see you. Above all things, send me some paper and a pencil.'

As Fabrizio had hoped, the extreme terror which he read in Clelia's face prevented the girl from breaking off the conversation after this very bold statement: 'I love you.' She contented herself with showing great annoyance. Fabrizio was clever enough to add: 'With the high wind blowing today I can only catch very faintly the advice you are so kind as to give in your singing; the sound of the piano drowns your voice. What is this poison, for instance, of which you speak?'

At these words the girl's terror reappeared in all its intensity. She hurriedly began to trace large letters in ink on pages which she tore out of a book, and Fabrizio was beside himself with joy on seeing at length established, after three months of effort, this method of correspondence for which he had so vainly begged. He was careful not to abandon the little ruse which had proved so successful. His aim was to begin a correspondence with her, and he kept on pretending not to catch the sense of the words, the letters of which Clelia was holding up in turn before his eyes.

She was obliged to leave the aviary and run off to seek her father. She feared more than anything that he might come to look for her. His suspicious nature would not have been at all satisfied by the close proximity of the aviary window to the shutter that masked the window of the prisoner's cell. A few minutes earlier, when Fabrizio's failure to appear had been causing her such acute anxiety, Clelia herself had had the idea that it might be possible to throw a small stone wrapped in a piece of paper over the top of this shutter. If by a lucky chance the gaoler set to guard Fabrizio should not happen to be in his cell at that moment, it would be a reliable method of corresponding with him.

Our prisoner hastened to make a sort of line out of his linen; and that evening, shortly after nine, he distinctly heard a faint tapping on the tubs of the orange-trees which stood beneath his window. He let down his line which brought back a very long, thin cord, by means of which he drew up first of all a supply of chocolate, and next, to his inexpressible satisfaction, a roll of paper and a pencil. In vain did he let out his cord again, he received nothing more; apparently the sentries had drawn near to the orange-trees. But he was wild with joy. He hastened to write Clelia a letter of infinite length:

no sooner was it finished than he attached it to the cord and let it down. For more than three hours he waited vainly for her to come and take it, and several times drew it up again to make alterations. 'If Clelia does not see my letter tonight,' he thought, 'while she is still excited by her thought of poison, tomorrow morning, perhaps, she will utterly reject all ideas of receiving a letter.'

The fact was that Clelia had been unable to get out of going down into the city with her father. Fabrizio almost guessed as much when, about half past twelve, he heard the General's carriage return; he recognized the sound of the horses' hooves. How great was his joy when, a few minutes after he had heard the General crossing the terrace and the sentries presenting arms to him, he felt a quiver of the cord which he had kept all the time wound round his arm! A heavy weight was attached to this cord, two little jerks on it gave him the signal to draw it up. He had considerable difficulty in getting this weighty object he was pulling up past a cornice which jutted out a long way just underneath his window.

This object which he had so much difficulty in pulling up was a water-bottle full to the brim and wrapped in a shawl. It was with ecstasy that this poor young man, who had been living for so long in such utter solitude, covered this shawl with kisses. But we must give up the attempt to describe his emotion when at last, after so many days of fruitless hoping, he discovered a little scrap of paper which was fastened to the shawl by a pin.

'Drink nothing but this water; keep yourself going on the chocolate. Tomorrow I shall do everything in the world to get some bread to you. I will mark it on all sides with little crosses in ink. It is frightful to have to say it, but you must be told, Barbone may possibly have orders to poison you. How was it you did not feel that the subject you touched on in your pencilled letter was bound to displease me? Consequently I should not be writing to you if it were not for the very grave danger that threatens us. I have just seen the Duchessa; she is well and so is the Conte, but she has grown very thin. Don't write to me any more about that subject. Do you want to make me angry?'

It required a great effort of virtue on Clelia's part to write the last line but one of this letter. Everyone among the society at court alleged that her Grace the Duchessa Sanseverina was becoming extremely friendly with Conte Baldi, that handsome young man, the former friend of the Marchesa Raversi. What was certain was that he had broken in the most scandalous way with the said Marchesa, who for six years had been a second mother to him and had helped him to take a good position in society.

Clelia had been obliged to begin this hastily written little note all over again, since in her first draft there had been some hint of the new love affair with which public spite had credited the Duchessa.

'How mean of me,' she had exclaimed, 'to say things to Fabrizio against the woman he loves!'

The following morning, long before it was light, Grillo came into Fabrizio's cell, put down a fairly heavy parcel, and vanished without saying a word. This parcel contained a fair-sized loaf of bread, marked on every side with little crosses traced with a pen. Fabrizio covered them with kisses; he was very much in love. With the loaf there was a roll of something wrapped in several thicknesses of paper; it contained sequins to the value of six thousand lire. Last of all Fabrizio found a handsome breviary, quite new; a hand which he was beginning to know had traced these words in the margin: '*Poison!* Beware of water, wine, everything; live on chocolate. Get the dog to eat the meal you will have left untouched. You must not appear to suspect anything, the enemy will try some other plan. Don't be foolish, for heaven's sake! and don't take things too lightly!'

Fabrizio made haste to rub out these precious words, which might compromise Clelia, and to tear out a large number of pages from the breviary, with the help of which he made several alphabets. Each letter was neatly traced by means of crushed charcoal soaked in wine. These alphabets were dry when at a quarter to twelve Clelia appeared a foot or two away from the aviary window. 'The great thing now,' said Fabrizio to himself, 'is to get her to agree to make use of them.' But luckily for him, as it happened, she had a great many things to say to the young prisoner about the attempt to poison him; a dog belonging to one of the maidservants had died after eating a dish that was intended for Fabrizio. Clelia, so far from raising any objection to using the alphabets, had prepared a magnificent one of her own sketched in ink. The conversation carried on by this method, a little awkwardly in the first few moments, lasted no less than an hour and a half, that is to say for as long as Clelia was able to stay in the aviary. Two or three times, when Fabrizio ventured on forbidden topics, she made no reply, and turned away for a moment or two to give the necessary attention to her birds.

Fabrizio had got her to promise that, in the evening, when she sent him some water, she would at the same time send him one of her own alphabets, written out in ink, which was much more easily visible. He did not fail to write her a very long letter from which he took care to exclude all expressions of affection, or at any rate those of a kind to give offence. This method proved successful; his letter was accepted.

Next day, in their exchange of conversation by alphabets, Clelia made him no reproaches. She told him that the danger of poison was growing less; Barbone had been attacked and almost killed by the men who were keeping company with the kitchenmaids in the governor's house; probably he would not dare to venture into the kitchens again. Clelia confessed to Fabrizio that, for his sake, she had dared to steal an antidote from her father. She was sending it to him. The essential thing was for him to reject at once any food in which he could detect an unusual taste.

Clelia had questioned Don Cesare closely, but without succeeding in discovering who had sent the six thousand lire which Fabrizio had received. In any case it was an excellent sign; supervision was becoming less strict.

This episode of the poison furthered our prisoner's interests enormously. All the same, he could never obtain the least avowal of anything that looked like love; but he had the happiness of living on the most intimate terms with Clelia. Every morning, and often in the evening, there was a long conversation with the alphabets. Every evening, at nine o'clock, Clelia accepted a long letter, and sometimes wrote him a few words in reply. She also sent him the newspaper and several books. Last of all, Grillo had been won over to the extent of bringing Fabrizio bread and wine, which were handed over to him every day by Clelia's maid. Grillo had concluded from this that the governor was not acting in concert with those people who had given Barbone instructions to poison the young Monsignore, and he was very glad of it, as were all his fellows, for it had become a by-word in the prison that you had only to look Monsignore del Dongo in the face for him to give you money.

Fabrizio had grown very pale. The complete lack of exercise was affecting his health; apart from this, he had never felt so happy. The tone of the conversation between Clelia and himself was intimate, and at times very gay. The only moments in Clelia's life that were not haunted by grim forebodings and self-reproach were those she spent in talking to him.

One day she was so rash as to say to him: 'I admire your delicacy. Seeing I am the Governor's daughter, you never speak to me of your desire to regain your freedom.'

'That is because I take good care to have no such absurd desire,' replied Fabrizio. 'Once I got back to Parma, how should I see you again? And life would become unbearable if I could not tell you all my thoughts. ... No, not exactly all my thoughts, you take good care of that. But still, in spite of your unkindness, to live without seeing you every day would be for me far greater torture than this prison. In all my life I have never been so happy! Isn't it a comical thing to find that happiness should have been awaiting me in a prison?'

'There is a great deal to be said on that subject,' answered Clelia, suddenly assuming an air of extreme gravity that was almost sinister.

'What!' cried Fabrizio, greatly alarmed, 'am I in danger of losing that tiny corner I have managed to win in your heart, which is for me the only joy I have in the world?'

'Yes,' she replied. 'I have every reason to believe you are not acting honestly with me, although by the outside world you are considered a man of honour. But I do not wish to discuss this subject today.'

This singular opening introduced a good deal of awkwardness into their conversation, and often both of them had tears in their eyes.

Chief Justice Rassi was still pining to change his name. He was extremely tired of the one he had made for himself, and was anxious to become Barone Riva. Conte Mosca, for his part, was toiling, with all the skill in his power, to bolster up this venal judge's passion for a barony, just as he was seeking to increase the Prince's insane hope of making himself constitutional King of Lombardy. These were the only means that he could discover of delaying Fabrizio's execution.

The Prince said to Rassi: 'A fortnight's despair, a fortnight's hope – it is by this treatment, patiently applied, that we shall succeed in subduing that haughty woman's spirit. It is by such alternations of gentleness and severity that one manages to break in the most savage horses. Apply the caustic unsparingly.'

And, indeed, every fortnight saw a fresh report of Fabrizio's approaching death spring to life in Parma. These rumours plunged the unhappy Duchessa in the depths of despair. Faithful to her resolution not to involve the Conte in her downfall, she would not see him more than twice a month; but she was punished for her cruelty towards that poor man by the continually recurring moods of dark despair in which her life was spent. In vain did Conte Mosca, overcoming the bitter jealousy inspired in him by the diligent attentions of that handsome man, Conte Baldi, write to her when he could not see her, and hand on to her all the information that he owed to the zeal of the future Barone Riva. The Duchessa, to be capable of bearing up against the frightful rumours that were incessantly circulating with regard to Fabrizio, would have needed to live in constant contact with a man of intelligence and of heart like Conte Mosca. Baldi's total lack of personality, leaving her alone with her thoughts, condemned her to lead a frightful existence, and Conte Mosca could not succeed in imparting to her his own reasons for hope.

By means of various rather ingenious pretexts this Minister had induced the Prince to agree to having deposited in a friendly castle in the very heart of Lombardy, in the neighbourhood of Saronno, the documents relating to all the highly complicated intrigues by means of which Ranuccio-Ernesto IV fostered his extravagantly mad hopes of making himself constitutional monarch of that fair country.

More than a score of these extremely compromising documents were in the Prince's hand or bore his signature, and in the event of Fabrizio's life being seriously threatened the Conte planned to announce to His Highness that he was going to place these documents in the hands of a great Power that could crush him with a single word.

Conte Mosca believed he could rely upon the future Barone Riva, the only thing he feared was poison. Barbone's attempt had greatly alarmed him, and to such a point that he had determined to risk taking a step which, to all appearances, was an act of madness. One morning he presented himself at the gate of the citadel and sent for General Fabio Conti, who came down as far as the bastion above the gate. There, as they walked up and down in a friendly way together, the Conte, after a brief preamble, acid in tone but still quite civil, did not hesitate to say to him: 'If Fabrizio should die in any manner likely to cause suspicion, his death might be laid at my door. I shall be thought to have acted out of jealousy; that would expose me to the most odious ridicule, and this I am determined not to allow. So, to clear myself in the matter, if he dies of any illness, *I shall kill you with my own hands*; you may count on that.' General Fabio made a magnificent reply and spoke of his own valour, but the look on the Conte's face remained present in his mind.

A few days later, and as though he were working in concert with the Conte, Chief Justice Rassi ventured on an act of imprudence which was strange indeed in a man of his sort. The public scorn that clung to his name and made it a byword among the rabble was making him ill, now that he had a reasonable hope of shaking himself free of it. He addressed to General Fabio Conti an official copy of the sentence condemning Fabrizio to twelve years in the citadel. According to the law, this is what should have been done on the very day after Fabrizio's admission to prison. But what was unheard of in Parma, in that region of secret measures, was that legal authority should allow itself to take such a step without express orders from the Sovereign. For how indeed could the hope of re-doubling the Duchessa's alarm and subduing her proud spirit, as the Prince expressed it, be kept alive, once an official copy of the sentence had been issued from the Chancellery of Justice.

On the day before that on which General Fabio Conti received the official document from the Chief Justice, he learnt that the clerk Barbone had been given a thorough thrashing on his way back to the citadel. He concluded from this that there was no longer any question, in a certain quarter, of getting rid of Fabrizio; and, by a stroke of prudence which saved him from the immediate consequences of his folly, Rassi said nothing to the Prince, in the next audience he had with him, about the official copy of Fabrizio's sentence which had been transmitted to him. Fortunately for the poor Duchessa's peace of mind, the Conte had discovered that Barbone's clumsy attempt had merely been a desire for personal revenge, and he had caused the clerk to be given the warning recently mentioned.

Fabrizio was very agreeably surprised when, after one hundred and thirty-five days of confinement in a rather narrow cage, the good chaplain came to him one Thursday to take him for an airing on top of the Farnese Tower. He had not been there ten minutes before, overcome by the unaccustomed freshness of the air, he began to feel faint.

Don Cesare made this accident an excuse for allowing him half an hour's exercise every day. This was a mistake; these frequent outings had soon restored to our hero a strength which he abused.

There were several more serenades. The punctilious governor allowed them only because they created an engagement between the Marchese Crescenzi and his daughter Clelia, whose character alarmed him. He was vaguely conscious that there was no point of contact between himself and his daughter, and was always in dread of some mad freak on her part. She might take refuge in a convent, and he would be left helpless. The General was afraid, however, that all this music, the sound of which could penetrate right down into the deepest dungeons reserved for the blackest Liberals, might contain signals. The musicians, too, gave him some uneasiness on their own account. And so, no sooner had the serenade come to an end than they were locked up in the large, low-ceilinged rooms in the Governor's residence which by day served as offices for the staff, and the doors were not opened until broad daylight on the following morning. It was the Governor himself who, stationed on the Slaves' Bridge, had them searched in his presence and gave them their liberty, though not without repeating to them several times over that he would have hanged at once any one among them who had the audacity to undertake the smallest commission for any prisoner. And they knew that, in his fear of giving offence, he was a man who would keep his word, so that the Marchese Crescenzi was obliged to pay thrice the usual fee to his musicians, who were greatly upset at having to spend this night in prison.

All that the Duchessa could obtain, and that with great difficulty, from the pusillanimity of one of these men was that he should take with him a letter to be handed to the Governor. The letter was addressed to Fabrizio; in it the writer lamented the mischance which had made it impossible, during all the five months and more that he had been in prison, for his friends from outside to establish any communication with him.

On entering the citadel, the suborned musician flung himself at the feet of General Fabio Conti, and confessed to him that a priest, who was unknown to him, had so insisted on his taking charge of a letter addressed to Signor del Dongo that he had not dared to refuse; but, faithful to his duty, he now hastened to place it in His Excellency's hands.

His Excellency was highly flattered; he knew the resources at the Duchessa's disposal and was greatly afraid of being made the victim of some trick.

In his joy, the General went to submit this letter to the Prince, who was highly delighted.

'So the firmness of my administration has finally managed to avenge me! For five whole months that proud woman has been in anguish! But one of these days we are going to have a scaffold erected, and her wild imagination will not fail to convince her that it is intended for young del Dongo.'

CHAPTER 20: *Plans for Escape*

ONE night, towards one o'clock, Fabrizio, leaning up against the window-sill, had thrust his head through the little door he had made in the shutter and was gazing at the stars and the vast horizon open to view from the top floor of the Farnese Tower. His eyes, roaming over the country in the direction of the lower Po and Ferrara, chanced to notice an extremely small but quite brilliant light which seemed to be coming from the top of a tower. 'That light cannot be visible from the plain,' thought Fabrizio. 'The thickness of the tower prevents it from being seen from below; it must be a signal to some distant point.' All at once he noticed that this light kept on appearing and disappearing at very short intervals. 'It is some young woman speaking to her lover in the neighbouring village.' He counted nine flashes in succession. 'That is an I,' he said to himself, 'since I is in fact the ninth letter of the alphabet.' There followed, after a pause, fourteen flashes: 'That's an N'; then, after another pause, a single flash: 'That's an A; the word is *Ina*.'

What were his joy and surprise when the next series of flashes, still separated by short pauses, ended by making up the following words:

INA PENSA A TE

Evidently 'Gina is thinking of you!'

He replied at once by a series of flashes with his own lamp through the opening he had made:

FABRIZIO T'AMA (' Fabrizio loves you.')

The conversation continued until daybreak. This night was the one hundred and seventy-third of his imprisonment, and he was informed that for the past four months they had been making these signals every night. But anyone might see and interpret them; so that very night they began to arrange a system of abbreviations. Three flashes in very quick succession would stand for the Duchessa; four, the Prince; two, Conte Mosca; two quick flashes followed by two slow ones would signify 'escape'. They agreed to use in future the old alphabet *alla Monàca*, which, so as to baffle inquisitive observers, changes the usual sequence of the letters, and gives them another, arbitrary, order. A, for instance, is represented by 10, B by 3;

that is to say, three consecutive intermissions of the light mean B, ten consecutive intermissions A, and so on. A short interval of darkness marks the separation of the words. An appointment was made for one o'clock on the following night, and that night the Duchessa came to the tower, which was a quarter of a league out of town. Her eyes filled with tears as she saw the signals made by Fabrizio, whom she had so often given up for dead. She told him herself by flashes of the lamp: 'I love you – have courage – health – hope! Exercise your muscles in your cell, you will have need of strength in your arms. – I have not seen him,' said the Duchessa to herself, 'since that concert with Fausta, when he appeared at the door of my drawing-room dressed as a footman. Who would have said then what a fate was in store for us!'

The Duchessa had signals sent which informed Fabrizio that he was soon to be set free, THANKS TO THE PRINCE'S GRACIOUS KINDNESS (these signals might be read). Then she returned to sending messages of affection; she could not tear herself away from him! Only the remonstrances of Lodovico, who, on account of his services to Fabrizio, had become her factotum, could induce her, when it was already on the point of daybreak, to discontinue signals which might attract the attention of some ill-disposed person. This announcement, several times repeated, of his approaching release plunged Fabrizio in a mood of deepest sorrow. Clelia, noticing this the next day, was so imprudent as to enquire the cause of it.

'I can see myself on the point of giving the Duchessa serious grounds for displeasure.'

'And what can she demand of you that you would refuse her?' exclaimed Clelia, carried away by the most lively curiosity.

'She wants me to leave this place,' he answered, 'and that is what I will never consent to do.'

Clelia could not reply; she looked at him and burst into tears. If he had been able to speak to her at close quarters, then he would perhaps have obtained from her an avowal of feelings, his uncertainty as to which often plunged him in the deepest discouragement. He was keenly conscious that life without Clelia's love could be for him only a long round of bitter griefs or insupportable dullness. He felt that it was no longer worth his while to live only to re-experience those same pleasures that had seemed to him interesting before he had known what it was to love, and although suicide has not yet become the fashion in Italy, he had thought of it as a possible resource, if fate should happen to part him from Clelia.

Next day he received a long letter from her:

You must, my friend, be told the truth: many a time, since you have been here, it has been believed in Parma that your last day had come. It is true that you were sentenced only to twelve years in a fortress; but it is, unfortunately, impossible to doubt that an all-powerful hatred inexorably pursues you, and I have trembled a score of times for fear lest poison should put an end to your life. You must therefore snatch at every possible means of escaping from this place. You will see that for your sake I am failing in my most sacred duties; judge of the imminence of the danger by the things which I venture to say to you and which are so out of place on my lips. If it is absolutely necessary, if there is no other way of safety, fly. Every moment you spend inside this fortress may place your life in the greatest peril; bear in mind that there is a party at court whom the prospect of crime has never checked in its designs. And do you not see all the plans of that party constantly foiled by Conte Mosca's superior skill? Well, they have found a sure way of banishing him from Parma, that is to say, the Duchessa's despair; and are they not only too sure of driving her to such despair by the death of a certain young prisoner? This point alone, which is unanswerable, ought to enable you to judge how you stand.

You say that you feel some affection for me. Consider, in the first place, what insurmountable obstacles stand in the way of that feeling ever becoming firmly established between us. We may have met in our youth, we may each have held out a helping hand to the other in a time of trouble; fate may have set me in this cruel place to mitigate your sufferings, but I should never cease to reproach myself if illusions, which nothing justifies or will ever justify, should incline you not to seize every possible opportunity of removing your life from so terrible a peril. I have lost all peace of mind through the cruel folly I have committed in exchanging with you certain signs of good friendship. If our childish games with alphabets should have led you to form illusions so ill-founded and which may be so fatal to yourself, it would be vain for me to justify myself by recalling Barbone's attempt on you. It would mean that I had thrown you into far more frightful, far more certain peril, in the idea of saving you from a momentary danger; and my imprudent actions are for ever unpardonable if they have given rise to feelings which may lead you to reject the Duchessa's advice. See what you oblige me to repeat to you: Make your escape, I command you ...

This letter was very long. Certain passages, such as the 'I command you', which we have just transcribed, afforded some exquisite moments of hope to Fabrizio's love. It seemed to him that the underlying feelings in the letter were quite tender, even if the form of expression was remarkably prudent. At other moments, he paid the penalty for his total ignorance of this kind of warfare; and saw nothing but plain friendliness, or even a very ordinary feeling of humanity, in this letter of Clelia's.

Otherwise, nothing that she told him made him change his intentions for an instant. Even supposing that the perils which she depicted were indeed real, was it much to purchase, at the cost of a few momentary dangers, the happiness of seeing her every day? What sort of life would he lead when he had once more taken refuge in Bologna or in Florence? For, if he escaped from the citadel, he had not the least hope of getting permission to live in Parma. And even if the Prince should change his mind so far as to set him at liberty (which was extremely unlikely, seeing that he, Fabrizio, had become, for a powerful faction, a means of overthrowing Conte Mosca) what sort of life would he lead in Parma, separated from Clelia by all the hatred that divided the two parties? Once or twice in a month, perhaps, chance would place them in the same drawing-room; but even then, what sort of conversation could he hold with her? How could he recapture that perfect intimacy he now enjoyed for several hours every day? What would be the conversation of the drawing-room compared with that they were carrying on by means of alphabets? 'And even if I had to pay for this life of exquisite delight and this unique chance of happiness with a few trifling risks, where is the harm in that? And would it not be a further happiness thus to find a slight opportunity of giving her a proof of my love?'

Fabrizio saw nothing in Clelia's letter but an excuse for asking her for a meeting; this was the one and constant object of all his desires. He had only spoken to her once, and then for a brief moment, just at the time of his entry into prison; and that was now more than two hundred days ago.

An easy way of meeting Clelia offered itself. The excellent Don Cesare allowed Fabrizio half an hour's exercise on the terrace of the Farnese Tower every Thursday, during the daytime. On the other days of the week, however, this airing, which might be observed by all the inhabitants of Parma and the neighbourhood, and might seriously compromise the governor, took place only at nightfall. To get up on to the terrace of the Farnese Tower there was no other stair but that of the little belfry of the chapel so lugubriously decorated in black and white marble, which the reader may perhaps remember. Grillo would escort Fabrizio to this chapel and open the little stair to the belfry for him. It should have been his duty to accompany him but, as the evenings were beginning to get chilly, the gaoler allowed him to go up by himself, locked him into this belfry which communicated with the terrace and went back to keep himself warm in his room. Well then, one evening, could not Clelia contrive to appear, accompanied by her maid, in the black marble chapel?

The whole of the long letter in which Fabrizio replied to Clelia's was calculated to obtain this meeting. For the rest, he confided to her, with perfect sincerity, and as though it were a matter concerning some other person, all the reasons which had made him decide not to leave the citadel.

I would expose myself to the prospect of a thousand deaths every day to have the happiness of talking to you with the help of our alphabets, which now never hold us up for a moment; and you wish me to commit the silly mistake of exiling myself in Parma, or perhaps in Bologna, or even in Florence! You wish me to walk out of here so as to get farther away from you! Understand that any such effort is impossible for me. It would be useless for me to give you my word, I could never keep it.

The result of this request for a meeting was an absence on Clelia's part which lasted for no fewer than five days. For five whole days she did not come to the aviary except at times when she knew that Fabrizio could not make use of the little opening cut in the shutter. Fabrizio was in despair. He concluded from this absence that in spite of certain glances which had stirred wild hopes in him, he had never inspired in Clelia any feelings other than those of plain and simple friendship. 'In that case,' he said to himself, 'what good is life to me? Let the Prince take it from me, he will be welcome; one reason more for not leaving the fortress.' And it was with a deep sense of distaste for everything that, every night, he replied to the signals of the little lamp. The Duchessa thought him completely out of his mind when she read, on the record of signals transmitted which

Lodovico brought to her every morning, the strange words: '*I do not wish to escape; I wish to die here!*'

During these five days, so cruel for Fabrizio, Clelia was more unhappy than he. She had conceived the idea, so intensely painful to a warm-hearted nature: 'My duty is to take refuge in some convent, far from the citadel. When Fabrizio learns that I am no longer here, and I shall see to it that Grillo and all the other gaolers tell him, then he will decide upon an attempt at escape.' But going to a convent meant giving up all hopes of ever seeing Fabrizio again. And how could she give up the idea of seeing him now that he was offering her so clear a proof that the feelings which might at one time have bound him to the Duchessa no longer existed? What more touching proof of love could a young man give? After seven long months in prison, which had seriously affected his health, he now refused to regain his liberty. A man of frivolous nature, such as the talk of the courtiers had depicted Fabrizio, in Clelia's eyes, as being, would have sacrificed a score of mistresses for the chance of getting out of the citadel one day earlier; and what would such a man not have done to escape from a prison where poison might any day put an end to his life!

Clelia's courage failed her; she made the gross mistake of not seeking refuge in a convent, a step which would at the same time have furnished her with a quite natural means of breaking with the Marchese Crescenzi. Once this mistake was made, how was she to resist this young man – so attractive, so natural, so tender – who was exposing his life to frightful perils merely to gain the happiness of looking at her from one window to another? After five days of fearful conflicts, interspersed with fits of self-contempt, Clelia made up her mind to reply to the letter in which Fabrizio pleaded for the happiness of speaking to her in the black marble chapel. To tell the truth, she rejected his plea, and in terms that were somewhat cruel; but from that moment all peace of mind was lost to her. At every instant her imagination portrayed to her Fabrizio succumbing to the attempts to poison him; she came up six or eight times a day to her aviary, she felt a passionate need of assuring herself with her own eyes that Fabrizio was alive.

'If he is still in the fortress,' she said to herself, 'if he is exposed to all the horrible things which the Raversi faction are possibly plotting against him with the object of driving out Conte Mosca, it is solely because I have been so cowardly as not to flee to a convent! What excuse could he have for remaining here once he was certain that I had gone away for ever?'

This girl, at once so timid and so proud, came to the point of running the risk of a refusal on the part of the gaoler Grillo. What was even more, she laid herself open to all the comments which the man might venture to make upon the extraordinary nature of her behaviour. She stooped to the degree of humiliation involved in sending for him, and telling him in tremulous tones which gave away her whole secret, that within a few days Fabrizio was going to obtain his liberty; that the Duchessa Sanseverina, in the hope of this, was taking the most active measures; that it was frequently necessary to have the prisoner's immediate reply to certain proposals that were being put forward, and that she urged him, Grillo, to allow Fabrizio to make an opening in the shutter which masked his window, so that she might communicate to him by signs the instructions which she received several times a day from the Duchessa Sanseverina.

Grillo smiled and assured her of his respect and obedience. Clelia felt deeply grateful to him for not saying anything further; it was evident that he was fully aware of all that had been going on for the last few months.

Hardly had the gaoler left her when Clelia made the signal by which she had agreed to call Fabrizio upon important occasions; she confided to him all that she had just been doing. 'You are determined to perish by poison,' she added. 'I hope to have the courage, one of these days, to leave my father and escape to some remote convent; that is my bounden duty to you. And then I hope that you will no longer oppose the plans that may be suggested to you for getting you out of this place. So long as you are here, I have moments of frightful and unreasonable anxiety. Never in my life have I helped to do harm to anybody, and now I feel that I am to be the cause of of your death. The idea of such a thing, in the case of a perfect stranger, would drive me to despair. Imagine then what I feel when I picture to myself that a friend, whose unreasonableness gives me serious cause for complaint, but whom, after all, I have been seeing for so long every day, may be at this very moment a victim to the pangs of death. At times I feel the need to hear from your own lips that you are alive.

'It was to escape from this frightful anguish that I have just lowered myself so far as to ask a favour of an inferior who might have refused it me, and may yet betray me. And indeed, I should perhaps count myself happy if he did go and denounce me to my father. I should leave at once for the convent, and I should no longer be the most unwilling accomplice of your cruel folly. But, believe me, this cannot go on for long, you will obey the Duchessa's orders. Are you satisfied, my cruel friend? It is I who am begging you to betray my father! Send for Grillo, and give him a tip.'

Fabrizio was so deeply in love, the simplest expression of Clelia's wishes plunged him in such fear, that even this strange communication gave him no certainty that he was loved. He called Grillo, whom he paid generously for his kindnesses in the past, and told him that, with regard to the future, for every day on which he allowed him to make use of the opening cut in the shutter, he should receive a sequin. Grillo was delighted with these terms.

'Monsignore,' he said, 'I am going to speak to you quite frankly and honestly; will you agree to put up with eating a cold dinner every day? That is a very simple way of avoiding the risk of poison. But I ask you to use the utmost discretion; a gaoler has to see everything and guess nothing,' and so on. 'Instead of keeping one dog, I shall have several, and you yourself will make them taste every dish you intend to eat. As for wine, I will give you some of my own, and you will touch no bottle except those from which I have drunk myself. But if your Excellency wishes to ruin me for ever, you have only to confide these details even to Signorina Clelia herself. Women will always be women; if tomorrow she quarrels with you, the day after, to have her revenge, she will relate the whole contrivance to her father, whose greatest delight would be to find some excuse for having a gaoler hanged. Next to Barbone he is perhaps the most spiteful man in the fortress, and that is where the real danger of your position lies. He knows how to handle poison, you can be sure of that, and he would never forgive me for this idea of keeping three or four little dogs.'

Meanwhile there was another serenade. Grillo was now ready to answer all Fabrizio's questions; he had, however, resolved to be always discreet, and not to betray Signorina Clelia, who, to his mind, while on the point of marrying the Marchese Crescenzi, the richest man in the State of Parma, was none the less carrying on a love affair, so far as prison walls allowed, with the charming Monsignore del Dongo. He was answering the latter's final questions about the serenade when he made the blunder of adding: 'People think that he will marry her soon.' One can imagine the effect of the simple statement on Fabrizio. That night he made no reply to the signals from the lamp except to say he was ill. The following morning, on Clelia's appearance in the aviary on the stroke of ten, he asked her, in a tone of formal politeness quite new between them, why she had not told him frankly that she loved the Marchese Crescenzi, and that she was on the point of marrying him.

'Because there is not a word of truth in all that,' replied Clelia, in a tone of impatience. It is true, indeed, that the rest of her answer was less precise. Fabrizio pointed this out to her, and took advantage of the occasion to renew his request for a meeting. Clelia, seeing her sincerity called in question, granted this almost immediately, while pointing out to him at the same time that she was dishonouring herself for ever in Grillo's eyes.

That evening, when it was quite dark, she appeared, accompanied by her maid, in the black marble chapel. She stopped in the middle, beside the night-lamp; the maid and Grillo retired thirty paces towards the door. Clelia, who was trembling all over, had prepared a fine speech. Her object was to make no compromising admission, but the logic of passion is insistent; the deep interest it takes in discovering the truth does not allow it to keep up vain pretences, while at the same time the intense devotion that it feels for the object of its love frees it from all fear of giving offence. At first Fabrizio was dazzled by Clelia's beauty; for nearly eight months he had seen no one at such close range but his gaolers. But the name of the Marchese Crescenzi revived all his fury, which increased when he saw quite clearly that Clelia was answering only with the utmost circumspection. Clelia herself realized that she was increasing his suspicions instead of dispelling them. This sensation was too painful for her to bear.

'Would it make you really happy,' she said to him with a sort of anger and with tears in her eyes, 'to have made me overlook all that I owe to myself? Until the third of August last year I had never felt anything but aversion for those men who sought to please me. I had a boundless and probably exaggerated contempt for the character of a courtier, and everyone who was happy at this court I disliked intensely. I found, on the other hand, exceptional qualities in a prisoner who was brought to this citadel on the third of August. I suffered, though at first unaware of it, all the torments of jealousy. The attractions of a charming woman, and one whom I knew well, were like dagger-thrusts in my heart, because I believed, and am still inclined to believe, that this prisoner was attached to her. Soon the importunate attentions of the Marchese Crescenzi, who had sought my hand, redoubled. He is very rich and we have no fortune at all. I was rejecting these advances with the greatest independence of mind when my father uttered the fatal word "convent". I realized that if I left the citadel I should no longer be able to watch over the life of the prisoner in whose fate I was interested. The masterstroke of my precautions had been that up to that moment he had not the slightest suspicion of the frightful dangers that had threatened his life.

'I had indeed promised myself never to betray either my father or my secret; but that woman of marvellous energy, superior intelligence, and so terrible a will, who is protecting this prisoner, offered him, or so I suppose, some means of escape. He rejected them, and tried to persuade me that he was refusing to leave the citadel in order not to be separated from me. Then I made a great mistake. I fought with myself for five days; I ought to have fled at once to the convent and to have left the citadel; that course offered me a very easy method of breaking with the Marchese Crescenzi. I had not the courage to leave the citadel and I am now a lost girl. I have attached myself to a man of fickle character. I know what his conduct was like in Naples; and what reason should I have to believe that his character has altered? Confined in a harsh prison, he has made love to the only woman he could see, she has been a distraction for him in his boredom. As he could not speak to her without a certain amount of difficulty, this amusement has assumed a false appearance of passion. This prisoner, having made a name for himself in the world by his courage, imagines himself to be proving that his love is something more than a mere passing fancy by exposing himself to rather considerable dangers in order to go on seeing the person whom he believes he loves. But as soon as he is back in some great city, surrounded again by the seductions of society, he will once more become what he has always been – a man addicted to dissipation and to gallantry – and the poor companion of his prison will end her days in a convent, forgotten by this frivolous creature, and with eternal regret for having made him a confession of her love.'

This historic speech, of which we give only the principal points, was, as one can well imagine, interrupted a good score of times by Fabrizio. He was desperately in love; he was also perfectly convinced that before seeing Clelia, he had never loved, and that the destiny of his life was to live for her alone.

The reader will doubtless imagine the fine speeches he was making when the maid warned her mistress that it had just struck half past eleven, and that the General might be coming home at any moment. The parting was most painful.

'I am seeing you for the last time, perhaps,' said Clelia to the prisoner. 'A measure which is evidently in the interests of the Raversi cabal may provide you with a most cruel way of proving that you are not inconstant.' Choked by her sobs, and sick with shame at not being able to conceal them altogether from her maid, nor, more especially, from the gaoler Grillo, Clelia parted from Fabrizio. A second conversation would be possible only when the Governor should announce that he was going to spend the evening out. And as, since Fabrizio's imprisonment, and the interest it awakened in the minds of curious courtiers, he had found it prudent to give himself out as suffering from an almost continuous attack of gout, these expeditions to the city, governed by the requirements of a skilful policy, were frequently not decided upon until the very moment of his getting into his carriage.

Ever since that evening in the marble chapel, Fabrizio's life had been a long succession of transports of joy. Serious obstacles, it is true, seemed still to stand in the way of his happiness; but at all events he had that supreme and hardly hoped-for joy of being loved by the heavenly creature who occupied all his thoughts.

On the third day after this meeting, the signals from the lamp stopped very early, close upon midnight. At the moment of their coming to an end Fabrizio almost had his skull fractured by a huge ball of lead which was thrown over the upper part of the shutter on his window, came crashing through the paper panes, and fell into his room.

This extremely bulky ball was by no means so heavy as its size suggested. Fabrizio succeeded in opening it quite easily, and found inside a letter from the Duchessa. Through the agency of the Archbishop, whom she had charmed by assiduous flattery, she had won over a soldier belonging to the garrison of the citadel. This man, an expert in the use of a catapult, had either eluded the sentries posted at the corners and outside the door of the Governor's residence, or had come to terms with them.

You must escape by means of ropes. I shudder as I give you this strange advice. I have hesitated for more than two whole months before telling you as much: but the outlook on the official side grows darker every day, and we may expect the worst. By the way, start signalling again at once with your lamp, to prove to us that you have received this dangerous letter. Signal P – B – G *alla Monaca, that is to say four, twelve, and two. I shall not breathe freely until I see this signal. I am on the tower, we shall answer* N – O, *i.e., seven and five. Once you have received the answer, send no other signals, concentrate solely on making out the sense of my letter.*

Fabrizio hastened to obey, and sent the signals arranged, which were followed by the promised reply; then he went back to reading the letter.

We may expect the very worst; so I have been assured by the three men in whom I have the greatest confidence, after I had made them swear on the Gospels to tell me the truth, however painful it might be to me. The first of these men threatened the surgeon at Ferrara who denounced you that he would fall upon him with an open knife in his hand; the second told you, on your return from Belgirate, that it would have been more strictly prudent to have aimed a pistol shot at the footman who came singing through the wood leading a fine horse, who was a trifle too lean. You don't know the third; he is a highway robber of my acquaintance, a man of action if ever there was one, and as full of courage as yourself; that is the chief reason why I asked him to tell me what you ought to do. All three of them assured me, without knowing, any one of them, that I was consulting the other two, that it is better for you to risk breaking your neck than to spend eleven years and four months more in continual dread of a highly probable dose of poison.

You must for the next month practise climbing up and down a knotted rope in your cell. Then, on the night of some feast day when the garrison of the citadel will have received an extra ration of wine, you will make the great attempt. You will have three ropes of silk and hemp, of the thickness of a swan's quill, the first of eighty feet to carry you down the thirty-five feet from your window to the orange-trees, the second of three hundred feet — and that is where the difficulty will be, on account of the weight — to carry you down the hundred and eighty feet which is the height of the wall of the great tower; a third of thirty feet will help you get down from the ramparts. I spend my whole time studying the great wall on the east, that is to say on the side towards Ferrara: a fissure caused by an earthquake has been filled up by means of a buttress which forms an inclined plane. *My highwayman assures me that he would undertake to climb down on that side without much difficulty and at the risk of a few scratches only, by letting himself slide down the inclined plane formed by this buttress. The vertical drop is no more than twenty-eight feet to the very bottom; this side is the least well guarded.*

However, all things considered, my robber – who has escaped three times from prison, and whom you would like if you knew him, though he abominates people of your class – my highway robber, I say, who is as agile and nimble as you are, thinks that he would rather come down on the western side, exactly opposite the little palazzo formerly occupied by Fausta, which you know well. What would make him choose that side is that the wall, although only slightly inclined, is almost entirely covered with little bushes and brambles. There are twigs on these, as thick as your little finger, which may easily take your skin off if you are not careful, but which are also ex-cellent things to hold on to. Only this morning I was looking at this west side through an excellent spy-glass. The place to choose is the one just below a new bit of stone which was fixed on top of the parapet some two or three years ago. Directly beneath this stone you will find first of all a bare space of some twenty feet. You must go very slowly here (you can imagine how my heart trembles in giving you these terrible instructions, but courage consists in knowing how to choose the lesser evil, however frightful it may be). After the bare space, you will come upon eighty to ninety feet of very big bushes, in which one can see birds fluttering; then a space of thirty feet where there is nothing but grass, wall-flowers, and other rock-plants. Next, as you come near the ground, twenty feet of bushes, and last of all twenty-five or thirty feet of newly plastered wall.

What would make me choose this side is that, directly below the new bit of stone on the parapet at the top, there stands a wooden hut, built by one of the soldiers in his garden, and which the captain of engineers employed at the fortress is trying to force him to pull down. It is seventeen feet high, it has a thatched roof, and this roof comes close up against the great wall of the citadel. It is this roof that attracts me; in the dreadful event of an accident it would break your fall. Once you get there, you will be within the circle of the ramparts, which are none too carefully guarded. If anyone should stop you there, let fly with your pistols and defend yourself for a few minutes. Your friend from Ferrara and another stout-hearted fellow, the one I call the highwayman, will have ladders, and will not hesitate to scale this fairly low rampart and fly to your help.

The rampart is only twenty-five feet high, and has a considerable slope. I shall be at the foot of this last wall with a good number of armed men.

I hope to be able to send you five or six letters by the same channel as this one. I shall continue to repeat the same things in different terms, so that we may act in perfect harmony. You can guess what I feel when I tell you that the man who wanted you to shoot the footman, and who is, after all, the best of men, and is half-killing himself with remorse, thinks that you will get off with a broken arm. The highwayman, who has more experience of this sort of enterprise, thinks that, if you will only agree to climb down very slowly, and, above all, without hurrying, your liberty will not cost you any more than a few grazes. The great difficulty is to get hold of some ropes; and this is what has been the sole object of my thoughts for the fortnight during which this grand scheme has taken up every moment of my time.

I make no attempt to reply to your crazy notion, the only senseless thing you have said in all your life: 'I do not wish to escape!' The man who would have had you fire on the footman exclaimed that boredom had driven you mad. I shall not hide from you the fact that we fear a very imminent danger, which will perhaps hasten the day of your flight. To warn you of this danger, the lamp will signal several times in succession: The castle is on fire! You will reply: Are my books burnt?

This letter contained five or six pages more of details; it was written in microscopic characters on extremely thin paper.

'All that is very fine and very well thought out,' said Fabrizio to himself. 'I owe an eternal debt of gratitude to the Conte and the Duchessa; they will think perhaps that I am afraid, but I have no intention of escaping. Did anyone ever escape from a place where he was at the height of happiness, to rush into the most frightful exile where everything would be lacking, even air fit to breathe? What should I do at the end of a month spent in Florence? I should put on a disguise to come and prowl round the gate of this fortress, and try to catch a stray glance from her!'

Next day Fabrizio had a fright. He was at his window, about eleven o'clock, looking at the magnificent view and waiting for the happy moment when he should see Clelia, when Grillo rushed into his cell, quite breathless. 'Quick! Quick! Monsignore, fling yourself on your bed, pretend to be ill. There are three judges coming up! They are going to question you; think well before you speak; they are coming to *entangle* you.'

As he spoke Grillo hurried to close the little trap-door in the shutter. He thrust Fabrizio back on his bed, and threw two or three cloaks on top of him.

'Tell them that you are in great pain and don't talk much. Above all things, make them repeat their questions so that you may have time to think.'

The three judges entered. 'Three escaped gaolbirds,' said Fabrizio to himself on seeing their mean faces, 'not three judges.' They wore long black gowns. They bowed gravely and took possession, without saying a word, of the three chairs that were in the room.

'Signor Fabrizio del Dongo,' said the eldest of the three, 'we are distressed by the sad mission which we come to fulfil by this visit to you. We are here to announce to you the decease of His Excellency the Marchese del Dongo, your father, Second Grand Majordomo of the Lombardo-Venetian Kingdom, Knight Grand Cross of the Orders of ...,' and so forth. Fabrizio burst into tears.

The judge went on: 'Her Ladyship the Marchesa del Dongo, your mother, informs you of this event in a personal letter; but since she has added to this fact certain improper reflections, the Court of Justice, by a ruling issued yesterday, has decided that you should only be given an extract of this letter, and it is this extract which the clerk of the Court, Signor Bona, is now going to read to you.'

This reading finished, the judge came over to Fabrizio, who was still lying down, and made him follow on his mother's letter the passages of which copies had just been read to him. Fabrizio saw in the letter the words 'unjust imprisonment ... cruel punishment for a crime which is no crime at all', and understood the motive of the judges' visit. However, in his contempt for magistrates of no integrity, he said nothing at all to them except these few words: 'I am ill, gentlemen, I am half-dead with weakness, and you must excuse me if I am unable to rise.'

When the judges had gone, Fabrizio shed many more tears, then said to himself: 'Am I a hypocrite? I used to imagine I did not love him at all.'

On that day, and the days that followed, Clelia was very sad. She called him several times, but had barely the courage to say a few words to him. On the morning of the fifth day after their first meeting she told him that she would come that evening to the marble chapel.

'I can only say a few words to you,' she told him as she entered. She was trembling so much that she had to lean on her maid. After sending the latter back to the door of the chapel, she added in a voice that was barely audible: 'You will give me your word of honour that you will obey the Duchessa, and will attempt to escape on the day she orders you to and in the way she will indicate to you, or else tomorrow morning I shall fly to a convent, and I swear to you, here and now, that never in my life will I speak a word to you again.'

Fabrizio remained silent.

'Promise,' said Clelia with tears in her eyes and as if beside herself, 'or else we are speaking to each other here for the last time. The life you have created for me is horrible. You are here on my account, and each day is perhaps the last of your existence.' At that moment Clelia felt so weak that she was obliged to seek the support of an enormous armchair which had been placed long ago in the middle of the chapel, for the use of the imprisoned prince; she was nearly fainting.

'What must I promise?' asked Fabrizio, looking quite overcome.

'You know that.'

'I swear then to fling myself with my eyes open into a state of atrocious misery, and condemn myself to live far removed from all that I love in the world.'

'Promise something definite.'

'I swear to obey the Duchessa, and to make my escape on the day she wishes and as she wishes. And what is to become of me once I am far away from you?'

'Swear to escape, whatever may happen.'

'What! have you made up your mind to marry the Marchese Crescenzi as soon as I am no longer here?'

'Oh, heavens! What sort of creature do you think I am? ... But swear, or I shall never have a moment's peace of mind any more.'

'Very well, I swear to escape from here on the day on which her Grace the Duchessa shall order me to do so, and whatever may happen between now and then.'

Having obtained this oath, Clelia felt so faint that she was obliged to retire after thanking Fabrizio.

'Everything was in readiness for my flight tomorrow morning,' she told him, 'if you had insisted on staying here. I should have been seeing you at this moment for the last time in my life, I had vowed as much to the Madonna. Now, as soon as I can leave my room, I shall go and examine the terrible wall below the new stone in the parapet.'

On the following day he found her so pale as to cause him keen distress. She said to him from her aviary window: 'Let us be under no illusion, my dear friend; as there is sin in our friendship, I have no doubt that it will bring us some misfortune. You will be discovered while seeking to make your escape, and ruined for ever, if no worse. However, we must satisfy the demands of human prudence, which orders us to make every effort. To get down the outside of the great tower, you will need a stout rope more than two hundred feet long. In spite of all the trouble I have taken since I learnt of the Duchessa's plan, I have only been able to get hold of ropes that together amount to barely fifty feet. By an order issued by the Governor, every rope to be found inside the fortress has been burnt, and every evening they remove the well-ropes, which for that matter are so frail that they often break when drawing up the light weight they carry. But pray to God to grant me forgiveness; I am betraying my father, and working, unnatural daughter that I am, to cause him undying grief. Pray to God for me, and if your life is saved, make a vow to consecrate every moment of it to His Glory.

'Here is an idea which has occurred to me. In a week from now I shall be leaving the citadel to be present at the wedding of one of the Marchese Crescenzi's sisters. I shall come back that night, as is fitting, but I shall do all in my power not to return home until very late, and perhaps Barbone will not examine me too closely. All the greatest ladies of the court will be at this wedding of the Marchese's sister, and no doubt the Duchessa Sanseverina among them. In heaven's name, arrange for one of these ladies to hand me a bundle of ropes tightly packed, not too large, and reduced to the smallest possible size. If I have to expose myself to the risk of a thousand deaths, I shall use every means, even the most dangerous, to introduce this bundle of ropes into the citadel, in defiance, alas, of all my duties. If my father gets to know of it, I shall never see you again. But whatever fate awaits me, I shall be happy, within the limits of sisterly affection, if I can help to save you.'

That same evening, in their nocturnal correspondence by means of lamps, Fabrizio informed the Duchessa of the unique opportunity that would be offered of getting into the citadel a sufficient amount of rope. But he begged her to keep this secret even from the Conte, a thing which seemed to her odd. 'He is mad,' thought the Duchessa. 'Prison has altered him, he takes a tragic view of things.' Next day a ball of lead, thrown by the slinger, brought the prisoner news of the greatest possible peril: the person who was undertaking to get the ropes in, he was told, would be really and actually saving his life. Fabrizio hastened to impart this news to Clelia. This leaden ball brought Fabrizio also a very careful plan of the western wall by which he was to descend from the top of the great tower into the space enclosed within the bastions. From this spot it would be easy to effect the rest of his escape, the ramparts being only twenty-three feet in height and none too carefully guarded. On the back of the plan was written a magnificent sonnet, in a small delicate hand. A generous heart exhorted Fabrizio to take to flight, and not to allow his soul to be debased and his body worn out by the eleven years of captivity which he had still to undergo.

At this point an essential detail, and one that explains the courage that the Duchessa found to recommend to Fabrizio so dangerous a flight, obliges us to interrupt for a moment the story of this bold enterprise.

Like all parties which are not in power, the Raversi party was not very closely united. Cavaliere Riscara detested Chief Justice Rassi, whom he accused of having made him lose an important suit, in which, as a matter of fact, he, Riscara, had been in the wrong. Through Riscara's agency, the Prince received an anonymous message informing him that a copy of Fabrizio's sentence had been officially addressed to the Governor of the citadel. The Marchesa Raversi, that clever party leader, was exceedingly annoyed by this false move, and at once sent word of it to her friend the Chief Justice. She thought it quite natural that he should have wished to get something out of the Minister Mosca while Mosca remained in power. Rassi presented himself boldly at the Palace, convinced that he would be let off with a few kicks. The Prince could not do without a skilled jurisconsult, and Rassi had procured the banishment, as Liberals, of a judge and a barrister, the only men in the principality who could have taken his place.

The Prince, beside himself with rage, heaped insults upon him and advanced towards him to strike him.

'Why, it is only a silly mistake of some clerk,' replied Rassi, with the utmost coolness. 'The matter is laid down by law. It should have been done the day after Signor del Dongo was confined in the citadel. The clerk in his zeal thought it had been overlooked, and must have made me sign the covering letter as a matter of form.'

'And you expect to make me believe such clumsy lies!' cried the Prince in a fury. 'Why not say that you have sold yourself to that rascal Mosca, and that this is why he gave you the Cross. But upon my soul, you shall not get off with a thrashing; I shall have you brought before the courts, I shall disgrace you publicly.'

'I defy you to have me tried!' replied Rassi boldly. He knew that this was a sure way of calming the Prince. 'The law is on my side, and you have no second Rassi to find you a way of getting round it. You will not remove me from office, because there are moments when you are by nature severe; then you thirst for blood, but at the same time you are anxious to retain the esteem of level-minded Italians; that esteem is a *sine qua non* for your ambition. In short, you will recall me at the first act of severity which your nature feels the need for, and as usual I shall procure you a strictly regular sentence passed by timid judges who are fairly honest men, and one that will satisfy your passions. Find another man in your dominions as useful as myself!'

So saying, Rassi fled. He had got off with one well-directed blow from a ruler and half-a-dozen kicks. On leaving the Palace he set off for his estate of Riva. He had some apprehensions of a dagger-thrust in the first impulse of anger, but he had no doubt that before a fortnight was up a courier would summon him back to the capital. He employed the time he spent in the country in organizing a safe method of corresponding with Conte Mosca. He was madly in love with the title of Barone, and thought the Prince set too high a value on that once sublime thing, nobility, ever to confer it upon him; whereas the Conte, who was extremely proud of his own birth, respected nothing but nobility proved by titles prior to the year 1400.

The Chief Justice had not been mistaken in his forecast. He had hardly been a week on his estates when one of the Prince's friends, who came there by chance, advised him to return to Parma without delay. The Prince received him with smiles, then assumed a very solemn air, and made him swear on the Gospels that he would keep secret what was going to be confided to him. Rassi swore most solemnly, and the Prince, his eyes aflame with hatred, cried out that he would never be master in his own house so long as Fabrizio was alive.

'I cannot,' he added, 'either drive the Duchessa away or endure her presence; her glances defy me and poison all my life.'

Having allowed the Prince to explain himself at great length, Rassi, affecting extreme embarrassment, finally exclaimed: 'Your Highness shall be obeyed, of course, but the matter is one that presents the most frightful difficulties. There is no possibility of condemning a del Dongo to death for the murder of a Giletti; it is already an astonishing feat to have got twelve years in the citadel out of it. Besides, I suspect the Duchessa of having discovered three of the peasants who were working on the excavations at Sanguigna, and who happened to be outside the trench at the moment when that ruffian Giletti attacked del Dongo.'

'And where are these witnesses?' said the Prince angrily.

'Hiding in Piedmont, I suppose. It would require a conspiracy against your Highness's life ...'

'That method is somewhat dangerous,' said the Prince, 'it puts the idea of the real thing into people's heads.'

'However,' said Rassi with a show of innocence, 'that is the whole of my official arsenal.'

'There remains poison ...'

'But who is to give it? That fool of a Conti?'

'Well, from what people say, it would not be his first attempt ...'

'He would have to be roused to anger,' Rassi went on; 'and besides, when he made away with the captain he was under thirty, and he was desperately in love, and infinitely less chicken-hearted than he is today. Everything, no doubt, must give way to reasons of State; but taken unawares as I am now and at first sight, I can think of no one to carry out the Sovereign's orders but a certain Barbone, the clerk in charge of the records at the prison, whom Signor del Dongo felled with a box on the ear on the day of his admission there.'

Once the Prince had been put at his ease, the conversation went on endlessly; he brought it to a close by granting his Chief Justice a month's respite; Rassi would have liked to have two. The following day he received a secret gift of a thousand sequins. For three days he thought the matter over; on the fourth he came back to his original argument, which seemed to him self-evident: 'Conte Mosca alone will have the heart to keep his word to me, because, in making me a Barone, he does not give me anything he thinks of value; secondly, by warning him, I probably save myself from committing a crime for which I am practically paid in advance; thirdly, I have my revenge for the first humiliating blows which Cavaliere Rassi has received.' The following night he communicated to Conte Mosca the whole of his conversation with the Prince.

The Conte was paying court to the Duchessa in secret. It is true that he still did not see her at her home more than once or twice in a month, but nearly every week, and whenever he managed to create an occasion for speaking of Fabrizio, the Duchessa, accompanied by Cecchina, would come, very late in the evening, to spend a few moments in the Conte's garden. She managed even to deceive her coachman, who was devoted to her, and believed her to be paying a visit to some neighbouring house.

One can imagine whether the Conte, after receiving the Chief Justice's terrible confidence, immediately made the signal pre-arranged with the Duchessa. Although it was the middle of the night, she sent Cecchina to beg him to come at once to her house. The Conte, as delighted as any lover by this semblance of intimacy, hesitated, all the same, to tell the Duchessa everything; he was afraid of seeing her driven mad with grief.

However, after trying to find veiled words by which to mitigate the fatal announcement, he ended by telling her all; it was not in his power to keep back a secret which she asked him to tell her. In the last nine months her extreme misery had had a great influence on this eager, impulsive spirit, and given it strength; the Duchessa did not give way to sobs or lamentations.

On the following evening she had the signal of great danger sent to Fabrizio:

'THE CASTLE IS ON FIRE.'

He answered very clearly:

'ARE MY BOOKS BURNT?'

The same night she was fortunate enough to have a letter conveyed to him in a leaden ball. It was a week after this that the wedding of the Marchese Crescenzi's sister took place, on which occasion the Duchessa was guilty of a monstrous act of imprudence of which we shall give an account in due course.

ALMOST a year before the period of her misfortunes, the Duchessa had made the acquaintance of a curious individual. One day when she had a 'touch of the moon', as they say in those parts, she had gone on a sudden impulse to her villa at Sacca, beyond Colorno, on the hill overlooking the Po. She took a delight in improving this property; she loved the vast forest which crowns the hill and stretches right up to the house; she busied herself with laying out paths running through it in various picturesque directions.

'You will get yourself carried off by brigands, my fair Duchessa,' the Prince said to her one day. 'It is impossible that a forest in which you are known to walk should remain deserted.' The Prince cast a glance at the Conte, whose jealousy he hoped to excite.

'I never feel afraid, your Serene Highness,' replied the Duchessa with an air of innocence, 'when I am out walking in my woods. I reassure myself with this thought: I have done no harm to anyone, who then could possibly hate me?' This remark was considered daring; it recalled the insults offered by the Liberals of the principality, a most insolent set of people.

On the day of the walk in question, the Prince's words came back to the Duchessa's mind as she noticed a very poorly dressed man who was following her at a distance through the wood. At a sudden turn the Duchessa made in the course of her walk, this unknown person came so close to her that she felt alarmed. Her first impulse was to call her gamekeeper whom she had left about half a mile away, in the flower-garden close to the house. The stranger had time to come up to her, and fling himself at her feet. He was young, extremely good-looking, but miserably dressed; his clothes had rents in them about a foot long, but his eyes burned with the fire of an ardent soul.

'I am under sentence of death; I am Dr Ferrante Palla; I am dying of hunger and so are my five children.'

The Duchessa had noticed that he was terribly thin; but his eyes were so fine and filled with such tender enthusiasm that they acquitted him of any suspicion of criminal intent. 'Palagi,' she thought, 'might well have given eyes like those to the Saint John in the Desert he has just placed in the Cathedral.' The idea of Saint John was suggested to her by Ferrante's incredible thinness. The Duchessa gave him three sequins which she had in her purse, apologizing for offering him so little on the score of having just paid her gardener's account. Ferrante thanked her effusively. 'Alas!' he said to her, 'once I lived in towns, I used to meet women of some refinement; now that in fulfilment of my duties as a citizen I have got myself sentenced to death, I live in the woods, and I was following you, not to ask alms of you nor to rob you, but like a savage fascinated by an angelic beauty. It is so long since I have seen a pair of lovely white hands!'

'Please get up,' the Duchessa said to him, for he had remained on his knees.

'Allow me to remain like this,' said Ferrante. 'This position proves to me that I am not at this present moment engaged in stealing, and that calms me. For you should know that I steal for a living, now that I am prevented from practising my profession. But at this moment I am a simple mortal who is adoring sublime beauty.' The Duchessa gathered that he was slightly mad, but she was not at all afraid; she read in this man's eyes that he had a kindly, eager soul, and besides she felt no aversion to people of peculiar appearance.

'I am a physician, then, and I made love to the wife of the apothecary Sarasine, of Parma. He took us by surprise and drove her out of his house, as well as three children whom he supposed, and rightly, to be mine and not his. I have had two since then. The mother and the five children are living in the most utter poverty, in a sort of hut which I built with my own hands a league from here, in the wood. For I have to keep out of the way of the police, and the poor woman refuses to be parted from me. I was sentenced to death, and quite justly; I was conspiring. I loathe the Prince, who is a tyrant. I did not take to flight for want of money. My misfortunes have greatly increased, and I would have done a thousand times better to have killed myself. I no longer love the unhappy woman who has borne me these five children and has ruined herself for me; I love another. But if I kill myself, the five children and their mother will literally starve to death.' The man spoke with an accent of sincerity.

'But how do you live?' asked the Duchessa, moved to pity.

'The children's mother spins; the eldest girl is kept in a farm owned by some Liberals, where she tends the sheep; as for me, I rob people on the road from Piacenza to Genoa.'

'How do you reconcile robbery with your Liberal principles?'

'I keep a note of the people I rob, and if ever I have anything, I shall give them back the sums I have stolen. I consider that a Tribune of the People like myself is performing work which, by reason of its danger, is well worth a hundred lire a month; and so I am careful not to take more than twelve hundred lire in a year. No, I am wrong! I steal a small sum over and above this, for in that way I am able to meet the cost of printing my works.'

'What works?'

'*Will — ever have a Chamber and a Budget?*'

'What!' cried the Duchessa in amazement, 'it is you, sir, who are one of the greatest poets of this age, the famous Ferrante Palla?'

'Famous, perhaps, but most unfortunate, that is certain.'

'And a man of your talent, sir, is obliged to steal in order to live?'

'That is perhaps the reason why I have some talent. Up till now all our authors who have made a name for themselves have been people paid by the government or the religion which they sought to undermine. Now I, in the first place, risk my life; in the second place, think, Signora, of the reflections that stir within my mind when I go out to rob! "Am I in the right?" I ask myself. "Does the office of Tribune render services that are really worth a hundred lire a month?" I have two shirts, the coat you see me wearing, a few poor weapons, and I am sure to finish at the end of a rope. I venture to think I am disinterested. I should be happy but for this fatal love which no longer allows me to feel anything but misery in the company of the mother of my children. Poverty weighs me down by its ugliness; I like fine clothes, white hands. . . .' He looked at the Duchessa's in such a way that fear seized hold of her.

'Good-bye, sir,' she said to him. 'Can I be of any service to you in Parma?'

'Give a thought now and then to this question: His task is to awaken men's hearts and to prevent their being lulled to sleep by that false and wholly material happiness which monarchies provide. Is the service he renders his fellow citizens worth a hundred lire a month? . . . It is my misfortune to love,' he said very gently, 'and for nearly two years my heart has been occupied by you alone, but until now I have seen you without causing you alarm.' And he took to his heels with a prodigious speed which both astonished the Duchessa and reassured her. 'The police would find it difficult to catch him,' she thought. 'He certainly is quite mad.'

'He is indeed mad,' her servants told her. 'We have all known for a long time that the poor fellow was in love with the Signora. When the Signora is here we see him wandering about in the highest parts of the woods, and as soon as the Signora has gone he never fails to come and sit in the very places where she has rested. He is careful to pick up any flowers which have fallen from her nosegay, and keeps them for a long time stuck in his shabby hat.'

'And you have never spoken to me of these follies,' said the Duchessa, almost in a tone of reproach.

'We were afraid that the Signora might tell the Minister Mosca. Poor Ferrante is such a good fellow! He has never done harm to anyone, and just because he loves our Napoleon they have sentenced him to death.'

She did not say a word to the Minister about this meeting, and as, for four whole years, it was the first secret she had kept from him, half a score of times she was obliged to stop short in the middle of a sentence. She returned to Sacca bringing with her some gold; Ferrante did not appear. She came back again a fortnight later. Ferrante, after following her for some time, skipping along through the wood about a hundred paces from her, bore down upon her with the lightning speed of a sparrow-hawk, and fell at her feet as on the previous occasion.

'Where were you a fortnight ago?'

'In the mountains beyond Novi, robbing some muleteers who were returning from Milan, where they had been selling oil.'

'Take this purse.'

Ferrante opened the purse, took from it a sequin which he kissed and thrust into his bosom, then handed it back to her.

'You give me back this purse, and you are a robber!'

'Why certainly. My rule is that I must never possess more than a hundred lire. Now, at this moment, the mother of my children has eighty lire, and I have twenty-five; I have five more lire than I ought, and if they were to hang me now I should feel remorse. I took this sequin because it comes from you and I love you.'

The tone of this simple speech was faultless. 'He is really in love,' the Duchessa said to herself.

That day he appeared quite distracted. He said that there were people in Parma who owed him six hundred lire, and that with that sum he could repair his hut, in which at present his poor little children were continually catching cold.

'But I will make you a loan of these six hundred lire,' said the Duchessa, deeply moved.

'But then, since I am a man in a public position – wouldn't the opposite party be able to slander me, and say that I am selling myself?'

The Duchessa, deeply touched, offered him a hiding-place in Parma if he would swear that for the time being he would not exercise his judicial functions in that city, and above all would not carry out any of the sentences of death which, so he said, he had secretly in mind.

'And if they hang me as a result of my rashness,' said Ferrante gravely, 'all those scoundrels, who work such harm to the common people, will live on for many long years to come, and whose fault will it be? What will my father say when he greets me up above?'

The Duchessa talked to him a great deal about his young children, who might be taken with some fatal illness on account of the damp. He ended by accepting her offer of a hiding-place in Parma.

The Duca Sanseverina, during the single half-day which he had spent in Parma after his marriage, had shown the Duchessa a very curious hiding-place which exists in the southern corner of the *palazzo* which bears his name. The outer wall, which dates from the middle ages, is eight foot thick. It has been hollowed out inside, and in this cavity is a secret chamber twenty feet in height, but only two feet in width. Close beside it one can admire that reservoir mentioned in all books of travels, a famous work of the twelfth century, constructed at the time of the siege of Parma by the Emperor Sigismund, and enclosed, at a later date, within the walls of the Palazzo Sanseverina.

Access to this hiding-place is obtained by moving aside an enormous stone which turns on an iron pivot running through the middle of the block. The Duchessa was so deeply moved by Ferrante's madness and by the sad lot of his children, for whom he obstinately refused any present of any value, that she gave him permission to make use of this hiding-place for a fairly considerable time. She saw him again a month later, still in the woods of Sacca, and as on that day he was slightly more composed, he recited to her one of his sonnets, which seemed to her equal, if not superior, to any of the finest work produced in Italy in the last two centuries. Ferrante obtained several interviews; but his love grew more ardent, became importunate, and the Duchessa realized that this passion was conforming to the rules of all love-affairs which are given a possible chance of entertaining a glimmer of hope. She sent him back to his woods, forbidding him to speak to her again; he obeyed her instantly and with perfect sweetness of temper.

Things had reached this point when Fabrizio was arrested. Three days later, at nightfall, a Capuchin friar presented himself at the door of the Palazzo Sanseverina. He had, he said, an important secret to communicate to the mistress of the house. She was feeling so miserable that she had him admitted: it was Ferrante. 'Some fresh iniquity of which the Tribune of the People ought to take cognizance is happening here,' said this man mad with love. 'On the other hand, acting as a private individual,' he added, 'I have nothing to give Her Grace the Duchessa Sanseverina but my life, and I place it in her hands.'

Such true devotion on the part of a thief and a madman touched the Duchessa keenly. She talked for a long time to this man who was considered the greatest poet in Northern Italy, and shed many tears. 'Here is a man who understands my heart,' she thought. The following day he reappeared, again at the hour of the Angelus, disguised as a servant in livery.

'I have not left Parma; I have heard tell of an atrocity which my lips shall not repeat; but here I am. Think, Signora, of what you are refusing! The being you see before you is no court puppet, but a man!' He was on his knees as he spoke these words in a tone that gave them full value. 'Yesterday,' he added, 'I said to myself: She wept in my presence; therefore she is a little less unhappy!'

'But consider, sir, what dangers surround you; you will be arrested in this city!'

'The Tribune will say to you: "Signora, what is life when duty calls?" The unhappy man, who suffers the pain of no longer feeling any passion for virtue now that love consumes him, will add: "Your Grace, Fabrizio, a man of spirit, is perhaps about to perish; do not repulse another man of spirit who offers himself to you! Here is a body of iron and a heart that fears nothing in the world save your displeasure." '

'If you speak to me again of your feelings, I will close my doors to you for ever.'

The Duchessa had some thoughts that evening of telling Ferrante that she would provide a small annuity for his children; but she was afraid he would go straight out and kill himself.

No sooner had he left her than, filled with gloomy presentiments, she said to herself: 'I, too, may die, and would to God I might, and soon! If I could only find a man worthy of the name to whom I might commend my poor Fabrizio.'

An idea struck the Duchessa. She took a sheet of paper and drafted an acknowledgement, into which she introduced the few legal terms that she knew, that she had received from Signor Ferrante Palla the sum of 25,000 lire, on the express condition of paying every year a life-annuity of 1,500 lire to Signora Sarasine and her five children. The Duchessa added: 'I further bequeath a life-annuity of 300 lire to each of these five children, on condition that Ferrante Palla gives his professional services as a physician to my nephew Fabrizio del Dongo, and acts as a brother to him. This I beg him to do.' She signed the document, ante-dated it by a year, and put it safely away.

Two days later, Ferrante reappeared. It was at the moment when the whole city was stirred by the rumour of the imminent execution of Fabrizio. Would this painful ceremony take place in the citadel or under the trees of the public promenade? Many of the humbler citizens took a walk that evening past the gates of the citadel, to try and see whether the scaffold was being erected; this spectacle had moved Ferrante. He found the Duchessa in floods of tears, and quite unable to speak; she greeted him with a wave of her hand and pointed to a chair. Ferrante, disguised that day as a Capuchin, behaved magnificently; instead of seating himself he knelt down and addressed a devout prayer to God in an undertone. At a moment when the Duchessa seemed slightly more composed, without changing his posture, he broke off his prayer for an instant to say these words: 'Once again he offers his life.'

'Consider what you are saying,' cried the Duchessa, with that haggard look in the eye, which, after a fit of sobbing, indicates that anger is getting the better of more tender emotions.

'He offers his life to place an obstacle in the way of Fabrizio's doom, or to avenge it.'

'There are certain circumstances,' replied the Duchessa, 'in which I could accept the sacrifice of your life.'

She looked at him with careful scrutiny. A gleam of joy shone in his eye; he rose swiftly to his feet and stretched out his arms towards heaven. The Duchessa went to fetch a paper hidden in the secret drawer of a big walnut cabinet.

'Read this,' she said to Ferrante. It was the deed of gift in favour of his children, which we have mentioned.

Tears and sobs prevented Ferrante from reading it to the end; he fell on his knees.

'Give me back the paper,' said the Duchessa, and, in front of his eyes, she burnt it in the flame of a candle.

'My name,' she added, 'must not appear if you are taken and executed, for this is a matter in which your life will be at stake.'

'It will be my joy to die in harming the tyrant, a far greater joy to die for you. Now that this is stated and clearly understood, be so kind as to make no further mention of this trifling matter of money. I should see in it doubts insulting to myself.'

'If you are compromised, I may be compromised too,' replied the Duchessa, 'and Fabrizio as well as myself. It is for that reason, and not because I have any doubts of your courage, that I insist that the man who is wounding me to the heart shall be poisoned and not stabbed. For the same reason, which is of such great importance to me, I order you to do everything in the world to save your own life.'

'I will carry out everything faithfully, punctiliously, and prudently. I foresee, your Grace, that my revenge will be bound up with yours; even were it otherwise, I should still obey you faithfully, punctiliously, and prudently. I may not succeed, but I shall use all the strength that I possess as a man.'

'It is a question of poisoning Fabrizio's murderer.'

'So I had guessed; and during the twenty-seven months I have been leading this odious, vagabond life, I have often thought of a similar action on my own account.'

'If I am found out and condemned as an accomplice,' the Duchessa went on in a tone of pride, 'I do not wish to have it imputed to me that I have led you astray. I order you to make no further attempt to see me before the hour comes for our revenge; there must be no question of putting him to death before I have given you the signal. His death at this moment, for instance, far from being of service to me, would be disastrous. Probably his death will not have to occur until several months from now, but it will occur. I insist on his dying by poison, and I would rather let him live than see him killed by a bullet. For considerations which I do not choose to explain to you, I insist that your own life must be saved.'

Ferrante was delighted by the tone of authority which the Duchessa adopted with him; the keenest joy gleamed in his eyes. As we have said, he was horribly thin; but one could see that he had been very handsome in his youth, and he imagined himself to be still what he once had been. 'Am I quite mad?' he asked himself, 'or does the Duchessa really intend one day, when I have given her this proof of my devotion, to make me the happiest of men? And why not, after all? Am I not worth as much as that popinjay Conte Mosca who, when the time came, could do nothing for her, not even enable Monsignore Fabrizio to escape?'

'I may even desire his death tomorrow,' the Duchessa continued, still with the same air of authority. 'You know that huge reservoir at the corner of the *palazzo*, close to the hiding-place which you have sometimes occupied? There is a secret way of letting all the water run out into the street: well, that will be the signal for my revenge. You will see, if you are in Parma, or hear, if you are living in the woods, that the great reservoir of the Palazzo Sanseverina has burst. Act at once, but by means of poison, and above all risk your own life as little as possible. No one must ever know that I have had a hand in this affair.'

'Words are useless,' replied Ferrante, with an enthusiasm he could hardly restrain: 'I have already fixed on the means I shall employ. That man's life has become more odious to me than before, since, as long as he is alive, I shall not dare to see you. I shall await the signal of the burst reservoir pouring its water into the street.' He bowed abruptly and left the room. The Duchessa watched him go.

When he was in the next room she called him back.

'Ferrante!' she cried; 'you magnificent man!'

He came back, seemingly impatient at being detained; his face at that moment was superb.

'And your children?'

'Signora, they will be richer than I; you will perhaps allow them some small pension.'

'Look,' said the Duchessa as she handed him a sort of large case of olive wood, 'here are all the diamonds I have left; they are worth 50,000 lire.'

'Ah, Signora, you humiliate me! . . .' said Ferrante with a gesture of horror; and his whole expression changed completely.

'I shall never see you again before the deed is done. Take them, I insist,' added the Duchessa with an air of pride which left Ferrante thunderstruck. He put the case in his pocket and left the room.

He had closed the door behind him. The Duchessa called him back once again; he came in looking rather uneasy. The Duchessa was standing in the middle of the room; she threw herself into his arms. A moment later, Ferrante almost fainted with happiness. The Duchessa withdrew herself from his embraces, and with her eyes showed him the door.

'There goes the only man who has ever understood me,' she said to herself. 'That is how Fabrizio would have acted, if he could have known what I felt.'

There were two particular traits in the Duchessa's character: what she had once willed, she willed for ever, and she never reconsidered what she had once decided. She used to quote in this connexion a saying of her first husband, the charming General Pietranera: 'What an insult to myself!' he used to say. 'Why should I imagine that I have more sense today than when I made this decision?'

From that moment a sort of gaiety reappeared in the Duchessa's character. Before that fatal resolution, at each step taken by her mind, at each new thing she noticed, she had had a feeling of her own inferiority to the Prince, of her own weakness and her gullibility. The Prince, in her opinion, had basely deceived her, and Conte Mosca, as a result of his courtier's temperament, had, although innocently, backed up the Prince. Once she had resolved to avenge herself, she felt her strength, and every step her mind suggested brought her happiness. I am rather inclined to think that the immoral delight which the Italians take in revenge derives from the strength of imagination in that people. The natives of other countries do not properly speaking forgive – they forget.

The Duchessa did not see Palla again until round about the last days of Fabrizio's imprisonment. As the reader may perhaps have guessed, it was he who suggested the idea of his escape. There was in the woods, two leagues from Sacca, a medieval tower, half in ruins, and more than a hundred feet high. Before speaking a second time to the Duchessa of an escape, Ferrante begged her to send Lodovico, with some trustworthy men, to arrange a series of ladders up against this tower. In the Duchessa's presence, he climbed up by means of the ladders, and came down again by an ordinary knotted rope; he repeated the experiment three times, then explained his idea again. A week later, Lodovico also tried his hand at descending from this old tower by a knotted rope. It was then that the Duchessa communicated this idea to Fabrizio.

During the last few days preceding this attempt, which might lead to the death of the prisoner, and in more ways than one, the Duchessa never knew a moment's peace save when she had Ferrante by her side. The courage of this man electrified her own; but it will be easily understood that she had to hide this strange association from the Conte. She was afraid, not that he would be shocked by it, but that she would have been plagued by his objections, which would have increased her own anxiety. 'What! take as one's close counsellor a madman recognized as such, and under sentence of death! And,' added the Duchessa, speaking to herself, 'a man who, in the future, might do such very strange things!'

Ferrante happened to be in the Duchessa's drawing-room at the moment when the Conte came to acquaint her with the conversation the Prince had had with Rassi; and when the Conte had left she had great difficulty in preventing Ferrante from proceeding straight away to the execution of a frightful plan!

'I am strong now,' cried this madman, 'I have no longer any doubt as to the lawfulness of the act!'

'But, in the outburst of indignation which must inevitably follow, Fabrizio would be put to death!'

'Yes, but in that way he would be spared the dangers of this descent. It is possible, even easy,' he added, 'but the young man lacks experience.'

The marriage of the Marchese Crescenzi's sister was celebrated, and it was at the party given on that occasion that the Duchessa met Clelia and was able to talk to her without arousing any suspicions on the part of the fashionable onlookers. In the garden, where the two ladies had gone to get a moment's breath of air, the Duchessa herself handed over the bundle of ropes to Clelia. These ropes, woven with the greatest care of hemp and silk in equal parts and knotted, were very slender and fairly flexible. Lodovico had tested their strength, and throughout their whole extent they could bear without breaking a load of eight hundredweight. They had been tightly packed together in such a way as to form several packets, each of the size and shape of a quarto-volume. Clelia took charge of them, and promised the Duchessa that everything that was humanly possible would be done to get these packets into the Farnese Tower.

'But I am afraid of the timidity of your character; and besides,' the Duchessa added politely, 'what interest can you feel in a man you do not know?'

'Signor del Dongo is in distress, *and I promise you that he shall be saved by me!*'

But the Duchessa, placing only a very moderate reliance on the presence of mind of a young person of twenty, had taken other precautions which she took good care not to reveal to the Governor's daughter. As might naturally be expected, this Governor was present at the party given for the marriage of the Marchese Crescenzi's sister. The Duchessa said to herself that, if she could arrange for him to be given a powerful narcotic, it might be supposed, at first, that he had had an apoplectic fit, and then, instead of his being put into his carriage to take him back to the citadel, it might, with a little artful management, be possible to make it seem a better idea to use a litter, which would happen to be in the house where the party was being given. There, too, would be gathered a certain number of men with their heads about them, dressed as workmen engaged for the party, who, in the general confusion, would obligingly offer to bear the sick man back to his very lofty *palazzo*. These men, under the direction of Lodovico, carried a fairly considerable amount of ropes, cleverly concealed beneath their coats.

It can be seen that the Duchessa's mind had become really un-balanced since the time she had begun to think seriously of Fabrizio's escape. The peril threatening this beloved being had proved too much for her spirit, and above all had lasted too long. By the very excess of her precautions, she nearly, as we shall presently see, brought about the failure of this escape. Everything went off as she had planned, with this one difference, that the narcotic had too powerful an effect. Everyone, including members of the medical profession, believed that the General had had an apoplectic fit.

Fortunately Clelia, who was in despair, had not the slightest suspicion of so criminal an attempt on the part of the Duchessa. The confusion was such at the moment when the litter in which the General was lying half dead entered the citadel, that Lodovico and his men passed in without challenge; they were subjected to a formal search only on the Slaves' Bridge. When they had carried the General to his bedroom, they were taken to the kitchen quarters, where the servants entertained them very well. But after this meal, which did not end until it was very nearly morning, it was explained to them that the rule of the prison required that, for the remainder of the night, they should be locked up in the basement of the *palazzo*; in the morning, at daybreak, they would be released by the Governor's deputy.

These men had found an opportunity of handing to Lodovico the ropes they had taken charge of, but Lodovico had great difficulty in attracting Clelia's attention for a moment. At length, as she was passing from one room to another, he managed to make her see that he was laying down packets of rope in a dark corner of one of the drawing-rooms on the first floor. Clelia was greatly struck by this strange circumstance, and at once began to harbour frightful suspicions.

'Who are you?' she asked Lodovico, and, on receiving his highly ambiguous reply, she added: 'I ought to have you arrested; you or your men have poisoned my father! . . . Confess at once the nature of the poison you have used, so that the citadel doctor can administer the proper remedies! Confess this instant, or else you and your accomplices shall never leave this citadel!'

'The Signorina does wrong to be alarmed,' replied Lodovico, with perfect grace and politeness. 'There's no question at all of poison. Someone has been imprudent enough to administer a dose of laudanum to the General, and it appears that the servant ordered to perform this criminal act put a few drops too many into the glass. This we shall eternally regret, but the Signorina may rest assured that, thanks to heaven, there is no possible sort of danger. His Excellency the Governor should be treated as having taken an over-dose of laudanum by mistake. But I have the honour to repeat to the Signorina, the lackey responsible for the crime made no use of real poisons, as Barbone did, when he tried to poison Monsignore Fabrizio. This was no attempt to avenge the peril incurred by Monsignore Fabrizio; nothing was given to this clumsy lackey but a bottle containing laudanum, that I swear to the Signorina! But it must be clearly understood that if I were to be questioned officially I should deny everything.

'Besides, if the Signorina should speak to anyone in the world of laudanum and poison, even to the excellent Don Cesare, Fabrizio would be killed by the Signorina's own hand. She would render for ever impossible any plan of escape; and the Signorina knows better than I that it is not merely with laudanum that they wish to poison Monsignore; she knows also that a certain person has granted only a month's delay for that crime, and that already more than a week has gone by since the fatal order was given. Therefore, if she has me arrested, or if she merely says a word to Don Cesare or to anyone else, she will delay all our undertakings for very much more than a month, and I have reason to say that she will be killing Monsignore Fabrizio with her own hand.'

Clelia was horrified by Lodovico's strange composure.

'So here am I,' she said to herself, 'in actual conversation with my father's poisoner, who employs polite turns of speech in addressing me! And it is love which has led me into all these crimes! . . .'

Her remorse hardly left her strength to speak, but she said to Lodovico: 'I am going to lock you into this room. I shall run and tell the doctor that it is only a question of laudanum. But, good heavens! how shall I explain to him that I discovered this myself? I shall come back afterwards and release you. But,' said she, running back as she got to the door, 'did Fabrizio know anything about this laudanum?'

'Good heavens, no, Signorina, he would never have allowed it. And, besides, what was the good of making an unnecessary confidence? We are acting with the strictest caution. It is a question of saving the life of Monsignore, who is due to be poisoned in three weeks from now. The order has been given by a person who is not accustomed to find any opposition to his will; and, if the Signorina must know all, they say it is that terrible Chief Justice Rassi who has been given this commission.'

Clelia fled in terror. She could so rely on Don Cesare's perfect integrity that, using a certain amount of caution, she ventured to tell him that the General had been given laudanum, and nothing else. Without answering, without asking a single question, Don Cesare hurried off to see the doctor.

Clelia went back to the room into which she had locked Lodovico, intending to ply him with questions about the laudanum. She did not find him there: he had managed to escape. She saw a purse filled with sequins lying on a table, and a little box containing different kinds of poison. The sight of these poisons made her shudder. 'How can I tell,' she thought, 'that they have given nothing but laudanum to my father, and that the Duchessa has not tried to avenge herself for Barbone's attempt?'

'Good God!' she cried, 'here am I in touch with my father's poisoners! And I allow them to escape! And perhaps that man, if put to the question, would have confessed to something other than laudanum!'

Clelia sank at once to her knees, burst into tears, and addressed a fervent prayer to the Madonna.

Meanwhile the citadel doctor, greatly surprised by the information he had received from Don Cesare, according to which he had only laudanum to deal with, administered the appropriate remedies, which soon removed the most alarming symptoms. The General came to himself a little as day was beginning to break. His first act that showed he was regaining consciousness was to hurl a string of abuse at the Colonel who was second in command of the citadel, and had taken upon himself to issue orders of the simplest description in the world while the General lay unconscious.

The Governor next flew into a most violent rage with a kitchen-maid who, when bringing him a bowl of broth, had ventured to utter the word 'apoplexy'.

'Am I of an age,' he cried, 'to have apoplexies? It is only my deadliest enemies who could find pleasure in spreading such reports. And besides, have I been bled, that slander itself should dare talk of apoplexy?'

Fabrizio, entirely absorbed in preparations for his escape, could not imagine the reason for the strange sounds that filled the citadel at the moment when the Governor was brought back to it half dead. At first he had some idea that his sentence had been altered, and that they were coming to put him to death. But later, seeing that no one came to his cell, he thought that Clelia had been betrayed, that on her return to the fortress they had taken from her the ropes she was probably bringing back with her, and that, in fact, all his plans for escape were for the future impossible. Next morning, at daybreak, he saw come into his room a man unknown to him, who, without saying a word, put down a basket of fruit; beneath the fruit was hidden the following letter:

Filled with the keenest remorse for what has been done, not, thank heaven, by my consent, but as a result of an idea that I had, I have made a vow to the Most Holy Virgin that if, by the effect of her blessed intercessions, my father is saved, I will never refuse to obey any of his orders. I shall marry the Marchese Crescenzi as soon as he requires me to do so, and I shall never see you again.

All the same, I consider it my duty to finish what has been begun. Next Sunday, on your return from Mass, to which you will be taken at my request (remember to prepare your soul, you may lose your life in that difficult undertaking) – on your return from Mass, I say, put off as long as possible going back to your room; you will find there what you need for the enterprise you have in mind. If you perish, my heart will be broken! Will you be able to accuse me of having contributed to your death? Hasn't the Duchessa herself repeated to me upon several occasions that the Raversi faction is getting the upper hand? They wish to bind the Prince by an act of cruelty that will separate him for ever from Conte Mosca. The Duchessa, in floods of tears, has sworn to me that there remains only this resource; if you make no attempt, you perish.

I cannot look at you again, I have made a vow not to. But if on Sunday, towards evening, you see me dressed all in black, at the usual window, that will be the signal that when night comes everything will be ready so far as my feeble means allow. After eleven, possibly not before midnight or one o'clock, a little lamp will appear in my window; that will be the decisive moment. Commend yourself to your patron saint, put on as quickly as possible the priestly habit provided for you, and be off.

Farewell Fabrizio! I shall be praying for you, and shedding the most bitter tears, you may be sure, while you are running such great risks. If you perish, I shall not survive you – Good God! what am I saying! – but if you succeed, I shall never see you again. On Sunday, after Mass, you will find in your prison the money, the poison, the ropes, sent by that terrible woman who loves you to distraction, and who has assured me, three times over, that this course must be adopted. May God and the Blessed Madonna preserve you!

Fabio Conti was a gaoler who was always ill at ease, always troubled, always seeing in his dreams one or other of his prisoners escaping his clutches. Everyone in the citadel loathed him; but since misfortune suggests the same decisions to all men, the poor prisoners, even those chained up in dungeons three feet high, three feet wide, and eight feet long, in which they could neither stand nor sit upright, all the prisoners, even these, I say, had the idea of ordering a *Te Deum* to be sung at their own expense when they heard that their Governor was out of danger. Two or three of these poor wretches composed sonnets in honour of Fabio Conti. Oh, the effect of misery upon these men! May that man who blames them be led by his destiny to spend a year in a cell three feet high, with eight ounces of bread a day, and *fasting* on Fridays!

Clelia, who never left her father's room except to go and pray in the chapel, said that the Governor had decided that the rejoicings should not take place until the following Sunday. On the morning of that Sunday, Fabrizio was present at Mass and the *Te Deum*. In the evening there were fireworks, and the soldiers in the lower rooms of the palazzo received a ration of wine which was four times that which the Governor had ordered for them; some unknown person had even sent in several barrels of brandy which the soldiers broached. The generous spirit of those soldiers who were getting tipsy would not allow their five comrades who were on sentry duty outside the *palazzo* to suffer by this circumstance; as fast as they arrived at their sentry-boxes, a trusty servant gave them wine, and it was not known from what hand each of those who came on duty from midnight until morning received also a glass of brandy, while the bottle was in each case forgotten and left beside the sentry-box (as was proved at the ensuing court-martial).

The general state of confusion lasted longer than Clelia had expected, and it was not until nearly one o'clock that Fabrizio, who, more than a week earlier, had sawn through two bars of his window, the one that did not look out on the aviary, began to take down the shutter. He was working almost over the heads of the sentries who were guarding the Governor's residence; but they heard nothing. He had made some fresh knots only in the enormously long rope necessary for descending from that terrible height of one hundred and eighty feet. He coiled this rope like a bandolier around his body; it embarrassed him greatly, its bulk was enormous; the knots prevented it from forming a compact mass, and it stood out more than eighteen inches from his body. 'Here's my chief obstacle,' said Fabrizio to himself.

Having arranged this cord as best as he could, Fabrizio took up the one with which he counted on getting down the thirty-five feet which separated his window from the terrace on which the Governor's residence stood. But since, however drunk the sentries were, he could not all the same descend exactly over their heads, he climbed out, as we have said, by the other window of his room, that which looked out on the roof of a sort of vast guard-room. Out of some sick man's whim, as soon as General Fabio Conti was able to speak, he had ordered up two hundred soldiers into this old guard-room, out of use for over a century. He said that after poisoning him they would try to murder him in his bed, and these two hundred soldiers were to guard him. One may judge of the effect of this unexpected measure on Clelia's heart. That piously-minded girl was fully conscious of the extent to which she was betraying her father, and a father who had just been nearly poisoned in the interests of the prisoner whom she loved. She almost saw in the unexpected arrival of these two hundred men a decree of Providence which forbade her to go any farther and to give Fabrizio his freedom.

But everyone in Parma was talking of the imminent death of the prisoner. This melancholy subject was still being discussed even at the party given on the occasion of the marriage of Signora Giulia Crescenzi. Since for such a mere trifle as a misplaced sword-thrust given to an actor a man of Fabrizio's birth had not been set at liberty at the end of nine months' imprisonment, and when he was under the protection of the Prime Minister, it must be that a question of politics was involved in his affair. In that case, people said, it was useless to trouble their heads about him any more. If it did not suit those in authority to put him to death in a public place, he would soon die of sickness. A locksmith who had been summoned to General Fabio Conti's palazzo spoke of Fabrizio as a prisoner long since disposed of, and whose death was being kept secret for reasons of policy. This man's words decided Clelia.

DURING the day Fabrizio had been assailed by serious and disagreeable misgivings; but as he heard the hours strike which brought him nearer to the moment of action he began to feel alert and cheerful. The Duchessa had written to warn him that the fresh air would take him unawares, and that as soon as he was out of his prison he might find it impossible to press on. In that case it was better to run the risk of being recaptured than to let himself fall from the top of a wall a hundred and eighty feet high. 'If this misfortune overtakes me,' thought Fabrizio, 'I shall lie down close to the parapet, I shall sleep for an hour, then I shall start again. Since I have given my solemn word to Clelia, I would rather fall from the top of a rampart, however high, than be continually forced to ponder over the taste of the bread I eat. What horrible pains one must feel before the end, when one dies of poison! Fabio Conti won't stand on ceremony; he'll have me given a dose of the arsenic with which they kill the rats in his citadel.'

Towards midnight one of those thick white fogs in which the Po sometimes swathes its banks spread at first all over the city, and then reached the terrace and the bastions from the midst of which the great tower of the citadel rises. Fabrizio estimated that the little acacias surrounding the gardens laid out by the soldiers at the base of the hundred and eighty foot wall would no longer be visible from the parapet of the platform. 'That's capital,' he thought.

Shortly after half past twelve had struck, the signal of the little lamp appeared in the aviary window. Fabrizio was ready for action; he crossed himself, then fastened to his bed the short rope intended to carry him down the thirty-five feet that lay between him and the platform on which the palazzo stood. He landed without any hitch on the roof of the guard-room occupied since the previous night by the reinforcement of two hundred soldiers of which we have spoken. Unfortunately at that hour – a quarter to one in the morning – the soldiers were not yet asleep; while he was creeping on tiptoe over the roof of large curved tiles, Fabrizio heard them saying that the devil was on the roof and they must try to kill him with a shot from a musket. Certain voices asserted that such a desire was grossly impious; others said that if a shot were fired without killing anyone the Governor would put them in prison for having alarmed the garrison unnecessarily. The effect of all this fine discussion was that Fabrizio hurried across the roof as quickly as possible and made a great deal more noise. As a matter of fact, at the moment when, hanging by his rope, he passed in front of the windows, luckily for him at a distance of four or five feet on account of the projecting edge of the roof, they were bristling with bayonets. Certain people maintain that Fabrizio, always a madcap, had the idea of playing the part of the devil, and that he flung these soldiers a handful of sequins. What is certain is that he had scattered sequins over the floor of his room, and that he scattered more on his way from the Farnese Tower to the parapet, on the chance of their distracting the attention of the soldiers who might come in pursuit of him.

After landing on the platform, where he was surrounded by soldiers on guard who normally called out every quarter of an hour the whole sentence: 'All's well round my post', he made his way towards the western parapet, and looked about him for the new stone.

What appears incredible, and might make one doubt the truth of the story, if the result had not had a whole city as witnesses, is that the sentries posted along the parapet did not see and arrest Fabrizio. As a matter of fact the fog we have mentioned was beginning to spread upwards, and Fabrizio said later that when he was on the platform the fog seemed to him to have come already half-way up the Farnese Tower. But this fog was by no means thick, and he could easily see the sentries, some of whom were walking up and down. He added that, as if impelled by some supernatural force, he went and placed himself boldly between two sentries who were quite near each other. He calmly unwound the big rope which he had round his body and which got entangled twice; it took him a long time to disentangle it and spread it out upon the parapet. He heard the soldiers talking all round him, and was quite determined to stab the first who advanced upon him. 'I was not in the least worried,' he said, 'I felt as though I were performing some ceremony.'

He fastened his rope, when he had finally disentangled it, to an opening cut in the parapet to let the rain-water escape. He climbed on to the said parapet and addressed an earnest prayer to God; then, like a hero of the days of chivalry, he thought for a moment of Clelia. 'How different I am,' he said to himself, 'from the fickle, libertine

Fabrizio who entered this place nine months ago!' At length he began to descend that astounding height. He acted mechanically, he said, and as he would have done if he had been climbing down in broad daylight, in the presence of his friends, to win a wager. About half-way down, he suddenly felt his arms lose their strength; it seemed to him, looking back, that he even let go of the rope for an instant, but he soon caught hold of it again. Possibly, he said, he had held on to the bushes into which he slipped and which tore his skin. From time to time he felt an agonizing pain between his shoulders which actually took his breath away. There was an extremely uncomfortable swaying motion; he was constantly flung backwards and forwards from the rope to the bushes. He was brushed by several birds of considerable size which he roused from their slumbers, and which dashed out upon him as they flew away. The first few times he thought he had been overtaken by men in pursuit of him who had come down from the citadel by the same way as himself, and he made ready to defend himself. At last he arrived at the base of the great tower without any ill consequence save that his hands were bleeding. He related that, from half-way down the tower, the slope it forms was of great help to him; he kept close to the wall as he went down, and the plants which grew between the stones often kept him from slipping. When he reached the bottom, among the soldiers' gardens, he fell on to an acacia which, looked at from above, had seemed to him to be four or five feet, but was really fifteen or twenty. A drunken man who was lying asleep beneath it took him for a robber. In his fall from this tree, Fabrizio nearly dislocated his left arm. He started to run towards the rampart, but, as he afterwards said, his legs felt made of wadding; he had no strength left.

In spite of the danger he sat down and drank a little brandy which still remained to him. He dozed off for a few minutes, so soundly as not to know where he was; on waking up he could not understand how, being in his cell, he saw trees. At length the terrible truth flashed into his mind. He immediately started to walk towards the rampart; he climbed to the top up a wide flight of steps. The sentry, who was posted quite near to it, was snoring away in his box. He came upon a cannon lying flat on the grass, and fastened his third rope to it. It proved to be a little too short, and he fell into a muddy ditch in which there was about a foot of water. As he was picking himself up and trying to get his bearings, he felt two men seize hold of him. For a moment he was alarmed; but the next minute he heard a voice close to his ear whisper very softly: 'Ah! Monsignore, Monsignore!' He gathered vaguely that these men belonged to the Duchessa, and immediately went off in a dead faint. A little while after, he became aware he was being carried by men who were walking in silence and very fast. Then they stopped, which caused him great uneasiness; but he had not the strength either to speak or to open his eyes. He felt someone clasp him tightly; suddenly he recognized the scent of the Duchessa's clothes. This scent revived him; he opened his eyes; he was able to utter the words: 'Ah! dear friend!' Then once again he fainted dead away.

The faithful Bruno, with a squad of police all devoted to the Conte, stood in reserve two hundred paces away – the Conte himself was in hiding in a small house quite close to the place where the Duchessa was waiting. He would not have hesitated, had the need arisen, to take his sword in hand, with a party of half-pay officers, his intimate friends. He considered himself as bound to save Fabrizio's life, since he believed him to be exposed to the gravest danger, and felt that the Prince would have signed his pardon a long time back if he, Mosca, had not been guilty of the folly of seeking to save his Sovereign from writing something absurd.

Ever since midnight the Duchessa, surrounded by a body of men armed to the teeth, had been pacing up and down in deep silence outside the ramparts of the citadel. She could not stay still anywhere; she thought she would have to fight to rescue Fabrizio from the men who would pursue him. This eager, imaginative spirit of hers had suggested her taking a hundred precautions, too many to enumerate here, and all incredibly imprudent. It has been reckoned that more than eighty agents were on foot that night, expecting to have to fight in some extraordinary emergency. Fortunately Ferrante and Lodovico were at the head of all these, and the Minister of Police was not hostile. But the Conte in person took care to see that the Duchessa was not betrayed by anyone, and that he himself, in his ministerial capacity, knew nothing.

The Duchessa went completely off her head on seeing Fabrizio again; she clasped him convulsively in her arms, then was in despair on seeing her dress all covered in blood. It was the blood from Fabrizio's hands; she had thought that he was dangerously wounded. Helped by one of her men, she was taking off his coat to attend to his injuries, when Lodovico, who fortunately happened to be on the spot, firmly put her and Fabrizio into one of the little carriages which were hidden in a garden near the gate of the city, and they set off at full gallop to cross the Po near Sacca. Ferrante, with a score of well-armed men, formed the rear-guard, and had staked his life that he would stop all pursuit. The Conte, alone and on foot, did not leave the neighbourhood of the citadel until two hours later, when he saw that no one was stirring. 'Here am I, committing high treason!' he said to himself, wild with joy.

Lodovico had hit upon the excellent idea of putting in one of the carriages a young surgeon attached to the Duchessa's household, who was of much the same build as Fabrizio.

'Make your escape,' he said to him, 'in the direction of Bologna. Behave very stupidly, try to get yourself arrested, then contradict yourself in your answers, and finally admit that you are Fabrizio del Dongo; above all, gain time. Use all your skill in making yourself awkward. You will get off with a month's imprisonment, and the Signora will give you fifty sequins.'

'Does anyone think of money when one is serving her Grace?'

He set off, and was arrested a few hours later, an event which gave the greatest joy to General Fabio Conti and also to Rassi, who, at the same time as Fabrizio's peril, saw his Barony taking flight.

The escape was not known at the citadel until about six o'clock in the morning, and it was not until ten that anyone dared inform the Prince. The Duchessa had been so well served that, in spite of Fabrizio's deep sleep, which she mistook for a dead faint, and consequently had the carriage stopped three times, she crossed the Po in a boat at four o'clock in the morning. Relays were waiting on the opposite bank; they covered two leagues at great speed, then they were stopped for more than an hour while their passports were examined. The Duchessa had every variety of these, both for herself and Fabrizio; but she was mad that day, and took it into her head to give ten napoleons to the clerk of Austrian police, and to clasp his hand and burst into tears. This official, greatly alarmed, began the examination all over again. They then travelled post; the Duchessa paid so lavishly that, in a country where every foreigner is suspect, she aroused suspicions everywhere they went. Lodovico once more came to the rescue; he said that her Grace the Duchessa was beside herself with grief on account of the protracted fever of young Conte

Mosca, son of the Prime Minister of Parma, whom she was taking with her to Pavia to consult the doctors there.

It was not until they were ten leagues beyond the Po that the prisoner became really wide awake; he had a dislocated shoulder and any number of scratches. The Duchessa again behaved in so extraordinary a fashion that the landlord of a village inn where they dined thought he was entertaining a Princess of the Imperial House, and was about to pay her the honours which he considered were her due, when Lodovico told him that the Princess would not fail to put him in prison if he thought of ordering the bells to be rung.

At length, at six o'clock in the evening, they reached Piedmontese territory; there for the first time Fabrizio was in perfect safety. He was taken to a little village well away from the main road, the scratches on his hands were dressed, and he slept for several hours more.

It was at this village that the Duchessa allowed herself to take a step that was not only horrible from a moral point of view but also fatal to her peace of mind for the rest of her life. A few weeks before Fabrizio's escape, on a day when the whole of Parma had gone to the gate of the citadel to try and catch a glimpse of the scaffold that was being erected in the courtyard for his benefit, the Duchessa had shown Lodovico, now her household factotum, the secret by which one of the stones forming the floor of the famous reservoir of the Palazzo Sanseverina, a work of the thirteenth century to which we have already referred, could be slipped out of a little iron frame, very cleverly concealed. While Fabrizio was lying asleep in the *trattoria* (tavern) of this little village, the Duchessa sent for Lodovico; there was something so strange in the way she looked at him that he thought she was out of her mind.

'You may indeed have expected,' she said to him, 'that I was going to give you a few thousand lire; well, I am not. I know you, you are a poet, you would soon have squandered this money. I am giving you the small property of La Ricciarda, a league from Casalmaggiore!' Beside himself with joy, Lodovico flung himself at her feet, protesting in heartfelt accents that it was not with any thought of gaining money that he had helped to save Monsignore Fabrizio; that he had always loved him with a special affection ever since he had once the honour of driving him in his capacity as her Grace's third coachman. When this man, who was genuinely warm-hearted, thought he had taken up enough of the time of so great a lady, he took his leave; but she, with flashing eyes, said to him: 'Stay here'.

She paced the floor of this inn without saying a word, from time to time glancing at Lodovico with an incredible expression in her eyes. At last the man, seeing that this strange exercise showed no sign of coming to an end, felt it was up to him to address his mistress.

'The Signora has made me such an extravagant gift, so far beyond anything that a poor man like me could have imagined, and above all so much greater than the poor services I have had the honour of doing her, that I feel it against my conscience to accept this property of La Ricciarda. I have the honour to return this land to the Signora, and to beg her to grant me a pension of four hundred lire.'

'How many times in your life,' she said to him with the most mournful air of disdain, 'how many times have you heard it said that I relinquished a plan once I had declared my intentions?'

After uttering these words, the Duchessa continued to pace the floor of the room for some minutes; then suddenly stopping, exclaimed: 'It is by accident, and because he managed to take that young girl's fancy that Fabrizio's life has been saved! If he had not been charming, he would have died. Can you deny that?' she asked, advancing on Lodovico with eyes in which the most sinister fury blazed. Lodovico stepped back a few paces, thinking her mad, an idea that caused him grave uneasiness as to his ownership of the estate of La Ricciarda.

'Well,' continued the Duchessa, in the gentlest and most light-hearted manner, with a complete change of mood, 'I want my good people of Sacca to enjoy a madly exciting day, and one which they will long remember. You are to return to Sacca; have you any objection? Do you think you will be running any risk?'

'Nothing to matter, Signora; none of the people of Sacca will ever say that I was in Monsignore Fabrizio's service. Besides, if I may venture to say so to the Signora, I am burning to see *my* property at La Ricciarda. It seems so odd for me to be a landowner!'

'Your joy delights me. The farmer at La Ricciarda owes me, I think, some three or four years' rent. I will make him a present of one half of what he owes me, and the other half of all these arrears I give to you, but on this condition: You will go to Sacca, you will say that the day after tomorrow is the feast of one of my patron saints, and, the evening after your arrival, you will have my house illuminated in the most splendid fashion. Spare neither money nor pains; remember that this has to do with the greatest happiness of my life.

'I have made my preparations for this illumination a long time in advance. For more than three months I have been collecting in the cellars of the house everything that will be of use for this noble celebration. I have put in the gardener's keeping all the fireworks necessary for a magnificent display; you will have them let off from the terrace overlooking the Po. I have eighty-nine great barrels of wine in my cellars; you will set up eighty-nine fountains of wine in my park. If the next day so much as a single bottle of wine remains undrunk, I shall say that you do not love Fabrizio. When the fountains of wine, the illuminations, and the fireworks are in full swing, you will slip away cautiously, for it is possible, and it is my hope, that in Parma all these fine doings will appear as an act of insolence.'

'That is not merely possible, but certain; as it is also certain that Chief Justice Rassi, who signed Monsignore's sentence, will be bursting with rage. And also . . .' added Lodovico timidly, 'if the Signora wished to give more pleasure to her humble servant than by bestowing on him half the arrears of La Ricciarda, she would give me leave to play a little joke on that man Rassi. . . .'

'You are a good fellow!' exclaimed the Duchessa in high glee. 'But I forbid you absolutely to do anything at all to Rassi; I have a plan for having him publicly hanged, later on. As for you, try not to get yourself arrested at Sacca; everything would be spoilt if I lost you.'

'Me, Signora! Once I have said that I am celebrating the feast of one of Signora's patron saints, if the police sent thirty constables to upset anything, you may be sure that before they had reached the red Cross in the middle of the village, not one of them would be on his horse. They're not men to be trifled with, the people of Sacca; expert smugglers all of them, and they worship the Signora.

'Finally,' continued the Duchessa in a curiously casual manner, 'if I give wine to my good people of Sacca, I wish to drench the inhabitants of Parma with water. That same evening on which my house is illuminated, take the best horse in my stables, dash to my *palazzo* in Parma, and open the reservoir.'

'Ah! that's a capital idea of the Signora's!' cried Lodovico, in fits of laughter. 'Wine for the good people of Sacca, water for the smug citizens of Parma, who were so sure, the wretches, that Monsignore Fabrizio was going to be poisoned like poor L —'

Lodovico's joy knew no end; the Duchessa complaisantly watched his wild bursts of laughter. He kept on repeating: 'Wine for the people of Sacca, water for the people of Parma. The Signora knows better than I that when they rashly emptied the reservoir, twenty years ago, there was as much as a foot of water in several of the streets of Parma.'

'And water for the people of Parma,' echoed the Duchessa laughing. 'The public square in front of the citadel would have been filled with people if they had cut off Fabrizio's head. ... Everyone calls him the *great culprit*. ... But, above all things, carry the matter through skilfully, so that not a living soul knows that this flooding was either your work, or was ordered by me. Fabrizio, even the Conte himself, must be left in ignorance of this mad prank. ... But I was forgetting my poor people at Sacca. Go and write a letter to my agent, which I will sign. You will tell him that, for the feast of my holy patron, he is to distribute a hundred sequins among the poor of Sacca and that he is to obey you in everything to do with the illuminations, the fireworks, and the wine, and take particular care yourself that there is not one full bottle left in my cellars the next morning.'

'The Signora's agent will have no difficulty except on one point: in the five years that the Signora has had the villa, she has not left ten poor persons in Sacca.'

'*And water for the people of Parma!*' repeated the Duchessa, in a sing-song. 'How will you carry out this joke?'

'My plans are all made. I shall leave Sacca about nine o'clock. At half past ten my horse will be at the inn of "The Three Numskulls", on the road to Casalmaggiore and *my* property of La Ricciarda. At eleven, I shall be in my room in the *palazzo*, and at a quarter past eleven there will be water for the people of Parma, and more than they want, to drink the health of the "great culprit". Ten minutes later I shall leave the town by the Bologna road. I shall make, as I pass by, a low bow to the citadel, which Monsignore's courage and the Signora's cleverness have just disgraced; I shall take a cross-country path, which I know well, and so make my entry into La Ricciarda.'

Lodovico raised his eyes and looked at the Duchessa; he was

startled. She was staring fixedly at the bare wall six paces away from her, and her expression, it must be admitted, was terrible. 'Ah! my poor property!' thought Lodovico, 'the truth of it is, she is mad!' The Duchessa looked at him and read his thoughts.

'Ah! Signor Lodovico the great poet, you wish for a deed of gift in writing. Run and fetch me a sheet of paper.' Lodovico did not wait to be told twice, and the Duchessa wrote out in her own hand a lengthy form of receipt, antedated by a year, in which she declared that she had received from Lodovico San Micheli the sum of eighty thousand lire, and had given him as security for it the property of La Ricciarda. If after the expiration of twelve months the Duchessa had not repaid the said eighty thousand lire to Lodovico, the lands of La Ricciarda were to remain his property.

'It is a fine thing,' the Duchessa said to herself, 'to give to a faithful servant nearly a third of what is left to me.

'Now then,' she said to Lodovico, 'after this joke with the reservoir, I give you just two days to enjoy yourself at Casalmaggiore. For the conveyance to hold good, say that it is a matter which dates back more than a year. Come back and join me at Belgirate, and that without the slightest delay. Fabrizio may possibly be going to England, where you will follow him.'

Early the next day the Duchessa and Fabrizio were at Belgirate.

They settled down in that enchanting village; but agonizing grief awaited the Duchessa beside this beautiful lake. Fabrizio was entirely changed. From the very first moments of his awakening, still somewhat lethargic, out of the sleep which had followed on his escape, the Duchessa had become aware that something out of the ordinary was going on inside him. The deep-lying feeling which he took such pains to conceal was a somewhat odd one – it was nothing less than this: he was in despair at being out of prison. He took good care not to admit to this cause of his melancholy, which would have given rise to questions which he did not wish to answer.

'But, in heaven's name!' the Duchessa said to him in amazement, 'that horrible sensation when hunger forced you to feed, so as not to drop down fainting from exhaustion, on those loathsome dishes supplied by the prison kitchen, that feeling: "Is there some curious taste in this, am I poisoning myself at this moment?" – didn't that sensation fill you with horror?'

'I thought of death,' replied Fabrizio, 'as I suppose soldiers think of it: it was a possibility which I fully thought to avoid by my own skill.'

What disquietude therefore, what grief for the Duchessa! This being so dearly loved, so exceptional, lively, and original, was now, before her eyes, a prey to all-absorbing day-dreams. He actually preferred solitude to the pleasure of talking about all kinds of things, freely and frankly, to the best friend he had in the world. At all times he was good-tempered, attentive, and full of gratitude in his behaviour towards the Duchessa. He would, as before, have given his life for her a hundred times over. But his heart was elsewhere. They often sailed four or five leagues over that beautiful lake without uttering a word to each other. General conversation, the cold exchange of ideas which, from now on, was all that was possible between them, might perhaps have seemed pleasant to other people. But they remembered still, and the Duchessa in particular, what their conversations had been before that fatal fight with Giletti which had kept them apart from each other. Fabrizio owed the Duchessa an account of the nine months spent in a horrible prison, and now it appeared that he had nothing to say about his stay there save a few brief and fragmentary sentences.

'This is what was bound to happen sooner or later,' the Duchessa told herself, in sullen grief. 'Sorrow has aged me, or else he is really in love, and I now hold only second place in his heart.' Humiliated, utterly overwhelmed by the greatest of all possible sorrows, the Duchessa would say to herself at times: 'If Heaven had so willed it that Ferrante had gone completely mad, or that he had been lacking in courage, it seems to me that I should be less miserable.' From that moment this faint stirring of remorse poisoned the respect that the Duchessa had for her own character. 'So,' she said to herself bitterly, 'I am repenting of a resolution I have already made! Then I am no longer a del Dongo!

'It is the will of Heaven,' she would add: 'Fabrizio is in love, and what right have I to wish he were not in love? Has one single word of real love ever been exchanged between us?'

This extremely sensible reflection robbed her of sleep, and as a matter of fact – a thing which showed how old age and a certain deterioration of spiritual force had overtaken her with the prospect of wreaking a glorious revenge – she was a hundred times more unhappy at Belgirate than she had been in Parma. As regards the identity of the person who might be responsible for Fabrizio's strange absorption, it was hardly possible to entertain any reasonable doubt. Clelia Conti, that very pious girl, had betrayed her father, since she had consented to make the garrison drunk, and Fabrizio never made any mention of Clelia! 'But,' added the Duchessa, beating her breast in desperation, 'if the garrison had not been made drunk, all my ingenious arrangements, all my pains would have proved useless: therefore it is she who saved him!'

It was with the most extreme difficulty that the Duchessa obtained from Fabrizio any details of the events of that night, which, so she told herself, 'would once have been the subject of endlessly renewed conversations between us! In those happy times, he would have talked the whole day long, with an unceasing flow of zest and gaiety, about the slightest trifle it occurred to me to bring forward.'

As it was necessary to provide for any emergency, the Duchessa had installed Fabrizio at the port of Locarno, a Swiss town at the further end of Lake Maggiore. Every day she went to fetch him in a boat for long excursions over the lake. Well, on one occasion when she took it into her head to go up to his room, she found the walls covered with a number of views of the city of Parma, for which he had sent to Milan, or even to Parma itself, a place which he should have held in abhorrence. His little sitting-room, converted into a studio, was littered with all the apparatus of a painter in water-colours, and she found him finishing a third sketch of the Farnese Tower and the Governor's house.

'All you need to do now,' she said to him with an air of annoyance, 'is to make a portrait from memory of that charming Governor who merely wished to poison you. But, now I think of it,' she went on, 'you ought to write him a letter of apology for having taken the liberty of escaping and making his citadel look foolish.'

The poor woman little thought how true her words were. No sooner had he arrived in a place of safety than Fabrizio's first care had been to write General Fabio Conti a perfectly polite and, in a sense, a highly ridiculous letter, in which he begged his pardon for having escaped, alleging as an excuse that a certain person in a subordinate position in the citadel had been ordered to give him poison. Little did Fabrizio care what he wrote, his hope was that Clelia's eyes would see this letter, and his cheeks were wet with tears as he wrote it. He ended it with a highly amusing sentence: he ventured to say that, now he found himself at liberty, he frequently found himself regretting his little room in the Farnese Tower. This was the principal idea of his letter, he hoped that Clelia would understand it.

Still in the mood for writing, and always in the hope of being read by 'someone', Fabrizio expressed his thanks to Don Cesare, the kindly chaplain who had lent him books on theology. A few days later Fabrizio persuaded the owner of the small bookshop in Locarno to make the journey to Milan, where this bookseller, a friend of the celebrated bibliomaniac Reina, bought the most magnificent editions he could find of the works that Don Cesare had lent Fabrizio. The good chaplain received these books and a handsome letter which informed him that, in moments of impatience, pardonable perhaps in a poor prisoner, the writer had covered the margins of these books with some rather nonsensical notes. He begged him, therefore, to replace them in his library by the volumes which, with the most lively sense of gratitude, he took the liberty of presenting to him.

It was very generous of Fabrizio to give the simple name of notes to the endless scribblings with which he had covered the margins of a folio volume of the works of Saint Jerome. In the hope that he might be able to return this book to the worthy chaplain and exchange it for another, he had written day by day on its margins a very exact diary of everything that had happened to him in prison. The great events were nothing else than ecstasies of *divine love* (this word *divine* took the place of another which he dared not write). At one moment this 'divine love' drove the prisoner into the depths of despair, at others a voice carried across the air restored some hope to him, and gave rise to transports of joy. All this, fortunately, was written in prison ink, made up of wine, chocolate, and soot, and Don Cesare had done no more than cast an eye over it when putting the volume of Saint Jerome back on his shelves. If he had studied the margins he would have seen that one day the prisoner, believing himself to have been poisoned, was congratulating himself on dying at a distance of less than forty paces from what he had loved best in the world. But other eyes than the good chaplain's had read this page since Fabrizio's escape. That fine idea: *To die near what one loves!* expressed in a hundred different ways, was followed by a sonnet which portrayed this soul, parted, after atrocious torments, from the frail body it had inhabited for three-and-twenty years, and impelled by that instinctive desire for happiness natural to everything that has once had life, refusing to mount to heaven to mingle with the choirs of angels as soon as it should be free, and provided the dread Judge should grant it pardon for its sins; but that, more fortunate after death than it had been in life, it would go a short distance away from the prison, where for so long it had groaned, to be united with all that it had loved in this world. 'And so,' said the last line of this sonnet, 'I shall have found my paradise on earth.'

Although Fabrizio was never referred to in the citadel as anything but an infamous traitor who had violated the most sacred laws of duty, the worthy priest Don Cesare was none the less delighted by the sight of the fine books which an unknown hand had sent him; for Fabrizio had been careful not to write to him until a few days after sending them, for fear lest his name might cause the whole consignment to be indignantly rejected. Don Cesare said no word of this kind attention to his brother, who flew into a rage at the mere mention of Fabrizio's name. But since the prisoner's escape, he had resumed all his old intimacy with his charming niece, and as he had once taught her a few words of Latin, he showed her the fine books he had received. Such had been the traveller's hope. Suddenly Clelia blushed deeply; she had just recognized Fabrizio's hand-writing. Long and very narrow strips of yellow paper had been inserted by way of bookmarkers in various places in the volume. And as it is true to say that amidst the sordid pecuniary interests and the the cold and colourless vulgarity of the thoughts that fill our lives, the actions inspired by a genuine passion rarely fail to produce their effect, so, as though a propitious deity were taking trouble to lead her by the hand, Clelia, guided by this instinct, and by the thought of one thing only in the world, asked her uncle if she might compare the old copy of Saint Jerome with the one that he had just received. How can I describe her rapture in the midst of the dark grief in which Fabrizio's absence had plunged her, when she found on the margins of that old copy of Saint Jerome the sonnet we have mentioned, and the record, day by day, of the love that he had felt for her.

From the very first day she knew that sonnet by heart; she would sing it, leaning on her window sill, opposite that window, now deserted, where she had so often seen a little opening appear in the shutter. This shutter had been taken down to be placed on the judge's desk in the criminal court and to serve as evidence in a ridiculous suit which Rassi was instituting against Fabrizio, accused of the crime of having escaped, or, as the Chief Justice said, laughing inwardly as he said it, 'of having removed himself from the clemency of a magnanimous Prince!'

Every step that Clelia had taken was for her a subject of keen remorse, and now that she was unhappy, her remorse was all the keener. She tried in some slight degree to still the reproaches she addressed to herself by reminding herself of her vow *never to see Fabrizio again*, which she had made to the Madonna at the time when the General was nearly poisoned, and since then had renewed daily.

Fabrizio's escape had made her father ill, and, in addition, had brought him very near to losing his post when the Prince, in his fury, dismissed all the gaolers of the Farnese Tower, and sent them as prisoners to the city gaol. The General had been partly saved by the intercession of Conte Mosca, who preferred to see him shut up at the top of his citadel rather than find him an active and intriguing rival in court circles.

It was during the fortnight of uncertainty as to the disgrace of General Fabio Conti, who was really ill, that Clelia found courage to carry out the sacrifice which she had announced to Fabrizio. She had the sense to be ill on the day of general rejoicing, which was also that of the prisoner's escape, as the reader may possibly remember. She was ill also on the following day, and, in short, managed things so well that, with the exception of the gaoler Grillo, whose special duty was to look after Fabrizio, no one had any suspicion of her complicity, and Grillo kept his mouth shut.

But as soon as Clelia had no longer any anxiety in that direction she was even more cruelly disquieted by her rightful feelings of remorse. 'What argument in the world,' she would ask herself, 'can lessen the crime of a daughter who betrays her own father?'

One evening, after a day spent almost entirely in the chapel, and in tears, she begged her uncle, Don Cesare, to come with her to the General, whose outbursts of rage terrified her all the more since on every occasion he introduced imprecations against Fabrizio, that abominable, perfidious wretch.

Having come into her father's presence, she had the courage to say to him that if she had refused to give her hand to the Marchese Crescenzi it was because she did not feel any inclination towards him, and that she was convinced she would find no happiness in that union. At these words the General flew into a rage, and Clelia had some difficulty in carrying on with what she had to say. She added that if her father, tempted by the Marchese's great wealth, felt himself obliged to give her a formal order to marry him, she was prepared to obey. The General was quite astonished by this conclusion, which he had been far from expecting; he ended, however, by rejoicing at it. 'So,' he said to his brother, 'I shall not be reduced to living in rooms on a second floor, after all, even supposing that scoundrel Fabrizio's vile behaviour makes me lose my post.'

Conte Mosca did not fail to make a show of being deeply shocked by the escape of that *good-for-nothing fellow* Fabrizio, and repeated, when opportunity offered, the expression coined by Rassi with regard to the pointless behaviour of this young man – a very commonplace fellow by the way – who had fled away from the Prince's clemency. This witty remark, to which high society gave its blessing, did not in any way impress the lower orders. Left to their own good sense, while entirely convinced that Fabrizio was highly guilty, they admired the determination necessary for flinging oneself down from the top of so high a wall. Not a soul at court appreciated this courage. As for the police, greatly humiliated by this blow, they had officially discovered that a band of twenty soldiers, won over by the money distributed by the Duchessa, that horribly ungrateful woman whose name was no longer uttered save with a sigh, had given Fabrizio four ladders roped together, and each of them forty-five feet long. Fabrizio, having let down a cord which they had fastened to these ladders, had had only the quite commonplace distinction of pulling the ladders up to his cell. Certain Liberals notorious for their imprudence, and among them a Dr C —, an agent personally employed by the Prince, added, but compromised themselves by doing so, that these atrocious police had had the barbarity to order the shooting of eight of the unfortunate soldiers who had made it easier for that objectionable Fabrizio to escape. Thereupon he was blamed, even by genuine Liberals, as being responsible through his imprudence for the death of eight poor soldiers. It is thus that petty despotisms reduce to nothing the value of public opinion.

CHAPTER 23: *Death of a Prince*

AMIDST the general outcry against him, Archbishop Landriani alone showed himself faithful to his young friend's cause. He ventured to repeat, even at the Princess's court, that axiom of jurisprudence according to which, in every trial, justice must lend an entirely unprejudiced ear to the arguments in defence of an absent party.

The day after Fabrizio's escape a number of people had received a rather indifferent sonnet acclaiming this escape as one of the fine actions of the age, and comparing Fabrizio to an angel alighting upon the earth with outspread wings. Two evenings later, the whole of Parma was repeating a magnificent little poem. It set forth Fabrizio's soliloquy as he let himself slide down the rope, passing comment, meanwhile, on the various incidents of his life. This sonnet gave him a high place in public estimation by reason of two magnificent lines; every connoisseur of poetry recognized the style of Ferrante Palla.

But here I myself must have recourse to an epic style. Where can I find colours vivid enough to paint the torrents of indignation which suddenly flooded every politically right-minded heart when news came of the frightful insolence of that illumination of the house at Sacca? One single cry of horror went up against the Duchessa; even genuine Liberals considered that such an action endangered in an outrageous fashion the safety of poor suspects detained in the various prisons, and needlessly exasperated the Sovereign's temper. Conte Mosca declared that only one course was left to the Duchessa's old friends – to forget her. The chorus of execration was therefore unanimous; a stranger passing through the town would have been struck by the vehemence of public opinion. Yet, in this land of Italy, where people know how to appreciate the pleasures of revenge, the illuminations at Sacca and the marvellous feast given in the park to more than six thousand peasants had an immense success. Everyone in Parma was talking of how the Duchessa had distributed a thousand sequins among her peasantry; it was thus they accounted for the somewhat rough reception given to a party of some thirty constables whom the police had been so foolish as to send to that little village, thirty-six hours after the splendid evening's entertainment and the general drunkenness that had ensued. The constables, greeted with showers of stones, had turned and fled, and two of them, who had fallen off their horses, were flung into the Po.

As for the bursting of the great reservoir of the Palazzo Sanseverina, it had passed almost unnoticed. It was during the night that several streets had been flooded, by morning one would have said that it had been raining. Lodovico had taken care to break the panes of one of the windows in the *palazzo*, in a manner suggesting that thieves had broken in. A little ladder had actually been found there. Conte Mosca alone recognized his friend's inventive genius.

Fabrizio was fully determined to get back to Parma as soon as he could. He sent Lodovico with a long letter to the Archbishop, and this faithful servant came back to post at the first village in Piedmont, San Nazzaro, to the west of Pavia, a Latin epistle which the worthy prelate had addressed to his young protégé. We will here add a detail which, like many others, no doubt, may seem tedious to people in countries where there is no longer any need of precautions. The name of Fabrizio del Dongo was never written; all letters intended for him were addressed to Lodovico San Micheli, either at Locarno in Switzerland, or at Belgirate in Piedmont. The envelope was made of coarse paper, the seal carelessly applied, the address was scarcely legible and adorned at times with recommendations worthy of a cook; all the letters were dated, as from Naples, six days before their actual date.

From the Piedmontese village of San Nazzaro, near Pavia, Lodovico returned with all possible speed to Parma; he was charged with a mission to which Fabrizio attached the greatest importance. This was nothing less than to convey to Clelia Conti a silk handkerchief on which was printed one of Petrarch's sonnets. One word, it is true, had been altered in this sonnet. Clelia found it on her table two days after she had received the thanks of the Marchese Crescenzi, who declared himself the happiest of men. There is no need to say what impression this mark of still constant remembrance made on her heart.

It was Lodovico's business to procure all possible details of what was happening at the citadel. It was he who brought Fabrizio the sad news that the Marchese Crescenzi's marriage now appeared to be definitely settled; hardly a day passed without his providing some form of entertainment for Clelia inside the citadel. A decisive proof of the marriage was that this Marchese, who was immensely rich and in consequence, as is usual among wealthy people in Northern Italy, extremely stingy, was making huge preparations, and yet he was marrying a *portionless* girl. It is true that General Fabio Conti, whose vanity was greatly wounded by this observation, the first to spring to the minds of all his compatriots, had just bought a property worth more than three hundred thousand lire, and for this property he, who had nothing of his own, had paid cash down, presumably out of the Marchese's money. Moreover, the General had given out that he was bestowing this property on his daughter as a marriage portion. But the charges for the deed of gift and other documents, which amounted to more than twelve thousand lire, seemed a most ridiculous outlay to the Marchese, a man of an eminently logical mind.

He for his part was having woven for him in Lyons a set of magnificent tapestries of admirably blended colours, well calculated to delight the eye, designed by the famous Bolognese painter Palagi. These tapestries, each of which embodied some details of the armorial bearings of the Crescenzi family which, as all the world knows, is descended from the famous Crescentius, Roman Consul in the year 985, were to furnish the seventeen reception rooms composing the ground floor of the Marchese's *palazzo*. The tapestries, clocks, and crystal chandeliers sent to Parma cost over three hundred and fifty thousand lire; the value of the new mirrors, added to those which the house already contained, came to two hundred thousand lire. With the exception of two drawing-rooms, decorated by the famous Parmigianino, the greatest painter of the locality after the divine Correggio, all the rooms on the first and second floor were now occupied by the leading painters of Florence, Rome, and Milan, who were adorning them with frescoes. Fokelberg, the great Swedish sculptor, Tenerani of Rome and Marchesi of Milan had been working for a year on ten bas-reliefs representing as many noble deeds of Crescentius, that truly great man. The majority of the ceilings, also painted in fresco, offered some other allusions to his life. General admiration was expressed for the ceiling on which Hayez of Milan had represented Crescentius being greeted in the Elysian Fields by Francesco Sforza, Lorenzo the Magnificent, King Robert, the Tribune Cola di Rienzi, Machiavelli, Dante, and other great men of the middle ages. The admiration shown for these chosen spirits was taken to be a witty reflection on those people actually in power.

All these sumptuous details absorbed the whole attention of the nobility and the bourgeoisie of Parma, and wounded our hero to the heart when he read of them, described with artless admiration, in a long letter of more than twenty pages which Lodovico had dictated to a customs-officer at Casalmaggiore.

'And I, who am so poor!' thought Fabrizio, 'with an income of four thousand lire in all, and for all! It is utter impertinence on my part to dare to be in love with Clelia Conti for whom all these miracles are being performed.'

A single paragraph of Lodovico's long letter, but this written out in his own wretched hand, informed his master that one evening he had run into poor Grillo, his former gaoler, who had been thrown into prison and subsequently released, and was now apparently in hiding. Grillo had begged him for a sequin, out of charity, and Lodovico had given him four in the Duchessa's name. The old gaolers, twelve in all, who had been recently released, were preparing to give a rousing reception with their knives (*un trattamento di cortellate*) to their successors the new gaolers, should they ever succeed in meeting them outside the citadel. Grillo had said that almost every night there was a serenade at the fortress, that Signorina Clelia looked extremely pale, was often ill, *and other things of that sort*. As a consequence of this foolish remark Lodovico received order by return of post to come back to Locarno. He returned, and the details he supplied by word of mouth were even more distressing to Fabrizio.

One can imagine how pleasant he made himself to the poor Duchessa; he would rather have died a thousand deaths than utter the name of Clelia Conti in her presence. The Duchessa loathed Parma, whereas, for Fabrizio, everything that reminded him of that city was at once sublime and moving.

The Duchessa had less than ever put ideas of her revenge out of her mind; she had been so happy before the incident of Giletti's death – and now, what a fate was hers! She was living in expectation of a dire event of which she took good care not to say a word to Fabrizio, she who once, at the time of her arrangement with Ferrante, had thought that she would at some future date delight Fabrizio so much by telling him that one day he would be avenged.

We can now form some idea of the pleasantness of Fabrizio's intercourse with the Duchessa: a gloomy silence reigned almost always between them. To make their relations with each other more enjoyable, the Duchessa had yielded to the temptation of playing a trick on this too beloved nephew. The Conte wrote to her almost every day; apparently he still sent them by courier as in the days when their love was new, for his letters always bore the postmark of some little town in Switzerland. The poor man racked his brains so as not so speak too openly of his affection, and to compose amusing letters; they barely received a casual glance from her eye. Of what avail, alas, is the fidelity of a lover she esteems to a woman whose heart is broken by the coldness of the man she prefers to him.

In the space of two months the Duchessa answered him only once, and that was to request him to find out how the land lay with regard to the Princess, and to see whether, in spite of the insolence of the display of fireworks, a letter from herself would be received with pleasure. The letter he was to present, if he thought fit, requested the post of Lord-in-waiting to the Princess, which had lately fallen vacant, for the Marchese Crescenzi, and expressed the wish that it might be conferred upon him in consideration of his marriage. The Duchessa's letter was a masterpiece; it was a model of the most tender respect expressed in the most admirable terms. In this courtly style not a single word was allowed to intrude which might have given rise to consequences, even the most remote, which could have proved disagreeable to the Princess. The reply to it, moreover, breathed a tender affection, that was being tortured by the absence of a friend.

My son and I [the Princess told her] *have not spent one fairly tolerable evening since your departure. Does my dear Duchessa no longer remember that it is to her I owe a consulting voice in the nomination of the officers of my household? Does she then feel herself obliged to give me reasons for the Marchese's appointment, as if the expression of her desire were not the best of reasons for me? The Marchese shall have the post, if I have any say in the matter, and there will always be a place in my heart, and that the first, for my charming Duchessa. My son expresses himself in absolutely the same terms, a trifle strong perhaps on the lips of a great fellow of one-and-twenty, and asks you for specimens of minerals from the Val d'Orta, near Belgirate. You may address your letters, which will I hope, be frequent, to the Conte, who is still in a furious temper with you, and whom I particularly like on account of such feelings. The Archbishop too has remained faithful to you. We all hope to see you come back some day; remember, you really must. The Marchesa Ghisleri, my Mistress of the Robes, is preparing to leave this world for a better one. The poor woman has given me a great deal of trouble; she annoys*

me still further by departing so inopportunely. Her illness makes me think of
the name which I should once have had so much pleasure in substituting for
hers, if, that is, I could have obtained that sacrifice of her independence from
the matchless woman who, in running away from us, has taken with her all
the joy of my little court [and so on].

It was therefore with the consciousness of having sought to hasten, so far as it lay in her power, the marriage which was filling Fabrizio with despair, that the Duchessa saw him every day. Thus they sometimes spent four or five hours sailing in each other's company over the lake, without exchanging a single word. On Fabrizio's side there was complete and perfect good-will; but he was thinking of other things, and his artless, simple nature supplied him with nothing to say. The Duchessa saw this; and it was anguish to her.

We have forgotten to mention, in its proper place, that the Duchessa had taken a house at Belgirate, a charming village and one which fulfils all the promise of its name (i.e. the view of a beautiful bend in the lake). From the french window of her drawing-room, the Duchessa could step out into her boat. She had chosen a quite simple one for which four rowers would have sufficed; she hired twelve, and arranged things so as to have a man from each of the villages situated in the neighbourhood of Belgirate. The third or fourth time that she found herself in the middle of the lake with all of these well-chosen men, she made them stop rowing.

'I look upon you all as friends,' she said to them, 'and I wish to let you into a secret. My nephew Fabrizio has escaped from prison; and possibly, in some treacherous way, they will seek to recapture him, even though he is on your lake, in a place where men are free. Keep your ears open and give me warning of everything you hear. I give you leave to enter my room by day or night.'

The rowers responded enthusiastically; she knew how to make people love her. But she did not think that there was any likelihood of Fabrizio's being recaptured; it was for herself that she took all these precautions, and, before the fatal order to open the reservoir of the Palazzo Sanseverina, she would not have dreamt of doing such a thing.

Her prudence had led her also to take lodgings for Fabrizio at the port of Locarno; every day he either came to see her, or she herself crossed over into Switzerland. The amount of pleasure they found in each other's constant society may be guaged from the following detail. The Marchesa and her daughters came twice to see them, and the presence of these strangers was a pleasant relief to them; for even where ties of blood exist, we can apply the name of 'stranger' to a person who knows nothing of our dearest interests and whom we see but once a year.

The Duchessa happened to be one evening in Fabrizio's rooms in Locarno with the Marchesa and her two daughters. The archpriest of the district and the parish priest had both come to pay their respects to these ladies. The former, who had an interest in some business concern, and kept closely up to date with the news, suddenly took it into his head to say: 'The Prince of Parma is dead!'

The Duchessa turned very pale. She could hardly summon up the courage to say: 'Do they give any details?'

'No,' replied the archpriest. 'The report is confined to the announcement of his death, which is quite certain.'

The Duchessa looked at Fabrizio. 'I have done this for him,' she said to herself. 'I would have done things a thousand times worse. And there he stands in front of me indifferent, and with his mind on another woman!' It was beyond the Duchessa's strength to endure this frightful thought; she fell into a dead faint. Everyone hastened to her assistance; but, on coming round, she noticed that Fabrizio was bestirring himself far less than the archpriest and the curé; he was dreaming as usual.

'He is thinking of returning to Parma,' the Duchessa said to herself, 'and perhaps of breaking off Clelia's marriage to the Marchese; but I shall manage to prevent him.' Then, remembering the presence of the two priests, she made haste to add: 'He was a great Prince, and one who has been sorely maligned! It is an immense loss for us all!'

The two priests took their leave, and the Duchessa, in order to be alone, announced that she was going to bed.

'No doubt,' she said to herself, 'prudence ordains that I should wait a month or two before returning to Parma; but I feel that I should never have the patience; I am suffering too keenly here. Fabrizio's continual absorption and his silence are more than my heart can bear. Who would have said that I would ever find it wearisome to be skimming over this charming lake, the two of us alone together, and at a moment when, to avenge him, I have done more than I can ever let him know! After such an experience as that, death is nothing. It is now that I am paying for the transports of happiness and childish delight which I felt in my palazzo in Parma when I welcomed Fabrizio there on his return from Naples. If I had said a word, all would have been settled, and it may be that, once he was bound to me, he would never have given a thought to that young Clelia; but that word was horribly repugnant to me. Now she triumphs over me. What more natural? She is only twenty; while I for my part, changed from what I was by my troubles, and sick as well, am twice her age! ... I must die, I must make an end of things! A woman of forty is no longer of any account save to the men who loved her in her youth. Now I shall find nothing left to me but the pleasures of vanity. And do they make life worth living? All the more reason for going to Parma, and amusing myself. If things took a certain turn, I should lose my life. Well, what's the harm in that? I shall make a magnificent end, and before it's all over, but only then, I shall say to Fabrizio: "Ungrateful creature; this is for your sake!" ... Yes, I can find no occupation for what little life remains to me save in Parma; I shall play the great lady there. What a happy thing if I could now appreciate all those honours which used to make that woman, the Marchesa Raversi, so miserably jealous! In those days, in order to see my happiness, I had to look in the eyes of envious people ... My vanity has one cause for satisfaction. With the possible exception of the Conte, no one can have guessed what event it was that has left my heart cold and lifeless ... I shall love Fabrizio, I shall be devoted to his interests; but he must not break off Clelia's marriage, and end by marrying her himself ... No, that shall never happen!'

The Duchessa had reached this point in her mournful soliloquy when she heard a great noise in the house.

'Good!' she said to herself, 'they are coming to arrest me. Ferrante has let himself be caught, he must have confessed. Well, so much the better! I shall have something to do; I am going to fight with them for my life. But in the first place, I must not let myself be taken.'

Half-dressed, the Duchessa fled to the bottom of her garden. She was already thinking of climbing over a little wall and escaping into the open country, when she saw someone going into her room. She recognized Bruno, the Conte's confidential servant; he was alone with her maid. She went up to the french window. The man was telling her maid of the injuries he had received. The Duchessa came back into the house. Bruno almost flung himself at her feet, imploring her not to tell the Conte of the preposterous hour at which he had arrived.

'Immediately after the Prince's death,' he added, 'his Lordship the Conte issued orders to all the post-houses not to supply horses to subjects of the State of Parma. Consequently I travelled as far as the Po with horses from our own stables; but as I was getting out of the boat my carriage was overturned, broken, and smashed to pieces, and I had such bad bruises that I couldn't get on a horse, as would have been my duty.'

'Well,' said the Duchessa, 'it's three o'clock in the morning. I shall say that you arrived at midday; but don't go and contradict me.'

'That's just like the Signora's kindness!'

Politics, in a literary work, are like a pistol-shot in the middle of a concert, something loud and out of place, yet something all the same to which we cannot refuse to pay attention.

We are about to speak of very ugly matters, concerning which, for more than one reason, we should like to keep silent; but we are obliged to mention events which come within our province, since they have for their theatre the hearts of actors in our story.

'But, in heaven's name,' said the Duchessa to Bruno, 'how did that great Prince come to die?'

'He was out shooting birds of passage in the marshes alongside the Po, two leagues from Sacca. He fell into a hole hidden by a tuft of grass; he was all in a sweat, and caught a chill. They carried him to a lonely house, where he died within a few hours. Some say that Signor Catena and Signor Borone are dead as well, and that the whole accident arose from the copper saucepans in the peasant's house they went to, which were full of verdigris. They had their lunch there. As a matter of fact those hot-heads, the Jacobins, who say whatever suits them, talk of poison. I know that my friend Toto, a quartermaster in the Royal Guard, would have died but for the kind attention of a yokel who appeared to know a great deal about medicine, and made him take some very curious remedies. But they've ceased to talk about the Prince's death already; after all, he was a cruel man. As I was leaving, the people were gathering together to go and slaughter Chief Justice Rassi; they also wanted to set fire to the gates of the citadel, to enable the prisoners to escape. But some declared that Fabio Conti would fire his guns. Others swore that the gunners at the citadel had poured water on their powder, and refused to massacre their fellow-citizens. But here is something far more interesting: while the surgeon of Sandolaro was attending to my poor arm, a man from Parma came in and told us that the mob, having come upon Barbone, that precious clerk from the citadel, in the street, had thrashed him mercilessly and then hanged him from the tree on the public square which is nearest to the citadel. The mob were marching to smash that fine statue of the Prince which is in the Palace gardens. But his Lordship sent for a battalion of the Guard, had them drawn up in front of the statue, and sent word to the people that no one who came into the gardens should go out of them alive, and the people were frightened. But what is a very curious thing, and what the man from Parma, who is a retired constable, repeated to me several times, is that his Lordship kicked General P—, the commander of the Royal Guard, and after tearing off his epaulettes, had him marched out of the gardens by two fusiliers.'

'That's just like the Conte!' cried the Duchessa in a transport of joy which she would not have believed possible a few minutes earlier. 'He would never allow anyone to insult our Princess; and as for General P—, in his devotion to his rightful masters, he would never consent to serve the usurper, whereas the Conte, whose feelings were less delicate, fought in all the Spanish campaigns, a thing for which he has often been adversely criticized at court.'

The Duchessa had opened the Conte's letter, but kept interrupting her reading of it to ask Bruno innumerable questions.

The letter itself was very amusing; the Conte made use of the most lugubrious expressions, and yet the keenest joy broke out in every word. He avoided all details about the Prince's death, and ended his letter with the following words:

You will no doubt come back, my dear angel, but I advise you to wait a day or two for the courier whom the Princess will send you, or so I hope, today or tomorrow. Your return must be as imposing as your departure was bold. As for the 'great culprit' who is with you, I fully count upon having him tried by a dozen judges selected from every party in this State. But to have the young villain punished as he deserved I must first be able to tear the first sentence to ribbons, if it still exists.

The Conte had opened his letter to add:

Now for a very different matter. I have just issued ammunition to the two battalions of the Guard; I am going to fight and do my best to deserve the nickname of 'Cruel' with which the Liberals have favoured me for so long. That old fossil, General P— has dared to speak in the barracks of parleying with the townsfolk, who are more or less in a state of revolt. I am writing to you out in the street; I am on my way to the palace, which they shall not enter save over my dead body. Goodbye! If I die it will be as I have lived, still worshipping you in spite of everything! Do not forget to draw the 300,000 lire deposited in your name with D— in Lyons.

Here comes that poor devil Rassi pale as death, and without his wig. You've no idea what he looks like! The townsfolk are absolutely bent on hanging him; that would be doing him a great wrong, he deserves to be drawn and quartered. He fled for safety to my house, and has now run after me into the street. I hardly know what to do with him ... I don't want to take him to the Prince's Palace; that would bring about a revolt in that quarter. F— shall see whether I love him: my first words to Rassi were: 'I must have the sentence passed on Signor del Dongo, and any copies you may have of it; and say to all those unjust judges, who are the cause of this revolt, that I will have the lot of them hanged and you as well, my dear fellow, if they breathe a word of that sentence, which never existed.' I am sending a company of grenadiers in Fabrizio's name, to the Archbishop. Goodbye, dear angel! My house will be burned, and I shall lose those charming portraits I have of you. I am hurrying off to the Palace to get that infamous General G—, who is up to some tricks, cashiered. He is basely toadying to the people, as he once used to toady to the late Prince. All these generals are in the devil of a fright; I think I'll have myself made Commander-in-Chief.

The Duchessa was unkind enough not to send to waken Fabrizio. She felt a glow of admiration for the Conte which was closely akin to love. 'All things considered,' she said to herself, 'I shall really have to marry him.' She wrote to him at once, and sent off one of her men. That night the Duchessa had no time to feel unhappy.

Next day, about noon, she saw a boat manned by six rowers plying rapidly through the waters of the lake; Fabrizio and she soon recognized a man wearing the livery of the Prince of Parma. It was in fact, one of his couriers who, before landing, called out to the Duchessa: 'The revolt has been quelled!' This courier handed her several letters from the Conte, a charming one from the Princess, and an order of Prince Ranuccio-Ernesto V, inscribed on parchment, creating her Duchessa di San Giovanni and Mistress of the Robes to the Princess-Mother. The young Prince, an expert in mineralogy, whom she regarded as a simpleton, had had enough intelligence to write her a short note, but there was a hint of love at the end of it.

The note began thus:

The Conte says, your Grace, that he is pleased with me. The fact is that I stood up to a few musket shots at his side, and my horse was hit. Seeing the fuss made over so small a matter, I long to take part in a real battle, but not against my own subjects. I owe everything to the Conte; all my Generals, who have never been to war, ran like hares; I believe two or three of them fled as far as Bologna. Since the day when a great and deplorable event called me to power, I have signed no order which has given me so much pleasure as this which appoints you Mistress of the Robes to my mother. She and I both remembered how one day you admired the fine view one has from the villa of San Giovanni, which once belonged to Petrarch, or so at least it is said. My mother wished to give you that little property: and I, not knowing what to give you, and not daring to offer you all that is your due, have made you a Duchessa in my own principality. I do not know whether you are so much of a scholar as to be aware that Sanseverina is a Roman title. I have just given the Grand Cordon of my Order to our worthy Archbishop, who has shown a firmness very rare in a man of seventy. You will not be vexed with me for having recalled all the ladies who were banished. I am told that in future I must never sign my name without first writing the words 'Your affectionate'. It grieves me that I should be forced to make such lavish use of a protestation which is only completely true when I write to you ...

Your affectionate,
Ranuccio-Ernesto

Who would not have said, judging by such language, that the Duchessa was about to enjoy the highest favour? All the same, she found something very odd in other letters from the Conte, which reached her two hours later. He advised her, without further explanation, to postpone her return to Parma for some days, and to write to the Princess that she was seriously unwell. Notwithstanding this, the Duchess and Fabrizio set off for Parma immediately after dinner. The Duchessa's object, which, however, she did not admit to herself, was to hasten the Marchese Crescenzi's marriage. Fabrizio, for his part, spent the journey in a state of wild, ecstatic happiness, which seemed to his aunt quite absurd. He was in hopes of seeing Clelia again very soon; he fully reckoned on carrying her off, even against her will, if there should be no other way of breaking off this marriage.

The journey of the Duchessa and her nephew passed off very gaily. At the last stage before Parma, Fabrizio stopped for a moment or two to resume his clerical habit; usually he dressed as a layman in mourning. When he returned to the Duchessa's room she said to him: 'There seems to me something dubious and inexplicable in the Conte's letters. If you will take my advice you will stay here for a few hours. I'll send you a courier as soon as I have had a talk with that important Minister.'

It was with a great deal of reluctance that Fabrizio agreed to yield to this sensible advice. Transports of joy worthy of a boy of fifteen marked the welcome which the Conte accorded to the Duchessa, whom he addressed as his wife. It was a long time before he would consent to speak of politics, and when at length they came down to cold common sense he said to her: 'You acted very wisely in preventing Fabrizio from making a public appearance; we are in the full swing of a reaction here. Just guess who is the colleague whom the Prince has given me as Minister of Justice! It's Rassi, my dear, Rassi, whom I treated like the beggarly knave he is, at the time of our great undertaking. By the way, I must warn you that everything that has happened here has been suppressed. If you read our *Gazette* you will see that a clerk from the citadel, named Barbone, has died as the result of falling from a carriage. As for the sixty odd rogues whom I had picked off with musket shots when they were attacking the Prince's statue in the gardens, they are in very good health, but are on their travels. Conte Zurla, the Minister of the Interior, has gone in person to the house of each of these unfortunate heroes, and has handed fifteen sequins to his family or his friends, with orders to say that the deceased was on his travels, and a very definite threat of imprisonment to anyone who should let it be understood that he had been killed. A man from my own Ministry for Foreign Affairs has been sent on a mission to the journalists of Milan and Turin, so that they shall not make any mention of the "unfortunate incident" – that is the accepted expression. This man is to push on as far as Paris and London, to publish a semi-official denial in all the newspapers of anything that they may say about our troubles. Another agent has made his way to Bologna and Florence. I just shrugged my shoulders.

'But the comical thing, at my age, is that I felt a momentary thrill of enthusiasm when I was speaking to the soldiers of the Guard, and when I tore the epaulettes off that contemptible fellow, General P—... At that moment, I would have given my life for the Prince, without the least hesitation: I admit now that it would have been a very silly way of ending it. Today the Prince, excellent young fellow as he is, would give a hundred scudi to see me carried off by some illness or other. He has not yet dared to ask for my resignation, but we speak to each other as seldom as possible, and I send him a number of little reports in writing, as I used to do with the late Prince after Fabrizio was imprisoned. By the way, I have not yet torn to ribbons the sentence passed against him, for the very good reason that that scoundrel Rassi has not let me have it. You have therefore acted very wisely in preventing Fabrizio from putting in a public appearance here. The sentence is still in force; however, I do not think that Rassi would dare to have our nephew arrested at this moment, though he possibly may in another fortnight. If Fabrizio absolutely insists on returning to town, let him come and stay with me.'

'But what's the reason for all this?' cried the Duchessa in amazement.

'They have persuaded the Prince that I am giving myself airs as a dictator and a saviour of his country, and that I wish to guide him as if he were a mere child; what is more, in speaking of him, I seem to have uttered the fatal words "that child". This may be true; I was greatly excited that day. For instance, I looked on him as a proper man, because he was not unduly frightened in face of the first musket shots he had ever heard fired in his life. He's not lacking in intelligence, he has even more quality than his father: in fact – I cannot repeat it too often – in his heart of hearts he is both honest and good. But this honest, young heart is moved to anger when he is told of any dastardly trick, and he reckons that he must have a very dark soul himself to so much as notice such things! Just think of the upbringing he has had!'

'Your Excellency should have remembered that one day he would be our master, and have appointed a man of intelligence to be with him.'

'In the first place, we have the example of the Abbé de Condillac, who, when appointed by the Marchese di Felino, my predecessor, made nothing more of his pupil than a King of Fools. He walked in religious processions, and, in 1796, he failed to come to terms with General Bonaparte, who would have tripled the size of his dominions. In the second place, I never expected to remain as Prime Minister for ten successive years. Now that I am completely disillusioned, as I have been for a month past, I intend to amass a million lire before I leave this bear-garden, which I have saved, to its own devices. But for me, Parma would have been a Republic two months ago, with the poet Ferrante Palla as Dictator.'

This remark made the Duchessa blush; the Conte knew nothing of what had happened.

'We are about to fall back into a regular eighteenth-century monarchy: the confessor and the mistress. At heart, the Prince cares for nothing but mineralogy, and possibly, my dear lady, for you. Since he began to reign, his valet – whose brother I have just made a captain, this brother having completed nine months' service – his valet, I say, has gone and stuffed his head with the idea that he ought to be the happiest of men because his profile is going to appear on the scudi. This bright idea has brought boredom in its train.

'Now he has to have an aide-de-camp to cure him of his boredom. Well, even if he were to offer me that precious million which we need to live in comfort in Naples or Paris, I would not choose to be the remedy for his boredom, and spend four or five hours in His Highness's company. Besides, since I have more intelligence than he, by the end of a month he would regard me as a monster.

'The late Prince was spiteful and jealous, but he had been on active service, and had commanded troops, which had given him a certain dignity of bearing. One saw in him the making of a Prince, and with him I could be a more or less competent Minister. With this honest, frank, and really well-meaning son of his I am forced to be an intriguer. Here am I now the rival of the most insignificant little woman in the Palace, and a very inferior rival at that, for I shall certainly disregard a host of essential details. For instance, three days ago one of these women who put out clean towels every morning in the rooms took it into her head to mislay the key of one of the Prince's English writing-desks. Whereupon his Highness refused to deal with any business, the papers relating to which were inside this desk. As a matter of fact, for twenty lire, they could have removed the wooden back, or made use of a skeleton key. But Ranuccio-Ernesto V said to me that that would be teaching the court locksmith bad habits.

'Up to the present it has been absolutely impossible for him to be of the same mind for three days running. If he had been born Marchese so-and-so, with an ample fortune, this young Prince would have been one of the most estimable men about his court – a sort of Louis XVI. But how, with that pious simplicity of his, will he manage to escape all the cunningly laid snares that surround him? And so the salon of your enemy the Marchesa Raversi is more powerful than ever. They have discovered there that I, who gave the order to fire on the people, and was determined to kill three thousand men if necessary, rather than let them desecrate the statue of the Prince who had been my master, I am a red-hot Liberal; that I tried to make him sign a Constitution, and a hundred such absurdities. With all this talk of a Republic, certain fools would prevent us from enjoying even the best of Monarchies ... In short, my dear lady, you are the only member of the present Liberal party, whose head my enemies make me out to be, of whom the Prince has not spoken in offensive terms. The Archbishop, always a perfectly honourable man, is in deep disgrace for having spoken in reasonable terms of what I did on "the unhappy day".

'On the morrow of the day which was not as yet called "unhappy", and while it was still accepted that a revolt had really taken place, the Prince told the Archbishop that, so that you should not have to take an inferior title on marrying me, he would make me a Duca. Today I fancy it is Rassi, whom I ennobled when he sold me the late Prince's secrets, who is going to be made a Conte. In the face of such a promotion as that I shall be made to look a fool.'

'The poor Prince will cut a sorry figure.'

'No doubt; but after all he is *our master*, a distinction which, in less than a fortnight, eliminates any element of ridicule. So, dear Duchessa, let us act as if we were playing backgammon – *let us withdraw.*'

'But we shall not be exactly rich.'

'After all, neither you nor I have any need of luxury. If you give me, in Naples, a seat in a box at the San Carlo and a horse, I shall be more than satisfied. It will never be a more or less luxurious style of living which will give you and me a position in society, but the pleasure which intelligent people of that place may possibly find in coming to drink a cup of tea at your house.'

'But,' the Duchessa put in, 'what would have happened on the "unhappy day" if you had held aloof, as I hope you will in future?'

'The troops would have fraternized with the townsfolk, there would have been three days of bloodshed and incendiarism (for it would take a hundred years in this principality for a Republic to be anything but an absurdity), then a fortnight of looting, until two or three regiments supplied by a foreign power came to put a stop to it. Ferrante Palla was in the midst of the mob, as full of courage and as uproarious as usual. He had probably a dozen friends who were acting in collusion with him, which Rassi will make into a superb conspiracy. What is certain is that, while wearing an incredibly tattered coat, he was scattering gold by handfuls.'

Astounded by all this news, the Duchessa went off in haste to thank the Princess. As she entered the room the Lady of the Bed-chamber handed her the little gold key which is worn at the waist, and is the badge of supreme authority in that part of the Palace over which the Princess has control. Clara Paolina hastened to dismiss all the company; and, once she was alone with her friend, she persisted for some moments in expressing herself a trifle obscurely. The Duchessa was not very clear as to what it all meant, and only gave very cautious answers. At length the Princess burst into tears and, flinging herself into the Duchessa's arms, exclaimed: 'My days of unhappiness are going to begin all over again. My son will treat me worse than his father did!'

'I shall see that does not happen,' the Duchessa answered hotly. 'But first of all,' she went on, 'I must beg your Serene Highness to deign to accept here and now this tribute of all my gratitude and my profound respect.'

'What do you mean?' cried the Princess, full of uneasiness and apprehending a resignation.

'What I mean is that whenever your Serene Highness gives me leave to turn the nodding chin of that comical Chinese figure on her chimneypiece to the right, she will permit me also to call things by their proper names.'

'Is that all, my dear Duchessa?' cried Clara Paolina, rising from her seat and hastening herself to put the creature's head in the right position. 'Now, my dear Mistress of the Robes,' she said in a charming tone of voice, 'you may speak as freely as you like.'

'Madam,' the Duchessa went on, 'your Highness has grasped the situation perfectly; you and I are both in the greatest danger. The sentence passed on Fabrizio has not been revoked; consequently, on the day when they wish to rid themselves of me and to insult you, they will put him back into prison. Our position is as bad as ever. As regards myself, I am marrying the Conte, and we are going to settle down in Naples or in Paris. The final stroke of ingratitude of which the Conte is at this moment the victim has entirely disgusted him with public affairs, and were it not a question of your Serene Highness's interests, I should advise him not to remain in this mess unless the Prince were to give him an enormous sum of money. I will ask your Highness's leave to explain that the Conte, who had a hundred and thirty thousand lire when he came into office, has today an income of barely twenty thousand. For a very long time I have vainly urged him to give some thought to his fortune. In my absence, he picked a quarrel with the Prince's Farmers-General, who were scoundrels; he has replaced them by other scoundrels, who have given him eight hundred thousand lire.'

'What!' cried the Princess in surprise. 'Good heavens, I am sorry to hear that!'

'Madam,' replied the Duchessa with the greatest coolness, 'must I turn the figure's nose to the left?'

'Good gracious, no,' exclaimed the Princess; 'but I am sorry that a man of the Conte's character should have considered that sort of gain.'

'But for this speculation he would be despised by all well-bred people.'

'Good heavens! Is it possible!'

'Madam,' replied the Duchessa, 'except for my friend the Marchese Crescenzi, who has an income of three or four hundred thousand lire, everyone here steals. And how should they not steal in a principality where gratitude for the greatest services lasts for hardly a month? There is therefore nothing real, or capable of surviving disgrace, save money. I am going to take the liberty, Madam, of venturing on some terrible truths.'

'You have my permission,' said the Princess, sighing deeply, 'and yet I find them painfully unpleasant.'

'Well then, Madam, the Prince your son, a perfectly upright man, is capable of making you far more unhappy than his father ever did. The late Prince had a character more or less like any other man's;

our present ruler is never sure of wanting the same thing for three days on end. Consequently, in order to make sure of him, you must live all the time in his company and never allow him to speak to anyone else. As this truth is not difficult to fathom, the new *Ultra* Party, controlled by those two clever people, Rassi and the Marchesa Raversi, are going to try to provide a mistress for the Prince. This mistress will have permission to line her own pocket and to dispose of some minor posts; but she will be responsible to the Party for keeping the master in the same frame of mind.

'For my part, to feel properly established at your Highness's court, I must have that man Rassi banished and disgraced. Furthermore, it is my earnest wish that Fabrizio should be tried by the most honest judges that can be found. If these gentlemen, as I hope, recognize that he is innocent, it will be natural to grant his Grace the Archbishop's desire that Fabrizio should be his Coadjutor with eventual succession. If I fail, the Conte and I will retire from the field. In that case, I leave this parting advice with your Serene Highness: you must never forgive Rassi, nor must you ever leave your son's dominions. So long as you are near him this dutiful son will never do you any serious harm.'

'I have followed your arguments with all due attention,' replied the Princess, smiling. 'But ought I, then, to take upon myself the responsibility of finding a mistress for my son?'

'Certainly not, Madam. But make it your first care to see that your drawing-room is the only one which he finds entertaining.'

On this topic the conversation continued endlessly. The scales were falling from the eyes of the innocent and intelligent Princess.

One of the Duchessa's couriers went to tell Fabrizio that he might enter the city, but must keep himself hidden. He was barely noticed. He spent his whole time, disguised as a peasant, in the wooden-booth of a chestnut-vendor, put up just opposite the gates of the citadel, beneath the trees in the public promenade.

CHAPTER 24 : *Court Entertainments*

THE Duchessa organized some delightful evening parties at the Palace, which had never seen such gaiety. Never had she been more charming than she was that winter, and yet she was living in circumstances of the greatest danger. All the same, during this critical period, she only once or twice happened to think with a certain degree of sadness of the strange alteration in Fabrizio's character.

The young Prince used to appear very early at his mother's delightful parties, where she would always say to him: 'Go away, do, and attend to your governing. I'm almost certain there are more than a score of reports on your table just waiting for acceptance or rejection and I don't want the rest of Europe to accuse me of making you a King of sluggards in order to reign in your stead.'

These counsels had the disadvantage of being offered always at the most inopportune moments, that is to say when the Prince, having overcome his shyness, was taking part in some current charade which amused him greatly. Twice a week there were parties in the country to which, on the pretext of winning the affection of the people for their new ruler, the Princess invited the prettiest women of the middle class. The Duchessa, who was the life and soul of this joyous court, was in hopes that these fair plebeians, all of whom looked with a bitterly envious eye on the great success of their fellow townsman Rassi, would tell the Prince of some of that Minister's countless rascally tricks. For, among other childish notions, the Prince entertained the idea that he had a *moral* ministry.

Rassi had too much sense not to realize how dangerous these brilliant evenings at the Princess's court, under the direction of the woman who hated him, were to himself. He had not chosen to hand over to Conte Mosca the perfectly legal sentence passed on Fabrizio. It was therefore necessary that either the Duchessa or he should vanish from the court.

On the day of that popular rising, the existence of which it was now the correct thing to deny, someone had distributed money among the populace. Rassi made this his starting-point. Dressed even more shabbily than usual, he climbed the stairs of the most wretched houses in the city, and spent whole hours in serious conversation with their poverty-stricken inhabitants. He was well rewarded for all his trouble: by the end of a fortnight of this kind of life he knew to a certainty that Ferrante Palla had been the secret leader of the insurrection, and what was more, that this man, a pauper all his life as a great poet should be, had sent nine or ten diamonds to be sold in Genoa.

Among others were mentioned five valuable stones which were actually worth more than forty thousand lire, and which, *ten days before the Prince's death*, had been sacrificed for thirty-five thousand, because, so the vendor said, the money was needed.

How can one describe the minister's rapture on making this discovery? He was aware that every day he was being made a laughing stock at the court of the Princess Dowager, and on several occasions the Prince, when discussing business with him, had laughed in his face with all the artless impudence of youth. It must be admitted that Rassi had some singularly plebeian habits. For instance, as soon as he grew interested in a discussion, he would cross his legs and clutch hold of one of his shoes; if his interest increased, he would spread his red cotton handkerchief over his knee, and so forth. The Prince had laughed heartily at the merry jest of one of the prettiest women of the middle class, who, knowing by the way that she had a very shapely leg, had set out to imitate this elegant gesture of the Minister of Justice.

Rassi craved a special audience and said to the Prince: 'Would Your Highness be willing to give a hundred thousand lire to know exactly in what manner your august father met his death? With that sum, the legal authorities would be in a position to arrest the guilty parties, if any exist.' The Prince's answer was a foregone conclusion.

Shortly after, Cecchina informed the Duchessa that she had been offered a large sum of money to allow her mistress's diamonds to be examined by a jeweller; she had indignantly refused. The Duchessa scolded her for having refused, and a week later Cecchina had the diamonds ready to show. On the day fixed for this exhibition of the diamonds the Conte posted a couple of reliable men at every jeweller's in Parma, and towards midnight he came to tell the Duchessa that the inquisitive jeweller was none other than Rassi's brother. The Duchessa was in a very merry mood that evening (they were performing at the Palace a *commedia dell'arte*, that is to say a piece in which each character invents the dialogue as he goes along, only the plot of the play being posted up in the wings). The Duchessa, who was playing a part, had as her lover in the comedy Conte Baldi, the former friend of the Marchese Raversi, who happened to be present. The Prince, who was the shyest man in his dominions, but an extremely handsome fellow and endowed with the tenderest of hearts, was studying Conte Baldi's part, which he intended to play at the second performance.

'I have very little time,' the Duchessa told the Conte, 'I am appearing in the first scene of the second act. Let us go into the guard-room.'

There, surrounded by a score of the body-guard, all very much on the alert and keenly attentive to the conversation between the Prime Minister and the Mistress of the Robes, the Duchessa said laughingly to her friend: 'You always scold me when I tell you unnecessary secrets. It was through me that Ernesto V was called to the throne. It was a question of avenging Fabrizio, whom I loved then far more than I do today, although always quite innocently. I know very well that you have not much belief in my innocence, but that does not matter, since you love me in spite of my crimes. Well, here is a real crime. I gave all my diamonds to a very interesting sort of lunatic, named Ferrante Palla, I even kissed him so that he should destroy the man who wished to have Fabrizio poisoned. What's the harm in that?'

'Ah! so that is where Ferrante had got the money for his rising!' said the Conte, slightly taken aback. 'And you tell me all this in the guard-room!'

'That's because I'm in a hurry, and now Rassi is on the track of the crime. It is quite true that I never mentioned an insurrection, for I loathe the Jacobins. Think it over, and let me have your advice after the play.'

'I will tell you at once that you must make the Prince fall in love with you ... But perfectly honourably, of course!'

The Duchessa was summoned to appear on the stage; she hurried away.

A few days later, the Duchessa received by post a long and absurd sort of letter, signed with the name of a person who had once been her maid. The woman asked to be employed at the court, but the Duchessa had realized at the first glance that it was neither in her hand-writing nor her style. On opening the sheet to read the second page, the Duchessa saw a little miraculous picture of the Madonna, folded in a printed leaf from an old book, fall to the ground at her feet. After glancing at the picture, the Duchessa read a few lines of the old printed page. Her eyes shone, for she found on it these words:

The tribune has taken one hundred lire and no more. With the rest he tried to rekindle the sacred flame in souls that through selfishness had grown cold as ice. The fox is on my track, that is why I have not sought to catch a last glimpse of the being whom I adore. I said to myself: 'She does not love the Republic, she who is as superior to me in mind as she is by her graces and her beauty. Besides, how is one to establish a Republic without republicans?' Can I be mistaken? In six months' time I shall be wandering, microscope in hand, and on foot, through the small towns of America. I shall see whether I ought still to love the sole rival you have in my heart. If you receive this letter, Baronessa, and no profane eye has read it before yours, break off a branch from one of the young ash trees planted twenty paces from the spot where I ventured to speak to you for the first time. I shall then bury, under the great box tree in the garden which you pointed out to me once in the days when I was happy, a box containing some of those things which lead to the slandering of men of my way of thinking. You may be sure that I should never have ventured to write if the fox were not hard on my trail and there were not a risk of his reaching that heavenly being. Look under the box tree in a fortnight's time.

'Since he has a printing press at his command,' said the Duchessa to herself, 'we shall soon have a volume of sonnets. Heaven knows what name he will give me in these!'

The Duchessa's coquettish instincts led her to make a trial of her charms; for a week she gave out that she was unwell, and the court had no more pleasant evenings. The Princess, greatly shocked by all that her fear of her son was obliging her to do in the first days of her widowhood, went to spend this week in a convent attached to the church where the late Prince had been buried. This interruption of the evening parties threw upon the Prince an enormous burden of leisure, and resulted in a considerable decrease in the influence of the Minister of Justice. Ernesto V realized all the boredom that threatened him if the Duchessa left the court, or merely ceased to shed gaiety upon it. The evening parties began again, and the Prince showed himself more and more interested in the *commedia dell'arte*. He had the intention of playing a part himself, but dared not confess this ambition. One day, blushing deeply, he said to the Duchessa: 'Why shouldn't I act too?'

'We are all at your Highness's orders here. If you will deign to give me the order, I will draw up the plot of a comedy. All your Highness's most striking scenes will be with me, and as on a first appearance everyone is a trifle shaky, if your Highness will please to watch me rather closely, I will tell you what answers you should make.' Everything was arranged and with infinite skill. The extremely shy Prince was ashamed of being shy; the care the Duchessa took not to let this innate shyness suffer made a deep impression on the young Sovereign.

On the day of his first appearance, the performance began half an hour earlier than usual, and there were in the drawing-room, at the time the company moved into the theatre, no more than nine or ten elderly women. These persons caused the Prince no particular alarm, and besides, as they had been brought up in Munich on true monarchical principles, they always applauded. Using her authority as Mistress of the Robes, the Duchessa turned the key in the door by which the rank and file of the courtiers were admitted to the performance. The Prince, who had a *literary* turn of mind and a handsome face, got through the first scenes very well. He rendered very cleverly the lines which he read in the Duchessa's eyes, or which she suggested to him in an undertone.

At a moment when the few spectators were applauding with all their might, the Duchessa made a sign; the door of honour was flung open, and the theatre filled in a moment with all the prettiest ladies of the court who, finding the Prince cut a charming figure and seemed very much at his ease, began to applaud. The Prince flushed with delight. He was playing the part of lover to the Duchessa. So far from having to suggest speeches to him, she was soon obliged to beg him to cut short his scenes. He spoke of love with an enthusiasm which frequently embarrassed the actress; his replies lasted for five minutes at a stretch.

The Duchessa was no longer the dazzling beauty of the year before: Fabrizio's imprisonment, and still more her stay by Lake Maggiore with a Fabrizio grown morose and silent, had added ten years to the fair Gina's age. Her features had grown sharper, they were at once more intelligent and less youthful. They no longer displayed, save on rare occasions, the eager animation of early youth; but on the stage, with the help of rouge and all the aids which art supplies to actresses, she was still the prettiest woman at court. The long, impassioned speeches uttered by the Prince put the courtiers on the alert; they were all saying to each other that evening: 'There is the Balbi of this new reign.' The Conte was inwardly revolted.

When the play ended, the Duchessa said to the Prince in front of all the court: 'Your Highness acts too well. People will say that you are in love with a woman of eight-and-thirty, and that will ruin my chances of marriage with the Conte. And so I will not act any more with your Highness, unless my Prince swears to me to address me as he would a woman of a certain age – her Ladyship the Marchesa Raversi, for instance.'

The same play was three times repeated. The Prince was wild with delight; but one evening he looked extremely worried. 'Unless I am greatly mistaken,' said the Mistress of the Robes to the Princess, 'that man Rassi is trying to play some trick on us. I should advise your Highness to suggest a performance for tomorrow; the Prince will act badly, and in his despair, he will tell you something.'

The Prince did in fact act very badly; he could hardly be heard, and he no longer knew how to end his sentences. At the close of the first act he was almost in tears. The Duchessa remained beside him, but cold and unmoved. The Prince, finding himself alone with her for a moment in the green-room, went and shut the door. 'I shall never be able to get through the second and third acts,' he said to her. 'I absolutely decline to be applauded out of mere politeness; the applause they gave me this evening cut me to the heart. Give me your advice. What ought I to do?'

'I will go back to the stage, make a deep curtsy to Her Highness, another to the audience, like a real stage manager, and say that the actor who was playing the part of Lelio having suddenly been taken ill, the performance will conclude with a few pieces of music. Conte Rusca and little Signora Ghisolfi will be delighted to have a chance of showing off their thin, squeaky voices in front of such a distinguished company.'

The Prince took the Duchessa's hand and kissed it with rapture. 'Why aren't you a man?' he said to her. 'You would give me good advice. Rassi has just laid on my writing-table one hundred and eighty-two depositions against the alleged murderers of my father. Apart from the depositions, there is also a formal indictment of more than two hundred pages. I shall have to read all that, and, on top of it, I have given my word not to say anything about it to the Conte. All this is leading straight to executions. Already he wants me to have Ferrante Palla, that great poet whom I admire so much, arrested and brought back from France, from a place near Antibes. He is living there under the name of Poncet.'

'The day on which you have a Liberal hanged, Rassi will be bound to his ministry by chains of iron, and that is what he particularly desires. Your Highness, however, will no longer be able to announce two hours in advance that you are going anywhere outside the Palace. I shall say nothing to the Princess or the Conte of the cry of distress which has just escaped you; but since my oath forbids me to keep anything secret from the Princess, I should be glad if your Highness would tell your mother the very same things that you let slip when talking to me.'

This idea diverted the Sovereign's mind from the distress with which his failure as an actor had overwhelmed him.

'Very well, go and warn my mother. I am going straight to her big sitting-room.'

The Prince left the wings, crossed the drawing-room which gave entry to the theatre, and gruffly dismissed the High Chamberlain and the aide-de-camp in waiting, who were following him. The Princess, for her part, hurriedly left the play. As soon as she reached the sitting-room the Mistress of the Robes curtsied low to mother and son, and left them alone. One may imagine the excitement of the courtiers; it is things of this sort that make life at court so amusing. At the end of an hour the Prince himself appeared at the door of the sitting-room, and summoned the Duchessa. The Princess was in tears, her son's face looked quite haggard.

'Here,' thought the Mistress of the Robes, 'are two weak characters in a bad temper seeking an excuse to vent their anger on somebody.' At first both mother and son took the words out of each other's mouth in an attempt to relate every detail to the Duchessa, who was careful not to put forward any idea in her replies. For two mortal hours the three actors in this tedious scene did not step outside the roles we have indicated. The Prince himself went to fetch the two enormous portfolios which Rassi had deposited on his table; on coming out of his mother's sitting-room he found the whole court awaiting him. 'Go away, and leave me in peace!' he cried in a most uncivil tone and one they had never known him to use. The Prince did not wish to be seen carrying the two portfolios himself; a prince must never carry anything. In the twinkling of an eye the courtiers vanished. On his way back the Prince found nobody about except the footmen who were snuffing out the candles. He packed them off in a rage, and the same with poor Fontana, the aide-de-camp in waiting, who, in his zeal, had been so tactless as to stay behind.

'Everyone is doing his best to try my patience this evening,' he said crossly to the Duchessa as he was coming back into the room. He credited her with great intelligence and he was furious with her for her obvious determination not to offer any opinion. She, on her part, was resolved to say nothing so long as she was not asked for her opinion *quite expressly*. Another long half hour elapsed before the Prince, who had a sense of his own dignity, could make up his mind to say to her: 'But you are saying nothing, madam.'

'I am here to serve the Princess, and to forget very quickly what is said in front of me.'

'Well then, madam,' said the Prince getting very red, 'I order you to give me your opinion.'

'Crimes are punished with the object of preventing their recurrence. Was the late Prince poisoned? That is very doubtful. Was he poisoned by the Jacobins? That is what Rassi would very much like to prove, for then he becomes for your Highness a permanently essential instrument. In that case your Highness, whose reign is just beginning, can promise himself many evenings like this one. Your subjects say on the whole, and this is quite true, that your Highness has a kindly disposition. So long as your Highness has not had any Liberal hanged you will enjoy this reputation, and most certainly no one will think of planning to poison you.'

'Your conclusion is quite obvious,' cried the Princess with a touch of ill-humour. 'You do not wish the murderers of my husband to be punished.'

'That is because, Madam, I am seemingly bound to them by ties of tender affection.'

The Duchessa could see in the Prince's eyes that he believed her to be perfectly in accord with his mother on some line of conduct to be dictated to him. A fairly rapid succession of acid repartees now followed between the two women, at the end of which the Duchessa protested that she would not utter another word more, and adhered to her resolution. But the Prince, after a long discussion with his mother, ordered her once more to express her opinion.

'I assure your Highnesses I will do no such thing!'

'But this is mere childishness!' exclaimed the Prince.

'I beg you to speak, Duchessa,' said the Princess with an air of dignity.

'That is what I implore you to excuse me from doing, Madam. But,' added the Duchessa, addressing the Prince, 'your Highness reads French perfectly. To calm our agitated minds, will you read *us* a fable by La Fontaine?'

The Princess thought this *'us'* extremely impertinent, but she looked both astonished and amused when the Mistress of the Robes, who had gone with the utmost coolness to open the bookcase, came back with a volume of La Fontaine's *Fables*. She turned over the pages for a minute or two, then said to the Prince, as she handed him the book: 'I beg your Highness to read *the whole* of the Fable.'

THE GARDENER AND HIS LORD

A countryman, half yeoman and half hind,
A garden-lover too, had set his mind
On tending, from the noisy world concealed,
A tidy garden, with adjacent field.
A quickset hedge enclosed it all around,
Lettuce and sorrel flourished on the ground,
While leaving still a place for flowers to spring
Wherewith to make a pretty offering,
A posy of sweet thyme, a jessamine spray,
For Margery upon her natal day.
His paradise invaded by a hare,
Straightway our man doth to his lord repair,
Complaining loudly that th'accursèd beast
Morning and night of his best crops makes feast.
No snares avail to catch him. Stones and sticks
All fail to get the better of his tricks.
'Sure 'tis a warlock!' 'Zounds!' replies his lord,
'Were he old Nick himself, I'll pledge my word,
For all his cunning, my own trusty hound
Will stop his gambols with a single bound.
I'll rid you of him, 'pon my life, I say.'
'But when?' 'Tomorrow without more delay.'
Next day the lord appears with all his men,

Surveys the goodman's little plot, and then
Before they start, he cries, in accents gruff:
'We'll lunch, but see your fowls are not too tough.'
When luncheon's done the lively crowd troops in
To hunt their quarry, but with such a din
Of horns and trumpets that the goodman stands
Aghast, and stops his ears with both hands.
But worst of all things was the piteous plight
Of that poor garden, once his heart's delight.
Farewell to all those well-tilled, tidy beds,
Where chicory, leeks, etc., raised their heads.
His herb-plot ravaged by this wanton troop,
Farewell to all those things that flavour soup.
The goodman murmurs: 'Here's the sport of kings,'
But no one listens to his mutterings;
And dogs and men in one hour's frolic spoil
The fruit of all his years of loving toil,
Doing more hurtful damage to his ground
Than if the hares from all the country round
Had set themselves to nibble greedily
Within his garden for a century.

Princelings, resolve your private bickerings
Yourselves. 'Tis folly to resort to kings.
Fight your own battles, form your own opinions,
And keep all strangers out of your dominions.

This reading was followed by a long silence. The Prince paced up and down the room, after going himself to put the volume back in its place.

'Well, madam,' said the Princess, 'will you deign to speak?'

'No indeed, Madam, so long as His Highness has not made me his Minister; by speaking here I should run the risk of losing my place as Mistress of the Robes.'

A fresh silence, lasting a full quarter of an hour. Finally the Princess began to ponder over the part once played by Marie de' Medici, the mother of Louis XIII. For some days past the Mistress of the Robes had arranged for a lady-in-waiting to read aloud the excellent *History of Louis XIII*, by M. Bazin. The Princess, although greatly annoyed, reflected that the Duchessa might easily leave the principality, and then Rassi, of whom she was horribly afraid, might quite well imitate Richelieu and persuade her son to banish her. At that moment, the Princess would have given everything in the world to humiliate her Mistress of the Robes; but she could not. She rose and came, with a smile that was slightly forced, to take the Duchessa's hand and say to her: 'Come, madam, prove your affection for me by speaking.'

'Very well!' Two words and no more. 'Burn, in the grate over there, all the papers collected by the viper Rassi, and never reveal to him that they have been burnt.'

She added in a whisper, and in a familiar tone, in the Princess's ear: 'Rassi may be a Richelieu!'

'But, damn it,' cried the Prince angrily, 'these papers cost me more than eighty thousand lire!'

'Prince,' replied the Duchessa firmly, 'now you see what it costs you to employ scoundrels of low birth. Would to God you might lose a million, rather than you should ever put your trust in the base rascals who kept your father from sleeping during the last six years of his reign.'

The words 'low birth' had greatly pleased the Princess, who felt that the Conte and his friend had too exclusive a regard for intelligence – always in some sort close cousin to Jacobinism.

During the short interval of deep silence filled by the Princess's reflections the Palace clock struck three. The Princess rose, made a low curtsy to her son, and said: 'My health does not permit me to prolong the discussion any further. Never have a Minister of *low birth*. You will never make me give up the idea that your Rassi has robbed you of half the money he has made you spend on your secret service.' The Princess took two candles out of their candle-sticks and set them in the fireplace in such a way that they should not blow out. Then, going up to her son, she added: 'La Fontaine's fable, to my mind, overrides my rightful desire to avenge my husband. Will your Highness permit me to burn *these documents*?' The Prince stood motionless.

'He really has a stupid face,' the Duchessa said to herself. 'The Conte is right: the late Prince would never have kept us out of our beds until three o'clock in the morning before making up his mind.'

The Princess, still standing, added: 'That little attorney would feel very proud, if he knew that his wretched papers, stuffed with lies and adjusted in a way to secure his own advancement, had kept the two greatest personages in the State up all night.'

The Prince snatched up one of the portfolios like a madman, and emptied its contents into the fireplace. The mass of papers very nearly extinguished the two candles; the room was filled with smoke. The Princess gathered from her son's eyes that he was tempted to seize a jug of water and save these papers, which cost him eighty thousand lire.

'Open the window, do!' she cried angrily to the Duchessa. The Duchessa made haste to obey. Immediately all the papers burst simultaneously into flames; there was a great roar in the chimney and it soon became evident that it was on fire.

The Prince had a petty nature in everything to do with money. He thought to see his Palace in flames, and all the treasures it contained destroyed; he ran over to the window and called to the guard in a voice entirely unlike his usual one. The soldiers having rushed in wild confusion into the courtyard at the sound of the Prince's voice, he returned to the fireplace which was drawing in the air from the open window with a really alarming noise. He grew impatient, swore, took two or three turns up and down the room like a man quite out of his mind, and finally rushed away.

The Princess and her Mistress of the Robes remained standing, face to face with each other, and preserving complete silence.

'Is there going to be a fresh outburst of anger?' the Duchessa wondered. 'Upon my word, I've won my case.' And she was preparing to be highly impertinent in her replies, when a sudden thought struck her; she saw the second portfolio left intact. 'No, my case is only half won.' In a rather cold tone of voice she said to the Princess 'Does your Highness order me to burn the rest of these papers?'

'And where will you burn them?' said the Princess crossly.

'In the drawing-room fireplace; if they are thrown in one by one there is no danger.'

The Duchessa thrust the portfolio, bursting with papers, under her arm, seized a candle, and went into the adjoining drawing-room. She gave herself time to make sure that this portfolio was the one containing the depositions, put five or six bundles of papers under her shawl, burnt the rest very carefully, then slipped away without taking leave of the Princess.

'There's a fine piece of impertinence,' she said to herself laughing, 'but with her posing as an inconsolable widow she came near to making me lose my head on a scaffold.'

On hearing the sound of the Duchessa's carriage, the Princess grew mad with rage against her Mistress of the Robes.

In spite of the lateness of the hour, the Duchessa sent for the Conte. He had gone to see the fire at the Palace, but soon appeared with the news that it was all over. 'That young Prince really showed great courage, and I complimented him heartily upon it.'

'Take a very quick look at these depositions, and let us burn them as soon as possible.'

The Conte read them, and turned pale.

'By Jove, they have come very near to the truth. They have managed the whole business very cleverly. They are hot on Ferrante Palla's tracks; and, if he talks, we shall be in a tight fix.'

'But he won't talk,' cried the Duchessa. 'He is a man of honour. Burn them! burn them!'

'Not just yet. Allow me to take down the names of twelve or fifteen dangerous witnesses, whom I shall take the liberty of removing, if that fellow Rassi ever tries to reopen the case.'

'Let me remind your Excellency that the Prince has given his word to say nothing to his Minister of Justice about our adventure tonight.'

'Out of cowardice and fear of a scene he will keep it.'

'Now my friend, this is a night which has greatly hastened our marriage. I should not have wished to bring you a trial in the criminal courts as my dowry, still less one for an offence which I was led to commit by my interest in another man.'

The Conte was moved with love for her. He took her hand with a cry of protest; there were tears in his eyes.

'Before you go, give me some advice as to how I ought to behave with the Princess. I am utterly worn out, I have been playing a part for an hour on the stage, and for five hours in her room.'

'You have avenged yourself quite sufficiently for the Princess's acid remarks, which were only a sign of weakness, by the impertinent way in which you left her. Adopt with her tomorrow the same tone you used this morning. Rassi is not yet in prison or in exile, and we have not yet torn up Fabrizio's sentence.

'You were asking the Princess to come to a decision; that is a thing which always puts Princes, and even Prime Ministers, in a bad temper. After all, you are her Mistress of the Robes; in other words her humble servant. By a revulsion of feeling which is inevitable with weak natures, Rassi will be in greater favour than ever in three days' time. He will try to have someone hanged. But so long as he has not compromised the Prince he can be sure of nothing.

'There was a man injured in this fire tonight; he is a tailor who, upon my word, showed the most remarkable fearlessness. Tomorrow I am going to persuade the Prince to take my arm and come with me to pay this tailor a visit. I shall be armed to the teeth, and shall keep a sharp look-out; but anyhow, this young Prince is not hated as yet. For my part, I want to get him accustomed to walking in the streets; that is a trick I am playing on Rassi, who is certainly going to succeed me, and will not be able to allow such imprudent proceedings any longer. On our way back from the tailor I shall take the Prince past his father's statue. He will notice the marks of the stones which have broken the Roman toga in which the fool of a sculptor dressed it up; and, in short, the Prince will have to be very unintelligent if he doesn't of his own accord make the comment: "That is what one gains by having Jacobins hanged." Whereupon I shall reply: "You must either hang ten thousand or none at all; the massacre of Saint Bartholomew wiped out the Protestants in France."

'Tomorrow, my dear, before this excursion, send in your name to the Prince, and say to him: "Yesterday evening, I performed the duties of a Minister to you; I gave you advice, and in obeying your orders I incurred the Princess's displeasure. You ought to pay me for it." He will expect a demand for money, and begin to frown. You will leave him absorbed by this unpleasing thought for as long as you possibly can; then you will say: "I entreat your Highness to order that Fabrizio's case shall be given a *full hearing* (that means when he himself is present) by the twelve most respected judges in your States." Then, without a moment's delay, you will present for his signature a short statement written out by your own fair hand, and which I am going to dictate to you. I shall of course include a clause to the effect that the first sentence is revoked. To this there is only one objection; but, if you carry things through briskly, it will not strike the Prince. He may say to you: "Fabrizio must first get himself committed to the citadel prison". To which you will reply: "He will get himself committed to the city gaol" (you know that I am the master there, and your nephew will come to see you every evening). If the Prince answers: "No, his escape has cast a slur on the honour of my citadel, and I insist, as a matter of form, on his going back to the cell in which he was," you in turn will answer: "No, for there he would be at the mercy of my enemy Rassi." And, in one of those feminine ripostes which you can deliver so skilfully, you will give him to understand that, to make Rassi yield, you might possibly tell him of tonight's *auto-da-fé*. If he insists, you will announce that you are going to spend a fortnight at your place at Sacca.

'You will send for Fabrizio and consult with him about this step, which may land him in prison. If, to anticipate everything, Rassi should grow too impatient while he is under lock and key, and have me poisoned, Fabrizio may be in some danger. But that is hardly probable. I have, as you know, imported a French chef, who is the merriest of men and given to making puns; well, punning is incompatible with murder. I have already told our friend Fabrizio that I have managed to find all the witnesses of his fine and courageous action; it is clear that it was Giletti who tried to murder him. I have not spoken to you of these witnesses, because I wanted to give you a surprise. The plan however has failed; the Prince refused to sign. I have told our dear Fabrizio that I should certainly procure him a high ecclesiastical office; but I shall find that very difficult if his enemies can bring the objection of a charge of murder before the Papal Court.

'Do you realize, madam, that, if he is not tried and judged in the most formal manner, the name of Giletti will be a source of unpleasantness for him all his life? It would be an extremely poor-spirited thing to avoid a trial when one is sure of one's innocence. Besides, even if he were guilty, I should manage to have him acquitted. When I spoke to him, the hot-headed young man would not let me finish; he picked up the official directory and we went through it together choosing the names of the twelve most upright and learned judges. After making the list, we struck out six of the names to replace them by those of six expert lawyers who are my personal enemies, and, as we could discover only two enemies, we made up the number with four rascals who are devoted to Rassi.'

This proposal of the Conte's very greatly alarmed the Duchessa, and not without cause. At length she listened to reason and, at the Minister's dictation, wrote out the order appointing the judges.

The Conte did not leave her until six o'clock in the morning. She tried to sleep, but in vain. At nine o'clock she had breakfast with Fabrizio, whom she found consumed with eagerness to be tried; at ten o'clock she waited on the Princess, who was not visible; at eleven she saw the Prince, who was holding his levee, and who signed the order without making the slightest objection. The Duchessa sent the order to the Conte, and retired to bed.

It would be amusing perhaps to tell of Rassi's fury when the Conte obliged him to add his signature, in the Prince's presence, to the order his Highness had signed that morning; but events oblige us to hurry on.

The Conte discussed the merits of each judge and offered to change the names. But the reader is perhaps a little tired of all these details of legal procedure, no less than of all these court intrigues. From all such business we can draw this moral, that the man who gets within close range of a court endangers his happiness, if he is happy, and, in any case, makes his future depend on the intrigues of some chamber-maid or other.

On the other hand, in a republic such as America, one is forced to bore oneself the whole day long by paying serious court to the shop-keepers in the street, and become as dull and stupid as they are; and over there, one has no Opera.

On rising from her bed that evening, the Duchessa experienced a moment of keen anxiety; Fabrizio was not to be found. In the end, towards midnight, during the performance of a play at court, she received a letter from him. Instead of making himself a prisoner *at the city gaol*, where the Conte was in authority, he had gone back to occupy his old cell in the citadel, only too happy to be living within a few feet of Clelia.

This was an event of enormous import; in this place he was more than ever exposed to the risk of being poisoned. This act of folly filled the Duchessa with despair; she forgave the cause of it – his mad love for Clelia – because in a few days' time the girl was going to marry the rich Marchese Crescenzi. By this mad act Fabrizio recovered all his former influence over the Duchessa's heart.

'It is that cursed paper which I made the Prince sign that will bring about his death! What fools men are with their ideas of honour! As if one needed to consider honour under absolute governments, in States where a man like Rassi is Minister of Justice! We ought to have accepted without more ado the pardon which the Prince would have signed just as readily as he signed the order convening that special tribunal. What does it matter, after all, that a man of Fabrizio's birth should be more or less accused of having taken a sword to kill an actor like Giletti with his own hand!'

No sooner had the Duchessa received Fabrizio's letter than she hurried off to see the Conte, whom she found pale as death.

'Good God! my dear,' he cried, 'I am most unlucky in my handling of this poor boy, and you will be angry with me again. I can give you proof that I sent for the keeper of the city gaol yesterday evening; every day your nephew would have come to take tea with you. The frightful thing about it is that it is impossible for either you or me to say to the Prince we are afraid of poison, and poison administered by Rassi; he would regard such a suspicion as the height of immorality. However, if you insist, I am ready to go up to the Palace; but I am certain of the answer. I am going to say more; I offer you a measure which I would not resort to for myself. Since I have held authority in this State, I have not caused the death of a single man, and you know that I am so idiotically sensitive in that respect that sometimes, at the close of day, I still think of those two spies whom I had shot, a little too light-heartedly, in Spain. Well now, do you wish me to get rid of Rassi for you? There are no limits to the risk he is making Fabrizio run. He has in this a sure way of forcing me to clear out.'

This proposal pleased the Duchessa extremely, but she did not adopt it.

'I do not want you,' she said to the Conte, 'in our retirement, under that beautiful sky of Naples, to have dark thoughts to sadden your evenings.'

'But, my dear, it seems to me we are left with nothing but dark thoughts to choose from. What will become of you, what indeed will become of me, if Fabrizio is carried off by some illness?'

Discussion continued with fresh vigour on this point, and the Duchessa closed it with these words: 'Rassi owes his life to the fact that I love you better than I do Fabrizio. No, I do not wish to poison all the evenings of the old age we are going to spend together.'

The Duchessa hurried to the fortress. General Fabio Conti was delighted to confront her with the precise terms of military regulations: 'No one may enter a State prison without an order signed by the Prince.'

'But the Marchese Crescenzi and his musicians come to the citadel every day.'

'That is because I obtained an order for them from the Prince.'

The poor Duchessa was unaware of the full extent of her misfortunes. General Fabio Conti had regarded himself as personally dishonoured by Fabrizio's escape. When he saw him arrive at the citadel, he ought not to have admitted him, for he had no order to that effect. 'But,' said he to himself, 'it is Heaven that is sending him to me to restore my honour and to save me from the ridicule which would blight my military career. I must take care not to lose this opportunity; doubtless he will be acquitted, and I have only a few days in which to take my revenge.'

T HE arrival of our hero filled Clelia with despair. The poor girl, deeply religious and strictly honest with herself, could not shut her eyes to the fact that there would never be any happiness for her apart from Fabrizio; but she had made a vow to the Madonna, at the time when her father was nearly poisoned, that she would offer him the sacrifice of marrying the Marchese Crescenzi. She had made a vow that she would never see Fabrizio again, and already she was suffering the most frightful pangs of conscience over the admission she had been led to make in the letter she had written to Fabrizio on the eve of his escape. How can I depict the feelings aroused in that sorrowful heart when, as she sadly watched her birds flit to and fro, and raised her eyes from habit, and with affection, towards that window from which Fabrizio once used to look at her, she saw him standing there again and greeting her with the tenderest respect?

She imagined it to be a vision which Heaven had allowed as a punishment; then the hideous truth dawned on her mind. 'They have caught him again,' she said to herself, 'and he is lost!' She called to mind the comments made in the fortress after his escape; the very humblest of the gaolers had regarded themselves as mortally insulted. Clelia looked at Fabrizio, and in spite of herself that glance portrayed in full the passion that was driving her to despair. 'Do you suppose,' she seemed to be saying to Fabrizio, 'that I shall find happiness in that sumptuous palace which they are making ready for me? My father keeps on telling me, till I am sick to death of hearing it, that you are as poor as we are; but, good God! how gladly would I share that poverty. But alas! we must never see each other again!'

Clelia had not the strength to make use of the alphabets. As she gazed at Fabrizio she grew faint and sank into a chair beside the window. Her head rested upon the ledge of this window, and as she had wanted to see him right up to the last moment, her face was turned towards Fabrizio, who had a perfect view of it. When, after a few moments, she opened her eyes again, her first glance was at Fabrizio. She saw tears in his eyes, but those tears sprang from utter happiness; he saw that absence had not caused her to forget him. The two poor young things remained for some time as though spell-bound by the sight of each other. Fabrizio ventured to sing, as if he were accompanying himself on the guitar, a few improvised lines which conveyed the message: '*It is to see you again* that I have returned to prison: they are going to try me.'

These words seemed to arouse all Clelia's virtuous instincts. She rose quickly to her feet, hid her eyes, and, by means of the most expressive gestures, sought to convey to him that she must never see him again. She had promised this to the Madonna, and had looked at him inadvertently just now. Fabrizio venturing still to express his love, Clelia fled from the room indignant, and swearing to herself that never would she see him again. For such were the precise terms of her vow to the Madonna: '*My eyes shall never look on him again.*' She had written them on a little slip of paper which her uncle Don Cesare had allowed her to burn upon the altar at the moment of the offertory, while he was saying Mass.

All the same, no matter what the vow that bound her, Fabrizio's presence in the Farnese Tower brought Clelia to resume her former habits and activities. She had become accustomed to spending the whole day alone in her room. No sooner had she recovered from the unlooked-for agitation which the sight of Fabrizio had provoked in her, than she began to move about the house and renew acquaintance, so to speak, with all her humbler friends. A very garrulous old woman, employed in the kitchen, said to her with an air of mystery: 'This time Signor Fabrizio will not get out of the citadel.'

'He will not make the mistake of getting over the walls again,' said Clelia, 'but he will go out by the door, if he is acquitted.'

'I tell your Excellency, and I know what I am saying, that he will not leave the citadel except feet first.'

Clelia turned extremely pale; the old woman remarked it, and promptly held her tongue. She said to herself that she had been guilty of an imprudence in speaking thus in front of the Governor's daughter, whose duty it would be to tell everybody that Fabrizio had died a natural death. As she was going up to her room Clelia met the prison doctor, an honest, but timid, sort of man, who told her with an air of great alarm that Fabrizio was seriously ill. Clelia could hardly keep on her feet; she looked everywhere for her uncle, the good Don Cesare, and at last found him in the chapel, engaged in fervent prayer; his face betrayed extreme distress. The dinner bell rang. During the meal not a word was exchanged between the two brothers; but, towards the very end of dinner, the General addressed a few very harsh words to his brother. The latter looked at the servants, who left the room.

'General,' said Don Cesare to the Governor, 'I have the honour to inform you that I am leaving the citadel; I am sending in my resignation.'

'Bravo! Bravissimo! to cast suspicion on me! ... And your reason, if you please?'

'My conscience.'

'Go on, you are only a snivelling priest! You know nothing about honour.'

'Fabrizio is dead,' thought Clelia. 'They have poisoned him at dinner, or they'll do it tomorrow.' She ran to the aviary, resolved to sing, accompanying herself on the piano. 'I shall go to confession,' she said to herself, 'and I shall be forgiven for breaking my vow to save a man's life.' What was her consternation when, on reaching the aviary, she saw that the shutters had been replaced by boards affixed to the iron bars! Utterly frantic, she tried to give the prisoner a warning by a few words shouted rather than sung. There was no response of any sort; a deathly silence already reigned within the Farnese Tower. 'It's all over,' she thought. Quite beside herself, she went downstairs, then came up again to collect what little money she had, and some tiny diamond earrings. On her way out she also took some bread left over from dinner, which had been put away in a sideboard. 'If he is still alive, my duty is to save him.'

She made her way with a haughty air towards the door of the tower. This door was standing open, and eight soldiers had been posted only a moment or two before in the pillared hall on the ground floor. Clelia faced these soldiers boldly. She was counting on speaking to the sergeant who would be in charge of them; but this man was not there. Clelia darted on to the little iron staircase which wound round one of the pillars; the soldiers gazed at her with mouths wide open, but, presumably on account of her lace shawl and her bonnet, did not dare say anything to her. There was nobody at all on the first floor; but when she reached the second, at the entrance to the corridor which, as the reader may remember, was closed by three iron-barred doors and led to Fabrizio's cell, she found a turnkey whom she did not know and who said to her with a startled air: 'He hasn't yet had his dinner.'

'I am quite aware of that,' said Clelia haughtily. The man did not dare stop her. Twenty paces farther on, Clelia found sitting on the first of the six steps which led to Fabrizio's cell another turnkey, very elderly and with a very red face, who said to her firmly: 'Signorina, have you an order from the Governor?'

'Don't you know who I am?'

Clelia at that moment was possessed by a sort of supernatural force; she was really out of her mind. 'I am going to save my husband,' she said to herself.

While the old turnkey was exclaiming: 'But my duty doesn't allow me ...' Clelia ran swiftly up the six steps. She hurled herself against the door; an enormous key was in the lock; she needed all her strength to turn it. At that moment the old turnkey, who was half drunk, clutched at the hem of her dress. She dashed into the room, shut the door behind her, tearing her gown, and, as the turnkey was pushing against the door to get in after her, she closed it with a bolt that was just under her hand. She looked round the cell and saw Fabrizio seated at a tiny table on which his dinner was laid. She rushed up to the table, overturned it, and seizing Fabrizio by the arm, said to him: 'Oh, my dear, have you eaten anything?'

The note of tenderness in these words filled Fabrizio with joy. In her agitation, Clelia for the first time in her life forgot her feminine reserve, and let her love appear.

Fabrizio had been on the point of beginning this fatal meal. He took her in his arms and covered her with kisses. 'This dinner was poisoned,' he thought. 'If I tell her I haven't touched it, religion will reassert its rights, and Clelia will disappear. If, on the other hand, she regards me as a dying man, I shall manage to persuade her not to leave me. She is anxious to find some way of breaking off her hateful marriage; chance offers us this one. The gaolers will soon collect; they will break down the door, and there will be such a scandal that the Marchese Crescenzi will possibly be scared by it, and the marriage will be broken off.'

During the moment of silence occupied by these reflections Fabrizio felt that Clelia was already trying to free herself from his embraces.

'I don't feel any pain as yet,' he said to her, 'but presently it will prostrate me at your feet. Help me to die.'

'O my only friend,' she answered, 'I will die with you.'

She was so beautiful, with her gown half torn off, and stirred to such a pitch of passion, that Fabrizio could not refrain from following an almost unconscious impulse. No resistance was offered him.

In the ecstasy of passion and generous emotion which follows on extreme happiness he said to her somewhat rashly: 'I must not allow the first moments of our happiness to be sullied by a base lie. But for your courage I should now be just a corpse, or writhing in the most atrocious agony. But I was just about to begin my dinner when you came in. I have not touched any one of these dishes.'

Fabrizio began to dilate upon these imaginary horrors to dispel the indignation which he could already read in Clelia's eyes. She looked at him for some moments, two violent and conflicting emotions at war within her, then flung herself into his arms. They heard a great noise in the corridor, the three iron doors were violently opened and shut, voices shouted.

'Ah! If I had arms!' cried Fabrizio. 'They made me hand them over before they would let me in. No doubt they are coming to finish me off. Goodbye, my Clelia, I bless my death since it has been the cause of my happiness.' Clelia embraced him and gave him a little dagger with an ivory handle and a blade not much larger than that of a pen-knife.

'Don't let them kill you,' she said to him; 'defend yourself to the very last moment. If my uncle hears the noise, he is brave and good, he will save you. I'm going out to speak to them.' As she said these words she rushed towards the door.

'If you are not killed,' she said, tense with emotion, her hand on the bolt of the door and her head turned towards him, 'let yourself die of hunger rather than touch any sort of food whatever. Keep this bread always in your pocket.'

The noise was coming nearer. Fabrizio caught hold of her round the waist, took her place by the door, and throwing it open violently, dashed down the six steps of the wooden stairs. He had hold of the dagger with the ivory handle and very nearly thrust it into the waistcoat of General Fontana, aide-de-camp to the Prince, who promptly retreated, crying out in a panic: 'But I have come to save you, Signor del Dongo.'

Fabrizio went back up the six steps and called into the cell: 'Fontana has come to save me.' Then, turning back down the wooden steps to approach the General, he discussed the situation coldly with him. He begged him at great length to forgive him a first impulse of anger. 'They were trying to poison me; this dinner you see placed in front of me is poisoned. I had the sense not to touch it,' but I will confess that such a proceeding has given me a shock. When I heard you coming up the stairs, I thought they were coming to finish me off with their daggers. ... I request you, my dear General, to give orders that no one shall enter my cell. They would remove the poison, and our good Prince must be informed of all the circumstances.'

The General, very pale and completely taken aback, passed on the orders suggested to the picked body of gaolers who were following him. These men, quite crestfallen at finding the poison discovered, lost no time in getting down the stairs. They went in front, ostensibly to leave the way clear for the Prince's aide-de-camp on the very narrow stairway, but actually in order to escape and retire from sight. To the great surprise of General Fontana, Fabrizio lingered for a full quarter of an hour on the little iron staircase which ran round the pillar on the ground floor. He wanted to give Clelia time to hide herself on the floor above.

It was the Duchessa who, after several wild attempts, had succeeded in getting General Fontana sent to the citadel; it was only by chance that she managed it. On leaving Conte Mosca, as much alarmed as she was herself, she had rushed off to the Palace. The Princess, who had a marked repugnance for any display of energy, which seemed to her vulgar, thought her mad and did not appear at all disposed to take any unusual steps to help her. The Duchessa, quite distracted, was shedding bitter tears; she could do nothing but reiterate at every moment: 'But, Madam, in a quarter of an hour, Fabrizio will have died of poisoning!'

At the sight of the Princess's perfect composure, the Duchessa became mad with grief. She did not make that moral reflection which would not have escaped a woman brought up in one of those Northern religions which allow self-examination: 'I was the first to use poison, now poison is destroying me.' In Italy reflections of that sort, in moments of passion, appear as much the mark of a vulgar mind as a pun would seem in Paris in similar circumstances.

The Duchessa, in desperation, risked going into the drawing-room where the Marchese Crescenzi, who was in waiting that day, happened to be at that moment. On her return to Parma he had thanked her effusively for the post of Lord-in-waiting, to which, but for her, he could never have aspired. Protestations of unbounded devotion had not been lacking on his part.

The Duchessa addressed these words to him: 'Rassi is going to have Fabrizio, who is in the citadel, poisoned. Take with you in your pocket some chocolate and a bottle of water which I shall give you. Go up to the citadel, and save my life by telling General Fabio Conti that you will break off your marriage with his daughter if he does not allow you to hand this water and this chocolate to Fabrizio yourself.'

The Marchese turned pale, and his features, so far from showing any animation at these words, presented a picture of the most foolishly stolid embarrassment. He could not believe in the possibility of so shocking a crime in so moral a city as Parma, and one where such a great Prince was reigning, and so forth; moreover, he uttered these platitudes very slowly. In a word, the Duchessa found an honest man, but weak to a degree, and quite unable to make up his mind to act. After a score of similar remarks interrupted by cries of impatience from the Duchessa, he hit upon an excellent idea; the oath he had sworn as Lord-in-waiting forbade him to take part in any intrigues against the government.

Who can picture the anxiety and the despair of the Duchessa, who felt that time was flying?

'But, at all events, go and see the Governor; tell him that I will hunt down Fabrizio's murderers as far as hell itself! . . .'

Despair increased the Duchessa's natural eloquence; but all this fire only made the Marchese more alarmed and left him doubly hesitant. At the end of an hour he was less disposed to act than he had been at first.

This unhappy woman, who had reached the uttermost limits of despair, and knew well that the Governor would refuse nothing to so rich a son-in-law, went so far as to fling herself at his feet. At this the Marchese's pusillanimity seemed to increase still further; at the sight of this strange spectacle he was filled with fear of being compromised himself, all unwittingly. But then an odd thing happened. The Marchese, a kind enough man at heart, was touched by the tears and by the position, at his feet, of so beautiful and, above all, so influential a woman.

'I myself, rich and noble as I am,' he thought, 'may perhaps one day be at the feet of some Republican!' The Marchese burst into tears, and finally it was agreed that the Duchessa, in her capacity as Mistress of the Robes, should present him to the Princess, who would give him permission to convey to Fabrizio a little hamper, the contents of which he would declare he knew nothing about.

The previous evening, before the Duchessa knew of Fabrizio's act of folly in going to the citadel, they had performed a *commedia dell'arte* at court, and the Prince, who always reserved for himself the part of playing lover to the Duchessa, had been so passionate in speaking to her of his love that he would have seemed ridiculous, if, in Italy, a passionate man or a Prince could ever be thought so!

The Prince, extremely shy, but always intensely serious in matters of love, happened, in one of the Palace corridors, to meet the Duchessa as she was carrying off the Marchese, in a great state of worry, to see the Princess. He was so surprised and dazzled by the touching beauty which her despair bestowed upon the Mistress of the Robes, that for the first time in his life he showed some force of character. With a more than imperious gesture he dismissed the Marchese, and began to make a formal declaration of love to the Duchessa. The Prince had doubtless prepared this speech a long time beforehand, for certain things about it were fairly sensible.

'Since the conventions of my rank forbid me to give myself the supreme happiness of marrying you, I will swear upon the Blessed Sacrament never to marry without your written consent. I am well aware,' he added, 'that I am making you forfeit the hand of a Prime Minister, a clever and extremely charming man; but after all he is fifty-six, and I am not yet twenty-two. I should consider myself to be insulting you, and to deserve your refusal if I spoke to you of advantages that have no connexion with love. But everyone at my court who is interested in money speaks with admiration of the proof of his love which the Conte gives you in leaving everything he possesses in your hands. I shall be only too happy to copy him in that respect. You will make better use of my fortune than I, and you shall have the entire disposal of the annual sum which my Ministers hand over to the Intendant General of my Crown. Thus it will be you, my dear Duchessa, who will decide upon the sums which I may spend each month.' The Duchessa found all these details very long and tedious; the risks Fabrizio was meanwhile running cut her to the heart.

'You don't seem to know, your Highness,' she cried, 'that at this

very moment they are poisoning Fabrizio in your citadel! Save him!
I'll take your word for everything.'

This presentation of her thoughts was impolitic in the extreme. At
the mere mention of poison all the ease, all the sincerity which this
poor, high-minded Prince had introduced into this conversation
vanished in the twinkling of an eye. The Duchessa did not realize
her blunder until it was too late to remedy it, and her despair was
intensified, a thing she had not thought possible: 'If I had not spoken
of poison,' she said to herself, 'he would have granted me Fabrizio's
liberty. O my dear Fabrizio,' she added, 'it is fated then that I should
be the one to stab you to the heart through my stupidity!'

It took the Duchessa a long time and much exercise of charm to
bring the Prince back to his talk of passionate love, but he still
remained deeply offended. It was his mind alone that spoke; his heart
had been frozen, first of all by the idea of poison, and then by this
other idea as unpleasing as the first was terrible. . . . 'They administer
poison in my dominions, and that without telling me! So Rassi
wishes to dishonour me in the eyes of Europe! And God knows what
I shall read next month in the Paris newspapers!'

Suddenly the heart of this shy young man was silent, his mind
had hit on an idea.

'Dear Duchessa! you know how much I am attached to you.
Your horrible notion of poison, or so I would like to believe, is
unfounded. But after all it also sets me thinking, and makes me almost
forget for an instant the passion I feel for you, the only one I have
experienced in all my life. I feel I am not attractive; I am only a boy
who is deeply in love. But, anyhow, put me to the test.'

The Prince became quite animated in using this sort of language.

'Save Fabrizio, and I'll believe anything you say! No doubt I am
carried away by a mother's foolish fears. But send at once to fetch
Fabrizio from the citadel, so that I may see him. If he is still alive
send him from the Palace to the city gaol, where he can remain for
months on end, if your Highness requires it, until his trial.'

The Duchessa saw with despair that the Prince, instead of briefly
granting so simple a request, had turned moody. He was very red;
he looked at the Duchessa, then lowered his eyes, and his cheeks
grew pale. The idea of poison, put forward so inopportunely, had
suggested to him an idea worthy of his father or of Philip II; but
he did not dare to put it into words.

'Listen, madam,' he said at length, as though forcing himself to speak, and in a tone that was scarcely gracious. 'You scorn me as a mere youngster, and, what is more, a person without any power to charm you. Well now, I am going to say something horrible, but which has just been suggested to me, this instant, by the deep and genuine passion which I feel for you. If I had the very least belief in the idea of poison, I should already have taken action, as my duty would have dictated. But I see nothing in your request save a fancy inspired by passion, the implications of which, I beg leave to say, I do not fully grasp. You wish me, who have been reigning for barely three months, to act without consulting my Ministers! You ask me to make a serious exception to my usual manner of procedure, which, I must admit, seems to me a highly rational one. It is you, madam, who, at this moment, are absolute sovereign here, you give me grounds for hope in a matter which means everything to me. But, in an hour's time, when this fanciful dream of poison, this nightmare of yours, has vanished, my company will become irksome to you, I shall be out of favour with you, madam. Well then, I require an oath. Swear to me, madam, that if Fabrizio is restored to you safe and sound, I shall obtain from you, within three months from now, all the highest bliss that my love can desire; that you will ensure the happiness of my whole life by placing at my disposal one hour of yours, and that you will be wholly mine.'

At that moment the Palace clock struck two. 'Ah! it is too late, perhaps,' thought the Duchessa.

'I swear it,' she cried, with a wild look in her eyes.

The Prince immediately became a different man; he ran to the far end of the gallery, where the aides-de-camp had their room.

'General Fontana, gallop at full speed to the citadel; go up as fast as you can to the cell where Signor del Dongo is confined, and bring him to me. I must speak to him within twenty minutes, or fifteen, if possible!'

'Ah! General,' cried the Duchessa, who had followed the Prince. 'One minute may decide my life. A report, which is doubtless false, makes me fear poison for Fabrizio. The moment you are within earshot call out to him not to eat. If he has begun his meal, see that you make him sick. Tell him it is I who wish it, employ force if necessary. Tell him that I am following close behind you, and, believe me, I shall be indebted to you all my life.'

'Your Grace, my horse is saddled, I am generally considered a good horseman, and I will gallop off at full speed. I shall be at the citadel eight minutes before you.'

'And I, madam,' cried the Prince, 'I ask you for four of those eight minutes.'

The aide-de-camp had vanished; he was a man whose only merit was that he knew how to ride. No sooner had he shut the door than the young Prince, who seemed to have some force of character, seized the Duchessa's hand.

'Be so good, madam,' he said to her in a voice full of passion, 'as to come with me to the chapel.' The Duchessa, at a loss for the first time in her life, followed him without uttering a word. The Prince and she hurried down the whole length of the gallery, the chapel being at the other end. On entering the chapel, the Prince fell on his knees, almost as much before the Duchessa as before the altar.

'Repeat the oath!' he said with passion. 'If you had had a sense of justice, if the unlucky fact of my princely rank had not stood in my way, you would have granted me out of pity what now you owe because you have sworn it.'

'If I see Fabrizio again, and not poisoned; if he is alive a week from now, if your Highness will appoint him Coadjutor to Archbishop Landriani and his ultimate successor, my honour, my womanly dignity, everything shall be trampled under foot, and I will give myself to your Highness.'

'But, *my sweet friend*,' said the Prince, with a blend of timorous anxiety and affection that was distinctly droll, 'I am afraid of some secret danger whose nature I cannot gather, and which may wreck my happiness; that would kill me. If the Archbishop opposes me with one of those ecclesiastical arguments which keep things dragging on for years on end, what will become of me? You see that I am behaving to you with entire good faith; are you going to behave to me like a little Jesuit?'

'No; in all good faith. If Fabrizio is saved, if, so far as it lies in your power, you make him a Coadjutor and a future Archbishop, I sacrifice my honour, and I am yours ... Your Highness undertakes to write *"approved"* on the margin of a request which His Grace the Archbishop will present to you in a week from now?'

'I will sign you a blank sheet of paper; reign over me and over my dominions!' cried the Prince, flushing red with happiness, and really beside himself. He insisted on a second oath. He was so deeply moved that he forgot the shyness that was so natural to him, and, in this chapel where they were alone, he murmured to the Duchessa things which, uttered three days earlier, would have altered the opinion that she held of him. But in her heart the despair aroused by Fabrizio's danger had given place to horror at the promise that had been wrung from her.

The Duchessa was thoroughly upset by what she had just done. If she was not yet fully conscious of all the fearful bitterness of the word she had given, it was because her attention was centred on the question of whether General Fontana would be able to reach the citadel in time

To free herself from the madly tender speeches of this stripling, and to turn the conversation a little, she praised a famous picture by Parmigianino, which hung over the high altar of this chapel.

'Be so good as to permit me to send it to you,' said the Prince.

'I accept,' replied the Duchessa; 'but give me leave to hurry off to meet Fabrizio.'

Looking quite demented, she told her coachman to put his horses into a gallop. On the bridge over the citadel moat she met General Fontana and Fabrizio, who were coming out on foot.

'Have you eaten anything?'

'No, by a miracle.'

She flung her arms round Fabrizio's neck, and fell into a faint which lasted for an hour, and gave rise to fears for her life and afterwards for her reason.

Governor Fabio Conti had turned white with rage at the sight of General Fontana. He had been so slow in obeying the Prince's orders, that the aide-de-camp, who assumed that the Duchessa was going to occupy the position of reigning mistress, had ended by losing his temper. The Governor had reckoned upon making Fabrizio's illness last for two or three days, 'and now,' he said to himself, 'the General, a man from the court, will find that insolent fellow writhing in the agony which is to avenge me for this escape.'

Fabio Conti, absorbed in thought, stopped in the guard-room of the Farnese Tower, from which he hastily dismissed the soldiers. He did not wish to have any witnesses of the scene about to begin. Five minutes later he was petrified with astonishment on hearing Fabrizio's voice, and seeing him, lively and alert, giving General Fontana a description of the prison. He made himself scarce.

Fabrizio showed himself a perfect 'gentleman' in his interview with the Prince. For one thing, he did not want to appear like a child who takes fright at the merest trifle. When the Prince inquired kindly how he felt, he answered: 'Like a man, your Serene Highness, who is dying of hunger, having luckily neither breakfasted nor dined.' After having had the honour of thanking the Prince, he requested permission to visit the Archbishop before presenting himself at the city gaol.

The Prince had turned amazingly pale when his childish brain began to gather some idea that this poison was not entirely a wild fantasy of the Duchessa's imagination. Absorbed in this cruel thought, he did not at first reply to the request to see the Archbishop which Fabrizio addressed to him; then he felt himself obliged to atone for his inattention by excessive graciousness.

'Go out alone, sir, and walk through the streets of my capital unguarded. About ten or eleven o'clock you will present yourself at the prison, where I hope you will not have to stay very long.'

On the morrow of this great day, the most remarkable in his life, the Prince fancied himself a little Napoleon; he had read that this great man had been kindly treated by several of the beauties of his court. Once established as a Napoleon by his success in love, he recalled that he had also been a Napoleon under fire. His heart was still thrilled by the firmness of his conduct with the Duchessa. The consciousness of having accomplished something difficult made him a different man altogether for the space of a fortnight; he became susceptible to generous considerations; he showed some force of character.

He began that day by burning the patent creating Rassi a Conte, which had been lying on his table for a month. He dismissed General Fabio Conti, and demanded from Colonel Lange, his successor, the truth about the poison. Lange, a gallant Polish officer, struck fear into the gaolers' hearts, and reported to the Prince that there had been a plan to poison Signor del Dongo's breakfast, but too many persons would have had to be let into the secret. For his dinner more careful measures had been taken; and, but for the arrival of General Fontana, Signor del Dongo would have died. The Prince was aghast; but, as he was really very much in love, it was a consolation for him to be able to say to himself: 'It turns out that I really did save Signor del Dongo's life, and the Duchessa will not dare fail to keep the word she has given me.' Another idea occurred to him: 'My calling is a great deal more difficult than I imagined. Everyone is agreed that the Duchessa is a woman of infinite intelligence, and here my political interests and my heart are in harmony with each other. It would be heavenly for me if she would consent to be my Prime Minister.'

That evening the Prince was so revolted by the horrors he had discovered that he refused to take part in the play.

'I should be more than happy,' he said to the Duchessa, 'if you would rule over my dominions as you rule over my heart. To begin with, I am going to tell you how I have spent my day.' He then gave her an exact account of everything; the burning of Rassi's patent, the appointment of Lange, the latter's report on the poisoning, and so on. 'I feel that I have very little experience of how to rule. The Conte humiliates me with his jokes; he even jokes at meetings of the Council, and, in society, he says things the truth of which you will dispute. He says I am a mere child whom he leads wherever he chooses. Even if I am a Prince, madam, I am none the less a man, and such things annoy me. In order to give an air of improbability to any stories Conte Mosca may concoct, I have been induced to summon that dangerous rascal Rassi to the Ministry; and now I have that General Conti believing him still so powerful that he dare not admit that it was Rassi or the Marchesa Raversi who suggested his making away with your nephew. I have a good mind to send General Fabio quite simply before the court; the judges will see whether he is guilty of an attempt at poisoning.'

'But, your Highness, have you any judges?'

'What!' said the Prince in astonishment.

'You have clever legal experts, who parade the streets with an air of solemnity; apart from that they will always pronounce sentence in a way to please the dominant party at your court.'

While the young Prince, thoroughly shocked, was making remarks which showed his candour far more than his sagacity, the Duchessa was saying to herself: 'Does it really suit me to have Conti disgraced? No, certainly not, for then the marriage of his daughter with that honest dullard the Marchese Crescenzi becomes impossible.'

On this topic there followed an endless discussion between the Duchessa and the Prince. The Prince was dazed with admiration. In consideration of the marriage of Clelia Conti to the Marchese Crescenzi, but on that express condition, which he himself announced in angry tones to the ex-Governor, the Prince pardoned him his attempt at poisoning; but, on the Duchessa's advice, he banished him until the date of his daughter's wedding. The Duchessa imagined that she was no longer really in love with Fabrizio, but she was still passionately anxious for the marriage of Clelia Conti with the Marchese Crescenzi. This afforded her some vague hope that gradually she might see Fabrizio's preoccupation disappear.

The Prince, off his head with joy, would have liked, that evening, to strip Rassi of all his honours in public. The Duchessa said to him laughing: 'Do you know a saying of Napoleon's? "A man placed in an exalted position, on whom all men's eyes are fixed, ought never to give way to a violent impulse." But anyhow, this evening it is too late; let us put off all business until tomorrow.'

She wished to give herself time to consult the Conte, to whom she gave a very exact account of the whole of that evening's conversation, suppressing, however, the Prince's frequent allusions to a promise which was poisoning her life. The Duchessa hoped to make herself so indispensable that she would be able to obtain an indefinite adjournment by saying to the Prince: 'If you have the barbarity to insist upon subjecting me to that humiliation, which I will never forgive you, I shall leave your principality the day after.'

Consulted by the Duchessa as to Rassi's fate the Conte proved himself most sagacious. General Fabio Conti and the ex-minister went on their travels together to Piedmont.

A singular difficulty arose in connexion with Fabrizio's trial: the judges wished to acquit him by acclamation, and at the first sitting of the court. The Conte was obliged to use threats to ensure that the trial should last for at least a week, and that the judges should take the trouble to hear all the witnesses. 'These fellows are all alike,' he said to himself.

The day after his acquittal Fabrizio del Dongo took possession at last of the office of Vicar-general to the worthy Archbishop Landriani. That same day, the Prince signed the official letters necessary to obtain Fabrizio's nomination as Coadjutor with eventual succession, and less than two months after he was installed in that post.

Everyone complimented the Duchessa on her nephew's grave demeanour; the fact was that he was in despair. The day after his deliverance, which was followed by the dismissal and banishment of General Fabio Conti and the Duchessa's coming into high favour, Clelia had taken refuge with her aunt, Contessa Contarini, an extremely rich and extremely aged lady, occupied exclusively with looking after her own health. Clelia could, had she wished, have seen Fabrizio; but anyone acquainted with her previous activities who had seen her present mode of behaviour might well have thought that with the passing of her lover's danger her love for him had also ceased. Not only did Fabrizio pass as often as he decently could in front of the Palazzo Contarini, but he had also succeeded, after endless trouble, in taking a little apartment opposite the windows of its first floor. On one occasion Clelia, having gone to the window without thinking, to see a procession pass, drew back at once, as though terror-stricken. She had caught sight of Fabrizio, dressed in black, but as a workman in very poor circumstances, looking at her from one of the windows of his wretched lodgings which were filled with oiled paper, like those of the Farnese Tower. Fabrizio would much have liked to persuade himself that Clelia was avoiding him as a consequence of her father's disgrace, which public report attributed to the Duchessa. But he was only too well aware of another cause for her keeping him at a distance, and nothing could rouse him out of his melancholy.

Neither his acquittal, nor his installation in an office entailing the performance of important functions, the first he had been called upon to fulfil in his life, nor his fine position in society, nor, indeed, the assiduous court that was paid to him by all the clergy and all devout persons in the diocese, had moved him in the least. The charming rooms he had in the Palazzo Sanseverina were no longer sufficient for him. The Duchessa, to her great delight, was obliged to give to him the whole of the second floor in her *palazzo* and two fine drawing-rooms on the first floor, which were always full of people awaiting an opportunity to pay their respects to the young Coadjutor. The clause securing his eventual succession had produced an amazing impression in the principality. All those resolute traits in Fabrizio's character, which formerly had so greatly shocked the poor, foolish courtiers, were now accounted to him as virtues.

It was a great lesson in philosophy for Fabrizio to find himself completely indifferent to all these honours, and far more unhappy in these magnificent rooms, with ten lackeys wearing his livery, than he had been in his wooden cell in the Farnese Tower, surrounded by hideous gaolers and in continual fear for his life. His mother and his sister, the Duchessa V —, who came to Parma to see him in his glory, were struck by his profound melancholy. The Marchesa del Dongo, now the least romantic of women, was so greatly alarmed by it that she imagined he must have been given some slow poison while in the Farnese Tower. Despite her extreme discretion, she felt it her duty to speak to him about this most unusual melancholy, and Fabrizio answered her only with tears.

A host of advantages, arising out of his brilliant position, produced no other effect on him save to make him out of temper. His brother, that vain soul consumed by the canker of the vilest selfishness, wrote him an almost official letter of congratulation, and with this letter enclosed a draft for fifty thousand lire, to enable him, so the new Marchese wrote, to buy himself horses and a carriage worthy of his name. Fabrizio sent this money to his younger sister, who was poorly married.

Conte Mosca had ordered a fine translation to be made, in Italian, of the genealogy of the Valserra del Dongo family, originally published in Latin by Fabrizio, Archbishop of Parma. He had it printed in a magnificent style, with the Latin text on alternate pages; the engravings had been reproduced as superb lithographs, done in Paris. The Duchessa had asked that a fine portrait of Fabrizio should be placed opposite that of the old Archbishop. This translation was published as being the work of Fabrizio during his first period of imprisonment. But every feeling had been crushed out of existence in our hero, even that vanity which is so natural to man. He did not deign to read a single page of this work attributed to himself. His social position made it incumbent upon him to present a magnificently bound copy to the Prince, who, feeling that he owed him some compensation for the cruel death to which he had come so near, accorded him the right of entry to his grand levee, a favour which confers the title of *Excellency*.

CHAPTER 26: *An Evening at Court*

THE only moments in which Fabrizio had some chance of rousing himself out of his deep melancholy were those which he spent hidden behind a pane of glass which he had substituted for a square of oiled paper in a window of his lodgings facing the Palazzo Contarini, in which, as we know, Clelia had taken refuge. On the few occasions on which he had seen her since his leaving the citadel he had been deeply distressed by a striking change in her, which seemed to him to augur ill. Since her one lapse, Clelia's face had assumed a character of nobility and gravity that was truly remarkable; one would have taken her for a woman of thirty. In this extraordinary change, Fabrizio saw the reflection of some steadfast resolution. 'At every moment of the day,' he said to himself, 'she is swearing inwardly to be faithful to the vow she has made to the Madonna, and never see me again.'

Fabrizio guessed only a part of Clelia's troubles. She knew that her father, having fallen into deep disgrace, could not return to Parma and reappear at court (without which life for him was impossible) until the day of her marriage to the Marchese Crescenzi. She wrote to tell him that she desired this marriage. The General was in retirement at Turin, and ill with grief. As a matter of fact, the effect of this heroic decision had been to add ten years to her age.

She was well aware that Fabrizio had a window facing the Palazzo Contarini; but she had only once been so unfortunate as to look at him. As soon as she noticed a certain turn of the head or the shape of a figure in any way resembling his, she immediately shut her eyes. Her deep piety and her trust in the Madonna's aid were from henceforth her only resources. She had to endure the pain of feeling no respect for her father; her future husband's character seemed to her perfectly commonplace and in conformity with the usual standards of taste and feeling in high society; lastly she adored a man whom she must never see again, and who all the same had certain claims on her. This combination of things ordained by fate seemed to her the height of misery, and we must acknowledge she was right. What she needed, after her marriage, was to go and live two hundred leagues from Parma.

Fabrizio was aware of Clelia's intense modesty; he knew how much any unusual enterprise, which might, if it were discovered, form a subject for gossip, was bound to displease her. None the less, provoked beyond endurance by his own excessive melancholy and by Clelia's constant habit of turning her eyes away from him, he ventured on an attempt to bribe two of the servants of her aunt, Contessa Contarini. One day, as night was falling, Fabrizio, dressed as a well-to-do countryman, presented himself at the door of the *palazzo*, where one of the servants whom he had bribed was waiting for him. He announced himself as coming from Turin and bearing letters for Clelia from her father. The servant went to deliver the message and then showed him up into a huge anteroom on the first floor of the *palazzo*. It was here that Fabrizio spent what was perhaps the most anxious quarter of an hour in his life. If Clelia refused to see him there was no more hope of peace of mind for him. 'To put an end to those irksome labours which my new dignity heaps upon me, I shall rid the Church of an unworthy priest, and, under an assumed name, seek refuge in some Carthusian monastery.' At length the servant came to inform him that Signorina Clelia Conti was willing to receive him. Our hero's courage failed him completely; he almost collapsed with fear as he went up the stairs to the second floor.

Clelia was sitting at a little table on which stood a single candle. No sooner had she caught sight of Fabrizio than she rushed away and hid herself at the far end of the room.

'This is how you care for my salvation,' she cried to him, hiding her face in her hands. 'Yet you know that when my father was at the point of death after taking poison I made a vow to the Madonna that I would never see you. I have never failed to keep that vow save on that day, the most wretched day of my life, when I felt myself bound by my conscience to rescue you from death. It is already a great thing, if by a strained and no doubt criminal interpretation of my vow, I consent to listen to you.'

This last remark surprised Fabrizio so much that it took him a few seconds to feel jubilant about it. He had expected to meet with the keenest anger, and to see Clelia fly from the room; at length he recovered his presence of mind and extinguished the one candle. Although he believed he had really understood Clelia's orders he was trembling from head to foot as he advanced towards the end of the room, where she had taken refuge behind a sofa. He did know whether it would offend her if he kissed her hand; she herself was trembling, too, with love, and flung herself into his arms.

'Dear Fabrizio,' she said to him, 'how slow you have been in coming! I can only speak to you for a moment, for it is certainly a great sin, and when I promised never to see you, no doubt I also implied that I promised not to speak to you. But how could you so barbarously pursue my poor father's idea of revenging himself? For, after all, it was he who was first nearly poisoned to help you make your escape. Ought you not to do something for me, who have exposed my reputation to such great risks in order to save you? And besides you are now altogether committed to Holy Orders; you could not marry me, even if I found a way of getting rid of that odious Marchese. And then, how could you dare, on the evening of the procession, try to see me in broad daylight, and so violate, in the most flagrant manner, the sacred promise I have made to the Madonna?'

Fabrizio clasped her in his arms, beside himself with joy and surprise.

A conversation that began with such a quantity of things to be said could not finish quickly. Fabrizio told Clelia the exact truth about her father's banishment. The Duchessa had had no part in it whatsoever, for the simple reason that she had not for a single moment believed that the idea of poison had originated with General Conti. She had always thought it to be a cunning stroke on the part of the Raversi faction, who were bent on driving out Conte Mosca. This incontrovertible fact, developed at great length, made Clelia very happy; she had been deeply distressed at having to hate anyone who belonged to Fabrizio. She no longer now regarded the Duchessa with a jealous eye.

The state of happiness created by that evening lasted only a few days.

The worthy Don Cesare arrived back from Turin, and, drawing courage from the perfect integrity of his heart, ventured to call on the Duchessa. After asking her to give him her word that she would not abuse the confidence he was about to repose in her, he admitted that his brother, led astray by a false point of honour, and believing himself defied and disgraced in the eyes of the public by Fabrizio's escape, had felt bound to revenge himself.

Don Cesare had not been speaking for two minutes before he had won his case: his perfect goodness had touched the Duchessa, who was by no means accustomed to such exhibitions. He appealed to her as a novelty.

'Hasten the marriage between the General's daughter and the

Marchese Crescenzi, and I give you my word that I will do all in my power to have the General received as though he were just returning from his travels. I shall invite him to dinner; does that satisfy you? No doubt there will be some coolness at the beginning, and the General must on no account be in a hurry to ask to be reinstated in his post as Governor of the citadel. But you know that I have a friendly feeling for the Marchese, and I shall not harbour any sort of grudge against his father-in-law.'

Fortified by these words, Don Cesare came to tell his niece that she held in her hands the life of her father, who was sick with despair. For several months he had not appeared at any court.

Clelia made up her mind to go to visit her father, who was hiding under an assumed name in a village near Turin; for he had taken it into his head that the court of Parma would lay a demand for his extradition before the court of Turin, so that he might be brought to trial. She found him ill, and almost out of his mind. That same evening she wrote a letter to Fabrizio announcing their eternal separation. On receiving this letter Fabrizio, who was developing a character exactly resembling that of his mistress, went into retreat at the monastery of Velleia, situated in the mountains, ten leagues from Parma. Clelia wrote him a letter of ten pages. She had sworn to him some time before that she would never marry the Marchese without his consent; now she asked him for it, and Fabrizio granted it from the depths of his retreat at Velleia, in a letter full of the purest friendship.

On receiving this letter, the friendly tone of which, it must be admitted, vexed her, Clelia herself fixed the day of her wedding, the festivities attending which enhanced still further the splendour which distinguished the court of Parma during that winter.

Ranuccio-Ernesto V was a miser at heart; but he was desperately in love, and he hoped to establish the Duchessa permanently at his court. He begged his mother to accept a very considerable sum of money, and to give entertainments. The Mistress of the Robes contrived to make an admirable use of this additional capital; the entertainments in Parma that winter recalled the great days of the court of Milan and of that charming Prince Eugène, Viceroy of Italy, whose kindness and generosity has left so lasting a memory behind him.

His duties as Coadjutor had summoned Fabrizio back to Parma; but he announced that, for reasons connected with religion, he would continue his retreat in the small suite of rooms which his patron,

Monsignore Landriani, had insisted on his occupying in the Arch-bishop's Palace; and he went to shut himself up there, attended by a single servant. Thus he was present at none of the brilliant fes-tivities of the court, a circumstance which won for him in Parma, and throughout his future diocese, an immense reputation for saintliness. An unexpected consequence of this retirement, inspired in Fabrizio solely by his profound and hopeless melancholy, was that the good Archbishop Landriani, who had always loved him, and who, in fact, had himself originally conceived the idea of making him a Coadjutor, began to feel slightly jealous of him. The Archbishop, and rightly too, considered it his duty to attend all the festivities at court, as is the custom in Italy. On these occasions he wore his ceremonial costume, which was more or less the same as that in which he was to be seen in the choir of his cathedral. The hundreds of servants gathered in the pillared ante-chamber of the Palace never failed to rise and ask for a blessing from Monsignore, who would kindly stop to bestow it on them. It was during one of these moments of solemn silence that Monsignore Landriani heard a voice say: 'Our Archbishop goes out to balls, and Monsignore del Dongo never leaves his room!'

From that moment the immense favour that Fabrizio had enjoyed in the Archbishop's Palace was at an end; but he was able now to stand on his own feet. All this behaviour, which had been inspired solely by the despair in which Clelia's marriage had plunged him, was regarded as due to a simple and sublime piety, and devout souls were reading, as a work of edification, the translation of the genealogy of his family, in which the most absurdly foolish vanity was displayed. The booksellers prepared a lithographed edition of his portrait, which was bought up in a few days, mainly by people of the lower classes. The engraver, in his ignorance, had reproduced round Fabrizio's portrait a number of ornamental designs which ought only to be found on the portraits of bishops, and to which a coadjutor could have no claim.

The Archbishop saw one of these portraits, and his fury knew no bounds. He sent for Fabrizio and said the harshest things to him, and in terms which his passion rendered at times extremely coarse. It required no effort on Fabrizio's part, as may well be imagined, to behave as Fénelon would have done in similar circumstances. He listened to the Archbishop with all possible humility and respect; and when the prelate had finished speaking, he told him the whole story of the translation of this genealogy made by Conte Mosca's orders, at the time of his first period in prison. It had been published with a worldly object, which had always seemed to him hardly befitting a man of his own calling. As for the portrait, he had had nothing to do with the first edition, and the same with the second; and the bookseller having sent to him, at the Archbishop's Palace, while he was in retirement, twenty-four copies of this second edition, he had sent his servant to buy a twenty-fifth. Having learnt in this way that the portrait was being sold for thirty soldi, he had sent a hundred lire in payment for the twenty-four copies.

All these arguments, although set forth in the most reasonable manner by a man who had many other sorrows in his heart, excited the Archbishop's anger to the verge of madness. He even went so far as to accuse Fabrizio of hypocrisy.

'That is what people of the lower classes are like,' thought Fabrizio, 'even when they have some intelligence!'

He had at the time a more serious cause for worry; this was his aunt's letters, in which she absolutely insisted on his coming back to occupy his rooms in the Palazzo Sanseverina, or at least paying her an occasional visit. There Fabrizio was certain of hearing talk of the splendid entertainments given by the Marchese Crescenzi on the occasion of his marriage; and he was not sure of being able to endure this without making an exhibition of himself.

When the marriage ceremony took place, Fabrizio had already for a week past maintained utter and complete silence, after giving orders to his servant and to those members of the Archbishop's household with whom he had any dealings never to say a single word to him.

When Monsignore Landriani learnt of this new piece of affectation he sent for Fabrizio far more often than was his usual custom, and tried to engage him in long conversations. He even obliged him to hold conferences with certain canons from the country, who claimed that the Archbishop had infringed their privileges. Fabrizio took all these things with the perfect indifference of a man who has other things on his mind. 'It would be better for me,' he thought, 'to become a Carthusian. I should suffer less among the rocks of Velleia.'

He went to see his aunt, and could not restrain his tears as he embraced her. She found him so greatly altered; his eyes, seeming larger than ever on account of his excessive thinness, looked as though they were starting out of his head, and he himself presented such a sickly and miserable appearance in a little threadbare black cassock such as a humble priest would wear, that at her first sight of him she could hardly keep back her own tears. But a moment later, when she reminded herself that all the changes in this handsome young man's appearance were due to Clelia's marriage, her feelings were almost equal in vehemence to those of the Archbishop, although more skilfully controlled. She was cruel enough to dilate at length on certain picturesque details which had distinguished the delightful entertainments given by the Marchese Crescenzi. Fabrizio made no reply; but his eyes half-closed with a convulsive movement, and he became even paler than he already was, which at first sight might have seemed impossible. In these moments of keen anguish his pallor assumed a greenish hue.

Conte Mosca happened to come in, and what he saw—a thing which seemed to him incredible—cured him for good and all of that jealousy which Fabrizio had never ceased to arouse in him. This able man employed the most delicate and ingenious turns of phrase in an attempt to restore to Fabrizio some interest in mundane things. The Conte had always felt much esteem and a certain degree of affection for him; this affection, being no longer counter-balanced by jealousy, became at that moment something approaching devotion. 'There's no doubt he has paid dearly for his fine position,' he said to himself, going over the tale of Fabrizio's misfortunes in his mind.

On the pretext of showing him the picture by Parmigianino which the Prince had sent to the Duchessa the Conte drew Fabrizio aside. 'Now then, my friend, let us speak as man to man. Can I help you in any way? You need not be afraid of any questions on my part. Still, can money be of use to you, can influence help you? Speak freely, I am at your orders; if you prefer to write, then write to me.'

Fabrizio embraced him tenderly and made remarks on the picture.

'Your conduct is a masterpiece of the subtlest policy,' the Conte said to him, reverting to the normal light tone of conversation. 'You are laying up for yourself a most agreeable future. The Prince respects you, the people venerate you, your little threadbare black cassock gives Monsignore Landriani some bad nights. I have some experience of things, and I can assure you that I should not know what advice to give you to improve upon what I see. Your first step in society at the age of twenty-five has carried you to perfection. You are very much talked of at court; and do you know to what you owe that distinction: unique at your age? To your shabby little black cassock. The Duchessa and I, as you know, have at our disposal Petrarch's old house on that fine hill in the middle of the forest, near the Po. It has struck me that if ever you grow weary of the pettiness and spite of envious people, you might become Petrarch's successor, whose fame will enhance your own.' The Conte was racking his brains to raise a smile on that ascetic's face, but he could not manage to do so. What made the change more striking was that, until latterly, if Fabrizio's features had any defect, it was that of occasionally presenting, at the wrong moment, an expression of sensuous delight and gaiety.

The Conte did not let him go without telling him that, notwithstanding his being in retreat, it would perhaps look somewhat affected if he did not appear at court on the following Saturday, which was the Princess's birthday. This remark was like a dagger-thrust to Fabrizio. 'Good God!' he thought, 'why on earth did I come to this house!' He could not think without shuddering of the meeting which might occur at court. This idea absorbed all others. He felt that his only remaining chance was to arrive at the Palace at the precise moment at which the doors of the reception rooms were thrown open.

And as a matter of fact, the name of Monsignore del Dongo was one of the first to be announced on the evening of this festive occasion, and the Princess received him with the utmost possible politeness. Fabrizio kept his eyes glued to the clock, and at the moment at which it marked the twentieth minute of his presence in the room he was rising to take his leave when the Prince came in to join his mother. After paying his respects to him for some minutes, Fabrizio was cleverly manoeuvring to reach the door, when one of those trifling incidents of court life which the Mistress of the Robes knew so well how to handle happened suddenly to occur at his expense. The Chamberlain in waiting ran after him to tell him that he had been chosen to join the Prince at whist. In Parma this was a signal honour, and far above the rank which the Coadjutor held in society. To play whist with the Prince was a marked honour even for the Archbishop. At the Chamberlain's words Fabrizio felt cut to the heart, and although he had a rooted abhorrence of making a scene in public he was on the point of going up to him to tell him that he was seized with a sudden fit of dizziness, but he reflected that he would be exposed to questions and polite expressions of sympathy, more intolerable even than the game itself. That day he felt a horror of speaking.

Fortunately the Superior General of the Franciscan Friars happened to be among the important personages who had come to pay their respects to the Princess. This friar, a very learned man, a worthy emulator of such men as Cardinal Fontana or Bishop Duvoisin, had taken up his position in a far corner of the room. Fabrizio placed himself in front of him, so that he could not see the door, and began to discuss theology. But he could not prevent his ears from hearing a servant announce the Marchese and the Marchesa Crescenzi. Contrary to his own expectation, Fabrizio felt a violent impulse of anger.

'If I were Borso Valserra,' he said to himself (this being one of the generals of the first Sforza), 'I should go and stab that lout of a Marchese, and with that very same dagger with the ivory handle which Clelia gave me on that happy day, and I would teach him to have the insolence to present himself with his Marchesa in a place where I happen to be!'

His expression changed so completely that the Superior of the Franciscans asked him: 'Does your Excellency feel unwell?'

'I have a shocking headache ... the light hurts me ... and I am only staying here because I have been chosen to join the Prince's whist-party.'

At these words the Superior of the Franciscans, who was of middle-class extraction, was so disconcerted that, not knowing what to do, he began bowing to Fabrizio, who, for his part, being far more disturbed than his companion, began to talk with extraordinary volubility. He noticed that a great silence had fallen on the room behind him, but he would not look round. Suddenly a violin bow was rapped against a music-stand; a *ritornello* was played, and the famous Signora P— sang that air by Cimarosa, once so popular: *Quelle pupille tenere!*

Fabrizio held out for the first few bars, but soon his anger melted away, and he felt a strong compulsion to burst into tears. 'Good God!' he said to himself, 'what a ridiculous scene! and for a man of my cloth too!' He felt it wiser to talk about himself.

'These violent headaches of mine, when I fight against them as I am doing this evening,' he said to the Superior General, 'end in fits of tears which might provide food for scandal in a man of our calling. And so I beg that your illustrious Reverence will allow me to shed tears while I am looking your way, and not pay any sort of attention to it.'

'Our Father Provincial at Cantazaro suffers from the same disability,' said the Franciscan. And he began a very lengthy story in a low tone of voice.

The absurdity of this story, which involved a detailed account of the Father Provincial's evening meals, made Fabrizio smile, a thing which had not happened to him for a very long time; but soon he ceased to listen to the Superior General. Signora P — was singing, most divinely, an air of Pergolese (the Princess had a fondness for old-fashioned music). There was a slight sound a few feet away from Fabrizio; for the first time that evening he looked round. The chair that had just caused this faint creaking of the parquet floor was occupied by the Marchesa Crescenzi, whose eyes, filled with tears, met the direct gaze of Fabrizio's, which were hardly in better case. The Marchesa bent her head. Fabrizio continued to gaze at her for some moments; he was making a study of that head laden with diamonds, but his glance expressed anger and disdain. Then, saying to himself, *and my eyes shall never look upon you*,' he turned back to the Superior General, and said to him: 'There now, my weakness is getting hold of me worse than ever.'

And indeed, for over half an hour Fabrizio shed hot tears. Fortunately, a symphony of Mozart, horribly mangled, as is customary in Italy, came to his rescue and helped to dry his tears.

He stood firm and did not turn his eyes towards the Marchesa Crescenzi. But Signora P — sang again, and Fabrizio's heart, relieved by his tears, attained a state of perfect repose. Then life appeared to him in a new light. 'How can I claim,' he said to himself, 'to be able to forget her entirely at the very outset? Would such a thing be possible for me?' Then this thought struck him: 'Can I be more unhappy than I have been for the last two months? And if nothing can make my anguish keener, why deny myself the pleasure of seeing her? She has forgotten her vows; she is light and fickle; aren't all women the same? But who could deny her a heavenly beauty? She has a look in her eyes which sends me into ecstasies, whereas I have to make an effort to force myself to cast a glance at women who are considered among the greatest beauties! Well, why not let myself be enraptured? It will at least be a moment's respite.'

Fabrizio had some knowledge of men, but no experience of the passions, otherwise he would have told himself that this momentary pleasure, to which he was about to yield, would render futile all the efforts he had been making for the past two months to forget Clelia.

That poor woman had only come to this party under compulsion from her husband. She would anyhow have tried to slip away after the first half hour, on a plea of feeling unwell, but the Marchese assured her that to send for her carriage to go away when many carriages were still arriving would be a most unusual proceeding, and one that might even be interpreted as an indirect criticism of the entertainment offered by the Princess.

'In my capacity as Lord-in-waiting,' the Marchese added, 'I have to remain in the drawing-room at the Princess's orders until everyone has gone. There may be, and no doubt will be, orders to be given to the servants, they are so careless! And would you have a mere Equerry usurp that honour?'

Clelia resigned herself; she had not seen Fabrizio; she still hoped that he might not have come to this party. But at the moment when the concert was about to begin, the Princess having given permission to the ladies to be seated, Clelia, who was not at all alert in that sort of thing, let all the best places near the Princess be snatched from her, and was obliged to go and look for a chair at the far end of the room, in the very corner to which Fabrizio had fled. As she reached her chair the brown frock of the Franciscan Superior General, an unusual costume in such a place, attracted her attention, and at first she did not notice the slim figure in a plain black suit who was talking to him. All the same a certain secret impulse brought her eyes to rest on this man. 'Everyone here is wearing either uniform or a richly embroidered coat. Who then is that young man in such a plain black suit?' She was gazing at him with profound attention when a lady, taking her seat beside her, caused her chair to move. Fabrizio turned his head; she did not recognize him, he was so altered. At first she said to herself: 'That is somebody like him, it must be his elder brother. But I thought he was only a few years older than Fabrizio, and that man must be forty.' Suddenly she recognized him by a movement of his lips.

'Poor fellow, how he has suffered!' She bent her head, bowed down by grief and not in fidelity to her vow. Her heart was convulsed with pity: 'after nine months in prison he did not look anything like that!' She did not look at him again; but, without actually turning her eyes in his direction, she could see every movement that he made.

After the concert, she saw him go up to the Prince's card-table, placed a few feet away from the throne. She breathed more freely when Fabrizio was thus removed some distance away from her.

But the Marchese Crescenzi had been greatly annoyed at seeing his wife relegated to a seat so far away from the throne. The whole of the evening he had been occupied in persuading a lady seated three chairs away from the Princess, and whose husband was under a financial obligation to him, that she would do well to change places with the Marchesa. Since the poor woman, as was natural, resisted, he went in search of the husband in debt to him, who made his better half listen to the sad voice of reason, and finally the Marchese had the pleasure of effecting the exchange.

He went to find his wife. 'You are always too modest,' he said to her. 'Why walk about as you do with downcast eyes? People will take you for one of those middle-class women who are quite amazed at finding themselves here, and whom everyone else is amazed to see here. That crazy Mistress of the Robes is always doing things like that! And they talk of checking the progress of Jacobinism! Remember that your husband holds the highest position among the gentlemen at the Princess's court, and that even if the Republicans should succeed in doing away with the court, and even with the nobility, your husband would still be the richest man in this State. That is an idea which you do not sufficiently keep in mind.'

The chair in which the Marchese had the pleasure of installing his wife was only six paces away from the Prince's card-table. She could see Fabrizio only in profile, but she found him grown so thin, he had, above all, an air of being so far above everything that might happen in this world – he who once would never let any incident pass without making his comment upon it – that she ended by coming to this frightful conclusion: Fabrizio had changed completely; he had forgotten her; if he had grown so thin, it was the effect of the severe fasting to which his piety subjected him. Clelia was confirmed in this sad idea by the conversation of everyone around her. The Coadjutor's name was on everyone's lips; they sought a reason for the signal favour which they saw conferred upon him: he, so young, to be invited to the Prince's card-table! They marvelled at his

polite indifference and the haughty air with which he flung down h
cards, even when he was trumping one of His Highness's.

'But this is incredible!' cried certain old courtiers. 'The favours
accorded to his aunt have quite turned his head ... But, thank
heaven, that sort of thing won't last. Our Sovereign doesn't like
people to assume such little airs of superiority.' The Duchessa went
up to the Prince; the courtiers, who kept at a very respectable distance
from the card-table, so that they could only catch a chance word or
two of the Prince's conversation, noticed that Fabrizio flushed deeply.
'His aunt will have been reading him a lesson,' they thought, 'about
his high-and-mighty airs of indifference.' Fabrizio had just caught the
sound of Clelia's voice; she was replying to the Princess, who, in
making her tour of the ball-room, had addressed a few words to the
wife of her Lord-in-waiting. The moment arrived when Fabrizio
had to change his place at the whist-table. He then found himself
directly facing Clelia, and gave himself up a number of times
to the pleasure of gazing at her. The poor Marchesa, feeling his eyes
upon her, became embarrassed. More than once she forgot what
she owed to her vow: in her desire to find out what was going on in
Fabrizio's heart, she fixed her eyes on him.

The Prince's game having ended, the ladies rose to go into the
supper room. There was some slight confusion. Fabrizio found himself close to Clelia. He was still quite determined, but he happened
to recognize a faint perfume she used on her clothes, and this sensation
overthrew all the resolutions he had made. He drew near to her,
and murmured softly, and as if speaking to himself, two lines from
that sonnet of Petrarch which he had sent her from Lake Maggiore,
printed on a silk handkerchief:

> 'What joy was mine when all the common crowd
> Believed me wretched. Now, how changed my lot!'

'No, he has not forgotten me,' said Clelia to herself, in an ecstasy
of joy. 'That noble heart is not inconstant!'

She ventured to repeat to herself these two lines from Petrarch:

> 'No, you will never see a change in me,
> Fair eyes, that taught my heart what love can be.'

The Princess withdrew immediately after supper; the Prince had
gone with her to her own apartments, and did not appear again in

the reception rooms. As soon as this became known, everyone tried to leave at once. There was complete confusion in the ante-rooms; Clelia found herself quite close to Fabrizio; the utter misery depicted on his face moved her to pity. 'Let us forget the past,' she said to him, 'and keep this reminder of *friendship*.' As she said these words she held out her fan so that he might take it.

Everything changed in Fabrizio's eyes: in an instant he was another man. The very next day he announced that his retreat was at an end, and returned to occupy his magnificent suite of rooms at the Palazzo Sanseverina. The Archbishop said, and believed, that the favour which the Prince had shown Fabrizio in inviting him to join his game had completely turned the head of this novice in sainthood: the Duchessa saw that he had come to an understanding with Clelia. This thought, coming to aggravate the misery caused her by the memory of a fatal promise, finally decided her to go away for a while. People marvelled at her folly. What! leave the court at the moment when the favour that she enjoyed appeared to have no limits!

The Conte, perfectly happy since he had seen that there was no question of love between Fabrizio and the Duchessa, said to his friend: 'This new Prince is the very personification of virtue, but I called him "*that child*": will he ever forgive me? I can see only one way of getting back into his good books again, and that is by absence. I am going to show myself a perfect model of charm and polite respect, after which I shall be ill, and shall ask leave to retire. You will allow me to do so, now that Fabrizio's career is assured. But will you make me the immense sacrifice,' he added, laughing, 'of changing the lofty title of Duchessa for a very much humbler one? For my own amusement, I am leaving everything here in an inextricable state of confusion. I had four or five hard-working men in my various ministries; I placed them all on the pension list two months ago, because they read the French newspapers; and I have filled their places with a set of first-class idiots.

'After our departure, the Prince will find himself in such difficulties that, in spite of the horror that he feels for Rassi's character, I have no doubt that he will be obliged to recall him, and I myself am only awaiting an order from the tyrant who holds my fate in his hands to write a letter of tender friendship to my friend Rassi, and tell him that I have every reason to hope that his merits will soon be appreciated at their true worth.'

CHAPTER 27: *An Evening in Church*

THIS serious conversation took place on the day after Fabrizio's return to the Palazzo Sanseverina. The Duchessa was still feeling the effects of the sudden flush of happiness which was only too plain in everything Fabrizio did. 'So,' she said to herself, 'that pious little creature has deceived me! She has not been able to hold out against her lover for even three months.'

The certainty of a happy conclusion had given that faint-hearted individual, the young Prince, courage to love. He had heard something of the preparations for departure that were being made at the Palazzo Sanseverina; and his French valet, who had little faith in the virtue of great ladies, bolstered up his courage with regard to the Duchessa. Ernesto V ventured on a step which was severely criticized by the Princess and by all sensible people at court; the townsfolk regarded it as setting the seal on the astonishing favour which the Duchessa enjoyed. The Prince came to see her at her house.

'You are leaving,' he said to her with an air of solemnity which the Duchessa thought in odious taste, 'you are leaving, you are going to play me false and violate your oath! And yet, if I had delayed ten minutes in granting Fabrizio's pardon, he would have been dead. And you leave me wretched! and but for your oath I should never have had the courage to love you as I do! Have you then no sense of honour?'

'Look at the matter sensibly, your Highness. In the whole of your life has there been any period equal in happiness to the four months which have just gone by? Your fame as a sovereign, and, I venture to think, your happiness as a man of kindly nature, have never reached such a pitch before. This is the compact that I propose; if you deign to agree to it, I shall not be your mistress for a passing moment, and by virtue of an oath extorted by fear, but I shall consecrate every moment of my life to procuring your happiness. I shall always be what I have been for the past four months, and perhaps, one day, love will come to crown friendship. I would not swear to the contrary.'

'Well then,' said the Prince, overjoyed, 'take on another role, be even more, reign at once over my heart and over my State, be my ime Minister. I offer you such a marriage as the unfortunate conventions of my rank permit. We have an example close at hand; the King of Naples has recently married the Duchessa di Partanna. I offer you all that I have to offer, a marriage of the same sort. I am going to add a distressing political consideration to show you that I am no longer a mere child, and that I have thought of everything. I will not lay stress on the condition which I impose on myself of being the last Sovereign of my race, nor on the sorrow of seeing, in my lifetime, the Great Powers take upon themselves to choose my successor. I count these very real disadvantages as a blessing, since they offer me additional means of proving to you my esteem for you and my passion.'

The Duchessa did not hesitate for an instant. The Prince bored her and the Conte seemed to her perfectly charming. There was only one man in the world who could be preferred to him. Besides, she ruled the Conte, and the Prince, controlled by the exigencies of his rank, would more or less rule her. And then, he might turn fickle and take mistresses; the difference of age between them would seem, in a very few years, to give him the right to do so.

From the first moment, the prospect of being bored had settled the whole question. However, the Duchessa, who was anxious to be as charming as possible, asked for leave to think the matter over.

It would take too long to set down here all the almost tender turns of speech and the infinitely gracious terms in which she managed to clothe her refusal. The Prince lost his temper; he saw all his happiness slipping through his fingers. What was to become of him when the Duchessa had left his court? Besides, what a humiliation to be refused! 'And then what will my French valet say when I tell him of my defeat?'

The Duchessa had enough skill to calm the Prince and bring the discussion back by degrees to the actual terms of her proposal.

'If your Highness deigns to consent not to press for the fulfilment of a fatal promise, and one that is horrible in my eyes, as exposing me to self-contempt, I will spend my whole life at your court, and that court shall always be what it has been this winter. Every moment of my time will be devoted to contributing to your happiness as a man, and to your glory as a ruler. If you insist on my keeping my oath, you will have blighted the rest of my life, and will see me leave your principality immediately, never to return. The day on which

I shall have lost my honour will also be the last day I shall ever see you.'

But the Prince, like all weak-spirited characters, was obstinate; moreover, his pride as a man and a sovereign was piqued by the refusal of his hand. He thought of all the difficulties he would have had to surmount to make this marriage generally acceptable, difficulties which, nevertheless, he was determined to overcome. For the next three hours the same arguments were repeated on either side, often accompanied by very sharp words.

'Do you then wish to convince me, madam,' cried the Prince, 'that you have no regard for honour? If I had hesitated as long on the day when General Fabio Conti was giving Fabrizio poison, you would now be occupied in erecting a tomb for him in one of the churches in Parma.'

'Not in Parma, certainly, in this city of prisoners.'

'Very well then, leave it, madam,' the Prince retorted angrily, 'and take my contempt with you.'

As he was going the Duchessa said to him beneath her breath: 'Very well, come here at ten o'clock this evening, in the strictest incognito, and you will be making a fool's bargain. You will have seen me for the last time, and I would have devoted my life to making you as happy as an absolute Prince can be in this age of Jacobins. And think what your court will be when I am no longer there to rescue it by force from its natural dullness and spite.'

'You, on your side, refuse the crown of Parma, and more than the crown. For you would not have been an ordinary sort of Princess whom one marries for reasons of politics, and does not love. My heart is wholly yours, and you would have seen yourself for ever the absolute mistress of my actions as of my government.'

'Yes, but the Princess, your mother, would have had the right to look on me as a vile, scheming woman.'

'Well then, I should have had the Princess banished with a pension.'

There followed a further three-quarters of an hour of cutting rejoinders. The Prince, who was naturally inclined to the weighing of scruples, could neither make up his mind to insist on his rights, nor to let the Duchessa go. He had been told that once the first point was gained, no matter how, women come round.

Driven from the house by the indignant Duchessa, he had the temerity to reappear, trembling all over and extremely miserable, at three minutes to ten. At half past ten the Duchessa stepped into her carriage and set off for Bologna. As soon as she was outside the Prince's territory she wrote to the Conte:

> *The sacrifice has been made. Do not ask me to be cheerful for a month at least. I shall not see Fabrizio again. I am waiting for you in Bologna and I will be Contessa Mosca whenever you choose. I ask you for one thing only: do not ever force me to appear again in the dominions I am now leaving, and remember always that instead of an income of a hundred and fifty thousand lire you are going to have thirty or forty thousand at the very most. All the fools have been watching you with gaping mouths, and for the future you will be respected only in so far as you choose to lower yourself to understand all their petty ideas.* 'You asked for it, Georges Dandin!'

A week later their marriage was celebrated at Perugia, in a church which contains the tombs of the Conte's ancestors. The Prince was in despair. The Duchessa had received from him three or four couriers, and had not failed to return his letters to him, enclosed in fresh envelopes, and with the seals unbroken. Ernesto V had bestowed a magnificent pension on the Conte, and had given the Grand Cordon of his Order to Fabrizio.

'That is what pleased me most in our farewells,' said the Conte to the new Contessa Mosca della Rovere. 'We parted the best of friends. He gave me the Grand Cordon of a Spanish Order, and diamonds which are worth quite as much as the Grand Cordon. He told me that he would have made me a Duca, if he did not wish to keep that in reserve as a way of bringing you back to his dominions. I am therefore commissioned to inform you – a fine commission for a husband – that if you will condescend to return to Parma, if only for a month, I shall be made a Duca, with whatever title you choose, and you shall have a fine estate.'

This the Duchessa refused with something like horror.

After the scene that had taken place at the court ball, and which seemed to be fairly conclusive, Clelia did not appear to retain any memory of the love which she had apparently shared for one brief moment. The most violent remorse had taken possession of that virtuous and Christian soul. This Fabrizio realized very clearly, and in spite of all the hopes he tried to entertain, his heart was none the less a prey to the blackest misery. This time, however, his misery did not drive him into retreat, as at the time of Clelia's marriage.

The Conte had begged 'his nephew' to keep him exactly informed of all that went on at court, and Fabrizio, who was beginning to realize all that he owed to him, had promised himself that he would carry out this commission faithfully.

In common with the city and the court, Fabrizio had no doubt that his friend entertained the idea of coming back to the Ministry, and with more power than he had ever had before. The Conte's forecasts were not long in giving proof of their accuracy. In less than six weeks after his departure, Rassi was Prime Minister, Fabio Conti Minister of War, and the prisons, which the Conte had nearly emptied, were beginning to fill up again. The Prince, in summoning these men to power, fancied that he was avenging himself on the Duchessa. His brain was turned by love, and he felt a particular hatred of Conte Mosca as his rival.

Fabrizio had a great deal on his hands. Monsignore Landriani, now seventy-two years old, had fallen into a state of great weakness, and as he now hardly ever left his Palace, it fell to his Coadjutor to take his place in almost all his functions.

The Marchesa Crescenzi, overcome by remorse, and frightened by her spiritual director, had found an excellent way of keeping out of Fabrizio's sight. Taking as an excuse the last period of a first pregnancy, she made herself a prisoner in her own *palazzo*; but this house had an immense garden. Fabrizio contrived to find his way into it, and placed, along the path which was Clelia's favourite walk, nosegays of flowers arranged in such a way as to form a message, like those she had once sent him every evening during the last days of his imprisonment in the Farnese Tower.

The Marchesa was greatly annoyed by this tentative venture. The motions of her soul were governed at one moment by remorse, at another by passion. For several months she would not allow herself to go down into her garden; she even felt scruples about casting a glance that way.

Fabrizio was beginning to think that he was parted from her for ever, and despair had also begun to take possession of his soul. The company among whom he spent his time disgusted him intensely, and if he had not been inwardly persuaded that the Conte could not find peace of mind so long as he was out of office, he would have gone into retreat in his little suite of rooms in the Archbishop's Palace. It would have been pleasant to him to live alone with his thoughts and never to hear a human voice again save in the exercise of his official duties. 'But,' said he to himself, 'in serving the interests of the Conte and Contessa Mosca, no one can take my place.'

The Prince continued to treat him with a marked politeness which placed him in the highest rank at this court, and this favour he owed in great measure to himself. The extreme reserve which, in Fabrizio's case, sprang from an indifference amounting to disgust for all the affectations or petty passions that fill the life of men, had acted as a spur to the young Prince's vanity; he would often remark that Fabrizio had as lively a spirit as his aunt. The Prince's candid soul had guessed a part of the truth: namely that no one else approached him with the same feelings in his heart as Fabrizio. What could not escape the notice even of the most dull-witted courtiers was that the consideration Fabrizio had won was not that accorded to a mere Coadjutor, but actually exceeded the respect which the Sovereign showed to the Archbishop. Fabrizio wrote to the Conte that if ever the Prince had enough intelligence to perceive the mess into which the Ministers, Rassi, Fabio Conti, Zurla, and others of like calibre had got his affairs, he, Fabrizio, would be the natural channel by which the Sovereign could make overtures, without unduly compromising his self-respect.

But for the recollection of those fatal words, 'that child' [he told Contessa Mosca], applied by a man of genius to an august personage, the august personage would already have cried: 'Return at once and rid me of these ragamuffins!' Even now, if the wife of this man of genius would condescend to make some advances, of however little significance, the Conte would be recalled with joy; but he will return in a far more brilliant manner, if he is willing to wait till the time is ripe. For the rest, everyone is bored to death at the Princess's receptions; there is nothing to amuse them there save the crazy pose of that man Rassi, who, now that he is a Conte, has developed a mania for noble birth. Strict orders have just been issued that anyone who cannot prove his claim to eight quarterings of nobility shall no longer dare to present himself at the Princess's evenings (these are the exact terms of the proclamation). All the men who already possess the right of entry to the great gallery in the mornings, and to be present when the Sovereign passes through on his way to Mass, will continue to enjoy this privilege; but all newcomers will have to show proof of their eight quarterings. In connexion with this it has been pointed out that Rassi 'cuts down men without quarter.'

It can be imagined that such letters were not entrusted to the post. Contessa Mosca replied from Naples:

We have a concert every Thursday and a conversazione on Sundays; it's impossible to move about in our drawing-rooms. The Conte is thrilled with his excavations, he devotes a thousand lire a month to them, and has just brought in labourers from the mountains of the Abruzzi that cost him only twenty-three soldi a day. You really ought to come and see us. This is more than the twentieth time, you ungrateful boy, that I have sent you this summons.

Fabrizio had no intention of obeying her. Even his daily letter to the Conte or the Contessa seemed to him an almost insupportable burden. The reader will forgive him when he learns that a whole year passed in this way without his being able to address a single word to the Marchesa. All his attempts to establish some kind of correspondence with her had been repulsed with horror. The habitual silence which, from sheer weariness with life, Fabrizio observed everywhere, except in the exercise of his functions and at court, added to the spotless purity of his conduct, had made him the object of such extraordinary veneration that he finally decided to follow his aunt's advice.

The Prince [she wrote] *has such deep veneration for you that you must expect to fall out of favour very soon. He will give abundant signs of his indifference, and the frightful contempt of the courtiers will follow in his lead. These petty despots, however honest they may be, are fickle as fashion and for the same reason – boredom. You will find no strength to resist the Sovereign's caprices except in preaching. You improvise so well in verse! Try to speak half an hour on religion. You will utter heresies at first; but pay some learned and discreet theologian to be present at your sermons, and point out your errors; you can put them right the next time.*

The kind of misery which a frustrated love engenders in the soul makes anything that calls for concentration or action a frightful burden. Fabrizio, however, told himself that his influence with the common people, if he acquired any, might one day be of use to his aunt and to the Conte, for whom his respect and admiration increased with every day in proportion as his experience of the world taught him to recognize the evil tendencies of mankind. He decided to preach, and his success, prepared for by his thin figure and his threadbare habit, was quite unparalleled. People found in his sermons a tincture of deep sadness which, combined with his pleasing countenance and the stories of the high favour which he enjoyed at court, made a conquest of every woman's heart; they invented the legend of his having been one of the bravest captains in Napoleon's army. Soon this ridiculous fiction passed for an undoubted fact. Seats in the churches where he was to preach were reserved beforehand; the poorer folk would take possession of them as a speculation from five o'clock in the morning.

Fabrizio's success was such that he finally conceived the idea, which put him in a completely different frame of mind, that, if only out of simple curiosity, the Marchesa Crescenzi might very well come one day to listen to one of his sermons. All at once the enraptured public became aware of a twofold increase in his talent. He allowed himself, when he was moved, to use imagery whose boldness would have made the most practised orators shudder. At times, forgetting himself completely, he would indulge in flights of impassioned inspiration, and his whole congregation would burst into tears. But his eager, questing eye sought in vain, among all the faces turned towards the pulpit, for that one face whose presence would have been so great an event in his life.

'But if I ever have that happiness,' he said to himself, 'either I shall faint, or I shall stop short altogether.' To ward against such an unlucky accident as the latter, he had composed a sort of tender and impassioned prayer which he always kept on a stool in his pulpit. His intention was to begin reading this piece, should the presence of the Marchesa ever place him at a loss for words.

One day he learnt through those of the Marchesa's servants who were in his pay that orders had been given to make ready the box of the *Casa Crescenzi* at the principal theatre for the following evening. It was a year since the Marchesa had been present at any performance, and it was a tenor whom everyone raved about and who filled the house every evening that was making her depart from her usual habits. Fabrizio's first reaction was one of deepest joy. 'At last I shall be able to look at her for a whole evening! They say she has grown very pale.' And he tried to imagine how that charming face would look, with its colours half dimmed by conflicts within the soul.

His friend Lodovico, in utter consternation at what he termed his master's madness, secured with great difficulty a box on the fourth tier, almost opposite the Marchesa's. An idea occurred to Fabrizio: 'I hope to put it into her head to come to the sermon, and I shall choose a church which is quite small, so as to be able to see her properly.' As a rule, Fabrizio preached at three o'clock. On the morning of the day on which the Marchesa was to attend the performance, he gave notice that as he would be detained at the Archbishop's Palace all day by some duty connected with his office, he would preach, as a special exception, at half past eight in the evening, in the little church of Santa Maria della Visitazione, situated precisely opposite one of the wings of the Palazzo Crescenzi. Lodovico, on his behalf, presented an enormous quantity of candles to the nuns of the Visitation, with the request that they would illuminate the church as brightly as possible. He got hold of a whole company of Grenadier Guards, and a sentry, with fixed bayonet, was posted outside each chapel, to prevent anything being stolen.

The sermon was announced for half past eight only, and by two o'clock the church was completely filled. One may imagine the din there was in that quiet street with the noble structure of the Palazzo Crescenzi towering above it. Fabrizio had announced that, in honour of Our Lady of Pity, he would preach on the pity which a generous soul should feel for anyone in misfortune, even when he is guilty.

Disguised with all possible care, Fabrizio reached his box at the theatre at the moment when the doors were opened, and when there were still no lights. The performance began about eight o'clock, and a few minutes later he experienced that joy which no heart that has not felt it can conceive – he saw the door of the Crescenzi box open. A moment or two later, the Marchesa entered; he had not had so clear a view of her since the day on which she had given him her fan. Fabrizio thought that his joy would choke him. He was conscious of such extraordinary sensations that he said to himself: 'Perhaps I am going to die! What a charming way of ending so sad a life! Perhaps I am going to collapse in this box. The faithful gathered at the Church of the Visitation will wait in vain for me to arrive, and tomorrow they will learn that their future Archbishop got lost in a box at the Opera, disguised as a servant, moreover, and wearing livery! Goodbye then to all my reputation! But what does my reputation mean to me?'

However, towards a quarter to nine, Fabrizio made an effort to pull himself together. He left his box on the fourth tier and had the greatest possible difficulty in reaching, on foot, the place where he was to take off his livery and put on more suitable attire. It was not until nearly nine o'clock that he arrived at the Convent of the Visitation, in such a state of pallor and weakness that the rumour went round the church that the reverend Coadjutor would not be able to preach that evening. One can imagine the attention that was lavished on him by the sisters, through the grating of their inner parlour to which he had retired. These good ladies talked incessantly. Fabrizio asked to be left alone for a few moments, then hastened to take his place in the pulpit. One of his assistants had told him, round about three o'clock, that the Church of the Visitation was completely filled, but with people of the lowest class, attracted apparently by the sight of the illuminations. On entering the pulpit, Fabrizio was agreeably surprised to find all the seats occupied by young men of fashion and by persons of the highest distinction.

He began his sermon with a few words of apology which were received with suppressed cries of admiration. Then followed an impassioned description of the unfortunate wretch whom one must pity in order to pay due honour to Our Lady of Pity, who herself had suffered so greatly while on earth. The orator was deeply stirred; there were moments when he could barely pronounce his words so as to be heard in every part of this little church. In the eyes of all the women, and of a good number of the men, he seemed himself to have the air of the unhappy wretch whom one ought to pity, so extremely pale was his face. A few minutes after the words of apology with which he had begun his discourse, people noticed that he was not in his normal state; it was felt that his melancholy, this evening, was more than usually tender and profound. At one moment he was seen to have tears in his eyes; immediately there rose from the whole congregation a single sob, and so loud that the sermon was completely interrupted.

This first interruption was followed by half a score of others. There were cries of admiration, there were outbursts of tears; at every moment could be heard such exclamations as: '*Ah! Santa Madonna!*' '*Ah! Gran Dio!*' So universal and so irresistible was the emotion felt by this select congregation, that no one was ashamed of uttering these cries, and the people who gave way to this impulse did not seem at all absurd to their neighbours.

During the interval for rest which it is customary to take in the middle of a sermon, Fabrizio was informed that there was absolutely no one left in the theatre. One lady only, the Marchesa Crescenzi, was still to be seen in her box. During this brief interval a sudden loud clamour made itself heard in the main body of the church; it came from the congregation, who were proposing to erect a statue to his Reverence the Coadjutor. The second part of his discourse was acclaimed in so wild and worldly a fashion, the outbursts of Christian contrition gave place so completely to cries of admiration which were altogether profane, that he felt it his duty, on leaving the pulpit, to address some kind of reprimand to his hearers. Whereupon they all walked out of the church at once in a singularly formal fashion and, on reaching the street, all began to clap madly, and to shout, '*Evviva del Dongo!*'

Fabrizio hurriedly glanced at his watch and ran over to a little barred window which lighted the narrow passage from the organ loft to the interior of the convent. Out of civility to the incredible and unprecedented crowd which filled the street, the porter of the Palazzo Crescenzi had placed a dozen torches in those iron sconces which we see projecting from the front walls of great houses built in the Middle Ages. After some minutes, and long before the shouting had ceased, the event for which Fabrizio was waiting with such anxiety occurred—the Marchesa's carriage, returning from the theatre, appeared in the street. The coachman was obliged to stop, and it was only at a crawling pace, and by dint of shouting, that the carriage was able to reach the door.

The Marchesa had been touched by the sublime sweetness of the music, as is the way with sorrowing hearts, but was far more affected, once she had learnt the reason for it, by the utter solitude around her in the theatre. In the middle of the second act, and while the marvellous tenor himself was on the stage, even the people in the pit had suddenly left their seats to try their luck at forcing their way into the Church of the Visitation. The Marchesa, finding herself stopped by the crowd outside her door, burst into tears. 'I did not make a bad choice!' she said to herself.

But precisely on account of this momentary yielding to tenderness she firmly resisted the pressure put upon her by the Marchese and all the friends of the family, who could not imagine why she did not go to hear so astonishing a preacher. 'Why,' said they, 'he is better by far than even the best tenor in Italy!' 'If I see him, I am lost!' said the Marchesa to herself.

In vain did Fabrizio, whose talent seemed to grow more brilliant with each day, preach several times more in that same little church, close to the Palazzo Crescenzi. He never caught a glimpse of Clelia, who even ended by feeling annoyed at his presuming to come and disturb her quiet street, after she had already driven him out of her garden.

In letting his eye run over the faces of the women who came to hear him, Fabrizio had for some time past observed the face of a little brunette, a very pretty one, with eyes that darted fire. These glorious eyes were usually bathed in tears by the time he reached the ninth or tenth sentence of his sermon. When Fabrizio was obliged to say things that he himself found long and boring, he would very readily let his own eyes rest on that head, whose youthfulness appealed to him. He learnt that this young person was a certain Annetta Marini, the only daughter and heiress of the richest cloth merchant in Parma, who had died a few months before.

Presently the name of this Annetta Marini, the cloth merchant's daughter, was on everyone's lips; she had fallen desperately in love with Fabrizio. When the famous sermons began, her marriage had been arranged with Giacomo Rassi, the eldest son of the Minister of Justice, who was by no means unattractive to her. But she had barely listened twice to Monsignore Fabrizio before she declared that she no longer wished to marry; and when she was asked a reason for so extraordinary a change of mind, she replied that it was not fitting for a virtuous girl to marry one man when she felt so desperately in love with another. Her family tried to discover, at first without success, who this other man might be.

But the burning tears which Annetta shed during the sermons put them on the track of the truth. Her mother and her uncles having asked her whether she loved Monsignore Fabrizio, she answered boldly that since they had discovered the truth, she would not lower herself so far as to tell a lie. She added that, having no hope of marrying the man whom she adored, she wished at least no longer to have her eyes offended by the sight of Contino Rassi's ridiculous figure. This mockery of the son of a man who attracted the envy of every middle-class citizen became in a couple of days the talk of the whole town. Annetta Marini's reply was thought charming, and everyone repeated it. It was talked of at the Palazzo Crescenzi as everywhere else.

Clelia was very careful not to open her lips on such a topic in her drawing-room. But she questioned her maid about it, and the following Sunday, after attending Mass in her private chapel, she took her maid with her in her carriage, and went to hear a second Mass in Signorina Marini's parish church. Here she found assembled all the fops of the town, attracted there by the same object; these gentlemen were standing round the door. Presently, from the great commotion among them, the Marchesa gathered that this Signorina Marini was entering the church. She found herself excellently placed to see her, and, for all her piety, paid little attention to the Mass. Clelia found in this middle-class beauty a certain slight air of self-confidence which, to her thinking, would at most have been appropriate in a woman already married for several years. Otherwise, she was admirably proportioned for a woman of small stature and her eyes, as they say in Lombardy, seemed to be holding conversation with everything they looked at. The Marchesa slipped away before the end of Mass.

The following day, the friends of the Crescenzi family, who came regularly to spend the evening with them, had a fresh story to tell of Annetta Marini's absurd behaviour. As her mother, afraid of some foolish action on her part, left only a small amount of money at her disposal, Annetta Marini had gone to offer a magnificent diamond ring, a gift from her father, to the famous Hayez, who was at the time in Parma decorating the drawing-rooms of the Palazzo Crescenzi, and had asked him to paint a portrait of Signor del Dongo. She wished however this portrait to show him dressed simply in black, and not in a cassock. Consequently, on the previous evening, young Annetta's mother had been greatly surprised, and even more highly shocked, to find in her daughter's bedroom a magnificent portrait of Fabrizio del Dongo, set in the finest frame that had been gilded in Parma in the last twenty years.

SWEPT away by the current of events, we have had no time to give a sketch of the comical race of courtiers that swarmed at the court of Parma and made the oddest comments on the incidents which we have related. In that principality, what made a member of the lesser nobility, furnished with an income of three or four thousand lire, worthy to figure in black stockings at the Prince's levees, was first and foremost the fact that he had never read Voltaire and Rousseau; this condition was not very difficult to fulfil. He must next know how to speak with some feeling of the Sovereign's cold, or of the latest case of mineral specimens he had received from Saxony. If after this our noble never missed attending Mass for a single day in the year, if he could reckon two or three fat monks among his intimate friends, the Prince would condescend to address a few words to him once in every year, a fortnight before or a fortnight after the first of January, an honour which gave him good standing in his parish, and the tax collector would not dare to press him unduly if he was in arrears with the annual sum of one hundred lire that was levied on his small estate.

Signor Gonzo was a poor devil of this sort, a man of very noble birth, who, apart from possessing some small fortune of his own, had obtained, through the Marchese Crescenzi's influence, a magnificent post which brought him in eleven hundred and fifty lire a year. This man could very well have dined at home, but he had a particular mania. He was never happy or at his ease except when he found himself in the drawing-room of some great personage who said to him from time to time: 'Hold your tongue, Gonzo, you're a perfect fool.' This judgement was prompted by ill-temper, for Gonzo had almost always more intelligence than the great personage himself. He could talk, and quite charmingly too, about every kind of topic: moreover, he was always ready to change his opinion whenever the master of the house made a grimace. As a matter of fact, although extremely shrewd as regarded his own interests, he had not a single idea in his head, and when the Prince did not happen to have a cold, he was sometimes at a loss for words on entering a drawing-room.

What had won for Gonzo a reputation in Parma was a magnificent cocked hat, adorned with a plume that was somewhat the worse for wear, which he donned even when he was in plain evening dress. But you ought to have seen the way in which he carried that plume, whether upon his head or in his hand; it was a combination of art and self-importance. He would enquire with genuine anxiety after the health of the Marchesa's little dog, and, if the Palazzo Crescenzi had happened to catch fire, he would have risked his life to save one of those fine armchairs in gold brocade, on which for so many years his silk breeches had got caught, whenever it so happened that he ventured to sit down in one of them for a moment.

Seven or eight individuals of this type appeared every evening in the drawing-room of the Marchesa Crescenzi. No sooner had they sat down than a lackey, magnificently attired in a daffodil-yellow livery plastered with silver braid, as was the red waistcoat which completed its magnificence, came to take the poor devils' hats and walking-sticks. He was immediately followed by a footman carrying an extremely minute cup of coffee, set in a holder of silver filigree, and every half hour a butler, wearing a sword and a magnificent coat in the French style, came to hand round ices.

Half an hour after the seedy little courtiers, some five or six officers would be seen to arrive, with a very martial air, talking at the tops of their voices, and usually discussing the number and type of buttons a soldier should wear on his uniform if his Commander-in-Chief was to win any victories. It would not have been prudent to quote a French newspaper in this drawing-room; for, even when the news was of the most agreeable kind, as for instance that fifty Liberals had been shot in Spain, the person reporting it would none the less remain convicted of having read a French newspaper. The highest achievement of all these people's skill consisted in obtaining an increase of a hundred and fifty lire in their emoluments every ten years. It is thus that the Prince shares with his nobility the pleasure of reigning over his subjects, peasants and townsfolk alike.

The chief figure in the Crescenzi drawing-room was beyond all question Cavaliere Foscarini, a perfectly honest man who had consequently been in prison, off and on, under every successive government. He had been a member of that famous Chamber of Deputies at Milan which had rejected the Registration Law presented by Napoleon, an action of very rare occurrence in history. Cavaliere Foscarini, after being for twenty years the friend of the Marchese's mother, had remained a person of great influence in the household.

He had always some amusing story to tell, but nothing escaped his shrewd perception; and the young Marchesa, who felt herself guilty at heart, trembled before him.

As Gonzo had a regular passion for great nobles who said rude things to him and reduced him to tears once or twice a year, he had a mania for seeking to render them small services. And if he had not been paralysed by those habits which come from excessive poverty, he might sometimes have succeeded, for he was not lacking in a certain degree of shrewdness and a far greater amount of effrontery.

This man Gonzo, such as we know him, rather despised the Marchesa Crescenzi, for never once in her life had she addressed a slightly uncivil remark to him. But after all she was the wife of the famous Marchese Crescenzi, the Princess's Lord-in-waiting, who once or twice in a month would say to Gonzo: 'Hold your tongue, Gonzo, you're a perfect fool!'

Gonzo noticed that everything that was said about young Annetta Marini drew the Marchesa for a moment out of the state of dreamy indifference in which she usually remained sunk until the clock struck eleven. Then she would make tea, and offer a cup of it to each of the men present, addressing him by name. After which, just before she retired to her room, she seemed to recover her spirits for a moment, and this was the time that people would choose for reciting to her some satirical sonnets.

Excellent things of this sort are composed in Italy: it is the one type of literature that has preserved some little vitality. As a matter of fact it is not subject to censorship, and the courtiers of the Crescenzi household invariably prefaced their sonnets with the words: 'Will Her Ladyship the Marchesa kindly permit us to recite a very poor sonnet in her presence?' And when the sonnet had been greeted with laughter and had been repeated several times, one of the officers would not fail to exclaim: 'His Excellency the Minister of Police ought really to have a few of the authors of such infamous verses hanged.' In middle class circles, on the other hand, these sonnets are greeted with the most open admiration, and copies of them are sold by lawyers' clerks.

From the sort of curiosity shown by the Marchesa, Gonzo imagined that too much had been said in front of her in praise of the beauty of young Signorina Marini, who also had a fortune of a million, and that she was jealous of her. As, with his perpetual smile and his utter insolence towards anyone who was not noble, Gonzo found admittance everywhere, on the very next day he made his appearance in the Marchesa's drawing-room, carrying his plumed hat with a certain triumphant air such as was only to be seen in him perhaps once or twice in a year, when the Prince had said to him: 'Goodbye, Gonzo.'

After bowing respectfully to the Marchesa, Gonzo did not withdraw, as was his usual custom, to take his seat on the chair which had just been pushed forward for him. He took his stand in the middle of the circle and exclaimed abruptly: 'I have seen the portrait of Monsignore del Dongo.' Clelia was so taken aback that she was obliged to lean upon the arm of her chair; she did her best to stand up against the storm, but presently was obliged to retire from the room.

'You must agree, my poor Gonzo,' exclaimed one of the officers haughtily, as he was finishing his fourth ice, 'that you have put your foot in it with a vengeance. How is it you don't know that the Coadjutor, who was one of the most gallant Colonels in Napoleon's army, lately played an abominable trick on the Marchesa's father by walking out of the citadel where General Conti was in command as he might have walked out of the Steccata?' (The Steccata is the principal church in Parma.)

'Indeed, I am ignorant of many things, my dear Captain, and I am just a poor imbecile who makes blunders all day long.'

This reply, very much to the Italian taste, raised a laugh at the smart officer's expense. The Marchesa soon returned; she had armed herself with courage, and was not without some vague hope of having a chance herself to admire this portrait, which was said to be excellent. She spoke with praise of the talent of Hayez, who had painted it. All unconsciously, she smiled in the most charming way at Gonzo, who cast sly glances at the officer. As all the other toadies of the house indulged in the same pastime, the officer took to flight, not without vowing a deadly hatred against Gonzo. The latter was triumphant, and later in the evening, as he took his leave, was invited to dinner on the following day.

'Here's another piece of news,' exclaimed Gonzo after that dinner, when the servants had left the room: 'it appears that our Coadjutor has fallen in love with the little Marini!'

One may judge of the agitation provoked in Clelia's heart on hearing so extraordinary an announcement. The Marchese himself was disturbed.

'But Gonzo, my good fellow, you are talking nonsense as usual! And you really should use a little more discretion in speaking of a man who has had the honour of playing whist eleven times with His Highness!'

'Well, your Lordship,' answered Gonzo, with the coarseness of men of his type, 'I'll dare swear he would just as soon play games with the little Marini. But it is enough that these details offend you. As far as I'm concerned they cease to exist, for above all things I am anxious not to shock my beloved Marchese.'

Regularly, after dinner, the Marchese used to retire to take a siesta. That day he felt no inclination to do so. But Gonzo would rather have cut out his tongue than have said a word more about the little Marini; and, every moment, he began some speech well calculated to make the Marchese hope that he was about to revert to the love affairs of this young middle-class beauty. Gonzo possessed, in a superior degree, that Italian kind of wit which consists in delaying, with an exquisite sense of delight, the utterance of the word the hearer longs for. The poor Marchese, dying of curiosity, was obliged to make advances. He remarked to Gonzo that whenever he had the pleasure of dining in his company he always ate twice as much as usual. Gonzo did not take the hint; he began to describe a magnificent gallery of pictures which the Marchesa Balbi, the late Prince's mistress, was in process of forming. Three or four times he spoke of Hayez, in lingering tones of the greatest admiration. 'Good!' said the Marchese to himself, 'now he's coming at last to the portrait ordered by the little Marini!' But this was what Gonzo took good care not to do. Five o'clock struck, to the great annoyance of the Marchese, who was in the habit of getting into his carriage at half past five, after his siesta, to drive to the Corso.

'This is what you do, with your silly chatter!' he said rudely to Gonzo. 'You are making me arrive at the Corso after the Princess when I am her Lord-in-waiting, and she may have orders to give me. Come along! Hurry up! Tell me in a few words, if you can, what is this so-called love affair of his Reverence the Coadjutor's?'

But Gonzo wished to keep this tale for the ears of the Marchesa, who had invited him to dinner. He therefore 'hurried up', and gave the asked-for story in a very few words, and the Marchese, half asleep, ran off to take his siesta. Gonzo adopted a wholly different manner with the poor Marchesa. She had remained so young and so ingenuous in spite of her great wealth and position that she felt it her duty to make amends for the rudeness with which the Marchese had just spoken to Gonzo. Charmed by this success, the latter recovered all his eloquence, and made it a pleasure, no less than a duty, to enter into endless details with her.

Young Annetta Marini was paying a sequin for each place that was reserved for her at the sermons. She invariably arrived with two of her aunts and her father's old bookkeeper. These seats, which she had reserved for her overnight, were generally selected almost facing the pulpit, but slightly in the direction of the high altar, for she had noticed that the Coadjutor often turned towards the altar. Now, what the congregation had also noticed was that, *not infrequently*, those speaking eyes of the young preacher would linger with a certain pleasure on this young heiress, in her appealing beauty. And apparently with some attention, too, for as soon as he had his eyes fixed on her his sermon became erudite. Quotations began to abound in it, there was no more sign in it of those emotions which spring from the heart; and the ladies whose interest faded almost immediately, would begin to look at Signorina Marini, and say unkind things about her.

Clelia made him repeat the whole of these curious details three times over. At the third repetition, she became lost in thought; she was reckoning up that it was exactly fourteen months since she had last seen Fabrizio. 'Would there be any great harm,' she wondered, 'in my spending an hour in a church, not to see Fabrizio, but to hear a famous preacher? Besides, I shall take a seat a long way from the pulpit, and I shall look at Fabrizio only once as I go in and once more at the end of the sermon ... No,' said Clelia to herself, 'it is not Fabrizio I am going to see, I am going to hear this amazing preacher!' In the midst of all these reasonings, the Marchesa felt some pangs of conscience; her conduct had been so exemplary for the last fourteen months! 'Well,' she said to herself, to quiet her conscience a little, 'if the first woman to arrive this evening has been to hear Monsignore del Dongo, I shall go too; if she has not been, I shall forgo the idea.'

Once she had come to this decision, the Marchesa filled Gonzo with delight by saying to him: 'Try to find out on what day the Coadjutor will be preaching, and in what church. This evening, before you go, I shall perhaps have some commission to give you.'

No sooner had Gonzo left to go to the Corso than Clelia went to take the air in the garden of her *palazzo*. She did not make any objection to this on the grounds that for ten months she had not set foot in it. She was lively and in good spirits; her cheeks had some colour. That evening, as each visitor entered her drawing-room, her heart throbbed with emotion. At length Gonzo was announced, and he realized at the first glance that for the next week he was going to be the one indispensable person. 'The Marchesa,' he said to himself, 'is jealous of the little Marini, and, upon my word, it would make a marvellously effective comedy with the Marchesa playing the leading part, little Annetta the lady's maid, and Monsignore del Dongo the lover! Upon my word, two lire would not be too dear a price for the tickets.'

He was beside himself with joy, and during the whole of the evening kept taking the words out of everyone's mouth and retailing the most preposterous pieces of gossip (as, for instance, about the famous actress and the Marquis de Pecquigny, which he had heard the day before from a French tourist). The Marchesa, for her part, could not stay in one place; she walked about the drawing-room, she moved into an adjoining gallery into which the Marchese had admitted no picture that had not cost more than twenty thousand lire. These pictures spoke to her in so clear a language that evening that they left the Marchesa's heart worn out with excess of feeling. At last she heard both sides of the great door flung open, and hurried back to the drawing-room. It was the Marchesa Raversi! But as Clelia was greeting her with the customary polite words of welcome, she felt her voice fail her. Twice over the Marchesa had to make her repeat the question: 'Have you heard the famous preacher?' which she had not caught at first.

'I used to think of him as a young intriguer, a worthy nephew of the notorious Contessa Mosca. But the last time he preached, which was, let me see, at the Church of the Visitation, opposite your house, he was so sublime that, with all my hatred for him vanished, I now regard him as the most eloquent man I have ever heard.'

'So you have been to one of his sermons?' said Clelia, trembling with happiness.

'Why, weren't you listening to me?' said the Marchesa, laughing. 'I wouldn't miss them for anything in the world. They say that his lungs are affected, and that soon he will have to give up preaching!'

No sooner had the Marchesa left than Clelia called Gonzo into the gallery.

'I have almost decided,' she said to him, 'to hear this much-vaunted preacher. When is he going to preach?'

'Next Monday, that is to say in three days from now; and one would say that he guessed your Excellency's intention, for he is coming to preach in the Church of the Visitation.'

There was more to discuss; but Clelia could no longer summon up enough voice to speak. She walked up and down the gallery five or six times without saying another word. Gonzo said to himself: 'I see the idea of vengeance working in her mind. How can anyone have such insolence as to escape from a prison, especially when he has the honour of being guarded by a hero like General Fabio Conti?'

'By the way,' he added aloud with a delicate touch of irony, 'you will have to hurry. His lungs are affected; I heard Dr Rambo say that he hasn't a year to live. God is punishing him for having broken his ban by treacherously escaping from the citadel.'

The Marchesa sat down on the couch in the gallery and made a sign to Gonzo to follow her example. After a few moments, she handed him a little purse in which she had a few sequins ready. 'Reserve four places for me.'

'Will it be permissible for your poor Gonzo to slip in in your Excellency's train?'

'Certainly; reserve five places ... I do not in the least mind,' she added, 'whether I am near the pulpit; but I should like to see Signorina Marini, who is said to be so pretty.'

The Marchesa could hardly live through the three days that separated her from the famous Monday, the day of the sermon. Gonzo, for whom it was a signal honour to be seen in public in the train of so great a lady, had put on his French coat with his sword. Nor was this all. Taking advantage of the proximity of the *palazzo*, he had had a magnificent gilt armchair carried into the church for the use of the Marchesa, a proceeding which was considered the last word in insolence by the townsfolk. It can be imagined how the poor Marchesa felt when she saw this armchair, which had been placed directly facing the pulpit. Clelia was in such confusion, with downcast eyes, and shrunk into a corner of this huge chair, that she had not even the courage to look at the little Marini, whom Gonzo pointed out to her with his hand with an effrontery that quite took her aback. Everyone not of noble birth was absolutely nothing in the eyes of this courtier.

Fabrizio appeared in the pulpit; he was so thin, so pale, so *wasted*, that Clelia's eyes immediately filled with tears. Fabrizio uttered a few words, then stopped, as though his voice had suddenly failed him. He vainly tried to begin a sentence or two and then he turned round, and took up a sheet of paper with writing on it.

'My brethren,' he said, 'an unhappy soul and one well deserving of your pity begs you, through my voice, to pray for the ending of his torments, which will cease only with his life.'

Fabrizio read the rest of his paper very slowly; but the tone of his voice was such that before he was half-way through the prayer everyone, even Gonzo himself was weeping. 'At any rate, I shall not be noticed,' thought the Marchesa, bursting into tears.

While he was reading the words on the paper, Fabrizio happened upon one or two ideas concerning the state of the unhappy man on whose behalf he had just begged the prayers of the congregation. Soon thoughts began to come to him in abundance. While seeming to address himself to the people in general, he spoke to the Marchesa alone. He ended his discourse a little sooner than usual, because, in spite of all his efforts, his own tears were getting so much the better of him that he could no longer articulate his words in an intelligible manner. The best judges found this sermon strange, but equal, at all events, in its pathos, to the famous sermon preached by the light of the candles. As for Clelia, she had hardly heard the first ten lines of the prayer read by Fabrizio before it seemed to her an atrocious crime to have been able to live through fourteen months without seeing him. On returning home she retired to bed to be able to think of Fabrizio with perfect freedom; and the next morning, fairly early, Fabrizio received a note couched in the following terms:

The writer relies on your honour. Find four stout rogues of whose discretion you can be sure, and tomorrow night, when the clock on the Steccata strikes twelve, be beside a little door which bears the number 19 in the Strada San Paolo. Remember that you may be attacked, and do not come alone.

On recognizing that heavenly handwriting, Fabrizio fell on his knees and burst into tears. 'At last,' he cried, 'after fourteen months and one week! Farewell to preaching.'

It would take too long to describe all the various kinds of folly to which, that day, the hearts of Fabrizio and of Clelia were a prey.

The little door indicated in the note was none other than that of the orangery of the Palazzo Crescenzi, and ten times in the course of that day Fabrizio found occasion to take a look at it. He armed himself, and alone, a little before midnight, was walking with rapid steps towards that door when to his inexpressible joy he heard a well-known voice say in a very low whisper: 'Come in here, dear heart.'

Fabrizio entered cautiously and found himself inside the orangery, but opposite a heavily barred window raised some three or four feet above the ground. The darkness was intense. Fabrizio had heard a slight sound inside this window, and he was exploring the bars with his hand when he felt another hand, slipped through the bars, take hold of his and carry it to lips which imprinted a kiss upon it.

'It is I,' said a beloved voice, 'who have come here to tell you that I love you, and to ask you if you are willing to obey me.'

One may imagine the answer, the joy, the astonishment of Fabrizio. After the first transports, Clelia said to him: 'I have made a vow to the Madonna, as you know, never to see you. That is why I receive you now in this complete darkness. I wish you to understand clearly that, should you ever force me to look at you in broad daylight, all would be over between us. But first of all, I do not wish you to preach in front of Annetta Marini, and do not go and think that it was I who was so stupid as to have an armchair carried into the House of God.'

'My dearest angel, I shall never preach again before anyone. I only preached in the hope that one day I might see you.'

'Do not speak like that! Remember that I, for my part, am not permitted to see you.'

*

At this point I will ask leave to pass over, without saying a single word about it, an interval of three years.

At the time when our story begins again, Conte Mosca had long since returned to Parma as its Prime Minister, and was more powerful than ever.

After these three years of divine happiness, Fabrizio's heart was possessed by a sudden tender caprice which came to alter everything. The Marchesa had a charming little boy two years old, Sandrino, who was his mother's joy. He was always with her or on the Marchese Crescenzi's knee; Fabrizio, on the other hand, hardly ever saw him.

He did not want the boy to become accustomed to loving another father, and conceived the idea of taking the child away before his memories had grown really distinct.

During the long hours of each day when the Marchesa could not be with her lover, Sandrino's company consoled her. For we have to confess a thing which will seem strange to those who live north of the Alps – in spite of her errors she had remained true to her vow. She had promised the Madonna, as the reader will doubtless remember, never to *see* Fabrizio; these had been her exact words. Consequently she received him only at night, and there was never any light in the room.

But every evening he was received by his mistress; and, what was remarkable, in the midst of a court devoured by curiosity and envy, Fabrizio's precautions had been so ably calculated that this *amicizia*, as it is called in Lombardy, had never even been suspected. Their love was too intense for them to have no quarrels; Clelia was extremely given to jealousy, but almost always their quarrels sprang from a different cause. Fabrizio had, for instance, taken unfair advantage of a public ceremony to be in the same place as the Marchesa and to look at her; she then seized upon some pretext for leaving the place quickly and for a long time afterwards kept her lover at a distance.

People at the court of Parma were amazed that no intrigue should be known on the part of a woman so remarkable for her beauty and the high quality of her mind. She awakened certain passions which inspired many acts of folly, and Fabrizio was often jealous himself.

The good Archbishop Landriani had long been dead. Fabrizio's piety, his exemplary morals, and his eloquence had caused him to be forgotten. The new prelate's elder brother was dead, and all the family possessions had reverted to him. From that time forward he distributed annually among the vicars and curates of his diocese the hundred thousand lire or so which the Archbishopric of Parma brought him in.

It would be difficult to imagine a life more honoured, more honourable and more useful than that which Fabrizio had made for himself when everything was upset by an unfortunate sentimental caprice.

'According to this vow of yours, which I respect and which nevertheless is the bane of my life, since you refuse to see me by day,' he said on one occasion to Clelia, 'I am obliged to live perpetually alone, with no other distraction save work; and even then I have not enough work on hand. In the course of this grim and dreary way of spending the long hours of each day, an idea has occurred to me, which is now tormenting me, and against which I have been struggling in vain for the past six months. My son will never get to love me; he never hears my name. Brought up amid all the pleasing luxury of the Palazzo Crescenzi, he barely knows me. On the rare occasions when I do see him I think of his mother, whose heavenly beauty, which I may never look at, he brings back to my mind, and he must find me a solemn sort of person, which, with children, means dull and gloomy.'

'Well,' said the Marchesa, 'what is all this alarming speech of yours leading up to?'

'To getting back my son. I want him to live with me; I want him to grow accustomed to loving me; I want to have full opportunity of loving him myself. Since a fatality without parallel in the world decrees that I should be deprived of that happiness which so many tender hearts enjoy, and forbids me to spend my life with all that I adore, I wish at least to have beside me a being who recalls you to my heart and who to some extent takes your place. Men and affairs are a burden to me in my enforced solitude. You know that ambition has always been an empty word to me, ever since the moment when I had the good fortune to be locked up by Barbone, and in the melancholy that overwhelms me when I am not with you, anything unconnected with the heart's emotions seems to me absurd.'

It is easy to understand the keen anguish with which her lover's grief filled poor Clelia's heart. Her sorrow was all the more intense because she felt that Fabrizio was in some degree justified. She went to the length of questioning whether she ought not to venture to break her vow. Then she would receive Fabrizio during the day like any other important member of society, and her reputation as a woman of virtue was too well established for anyone to gainsay it. She told herself that at the cost of a fair amount of money she could procure a dispensation from her vow; but she felt that this purely worldly transaction would not set her conscience at rest, and that an angry heaven might perhaps punish her for this fresh crime.

On the other hand, if she consented to yield to Fabrizio's very natural desire, if she tried not to bring unhappiness to that tender heart which she knew so well, and whose peace of mind was so strangely jeopardized by her peculiar vow, what chance was there of abducting the only son of one of the greatest nobles in Italy without the trick becoming known? The Marchese Crescenzi would spend untold sums of money, would himself conduct the investigations, and sooner or later the facts of the abduction would become known. There was only one way of guarding against this danger, and that was to send the child far away, to Edinburgh, for instance, or to Paris; but that was a course to which a mother's heart could never agree. The other plan proposed by Fabrizio, and certainly the more reasonable of the two, had something of a sinister omen about it, and was almost more alarming still in the eyes of this distracted mother. There would have to be, said Fabrizio, a feigned illness; the child would grow steadily worse and finally die while the Marchese Crescenzi was away from home.

Clelia's deep aversion to this plan, an aversion amounting to terror, caused a breach between them that could not last long.

Clelia maintained that they must not tempt God; that this beloved son was the offspring of a sin, and that if they provoked the divine anger any further, God would not fail to take the child back to Himself. Fabrizio spoke again of his strange destiny: 'The station in life to which chance has called me, together with my love,' he said to Clelia, 'condemn me to perpetual solitude. I cannot, like the majority of my fellows, enjoy the pleasures of intimate companionship, since you are only willing to receive me in the dark, which, so to speak, reduces to a few brief moments that part of my life which I may spend with you.'

Many tears were shed, and Clelia fell ill. But she loved Fabrizio too much to continue in her refusal to make the terrible sacrifice he demanded of her. To all appearances Sandrino fell ill. The Marchese sent in haste for the most eminent physicians, and Clelia was from that moment confronted with a most frightful difficulty which she had not foreseen. She had to prevent the child she adored from taking any of the remedies prescribed by the doctors; this was no easy matter.

The child, kept in bed longer than was good for his health, became really ill. How was she to explain to the doctor the real cause of his illness? Torn asunder by two conflicting interests both so dear to her, Clelia came very near to losing her reason. Must she agree to an apparent recovery and so sacrifice all the results of such long and painful dissimulation? Fabrizio, for his part, could neither forgive

himself the violence he was doing to his mistress's heart, nor abandon
his project. He had found a way of being admitted every night to
the sick child's room, and this had led to another complication. The
Marchesa would come to attend to her son, and Fabrizio was sometimes obliged to see her by candle-light, which seemed to Clelia's
poor sick heart a horrible sin and one that foreboded the death of
Sandrino. In vain had the most famous casuists, consulted as to the
keeping of a vow in a case where the observance of it would obviously do harm, replied that the vow could not be regarded as
broken in a sinful fashion, so long as the person bound by a promise to
the Deity failed to keep that promise, not, for the sake of some vain
sensual pleasure, but so as not to cause obvious harm. The Marchesa
was none the less in despair, and Fabrizio could see the moment
approaching when that fantastic idea of his would bring about both
Clelia's death and her son's.

He had recourse to his intimate friend Conte Mosca, who, hardened
old Minister as he was, was touched by this tale of love, the greater
part of which was unknown to him.

'I can manage to remove the Marchese for five or six days at least.
When do you want this to be?'

A short time after Fabrizio came to inform the Conte that everything was now in readiness for them to take advantage of the Marchese's absence.

Two days later, as the Marchese was riding home from one of his
estates in the neighbourhood of Mantua, a few stout ruffians, apparently paid to carry out some private act of vengeance, laid hands
on him, without maltreating him in any way, and put him into a
boat which took three days to travel down the Po, making the same
journey that Fabrizio had made long ago, after the famous affair with
Giletti. On the fourth day the ruffians landed the Marchese on a
lonely island in the Po, after taking care to rob him of all he had, and
to leave him no money or any object of the slightest value. It took
the Marchese two whole days before he could get back to his *palazzo*
in Parma. He found it draped in black and all his household in the
depths of grief.

This abduction, very skilfully carried out, had fatal consequences:
Sandrino, secretly installed in a large and handsome house where
the Marchesa came to see him almost every day, died within a few
months. Clelia imagined that just punishment had fallen upon her

for having been unfaithful to her vow to the Madonna; she had seen Fabrizio so often by candle-light, and even twice in broad daylight, and with such tender rapture, during Sandrino's illness. She survived her much-loved child by a few months only, but had the joy of dying in her lover's arms.

Fabrizio was too much in love and too earnest a believer to have recourse to suicide. He hoped to meet Clelia again in a better world, but had too much intelligence not to feel that there was much for which he must first atone.

A few days after Clelia's death he signed several settlements by which he assured a pension of one thousand lire to each of his servants, and reserved a similar pension for himself. He made over landed property, of an annual value of about one hundred thousand lire, to Contessa Mosca; a like sum to the Marchesa del Dongo, his mother, and such residue as there might be of his patrimony to that one of his sisters who was poorly married. On the following day, having forwarded to the proper authorities his resignation of his Archbishopric and of all the posts which the favour of Ernesto V and the Prime Minister's friendship had successively heaped upon him, he retired to the *Charterhouse of Parma*, which stands in the woods beside the Po, a couple of leagues from Sacca.

Contessa Mosca had strongly approved, at the time, of her husband's return to the Ministry, but she herself had never been willing to consent to set foot again in Ernesto V's dominions. She held her court at Vignano, on the left bank of the Po, and consequently within Austrian territory. In this magnificent palace of Vignano, which the Conte had built for her, she was at home every Thursday to all the best society in Parma, and every day to her own numerous friends. Fabrizio would not have let a day pass without going to Vignano. The Contessa, in short, combined in her life all the outward appearances of happiness, but she lived for a very short time only after Fabrizio, whom she adored, and who spent but one year in his Charterhouse.

The prisons of Parma were empty. The Conte was immensely rich, and Ernesto V adored by his subjects, who compared his rule to that of the Grand Dukes of Tuscany.

★

TO THE HAPPY FEW

FOR THE BEST IN PAPERBACKS, LOOK FOR THE

In every corner of the world, on every subject under the sun, Penguin represents quality and variety – the very best in publishing today.

For complete information about books available from Penguin – including Pelicans, Puffins, Peregrines and Penguin Classics – and how to order them, write to us at the appropriate address below. Please note that for copyright reasons the selection of books varies from country to country.

In the United Kingdom: For a complete list of books available from Penguin in the U.K., please write to *Dept E.P., Penguin Books Ltd, Harmondsworth, Middlesex, UB7 0DA*

In the United States: For a complete list of books available from Penguin in the U.S., please write to *Dept BA, Penguin, 299 Murray Hill Parkway, East Rutherford, New Jersey 07073*

In Canada: For a complete list of books available from Penguin in Canada, please write to *Penguin Books Canada Ltd, 2801 John Street, Markham, Ontario L3R 1B4*

In Australia: For a complete list of books available from Penguin in Australia, please write to the *Marketing Department, Penguin Books Australia Ltd, P.O. Box 257, Ringwood, Victoria 3134*

In New Zealand: For a complete list of books available from Penguin in New Zealand, please write to the *Marketing Department, Penguin Books (NZ) Ltd, Private Bag, Takapuna, Auckland 9*

In India: For a complete list of books available from Penguin, please write to *Penguin Overseas Ltd, 706 Eros Apartments, 56 Nehru Place, New Delhi, 110019*

In Holland: For a complete list of books available from Penguin in Holland, please write to *Penguin Books Nederland B.V., Postbus 195, NL–1380AD Weesp, Netherlands*

In Germany: For a complete list of books available from Penguin, please write to *Penguin Books Ltd, Friedrichstrasse 10 – 12, D–6000 Frankfurt Main 1, Federal Republic of Germany*

In Spain: For a complete list of books available from Penguin in Spain, please write to *Longman Penguin España, Calle San Nicolas 15, E–28013 Madrid, Spain*

FOR THE BEST IN PAPERBACKS, LOOK FOR THE

PENGUIN CLASSICS

Netochka Nezvanova   Fyodor Dostoyevsky

Dostoyevsky's first book tells the story of 'Nameless Nobody' and introduces many of the themes and issues which will dominate his great masterpieces.

Selections from the Carmina Burana   A verse translation by David Parlett

The famous songs from the *Carmina Burana* (made into an oratorio by Carl Orff) tell of lecherous monks and corrupt clerics, drinkers and gamblers, and the fleeting pleasures of youth.

Fear and Trembling   Søren Kierkegaard

A profound meditation on the nature of faith and submission to God's will which examines with startling originality the story of Abraham and Isaac.

Selected Prose   Charles Lamb

Lamb's famous essays (under the strange pseudonym of Elia) on anything and everything have long been celebrated for their apparently innocent charm; this major new edition allows readers to discover the darker and more interesting aspects of Lamb.

The Picture of Dorian Gray   Oscar Wilde

Wilde's superb and macabre novella, one of his supreme works, is reprinted here with a masterly Introduction and valuable Notes by Peter Ackroyd.

A Treatise of Human Nature   David Hume

A universally acknowledged masterpiece by 'the greatest of all British Philosophers' – A. J. Ayer

PENGUIN CLASSICS

Honoré de Balzac	**Cousin Bette**
	Eugénie Grandet
	Lost Illusions
	Old Goriot
	Ursule Mirouet
Benjamin Constant	**Adolphe**
Corneille	**The Cid/Cinna/The Theatrical Illusion**
Alphonse Daudet	**Letters from My Windmill**
René Descartes	**Discourse on Method and Other Writings**
Denis Diderot	**Jacques the Fatalist**
Gustave Flaubert	**Madame Bovary**
	Sentimental Education
	Three Tales
Jean de la Fontaine	**Selected Fables**
Jean Froissart	**The Chronicles**
Théophile Gautier	**Mademoiselle de Maupin**
Edmond and Jules de Goncourt	**Germinie Lacerteux**
J.-K. Huysmans	**Against Nature**
Guy de Maupassant	**Selected Short Stories**
Molière	**The Misanthrope/The Sicilian/Tartuffe/A Doctor in Spite of Himself/The Imaginary Invalid**
Michel de Montaigne	**Essays**
Marguerite de Navarre	**The Heptameron**
Marie de France	**Lais**
Blaise Pascal	**Pensées**
Rabelais	**The Histories of Gargantua and Pantagruel**
Racine	**Iphigenia/Phaedra/Athaliah**
Arthur Rimbaud	**Collected Poems**
Jean-Jacques Rousseau	**The Confessions**
	Reveries of a Solitary Walker
Madame de Sevigné	**Selected Letters**
Voltaire	**Candide**
	Philosophical Dictionary

FOR THE BEST IN PAPERBACKS, LOOK FOR THE 🐧

PENGUIN CLASSICS

Pedro de Alarcón	**The Three-Cornered Hat and Other Stories**
Leopoldo Alas	**La Regenta**
Ludovico Ariosto	**Orlando Furioso**
Giovanni Boccaccio	**The Decameron**
Baldassar Castiglione	**The Book of the Courtier**
Benvenuto Cellini	**Autobiography**
Miguel de Cervantes	**Don Quixote**
	Exemplary Stories
Dante	**The Divine Comedy** (in 3 volumes)
	La Vita Nuova
Bernal Diaz	**The Conquest of New Spain**
Carlo Goldoni	**Four Comedies (The Venetian Twins/The Artful Widow/Mirandolina/The Superior Residence)**
Niccolo Machiavelli	**The Discourses**
	The Prince
Alessandro Manzoni	**The Betrothed**
Giorgio Vasari	**Lives of the Artists** (in 2 volumes)

and

Five Italian Renaissance Comedies (Machiavelli/The Mandragola; Ariosto/Lena; Aretino/The Stablemaster; Gl'Intronatie/The Deceived; Guarini/The Faithful Shepherd)
The Jewish Poets of Spain
The Poem of the Cid
Two Spanish Picaresque Novels (Anon/Lazarillo de Tormes; de Quevedo/The Swindler)

FOR THE BEST IN PAPERBACKS, LOOK FOR THE 🐧

PENGUIN CLASSICS

Klaus von Clausewitz	**On War**
Friedrich Engels	**The Origins of the Family, Private Property and the State**
Wolfram von Eschenbach	**Parzival**
	Willehalm
Goethe	**Elective Affinities**
	Faust
	Italian Journey 1786–88
Jacob and Wilhelm Grimm	**Selected Tales**
E. T. A. Hoffmann	**Tales of Hoffmann**
Henrik Ibsen	**The Doll's House/The League of Youth/The Lady from the Sea**
	Ghosts/A Public Enemy/When We Dead Wake
	Hedda Gabler/The Pillars of the Community/The Wild Duck
	The Master Builder/Rosmersholm/Little Eyolf/John Gabriel Borkman/Peer Gynt
Søren Kierkegaard	**Fear and Trembling**
Friedrich Nietzsche	**Beyond Good and Evil**
	Ecce Homo
	A Nietzsche Reader
	Thus Spoke Zarathustra
	Twilight of the Idols and The Anti-Christ
Friedrich Schiller	**The Robbers and Wallenstein**
Arthur Schopenhauer	**Essays and Aphorisms**
Gottfried von Strassburg	**Tristan**
August Strindberg	**Inferno and From an Occult Diary**

FOR THE BEST IN PAPERBACKS, LOOK FOR THE

PENGUIN CLASSICS

Anton Chekhov

The Duel and Other Stories
The Kiss and Other Stories
Lady with Lapdog and Other Stories
Plays (The Cherry Orchard/Ivanov/The
    Seagull/Uncle Vanya/The Bear/The
    Proposal/A Jubilee/Three Sisters
The Party and Other Stories

Fyodor Dostoyevsky

The Brothers Karamazov
Crime and Punishment
The Devils
The Gambler/Bobok/A Nasty Story
The House of the Dead
The Idiot
Netochka Nezvanova
Notes From Underground and **The Double**

Nikolai Gogol

Dead Souls
Diary of a Madman and Other Stories

Maxim Gorky

My Apprenticeship
My Childhood
My Universities

Mikhail Lermontov

A Hero of Our Time

Alexander Pushkin

Eugene Onegin
The Queen of Spades and Other Stories

Leo Tolstoy

Anna Karenin
Childhood/Boyhood/Youth
The Cossacks/The Death of Ivan Ilyich/Happy
    Ever After
The Kreutzer Sonata and Other Stories
Master and Man and Other Stories
Resurrection
The Sebastopol Sketches
War and Peace

Ivan Turgenev

Fathers and Sons
First Love

FOR THE BEST IN PAPERBACKS, LOOK FOR THE

PENGUIN CLASSICS

Horatio Alger, Jr.	**Ragged Dick** and **Struggling Upward**
Phineas T. Barnum	**Struggles and Triumphs**
Ambrose Bierce	**The Enlarged Devil's Dictionary**
Kate Chopin	**The Awakening and Selected Stories**
Stephen Crane	**The Red Badge of Courage**
Richard Henry Dana, Jr.	**Two Years Before the Mast**
Frederick Douglass	**Narrative of the Life of Frederick Douglass, An American Slave**
Theodore Dreiser	**Sister Carrie**
Ralph Waldo Emerson	**Selected Essays**
Joel Chandler Harris	**Uncle Remus**
Nathaniel Hawthorne	**Blithedale Romance**
	The House of the Seven Gables
	The Scarlet Letter and Selected Tales
William Dean Howells	**The Rise of Silas Lapham**
Alice James	**The Diary of Alice James**
William James	**Varieties of Religious Experience**
Jack London	**The Call of the Wild and Other Stories**
	Martin Eden
Herman Melville	**Billy Budd, Sailor and Other Stories**
	Moby-Dick
	Redburn
	Typee
Frank Norris	**McTeague**
Thomas Paine	**Common Sense**
Edgar Allan Poe	**The Narrative of Arthur Gordon Pym of Nantucket**
	The Other Poe
	The Science Fiction of Edgar Allan Poe
	Selected Writings
Harriet Beecher Stowe	**Uncle Tom's Cabin**
Henry David Thoreau	**Walden and Civil Disobedience**
Mark Twain	**The Adventures of Huckleberry Finn**